A Gay and Melancholy Sound

A Gay and Melancholy Sound

By Merle Miller

Introduction by Nancy Pearl

Text copyright © 1961 Merle Miller
Introduction and Reading Group Guide copyright © 2012 Nancy Pearl
All rights reserved.

A Book Lust Rediscovery
Published by AmazonEncore
P.O. Box 400818
Las Vegas, NV 89140

ISBN-10: 1612182976
ISBN-13: 9781612182971

Introduction

I first read Merle Miller's *A Gay and Melancholy Sound* in the late fall of 1962. I was a freshman at St. John's College (the "Great Books" school) and finding the going very tough. The schoolwork demanded a kind of thinking that did not come naturally to me. I was not then, nor have I ever been, much of an analytical thinker, and that seemed to be the approach required for the assignments we were given. I felt inadequate intellectually, uncertain emotionally, and confused by the intricacies of the social life the college offered. I was just about to turn eighteen and felt lonely, alien, and terribly afraid I'd made a grave mistake in my choice of a college.

So I did what I'd done my whole life when I felt uncomfortable or depressed: I went to the library. Not the college library, but the public library in Annapolis. I understand there's a new library there now, but back then it was—at least as I remember it—small and dark (the better to match my mood, perhaps). I browsed the fiction shelves, looking for something that might take me out of my own life, and saw a title that intrigued me: *A Gay and Melancholy Sound*. It turned out to be the perfect book for that moment in my life. It became (and remains) one of my all-time favorite novels.

I'd never heard of Merle Miller, the author, but decided to give the book a try. From the very first paragraph, I was hooked by the narrator's voice:

I was presented with this tape recorder five years ago. It was the gift of a group of people—most of them actors, if you call actors people—I had helped keep off the streets and the unemployment lists for three wildly successful years.

I checked the book out and continued reading as I walked back to my dorm, heedless of traffic and Naval Academy cadets out and about. Once in my room, I deliberately ignored the reading assignment (probably Herodotus) for the next seminar. I was already too drawn into Joshua Bland's story to put it down.

Merle Miller (1919–1986) has written what I think is probably the purest example of the novel as autobiography that I've ever read. I found unforgettable his stark and stunning portrait of an Iowa-born former child prodigy whose inability to love stems from a lacerating self-hatred. Throughout his life, Joshua Bland has systematically destroyed whatever happiness could be his, knowing exactly what he was doing as he did it, but unable to stop himself. His behavior, which will perhaps be inexplicable to some readers, seemed all too understandable to me, then. (It still does.)

When I think about the narrator/protagonist of Miller's novel, it always brings to mind A. E. Housman's poem "In My Own Shire, If I Was Sad," in which the speaker describes many of the Londoners he meets as having "The mortal sickness of a mind/Too unhappy to be kind." That fits Joshua Bland's life to a T. Some of what he does is, perhaps, unforgivable, but even more, he doesn't *want* to be forgiven, doesn't want, or at least can't accept, kindness from people. That's the deep tragedy of his life: he feels he's never lived up to what was expected of him, what his genius IQ presaged, and therefore doesn't deserve to be liked, let alone loved.

I've now read *A Gay and Melancholy Sound* at least a dozen more times. My memory is that originally I couldn't bear to give the book back to the library, so I simply kept it, but knowing my—even then—reverence for libraries and what they stand for, perhaps that memory is apocryphal. More likely, I just kept checking it out, over and over, for those two unhappy years I spent in Annapolis. But somehow, I did end up with a copy of the novel, which I treasured until it fell apart from too many rereadings.

A Gay and Melancholy Sound is certainly grounded in the great historical events of the mid-twentieth century—the Second World War and McCarthyism, to take two notable examples. Yet, Miller's novel never feels dated or awkward: there's no strong whiff of the long-dead past emanating from its pages. Indeed, there's enough snark, emotional pain, and irony to satisfy even the most demanding twenty-first-century reader.

Early in 1971, ten years after *A Gay and Melancholy Sound* was published, and two years after the Stonewall riots marked the beginning of the modern gay pride movement, Miller very publicly came out, writing an article for the *New York Times Magazine* entitled "What It Means to Be a Homosexual." In it, he described the pain of inhabiting his theretofore well-closeted life. Knowing that Miller was a gay man gave my rereadings of the 1970s and 1980s an added depth and poignancy; Joshua Bland in *A Gay and Melancholy Sound* sounds an awful lot like Miller in the article. I could only wonder about the extent to which Miller's *A Gay and Melancholy Sound* was not only novel as autobiography, but also autobiography (at least emotional autobiography) as novel. (That magazine piece was later published in book form under the title *On Being Different*. Wonderfully and serendipitously, it's going to be reissued by Penguin Classics in 2012.)

For decades, though, *A Gay and Melancholy Sound* has been nearly impossible to find. It never attained the status of a "classic," so most libraries had long since weeded it from their collections. In all my searching, I'd only ever found one copy, about six years ago: it was at Renaissance Books, a used bookstore in Milwaukee's Mitchell International Airport. Naturally, I immediately bought it. When I was writing *Book Lust: Recommended Reading for Every Mood, Moment, and Reason* in 2002, it had been at least a decade since I'd gone back to Miller's novel. I knew I wanted to include it, but, worried that readers of *Book Lust* wouldn't find it as compelling as I remembered it being—or perhaps fearing not being as fond of it as I once was—I hedged my bets and listed it in a section called "Better Remembered Than Reread." Now, having reread it in order to make sure I wanted to include it in the Book Lust Rediscovery series, I see how foolish I was not to trust that earlier me, who found so much to admire and love in Miller's witty, smart, and viscerally powerful novel.

My favorite anecdote about my ongoing love for Merle Miller's novels took place in 1967. My husband and I had gotten a job with the University of Michigan's Institute for Social Research, along with almost two dozen other young married couples, to be part of a national study of undetected juvenile delinquency. Our assignment was to interview teens about crimes they may have committed that never went onto a police report. A roll of the dice determined where we were to be sent; in our case, it was to Sioux Falls, South Dakota, Chicago, and a few small towns in Iowa. By this time, I had read all of Miller's novels, but I was dying to own them as well, and even back then they were hard to come by. I noticed that one of the Iowa towns we were assigned to was not too far from Marshalltown, where Miller had grown up. I felt sure that any bookstore in that town would feature a complete complement of his books, new and older, since he was a native son who had (at least in my mind) gone on to fame and fortune. So, one sunny afternoon, we drove to Marshalltown and went into the bookstore. My conversation with the man behind the counter went like this:

"Do you have any of Merle Miller's books?"

The proprietor's brow furled for a moment, and then cleared. "Of course," he said, "I keep them in the window." The window! How thrilling! I went outside and looked at the window display. There, nestled near William Styron's *The Confessions of Nat Turner*, William Manchester's *The Death of a President*, and Chaim Potok's *The Chosen* (all bestsellers in 1967) were Henry Miller's *Tropic of Cancer* and *Tropic of Capricorn*.

Though I never met him, except through the pages of his books, I'm pretty sure that Merle Miller would have had a bitter laugh about that.

I hope you love this novel as much as I do.

Nancy Pearl

For Elly, who thought it was about time,
for Ruth, who helped with it, for John,
who was patient, and for Bill.

"...I always willingly acknowledge my own self as the principal cause of every good or evil which may befall me; therefore, I have always found myself capable of being my own pupil and ready to love my teacher."

THE MEMOIRS OF JACQUES CASANOVA

"Good sense is of all things in the world the most equally distributed, for everybody thinks himself so abundantly provided with it that even the most difficult to please in all other matters do not commonly desire more of it than they already have."

RENÉ DESCARTES

Although what follows is written in the first person singular, it is a work of fiction. None of the events related here actually happened.

Like the protagonist in these pages, the author was born in Iowa; he has served time in certain improbable areas of Southern California and Manhattan, and now lives in a house of glass somewhat north of New York City.

But there the resemblance ends.

As for the people I have known along the way, none of them will find themselves portrayed here. If any of them think they do, let them try to prove it.

M. M.

A Gay and Melancholy Sound

PART • ONE

NOTES·DICTATED·ON·THE·FIRST·DAY

(1) The beginning

I was presented with this tape recorder five years ago. It was the gift of a group of people—most of them actors, if you call actors people—I had helped keep off the streets and the unemployment lists for three wildly successful years.

Until now, I had thought the damn thing would be auctioned off with the rest, unwanted and unused. In fact, several times I had started to give it away, but there's more of my mother in me than I like to think. As she used to say, "A penny earned is a penny saved, and a stitch in nine saves time."

So this morning I unlocked the closet, and there this recorder was, gathering dust; there were also enough boxes of tape to start a tape store.

I'll start off with a quote from Romain Rolland that always impressed me, from *Jean Christophe*, I think:

> There are in life certain ages when there takes place a silently working organic change in a man; then body and soul are more susceptible to attack from without; the mind is weakened; its power is sapped by a vague sadness, a feeling of satiety, a sort of detachment from what it is doing, an incapacity for seeing any other course of action....

I first read those words twenty-five or more years ago, read them and remembered them.

I have forgotten almost everything else I ever read or learned or knew but never those words, and yesterday afternoon I realized that I had come to such a time in my own life.

Her telegram arrived at a little after three.

I held it in my hand for a moment, still hoping it would not say what it had to say.

Then I tore it open. It said, "Decree granted at ten this morning. Charley." Nothing else, no regards, no regrets, no good-byes, not even the full ten words.

I crumpled it and threw it in the wastebasket, and then I went for a walk. I cannot remember exactly where I went. My memory started disintegrating a little more than three months ago, shortly after the headaches began.

However, around five-thirty I found myself seated among the tired and peculiar people who make use of Bryant Park, directly behind the New York Public Library.

As I sat there, I thought of the afternoon almost three years ago when Charley and I were in the park for the first time, listening to the library luncheon concert. One of the pieces was a special favorite of Charley's, "The Cuckoo and the Nightingale." Charley and I held hands while it was played—a small woman of thirty-five who at first glance might have seemed plain and a nearly middle-aged man wearing a beard and a look of hope and apprehension.

I don't know how Charley felt, but I felt foolish and incredulous. I felt amazed and grateful, and I was filled with such a sense of awe. Who me, I kept thinking, me loved and loving? Oh, there must be some mistake here. The mistake will be rectified; such mistakes always are, but for the moment, for however many moments, I am grateful. I give thanks.

I remember Charley giggling rather girlishly and saying, "Let's go to Paris on our honeymoon; I've never been, and I can't think of anybody I'd rather go with." I said, "Is that the reason you're marrying me?" "One of the reasons," she said.

I remember that on that sultry summer afternoon three years ago I also prayed, to God and to the gods, that I would not fail Charley.

Yesterday, I finally admitted what has been apparent for some time. Except to me. Except to the leading non-facer of facts in this non-fact-facing time.

I failed Charley all right. I failed her as completely as I have failed every human being whose path has through some unlucky accident crossed mine. Including me. Oh, especially including me.

Yesterday, I thought, "I cannot love; therefore, I am not."

And I had that feeling of total abasement I have read about but never before experienced. I felt a complete collapse of self-esteem, and I knew what I have to do. I left unanswered the question of whether I will have the courage.

Yesterday, smelling of decay and defeat and humiliation, my thoughts were interrupted, *allegro vivace*, by the angry voice of a woman.

I looked up. The woman, who had the face of a befuddled cockatoo, was standing a little away from me, her sparse gray hair in wild disorder. She was shaking her fist at me, and on her thin, speckled arm was a great grease-stained purse out of which poked a graying, somewhat mangled half of a ham on rye.

"I know who you are," the woman shouted at me. "I recognize your kind. Every time."

A few people turned and looked at me, not many. Almost everyone in Bryant Park at that time of day has some disreputable activity of his own to attend to.

Nevertheless, I rose quickly and started out of the park, the woman's voice pursuing me.

"You can't fool me with a false beard," she screamed. "It isn't even a *good* false beard."

I walked away from the sound of late-summer madness, to the corner of Fortieth Street and Fifth Avenue, then stopped, looked behind me, and saw that the woman had not followed.

After that I laughed for a moment, and then I cried.

By the time I got back to my office, I decided that I was quite capable of taking my own life. Two questions remained, how and when.

I was surprised then and as I speak these words I am still surprised at how easily I made up my mind. Decisions come hard for me. In the morning I often find it difficult to decide which pair of socks to wear. I've often spent as much as half an hour just looking into my sock drawer, and I've sometimes compromised by wearing one each of two pairs.

After the sock decision, there is the egg decision. I never know whether to ask Louella to boil, bake, scramble or fry them.

Which will it be—vanilla or strawberry? Catsup or mustard? Rare or medium? Large or small? Decisions. Decisions. Decisions.

Why? Oh, I know *why*. I've spent thousands of hours and more thousands of dollars for expert guidance into the dark reasons for my indecisiveness, but what none of them—Adlerian, Jungian, or Freudian—has been able to tell me is how to stop.

Or how to love.

Anyhow, as I said, yesterday I made the most fundamental decision of my life in the few minutes it took me to walk from Fifth Avenue and Fortieth to my office, between Park and Lexington on Thirty-fourth.

Since it is no longer necessary to worry about lung cancer, I found a pack of cigarettes in my desk, lighted one, and inhaled. My first cigarette in months. Only an eye as familiar and expert as mine would have noticed the slight trembling of my hands.

I sat at my desk for a while. I had turned off the air-conditioner, and through the open window came the gentle sounds of an early August evening in the Murray Hill district.

Someplace a girl laughed. A boy with a prep-school voice said that he would be home after the second feature, and a woman's voice, old, cracked, yet mellowed, too, said, "I wish to *Christ* I could believe in some damn god or other."

I agreed, cherished the blasphemy, and waited for more, but there was no more.

(2) The list

Then I started a list.

I am a great list-maker. This habit comes from the fact that at an early age I became aware that whatever other qualities my mind might or might not have, its analytic ability was limited.

Yesterday on a piece of memo paper I wrote, *Item Number One*, and under that, *Benny the Philosopher*.

I'll tell about Benny first because he happened first. Monday week. This is a Saturday.

I was coming out of one of those restaurants in the East Fifties where they know how to attract celebrities and to overcharge but where they know nothing whatever about food.

Just outside the door, I was stopped by a sad, slack-jawed little derelict, male, pimpled, and no chin. At nine or thereabouts he had had life, and life had had him.

He pushed his underfed body against my leg, holding a stub of a pencil at the ready, keeping his black-rimmed thumb between the pages of a dilapidated autograph book.

"Hi, mister," he said, looking hopefully at me. "You anybody?"

Two girls, one of whom had blackheads on her forehead, leaned toward me, not expecting much.

"I'm afraid not," I said, and then, the look on the boy's face being so disappointed, I added, "I'm sorry," and I walked on.

Behind me, I heard one of the girls say, "Benny, with a beard like that if he was anybody, you'd *know*."

And the voice of Benny said, "I know, but you have to be careful. Van Johnson almost got away from me that time."

Benny's question has been haunting me ever since. Socrates couldn't have put it more succinctly.

I have kept answering Benny's question, too. I have kept saying to myself, "No, Benny. Nobody. Nobody at all."

I have said, "Nobody here but us nobodies, Benny."

Item Number Two. A week ago yesterday—on Friday afternoon—a young woman came to the apartment I keep on East Sixty-third. She is on the staff of a high-fashion magazine for girls which contains a small amount of editorial matter to separate a few of the advertisements.

She is not a pretty girl; they almost never are. She is too large and does not know how to handle it; she wore a suit that was well-cut but was too masculine, and her hair was too short, the horn-rimmed glasses too large. She gave the impression that if she hadn't been able to get into publishing, she could certainly have found an opening in professional wrestling.

She asked a great many questions, and a great many pictures were taken by another girl who was almost the same girl. The latter kept taking all kinds of crotch shots of me, and I kept thinking she was going to ask me to show her a little more leg.

The magazine was taking another look at six men—I was one—whose photographs had appeared in its pages shortly after the end of the Second World War; we had called ourselves The Crusaders, and if you stick around there'll be more about that. The magazine—this was in early 1946—called us, "Today's Hopefuls—Tomorrow's Leaders."

Anyway, Miss Callous—if that's what her name is—leaned toward me and, in a voice that reminded me of my neighbor Arthur Grayson calling in the cows for milking, she said, "Mr. Bland, how do you explain the fact that you didn't live up to your early promise?"

I doubt that that magazine will print my answer, but I see no reason why that girl shouldn't go straight to the top in the magazine business. She's got what I'd call one of the prime requirements, no empathy.

Item Number Three, which will take a little longer. This one has to do with saints.

On Monday of this week I got a letter from Jim Harkus, M.D., something, something Main Street, Niles, Michigan, and I thought, seeing it, who is Jim Harkus, and I thought the only person I ever heard of who came from Niles, Michigan, was Ring Lardner, who also did not live up to his early promise.

When I opened the letter, I remembered.

It said:

My wife and I and ye-gods five (count them) small Harkuses, three female, two male, are coming to New York in a couple of weeks. We are on our way to Tanganyika. No, not on vacation. We're going to *live* there. The *why* will take some telling, but right now all I can say is that I've given up my practice here in Niles and am going to try to help out there. I gather the natives are in desperate need of a doctor. Fortunately, I have an amenable wife and adventurous kids. As I say, I'll tell you all about it when I see you—if I see you. May I? Despite the fact that (I warn you) I'm coming begging? By the way, I immodestly assume you'll remember me. Do you?

As ever,
Jim Harkus

On Monday, after I read Jim's letter, I sat for a long time thinking about the day he and I met.

I was nine years old. Jim must have been eighteen or nineteen.

I had just become the Iowa winner of something I'm going to call the Harvey Jordan O'Connor Cranium Derby. Believe me, the real name was even more preposterous.

There were photographers in the living room of our house on Riverdale Avenue in New Athens, Iowa.

Mother was momentarily out of the room. I can't imagine why. She almost never left the room when there were photographers around.

Anyway, one of the photographers, from the *Cedar Rapids Gazette*, I believe, said to me, "You'll wear your brains out before you're eighteen, sonny boy."

People were always telling me I'd wear my brains out before I grew up, and it always seemed to make them happy.

Another photographer said, "The kid's probably a nance. They always are."

I had a vocabulary of nearly twelve thousand words at that time, but *nance* was not among them. I forget how I found out what it meant, but I did.

An extremely tall boy from the newspaper of a college I'm calling Pegasus leaned down from an immense height and winked at me. He looked at the other photographers and said, "You leave this kid alone. He's got more I.Q. in his little finger than the rest of us put together've got in our heads." Then he placed a large, reassuring hand on my shoulder. He said his name was Jim Harkus, and he said, "They're just envious."

After that, he smiled again and said, "But knowing people's motivations for being cruel is rather cold comfort, isn't it?"

I said that it was, and I looked carefully at him. He must have been six-three, and he had a smallish head on top of a long, awkward body. The neck made him look like an uneasy giraffe. Occasionally, his eyes glanced down at his lanky body as if to make sure it was still there.

His hair was thick and stubborn, and it grew like prairie grass all over the back of his neck.

His mouth was too small for the size of his face; his nose was too large, but when you penetrated beneath the jungle of his thick, joined eyebrows and the long lashes, you saw that his eyes were compassionate. And his smile—well, I have known only one other like it. Charley's. Both always momentarily convinced me that there was nobody else in the world so deserving of warmth and affection and understanding as I was.

Jim played the bassoon in the college orchestra, and his voice was rather like the instrument. You heard it rarely, but when you did, the sound surprised and pleased you. Me anyway.

However, when I was nine years old, I at first noticed only that Jim was ugly. Naturally, I said so. I said, "You're really quite unattractive, aren't you?"

Jim admitted it. "Does it bother you?" he asked.

"No," I said. "Ugly people are nicer than good-looking people as a general rule. You seem nice, but it's too early to tell. It's been my experience that contrary to the popular belief, first impressions are wrong more often than not."

Jim laughed, his eyes first and then his mouth, almost as an afterthought. I was impressed with that because I'd already noticed that with most people it was the other way around, if, in fact, their eyes joined in at all.

"Oh my, oh my," said Jim. "How is it that somebody didn't slug you years ago?"

"More than a few have considered it," I said. "Many more than a few."

"What're you going to do with all that I.Q.?" he asked.

People often asked me questions like that, usually because they felt they had to say *something* to me, and it wasn't easy to know just what.

But I felt Jim Harkus really wanted to know.

I said, "I'd like very much to become a saint. I've been reading *Lives of the Saints* and *The Varieties of Religious Experience*. The latter is by William James. He's a philosopher."

"Yes, I know," said Jim.

I blushed. I often blushed in those days.

"I'm sorry," I said. "That's one of my worst faults, assuming everybody else is an ignoramus. Forgive me."

Jim said that he would.

"At the moment, I happen to believe in God," I said, "incredible as that may seem."

Jim said that that didn't seem incredible to him, and he asked if there was any saint I wanted to be like.

"I think Saint Francis," I said, "although I have to admit his hygienic habits leave a great deal to be desired."

Jim must have said something to that. I can't remember what, though. I do remember that he asked if I went to church.

"Not really," I said. "I've shopped around a lot, but none of them seems to give me much. The Catholics seem to me the most spiritual, but I don't approve of most things they have stood for politically through the ages. I like the Unitarian minister quite a bit, Dr. Worthy, but he hardly ever talks about Jesus or God. It's usually about William Howard Taft or Senator LaFollette or somebody like that."

"I'm president of the Methodist Epworth League," said Jim. "Would you like to come on Sunday?"

I said that I would, and I did, but my friendship with the League didn't last long. The members of both sexes all wore steel-rimmed glasses, or so it seems to me now, and the glasses were often bent; the League members either looked at you from above their glasses or from below them. Either gave me the heebie jeebies. The girls were as ignorant of the use of the comb as the girls I came across many years later sitting around those lackluster coffeehouses in San Francisco. The boys in the Epworth League all wore a plentiful supply of dandruff. A few were planning to be ministers, and they were already working on their ecclesiastical monotones. Moist palms seemed to be a requirement of membership—Jim Harkus being the exception. These people were the kind of dolts who would have thought the books written by my enemy and neighbor (you'll meet him) were spiritual books, which they are not.

Jim Harkus would have spotted my neighbor as a flatulent fraud on first meeting, but Jim would have suffered him. Jim suffered many fools when I knew him, not gladly but with patience. Jim suffered little children, and he suffered me, whatever I was.

My friendship with Jim lasted until he was graduated and went back to Michigan. I remember I cried. I believe I knew then that in my whole life I'd never meet anybody nearly as kind as he was.

I saw him once more, in Germany, shortly after the war ended, at an army installation near Nuremberg. Jim and I had dinner at the officers' mess. Jim was a major in the medics; he had been with the First Division through Africa, Sicily, and all the way across from Normandy.

After dinner, we went outside to take a walk through the town. There was a long line of Germans, mostly old women and children, waiting near the garbage dump. The mess sergeant looked at them and then, with slow deliberation, poured gasoline over the garbage and lighted it. When a little boy tried to reach his hands into the flame, the mess sergeant started kicking at him, but Jim was there by then.

That evening in Nuremberg was the last I knew or heard of Jim for more than fourteen years, until his letter arrived last Monday. I sent him a check of some size and dictated a letter to him, wishing him and his family well in Africa. I said that, unfortunately, I would be out of the city while they were there, and so on.

"Too bad you can't see him," said my secretary Pan when I finished dictating the letter. "He sounds nice."

"Goddamn it, Pan," I said. "If I want your advice, I'll ask for it."

I saw the sudden sparkle of tears in Pan's eyes, and I said, "I'm sorry, I didn't mean to hurt your feelings."

"You haven't," said Pan. "You haven't hurt my feelings for quite a long time now."

So much for *Item Three*, which has to do with Jim Harkus and sainthood. Jim isn't a saint, of course, but for this place and this time, he comes close enough.

What ever happened to me, do you suppose? Where am I?

Item Number Four. This one has to do with the lunch I had day before yesterday with George Banning, artists' representative. I've known George since the far-off days when he was George Bansky the agent.

As usual, George bought the lunch, which was at Chambord.

While we were eating the magnificent food, George said, "Have you made up your mind about Shawn's play?"

I shook my head.

"What'd you think of it?" asked George.

"George," I said. "Stop it."

"All right, I've stopped. I just thought maybe you'd given up this—temporary insanity."

...I should explain here that for fourteen years now I have been in The Theater; I have been a producer. At least five years ago I realized that I was going through motions and that the motions were familiar and fatiguing. I realized that inertia, fatigue, and an increasing degree of hostility had taken the place of what at best had been no more than a mild enthusiasm for the way I made my living. It took me five years to do anything about it, and then after a series of disasters that were neither estimable nor profitable, and after Charley left me—which took the last of what was left of the juices in me—I announced that I was taking a sabbatical. A polite way of saying that I was through with the whole bloody mess. Russell Grierson, a man I once befriended in a desperate hour—an act for which he will understandably never forgive me—is taking over Joshua Bland Enterprises, Inc., and he is welcome to them. They deserve each other. And that's enough about the background of the lunch George and I had on Thursday....

"...insanity," said George. "There's no other word to describe it."

I said, "The papers will be drawn up on the fifteenth; and I am signing them that afternoon, and then I am taking off like a big-assed bird. But tomorrow is my last day at the office. So henceforth you will be dealing with my present partner and my successor."

"Grierson a producer," said George.

"Oh, indeed. He has every qualification. I remember exactly what you said those qualifications were when I got back from the wars in August 1945. I asked you what a producer did—and you said—"

"Please," said George. "There are certain past mistakes of yours I could mention."

"I think Russell will be a perfect producer. You'll both get very rich."

"Russell Grierson is a client of mine," said George, "so don't quote me, but—Russell Grierson is stupid, insensitive, and utterly without taste."

"That's exactly it," I said. "He will be a perfect producer. He will produce plays about nuns and Negroes and God and about how nuns and Negroes and God are just like anybody else once you get to know them; many of these plays will be in blank verse, and since you can't knock Negroes, nuns, God, or plays in blank verse I predict he will win all of the critics' awards. I see no reason at all—"

"Stop it," said George.

"Okay. I've stopped."

"And you still persist in this Nepal foolishness."

I nodded; you see, I have passage on a jet for India next Saturday, the 15th; I have always wanted to go to Nepal, which I am told is the most beautiful spot on earth. I wanted to see it before the end came (its and mine)—but I won't be on that plane on the 15th.

As I've said, I decided yesterday that I shall be taking off on a somewhat longer trip of indefinite duration.

"You'll be back in a week," said George. "A month. Six weeks at most."

I just sat there, and after a while George said, "Your trouble was you approached the theater as a shrine."

"If there is one thing I have never done, it is approach the theater as a shrine," I said. "An overpriced bordello, yes; a shrine, no."

"A shrine," said George. "All these plays by the German—what's-his-name. I never could remember. German names keep slipping my mind. All this how the world's going to hell in a breadbasket. No wonder you lost money hand over fist. What people want in the theater is a lot of girls or a lot of boys taking off their clothes. Am I right?"

"Indeed, yes," I said. "There's enough trouble in the world without having to go to the theater to see it."

George reached across and patted my hand. "You sonofabitch, I love you," he said.

"But you don't understand me."

"Not even remotely," said George, "though I understand this. You've always wanted to run away. When I first met you, when you were in the Army—how old were you? Eighteen? Twenty? You had New York at your feet, so to speak, but you couldn't wait to get back to Camp Whatyoumacallit in North Carolina. And when you got back from whatever you were doing in Europe, fighting or something, you got that play on the stage and right away you want to go straight back to Iowa, Ohio, whatever it's called. You spoke of getting yourself a doctor of philosophy degree. I brought you to this very restaurant for dinner, and I said, 'Josh, dear boy, what's your hurry? You're twenty-three years old. First make yourself a little cash money while the iron is still hot. Wait a year, maybe two.' You remember?"

"No, but if you want to remember it that way, I think it's fine."

"Well," said George, "the truth of the matter is you hadn't any intention of going in for a Ph.D. You were already hooked. You had on that cashmere jacket and a sea-island cotton shirt and tailor-made shoes, and I knew that you were not about to take off for someplace where you might work up to a salary of ninety-eight cents a year by the time you were sixty-five."

I laughed, and during the next few minutes George said almost everything I expected him to say as well as a few things I didn't expect. He said that my finances were in the worst shape they had ever been, not true but not unexpected. He said again that he did not understand me, also not unexpected and not true. George understands me very well, and he always has.

He said, "The contemplation of the navel has never interested me. I can't understand why it interests you."

He said, "Which are you going to be, Zen-Buddhist, a Yogi, a Beat?"

He said, "I realize, of course, that I am speaking to a child of thirty-seven. Look, darling [George recently returned from a month Out There], look, the last client of mine who took time off to look into his true nature was pulling down three hundred thousand dollars per annum not more than five years ago. You know where he is now? He has the twelve-to-three A.M. shift as disk jockey on a 250-watt radio station in San Luis Obispo, California."

He said, "Another four years, the way things are going, you'll be a rich man. You can spend the rest of your life searching for the ultimate truth. You can let your hair grow; you've already got the beard. You can take to the streets wearing sandals and a toga and carrying a sandwich board proclaiming what you have discovered. Most prophets need a rich widow to provide them with lichee nuts. You won't. You can sprinkle lichee nuts on your filet mignon. You'll be a rich prophet, a well-to-do wise man. People will know at a glance that you are wise because you can buy your togas at Sulka."

I nodded to the waiter, who refilled my demitasse.

"Believe me," said George. "I have been through this many, many times. I have held the hands of a great many of my clients while they were going through it. You are simply passing through male menopause, a period during which a man suddenly realizes that he has finished the major part of his life, that he is not immortal. Faced with this humbling thought, he occasionally makes up his mind to examine his navel, or he starts pinching an occasional bottom or takes a mistress, or starts drinking a little too much.

"For you I would suggest a third, charming try at matrimony. In the meantime—" George paused delicately—"I suggest a few days' rest. Take a few grains of Nembutal for a few nights."

"I've been doing that every night for five years now," I said, "the sleeping pills at night, the pep-up pills in the morning."

George sighed largely. "Maybe you'll change agents," he said. "It's part of the pattern. They come to me penniless and obscure. They say, 'Make me rich, Mr. Banning. Make me famous, if you please.' With some little co-operation from them, I do exactly that. Then along about menopause time, they abandon their latest headshrinker. They find Zen isn't all it was cracked up to be. They snap on a chastity belt, and they blame me for leading them away from The Actors Studio where their necks may have been dirty but their hearts were pure.

"If they're writers, they scream that if I hadn't corrupted them with a lousy swimming pool and a six-figure bank account and the kids at Groton and Yale and Bennington they'd be up for the Nobel Prize.

"Naturally, I have to be made to pay for said corruption. So they break their contracts with me, and after a short, disappointing run down the road to Damascus, they end up in the virginal arms of the William Morris Agency or the Music Corporation of America."

George motioned for the check and, as always, signed it without looking at it and, as always, overtipped the waiter.

"Myself, of course, I have none of these problems," he went on. "I am a barbarian. When I hear a young lady speak of her libido—as young ladies often do these days—I pretend to believe she is talking about an undergarment."

He sighed. "It was not always thus," he said. "In my youth I, too, was concerned with deeper meanings. When I was at N.Y.U., I used to wander around Washington Square at lunchtime—eager, energetic, argumentative. Why, there were times when, if no other possibilities were open to me, I'd stop somebody I'd never seen before and say, 'What about God? Take either side.'"

George leaned back and put a cigarette in the outrageous-looking holder he has been using lately. He didn't light the cigarette. He never does.

"Now except on those rare occasions when I am having lunch with a client *and* a friend," he said, making a bow in my direction, "I speak not of God but of Mammon. When I am having lunch with a producer from Out There, I say, 'At the mention of the figure one hundred thousand dollars, my client would laugh in your face.'"

George drew in on the unlighted cigarette. "I am no longer nineteen," he said, "and neither are you."

As he and I walked to the door of the Chambord, several waiters bowed, very low.

On the street, while we waited for cabs, George said, "I don't think I've mentioned this before, but I, too, once lusted for a Ph.D. I was a philosophy major."

He paused, thinking of it. Then he said, "Why don't you ask me what happened?"

"All right. What happened?"

George gave a short laugh. "Well, my father died, and after the funeral expenses were paid, his estate amounted to nine dollars and fifty-four cents, five pairs of pants customers hadn't called for, and a half-finished double-breasted suit not my size. Besides, I had met Shirley, who was also a student at N.Y.U., majoring in overthrowing the government, with a minor in picketing. We hopped into bed one night after Shirley convinced me that Clifford Odets and Karl Marx were the voices of the future. We got married; within six months, Jon was born, and I got the only job available at the moment, in the office of Fred Herman, actors' agent. In the beginning, I was going to devote my evenings to study. I still hoped to get my degree. I did study, too, for all of three months, but during that time I discovered that in the line of work I was in charm is more important than wisdom, so I began cultivating charm. It has paid off very, very handsomely."

"No regrets?" I asked.

"I leave the breast-beating and the soul-searching to my clients."

George made another short bow in my direction.

"Besides," he went on, "I don't despise money. I don't say it's the most important thing in the world, but, believe me, it's way ahead of whatever's next on the list. What's more, if they ever start up the bake ovens again, I'd like enough money to buy off the head baker. You know how I am about heat."

The doorman, who was holding the cab door open, gave George a look, and George gave him a dollar bill.

"To repeat, I predict you'll be back in the fray in a couple of weeks," George said. "You're too old to turn philosopher. You've been too old for about sixteen years now. Besides, kid, you never were a fellow that was satisfied to go around in a barrel, carrying a lantern."

He paused a moment, then said, "You know what your trouble is?"

Paraphrasing a speech from a play I wish I had produced—as if I hadn't already lost enough money that year—I said, "No, George, tell me what my trouble is."

"Your trouble is you should have been a preacher," said George. "You're always lecturing people on how they ought to shape up, and the only trouble is—"

I interrupted quickly. "The theater is not a pulpit," I said. "I know. I've been told."

"*Russell Grierson*," said George. "I'd rather do business with the commandant of Auschwitz."

I said, "I'll see you and Russ on the fifteenth then and don't be calling me all the time because I've got a lot of stuff to get ready, and don't be late because I've got a plane to catch."

"I am never late," said George. He touched me affectionately, another habit he picked up Out There. They are all big touchers Out There, but there isn't an ounce of affection in a carload of them. The reason people Out There touch you is that they want to see how tender you'll be when they get ready to eat you alive.

But this is not the place for my sermonette on Out There.

George got into the cab and was driven off. I stood on the sidewalk for a moment, watching.

So much for *Item Number Four*. Meaning? Why, that George confirmed what I already knew. It is too late for me to change. It has been too late for a very long time.

On Thursday I was not quite ready to face what you might call the ultimate fact. As I said, that came yesterday, shortly after I left Bryant Park.

Item Number Five, the last, also happened on Thursday afternoon. After I got back from Chambord, my secretary Pan came into my office. She was doing a word game; she is nearly always doing a word game. Pan is a great self-improver. This fall she will enroll in at least two courses at the New School, and she is studying Esperanto or something like that with the Berlitz folks, and she is studying guitar, and she regular-paints on Thursdays, and she fingerpaints on Fridays, and she is one of the most skilled game players of our time. She is also a pretty good secretary.

Anyway, Thursday afternoon she was doing a word game, and she said, "I've got one for you. What is the meaning of *insouciance*? That's one *everybody* gets wrong."

"What does *everybody* say?"

"*Almost* everybody says it means perky, lively, or sprightly, and Mr. Russell Grierson, your esteemed partner and successor, said it means officious."

"Mr. Russell Grierson, my partner and successor, is officious," I said. "*Officious* means volunteering one's services, or disposed to volunteer one's services where they are neither asked for nor needed, and that is Mr. Grierson all over. *Insouciance*, on the other hand, means want of concern, indifference, especially as an attitude of mind."

Pan said, "If anybody had told me I would end up working for an aging Quiz Kid, I would have shot anybody."

"I wasn't a Quiz Kid," I said. "It was called, 'Can You Top Them?' and I am only about thirty-five."

"Thirty-five is a very popular age this year," said Pan. "Practically every man I meet is thirty-five. It seems only yesterday that they were all thirty."

"Thirty-five," I said.

"Aging," said Pan.

At the door she turned and, trying to keep the emotion out of her voice, said, "Well, I say now what if I'd been in my right mind I'd have said on the first day I met you, some fourteen years ago. I say good-bye, Mr. Bland."

"I'll be in tomorrow. Won't you?"

"Uh-uh. I won't be in at all any more. I have quit."

"Pan, what's all this? We've been through all this before. You and Russ will get along all right. I've told you. Once you get to know him well, he's no more than despicable."

"Yes, I do remember your saying that. I remember your saying so many things. One sentence in particular. You said, 'I've never told anybody I loved them unless I meant it.' That was quite a sentence. I have sent it off to Bartlett's."

I rose and walked to where she was, but Pan eluded me.

"I think you're kidding," I said, knowing better.

"I'm not even married," said Pan. "I was just waiting for an excuse, and a couple of days ago Russ's wife entered the office, scented with frankincense and myrrh and the cloying odor of money, and she stood over my desk, all three graceless tons of her. She said, 'Get me Elizabeth Arden on the phone.' I said what I've often thought of saying but not said. I said—well, it's really too vulgar for your tender ears, but considering the size of everything visible about the lady, I see no reason why it wouldn't be a perfect fit. Then I quit."

After a moment, I said, "Pan, Russ didn't say anything about your quitting."

"I know. He was all set to go to Washington, where as one of the rulers and shakers of this proud era he is in charge of the committee to get everything in the hands of five or six people, and I told him to say nothing to you. I wanted to save that pleasure for myself, and I wanted to save it for last so that I wouldn't have to watch you go through all the nauseous motions of pretending to care."

Pan was crying, but when I tried to put my arm around her, she said, "I'd rather you wouldn't."

"I'm sorry," I said.

"There are very few things I'd have been willing to bet on, but that you'd say you were sorry was one of them."

"Pan, you mean you've been sitting in that office out there all these years, hating me?"

"Nope," said Pan. "I'm not what you'd call one of your big haters. I know that because I've been associated with an expert. No, for a long time I sat in that outer office loving you and hoping—silly girl—that you'd—well, change your mind. But not lately. Lately I haven't hoped, and I haven't been in love with you. What I have been is indifferent to you. I think that if they get up any competition to find the prize bastard of the world you ought to enter, because you'd at least get a very honorable mention. I think that, and I pity you, but that's all. That is absolutely all."

"I wish I'd known," I said.

Pan smiled at me. "I guess it's a good thing you think so."

"Pan, our extra-curricular—it's been over for more than five years now."

"Oh, indeed, and I'm not blaming you. I was over twenty-one, and no force was required on your part. No, my trouble was and still is that I'm willing to settle for the crumbs that drop off other people's tables."

She opened the door, and she said, "And don't say you'll be seeing me, because you won't. Not, as they say in Grand Island, Nebraska, which is where I come from, if I see you first."

I thought that that was Pan's exit line, but it wasn't. The last words she said were these: "If I didn't know better, I'd think they invented the word *insouciance* to describe you."

And that is the end of *Item Number Five*, which I'll call *The Meaning of Insouciance*.

You can see what I mean. They don't give it to you in dribs and drabs. Oh, no. They store these things up so you can have it all at once. These people, whoever they are, are very clever. They forget nothing.

But, getting back to yesterday afternoon, after writing down the five items I've just mentioned, I folded the sheet of memo paper and put it in my pocket.

I went through my desk, finding only one item I wanted to take with me, a letter from my daughter Taffy. I put that in my wallet.

I thought, How strange that after ten years in a room, there is nothing except one letter that I care about.

I thought, The walls are covered with pictures of a large number of people whose names are almost all Household Words, and all of them have autographed their pictures for me and have written messages proclaiming in one extravagant way or another that until they met me their lives were drab indeed. And I thought, There isn't one of them who on hearing that I have dropped out of the race will say much more than, "Oh? How did he do it?" Then they will all say something like, "Well, I never liked him anyway. Let's talk about *me*."

I looked at the photographs of all those prosperous and famous and always dissatisfied Household Words, including the one of the woman to whom I was married before I married Charley. I said, "So long, you worthless bastards."

I closed the door of what had been my office, and I locked it.

Then for the last time I left the house on Thirty-fourth Street.

Maybe you saw a picture of it in the white man's *Ebony*, lots of pictures. I was interviewed four or five years ago by a reportress from that publication, which is edited on the theory that one picture is worth a thousand words. Not so. None of the pictures in that magazine is worth a damn.

Anyway, this reportress wrote, "The brownstone house in the Murray Hill district of New York which is business headquarters for Joshua Bland is a reflection of his personality. More like a series of living rooms really."

I read that, and then I read it again, and then I said, not aloud (I hadn't started talking to myself yet), "Yes, yes, go on."

But that was all. That was it. Gives you something to think about, doesn't it? I've got a personality like a series of living rooms. Really.

She quoted me as saying, "Toots, when I was nine years old, my name appeared in a crossword puzzle in *The New York Times*. I was thirty-six horizontal. At the age of fourteen I was thirty-nine vertical in *The Chicago Tribune*, and not a hell of a lot of any importance has happened to me since."

The reportress hinted that I had been t-i-p-p-l-i-n-g. She didn't come right out and say so; she *hinted*. They're always *hinting* in that magazine.

Anyway, for the benefit of those who happened to see the pictures of my office and the simple words accompanying them, I hadn't been t-i-p-p-l-i-n-g. I had prepared for that interview by having a long talk with one of my oldest and best friends, a fellow by the name of Jack Daniel.

By the time the reportress arrived, I couldn't have pronounced *insouciance* for love or money. Especially not for love. I was stoned. I was d-r-u-n-k.

But to get back to yesterday afternoon, because that is what I was talking about when I started getting into what's wrong with the white man's *Ebony* and/or *Burden*.

After leaving my office, I walked to Grand Central, taking my time, watching the incredible number of people who on a humid evening in mid-August managed to appear happy, some of them even joyous.

A man of sixty or so who was wearing a handsome coconut straw hat spoke softly to a woman who was surely his wife. She smiled back. A girl who looked as if nothing had ever disappointed her leaned over and kissed the boy she was with. The boy looked contented.

It occurred to me then that I would never return to the city which, as you will see, has played so large a part in my life, but there was nothing I wanted to look at again, nobody I wanted to see.

Nothing in it belonged to me, and there was nothing to which I belonged, and nobody—which is the way with New York, I suppose. It is a city of displaced persons.

It is a city in which there are thousands of girls like Pan, now an admitted thirty-four, a refugee from a boy who was studying veterinary medicine at the University of Nebraska, who, according to Pan, was a very clean boy but who always smelled ever so slightly of sheep dip and, also unfortunately, admired the novels of Lloyd C. Douglas, while Pan was at the time an admirer—or said she was—of the early Henry James. Pan's nose is less sensitive now, and she would gladly adjust to the smell of sheep dip if only someone would ask her. Pan's bathroom in the one-room apartment on East Twenty-ninth Street is papered with old-fashioned comic valentines, and on a magazine rack beside the stool are copies of *Esquire* and *Playboy* and *Atlantic* and *Harper's*, and the trouble is that the only unmarried men Pan now knows prefer *Vogue*. And the married ones, according to Pan, "...talk a good divorce, but the minute you start suggesting, 'How about getting started, say, tomorrow?' off they go to Norwalk on the five-oh-seven, back to Freda Frigid and the kids."

What Pan said to me yesterday afternoon was no surprise. I knew all along that when, six years ago, I asked Pan to hop into bed with me, she thought I meant for keeps, or hoped as much. And I lied, of course; every time the word *love* has passed my lips, it has been a lie. Except once, and then it was too late.

There are a lot of me in The City, too. Hell a city much like Seville, as the Spanish say? Don't be silly. I've been in Seville.

Hell is Manhattan, between, say, Thirty-fourth and Fifty-ninth. Hell will hold no surprises for me, although I do hope they don't have Second Empire furniture in my cell, as Sartre says they sometimes do. Mine will be glass, I predict, a glass cell in the midst of an enchanted forest, and all the people I have spoken of love to, but not loved, will look in on me. They will not speak; they will only stare, and a woman named Elisia, whose dream I destroyed, will destroy me, over and over, day after day, forever.

Oh, yes, there are a lot of me in the Hell area of Manhattan, non-lovers who cannot love and know they cannot but who keep on testing. Testing, one, two, three, four. Testing, one, two, three, four....

On the northeast corner of Forty-second and Lex last evening, I threw the keys to my desk, my office, and the filing cabinet into the sewer opening. Let Russell Grierson sweat a little. Let Mr. Officious Himself in Person sweat a lot.

I stopped at the Doubleday shop on the Lexington side of Grand Central and bought a novel. I helped the clerk lift it off the table. He was tired; they are always tired.

At a newsstand I bought copies of each of what in New York in the afternoons pass for newspapers.

I got on the six-forty-five train, seating myself next to a perspiring fat man who had the face of a discredited angel. He said, not to me but in my direction, "I could of stayed right there in the cool Men's Bar at the Biltmore, and Mildred knows goddamn good and well I could of."

He said it a second time; then he fell into a sputtering slumber which lasted all the way to Valhalla. A solidly built, unsettlingly ugly woman who must have been Mildred waited for him by a Buick station wagon. She looked as if she knew everything goddamn good and well, and the minute she saw him she started telling him some of what she knew.

After that, I was alone on the seat.

And then, just this side of Chappaqua, an odd and disturbing incident occurred.

I was not dozing. I can no longer sleep without a pill.

Yet quite suddenly at seven forty-five last evening, I had what must have been a dream. A hallucination, then.

What happened was this:

I looked out the window of the coach, and the train was no longer on its way through the upper, richer reaches of Westchester. It was no longer a humid evening in August. It was a bright morning in April, and through the window I saw the sunbathed, blue-green hills of England.

In this dream—if it was a dream—I was sixteen and hopeful, not thirty-seven and finished. I was not on my way to a glass failure of a house where, when the time comes, I will end my life. I was on my way to spend a bank holiday with Professor Hollis Lindsay. Professor Lindsay taught me philosophy at the University of London and was the gentlest man and probably the best scholar I have ever known.

On that April morning more than twenty-one years ago I had in my hands a blue-bound copy of the collected poems of A. E. Housman, which I had bought a few hours earlier at a stall on Leicester Square.

I had chosen the Housman book as a house present for the Lindsays for the best possible reason. I wanted it for myself.

And on the long journey between London and Land's End, where the Lindsays had a summer place, I memorized all of "A Shropshire Lad." I thought that since I had to give the book away, at least no one could take those words from me.

Time did that, but at sixteen I was not familiar with its harsh demands.

Until last evening only four lines of "A Shropshire Lad" remained in my mind. That had been true for at least ten years, I'd say. Just these lines:

> This is the land of lost content,
> I see it shining plain,
> The happy highways where I went
> And cannot come again.

However, as I say, last evening, just this side of Chappaqua, a strange thing happened. First, I saw the limestone hills of Cornwall, and it was April. Then I looked at my hands and saw that they were no longer soft and old, no longer the hands of a man who indulges himself in a manicure twice a week. The hands I saw were those of a boy—brown, hard, somewhat dirty, the nails broken and unkempt.

And in them was not a current novel of no consequence. In them was a book of Housman poems, on the flyleaf of which was the stamp of the bookstore on Leicester Square.

I opened the phantom book to the first page, and there in clear Roman type were all the words I had thought were forever gone from my dwindling memory:

> From Clee to heaven the beacon burns,
> The skies have seen it plain,
> From north to south the sign returns
> And beacons burn again.

The entire poem was there on the ghost pages I held in my hands last evening, and the words are all in my memory now as I speak, down to:

> And fields will yearly bear them
> As light-leaved spring comes on,
> And luckless lads will wear them
> When I am dead and gone.

I cannot explain it.

Perhaps you can. Perhaps, when he listens to these tapes (as he surely will), Dr. Baron will be able to. He is the Adlerian, the one at the place in New Haven. He sat on a yellow chair, and I lay on a green couch, and there was a reproduction of a purple Picasso ceramic tacked to the bulletin board. The ceiling in his office was gray, and there was a stain in the shape of a snake or a ribbon, and I wanted Baron to die; I wanted that every day, but he didn't; he hasn't yet, and when I am gone, he will listen to these words, avidly.

But I digress; I digress. As one of the women who passed in and out of my life said, "Your whole life has been a digression, doll. All you never got to was the point."

Point: A dream or an hallucination on a filthy coach of the Harlem Division of the New York Central early last evening. What is amazing, unbelievable even, is the return of memory, particularly when these days I can almost never remember anybody else's name and sometimes am none too sure of my own.

Oh, well. It doesn't matter. I mention the Housman hallucination because it is another indication of what has been happening to me since shortly after Charley left me seven weeks ago.

(3) Sloane's Station—churches nearby

Last evening the spell was broken when the harsh, angry voice of the conductor announced that we had arrived in Sloane's Station, near which is the house of glass where I am now dictating these words.

As the conductor spoke, "Sloane's Sta-shun. Sloane's STA-shun," I looked once more at my hands. The imaginary Housman book was gone. In its place was the novel I'd bought at the Doubleday shop in Grand Central. The hands I saw were once more middle-aged, soft, and white. They were the hands of a man who had grown indifferent.

I rose, managing to avoid the eye of my enemy and neighbor, a fellow I'm calling the Rev. Pism C. Jackson. The name comes from a study of American names made by H. L. Mencken: "...the prize discovery is Pism C. Jackson—named by a devout mother after the Hundredth Psalm (Psalm C)."

Pism C. had been staring at me. Was it possible I had been reciting "A Shropshire Lad" aloud? Could he know? Had he guessed? The man is a cretin, of *course*, but cretins and children are often the most dangerous of all.

One thing sure. Pism C. will be glad when I'm gone. Pism C. has publicly and (I'm told) privately said that I am a dangerous element in Sloane's Station, a village near which live a lot of people so fancy that they can feel a pea through four mattresses, the kind of people who want a table for two for one.

What Pism C. means by saying I am dangerous is that I wrote a letter to *The Sloane's Station Banner* saying that despite the word from Wonderland, D.C., Strontium 90 isn't really awfully good for you.

Naturally, Hermia Brader at *The Banner* refused to print that letter. So I had it privately printed in White Plains and left contraband copies all over town, in Poole's Drugs and Sundries, in the supermarket, at Loretta's Diner, and so on.

As I say, Pism C. was staring at me on the train last evening; I decided, however, that even if I had been reciting the Housman aloud, he wouldn't have heard. He is another of the "Let's talk about *me*" fellows. In his life he has never heard any voice but his own.

Last evening I avoided his eye, and he avoided mine and preceded me off the train.

I watched while his chauffeur opened the door of his cream-colored Thunderbird, and while Pism C. worked his fat body through the door. The chauffeur reverentially closed the door behind him. Louella says that in her circles the chauffeur is called Uncle Tom. He lives in a two-room cabin in Silver Span, which is owned lock, stock, and barrel by Pism C. Uncle Tom, who gladly pays a hundred and fifty dollars' rent every month, wishes they hadn't abolished slavery. For that matter, so does Pism C.

Anyway, Uncle Tom drove off, and Pism C. leaned back on the leopard-skin upholstery and closed his eyes, his lips moving.

Pism C. was not praying; I can assure you of that.

He was probably calculating the day's take, church-wise, book-wise, Wall Street-wise, real-estate-wise, widow-and-orphan-wise. The reverend wouldn't stoop so low as to accept a mite from a widow, but he might let one of his more trustworthy deacons reach for it.

I see by the *Times* that the forthcoming book written by Pism C.'s unholy ghosts is to be called, "What God Thinks of You."

I have no idea what God if there is a God thinks of you, but I have a pretty fair notion what God thinks of Pism C.

I got into Carrie McCarthy's taxi. I have not been allowed to drive since that ridiculous episode Out There two years ago. But that's another story. All I need say here is that my driver's license was yanked away by a venal judge in Los Angeles. For life.

Going home with Carrie, who is widowed and who owns three taxis, is tiring, but it is also most informative.

On the ride from the station to my house, a distance of about eight miles, Carrie usually gives me just about the same amount of news as I get from the *Banner*, and Carrie's news is more interesting and more intimate than Hermia's news.

For instance, last night as Carrie and I passed the Dillon farm, Carrie asked if she had ever mentioned that the youngest Dillon boy, the one with the out-sized head, is the result of a drunken, impromptu union between Mother Dillon and her next-to-oldest son.

I said that Carrie never had. "It's like Greek tragedy," I said.

"There's no Greek in that family," said Carrie. "They're Irish from way back."

Then Carrie revealed that she had just read a *book*, name of *Peyton Place*.

She wanted to know was I familiar with it. I confessed that I was.

"The book's better'n the movie," said Carrie. "Boy, is that true to life."

Then she volunteered that her literary excursion had given her an idea. She said that if she just had the time she could write a book about Sloane's Station which would make *P.P.* look like *a kid's book*. She said that she understood that the woman responsible for *Peyton Place* had made a lot of money. I confirmed it. Then Carrie wanted to know whether I would be interested in collaborating with her on a book which would give the lowdown on Sloane's Station. I thanked her for the flattering suggestion but declined on the grounds that although I once committed a book, I am not a writer.

"But I'd tell you the whole thing," said Carrie. "All *you'd* have to do is write it down, and I'd be willing to split down the middle."

I smiled but again said no despite Carrie's most generous offer to split down the middle.

"It'd be like coining money," said Carrie, being careful to avoid my Dexter hybrids as she turned around in my driveway. Carrie and I have had several lively little discussions about the care and treatment of my rhododendrons.

"What do you hear from the missus?" asked Carrie.

"She's fine," I said. "She's just fine."

"Tell her how-de-do," said Carrie, slamming the door of the car and driving off.

"I'll tell her," I shouted into the grayness.

In the village they think Charley is on vacation, although I suppose the news of the divorce will be in the papers tomorrow.

"I'll tell Charley what you said," I shouted again.

Then I came into this sad defeat of a house. Louella had my dinner ready.

(4) The desecration

After I sent Louella home, I sat in complete darkness behind the glass wall of the living room and for a while looked out at the foothills of the Berkshires. There was only one light anywhere—in Hebe's barn, on the far side of what Hebe now calls Mount Olympus.

Hebe has converted her barn into a ceramics factory where her assistant goddesses and apprentice priests turn out, among other things, an unlovely line of imperfect vases and ash trays, which are sold at places like W. and J. Sloane. Eventually some of these artless objects make their way back here as gifts from the week-end locusts. One of the vases costs about as much as the gin a locust drinks *before* dinner on *Friday*.

Some of the ash trays are even more reasonable, but, of course, there are always those canisters of Kobu nuts a locust can pick up at the Vendome or some place like that on his or her way to Grand Central. A buck something, one double Martini's worth. I find that Kobu nut locusts are very often double-Martini drinkers, and one of the foundations may want to take a look into that situation. I have a number of suggestions for dandy ways for the foundations to spend their money. For instance, I'd like to see a study made of why people with hyphenated last names are invariably dishonest.

But back to Hebe.

To think that, as Louella says, Hebe is now "head of the whole shebang" over there on Olympus.

Not every girl from the wrong side of the tracks in Bucharest becomes a high priestess, but then not every Rumanian girl is able to find four husbands, each richer than the one before.

Hebe's fourth and, I imagine, final marital excursion was with a fellow who not only founded a new religion. He also invented a perpetual-motion machine. Something like that. Very profitable, whatever it was.

Shortly after marrying Hebe, he died of a very timely thrombosis, leaving both his religion and his loot to his bereaved widow.

If I thought there were any hope of her converting me, I would visit Hebe once more, but there isn't. I realize a man should have a god at a time like this. It was surely for such occasions that Voltaire or whoever it was took the trouble to invent one. But I'm afraid I must make my exit the way I made my entrance, naked and alone, wailing like a banshee. I have been told that God would forgive my uncounted transgressions if I went to Him now, hat in hand, but if I did that I would lose what little is left of my self-respect, and I can't see how He would think much of me either.

I don't know how long I'd been sitting in my darkened living room when the lights went off in Hebe's barn.

Suddenly I felt as if I were unalterably alone—not only in this house but in the universe. There was no car on the road, and nothing moved, not a leaf, not a blade of grass.

I felt as if I alone had survived some awful holocaust, and I wondered why me and wished it had not been me.

I have experienced that sensation several times before. At such a moment the ache of loneliness is almost impossible to endure.

I slid open the glass door and called softly for Absalom, but he was gone.

An awful moment passed, and then I walked to where Charley and I had hung the portrait of her painted by Loren Swearington. It was a good portrait, and some museum in Cincinnati wanted to buy it, not only because Loren was born and brought up in Cincinnati.

At the time I wouldn't sell. I gave Charley that portrait on our first wedding anniversary.

Last night I stood in front of it for a moment, then lifted it down, and took the painting itself from the frame. I walked through this study, which is at the back of the house, opened the glass panel to the left there, went across the deck, down the steps and into the stand of woods behind the house.

I laid the painting on the ground, quite tenderly, and after several unsuccessful attempts, I managed to set fire to it with my cigarette lighter. It burned quickly and well, and I brushed the ashes under a pile of pine needles.

I stood over the small mound of ashes for a time, and I wept. There were no stars, and there was no moon. There were only the dark, still shadows of the pines and the spruce.

Finally I came back into the house and undressed, my hands still trembling.

After I had brushed my teeth, I took three pills. I then decided that for the kind of coward I am, a man who tends to blanch at the mere mention of the word *pain*, the pills would be best. I have more than enough.

I also decided last night to spend the remaining time putting on tape as many memories as I have time for during these final few days. I will put them down just as they come to me; Stendhal felt that out of such spontaneity came truth. We'll see. I promise this. If I indulge myself in any second thoughts, I'll label them as such. Second thoughts are what people have when the truth gets a little rough for their delicate stomachs.

I am not one of those who think that by putting it all down they will find some *meaning* in their existence. No, I have read hundreds of such books, most of them written by senile old men of forty or thereabouts. Nothing written for a man searching for *meaning* in this time and this place is worth much. Here and now about all you can do is get through the day and hope that this won't be the one when the aging delinquents who own us, body and soul, and who are in charge of the hydrogen tinker toys decide to let 'er rip.

I came into the world in a disordered time and am leaving it at a moment when it is more disordered still. Out of disorder comes chaos, not meaning.

Nor is what I have in mind a *corrective punishment*, though Dostoevsky's *Notes from the Underground* impressed me in a way few books in my life have.

No. My purpose is much simpler. By dictating these disjointed fragments of memory into this machine I am trying nothing more than to—let's use the honest word here—stay *safe* until the end. Not sane, *safe*. Would a *sane* man have burned that canvas? For that matter, would a *safe* man?

You see, the list I made yesterday was like so many lists I have made. Truthful as far as it went—but it didn't go nearly far enough. Because I am by nature a coward, and by training and practice a liar, I left out the most important reason I cannot go on.

I composed that item before I drifted into unconsciousness last night; it is this:

Item Number Six. I have mentioned the headaches I have been having and euphemistically referred to the disintegration of my memory. The truth of the matter is I have been suffering from frequent blackouts recently, hours gone from my life, with no memory of where I have been or what I have been doing.

And that's not all. Several other small, familiar symptoms have returned, the ones I experienced before I was taken to the place in New Haven.

Let me mention only one other. For weeks now I have been afraid of looking into a mirror.

The last time, you see, at the end, I saw no reflection when I looked.

I decided a long time ago that I would take my life rather than go back to New Haven.

Oh, they are kind to you, and in the late afternoon a first-rate musician from the faculty at Yale plays the organ, and every cell in the place reverberates with the sound of the music—and sometimes, during the loud passages—of Bach, let us say—you cannot hear the screams at all. The women are the worst, really; they scream words that you have tried to blot out of your mind and words you never knew existed and didn't want to know.

No, I shall never return to the green couch in New Haven—or to the room with a death's head on the wall.

So much for *Item Number Six.*

Last night, before the pills made me unconscious, I said this, aloud: "Oh God, help me stay—safe until the end. Help me get through the days; help me past the hour of five in the afternoon, and, oh especially, God, help me through the terrifying hours of the night. Help me not to be afraid in the dark, God. Help me bear with this awful loneliness. Help me believe, God. In something. Almost anything will do. Give me some small faith. In something. Anything will do. And, oh God, if you deny me all else, please let me hurt no other living thing before the end. That will do. Just that...."

(5) Talk before you go!

It is now ten-thirty. Since getting up this morning, I have dictated on tape the above account of yesterday's and last night's events.

I haven't been up so early in years, but the effect of the pills wore off shortly before six, and I did not take the usual two or three aspirins to prolong the unconsciousness.

This morning I sat up in bed, opened the drawer of the night table, found some matches and some stale cigarettes, and lighted one.

After I had finished the cigarette, I felt pleasantly drunk, and I thought that a shot would be nice. When I was on the sauce, the only part of my day that really lived up to expectation was that morning shot. The juice of four oranges and two jiggers of vodka. Nothing like it to start off a day.

However, I am now sauceless, and for me there is no such thing as *one* drink. You see, I am now a member of The Brotherhood, and if I were just going to be around long enough, I would be eligible for an oak-leaf cluster for my merit badge.

I stubbed out the cigarette and then showered and dressed. I am wearing the slacks and the sport shirt Charley bought me in London last spring.

Could it have been last spring? Is it possible that such a short time ago she and I were eating fish and chips at a place within the sound of Bow bells and listening to an Irishman with one arm who sang for us?

It's seven-thirty in Las Vegas. Has Charley found peace, do you suppose?

That last night she said there had not been a single day of peace in this house. "There's been an hour of peace here and there," she said, "but not one complete day or night of it."

As X drove up the long, tree-lined road leading into the enchanted forest, soft lights from the house of glass shone out over the trees and the hills, making of the house a bright island of promise and warmth.

X went into the house and, as always, he called out her name—hopefully, fearfully, because even in the beginning X had known though not admitted that it would end and had known though not admitted how it would end.

She was sitting on a yellow chair which reminded him of another yellow chair, and she was wearing the black dress they had bought at Harrod's in London, and she had on the suggestion of a hat he had given her. A small black overnight case was on the carpet beside her, and her purse, nearly as large, was next to it.

He leaned over to kiss her, but she avoided his touch. Then he asked a question which he hoped she would not answer.

"What's the matter?" he asked.

"I'm leaving you," she said.

He had bought a very special book as a gift for her, but he let it fall to the floor, and he felt the sting of tears against his eyelids.

He asked why, and she said, "I'll try hard to make it clear and just for once listen to me. Just for once really hear me....

"I love you, darling, and I pity you, but I don't want to stay married to you. I'm too old and too tired and it's too much work."

She walked to the naked wall of glass and looked out.

"I thought maybe there'd be peace in this house," she said, "but there hasn't been. There's been an hour of peace here and there but not one complete day or night of it."

She said, "It's a beautiful house. The hills are beautiful, and the trees are beautiful, and there's peace on every side of us, but there's no peace here, and there never will be."

She said, "I know you tried, darling, as hard as you could, and I tried, too. I don't know which of us tried more. It doesn't matter. I just want out."

An eternity passed—or a moment or two.

Finally, someone standing where X was standing, said, "I guess it wouldn't do any good to say please don't. Or that I'll try harder. Or that I'll go back to Dr. Baron. I'll do anything you say. I'll do—anything, darling."

And the tight, small voice that must have been his said, "Please don't leave me."

The woman took X's hand in hers, and she said, "I've been going over it all in my mind for weeks now. What you'd do and say and what I'd say. What I'd say if you were angry and what it would do to me if you—cried. Oh, darling, don't turn your head from me and be ashamed. I'm sorry you never had a childhood. I'm sorry for all the hurts you felt and feel. I'm sorry that when somebody reaches out to caress you, you hit them before they can. I thought maybe I could help you, but I can't. Nobody ever will. Maybe if I were twenty, but I'm not. I'm thirty-eight years old, and I haven't got time."

X opened his mouth to speak, but the sound that emerged was half a moan and half a sob. Then X did manage to speak. "Are you sure?" he said.

She nodded. "And I'm not going to cry," she said, "not here and not later when I'm alone, not for the rest of my life, even if I'm always alone. I'm tired of crying, and, besides, I never cry at the big ones. I'm not going to get drunk either. This is drinking weather, but—I'm going to stay sober."

X said please, and he said that he loved her.

She said, "Oh, no. You would if you could, but you can't. You've tried, but you're not up to love. The ability got left out of you—or crushed out. I don't know.... Darling, you're sometimes so sweet and so generous and so kind and amusing and fun to be with and, oh dear, just about everything in the world I could want.... Except loving. Never that.... And that awful self-hatred of yours. Hours of it, days of it. That awful black despair that no matter how hard I try always drags me into it. Maybe if I were—healthier, I could escape it, but I'm not. I'm sorry."

She kissed X's hand, quite tenderly, and then she released it and picked up her bag and purse.

"I'll send for the rest of my things when I get settled," she said, "and I'll write when I get a permanent address. I'm going to stay with Maria and Wiz for the next few days."

"Is that—all?" asked X.

"That's all," she said.

She opened the black door; and X said, "Let me go. It's your house, after all. I built it for you."

"No, you didn't, darling," she said. "You built it for you. Everything was always for you."

She closed the black door behind her, and that was the end.

Later X burned the book he had bought for her, and he tried to burn the records they had bought together and listened to together. The records would not burn well, but for a while the fire in the woods lighted up the dark, despairing sky.

More than an hour appears to have passed since I dictated that account of the end of my life. Because the night seven weeks ago when Charley left me was the end. No question of that.

In the last hour I believe I have not moved from this chair. I believe I watched a blue jay—or else it was a robin; I believe the chipmunk came out of his home in the hollow log and looked for some of the sunflower seeds Charley used to leave for him and the birds. I believe a fawn came to the edge of the woods, stared curiously at me, and then ran off. I believe a cloud hid the sun for a while, but I cannot be sure.

What matters is that the sun is shining now, and I shall begin at the beginning. I'll get myself born.

(6) I am born

This will be a very short chapter, dealing only with three essentials—the place, the time, and the principals.

The place was New Athens, Iowa, which was founded by one of a dozen "educational missionaries" who got to Iowa in 1843. All of them were recent graduates of Andover Theological Seminary.

The founder was Robert Leith Kempton, my great-great-grandfather. He was a severe, scholarly man, and in the dark house in which I spent my childhood there was a dark portrait of him over the fireplace. He looked a little like Nathaniel Hawthorne—only not so handsome. I expect he cultivated that resemblance; he wore his hair long, and it was black, and so were his eyes. The way his eyes looked at you from that portrait—looked at me, anyway—you knew he knew *everything*.

R.L.—apparently everybody called him that—hoped that some day the place he named New Athens would be the state capital and would have the state university as well. He was wrong on both counts. Des Moines got the state government and Iowa City got the university.

At the time I was born, and still, the first sign you passed on the highway leading into town from the east said, "Welcome to New Athens, the Home of Twenty Thousand Friendly People."

There are two lies in that sentence. New Athens has never had a population of more than sixteen thousand, and few of those have ever been friendly.

A second sign says, "The Home of Uncle George's Kidney Beans. They Will Like You, and You Will Like Them." The truth of that depends on who *you* are. A third, "New Athens is the Headquarters of Radio Station KNAI. Two Hundred and Fifty *Powerful* Watts." I cannot deny it.

Finally, a fourth sign, "New Athens is the Home of Pegasus College. The Parthenon of the Prairies. A Very Special College for Very Special Young Men and Women."

When I was back in New Athens last year for the funeral of my Aunt Mettabel, the town seemed to me to have gone down hill, but then so had I. There is now an eleven-story King Korn Hotel named after a statewide contest in which out of more than eleven thousand entries *that* was the winning suggestion. There is a new J. C. Penney, two stories, and a new Monkey Ward, three. The young people who in my youth would have belonged to the Country Club have moved into a new development east of Pegasus, overpriced houses of poor design, Utrillo reproductions on the walls and hidden hi-fi, largely Sinatra and Sibelius. In my youth, the reproductions were usually

"The Song of the Lark," and *Humoresque* was a favorite Victrola record for those not lucky enough to have a player piano. Lots of the folks on West Main Street had Caruso regretting he was a clown. Whether Sibelius is an improvement on *Humoresque* I wouldn't care to say. As for the hi-fi as a cultural institution versus the player piano, that's a whole evening's discussion right there.

The Country Club is still there, but it's mostly for the aging. I never had much truck with the Country Club anyway. The only time in my youth that I was there, I was on exhibition the whole time. I do know that when I was fourteen and the biggest and also the smallest student at Pegasus I read John O'Hara's *Appointment in Samarra*, and I was convinced things at our country club were just the way he described them, though his was Pennsylvania and ours Iowa.

I never knew for sure, though. I do know this. Now the people in their late twenties, thirties, and early forties have barbecue pits in their back yards, and the one night I attended a get-together last year, there was lots of acrimony, lots of drunkenness, and enough adultery to go around. Whether nature copies art or it's the other way 'round is one of my many arguments I will no longer be able to participate in.

In my youth, West Main was where you lived if you *were* anybody in New Athens; now it's light-housekeeping rooms and doctors' offices, although the Lavendar place is still there, as forbidding as ever. The Lavendars still own Midwest Canning, where the likable kidney beans are put up; they own the *New Athens Times-Dispatch*, the city council, the school board, and the county's two state legislators. No change there.

That will be enough for now on New Athens and the Lavendars.

The time. I was born in 1921, the year after *Main Street* was published. I don't mean that the appearances of Sinclair Lewis's novel and me are of equal importance, but they are related.

If it hadn't been for *Main Street*, my mother might never have decided to produce a child. However, that novel made a profound impression on her. She was convinced that it was she who had inspired Mr. Lewis to create Carol Kennicott. True, she had never met him, but, "*He* certainly knows *all* about *me*. He may very well have observed me from afar."

She really talked like that—all the time, too.

Mr. Lewis's irony about Carol was lost on mother. To her, "Carol Kennicott represents the finer things in life, no *if*'s, *and*'s, and *but*'s about it." (And by the way, in case these notes are ever transcribed—and that's up to Dr. Baron—this is one of the house rules for any printer or typist: upper case for *Negro*, lower case for *mother*.)

My Aunt Mettabel, a woman of great gentleness who also hated my mother's guts, once told me that not long before mother became pregnant, she said, "Where Miss Kennicott made her big mistake was in not having a baby. A baby would have demonstrated her defiance of the Philistinians."

I am one of the world's leading authorities on insomnia, and during many sleepless nights I have tried to picture the scene in which my mother let my father in on the fact that she wanted a baby.

I could be wrong, but I picture her as saying something like, "Kendall, I have decided on a child."

I imagine my father protesting—slightly; he was a slight man. Perhaps he suggested that considering the strained relationship between him and my mother a child might not be desirable.

I know pretty well what Mother said back. "Kendall, in matters like this your position and my position always have been and always will be diabolically opposed."

And then she said, "I'll have a baby the like of which this town has never laid eyes on."

As was so often the case, she was right. She did just that.

No more than a few weeks after Old Doctor Llewellyn had confirmed her happy suspicions about the pregnancy, mother announced to the members of the New Athens Artsy-Craftsy Club that she was going to produce a genius.

"Jessica will be one of the most extraordinary women of her age," mother said.

One of the more courageous sisters then asked (my Aunt Mettabel told me this years later), "Celeste [that's *Mummy*], how can you be sure it'll be a girl?"

"Because I *want* a girl. I am *concentrating* on a girl. I do not *like* boys. It will *be* a girl. Moreover, I plan that Jessica will have the career I mistakenly gave up for marriage."

Mother went on to say, "Jessica will be musical, of course. My own voice is intact, as is my talent. My tones are fresh and clear. I shall simply teach Jessica what I know. She will sing, dance, and play, and unless I miss my guess and I won't she will be on the concert stage before she reaches her teens."

Why Jessica?

"It means Grace of God," said mother, "and rich. Jessica will be her mother's daughter, and she will be rich. You can bet your bottom dollar on that."

Mother's pregnancy must have been—well, hectic. I once heard her lecture on how she'd managed to give birth to a prodigy. Only one sentence remains in my mind. She said, "During the entire pregnancy I forced myself to think only the largest and most noble thoughts, and I ate a great deal of cottage cheese."

I would question the size and the quality of her thoughts.

Cottage cheese? Very probably. Mother was a food faddist. She went through the vitamins from A to Z and back again; she studied protein charts and I remember at one time she was convinced that a steak sandwich for breakfast would prevent cancer.

Wheat germ, black-strap molasses, yoghurt, we had them all long before people started making fortunes out of such nonsense.

Mother always felt she was ahead of her time, and maybe she was.

Once she went through a raw-fish period, and so did I, and so did Petrarch Pavan, to whom she was then married. My mother *shared* her enthusiasms.

"Raw fish are the original brain food," she announced. "This fact is well known throughout the Far East. How else can you explain Mahatma Gandhi?"

She had you there. How else could you?

During her pregnancy mother listened to classical records almost constantly. She played the piano, and she sang; *Main Street* was constantly at her side, and she may even have looked into a few other books. Mother was not much of a reader; she pecked at books, misunderstanding, mislabeling, and misremembering what little she did read; the rest she let lay. Nevertheless when literature was being discussed—which wasn't often where I was born and raised—mother always more than held up her end of the conversation.

Mother was not only an active Artsy-Craftsy girl; she was also the biggest thing that ever came along in the New Athens Eastern Star. Naturally, she called both groups in to assist with the delivery of Jessica.

I don't know *exactly* what the girls in the Star had in mind for when Jessica was delivered, but I believe (Aunt Mettabel again) the sisters intended to march into *Mummy's* bedroom as soon as was practicable thereafter, waving their arms. The Star sisters are always marching around, and they wave their arms about like so many semaphorists.

The frumps in the Artsy-Craftsy Club were planning to *serenade* Jessica's arrival. The songs they had in mind were "Joy to the World" and "Jingle Bells." You see, Jessica was scheduled for December 24. Mother had overlooked nothing.

Millicent Fairchild, who was *New Athens' Own World Renowned and Chatauqua-Celebrated Elocutionist*, was going to recite "The Night Before Christmas." If pushed, and the slightest shove would do, Millicent would probably also have run through "Over the Hills to the Poorhouse," which she had declaimed from the Chatauqua platform one thousand nine hundred and eighty-seven times.

Finally, the Star drill team was going to spell out Jessica's name.

Poor Jessica. She never knew what she missed.

You see, what happened was this. Jessica didn't show. I did, and I further complicated matters by not arriving on December 24 but on *October* 19, with *no* warning.

A line in a play in the Thirties went something like, "Oh, ye bright, ironic gods, laugh on. Laugh on." I never thought I'd be able to work that thought into a sentence, but it seems to fit perfectly here.

Laugh on, damn you; laugh on.

I was a seven months' baby, small, incomplete, and on arrival surrounded by hostility, a condition I have managed to keep going ever since.

There were no baby clothes, only a pink blanket in which to wrap me, an early gift from a sister Rebekah. Yes, mother was a Rebekah, too.

There was no time to summon the marchers, the singers, or Millicent, so the entertainment to greet Jessica's arrival had to be hurriedly improvised. On mother's orders, a Victrola in the next room was playing Schubert's *Serenade*. Mother had said, "No matter what, I want the sound of great music to be the first to reach her ears, and Schubert's *Serenade* is a song that will live forever."

I am positive that the first sounds to reach my ears were those of my own displeasure and resentment at being yanked, unready and unwilling, into a world I not only had never made but wanted no part of.

I can picture the scene. You'll have to take my word for it that I can.

Old Doctor Llewellyn must have said, "It's a boy, Mrs. Bland."

If I am any judge of my mother, and I most certainly am, she said, "A *boy! Impossible!*"

Old Doctor Llewellyn must then have said, "No, indeedy. A bouncing baby boy." All of his babies bounced.

"But I *insist* on a girl," mother said. "I've *planned* on a girl. I don't want a *boy*. I don't like *boys*."

"Goochy-goochy-goo," said Llewellyn, wagging a finger under my nose. "Handsome baby. Four pounds, thirteen ounces."

"But I've already *told* everybody it's going to be a girl," said mother.

She may even have asked Dr. Lewellyn to send me back. She was always sending something back. "It's inferior merchandise," she would say. "Don't try to palm your inferior merchandise off on me."

In my case, she must finally have recognized that the merchandise, inferior or not, was her own, and she may have wrinkled her nose at me. She often wrinkled her nose at what displeased her, and she often sighed and said, "Well, I guess I'll just have to make do."

She never did make do, though. She didn't know how.

After inspecting me critically, mother announced to my father, who was standing nearby, "It takes after you, Kendall. Go turn up the Victrola."

She may have hummed. She often hummed when she was upset.

Finally, using another of her favorite sentences, she may have said, "Well, nothing has ever non-pulsed me, and *Joshua* isn't going to either."

I spent several days after that in something that predated the incubator; it was called a "warming box." Of that I, of course, remember nothing, but I do know this. If I'd had any sense, I'd never have left it.

(7) An interruption

Louella came in while I was dictating what I'm pretty sure happened when I was served forth.

This being a Saturday, she didn't get here until one. She is now fixing my lunch.

When I finished dictating the above, I stood for a while by the glass wall, looking into the cool green pines, looking left to avoid the sight of that neat pile of needles.

Here and there were slivers of bright August sunlight. The air was cool and clear, and for a short time I had a feeling of well-being; for a moment I wished I could hold back time. "Keep it always now," Charley used to say.

Then I heard Louella's voice, warning me that she was on her way here.

"Jesus loves me; this I know. For the Bible tells me so. Little ones to Him will come..."

Those people all have a wonderful sense of rhythm, haven't they?

I ate the eggs, the ham, and the toast, and I glanced through the newspapers Louella had brought me from the village.

Not a word about Charley in Las Vegas, not even in *The News*.

Louella returned and asked if I wanted more coffee, and I said I didn't. She looked at me suspiciously, disapprovingly. Then she lowered her small, turtle-like head.

"Mr. Bland," she said. "The missus' picture has been stole."

"No, it hasn't," I said. "I took it down."

After digesting this, Louella said, "You want me to put it away some place?"

"No, thank you, Louella. I've taken care of it."

"You sure it's some place it won't get all moldy? You remember what happened with all those books that was downstairs last summer?"

I said that I was sure and that I remembered. I have put the frame of Charley's portrait in the closet over there.

Louella gave me a baleful glance, picked up the lunch tray, and left. I assume she has already started looking for the portrait, but that will take her some time. In addition to the glass and the brick, this house consists almost entirely of built-in cabinets and cupboards and drawers. It will take hours for Louella to go through them all. And, finally, she will have to conclude that the portrait is in one of the locked closets in this room.

Louella has many times hopefully asked if I don't want her to clean those closets, and I have an equal number of times told her thank you, no.

"Must be at least two feet a dust in there," Louella has said. "Easy two feet."

"Easy," I have said.

Lloyd Barlow, who is paid by us taxpayers to deliver the mail to those of us who live on Old South Friendly Road, has just roared up my driveway, scattering gravel on at least six of the Dexter hybrids.

Lloyd looks to see if anyone is watching. I am, but I am behind the Japanese screen.

Lloyd holds each of my letters up to the sun. He is now reading a postcard. He is a lip reader.

Having finished his labored look at my mail, Lloyd opened the door of the station wagon with an acned hand. He brought a special delivery letter to the house, and Louella signed for it.

Lloyd has now gone back to the station wagon, and he is relaxing for a moment, picking his nose.

Lloyd is a June graduate of our local high school, an institution which is without any frills whatsoever and also without much education. However, we were able to afford new uniforms for the football team last fall. All we had to do was cut the library appropriation ever so slightly.

Lloyd is hard of hearing, and he wears one of those very visible invisible hearing aids. Frank Lovelace, a boy who mows my lawn and pulls a few weeds when he can think of nothing less tiring to do, says that Lloyd was known in Sloane's Station High School as The Ear. Lloyd informed on the pupils to the teachers, on the teachers to the principal, and on the principal to his father, who is chairman of the Grand Old Party in this county as well as president of our budget-minded school board. Richard Barlow and his entire slate of candidates were elected because of their sensible, thought-provoking campaign slogan, "Balance the Budget and Education in Sloane's Station Will Balance Itself."

Lloyd has stopped picking his nose. Lloyd is now scratching himself furtively.

Nature's endowments to Lloyd Barlow are meager, but I see no reason to doubt that he has all the important qualifications to succeed his father in our local political and educational life, and possibly Lloyd may go above and beyond the old man. Richard Barlow suffers the grave political disadvantage of having gone to college, to Harvard in fact, though to hear him talk you'd never think he even could spell H-a-r-v-a-r-d. Lloyd, who couldn't spell the word r-e-g-e-n-t-s, let alone pass them, is not going any place to c-o-l-l-e-g-e. That's one great political advantage right there. No education. What's more, if you ask me, Lloyd's hearing aid is even more votes in the bank. Lately in this country we have taken to electing people to high office who have some malfunction or other, particularly in and around the head.

Oh, Lloyd may go far indeed. The school psychologist tells me he has an I.Q. of 74.

Now Lloyd is noisily turning the station wagon. It screams back down my road, scattering more gravel on more Dexter hybrids.

Lloyd's next stop will be at Ernestine Kraftall's, three quarters of a mile down Old South Friendly.

Lloyd will linger there for a while.

Ab is back; I believe he's been at Pism C.'s. Sacha, one of the Jackson poodles, is in heat. Ab is tired, but he looks happy.

My God, it is after three.

There was nothing much in the mail; the special-delivery letter was from an individual I shall identify only as America's Foremost Lady Novelist. Most of what she had to say is of no interest and of no importance. It never is. Why the special delivery then? Very simple. First-class mail is for *common* people. AFLN is all for common people so long as you understand she isn't one of them.

The last words in AFLN's letter were these:

"I never mentioned this to you before, darling, but I never cared much for Charley anyway. Too sweet for my taste. Too sweet to be real."

I put the letter in the garbage disposal. It disintegrated noisily, and I wish I could say as much for its author.

After I'd looked through the mail, Ab and I went for a walk, and we passed Filmore Grayson, who lives alone in a cabin in the woods over there. I spoke to Filmore, but he didn't speak back, and I'm sorry. Filmore is the only one of my neighbors I care a fig about knowing, but Filmore—a student of Thoreau—seldom speaks to anyone. He walks the seven miles to the village four times a year, buys the supplies he needs, and walks back; he will not accept a ride. Filmore is a little over seventy, and around here they say he is *strange*.

He seems to me to be most sensible. A couple summers ago Davy Bronson and Filmore met on Main Street in the village. Davy was wearing red trousers, an orange shirt, and blue shoes.

That's a fairly standard outfit Out There but unusual in Our Town.

According to Davy, Filmore stopped, looked Davy up and down, and said, "Young man, I don't know what line of work you're in, but, apparently, you have not learned the wise words of Henry David Thoreau, 'Beware of all enterprises that require new clothes.'"

Filmore Grayson must be one of the few people now living who does not know what line of work Davy is in.

Oh, damn. The phone.

(8) Conversation piece

Back again.

Just after Ab and I got back from our walk, Louella went to the village to shop. I thought I had told her to leave the phone off the hook, but I guess I hadn't. Anyway, she didn't. So when the phone rang, I answered it. I shouldn't have, but then my life has consisted largely of telephone calls I answered when I shouldn't have, of sentences I spoke when I ought to have kept my mouth shut, of opinions expressed when nobody asked me, when nobody even wanted to know.

My first wife, Letty, herself a noteworthy expert on volubility, once said (need I add in my presence?), "Joshua has the same feeling about silence that nature has about a vacuum."

Letty will miss me.

Anyway, speaking of volubility, one of this country's leading practitioners of that by no means lost art was on the phone when I answered, George Banning's wife, Shirley.

Shirley said she knew she wasn't supposed to call me; she said George had told her, but she couldn't resist asking me to come for dinner next Friday.

"I'm having several people up from Washington," Shirley said, "and government people just *love* to talk to someone of the opposite persuasion."

I told Shirley that it sounded like a simply wonderful evening, but, unhappily, I would not be available next Friday. Next Friday I shall be sitting in this room counting my pills and my final memories.

I couldn't help adding that for some time now I have not been of any persuasion at all politically.

"Oh, come now, Josh," said Shirley. "We all know you're a member of the Democrat Party, and that's what I *mean*."

I carefully explained to Shirley that I am not a member of the Democrat Party, that in fact if there is one thing I care less about than the Democrat Party, it is the Republic Party.

"But you're an American, after all," said Shirley. "You *have* to vote."

I did not tell Shirley that I am not at all sure I am an American, but I did say that I do not *have* to vote and further that there is no possibility of my being able to pass the *ache* test.

"What in the world is the *ache* test?" Shirley asked. "That sounds like a *fun* test."

I started to explain to Shirley about the ache meter which under the Bland Plan for Shaping Up the World would be installed in every voting booth, but then I stopped. I realized that if I went on I would probably burst into tears.

I passed on my regards to George and to Nina and Jonathan, their children, and then I hung up.

I want to say a few words about the Banning family, Shirley in particular. I have known them all very well and for a long time, and George has had a great influence on my life.

Shirley has come a long way from Washington Square, where she once asked George to sign a petition having to do with the Scottsboro boys. She has come even further from the cold-water flat where she was born and raised and from the cluttered apartment at Park Avenue and Eighty-ninth where she and George lived when I first knew them.

Not that Shirley has ever given any thought to herself. Shirley has devoted her life to Nina and Jonathan.

Admittedly, they are George's children, too, but in creating a family, it is the mother who produces a masterpiece, if it is a masterpiece, and in Shirley's case no other word will do.

What George did was provide the money, and bringing up Nina and Jonathan cost a good deal. It is costing still.

Just now, for example, George has to put up the money to support Nina through her final, expensive year at Smith, after which there will be Nina's costly wedding and the costly festivities to follow, probably at the Waldorf.

Next June Nina is going to marry a pleasant and handsome but, according to George, not very bright West Point cadet. I wish Nina wouldn't, but it's none of my business. Strictly speaking, it's none of George's business either, but, although he'd never tell her not to, George also wishes Nina wouldn't.

George went up to the Trade School on the Hudson last spring and, as George has said, "I asked this charming idiot Nina's going to marry what he thought of Proust."

George winked at me.

"I was just checking, you understand, because if there is anything I cannot stand, it's a lack of culture. That's why I get along so well Out There. They are up to their ass in culture Out There. Anyway, I was questioning this blond Adonis about Proust. You know what he said? He said, 'What war was General Proust in, sir?' Oh, my God. Nina will surely get tired of just looking at him."

I grinned ribaldly at George, and he said, "Well, even that gets dull after a while. What will they ever find to talk about?"

"General Marcel Proust," I said.

George smiled. Then he said, "Do you know what my father used to do? He used to spit on the ground every time a soldier passed. To him all soldiers of all countries were Cossacks. And you know something? I think he was right. And my grandfather. Oi."

George was hamming it up. "Nina not only has to marry a *goy* but a military *goy* at that. Believe me, the very worst kind. In Warsaw, a soldier seeing my grandfather might take it into his head to strike my grandfather on the head with the back of a sword. That would just be for a lark, you understand. If the soldier were drunk or mad at his wife or there had been an especially outspoken anti-Semitic editorial in the morning paper, the soldier might kill my grandfather on the spot and no questions asked. And now my daughter Nina is going to marry an officer Cossack. Oh, dear. Oh, dear."

"That's progress, George," I said. "That's what's made this country great."

Then, feeling bitchy, I added, "I'll bet Shirley's pleased."

George gave me a look, and then he said, "Now, darling, Shirley is very fond of you."

I said, "I know, and I'm very fond of Shirley."

"I didn't care much for whatshername, your first wife," said George, "but that's something else again."

"Has Nina any idea what it's like on an Army post?"

"I doubt it, although I tried to explain. I said to her, I said, 'Honey, have you any idea of life as it is lived in a place like Fort Sill, Oklahoma, or wherever it is, not that it matters; it's always the same.' I said, 'I'm saying nothing against Heath'—that's his name; it couldn't be, but it is—'but, baby, you'll have to kowtow to the wives of first lieutenants, and, believe me, they are invariably dowdy, those girls. Lieutenants—excepting for Heath, of course—always marry women as lieutenants that they regret when they are majors. It's in the manual; they have to. And as for the colonel's lady—baby doll, believe me, she is always Judy O'Grady. You'll be bored, honey.'"

George paused and sighed. "You know what Nina said? She said, 'Pop, I've had excitement and celebrities and first nights and Hollywood my whole life, and I'm up to here with them. I'm not ungrateful, understand, but I'll honestly welcome a little plain, honest boredom for a change.' And then she said, 'Besides, I happen to be mad about the boy.' Love, who can knock it?"

Nevertheless, despite the fact that George wouldn't think of interfering with Nina's wedding, it is still going to cost him a lot of money. George is going to have to invite a lot of the Smith girls who have been so very nice to Nina and a lot of newly commissioned second lieutenants who are fond both of Nina and of Heath. In addition, George will have to ask all of his clients, because all of George's clients are also George's personal friends. There will be people up from Wonderland, D.C., mainly Shirley's friends, and there will be dozens of people from Out There, producers, directors, other agents who started out with George and who have moved upward and onward, and if George can manage it, even two or three book writers. George likes to keep a handful of novelists on his small, select list of happy clients. True, without a movie sale or at the very least a television sale, book writers don't earn their salt in an agency, but they do lend a certain *éclat* to a wedding reception—if, that is, they don't drink too much, which, unless you are careful to pick the right book writer, the poor things are likely to do.

Oh, it will be quite a wedding all right and quite a reception, and thank God I will be unable to attend. Joshua Bland regrets.

Shirley's son Jonathan is now at Johns Hopkins, and it will be five more expensive years before Jon can set himself up in practice as an analyst, and Jon wants to spend two or three of those years abroad, which is going to cost George one hell of a lot of money.

Not that George resents the expense. Jon is a good boy and a smart boy and a hard-working boy, and although George can't understand why his son wants to fool around with a science—if it is a science—as inexact as psychology, that is Jon's business. George has never tried to make up his children's minds for them.

"The fact is," George once told me, "I haven't been able to speak to Jonnie since he was about five years old, and he's never had anything to say to me. The fact is Jon wishes he was a *goy*, and who can blame him? The fact is he is ashamed of me, and even the nose operation hasn't helped much. The fact is Jon wishes I would drop dead, and that I suppose is in the nature of things."

"The whole thing is as American as blueberry pie, George," I said. "A daughter who's going to marry an Army officer and a son who hates his old man. That's just about as American as you can get."

"Shirley has devoted her life to those kids," said George, "and I for one appreciate it."

I never could decide whether or not there was irony in George's voice.

"I'm a student," Shirley often says. "Learn, learn, learn. I'll never stop learning, because if one stops learning, one might just as well curl up one's toes and die, nest pa?"

"Nest pa," one says back. "Oh, undoubtedly nest pa."

Shirley has learned; it cannot be denied. Politically, for instance, if one were to mention to Shirley (and this one has) the days at N.Y.U., she would (does) smile sadly and say, "The fact that I have that silly little episode in my past is one of the very many reasons that I agree with J. Edgar Hoover in every word he says about the Communist menace. Fortunately, I saw the light in time, but there are other simple, unspoiled little girls who at this very moment and under our very eyes are being seduced by the Reds."

At this point, Shirley always sighs volubly, and if you don't think that is possible, you don't know Shirley.

"Every time I think of that part of my past, it makes me want to take a bawth," says Shirley.

Shirley has taken to speaking with an English-type accent. I believe this is the result of her having recently discovered that her given name was inspired by the Charlotte Brontë novel with that title.

Shirley considers Miss Brontë's *Shirley* a far more sensitive novel than that potboiler, *Jane Eyre*, which, according to Shirley, Miss Brontë wrote for—well, *money*. If there is anything that Shirley cannot stand, it is an artist who does things for *money*.

Shirley does have to admit, though, that *Shirley* very likely appeals only to a discriminating few.

Shirley, sad to say, does not read as much as she once did. For one thing, there simply are not any *really good* writers any more, and she knows that she shouldn't say this because George's list of clients includes several very competent craftsmen. But *great*?

"Where are the mighty oaks on today's literary horizon?" Shirley asks. "Saplings, yes, mighty oaks, no. Who since Joyce has been able to put two English sentences on paper? I ask you. Who?"

Shirley has asked me this question time and again, and I am always speechless. *Who*, I keep asking myself. *Where* are the mighty oaks?

At such times I always try to avoid the eye of any of George's competent clients who have heard Shirley and who are trying to pretend that they are plumbers.

Shirley is, of course, way past what you might call her salad and/or artificial sweet pea days when she and George lived at Park Avenue and Eighty-ninth. Nowadays, Shirley collects antiques and Hamiltonia.

Shirley often says that buying antiques is just the same as making very, very wise investments because, bad times or good, there are always people who can afford to and who will want to buy beautiful things, though if Shirley ever has to sell any of her treasures, it will simply kill her; it will just simply break her heart.

"There is nothing I love more than tradition," Shirley says, "and the beautiful old treasures I have collected over the years are tradition, and I do not see how it can be denied."

Up to now, I have never heard anybody deny that the lovely home near East Hampton in which George and his family spend their summers or the lovely home on East Thirty-sixth Street where Shirley and George spend their winters are rich in tradition, particularly the Thirty-sixth Street place.

During what Shirley refers to as the War of the American Revolution several important military conferences took place—or are said to have taken place, to Shirley the same thing—in the expensive living room which Shirley has tried so hard to keep the way They would have wanted it. *They* are our Glorious Forefathers, and Shirley's voice gets all vibrato when she speaks of Them. Shirley feels that their spirit is in her living room, and Shirley says, "Sometimes when I am alone at night in this room, meditating, I can hear their happy spirits saying, 'Shirley, thank you. Thank you for having it the way we remember it.'"

Shirley frequently adds, "That is the reason I am always so very, very careful who I invite to my dinners. There are certain clients of George's who may make his firm a very great deal of money and no two ways about it, but certain clients would just not fit into this lovely room. I can hear what They would say. They would say, 'Oh no, Shirley, oh no.'"

There are many jokes about where George Washington slept, and nobody seems to know for sure, but Shirley knows for sure that very often when Alexander Hamilton was simply too tired to go all the way down to his own town house near Sheridan Square, Mr. Hamilton slept in Shirley's lovely East Thirty-sixth Street house.

"The poor dear never rested more than a few minutes at a time," Shirley will tell you. "He was concerned, night and day, with the future of this great republic of ours."

Then Shirley will sigh one of her Englishy sighs. "They just don't make men like that any more," Shirley says. "They just aren't cut in the same pattern these days.

"People don't even *think* these days," Shirley says. "Most people don't anyway."

This latter clause clearly excludes Shirley, who thinks almost as much as Alexander Hamilton used to.

"Alexander Hamilton did a great deal of thinking at a desk in that corner, a desk very much like the beautiful old desk I have over there now. I got that desk at that place in West Tisbury I've told you about. Those two boys just don't know what they have—and I have simply robbed them blind.

"Alexander Hamilton may even have drafted the Declaration of Independence in the corner over there," Shirley goes on. "Oh, I know. Thomas Jefferson got the *credit* for writing it, but Alexander Hamilton was the author of the spirit of it, and don't try to argue with me. I've *read*."

I learned a long time ago never to argue with anybody who has *read*, and there is no question that Shirley has. She has simply doused herself in the history of Mr. Hamilton, who, in Shirley's opinion, made an incalculable contribution to the early days of this country's struggle for independence.

"Incalculable," says Shirley.

Naturally Shirley has become an ardent member of the Grand Old Party, and you can bet this has caused some very, very lively discussions in Shirley's gracious living room. Too many of Shirley's friends make their political decisions *emotionally* instead of *intellectually*, as Shirley does. They have not been willing to revise their opinions as one must do all through life if one wants to *grow and become a mature person*.

In the matter of the late Franklin Roosevelt, to use only one example—a president for whom Shirley used to have the greatest admiration and of whom many of Shirley's best friends still say, and I am quoting Shirley here, "the sun rose and set on the late Franklin Delano"—Shirley herself, after deep meditation and after the reading of many, many books, has decided that although he *may* have meant well, he did this country incalculable harm.

"Incalculable," says Shirley.

What's more, there is considerable evidence in some of the books Shirley has read indicating that Roosevelt did not even *mean* well.

Now you must understand, and you have to get this very, very straight, Shirley's admiration for Mrs. Roosevelt is just as strong as it ever was, though Shirley is terribly afraid that Mrs. R. simply does not understand politics, and Shirley would welcome the opportunity to discuss politics with Mrs. Roosevelt some time and try to straighten Mrs. Roosevelt out.

In one recent Campaign to Save the Republic, Shirley appeared on television with the President of the United States, who, for some reason, was running for re-election.

Shirley was one of the great cross-section of this great republic of ours. Shirley was Mrs. Average Housewife, and she spoke up loud and clear about high prices. She was against high prices.

George did his best to keep Shirley from getting into active politics. He insisted that it was simply not good business for her to do so, particularly since he and most of his clients are of what Shirley calls the opposite persuasion.

Nevertheless, Shirley realized that there was more than a little of Joan of Arc in her, and she damned the cost and the torpedoes and went right ahead. She was very active in the Athletes and Aesthetes for Him Committee.

And it just goes to show you. You have to have the courage of your convictions, because having the courage of your convictions is What Has Made This Country Great. Provided, of course, they are the right kind of convictions.

Happily, George did not lose a single client because of Shirley's political activity. Not only that. Shirley made herself some very good friends in the course of her arduous activities, and she has been rewarded by being made a member of the board of directors of a citizen's committee to outlaw the Democrat Party. Either that or it's a committee in favor of repealing the income tax and balancing the budget. Something like that.

As Shirley has so often said, "You take your average little man, and he simply has not the time nor the capacity to understand the *dichotomies*[1] and nuances of politics, and it is the privilege, and if I may so say, the duty of those of us who have studied and matured and learned to point the way for him.

"I don't care what you say," says Shirley. "I have found roots, and you have to have roots if you are to grow up."

One of Shirley's roots may or may not include Shirley's dear mother, whom Shirley loves very, very much. Shirley's mother, who brought Shirley up in the cold-water flat, is now just as happy as she can be in a lovely little home near the beach in Miami. Shirley sometimes visits her mother every year or so, and Shirley would visit her mother more often, except that Shirley does not fly, and Shirley cannot stand trains. So to visit her mother, Shirley has to drive, and, as Shirley points out, "There simply isn't a decent place to eat between New York and Palm Beach."

I have long since given up any hope of ever meeting Shirley's mother, and I'm sorry. I have always wanted to ask Mrs. Garfinkle how it was that she happened to name Shirley after a novel by Charlotte Brontë that is usually read only by candidates for Ph.D.'s in English literature.

And that is all I care to say at the moment about Shirley and her family. Since George is one of the two last people I will see before taking off for parts unknown, I will have more to say about him.

Ab is now asleep at my feet; he moans happily. He is probably chasing a phantom rabbit and, asleep as awake, never catching it.

It doesn't matter. The joy is all in the chase.

The next time around (and I am coming back) I would like to be a golden retriever, I believe—loving, simple-minded, always expecting the best but not broken-hearted at never getting it.

Almost all animals are better than almost any people anyway, especially dogs, and if I had just thought of it in time, I'll bet I could have become another Albert Payson Terhune. There's a lot

---

1   About that word *dichotomy*. I've spent a large part of my life making notes on the type person who uses that word; I'll bet I've got as many notes on *dichotomy-droppers* as the Kinsey people made on sex habits, and I'll tell you this. When you meet up with one, you should not only padlock the silver; you should put under lock and key everything else that isn't nailed down.

of loot in the dog-book racket, not as much as in the Jesus-book racket, but still plenty to make many tax problems for numerous *Writers*.

And just think how it would be if, in addition to the Disciples, Jesus had had a dog. A collie, say. Think of what that dog would have gone through The Day They Did It.

By the way, the last time I was Out There, I heard that a group of scientists at one of the universities is making a study of porpoises which seems to prove that not only are porpoises smarter than people. They are very much nicer, too.

(9) You are the cause of all this anguish—oh, my mother!

It is a little after nine in the evening, and I have to get on with it.

I've had dinner, Louella's chicken with orange sauce. Magnificent.

The evening is warm, and there is a slight breeze. I see the lights of an occasional car on the highway, and a plane is overhead. Both seem to make the night more lonely. I am not good with loneliness. You'd think I'd be used to it by now, wouldn't you?

I have just played back that part of the tape where I tell about getting born. It occurs to me that for what follows to make sense I will have to backtrack and say a few additional words about the woman who invented me, my mother, and about her unwilling partner in the enterprise, my father.

Mother was a small woman, about five-four. She was small-boned, too, and she looked a little like the early Janet Gaynor, which was probably not accidental. She saw *Seventh Heaven* at least a dozen times.

I have often wondered how a woman like my mother happened, and once, when I studied genetics, I hoped I'd come across a clue. I never did, though. I'm not sure there is an explanation.

Maybe some people are just born discontented. Why not? Some are born happy and some not.

I do know this; my mother ran all the way. From the cradle to the grave.

One of my early memories is of my father reading aloud to me from *Through the Looking Glass*.

Mother was in the room—not listening. Of course.

I can hear my father saying, "Listen to this, Celeste—"

Mother looked up from whatever she was doing and frowned.

My father read:

> ...and still the Queen cried, "Faster! Faster!" and dragged Alice along. "Are we nearly there?" Alice managed to pant out at last.
>
> "Nearly there," the Queen repeated. "Why, we passed it ten minutes ago. Faster...."
>
> ...suddenly, just as Alice was getting quite exhausted, they stopped, and she found herself sitting on the ground, breathless and giddy.
>
> The Queen propped her up against a tree and said kindly, "You may rest a little, now."
>
> Alice looked around her in great surprise. "Why, I do believe we've been under this tree the whole time. Everything's just as it was."
>
> "Of course it is," said the Queen. "What would you have it?"
>
> "Well, in *our* country," said Alice, still panting a little, "you'd generally get to somewhere else—if you ran very fast for a long time as we've been doing."
>
> "A slow sort of country," said the Queen. "Now, *here*, you see, it takes all the running *you* can do to keep in the same place."

There my father paused.

"Did you hear that, Celeste?" he asked.

Mother said, "Kendall, if I've told you once, I've told you a thousand times, I do not want to have sonny boy's head filled with all those myths. You are unwilling to face life, which is one of the many reasons you are under the weather so often, but life is real, and the grave is not the goal."

My father sighed. Then he continued reading:

> ...The most curious part of the thing was that the trees and other things round them never changed their places at all; however fast they went they never seemed to pass anything. "I wonder if all the things move along with us," thought poor, puzzled Alice....

"You read that part already, Pop," I said.

My father sighed again. "Oh, yes," he said. "I guess I did."

Faster! Faster!

So. My mother was a runner, but none of her seven brothers and sisters was. That doesn't mean they were contented; it just means they were too lazy to run. They cursed their fate sitting down.

There were three sisters and four brothers. Aunt Mettabel was the eldest, and I thought she was the nicest. I'll have more to say about her. Next in line were the twins, not identical, though I could never tell them apart. Fairfax was one; Farley was the other. Both were bulky, red-faced men, and together they raised cattle on the 320-acre "home place" that belonged to my grandfather. Their whole lives revolved around each other, and they hated each other, and both wives hated each other and also hated both husbands. I'm sure I didn't observe that fact; somebody must have told me, maybe my father; he looked on the entire human race with a jaundiced eye, particularly all members of mother's family.

I remember my father once said to me, "Josh, there is nothing in the world worse than gossip."

I nodded, and he winked at me. "There's nothing wrong in analyzing people, though," he said, and then we both laughed. We laughed a lot when we were alone together.

Anyway, Farley hated Fairfax and vice versa, and each waited hopefully for the other to die. Each lived to be eighty-some, and they died a few months apart, shortly after the end of the Second World War.

I will say a word about my Uncle Jebediah later, but of the others there is little of importance. They are all run-of-the-mill, Grade-B types, put on earth "simply to swell the crowd." Not one has yearned to achieve sainthood. Not one has ever laughed. Not one has ever read a book through for pleasure. They have snorted at the latest in scatology, giggled at the incestuous kind of joke-telling about Catholics and about Jews that in their barren minds passes for humor. But *laugh*? They wouldn't know how. Enjoy life? They wouldn't know where to begin.

They exchange subscriptions to the *Reader's Digest* for Christmas. They watch Lawrence Welk and Tennessee Ernie Ford.

They are members of the American Legion and its auxiliary. They are Methodists, and every four years they consider it their patriotic duty to vote, and if they are laggard in this regard, well-meaning fussbudgets from the League of Women Voters *urge* them to vote.

In short (and about time, too) the aunts and uncles and the cousins on my mother's side live in worlds bounded by the ends of their noses.

My Grandmother Kempton died long before I came along; she was a hearty peasant type and went off at forty, shortly after giving birth to my bachelor uncle, Robin, who would rather wash dishes than just about anything he can think of.

But I want to talk now about my grandfather. I may romanticize him a little. He may emerge here larger than life, but then I have probably made some of the people I've mentioned smaller than they are—difficult as that seems. Turn about.

I've mentioned R.L., my great-great-grandfather, and I will say more about him later. He accumulated a thousand acres of land—in Iowa a lot—and, since New Athens didn't get the state university, he and five other elders of the First Methodist Episcopal Church founded Pegasus. That was in 1857.

My great-grandfather lived to be thirty, and in those thirty years he managed to lose half of the thousand acres; he had no interest in the college. He imported Arabian horses. End of what I know about him.

My grandfather was six-two or thereabouts; he wore a Van Dyke beard; he carried himself with dignity, and he admired Shaw, Tolstoy, and Debs, which gave him a lot in common with my father, who also admired Shaw and Tolstoy and who had written about and known Debs when Debs was in jail during the First World War.

He attended Pegasus for two years and then had to drop out; by that time the college was on its last legs. What's more, my grandfather by then was already the father of Mettabel and the twins. He had wanted to go East to study at a theological seminary, but that didn't happen. He'd have been a good preacher, I think, and that's a compliment. The ministry seems to attract more incompetents than just about any other line of work—with the possible exception of the building trades.

It wasn't feasible to learn how to be a preacher at night, but my grandfather read law at night and, when he was forty, he gained admission to the Iowa bar. His law office was lined on four sides with books, floor to ceiling. That was unusual in Iowa at the time, and it would be unusual now.

He had a profitable practice for a small-town lawyer, even though he once defended a labor leader accused of trying to organize the canning factory. The organizing never happened, but my grandfather managed to get the labor leader out of town without a jail sentence—a considerable achievement.

My grandfather was elected to the state legislature twice, and on the Democratic ticket, an even more considerable achievement.

He was a lonely man—withdrawn, very much out of place in New Athens, but uncomplaining. His favorite story had to do with the time Thoreau went to jail rather than pay a tax of some kind. Emerson—I think it was—visited Thoreau and—according to the story—said, "What in the world are you doing in jail, Henry?" Thoreau allegedly said, "What in the world are you doing out of jail, Mr. Emerson?"

That story was one that not a single member of my grandfather's family came even close to understanding.

On at least two Sundays a month and on Easter and Christmas, all the members of the Kempton clan got together at my grandfather's house—and nothing on those occasions was the way it was in books—in Dickens, for instance. There were always just two kinds of people in Dickens' novels, those who laughed a lot and smiled a lot and sometimes even *sang*. Then there were the *villains*, but they were always colorful and you knew that deep down inside they had hearts of gold. Besides which, they almost always reformed, and at the end *everybody* was nice.

There were only two nice Kemptons—my grandfather and Aunt Mettabel, and there wasn't a colorful one among the others, all of them villains, not one with a heart of gold. What's more, I knew from the beginning that any hope of reform for any of them was out of the question.

God bless us everyone, said Tiny Tim.

When the Kemptons got together on Sundays and holidays, they talked about whichever member of the family wasn't there that day or had temporarily left the room. Or they talked about their crops, always bad. Or their ailments, always numerous, or about death or money.

In addition to the aunts and uncles, there were from ten to fifteen cousins in my grandfather's house on those occasions. The cousins played endless, noisy games with each other—but not with me. They called me names—*genius, four eyes* (did I say I started wearing glasses at the age of four?), *freak, sissy,* or *bookworm, bookworm, bookworm.* That last was their favorite and was clearly the meanest thing they could think of to say about *anybody.*

Once my cousin Pearl, who was five years my senior, and I did a little sexual exploration of each other. I was six, and the whole thing came to very little. Pearl was disappointed; I was stupefied.

My most consistent memory has to do with the walks my grandfather and I used to take when his house was full of his children and grandchildren and with talk and smoke and dissatisfaction and the lethargy that followed the midday meal.

After the food (children first sitting, adults second sitting), my grandfather always went to his study, lay on his black-leather couch, put the peach-colored sports section of the *Des Moines Register* over his face, and slept for exactly an hour.

Then he woke up, rose, and invariably said, "Where's my boy?"

His boy was me, and I had been waiting for him to get up, following every rise and fall of that peach-colored newsprint with the intensity of a spectator at a tennis match.

If it was winter, I was already bundled up for the walk. If it was summer, I was already perspiring with excitement.

"I'm ready," I would say, quietly, so that none of the cousins could hear me.

"Ready for what?" my grandfather would ask. He asked it every time.

"Aren't we going for a walk, Grandfather?" I'd say, anxiously. I was always pretty sure he was joking, but I was never sure enough.

"Well, now that you mention it," my grandfather would say, "if it isn't too much trouble for you, we might as well go for a walk."

I always assured him that it wasn't too much trouble for *me*.

Then, after putting on his overcoat if it was winter, and, winter or summer, picking up his malacca cane, my grandfather would look around at my cousins, who were usually screaming at each other, and say, rather softly, "Any of the rest of you children wish to accompany us?"

I always prayed that none of them would want to, and they almost never did.

Once in a while my father came with us, but not too often. You see, my father drank, and Sundays and holidays were his best drinking times; so he usually didn't come to my grandfather's house at all. Mother always took it upon herself to explain why. "Kendall was feeling under the weather this morning," she would say. "His kidneys. I just absolutely insisted he stay in bed."

On the walks, my grandfather and I usually went to the courthouse square where the inevitable old men were sitting on benches, whittling and gossiping and waiting to die.

The old men always said, "This one of your grand-young-uns, A.J.?"

My grandfather would nod and introduce me to each of the old men; he always knew all of their names.

"This is the one who's going to be president of the United States one of these days," my grandfather would say, and we would walk on.

We would go to the cemetery, and in summer I would feed the single swan on the lake. The cemetery was famous; a picture of the lake had appeared in *American* Magazine, a *whole page*.

We went to the zoo in the park, where there was one sleepy bear, two doltish monkeys, and an extremely cowardly lion.

We almost always went down to the railroad to watch the two-thirty train; it stopped for water on its way to Chicago. Very often there were people in the diner of that train, *eating*.

From the first time on I *knew* that as soon as I got big enough, in a year or so, I was going to travel on trains *all the time*, eating as many as ten or twelve meals a day. Eating on a train seemed to me the height of worldliness.

I hung on to this feeling until the railroads intensified their campaign to make passengers feel unwanted. The last time I was on the Twentieth Century I was kicked by two porters and kneed in the groin by the conductor. So were the other two passengers.

I doubt that my grandfather ever took a train trip. When I knew him, he drove everywhere, always in a black Packard sedan, as much a part of him as the malacca cane and the beard.

We never walked in that part of town where Pegasus was, and I don't believe we ever mentioned it. It was as if the place didn't exist.

Isn't it odd? I can't remember anything my grandfather and I talked about, or if we talked at all. He was not a garrulous man, and I was not then a talkative child. My garrulity came later.

Sometimes there was snow on the ground, and sometimes we were the first to walk on it, and then I used to pretend that there was no one in the world except my grandfather and me and, if he would only stay sober, my father.

I remember this, coming back to my grandfather's house with him on a summer Sunday afternoon. We stood on the sidewalk outside for a moment, listening to the voices of discontent coming from within. I remember his saying, "What in God's name did I ever do to deserve them?"

I wish I could think of some pertinent piece of advice he gave me; I can't. I wish I could pass along some piercing insight into his personality. I am unable to.

I remember that he sometimes preached on Sunday at the New Athens First Methodist Episcopal Church, usually when the regular preacher was on vacation or between preachers.

He had no Monotone; he just stood behind the lectern and talked; his text was sometimes from the Bible, more often not. Once it was from Emerson, "I cannot find language of sufficient energy to convey my sense of the sacredness of personal integrity." Not long before his death, it was Socrates' *Apology*, "And now it is time to go, to die and you to live, but which of us goes to a better thing is unknown to all but God."

My grandfather was going to baptize me, but he died before he had the chance, and that may be significant. Dr. Baron said it was.

I was later baptized by a man named Mayberry, one of a series of sanctimonious simpletons who tarried briefly at the New Athens First Methodist Episcopal Church, young men on their way up, old men on their way down. They were without exception chucklers and pear-shaped-tone fellows.

Mayberry got his fat hand wet, and he plumped it on top of my head, and he *leaned*. Then he went on for at least ten minutes about how from that moment on I would attend the Methodist Church. I remember thinking, A lot he knows. At least I *like* to remember thinking that, and I like to think that I said, "Take your clammy hand off my head, Mayberry, and stop *leaning*."

Well, now. I started to tell about mother, and I got off on my grandfather, who's a lot more interesting anyway. I seem to have concluded with a sermonette against one of the Protestant sects. Enough!

It seems hardly necessary to say that I have not stepped inside any church, particularly a Methodist one, for at least twenty-five years. Once, I did spend some time reading up on John Wesley, who was responsible for Methodism. If Wesley were around now, he'd be in a place like Wingdale, which, as I may have said, is the mental hospital not far from here.

Back to grandfather for one minute, then on to Celeste or Heavenly or *Mummy*.

Almost all of my memories of him are pleasant, and then there is this:

In May, 1927, shortly after he had made good a forged check my Uncle Jebediah had written, my grandfather went to every store in New Athens at which he had a charge account; he paid every bill he owed. Then he got into his Packard, and on a deserted country road he ran into a tree, dying shortly before that or shortly after that. The official cause of his death was heart failure. I have always thought it was really heartbreak.

He had wanted Pericles' funeral oration to the Athenians read at his funeral. I don't know why, but it didn't happen. I remember Aunt Amaryllis saying, "He must have been absolutely out of his mind, and people would think *we* were crazy if we allowed something like that.... Besides which the Greeks weren't Christians, so to speak...."

In any case, my grandfather's last wish was denied; instead, at the funeral, at which I did not cry, an old man with the dissatisfied face of a bank clerk said empty things for one of the longest and emptiest hours of my largely empty life.

At first, I didn't cry at the grave either.

I remember that it was on the crest of a low, green hill, and a white lilac tree bloomed nearby.

There were other graves in the Kempton plot, those of three cousins who had died young, my grandmother, and my great-grandfather.

I remember this. Just before the coffin was lowered into the grave, I ran to it, and for the first time I cried, and I also prayed that I could just once more see the peach-colored pages of the sports section of the *Des Moines Register* move rhythmically up and down on my grandfather's face.

After that, I ran away and hid in the duck house by the cemetery lake. I stayed there for what I hoped would turn out to be forever.

When I left the duck house, the sun had gone down, and it was cold. I stood over the grave for a while, and then I knelt beside it, and prayed. I prayed the Lord my grandfather's soul to keep.

By the time I got back to the crowded house in which my grandfather had lived, it was dark, and I heard the querulous voice of one of the twins saying, "You'd of thought he'd at least have left a little more insurance."

I needed my father that night. There were things about death that I wanted to know, but my father was back home, under the weather.

After all the others had gone, I went to bed, and my mother stayed in the parlor, and, without turning on the lights, she sang several hymns, and then she played and sang:

> With a hel-ping—h-ah-nd,
> I will under-sta-hnd,
> Oilways.

I listened to that, and then I cried myself to sleep.

Only now as I say these words does it occur to me that perhaps my mother cried that night, too.

My grandfather parceled out the land he still owned to various of my aunts and uncles; he left the house on Riverdale Avenue built by my great-great-grandfather to mother. Until then, we had lived in a small, cheerful bungalow on the east side of town.

The Riverdale Avenue house was really too large for us, and, as I may have said, it was dark. In the winter we closed off the entire upstairs; the bedrooms were never heated, and even the downstairs was never warm enough. I wore a sweater when I studied and was only comfortable in bed.

"We were all much healthier before we had furnaces," mother used to say. "After all, our ancestors lived in *caves*."

To me the house was never depressing, though, despite its size, its darkness, and the dampness that permeated everything from about the first of October until the following April. When I came on *Wuthering Heights* for the first time, I felt completely at home.

My grandfather left his library to me. It was a good, rather typical Nineteenth-Century library—his law books, sets of Dickens and Meredith and Hardy and Thackeray, the Harvard Classics, the Everyman Series, and so on. There were also two books that had belonged to R.L., as well as his journals.

I can still hear Aunt Amaryllis saying, "Those books would have brought a very good price at the auction, and don't you forget it. Instead, what happens? They go to some four-eyed little sissy that's always got his nose stuck in a book anyway."

Aaron, Aunt Amaryllis's oldest, then aged nine, was at the same time chanting, "Smarty, smarty had a party, and nobody came but a big, fat darky."

They all chanted that for my benefit, every one of the cousins. Aaron always ended his rendition with the highly original line, "And I don't care who knows it."

Then he would stick out his tongue.

My final remarks on mother's life before she came up with me will be brief, but here are a few things more it is necessary to know.

It is important to know that my mother was graduated from the New Athens High School at sixteen, two years under par. She was president of the class (thirty-five members), editor of the yearbook (*The Rock*), played the lead in the senior class play (*Green Stockings*), and gave the valedictory address, "All We Have to Look is Forward."

Does this mean my mother was a scholar? *False.* That she ever learned anything at all in school? *False.*

I believe I have already demonstrated that she had a tin ear; she exhibited that in nearly every sentence she spoke.

Naturally, she wanted to become a musician.

My grandfather had offered all of his daughters the chance to learn to play a musical instrument or, if they chose, to study singing. Only mother took him up on his offer. She not only took both piano and voice lessons, she *practiced.* She practiced four and sometimes five hours a day, *every* day.

"I can still hear her pounding away on that piano and bellering," Aunt Mettabel once told me. "That's what we used to call it. *Bellering.*"

Aunt Mettabel said that she had heard my grandfather speak the Lord's name in vain only once. It was after Sunday dinner. He was having his usual nap, and mother broke the house rule for silence; she must have been about twelve.

After a while, my grandfather woke up, rose, walked to the piano, looked down, and said, "For Jesus Christ's sweet sake shut the goddamn to hellitup. Forgive me, Lord. You had no daughters, and I believe it was Your good fortune that Your Son was not musically inclined."

Mother, according to Aunt Mettabel, said, "Father, I have my career to think of."

And there you have the nub of her musical interest. She felt no urgency to produce pleasing sounds; none. Her sole interest was in a career; she wanted to comport herself in public, and music happened to be the simplest available means to her.

You might and probably are saying that that is the motivation for a lot of art, good and bad.

Please don't say it to me, though. Not when I'm talking about my mother.

"Your mother stuck right to her music," Aunt Mettabel used to say. "Celeste played and sung through thick and thin, and you've got to give her credit for that."

Not me. I don't have to.

Persistence a virtue? *Ridiculous.* You should see some of the oddities I've come across in the the-ay-ter, anxious at twenty, hopeful at thirty, persevering at forty, tenacious at fifty, in there indefatigably punching away until the very end. That's creditable? *Ridiculous.*

Back now to *Mummy, pianissimo.*

She started playing the organ in the First Methodist Episcopal Church when she was fourteen and sometimes she sang with the choir, too. Both very *forte.*

Mother studied voice and piano with a booby named Lily Norton-White, and let me repeat that I have yet to come across anybody with a hyphenated name who didn't make me check the lock on the chicken house.

Miss Norton-White told mother, "I knew the minute I placed your piggly-wigglies on the keyboard that I had come across talent, and when I saw your little larynx quiver in song, I wanted to burst into tears of joy."

At least that's what mother claimed Norton-White told her, and I don't doubt it.

I met that odd mutation only once; I must have been six.

Norton-White took one look at me and brayed, "I always knew that with all your mother had in her, it would emerge somewhere."

Then she patted the emergence on the head.

Now Lily Norton-White wasn't alone in her feeling about *Mummy's* genius. The *Times-Dispatch* said of mother's piano playing, "...Brilliant...Those of us who have heard her rendition of Schubert's immortal *Serenade* will carry that lovely memory to our graves."

And of mother's singing, the *T-D* with its usual flair for the fresh phrase said, "A soprano voice like hers comes along once in a lifetime."

Naturally, mother had the clipping. *Naturally.*

I myself heard mother sing and play—oh, incessantly, it seems to me. Of her singing I will simply repeat a remark made by Mr. Samuel Clemens. He said, "You got the words, Octavia, but the melody ain't quite right."

Mother's piano playing? Let's not go into it.

However, is it any wonder that with the words of Norton-White and the *T-D* ringing loud in her receptive ears, mother announced long before she graduated from high school that she simply had to go East to study music? "I owe it to myself," she said. "The desert rose and all."

By *East* she meant Chicago.

Something called the Institute for Art in Chicago had awarded her *a partial scholarship*. Grandfather paid the rest of her tuition and gave her enough money to live in Chicago for a year.

"At the end of which time," said my mother, "I will, of course, be launched on my career, either in Chicago or New York, or perchance one of the far-flung capitals of Europe."

And so it was that on a bright September morning in 1909, mother set out for Chicago, nearly three hundred miles away.

Doesn't sound like much of a trip, does it?

Nevertheless, she had only been away from New Athens once before. She and the rest of the family had been taken by my grandfather to the Iowa Dairy Cattle Congress in Waterloo.

Mother often said, "I don't want you ever to forget, Joshua; your mother gave up a very, very brilliant career in your behalf."

Then she would show me the yellowed clipping that appeared on the front page of the *Times-Dispatch* the afternoon she left:

Miss Celeste Kempton, just turned seventeen and one of the brightest flowers ever to grace our fair city, left this morning to study at the Institute for Art in Chicago, Illinois, where she has been awarded a scholarship. Miss Kempton is to study voice and piano; her brilliance both as a pianist and as a soprano are well known to concert goers in New Athens.

The world will soon hear of this native daughter of whom we are all so justifiably proud, etc....

You understand, don't you, that the place to which mother had a scholarship was not the Chicago Art Institute? No, the Institute for Art in Chicago was far different. I have a feeling it may have been no more than a letterhead, an address, and a scheme to separate girls like mother from as much money as possible, but I'm only guessing. Perhaps it was a perfectly honest organization which performed the necessary but painful task of telling girls like mother that they had no t-a-l-e-n-t, to use mother's favorite phrase, "not a smidgin."

Mother said that of many people, "Not a smidgin of talent, of course." She said it of, among others, Caruso, Chaliapin, and Fritz Kreisler.

I have often thought how at ease mother would have been in the circles in which I have spent these last years of my life. That's about all those people talk about—how nobody has any talent any more except me and thee—and even thee....

Mother was in Chicago for five years. I have no idea what happened during that time, but she probably had it rough. It's rough for all those girlish refugees from reality who get off every train and every bus and every airplane in every large city every hour of every day, and who always will. I've mentioned Pan.

Mother always said, "My clippings tell the whole, entire story of my success in Chicago. I'll leave them all to you in my will, Joshua. They're all in the attic in that steamer trunk of your grandfather's."

After her death, there was no steamer trunk; there wasn't any attic either.

Mother's version of her triumphs was never twice the same. I won't bother with details of the variations except to say that she claimed "audiences were just simply mad for my whole, entire repertoire. I often thought they would just never stop cheering."

Why didn't she go on to challenge Alma Gluck, let's say?

"Madame *Cluck*, more like. That woman is an absolute fraud. Not a smidgin of talent to her name."

Well, mother was prevented by *agents* for one thing. The *agents*—"All Hebrew"—would have had her on the stage in a second if only she would agree to their lascivious suggestions, but she would not.

There were managers who almost swooned when they heard her perform, and they would have made her name immortal in the musical world—if it hadn't been for *the system*.

Mother would name several then-important musical figures, and she would say, "It was not *talent* that got *them* where they are today. Of that you can be sure. It cost each and every one of them hundreds of thousands of dollars, *hundreds of thousands*. If I heard it once, I heard it a thousand times. 'Celeste,' the managers would say, 'you could outshine them all, each and every one of them, but it would cost you a *fortune*.' Now your grandfather was well-fixed, Joshua, but he simply did not have that kind of money, not to speak of the fact that I was not a Hebrew, and, believe you me, they take care of their own, changing their names and all."

Or, "The musical world in Chicago is totally and exclusively in the hands of Hebrew rapists, 'scallions, and thieves, and no two ways about it. I understand in New York it's a different story, and they begged on bended knee for me to come. But—" here mother would smile waspishly—"romance entered my life, and I was a silly, headstrong little girl. I deserted my talent for your father, and I'll always regret it, always."

...I will under-sta-hnd,
Oil-ways.

Her letters home during this period were filled with vague references to success, and sometimes portions of them were printed in the *Times-Dispatch*. Once when I was in the newspaper library doing research on something or other, I read them.

I had never been in Chicago and knew nothing about the musical world, but I instinctively recognized that the letters were filled with half-truths and frequent total lies. The gaiety was forced and sad. It seems to me that there was a time when I wanted to tell my mother that I knew and that it didn't matter. I didn't do that, and, looking back on it now, I'm glad I didn't.

The structure of lies my mother had built needed every imagined brick. If a single one had been removed, it might have collapsed, and I have an awful feeling that she might have, too.

As I've said, I don't know what really happened in Chicago, but I'll bet she never performed professionally.

How did she support herself during the four years after my grandfather stopped? Clerking? At Marshall Field's? I don't know, but this clue: I once heard her say, "There was a brief time in my life when I worked out in the public all day, so don't try to tell me what *they're* like."

The people, sir, is a great beast.

All that matters here is that after five years in Chicago, mother came back to New Athens.

There must have been several people at the railroad station who hoped that the finest flower of New Athens had wilted away in Chicago. The hopers surely included several brothers and sisters— possibly including Aunt Mettabel.

They didn't know mother. She was born knowing how to turn an actual defeat into an imagined victory.

As she stepped from the train, she made an announcement.

"I have given up my career to make a home for a very important man. With Kendall and me it was love from the instant our eyes met."

Then she added, "If I hadn't met Kendall, I'd have gone on to New York. They were waiting for me there."

From the train, carrying the luggage, emerged a slight man with blue eyes, prematurely white hair, and a sad, kind smile that was to become sadder but no less kind as time went on.

Let's say his name was Kendall Bland. He turned out to be my father.

Mother was fond of describing father as "the former executive managing editor of the *Chicago Daily News*."

I don't believe I ever heard him contradict her about that. Or about anything else. Except once. She came through for perhaps the thousandth time with the line, "If I hadn't met Kendall, I'd have gone on to New York. They were waiting for me there."

On this occasion, I forget where it was or when, my father said, "Celeste, if you'd gone on to New York, you'd have just had that much further to come to get back here."

If memory serves, this was one of the few times in her life that my mother was silent.

It is now four o'clock—A.M.

For the first time in months, I'm exhausted.

I will save the memories of my father until I've had a little sleep. One pill should be enough.

NOTES·DICTATED·ON·
THE·SECOND·DAY

(1) Dear father, come home

One pill was enough.

It is a beautiful Sunday afternoon, and I feel very nearly rested. I'll tell you about my father.

I have no idea where he met mother or when or how he happened to agree to marry her. I'm sure that's the way it was, though. She did the asking.

Why should such a gentle failure of a man as my father agree to involve himself with a human tornado like my mother? I don't know.

Who understands anybody's marriage—including, very often, his own?

My own theory about my father's marriage, no better than anybody else's, is this:

I think he was a born patsy. If you're fancy, you call them Injustice Collectors. Except don't the latter complain? My father never complained. He just collected injustices.

Maybe he was simply unlucky.

One of the most haunting memories of my childhood is of a day—I was eight—when I heard my father say, half-aloud, "Oh, my God, why hast Thou deserted me?" And then I heard him cry. I'd never heard a man cry before; I didn't know they did.

My father didn't know I'd heard, and we never discussed it.

He was crying that morning because, without consulting my mother, he had invested $7,500 of the money in their joint bank account in what may have been the last sure thing of his life, a company that was making a premature plastic.

He lost every cent. I'll come back to that later.

The plastics fiasco took place in the fall of 1929, but it didn't take a stock-market crash to bring financial disaster to my father.

Four years earlier, in 1925, he had got in on the Florida land boom; he bought a hundred acres "less than half a mile from America's fastest growing city, Nirvana." It turned out Nirvana was an abandoned turpentine camp, and seventy-five of the hundred acres were sometimes under the Atlantic Ocean.

He invested in a roadside restaurant on U.S. Highway No. 30 because the Lincoln Highway was going to be the most important transcontinental highway in the country. The next year the route was changed, and the year after that the restaurant stood deserted beside an almost impassable country road.

He invested in a miniature golf course because there could be no doubt but that the people who couldn't afford the Country Club or who weren't asked would be interested in the next best thing, miniature golf. A few months after the golf course was finished, people in New Athens stopped playing miniature golf altogether.

There were many other such investments. Put it this way. My father would have been one of the last to get into the manufacture of glasses for three-D movies. Awhile back I thought—rather ruefully— that he might have got into the hoola-hoop business just before the end came. Maybe he was. You see, my father may still be alive.

Mother lied about my father having been a former executive managing editor of the *Chicago Daily News*. He had been a police reporter, probably not a very good one.

"I don't know about there being no such thing as a bad boy," he used to say. "I do know damn good and well there's no such thing as a good cop."

Like father, like son; I'm a born cop-hater.

My father got his job on the *Daily News* through a friend he met during his one year at the University of Chicago.... One year. Mother often said—not when father was around—"It embarrasses Kendall to have anybody mention his doctor of philosophy degree."

I know almost nothing about my father's family. It was large; they were Catholic, and they were poor. My father's mother had hoped that he would become a priest. He was the bookish one.

Instead, at the age of sixteen, Father left the Church, and at seventeen he managed a year at the university. If he had been able to continue, he would have majored in philosophy, and whenever I asked him a question he couldn't answer he would quote from *Quo Vadis*, "'The greater the philosopher a man is, the more difficult it is for him to answer the foolish questions of common people.'"

Then he would smile and wink, and I would run to him. He would swing me around over his head, and we would both laugh. If we were alone, that is.

Once I remember my father saying he thought he might have liked to be a librarian. "All those books," he said. "You just reach up and bring them down, all you want."

"Librarians are grossly exploited," I remember saying. "Teachers and librarians. Grossly."

Another time he said, "My trouble has always been I've never wanted anything enough. I never cared. You see that you care about something. The caring's what separates the men from the boys."

I also remember what I said to that. I said, "I'm going to be a scientist, of course." That was when I wanted to find a way to prevent polio.

Hughie Larrabee hadn't yet arrived in New Athens (Hughie was my best boyhood friend), and until he got there my one friend in school was a girl in a wheel chair. Was her name Lucille? She had had polio, and the two of us used to spend recesses together, us two cripples.

When my father first got to New Athens, there were no jobs on the *Times-Dispatch*. However, there was a small, apologetic weekly called *The New Athens Journal*. Its editor and publisher had died a few months before, and the *Journal* was for sale, cheap. My father borrowed enough money from the New Athens Farmers' and Merchants' Bank to make a down payment.

The savings bank, like everything else in New Athens, was controlled by the Lavendar family. I guess they figured neither my father nor the *Journal* was a threat to the *status quo*.

They were right.

However, my mother said, "Kendall will become the William Alfred White of the state of Iowa. On that I will bet my bottom dollar."

What she meant was that she saw herself as the Mrs. William Allen White of Iowa.

My mother was wrong.

In the first place, Father was never a good newspaper man. There were many reasons for that, among them the fact that he was impatient with what seemed to him unimportant, and very little that happened in New Athens seemed to him to be of consequence. For instance, he refused to print what he called *drivel*—"who is going where for the day, who had what bouquet of roses on the dining-room table when she entertained Priscilla Titlebottom, that kind of thing."

He was right, but that kind of *drivel* is what sells newspapers in small towns.

My father wouldn't print obituaries either, "unless it's somebody who's done something important." Since almost nobody in New Athens ever did anything worthwhile, there were few obits in the *Journal*.

Foolish, but nice.

Father was an honest man, a quality that at the time I took for granted.

He had courage, too, but he wasn't strong. As I've said, a born loser.

At first, the *Times-Dispatch* paid no attention to my father or to the *Journal*, even though Father started printing things that the *T-D* had been ignoring for years. For instance, Sheriff George Taliman—a Lavendar cousin, as I recall—was drunk all the time, and, occasionally, just for laughs, he would beat up a Negro or a tramp in the county jail. That's news? My father thought so, and every time anybody was beat up, my father found out about it and printed it. Councilman Fred Ellis was found with his hand in the town till. Ellis had enough relatives, Lavendar and otherwise, to keep him in office for life no matter what. Nevertheless, my father wrote an editorial saying that Fred Ellis was a common thief. Fred issued a statement in reply; Fred said, "I ain't puttin' nothin' out," and my father printed that, too.

So far, so good.

Then all hell broke loose. My father was campaigning for a municipally owned utility plant in New Athens. David Reasoner, a Lavendar son-in-law who was editor and publisher of the *Times-Dispatch* and chairman of the board of the privately owned utility plant, slipped a few hundred-dollar bills into the hands of a few state legislators. All they had to do in return was pass a law making municipally owned light and power plants illegal.

My father printed the whole thing on the front page of the *Journal*; that particular issue had the largest circulation in the history of the *Journal*—three thousand plus.

Well, that went too far. Reasoner immediately notified all of the *T-D*'s advertisers to stop advertising in the *Journal*. If they did, Reasoner said, they could no longer advertise in the *T-D*.

There's a law against that sort of thing, but in New Athens the Lavendars and the *Times-Dispatch* were (still are) above the law. The advertisers capitulated, to the man.

So, about six months later, did *The New Athens Journal*. The bank called in its loan, and Father couldn't pay it.

Nevertheless, Editor Reasoner was able to forgive my father, and a job on the *Times-Dispatch* was found for him. He was placed in charge of obituaries and the society page. The year was 1921. The salary was eighteen bucks a week.

My father immediately accepted the job. He had to; my mother was pregnant. With me.

Around then, my father started his really heavy drinking.

Which is pretty nearly where I come in.

(2) "And please do not quote me!"

First this, however. While my father collected his injustices, mother was by no means idle.

In the first place, she formed the Arts, Crafts, and Literature Society I've told you about. She was also president.

At first, mother dizzied the girls (and how easy that must have been) with hints that she might change her mind at any moment and resume what she called "my operatic career."

She would say, "Only yesterday I got a long-distance telephone message from New York City. The director of one of the most respected musical organizations in the whole wide and shining world and please do not quote me as saying it was the Metropolitan Opera begged me on bended knee to resound my decision to retire. 'Celeste Bland,' he said. 'I could have your name on every tongue and your voice in every home in the land.'"

Here my mother would pause so that the girls would get some idea of just who their president was and could, had she so chosen, have been.

Then she would go on. "Naturally, I said, 'No.' I said, 'My first loyalty is to my dear husband. Kendall has been under the weather recently, and he has had his own journey through Cavalry.'"

(Translator's note: Pop had become a bottle-and-a-half-a-day man.)

"My voice in every home," mother would say. "It gives me pause."

Me, too.

The girls in the Arts, Crafts, and Literature Society must have clucked sympathetically, knowing mother was lying through her teeth.

The purpose of the Artsy-Craftsy Club eludes me, but I do remember mother saying, "Our main interests are arts and letters, but we have our little sewing projects for the girls who have no special talents, the ones who simply like to be present when cultural ideas are being tossed about."

That means the ones who hadn't got their fill of gossip over the party line.

On Thanksgiving, they delivered baskets to the *deserving* poor. The recipients were expected to be grateful and to show it. If they didn't—well, I doubt that mother ever grabbed a basket away from an ingrate, but I do remember her saying to my father, "When I smell liquor on their breath, I just quietly fold my tents like the Arabs [that's a long A there, the Ah-rabs] and cross their names off my list."

Father, often sucking on a sen-sen, would nod.

Mother, who was a Grand Old Party member, wrote many letters, all printed in the *Times-Dispatch*, about WPA and PWA and what they were doing to *the moral fabric of our social structure*.

"As a result [of WPA], many of these individuals are becoming sullen to their betters," mother once wrote. "I can and if called upon will testify to this from personal experience."

Nobody ever called upon her to testify, not even her two brothers who were on WPA.

During the depression, the Artsy-Craftsy girls stopped their deliveries of Thanksgiving baskets. The depression hit New Athens very hard indeed. First, the canning factory closed, and the Lavendars all took off for Bermuda to wait out the storm.

The fact of the matter was that the Artsy-Craftsy girls didn't have a drumstick to spare during much of the depression, let alone a whole Thanksgiving basket. One of the New Athens' banks was the first in all of Iowa to go broke.

The depression struck our house early in 1927, shortly after the collapse of what mother called "the Florida land boon."

Mother, however, was above economics.

She used to say, "Of course, Kendall lost a veritable fortune in Florida. Until then, we lived like veritable kings."

She would often say this to women who knew good and well that before 1927 we had lived in the same catch-as-catch-can way as afterward.

Eventually, mother and the depression met head-on: my father's income and mother's outgo became blatantly disproportionate.

I don't know that all children are as conscious of the horrors of being *poor* as I was—but I'm inclined to think so. I've checked around. One of the nicest women I know—and seemingly the most secure—is the daughter of a Lutheran preacher, and she had to ask for "the clerical discount" when she went to the store for something. To this day she shudders at the memory of it.

And the only producer in New York who has taste any place but in his mouth gets the trembles when he remembers an early Thanksgiving in his life when he had to go to a convent to get a Thanksgiving basket. He couldn't afford a bus ride and had to carry the basket all the way from Second Avenue and Twenty-second to Second Avenue and Fifty-fourth, feeling that every eye in the world was watching, knowing that his family was poor.

My own trauma in this area has to do with day-old bread. In New Athens, fresh bread cost ten cents a loaf. Day-old bread was two cents cheaper. About the time my father's eighteen dollars a week started not reaching from Friday to Friday, mother discovered that day-old bread was *healthy*.

"The proof is right here in this book," she would say, waving a diet-and-health volume under my nose. "Right here. Fresh bread causes rickets and heartburn and *possibly* rheumatism."

And so Little Boy Blue traipsed down to the Holsum Bakery on East Main every afternoon after school. He waited until the bakery was deserted, which often meant a long wait, and then he sneaked in and in a frantic sotto voce would say, "Two loaves of bread, please," pointing to the stack of day-old bread. He couldn't possibly have said the words.

As Boy Blue walked home, even though the loaves were wrapped in brown paper, he was sure e-v-e-r-y-b-o-d-y could s-e-e that those brown-paper bundles had the mark of Cain upon them.

My second worst experience during the depression was a recurring one at the Hailey grocery.

"Run over to Hailey's," mother would say, "half a peck of potatoes, two pounds of prunes—Albert Einstein eats nothing else—and ask Mr. Hailey if he has any French ice cream."

Mr. Hailey did not have any French ice cream and mother knew it. He never had had any and never would have, but the addition of French ice cream to the potato-and-prune order made it possible for mother to persuade herself that we were still living grandly.

"Somebody has to keep up the standards. Somebody has to set an example for the lower classes."

I was the lower classman serving as liaison between my mother and Mr. Hailey, a sweet man who hated to mention the word *money*. All the worse for me.

After mother had given me the sentence about French ice cream, she would say, "And charge it, of course, and tell little Mr. Hailey that I don't believe he rendered a bill last month."

After about six months of bill-rendering and no response, Mr. Hailey, hating himself, would say to me, "Sonny, I wonder if you'd ask your mother if she could pay a little on account."

I would nod, hoping that the tears didn't show, and I would then run home with the potatoes and prunes and, if I was especially courageous, mention to mother what Mr. Hailey had said.

"A little on account!" mother would say. "The man must be stark, raving mad. We are overpaid if we are a cent."

Then she would render her Class-A sigh. "Well, there is nothing else to do, and the Haileys need the money, but I am afraid we shall simply have to take our patronage elsewhere."

And this:

A day my mother was having me fitted for a suit for school at the J. C. Penney store. The suit had been measured, and I was about to take it off.

"That's a charge, of course," said mother.

"Mrs. Bland," said the clerk, who was also the manager, "all our business is cash-and-carry."

Mother gave the theatrical pause I believe I've mentioned, and she said, "Sonny, take that suit off," and to the manager, "Don't try to palm your inferior merchandise off on me. If there is one thing I know, it is quality."

I took off the suit, but, even now, some thirty years later, I have not forgotten how nearly impossible it was for me to step out of the dark of the dressing room into the light of the store. Experiences like that have helped make me a perfect patsy for inferior merchandise. I step into a store—any store—and take whatever the clerk tries to palm off on me. The first suit. A cigarette hole burned in the jacket? Last year's style? Two sizes too large? No matter. I'll take it. Wrap it up. I've never been known to complain in this area—one of the few—and, naturally, clerks recognize my type at a glance.

I don't mean to underestimate what my mother probably felt on these occasions—or, let's face it, that my father never seemed to be around when the subject of money came up.

The depression left a mark on almost every member of my generation. That and the war. As a result, in these two areas there is always a lack of sympathy between me and those who didn't experience them.

Mother, undaunted by the depression, carried on. In addition to the activities already mentioned, she played the lead in nearly every play perpetrated by the New Athens Community Theater, which is no doubt one reason being in the same room with an actor or an actress gives me goose flesh.

As I've said, she was a Rebekah and a member of the P.E.O., whatever that is.

What's more, whenever two or more people gathered in a public place in or around New Athens, mother was usually on hand, playing or singing or both.

She also became president of the New Athens Woman's Club, and when the girls refused to amend their constitution so that she could run for a third term, mother and a handful of foolish followers seceded and formed the Woman's Club of New Athens, the motto of which was, "The only *Real* Woman's Club in Town."

There must have been other activities in her life. After all, there are twenty-four hours in a day.... Which leads me to mention another plank of the Bland Plan for Shaping Up the World—a semiannual check-up on everybody's thyroid. At the slightest hint of a hyper condition, out with the thyroid.

In any case, in 1921 mother was getting on toward thirty; like Alexander, she must have decided that there were no more worlds to conquer, not in New Athens anyway. So, as I've explained, she decided on pregnancy. "I'll have a baby the like of which this town has never laid eyes on."

But we've been through that.

Louella has brought me coffee and a sandwich.

"Now you relax and enjoy it, Mr. Bland," she said. "First thing you know the way you get worked up you'll pop off with a heart attack, and it's bad for your insides, eating and talking at the same time like that."

So I turned off the machine.

Louella left. She started singing. "Comfort, comfort ye my people. Speak ye peace, thus sayeth our God. Comfort those who sit in darkness...."

Comfort those who sit in darkness.

(3) Some childhood friends—real and imagined

It is evening now. The mild, pleasant afternoon has faded into a starless, muggy evening, and there is the smell of rain in the air. Rain depresses me. If I lived in Seattle, I'd be dead by now.

Louella has gone, and Ab is once more at Pism C.'s. I am again alone in my glass prison.

Just now as I put my solitary plate in the dishwasher I was thinking of all the childhood diseases I went through—diphtheria, small pox, measles (two kinds), whooping cough, scarlet fever, and a succession of common and uncommon colds.

I was thinking, too, that I have suffered from almost all of what cynical old men call adolescent diseases—idealism, pacifism, progressivism, socialism, and communism. After the next-to-final war, I was one of The Crusaders, and was an uncivil libertarian; twice I helped a man who wanted to be President, as well as right, succeed in being neither.

But for a long time now I've been a retired do-gooder, a former bleeding heart. All those who are still true believers have my blessing and my occasional check. I wish them well but do not expect much.

There will be no peace in the world, no real liberty, and right will not prevail so long as there are those of us who cannot love, so long as hatred blackens so many hearts, my own among them.

I want now to dredge forth some happy memories of my childhood. There were many.

First of all, there were always so many ways to lose myself. Once I spent a whole summer trying to find the rabbit hole the White Rabbit had used. I wanted to join him and Alice. I never found the hole, but looking for it was fun.

I once wrote a letter to Kim suggesting that he might want to change places with me for a couple weeks some summer. Kim never answered my letter, but I never gave up hope.

I remember once asking my father if Robert Louis Stevenson knew when I was bad; my father said he doubted it, which gave me the courage to write Mr. Stevenson suggesting that I was available for a possible second voyage to Treasure Island.

I never gave up expecting an answer to that one either.

Not surprisingly, my favorite escape has always been in books.

We had a Carnegie library in New Athens and a most unusual librarian. Her name was Evadne West, and she not only loved books, she liked to see people read them. It has been my experience that most librarians want to keep books locked up. Readers get them all *dirty*.

Not Evadne. I used to walk out of that cherished building with as many as ten books in my book bag, and at night, since my mother would probably have disapproved of all of them, I would wait until she and my father—or later, Pavan—were asleep, then turn on my bed lamp and read, usually until dawn. Miss West suggested and selected for me if I asked her—but I didn't very often.

Usually I went off on my own. I read everything from Thyra Samter Winslow to Kathleen Norris to Herman Melville (I had trouble with him at ten) to Laura Lee Hope to Saki (loved him at nine, never cared for her), to Kipling to Keats (Kipling was more my type at eight), Maugham to Moliere (I liked them both and still do).

I was never sure whether what I was reading was any good. All I could ever tell was whether I *enjoyed* it. Old-fashioned, but then....

In my youth at the New Athens Public Library I also learned that if there was a book I couldn't stand putting down and at the same time couldn't stand the thought of finishing, that, too, was a good book. For me, which was all that mattered.

I learned this further fact as well. If I could find a book that had a lot of peanut butter and jelly on its pages and if some of the pages were stuck together with some of somebody's breakfast egg, I had a book that nine times out of ten I was going to enjoy. Lots of other people already had.

And then there was the joy of discovering a new author. *The Thirteen* was the first book of Balzac's I happened on. I remember reading it at one sitting, though I doubt that I could have. I do know that the morning I finished it I hurried off to the library before I went to school. Miss West was already there, and she let me in, although the doors weren't officially opened.

I was breathless. "This Mr. Balzac," I think I said. "Did he write anything else besides this?"

Miss West took me by the hand and led me to the B fiction shelf, and there they all were, twenty-five more potential friends waiting to be met, hundreds of hours of entertainment and enlightenment and escape, just waiting for *me*.

So there were books, abundantly available. I don't imagine I'd have cared much for Andrew Carnegie personally, but he certainly left a lot of lovely monuments behind.

Most of my teachers were monstrous. Miss Velma, for instance, (more later of her), and there was Miss—I've forgotten her name. Deliberately, I'm sure.

Miss Forgotten taught Music Appreciation, and she had no ear for music, no knowledge of it, and no love for it, but then neither did I. My mother had already soured me on music.

I shall remember the first day in Miss Forgotten's class as long as I live, fortunately not long. I was seven, and I was late.

The other kids were all seated when I came into the room, all waiting, all watching as I walked the last mile to report to Forgotten's desk. Every eye watched my every step.

I got there; I stood more or less at attention. Miss Forgotten looked me up, and then she looked me down. Then she spoke. She said, "I hear you're supposed to be very smart. You want to know what I think?"

I said, "You want to tell me, and I have no objection to hearing it." (I had just read *Pride and Prejudice*.)

A flame appeared in each of Miss Forgotten's faded cheeks. "I think you're very stupid," she said.

"Well, it's a free country," I said. "You're entitled to your opinion. I'm entitled to mine."

I suspect this colloquy might have continued if Mr. Shay hadn't then come into the room. Mr. Shay was principal of our school.

"Go to your seat," said Miss Forgotten.

"I'll be happy to," I said, "but you seem to have neglected to tell me which one it is."

Forgotten told me, and I went to it.

"Is anything wrong?" Mr. Shay asked her.

"No, nothing," said Miss Forgotten. "We're just learning which are our little seats."

A little more on Frank Shay, a first-rate man and a real friend. He had been in real estate before he got to be principal of Arnold School. How he got the job I don't know, but I know what he did. Most unusual. He took being principal seriously. He learned as much as he possibly could about education. He saw to it that we had the best textbooks he could afford to buy, and, while his teaching staffs were not the best (e.g., Forgotten, Velma, and lots of others), they were the best his budget would allow.

What's more, Frank Shay was a *good* man, and he was an admirer of my father, which gave him a special place in my heart.

Miss Forgotten was a digression, though Frank Shay was not. These are happy memories.

We come now to Miss Ruth Auerbach and Miss Joyce Parkinson. Miss Auerbach taught American history and civics, and Miss Parkinson taught botany and chemistry. Both communicated that rare capacity which all of the few good teachers I've known have had, "a capacity of being astonished by the nature of things."

Miss Auerbach and Miss Parkinson lived together. Miss Auerbach was tall, wore her slate-colored hair cut short, and always had on a black wool skirt, ankle-length, and a severe white shirtwaist. Miss Parkinson was tiny; she wore her faded, once-red hair in two huge, loose, bunlike swirls, one over each ear. She also wore a spot of rouge redder than the rose on each cheek and a good deal of powder; the general effect of her face was that of a clown interrupted in mid-make-up. Miss Auerbach had the voice of a motherly top sergeant—and Miss Parkinson's voice was that of an off-key flute. You had to strain to hear her, but it was worth it. Miss Parkinson did all the cooking and all the housework, and Miss Auerbach did the gardening and in the winter chopped the wood for the fireplace and shoveled the sidewalk. She also painted the house in which they lived, white with orange shutters. Both were painted every two years.

The work division always seemed to me to be an ideal one.

Miss Parkinson and Miss Auerbach had met at a girls' school in Connecticut and had been best friends ever since. In their study was a framed sampler Miss Parkinson had made.

On it was embroidered this injunction from the headmistress of that school:

"I want all my girls to know how to shoot straight, speak the truth, and have a regard for the intellectual life."

"Ruth speaks the truth, and I have a regard for the intellectual life," Miss Parkinson would say, "but neither of us can shoot worth a damn."

Then we would all three go into gales of laughter.

Now mother, who never felt it necessary to be her brother's keeper, did insist on minding the business not only of all her brothers and sisters but of anybody else who ever hove into her nervous view.

Thus, "We all know what the Misses Auerbach and Parkinson are. The *messers* more like."

Did we? I didn't, and I don't think I ever even guessed what mother was talking about.

I loved those two women, and I learned from them. I used to go to their house after school. We would have tea and cookies and talk—about everything. I remember that although a dozen copies of the Sunday *New York Times* were bought in New Athens, Miss Auerbach and Miss Parkinson were the only people who got the *Times every* day of the week. We used to read stories aloud to each other, then discuss them.

I never mentioned these visits to my mother, but somehow she found out about them. Not hard to understand. New Athens was filled with pernicious gossips, one of the many things it had in common with Sloane's Station.

When mother found out, she said, "I *absolutely* forbid you to go to a house like *that*."

I didn't ask what she meant by *that*. I didn't want to know. But I never went back to their house. I never did what was *absolutely* forbidden by my mother.

Miss Parkinson suffered from arthritis. Mother said, "People like *that* spread arthritis, and I might add it is *highly* contagious."

I suppose Miss Auerbach and Miss Parkinson guessed why I stopped visiting them, but they never mentioned it. I'm sure they were hurt, and I'm sorry. Theirs was one of the three houses I was ever in in New Athens in which the people liked each other.

I learned as much as I was able to from Miss Parkinson, but that wasn't much. I shall die as ignorant of the sciences as when I was born. For instance, I've read as much as I could on the atom and still don't understand it, not to mention not understanding how we happened to make the mistake of splitting one. Nevertheless, Miss Parkinson always made the mysteries she was explaining sound exciting, and I always knew that if I didn't understand, the fault was mine, not hers.

With Miss Auerbach, I was more fortunate. She made me and just about everybody else in her classes love this preposterous country of ours, warts and all. Not what it was, what it could be.

"You have to work at democracy," Miss Auerbach kept saying. "*Work! Work! Work!* It's a full-time job."

I remember other things.

I remember Tony Genero, who smelled and who teased me mercilessly, calling me a series of unprintable names. Tony fought an unending battle against attempts to educate him. Yet Miss Auerbach got him to play George Washington in a play I wrote.

He remembered every line, and since I had written every line, I thought his performance was magnificent—a feeling I've found pretty common among playwrights.

"You were very good," I told him. "I hope you know that."

Tony smiled at me. "Thanks, Joshua," he said.

He never teased me again.

In Miss Auerbach's class we were always writing plays and acting them out, and we learned a lot of history and civics that way.

We pretended to be mayors and governors and senators, and I was once President of the United States for a day. I remember nothing of that experience except that we had a mock cabinet meeting that I opened by saying, "Well, gentlemen, the first thing we have to do is rewrite the Constitution."

Something else about Miss Auerbach. She *personally* paid for more than a hundred subscriptions to a little weekly news magazine called *Current Events. Personally.* I somehow found out and asked her why. She explained that she did it because there were always boys like Tony Genero who couldn't afford a subscription and because no matter how delicately these sensitive matters were arranged, somebody like Tony was always getting his feelings hurt.

So, she said, it seemed to her better to pay for everybody's subscription. Out of a salary of $1,500 a year.

Most other teachers weren't even aware that a boy like Tony had feelings. All they ever noticed was the smell.

I saw Miss Auerbach for the last time about five years ago. She was in New York for some meeting. She had long since retired.

Miss Parkinson was dead, but Miss Auerbach still seemed to be enjoying life immensely. We had lunch and discussed some of the Prominent Personalities then in Wonderland, D.C.

"They ought to be impeached," said Miss Auerbach.

She said it loud, and she said it clear, and people turned.

"Every damn one of them ought to be impeached," said Miss Auerbach.

I said a few minutes ago that there were three houses in New Athens in which people liked each other.

The second was Aunt Mettabel's and Uncle Dick's.

It wasn't until I was about thirty that Mettabel felt up to telling me what she really thought about my mother.

She said, "I shouldn't be saying this about my very own sister and your mother to boot, but I'm very much afraid that Celeste was a b-i-t-c-h."

Mettabel often spelled out things she felt were really better left unsaid. I remember once she told me that Spot, her fox terrier, had capriciously placed a bowel movement in my Uncle Dick's boater.

"Now don't l-a-u-g-h, darling," she said. "That will only e-n-c-o-u-r-a-g-e S-p-o-t."

Aunt Mettabel kept telling me that the doctor had brought me in his *little black bag*.

"That's where all babies come from," she would say. "The nice doctors bring them in their little black bags."

To me that sounded fishy. "How do they breathe?" I kept asking. "All cooped up in there, they couldn't breathe."

So Aunt Mettabel switched stories. "You really came from Monkey Ward," she said. "Your mother wanted a little b-a-b-y, and she wrote in to Monkey Ward and ordered you."

To that one I pointed out that there was no baby section in the Montgomery Ward catalogue; furthermore, if I had been mailed, I would have been shipped parcel post, and I would have been wrapped up, in which case, "How could I breathe? All wrapped up in a package, I couldn't breathe."

Finally, when I was four (just before I started to school), I got hold of a doctor book which had the whole explanation, *illustrated*. I went straight to Aunt Mettabel and told her in detail exactly where I had come from. She listened in silence and with great interest. I was probably wrong, but I had the feeling that most of what I said was news to Aunt Mettabel. She and Uncle Dick had no children.

Aunt Mettabel had the first radio in our family and the first electric refrigerator, and she always drove a Buick and, as was said by all the brothers and sisters, "she trades it in *every* year."

What's more, Aunt Mettabel had her hair "retouched." *Died* was a word that was never ever used in our family, no matter how you spelled it. No, *retouched* was what Mettabel had done, though she never admitted it. It was just something everybody knew, like the fact that Aunt Amaryllis was a kleptomaniac. The hair retouching was the reason Aunt Mettabel had such small bulbs in all the lamps in her living room and why she never turned on the ceiling lights. Aunt Amaryllis said that Aunt Mettabel *smoked in secret*. You couldn't prove it by me; during the month I stayed there, I never caught her at it, and I tried. She often did smell of tobacco, though. Uncle Dick smoked a pipe—but never in the house. Aunt Mettabel always said that if a man wanted to smoke he could do it in the garage or in the barn. He needn't smell up the house. In the house Uncle Dick chewed tobacco.

Mother said that Aunt Mettabel was a gadabout, but that seems to me a harsh judgment. Aunt Mettabel drove to Des Moines every two weeks; she went to the picture and the vaudeville show at the Orpheum, and she always had dinner at the Bishop's Cafeteria there, always with the pecan pie, which was famous, and she always bought something for her very extensive wardrobe, usually in Yonkers' Ready-to-Wear.

Aunt Mettabel was not a joiner like mother; in fact, the only place besides Des Moines she ever went was the New Athens First Methodist Episcopal Church. There she blossomed. I remember one Sunday during the month I stayed with her and Uncle Dick. She wore a bright red straw hat which had a cluster of purple flowers on the crown, a blue scarf, a dress that was neither pink nor red but a color somewhere in between that I had not seen before and have not seen since, high-heeled shoes as green as the meadow in the south forty, and a yellow linen coat.

I myself that day had on what I feel pretty sure was the first pair of horn-rimmed glasses ever to hit New Athens, and they were enormous, while I was small for my age.

The minister was a young man not long out of the theological seminary, and after the service he was standing at the door when Aunt Mettabel and I approached, hand in hand. He opened his mouth, closed it, opened it again, closed it, and, finally, in a high-pitched voice said, "Well, Mrs. Stryker [my aunt], you and little Joshua here are certainly a sight for sore eyes."

We must have been that.

The summer I'm going to tell about now was the summer before I entered Pegasus College.

I want to skip hurriedly over two points that I'll go into in some detail later. First point, my father was no longer living in New Athens. Second point, mother had just divorced him and had married Pavan. She and Pavan were in Chicago on their honeymoon—and, it turned out, on business. Monkey business.

"You could stay at Mettabel's while we're gone," I remember mother saying. "Not that Petrarch and I wouldn't love to have you come with us, of course."

"I'll stay at Aunt Mettabel's," I said.

Aunt Mettabel and Uncle Dick lived on the edge of New Athens. Uncle Dick was a truck farmer, which meant that he raised vegetables and trucked them into town, selling them at the college and at various groceries.

Uncle Dick raised particularly fine strawberries. He was, in fact, The Strawberry King of New Athens. It said so on the side of his truck.

I was there in strawberry time.

"You want to do a little work to earn your keep?" he asked me the day after I arrived. He smiled; he had hardly any teeth, but it didn't matter.

"You bet," I said, smiling back. My own smile isn't up to much, which is one of several reasons I wear a beard.

So Uncle Dick showed me how to pick strawberries.

In case there are a few non-strawberry pickers in the audience, I should explain that there is not a great deal to learn.

The green berries you don't pick. The pink ones—well, that takes a little judgment. Sometimes yes, sometimes no; depends on *how* pink they are. The red ones you do pick, and you place them in a basket, being careful not to bruise them. You also have to be careful not to damage the vines. All clear?

If it is and if you are patient, there is no reason you shouldn't have a successful career as a berry picker. Just be sure you get *all* the red ones. Otherwise, they rot.

That's the way Uncle Dick explained it to me, and I doubt if, despite automation, the technique has changed much in the twenty-odd years since.

Now in the scene coming up there are many other strawberry pickers, all grown except for a couple of high-school boys. In the spring of 1933 in New Athens, you could hire a good man for twenty-five cents an hour. True, in a strawberry patch you had to watch him; he might eat nearly as many berries as he put in the basket, and some rascals even tried to fill their pockets with berries so that they could take them home to their families. Many truck farmers around New Athens hired *foremen*, but the foremen were nothing more than watchers, meaning they just walked up and down in the strawberry patch to see that no berries were *eaten*. They earned thirty-five cents an hour. That kind of work always pays more.

My uncle never hired a foreman; he expected an hour's work for an hour's pay, but if berries were eaten by hungry men and if some were taken home to hungry families, my uncle never noticed. Not only that, the spring before (1932) he had been out on the Lincoln Highway helping dairy farmers who were his neighbors stop milk trucks that were trying to get into New Athens. My uncle helped empty the milk into roadside ditches. The idea was to keep the milk from being sold until the cost of production had been met.

I remember the *Times-Dispatch* had a picture on the front page, showing the milk being emptied. The caption said, "Outside agitators at the gates of New Athens."

New Athens had no gates, and my uncle voted straight Republican his whole life through. Herbert Hoover was a little radical for his taste.

I remember somebody—*who* doesn't matter—asking my uncle why he helped out the dairy farmers. "You're not a dairy farmer," Whoever said.

"You're right there," said my uncle, "but I'm a man."

I have one other depression memory of this—to me—extraordinary man. In a minute.

This is about berry-picking.

Uncle Dick showed me the row of berries he wanted me to pick, and he picked a few vines to demonstrate, and then I went to work.

He later told Aunt Mettabel, "Josh here looked like a little gray squirrel gathering nuts."

I had reached the end of my row, which must have been a good thirty feet long, before the other pickers had gone five feet in theirs. I noticed that they seemed to have as many berries in their baskets as I did, but I attributed this to the fact that Uncle Dick had given me a *difficult* row to pick.

I ran to Uncle Dick, carrying my half-filled basket of ripe, red berries.

"All finished," I said. "The whole row."

"Impossible," said Uncle Dick.

He glanced at my basket. "You didn't get them all," he said.

"Yes, I did. Every one that was ripe. Give me another row."

After that, I'm afraid I added, "I think I could handle the whole patch."

The whole patch was five acres, a lot of strawberries.

"You could no doubt dispense with their services," I said, pointing condescendingly to the other pickers.

"Let's take a look here," said my uncle, taking a look at my row.

"Don't look to me like you've been so awful thorough," he added, reaching into the first plant and coming up with three enormous red berries.

I would have sworn one of the other pickers had in a fit of jealousy hidden them there just to embarrass me.

Every plant my uncle examined had some ripe berries on it, all of them ostentatiously visible.

"Why don't you try another go at it?" asked my uncle, and I did.

The second time through I really took it slow; I made believe I was Sherlock Holmes and those berries were master criminals wanted by Scotland Yard.

When I finished that time, I was positive there wasn't a ripe berry on any of the vines.

I might add that most of the other pickers were by this time only halfway through their original rows.

Did that give me pause? Don't be silly.

I guess the end of the second try is clear enough. I went up that perverse row of strawberries for still a third time. This time I pretended I was King Alfred watching the spider spin its seven webs.

When I had finished, the third time turned out *not* to be a charm.

"You've still left too many," said Uncle Dick, kindly, smiling through what were left of his tobacco-stained teeth.

"I just don't think you're cut out to be a berry picker," he said. "You've got to be patient in this kind of work. You've got to learn to be patient."

He had something there, but I never learned it. Patience I never acquired, and that might be as good an epitaph as any. "You always ran all the way," Letty once said, "but what you never picked out is a direction. Who knows, if you had you might have got there first."

After that, Letty said what she said so often. "You're a failure," Letty said. "Ex-boy prodigy turns out to be a failure. A failure. A failure. A failure."

But this is about Uncle Dick.

He started loading a crate of berries into his truck. Then he looked at me. I was not looking at him. I was doing my best to look at nothing and not to cry.

"Look," said Uncle Dick. "You don't think I care about a thing like that, do you?"

"You well might," I said. "Mother says I'm no good at anything, and Pavan says I'm a stupid dunce."

I don't know what my uncle would have liked to say. What he did say, brusquely, was, "You like to ride into town with me and help me get rid of these berries?"

I said I would if he was sure I could really help him. He said he was sure.

On the way back, I had two Maid Rite hamburgers. They cost a *dime* each and were worth it. Whatever happened to the Maid Rite hamburger, do you suppose?

My uncle asked me if I'd consider a promotion. He said he needed somebody to help him keep books. Would I consider it?

I thought it over. "It's not just *made* work, is it?" I asked. I wasn't sure what *made* work was, but the *Times-Dispatch*, which was as much against WPA as mother was, kept saying that *made* work was the worst kind. "It saps the strength of our system," the *T-D* kept saying. I didn't want the strength of my system sapped.

Uncle Dick snorted. "I *need* somebody to help me keep the books," he said. "You'd be good at it. Some people are better at some things than at other things. You don't have to be good at everything."

"Mother says you do," I said. "She says I'm a genius, and she says geniuses are able to do everything if they just put their minds to it."

"Even your mother is perhaps sometimes wrong," said my uncle.

He said it gently. He was a gentle man.

So I accepted the bookkeeping job, and by the end of the month I was keeping all of my uncle's records with only an occasional suggestion from him. He was right. I was good at it.

I never did learn how to pick strawberries, though. And I never really learned to like baseball, and there are those—including a corrupt judge Out There—who claim that I cannot drive a car. You can see why I sometimes wonder if I am really an American. As for *driving*, I am what is known as a good *fast* driver. As we all know, it is your slow driver who causes all the trouble on the highways. All of the minor accidents I have been involved in have been the fault of *Sunday* drivers, and it doesn't matter what day or night of the week they happened on.

Anyway, after I had recovered from my failure as a berry picker, the month at Mettabel's and Dick's was one of the happiest of my life.

For one thing, I got along well with the other pickers. As soon as they found out I would never make a berry picker, they took me in.

"Why, I thought *anybody* could pick strawberries," they would say, smiling at the thought of their own superior skill. "Why, imagine *you* not being good at it and you're the one's so smart, in the papers and all."

People were always delighted when I failed at something and even more so when they found out they could do something better than I could.

They tried to teach me to pitch horseshoes, which is what everybody did at lunchtime. Eating the lunches they brought didn't take long.

I wasn't much good at horseshoe pitching either, which again only improved my popularity.

"All you have to do is like so," one of the high-school boys would say, showing me, and I would imitate what I thought I saw, but it was never right.

"I always figgered pitchin' horseshoes was easy," he would say. "Just goes to show. You see, with me it's as natural as breathing."

Then, breathing, he would pitch another ringer. "I guess it just ain't natural for you, huh?" he would say, and I would regretfully admit that it was not.

"I'd never even be in the same league with somebody like you," I would say.

"I guess you're probably right at that," he'd say, "though I'm not any too good at book learning or that kind of stuff."

I allowed my face to show what I thought of *book* learning.

Uncle Dick's hired man *talked* to me. I have never forgotten.

The hired man's name was Hank, and he was tall, built like an athlete, and very blond.

"Don't know where Hank's from and don't know how long he'll stay or what's his last name even," Uncle Dick had said. "He just come by and says could I use some good cheap help. Says he's good. I says I'd give him a go at it, and he's okay. He says to me, 'Morning' and he says to me 'Evening,' and when I hand him his pay on Saturday nights he says to me 'Thanks' and that's all he ever says to anybody. He ain't what you'd call much for talk."

Nevertheless, once he got started, Hank talked to me almost incessantly.

It happened this way.

I would watch Hank at work, currying the horses; my eyes would admiringly follow his every movement.

For several days neither of us said a word, and then I told him, somewhat diffidently, that he was the best horse currier I had ever come across, not mentioning that he was also the first. I said that I had been born wanting to know how to curry a horse properly but that until seeing him at work I had never found anyone I felt I could *trust* as a teacher.

Hank looked at me. Sincerity was in every inch of me, forty-eight of them.

"Why, now," said Hank, "there ain't an awful lot to curryin'. I mean if you want I should teach you I don't see no reason at all why a smart kid like you couldn't get the hang of it in no time. Of course, it ain't quite as easy as some thinks. I mean there are ways of curryin', and there are ways of curryin'. Some I've come across *thought* they was curryin' and didn't know the head of the horse from the ass in the first place like the feller says...."

He went right on from there. Speech flowed, oozed, sprang, leapt from Hank—last name Jacobsen.

He said I reminded him of his younger son, "smart as a whip," said Hank, "but he don't seem to cotton to farming."

Hank had owned a 640-acre wheat farm not far from Minneapolis; it had been foreclosed. "Damn Wall Street bankers are gonna own it all first thing you know." He was an ardent member of the Farmer-Labor party. His wife and three children were staying with *her* folks. *They* thought Hank was no good. They were *Republicans.* "I ain't never come across no Republicans I cared much for," said Hank.

One of his greatest fears was that they would turn Lars, the son I reminded him of, into a member of *that* party.

Hank earned fifteen dollars a week at Uncle Dick's, plus board and room, the room being the former haymow of the barn. Every Monday Hank sent his family a money order for fourteen dollars and fifty cents. How he squandered that fifty cents I don't remember.

The only book in Hank's library was Veblen's *The Theory of the Leisure Class*, and he spouted great chunks at me.

These two I remember—having just checked my own copy:

"The leisure class is in great measure sheltered from the stress of those economic exigencies which prevail in any modern, highly organized industrial community."

And—Hank was an atheist—"Sacred holidays and holidays generally are of the nature of a tribute leveled on the body of the people."

There were many more.

As for the currying, I got quite good, and I'll tell you this. There are ways of currying, and there are ways of currying.

Hank ate his meals with Aunt Mettabel, Uncle Dick, and me. He never said a word at meals, but then neither did we. At meals, you *ate*.

Occasionally Aunt Mettabel would ask, "What do you think of the strawberry pie, Richard?"

NOTES·DICTATED·ON·THE·SECOND·DAY

"Um.... Tasty," Uncle Dick would say, his mouth full of strawberry pie.

"Thank you, Richard," Mettabel would say. "I made it with very good strawberries."

"Um," Uncle Dick would say.

"Um," Hank would say.

"It tastes like more to me, Aunt Mettabel," I would say.

"Your eyes are bigger than your stomach, young man," Aunt Mettabel would say, but I knew she was pleased, and she would cut me another gigantic hunk of the pie.

I often ate more than my stomach could comfortably accommodate or my eyes really wanted, just to please Aunt Mettabel.

I remember I hardly cracked a book the whole time I was there. Pavan had given me a calculus text to study and a long reading list; I ignored both.

I must also have brought some books I wanted to read; I always did, but I didn't get into them that month.

I remember the entire library of Uncle Dick and Aunt Mettabel was on the living-room table; the Monkey Ward catalogue, a large pile of *Delineators*, and the Bible.

I remember that when I had finished making out the invoices and the checks and recording the day's transactions, Spot and I went on long walks.

There was a narrow stream in a neighboring field which whispered fascinating secrets, and I felt that if I could lean close enough and listen enough and keep Spot quiet long enough, I would find out what those secrets were, but I never did. Spot was largely fox terrier, with the nervousness of the breed.

And then there is this proud memory.

There were those—mother foremost among them, of course— who said my Uncle Dick had the first nickel he'd ever earned. Well, maybe. I know that despite his desire for a chew he would often hesitate before deciding whether to spend a nickel for a plug of tobacco. Still, he indulged Aunt Mettabel in her many fancies without, so far as I remember, a word of complaint.

Uncle Dick wasn't miserly; he was careful, and one result of his care with money was that there was never any talk of foreclosing his farm during the depression. He must have been one of the few farmers in the whole county who didn't even have a *first* mortgage. Nevertheless, he attended the foreclosure sales of all his neighbors—the ten-cent farm sales, they were called in the *Times-Dispatch*, which broadly hinted that they were inspired by *outside agitators* from some distant place like Chicago.

I asked a dozen times to go with my uncle to a sale, but he always said, "No, a thing like that wouldn't interest a boy like you."

Finally, I said what I said at the drop of a hat in those far-off days, "'...*humani nihil a me alienum*,' Uncle Dick. That means, 'Nothing human is alien to me.'" Oh, dear.

Finally, one day, my uncle said, "Well, your mother won't like it."

"My mother doesn't like much of anything," I said. "Besides, what she doesn't know won't hurt her. Let your conscience be your guide, Uncle Dick."

I guess he did, because he took me along.

The sale took place on an eighty-acre farm near Tama, a town not far from New Athens.

There were three beautiful children, two boys and a girl, all blond, and there was a mother who looked like—well, many years later I met Ingrid Bergman, and then I knew what that farmer's wife looked like. The farmer himself was a stocky man, built like a wrestler.

The household effects were piled in the yard, not many of them, but there was a gate-legged table (I don't know why I remember that) and several dark family portraits.

George Taleman, the sheriff, was type-cast—a huge-bellied, many-chinned man, and on one of his fat fingers was a diamond ring. At that time—and probably still—the position of sheriff was always a sinecure for a man not adequately endowed by nature to make an honest living. The voters are notoriously softhearted in this regard, and in general the practice does no real harm. It is only when such persons wind up in positions of power in Wonderland, D.C., that we are in for trouble.

Anyway, I remember that the afternoon of the sale Sheriff Taleman's face was a peculiar color; it had the yellowish hue of base-ball-park mustard, and it was years before I found out that what caused that odd color was fear.

There must have been fifty, maybe seventy-five other farmers around, and as the sheriff got out of his Buick, they stood in two straight lines, making a path for him. The silence was—well, again, let me bolster my childhood memory with something that came many years later. Once in Paris not long after V-E Day several thousand Frenchmen wearing the striped uniform of the German prison camp made a protest march up the Champs Elysées. Not a word was spoken the whole time, either by the spectators or by the gray-faced marchers. There was not even the sound of marching feet. Just the silence—of a quality that could not ever be forgotten.

The same—though on a much smaller scale—at the farm sale I'm talking about. The mustard-colored sheriff took the foreclosure notice out of his pocket and started to read it, but my uncle interrupted. He said that seeing as how everybody there knew why the sheriff was there, reading all that seemed a waste of time.

Then my uncle said to the other farmers, "Friends, the sheriff here is performing his duty, and we have all got a lot of respect for a man performing his duty. We all know the sheriff's a busy man; he's been having a lot of foreclosure sales these last few weeks, and he's just about tuckered out. So we're here to help him sell off Sven Sargent's belongings just as quick as we can so the sheriff can go about his business. Now what am I offered for that fine team of sorrels over there?"

The team, as I recall, went for fifteen cents; the gate-legged table brought a nickel, and the eighty acres and the house and out-buildings all together brought—as my uncle put it—"a plain silver dollar, one plain silver dollar. I hear a dollar once. I hear a dollar twice. Sold for one dollar."

As I remember it, the total price of everything on sale that day was less than three dollars. Naturally, the sheriff signed the bill of sale.

There was no violence of any kind, although on the edge of the crowd a neighbor of Mr. Sargent's did keep knotting and unknotting a rope.

After the sheriff left, everything was returned to the farmer, the wife who looked like Miss Bergman, and the three blond children.

Such foreclosure sales were common around New Athens that year, but that one is the only one I ever got to. I remember later a judge was practically hanged for trying to foreclose a mortgage; they even got the rope around his neck.

I also remember that on the way back to New Athens, my admiration for my Uncle Dick was almost impossible to contain.

I remember saying, "Uncle Dick, you'd have made a wonderful auctioneer."

"Umm," said my uncle, who when he was not being an auctioneer seldom uttered a complete sentence.

"Was a thing like that legal, Uncle Dick?" I asked.

"Don't look to me like anybody's going out of his way to prove to the contrary," said my uncle.

Aunt Mettabel and Uncle Dick lived in a bungalow with a bay window so close to the Lincoln Highway that the whole house shuddered every time a car passed. I would lie on the davenport with the towelling at each head rest and on the arms, playing a solitary game. I wanted to see one car from each state by the end of the month.

I didn't, though, only sixteen states.

But the way I looked at it I had plenty of time to watch for cars from the green davenport.

I had made up my mind that the month at Aunt Mettabel's was no more than a trial run. If I behaved myself and Mettabel and Dick liked me well enough, they were going to adopt me.

There had been many broad hints.

"I sure wish Dick and me had a boy like you around here," Aunt Mettabel would say as I wiped the dishes. "We could use a boy like you."

"Maybe you could have," I would say, wanting her to know I knew what was up. "I might very easily be persuaded to stay."

"Certainly do wish I had somebody like you around all the time to help out," Uncle Dick would say. "I'm no good at figgering and never was to speak of."

"Something like that could probably be arranged," I would say, smiling conspiratorially.

"You're getting to be easy the best horse currier I ever come across for your age," Hank would say. "The horses like you, too, especially Bessie. Gonna miss you when you leave."

"Bessie and all the rest of you may be in for some surprises," I would say.

It wasn't that Pavan and mother hadn't alluded to what I thought was afoot.

Once after some failure or other, mother said, "I don't blame you at all, Joshua. I think very possibly the whole thing is your father's fault. He was just not my intellectual equal. I was even *afraid* to inquire what his I.Q. was."

And then, reflectively, "Of course, Petrarch has one of the most splendid minds I have ever encountered."

And Pavan, "Since you are totally incapable of learning, I frankly fail to see why you feel it necessary to continue cumbering the earth."

And just a few days before they had left for Chicago, I had heard mother say to someone, I forget who, "If Pavan and I ever have any children, at least we'll know where we stand intellectually."

Whoever she said this to nodded in my direction, and mother said, "Joshua, go finish your Greek translations, and remember tonight you and Pavan have two hours of German."

I had discussed the whole matter of my adoption with Spot.

I said, "Spot, she and Pavan obviously got married so they could have kids of their own who will be some stupid geniuses or something, and they've got me here to find out how Aunt Mettabel and Uncle Dick like me. They don't give a damn how I feel about it. Well, for their information, Spot, I happen to like Mettabel and Dick. Very much."

I kept waiting for either Mettabel or Dick to bring up the matter of my adoption, but they didn't, and I decided they were just too shy.

One afternoon before supper, which was always at five, Aunt Mettabel said, "Well, young man, your mother and Mr. Pavan will be home from Chicago in the morning. I guess that makes you pretty happy, doesn't it?"

"It doesn't seem like a month," I said, which was true.

And I added, "But in some ways it seems like I've been here forever," also true.

"We've enjoyed having you," said Aunt Mettabel. "Dick and I were talking last night."

I then said what I had decided I would say when the time came. I was making it easy for Dick and Mettabel, pretending the whole thing was my idea.

"I don't suppose you and Uncle Dick would be interested in adopting me or having me stay here permanently or anything like that, would you?" I said.

Aunt Mettabel did not react at all the way I had expected. "Why, what a thing to say," she said, busying herself with the baking-powder biscuits.

"It happens all the time," I said, "kids getting adopted. Kids with parents and all. Pavan and she are no doubt going to want to have kids of their own, and I'll be somewhat in the way, I dare say. Besides, I'd be very useful around here. I mean even if I can't pick strawberries, I can keep the books and all, and Hank says I'm the best horse currier he's ever come across in his whole life, and I know Spot likes me, and I like you and Uncle Dick. I know I'm not easy to like; everybody says so, but if I worked hard, I could improve—"

Aunt Mettabel stooped and gathered me into her long, thin arms. "If I ever had a little boy, I'd want him to be exactly like you," she said, kissing me.

The kiss was dry, and her pointed chin jabbed into my cheek, and it hurt, but I kissed her back.

"Just don't get smart-alecky," she said. "If you do, I'll warm the seat of your britches. You hear that?"

I nodded.

"Nobody likes a smart-aleck, and don't you ever forget it."

"What about this adoption we were discussing?" I asked.

Aunt Mettabel went back to the biscuits. "Why, Joshua," she said. "We couldn't do anything like that. What would your mother say?"

"She'd say, 'Good riddance of bad rubbish.'"

A moment passed. I looked steadily at Mettabel. Was she avoiding my eye? It seemed so.

Then because I had to, I said, "You mean she never discussed the subject with you?"

"What subject?" asked Mettabel, more occupied with the biscuits than she had to be.

"Adopting me, of course," I said, "so she and Pavan can have the kind of kids they want which I am distinctly not."

"Why, Joshua. Your mother wouldn't do anything like that. What a thing to say."

She put the biscuits in the oven of the cook stove. "Besides, you don't want to be away from your very own mother."

"Oh, yes I do. Permanently if possible."

"You mustn't talk that way. It's not nice."

"It's true, though," I said.

"You must learn to love your mother, and you must keep it in mind that whatever she does, she does for you."

"Oh, sure. You bet."

Aunt Mettabel closed the oven door.

"In other words," I said, "the answer to my question about you and Uncle Dick adopting me is no."

Aunt Mettabel's voice sounded odd. She said that while the biscuits were baking she thought she would have herself a nice cool bath and why didn't I go out in the yard and play with Spot.

She ran a hand through my hair and said, "It's not always easy to understand God's will. Try and be nice to your mother."

While Aunt Mettabel was having her bath, I told Spot what had happened in the kitchen.

"They don't want me," I said. "That's obvious. They're nice enough while I'm here, but it's obvious they don't want me around here permanently. Not that you can blame them. I'm not everybody's dish of tea."

And I said, "I guess I'll have to go back there, Spot, for a year or so anyway, until I start making my own living."

And I said, "Maybe they'll both get killed in a bad train wreck on the way home from Chicago tonight. She and Pavan. It happens all the time, Spot."

The train wreck didn't happen, though.

The next afternoon mother and Pavan stepped off the train, he first; he was always first. He was wearing a new brown suit, a green Tyrolean hat, and he was carrying a cane.

"Chicago is not a windy city," he said. "It is an oversized village with many small, odorous breezes."

Mother had on a new dress, also brown, and a hat that looked like a bread basket. The luggage she carried was also new.

"Well, Mettabel," said mother, "and Dick."

"Pretty dress," said Mettabel.

"The saleslady at Marshall Field's said that not one woman in ten thousand could really wear this dress, really give it the *meaning* it deserves," said mother. Then she said, "Joshua darling."

She stooped; she bussed me; she even looked at me.

"You're brown as a berry. Did you have a good time?"

I nodded.

"He was busy as a one-armed paper hanger the whole time," said Uncle Dick. "Kept all my books."

"He ate so much you'd of thought he'd bust wide-open," said Aunt Mettabel.

"We've got the most wonderful surprise for you," said mother.

"Did you bring those books on Roman and Scandinavian mythology I asked you to bring me?" I asked.

Mother looked at Pavan, and Pavan looked at mother. Each started to say, "I told you—"

Mother recovered first. "We'll send for them. We'll just send for them."

"Thanks very much," I said.

I started away, and mother called after me. "You're going to be on the radio. Won't that be fun?"

"Coast to coast," said Pavan. "The Blue network."

"Coast to coast, huh," said Uncle Dick. "Well, well. He gonna crack jokes?"

I turned and looked first at mother and then at Pavan. "What's in it for you two?" I asked. "Besides the new glad rags?"

Aunt Mettabel said, "Now remember what we said about being smart-alecky."

"Oh, I'm used to that," said mother. "I'm used to no understanding from my son. It's one of the crosses I have to bear. The serpent's adder and all that sort of thing."

"This radio program will mean work," said Pavan. "Work, work, work, and then more work."

"You two bastards," I said. "You two rotten awful bastards."

I ran then. I ran up the railroad tracks until I came to a place where there were no more houses, and I went into a corn field, crouching there, waiting for them.

But nobody came, and when it was evening, I went to sleep.

When I woke up, I was hungry, and there was no place to go except to the house on Riverdale Avenue. So I started back. I could have run away, and I thought about it, but I didn't know where to run.

Patrolman Joe Dolan picked me up on West Main Street. "We been looking all over for you, young fellow," he said. "Your old lady's plenty worried about you."

He took me to the house on Riverdale Avenue, and, after he left, my mother fixed me some supper, and she said, "We are never going to mention what you said at the railroad station. We are not even going to think about it again."

That was the worst. What was not mentioned and not thought about was the worst kind of thing there was or could be.

Pavan came in from his study. "I see you're back," he said.

He carried a geography book. "They ask a lot of geographical questions on 'Can You Top Them,'" he said. "You are going to become as familiar with the geography of this planet as you are with the back of your hand."

He looked closely and critically at me. "Or are you at all familiar with the back of your hand?"

Mother, who was pouring a glass of milk for me, said, "Petrarch, leave him alone. He's had a bad day."

"Celeste, go to your room and get ready for bed," said Pavan.

Mother did, and the next morning I started learning geography.

These final words about Uncle Dick and Aunt Mettabel. My uncle died in 1942, when I was in the Army at Fort Jackson, South Carolina.

As I believe I mentioned, Aunt Mettabel died last year, and I returned to New Athens for the first time and the last to attend her funeral.

(4) "What is it happens with friends?"

And now Hughie.

In the afternoons in New Haven when I would go to Dr. Baron's office I would lie on the couch, staring hostilely at him or at the ceiling, and he would often say, "Tell me some more about Hughie Larrabee."

That would always start me talking. Always.

"He must have been a most unusual boy," Dr. Baron once said.

I don't suppose Hughie was, though I don't know. When I was young and hopeful, I liked to think there were a lot like him around. Now I'm not so sure.

I remember how happy mother was when she first heard that the house across the street from us had been sold to some people named Larrabee. The house had been abandoned for several years.

"They'll fix the place up, which has just been going to rack and ruin and running down property values," mother said. "Kendall, wasn't there a Larrabee in the philosophy department at the University of Chicago, didn't you say?"

"I didn't say," said my father. "I leave that sort of thing to you."

Forty-eight hours later, mother found out who the Larrabees were.

"*He* is nothing but a common, ordinary day laborer," she said to my father. "When I found out from the girls at the Star meeting last night, I came up to tell you, but you were—asleep, Kendall."

She paused a moment to get herself in hand.

"I was so upset that I took *ten* grains of aspirin," she said. "Heaven knows what having people like that in the neighborhood will do to sonny boy."

Later that morning, I looked at our bottle of aspirin. I was afraid that if mother had taken ten grains, there wouldn't be any left for my father, who daily ran through a great many aspirins. It turned out ten grains are two tablets.

Actually, Mr. Larrabee was the head of a repair crew for the telephone company and better paid than my father, obituary and social editor of *The New Athens Times-Dispatch.*

Mr. Larrabee was a pleasant, lean man who looked like a thinner, more assured Hughie. Mrs. Larrabee was overweight, garrulous, and she had almost no interests except the Church and the welfare of her two daughters, both nearly grown, and Hughie.

Hughie was nine when the Larrabees moved across the street from us.

They arrived on a Monday.

I don't know what Hughie did those first few days. I know what I did. At home I watched Hughie painfully, nervously, hopefully, from behind the living-room curtains. At school, I stalked him the way Richard Hannay stalked the man with the hooded eyes in *The Thirty-Nine Steps.*

Hughie was not a handsome boy. A fringe of soft blond hair sprawled over his forehead. His skin was always very white, always, no matter how much time he spent in the sun. He wore steelrimmed glasses which were held together with adhesive tape and hope, but the bright eyes behind the glasses dominated his face.

A girl once told Hughie that his eyes were a gentian blue. We both guffawed at that, and afterwards whenever Hughie was about to get out of hand, I would say, "What was it you were saying, Mr. Gentian Blue?" That nearly always stopped him. His eyes had a vast innocence which combined with the slightly crooked cupid's bow mouth and the bent stub of a nose and distended ears gave him a rakish, somewhat disreputable look.

But I had not observed these details the morning Hughie and I met for the first time. All I knew was that he was pleasantly ugly, that he was in the fourth grade, and that he was six inches taller and two years older than I was. I had also heard some of the boys in his grade say that he was a good baseball player, and I heard somebody call him "Four Eyes," which he didn't seem to mind. At least not the way I did when somebody called me that.

We met on the Saturday morning after the Larrabees moved in. I was lying on the porch swing trying to read when Hughie came across the street, dragging a bat and carrying a softball. He came into the yard and up to the porch and stood watching me. I pretended to be invisible.

"You read all the time?" he asked.

"When I feel like it," I said, looking down at my book.

"What do you want to be, the professor of all knowledge?" he asked. "You want to know all there is to know?"

"I know enough," I said.

"My mother said I ought to be nice to you," he said, giving the bat a tentative swing.

"Don't go out of your way," I said, getting up and starting toward the front door.

"Look, stuck up," said Hughie. "I wanted to talk to you on my own hook, too. I haven't got any friends yet, and maybe if everything works out, we could be friends."

I turned, one of the few times in my life I have. Hughie had a hopeful half-smile on his face, and his hand was extended slightly.

"Maybe we could," I said, smiling back. "You play checkers?"

Hughie shook his head. "You play baseball?"

"I'm not very good," I said. "I'm told I'm not any too well coordinated, but I'd like to get better at baseball. Around here, you have to play baseball."

"I'll show you how to play baseball, and you show me how to play checkers," said Hughie.

I closed my book and put it on the porch swing.

"Catch," said Hughie, throwing me the ball; awkwardly, I caught it.

"I thought you'd have a big head or be a freak or something like that," Hughie said.

"Well, I'm no freak," I said, throwing him the ball, which he expertly caught. "Why does everybody always think I'm going to be a freak or something?"

"Let's see you bat," said Hughie, throwing me the bat.

I batted.

"You bat like a freak," he said. "You'd better learn how to hold a bat in the first place, and then maybe some people won't think you're a freak."

He showed me how to hold a bat and how to catch, never expertly but less awkwardly.

"You're a quick learner," he said.

"You want me to help you with your school work?" I asked.

Hughie stopped showing me how to bat and gave me a look.

"Why should I want you to do a thing like that?" he asked, and then he said, "Your right hand goes lower. Like this."

Hughie was the best friend I ever had. You don't make real friends after a certain age.

Hughie and I spent a lot of time together. We went fishing, though I usually took a book along while Hughie did the fishing. Sometimes if Hughie didn't mind, and he usually didn't, I read aloud. On the other hand, we could and did spend hours together without exchanging a word.

We would watch the clouds change color and shape on a summer evening, and we would tell each other what the different shapes were, that one a lady dragon breathing pink fire, the second a bear with a cold reading a book, a third, Babe Ruth at bat, etc.

The latter invention was Hughie's. I was never much for baseball. Hughie was never much for literate bears or pink dragons.

We collected lightning bugs and snakes and let them die of neglect.

Hughie wasn't much for books either, but I did get him to read both Tom Sawyer and Huck Finn. He didn't like Tom much. He said that if Tom was around, he Hughie wouldn't want to play with him. He liked Huck, though.

"He'd like you," I said.

"You're not so bad when you get to know you," said Hughie.

Hughie said that Bunny Brown and his Sister Sue and the Rover Boys and Dick the Castaway all gave him pains in the ass and so did *Little Men* and *Penrod*, who was the worst of the lot.

"Is the guy that wrote that kidding?" Hughie used to ask. I wasn't sure myself.

Peter Pan, which I told him about but which Hughie refused to read, pained him all over, the whole idea of it.

I read sections of *Main Street* aloud to him.

"She's the biggest pain in the ass yet, that Carol Kennicott," said Hughie.

"Mother says she's just like Carol Kennicott herself," I said.

"You gonna play checkers or read that silly book?" asked Hughie.

I remember I used to talk about religion, and Hughie didn't mind listening. Hughie was Catholic, and he didn't have any interest in converting me or in explaining what Catholicism was all about.

However, at the time I was against Catholics and, in fact, against all Christianity. "It's pagan," I would say, "the whole thing, and I can prove it." Here my eyes would glisten darkly. "Hughie, if there really is a Christian God, how do you explain the fact that there are almost a billion Buddhists in the world?"

I would then smile at him triumphantly.

"Why don't you simmer down and shoot a basket?" Hughie would say.

I attended Mass with him a few times, but I never told mother, who sometimes called herself a freethinker and sometimes a Unitarian and who said she wanted me to make up my own mind, though I knew without asking that she would not want me to make up my own mind to be a Catholic. During the 1928 Presidential campaign, mother made several speeches in favor of Herbert Hoover. These speeches did not prevent Hoover from carrying New Athens by about three to one.

Mother said in her speeches that it was ridiculous to think that if Al Smith was elected there would be a direct pipeline from the Vatican to the White House, but her tone indicated that if Smith got in we might just as well make up our minds to having an indirect pipeline.

Mother identified the Democratic candidate only as *Smith*, making an epithet of the name. Common, mother hinted, anybody named *Smith!* There must have been a couple dozen Smiths in New Athens. I have a feeling they all voted Democratic in '28.

What's more, mother objected to the fact that *Smith* did not even know how to pronounce the word radio. "*Rah-di-o—rah-di-o*," mother would say, hamming it up. "Surely we do not want a mental pygmy like that in the hallowed shrine that is our White House.

Not to mention what people will think in the cultured courts and palaces abroad."

Nobody burned any crosses on Hughie's front lawn during the 1928 campaign, though crosses were burned on one or two other Catholic lawns in New Athens that year, and I remember that one morning when I went with Hughie to the Larrabee mailbox, there was something in it which made him blush angrily. He crumpled whatever it was and later burned it without letting me see.

"Filthy, rotten stuff," he said. "I wouldn't want my mother to see any filthy, rotten stuff like that."

I often had supper at the Larrabees', and sometimes I had Sunday dinner there, too; that was at noon. Mother was pained by this, particularly the Sunday part.

"People like that may very easily try to pervert you," she said, "especially on Sunday, all those priests hovering in the background."

Then she added, "I've been a freethinker all my life, and I don't care if Al Smith gets elected, and I am incinerated for it."

Mother admitted that Mrs. Larrabee was probably a good cook. "Peasants usually are," she said. "That's all they can do, cook and shell out babies."

I remember Mrs. Larrabee's fried chicken, which was better than the fried chicken of either Mrs. Hoadley, our sometime house-keeper, or Aunt Mettabel.

I was not company at the Larrabees'; I was family, and if there had ever been any need to hold back, I would have held back, but there was never any need.

Often when there was company, especially Father Malley, we would have fried chicken *and* ham *and* roast beef, mashed *and* sweet potatoes, garden peas *and* summer squash, and dessert, sometimes cherry pie made with the cherries Hughie and I had picked in the Larrabee orchard *and* the ice cream Hughie and I had frozen on the back porch, plus a huge chunk of store cheese.

Father Malley was the only priest I had ever met up to then, and he didn't hover, background or foreground. He drank his fill of bootleg whiskey and home brew, which Mr. Larrabee made in the basement, and he told funny stories about his boyhood in Ireland.

He had a round, red face with a fringe of white hair, and he seemed to enjoy every minute that passed.

I once heard mother tell one of her Eastern Star sisters, "We all know that they [Catholics] dissipate and have *orgies* in the basement."

She meant the basement of St. Mary's Church, next door to St. Mary's School.... Mother was a great one with the "we all know" routine. In fact, I never saw her equal until some of the early meetings of the United Nations when the Russian delegate would start an obvious whopper with the words, "We all know" or "It's a well-known fact." Mother would have made an awfully good Communist.

I used to look closely at Father Malley to see if there were any signs of dissipation on him. I never saw any.

But mostly what I remember is the Larrabee house. I don't mean its personal appearance, all gone from my mind except the Victorian ugliness of it and the fact that it always needed a coat of paint.

Mother said that the Larrabees had *discommoded* the entire neighborhood. "And that is only the beginning. We all know what Catholics are. They like to *crowd*."

The Larrabee house was not crowded, but it was the third of the three in New Athens in which people liked each other. It was a house in which kindness was taken for granted.

Eventually, in matters involving Hughie mother learned to keep her mouth as nearly shut as was psychologically and physically possible for her.

Hughie had her number, and mother had sense enough to know when her number was had.

I should perhaps say here that Hughie almost never mentioned her to me, and I never mentioned her to him. We had that kind of friendship.

The encounters between Hughie and mother were few and far between, but one of them I still remember:

I was in training for the national championship of the Harvey Jordan O'Conner Derby—"A $10,000 Cash Prize for America's Brightest Boy or Girl of the Year."

I had won the Iowa and the regional contests, and no one, including me, had the slightest doubt but that I would be the national champion as well.

I was on a study schedule so rigid that there wasn't a second of my eleven-hour day that wasn't accounted for, including a fifteen-minute rest and meditation period every two hours.

Mother would say, "Now remember, darling [I was *darling* during the entire O'Conner period], we mustn't let our minds stagnate for a single second, must we?"

Not only was I working very hard; my visitors were screened more carefully than those admitted to the White House.

"We don't want to upset the atmosphere with the wrong kind of people at a time like this," mother said.

Nevertheless, Hughie got in to see me. It was a couple of nights before the final O'Conner examination. I forget where mother and Pavan were; gone from the house, though.

I was at a huge desk piled high with books. A student lamp was at exactly the proper distance from my left shoulder and was the only light in the room.

Enter Hughie.

"Hi," he said. "How you doing?"

"Hi, Hughie," I said. "My, I'm glad to see you. I'm fine."

"You ever get outdoors?" asked Hughie. "You're pale as a ghost."

I must have looked—well, unusual. I wore a small green eye shade (made especially for me, *Compliments of the Hawkeye Eye Shade and Opticals, Inc., Council Bluffs, Iowa.*) I had on the enormous horn-rimmed glasses I've mentioned, and they kept slipping down on my nose, just as all their successors have. There were smudges of ink and pencil marks and dirt over my face (always smudges), and I had a long silver pencil behind my ear. I always wore that pencil behind my ear, outdoors and in. It was an election year in Iowa, and the pencil was a present from the governor, who was running for a second term, "From Governor, etc., to Master Joshua Bland, Proud Winner of the Harvey Jordan O'Conner, etc."

I had to wear the pencil. How else would you know it was me? ...Still got it, too. In that closet over there, the one on the left.

Anyway, when Hughie came in that night, I was pale, and when I took off my glasses, there were dark circles under my eyes. I was badly in need of a haircut, and I was nine years old and forty-three inches tall. A photographer from the *Des Moines Register* had measured my height. Is it necessary to add that the caption called me, "Iowa's Forty-Three-Inch Intellectual Giant"?

"It's just about over," I told Hughie, "and anyway as soon as I've won I'm going to take you at a game of checkers."

"That'll be the day," said Hughie. "Look, when you get this O'Conner crap out of your system, you better get yourself a little fresh air."

He handed me a brown paper bag in which there were four of Mrs. Larrabee's loganberry tarts.

"My mother says good luck," said Hughie.

"Thanks a lot," I said, removing the eyeshade. "I'll save them. I'm on a very strict scientific diet until day after tomorrow, all brain food of one kind or another."

"Lots of excitement around town," said Hughie. "They're all rooting for you to win."

I'm afraid I said, "That's very sweet of them."

In my defense, I plead youth and the fact that I was only forty-three inches tall.

"You're talking like a freak again," said Hughie, which is what he always said when I started getting more intolerable than usual.

"You coming to the banquet?" I asked.

"Huh-uh," said Hughie. "I don't go in for banquets."

I burst into tears. For weeks I had been going on nerves alone. The slightest thing would set me off.

"I thought you were my friend," I shouted.

"It's tough to be sometimes, but I am," said Hughie.

Then he said, "You don't mean I have to go to some fancy-pants banquet to prove I'm your friend, do you?"

I said no, and I perhaps should explain here that the banquet was to celebrate my winning the National Championship, which I hadn't yet done.

"I'm sorry," I said.

"I do wish you good luck, though," said Hughie.

"Thanks. I don't believe in luck myself. Just a lot of silly superstition."

And I added, "There's a radio broadcast, you know. Coast to coast. President Hoover will congratulate me. Himself."

Hughie came over to my desk and looked down at me. "Friend," he said, touching my shoulder lightly. "You might lose. You thought about that?"

"Don't say that. Mother says saying something like that just releases bad thoughts."

"Well, that's bright," said Hughie in one of his rare outbursts against mother. "That's very bright, I must say."

He grinned at me. "Look, kiddo," he said. "I think the whole thing's a bunch of crap anyway. But this town's all steamed up, and there's more crap floating around East Main Street than you can shake a stick at. If you lose—"

"Don't say—"

"If you lose," said Hughie, "a lot of people are gonna hate your guts. You know, like when the basketball team ended up last in the state tournament and everybody thought they were going to win. The way people around this town acted you'd of thought the guys on the team threw the game."

Then Hughie said, "I just want you to know that I don't care whether you win or not. You're my buddy. Okay?"

"Okay," I said.

"And if you do win, don't get any freakier than you already are."

"I won't," I promised.

A few minutes later mother sprang into the room.

I would describe her condition as *furied*. If you think my nerves were on edge, well—mother's were Way Out. Her thyroid was the most hyper I ever saw it.

"*What in the world are YOU doing here?*" she screamed at Hughie.

"Why, I'm talking to my friend Josh," said Hughie. "I should think anybody could see that."

"At a time like this," said mother. "At a time when the mantle of destiny is about to be laid on the shoulders of my son, you are *talking* to him."

Word of honor; she said *that*.

"Yup," said Hughie. "That's what I'm doing. Talking to him."

"Well, we'll excuse you, Mr. Larrabee," said mother.

"I was just going," said Hughie.

"What in the world do you call *these*?" mother screamed, swooping down on the bag of tarts.

"We call them loganberry tarts," said Hughie. "That's because they're tarts with loganberries in them."

Mother flung the bag of tarts into the wastebasket by my desk.

"Go, go, go," she cried at Hughie, "before I lose my temper."

"So long, Josh boy," said Hughie, squeezing my shoulder. "See you in the funny papers."

He winked at me and left.

"Entertaining *hoodlums* at a time like this," said mother.

She grabbed the tarts out of the wastebasket and waved them illustratively.

"I hope you haven't eaten any," she said. "They may be *poisoned*. There are no lengths to which some people won't go to prevent you from winning."

She touched my forehead. "Have you got a fever I don't doubt?"

"No," I said. "Have you?"

She started slamming up windows; it was January.

"Whew, whew," she said, fanning herself. "Whew. Whew. The air in here is all contaminated."

She threw open the door. "Whew, whew," she said. "People like that simply poison the cultural atmosphere of our nation. Whew. Whew."

Some more about Hughie.

Various analysts have over the years had various suggestions about the reasons for my friendship with Hughie, and Letty at one dark period of our dark marriage had a dark, direct suggestion of her own.

You'll get none from me. I don't know why Hughie put up with me; I am only grateful that on the day we met I turned back instead of slamming into the house. I'm glad I saw that shy, lopsided, hopeful smile on his face. I have a feeling I've missed a lot of smiles on a lot of people's faces.

All I know for sure is that my friendship with Hughie leaves a warm and wonderful memory.

When I was in Chicago for the "Can You Top Them?" program or in Iowa City, where I met Queen Marie of Rumania, or Out There, where, among others, I met Norma Shearer, I could always find comfort in the interminable hours before I went to sleep knowing that Hughie would still be in New Athens when I got back. Hughie would not exactly be waiting for me, but when he saw me, his preposterous face would light up with pleasure.

Hughie was never very curious about the great world outside New Athens.

Once somebody took a picture of me and a child movie star named Baby Eileen, who was sixteen if she was a day. The picture appeared in *The New Athens Times-Dispatch*.

I remember Hughie asked me if Baby Eileen was as big a pain in the ass in real life as she was in the movies. I said yes, only more so. Hughie said that's what he figured. He didn't ask anything about Queen Marie; he just said that it seemed to him she was doing an awful lot of sashaying around in this country and who was looking after things back in Rumania while she was doing all this sashaying around. The question had no doubt occurred to many Rumanians, but it had not occurred to me. If it had I would have asked the queen.

Hughie was friends with almost all the boys, but he was best friends with me, and the other kids mostly understood that and respected it.

The fact that he was not good-looking never seemed to bother any of the girls. Hughie could have gone with almost any of them, and he played the field.

I once heard a girl ask him, "Why do you pal around with that stuck-up drip?" Meaning me.

Hughie said, "I like him. That meet with your highness's approval?"

Hughie was better than I was at all games, baseball, tennis, and swimming; we swam in the Y.M.C.A. pool in our altogethers in the winter and in the pool at Riverdale Park in our bathing suits in the summer. Twice we went to the Y. camp at Coon Lake, and the second summer I persuaded myself that I would be chosen the *best all-around camper* and probably the *best-liked*. I didn't deserve to be either, but I wanted to be, and at that time wanting and getting seemed to me the same thing.

Hughie was both *best all-around camper* and the *best-liked*. I told him I was glad, which was a lie, but I did manage to forgive him.

Hughie was always being chosen *the most popular boy* or *the friendliest boy*, but he never seemed to care much one way or the other.

When I was graduated from Pegasus at the age of fifteen, I was chosen *the most likely to succeed* and *the most brilliant*. A girl named Matty Hare edited the yearbook; they always do. Miss Hare, whose palate was not quite cleft, wrote of me, "Little Joshua is going to be our own little shooting star."

I never wanted to be anybody's shooting star. I wanted to be *the most popular boy*. I never was, though. I never even came close.

That's about it—except for the big, final scene.

I was fifteen, and Hughie was eighteen. I'll later come to why I was leaving for England the next day.

Hughie came into my room above five the afternoon I'm telling about.

He was then just a little under six feet tall. I was very much shorter.

It was August. Hughie was eating an enormous sandwich which he had charmed out of Mrs. Hoadley, who was then our housekeeper.

Mother and Pavan were away. So I was home alone, getting ready for the greatest adventure of my life up to then, a trip to London. Oh, boy. Escape from *Mummy* and from Pavan. I was joyous. One of the few times in my life, completely so.

"Pret' near packed, huh?" said Hughie, taking a great bite out of the sandwich.

"Almost," I said, and I pointed to a pile of discarded clothes. "Take a look at that stuff, Hughie. Couple of practically new sweaters in there, and they'll stretch. If you don't want them, off they go to the Salvation Army. I'm getting me a couple of new cashmeres at Harrod's. That's the biggest department store in London."

Hughie may have looked at me strangely; I feel sure he did, but, as had happened before and was to happen many times again, I was far too engrossed in myself to notice.

What Hughie said was, "Gee, thanks. You are a generous bloke," but he did not look over the discarded pile of clothes.

"I'm generous to a fault," I said, handing him my Fowler's *King's English* and *Modern English Usage*.

"You can keep them," I said. "I want to get the India paper editions that Oxford University Press publishes."

Hughie had the books in the hand that had no sandwich, balancing them.

"It wouldn't do you any harm to study these books," I said—lightly, of course. "For somebody who's going to be a senior in high school your syntax leaves a lot to be desired."

I laughed to show that I was joking.

Hughie opened one of the books. "Subjunctives," he read aloud.

"'What care I how fair she be. Lose who may, I still can say, if ladies be but young and fair, et cetera.'"

He put both books down on my desk. "They'll be here when you get back," he said, "if you ever get back."

"I'll be back," I said. "Don't worry your pretty little head about that, and I'll buy you a pair of shoes at Harrod's and a cashmere sweater at Simpson's. That's the other big department store in London."

"Gee, thanks," said Hughie.

He finished the sandwich and went to my typewriter case and tapped the lock. "You get it fixed?"

I nodded, but Hughie examined the lock anyway. He never trusted me in mechanical matters, and he was right not to.

"You see the *Times-Dispatch* this afternoon?" he asked.

I shook my head. "What's in it?"

"Oh, nothing important," he said. "Don't let it worry you."

I looked closely at him. "Why should whatever it is worry me?"

"Whatever which is?" he asked.

I doubled my fists and started toward him, and he backed away in mock alarm.

"Have I reminded you lately of the penalty for hitting a man wearing glasses?" he asked.

Then he said, "Look, kid, it's probably nothing at all. I wouldn't worry about it. It probably won't hold up your trip more than six months or a year. One look at you and any jury would decide that you're not the one."

It was a moment before I could speak. I didn't know what he was talking about, but I had been expecting something like this all along. It had been my theory from the beginning that somebody or something would stop me from going to England and getting away from my mother for the first time in my life.

"Why, Hughie?" I asked again, fear in my voice. "What do you mean?"

Hughie was now testing a strap on my largest suitcase.

"It's just that Earl Bellamy's filed a paternity suit naming you," he said. "Earl alleges that Mildred is three and a half months gone and that—"

I went white. What he said couldn't be true, and I knew it couldn't be true, but I wasn't thinking.

"You're kidding," I said, grabbing Hughie's arm.

Hughie shook his head sadly. "Wish I was," he said. "I certainly do wish I was."

He sighed and shrugged. "I told you to quit banging that broad," he said. "But did you listen to your Uncle Hughie? You did not. I don't know what you—"

"But, Hughie, I didn't," I said. "I just said I did but I didn't. I didn't even kiss her much to speak of. I *told* you that."

Then I saw that he was grinning.

"You bastard," I said. "You rotten bastard."

And I said, "Oh, Hughie, I wish I weren't going."

"No, you don't," said Hughie. "What you're doing right now is standing there hating me because I'm staying home.

"You're spoiled now," he said. "Without me to bring you down a peg or two every once in a while I don't know what'll happen to you."

"Well," I said. "I've got to take a shower. You better get dressed. We've got to be at the Bakers' right after supper."

"You mean at President and Mrs. Horatio P. Baker's of Pegasus College?" asked Hughie.

"Nope," he went on. "It just so happens I have not got to be at the Bakers' for the shindig being given in your distinguished honor."

"How come?"

"What you mean is, how not come," said Hughie. "Maybe *your* syntax could stand a little improvement. The *how not come* is that I have not been invited to the Bakers. Lillian Baker, the virgin sturgeon very fine fish daughter of Mr. and Mrs. Horatio P., sort of sniffs the air every time I pass. She seems to think if your old man isn't on the Pegasus faculty you don't wash regular."

"That's ridiculous," I said. "That's the most ridiculous thing I ever heard of. I just assumed you were invited. Why didn't you tell me you weren't invited? Everybody knows you're my best friend."

"Want to know something?" said Hughie. "You didn't ask if I was invited. I seem to recall a couple of other times that happened."

"They were accidents both times, and I was sorry," I said.

"Uh-huh," said Hughie.

"Well, I'll call that old Baker biddy up right now," I said. "I'll tell her if you're not invited, I won't come either. After all, the party's being given for me."

I started for the stairs, but Hughie roughly grabbed my arm. He was very angry, and at the time I didn't know why.

"Don't do me any more favors," he said, shouting. "I've had enough of your favors."

He pushed past me and started down the stairs, two at a time.

I stood at the top of the stairs and said, "Now, look, Hughie, I'm not going to fight with you on my last night. I won't go. The Bakers can take their party and shove it. You stay to supper and we'll go to a movie or something. I mean after all it's my last night."

"No, thanks," said Hughie. "Go on to your triumph. And don't bother to write twice a week. Don't bother to write at all and don't send me any cashmere sweaters or shoes. Send them to the Salvation Army."

He stopped at the bottom of the stairs. He was not crying, but he was close to it.

"You don't even know my size," he shouted. "You never asked."

Then he said, "I hope you're going to see Miss Letty Novotny or whatever her name is in New York."

"As a matter of fact, I am," I said. "A lot."

"Good," said Hughie. "She's a phoney, and you're getting to be a phoney, and you two ought to get along swell together."

The remark was so uncharacteristic of Hughie that it silenced me for a moment, after which I said, "Hey, you forgot the Fowler books." There was no answer. So I shouted, "And you're staying for supper. It's roast chicken."

Since there was still no answer, I thought that Hughie had gone, and I shouted something else. "You're jealous," I shouted. "You're just like all the rest of them. You're so jealous you can taste it."

Hughie was not gone, though. He said two words, which were the last words he ever said to me. Then he slammed out the front door.

I took my shower, and while I dressed and ate the lonely supper that Mrs. Hoadley had fixed for me and Hughie, I kept listening for his step. I was sure he would come to his senses, and I was willing to forgive him.

"You didn't hardly touch the chicken or the baking powder biscuits, and you haven't ate a bite of the mashed potatoes and gravy," said Mrs. Hoadley, "and you didn't eat your gizzard, and there's Hughie's heart and liver."

I always ate the gizzard, and Hughie always ate the heart and liver.

"I don't want any dessert," I said, loud.

"But there's two kinds of ice cream and chocolate cake I baked special," said Mrs. Hoadley.

"Goddamn it, I don't want any," I said, shouting again.

"Now look here, young man, I won't be swore at and I won't be shouted at," said Mrs. Hoadley. "I'd of left this house without so much as a by-your-leave a long time ago if it hadn't been for you."

"I'm sorry," I said. "I'm very sorry."

"You're a little boy," said Mrs. Hoadley. "What they all forget is you're just a little boy."

"I'm almost sixteen years old," I said, and I said, "You've always been very nice to me, Mrs. Hoadley, and I hope you know I'm grateful."

She nodded. We were both close to tears.

"I'm going to send you those bedroom slippers I told you about," I said, and I quickly said, "I've got your size in my wallet. I won't forget."

"And my feet and I will thank you and more for them," said Mrs. Hoadley. "She'll just have to send them on is all."

She in our house always meant my mother.

"I haven't opened my mouth to her about this," Mrs. Hoadley said, "him neither when it comes to that, and they're two of a kind, but on Friday I'm taking my money, and I'm packing my bag, and I'll never darken her door again, and I don't care whether she likes it or lumps it. I'd rather go to the poor farm than work for her without you are around."

I smiled at her, and she started to clear the table, and she said, "Why don't you march yourself across the street there and tell Hughie you're sorry for whatever it was?"

"I've got nothing to be sorry about," I said.

"People with nothing to be sorry about get lonesome if they're not careful," said Mrs. Hoadley.

But I didn't march across the street, not until it was too late; it was always too late when I did it if I did it at all.

By the time I left for the farewell party at the Bakers' that evening, the Larrabees had gone off somewhere. I guessed to the movies. The *Casino* had Miriam Hopkins in *The Story of Temple Drake*.

I was bored and somewhat restive at the Bakers'. Still, the party was for me, and President Baker made a short speech. He said the entire campus was bursting at the seams with pride over me, and he said that one of these fine days my renowned name would add luster to Pegasus' crown.

President Baker was a mean man with a cliché; he had been a big man on the Chatauqua platform.

"You've given us many proud moments," said President Baker.

"Proud moments," said Mrs. Baker, a vague, unsettled woman who always wore a brown dress. Some people said it was always the same brown dress. Conversation with Mrs. Baker was difficult. She was a repeater. You would say, "Isn't it a beautiful day, Mrs. Baker?" And Mrs. Baker would reply, "Beautiful day." Or you would say, "Awfully glad to be here, Mrs. Baker." "Glad to be here," Mrs. Baker would say back. Letty Novotny was always threatening to say, "Just murdered my uncle, Mrs. Baker."

After his speech about the many proud moments, President Baker raised his glass, and a toast was drunk to me. The punch was straight ginger ale.

"Between you and I and the gatepost," President Baker said to me as I left that evening, "your being here has meant a lot to this campus. Your name and all. We're going to get that new football stadium yet."

It was after eleven when I got home, and the Larrabee house was dark. I looked across at it for a long time, but my telepathic message apparently never got there. The light in Hughie's room never went on.

The next morning, at Mrs. Hoadley's insistence and my own, I did cross the street, but Hughie had already left, and his mother didn't know where he'd gone.

"He leave any messages?" I asked.

Mrs. Larrabee said no, there weren't any messages. "Should there be?" she asked.

I said no, and I said, "Well, I better be moseying along, I guess."

"You're a good boy, Joshua," said Mrs. Larrabee, "and I'm glad Hughie got to know you."

"So'm I," I said.

I wanted to ask her to tell Hughie not to be angry with me and that I was sorry for what I'd said or hadn't said and that it was all my fault. I wanted to ask her to tell Hughie to wait for me to get back from England and that he was the best friend I'd ever had or ever would have and to thank him for trying to teach me how to play baseball, even though I'd never be any good at it. I wanted to say that I knew it had not been easy to be friends with me but that I was glad it had worked out that way, and ever so much more.

But I couldn't say any of those things to Hughie's mother.

I couldn't even have said them to Hughie, but if he had been there he would have sensed some of them.

"Well," I said. "I guess I better be going."

"Did you boys have a fight or something?" asked Mrs. Larrabee. I nodded.

"I knew it," she said. "Hughie acted funny all last night. We went to this awful terrible picture show and he fidgeted all the way through it, though I can't say as I blame him for that. Then this morning he didn't eat a bite of his breakfast, and then he went off someplace. I'll bet you dollars to doughnuts that boy won't even show up for work today. Your train soon?"

"Pret' near right now," I said. "Pavan's waiting right over there for me. He's back from Des Moines."

"And your mother away," said Mrs. Larrabee.

"She's getting installed as Worthy High Matron of the Eastern Star," I said. "Pavan drove her to Des Moines."

"You going off all alone at your age to a country that don't even talk the same language," said Mrs. Larrabee.

Then she reached out her arms, and I was in them. She kissed me, and she patted my head. "You're as nice a boy as anybody'd want to know anywheres," she said, "and you've had a tough row to hoe and don't let them tell you any different no matter what they say and what language they talk."

"It's English," I said. "I'm going to England."

"It doesn't matter where you're going," said Mrs. Larrabee. "You're going alone, and whatever they say about your mother around town I never have. You just be a good boy, and it's a pity for sure that you and Hughie have to have your spat the last thing before you go off."

"You tell Hughie I said good-bye," I told her, "and you tell him I said he better write me if he knows when his bread's well buttered."

"Hughie's not much for writing, but he'll be thinking about you," said Mrs. Larrabee. "You're the best friend far and away Hughie ever had, and he did better in his school work, too."

Then Pavan started honking the horn on the Chrysler, and Mrs. Larrabee kissed me once more.

"You tell Hughie I'm sorry," I said, "and say good-bye to the girls and Mr. Larrabee."

I crossed the street as slowly as I could, and as Pavan drove off, me in the seat beside him, I kept looking back at the Larrabee house, hoping that Hughie would show up.

He didn't though.

When I got on the train, I looked out the window, and as the train started, I saw a shadow in the station behind Mr. Durrell, the station master and ticket agent.

I have always thought that the shadow was Hughie, but I've never known.

Of course I could have jumped off the train and gone back to find out. All I'd have missed was the train, but I've never missed a train in my life.

I never saw Hughie again. The Larrabees moved to Eldora, Iowa, a few months later. I wrote once or twice, but there was no answer. Hughie was never much for writing.

In the fall of 1942 my Aunt Mettabel sent me the last I ever heard about Hughie Larrabee. It was a clipping from *The New Athens Times-Dispatch*, which I am able to quote in its entirety. It made a considerable impression on me at the time.

The item said:

Lieutenant Hugh Larrabee, formerly of this city, was recently killed when his plane was shot down in the Pacific Ocean near Guadalcanal. Larrabee is the son of Mr. and Mrs. Loren Larrabee, also once of this city, now residents of Eldora, Iowa.

Lieutenant Larrabee was a close personal boyhood friend of Joshua Bland, perhaps New Athens' most celebrated native son. Bland, himself now a soldier in the Army of the United States, was a student both in the public schools of New Athens and is a graduate of Pegasus College, having received his Bachelor of Arts degree at the age of fifteen, the youngest graduate in the history of Pegasus College. Bland is a member of Phi Beta Kappa and of the National Honor Society.

During his brilliant youth, educators from all over the world came to sit at the feet of the now Corporal Bland, whose late mother was the well-known local educator, lecturer, and Eastern Star leader, Celeste Bland.

Of course, Bland is now best known as the celebrated author of the currently hilarious and yet courageously outspoken account of Army life which is rapidly becoming one of the great best-sellers of all time, *Prodigy as Private*.

Bland was in his youth a permanent panel member of "Can You Top Them?", a radio predecessor of "The Quiz Kids." In addition, he won top honors in the Harvey Jordan O'Conner scholarship award competition.

Bland is married to a former Cedar Rapids girl, the former Letty Novotny, now a New York magazine editor.

Word reaches this newspaper from Eldora that memorial services for young Larrabee will be held in St. Patrick's Roman Catholic church there on Saturday next.

At the time I read that article I was in Beverly Hills, California, in a rather special foxhole, a bungalow of the Beverly Hills Hotel.

I knew at the time that I would never forget a word of the article about Hughie.

Finally, this:

In late December 1944, I was in Belgium, near the village of Spa. My jeep was stopped by two MP's; both of them were very nervous because the Battle of the Bulge had just begun, and nobody knew where the Germans were.

One of the MP's stuck an M-1 in my ribs and wanted to know the name of the capital of Illinois. I said Springfield.

The MP frowned and clicked the bolt of his rifle; so I changed my mind and said Chicago.

He nodded and then asked me several other questions, just to be sure.

I apparently answered them to his satisfaction, and he said, "Ain't trapped no Krauts yet, but we almost shot the ass off some queer from Paris I. and E. that didn't even know who won the World Series."

He and his buddy went to pieces over this sally, slapping their thighs and wheezing idiotically. I shifted more or less into first (gears elude me) and drove quietly on, trying to remember who had won the 1944 World Series. Or even who had played in it.

A little while later, I stopped the jeep, and I cried for a long time.

Several of the head fellows have nibbled at the edges of that one.

(5) The meaning of insouciance

And now I want to tell how I learned about the word having to do with the sickness of this time and this place.

I have said that my father was by nature a reticent man. As a result those rare times he did speak to me, I always listened carefully.

The afternoon I learned about insouciance, he and I were home alone. He was reading—and drinking.

I was working on what turned out to be my first and last novel. I was eight years old.

I expect my father was well into his second fifth of bootleg bourbon for the day.

Suddenly, he looked over to the dining-room table where I was typing. Then, as if the idea had just that minute occurred to him, he said, "Josh, most people are going to have to run like hell to get what you'll get just by standing still."

I nodded.

After another slug of the bourbon, he said, "Have you by any chance ever run across the word *insouciance?*"

I shook my head, rose, and went immediately to the Webster's Unabridged he had given me on my fifth birthday. That was S.O.P. in our house. If I didn't know the meaning of a word, I was honor-bound to look it up, no matter what, even if I came across it in reading something in the middle of the night. I usually did, too.

That afternoon after I had read aloud what Webster's had to say about *insouciance*, my father said, "If you do anything worthwhile with your life, they'll probably burn you at the stake or force you to drink the hemlock in one painful way or another, but if you become *insouciant* they'll reward you handsomely."

He paused a moment, then said, "Want something important, son; want something that matters."

"It's usually very hard to tell what's important," I said.

My father said, "No, it isn't. It's always very easy to tell."

He winked at me as if we were members of a happy conspiracy and then went off to write the obituaries and the *Social Notes from Around the Town* column for the *Times-Dispatch*.

I went back to work on the novel, which was about a group of blond, beautiful people who spent all their time just being nice to each other. A fairy tale, of course.

Upsidedown Land, both the setting of the novel and its title, was a place of endless wish fulfillment. Children stayed up all night, but adults were put to bed promptly at seven. Matches were played with, but nobody ever got burned. Cats and dogs were everywhere. In fact, they were *required* by law.

You see, mother disapproved of cats and dogs, and she pointed to Aunt Mettabel's Spot as a typical example of what happened if you had a pet.

"Why," she said, "if *we* had a dog, I'd be afraid to put on a hat. I'd never know *what* was in it."

She was convinced that cats carried deadly germs. I remember on one of the many occasions when she tried to get me to stop seeing Hughie, she said, "He smells of dog and cat, not to mention an I.Q. of a low eighty-eight. If that."

There was also a fifteen-hundred-room house in *Upsidedown Land*. The narrator—that was me—never ate or slept in a room more than once, which made it possible for him to ride up and down in a self-service elevator all the time without ever having to make beds or do the dishes. The idea for that must, to put it kindly, have been inspired by the Mad Hatter's tea party.

I made drawings of Upsidedown architecture. As I recall the buildings looked vaguely like Saul Steinberg's buildings—except that Mr. Steinberg can draw.

I invented an Upsidedown language, compiled a dictionary and made maps. I laid out cities and highways, and I built bridges with my erector set. I even drew up a constitution, more

British than American, and I issued a manifesto. *Everything* was socialized.

But what I liked best was the torture chamber in the basement of my fifteen-hundred-room house. There a woman was tortured constantly by naked giants *sixteen feet tall*.

This nameless harpy, who deserved every turn of the screw, bore a close spiritual and physical resemblance to Mignon Velma, my sixth-grade teacher.

Miss Velma was a bulging, nervous woman with another of the harmfully overactive thyroids I've mentioned. She chattered incessantly, aimlessly, loudly.

She was a great admirer of Henry Ford, not because of the automobile he manufactured but because he was not afraid to speak out against The Chosen People. According to Miss Velma and, I gathered, Mr. Ford, The Chosen People were responsible for practically everything wrong anywhere, knee-length skirts, farm foreclosures, adultery, and jazz.

Now I knew who The Chosen People were from the Bible, but I wasn't personally acquainted with any—except Old Jules, *Garfinkle's Junk and Hides*. On many Saturday afternoons Hughie and I took great piles of junk not technically ours to Old Jules. He never asked where we got it, and he always paid good prices.

Perhaps that is why I felt it incumbent on me to defend The Chosen People. More likely, though, it was because I liked to argue with Miss Velma. I nearly always won.

Of Henry Ford, though, I remember she said, "If what he says wasn't true, they'd sue," a remark which seemed so logical that I shut up at once.

It was one of the few times in my life I have shut up when the shutting was good. It was also the only argument I ever had with Miss Velma in which she scored a technical knockout.

If what Ford says isn't true, why don't they sue? I kept asking myself.

But I want to deal here only with one afternoon and one morning with Miss Velma because they have to do with *Upsidedown Land* and with my father and with a great change that was about to take place in my life.

Around three of the afternoon I have in mind Miss Velma told us sixth-graders that there was a mistake in our new biology books. On page 84, under *primates*, she said, were listed, one, the *ape*, and two, *man*.

This was clearly an error, she said. What the textbook should have said, was, one, primate, the ape, and two, man. Man was man and could not be classified with an ape, she said. She told us to ink in the correction.

Naturally, I challenged this. I said that the book was right and Miss Velma wrong. I'm sure I quoted an authority to prove my point. I nearly always did, and if I didn't know one, I made up one and quoted him, *loud*.

"Do you want to classify yourself with the apes?" asked Miss Velma.

"I most certainly do," I said, and the class giggled happily. Miss Velma and I were at it again.

"You can stay a half an hour after school," said Miss Velma.

"With pleasure," I said.

"An hour," she said.

Miss Velma did not like me, which was not unusual, but she didn't even pretend to like me, which was unforgivable.

I once heard Irma Beardsley tell Miss Velma, "It's not Joshua Bland's fault he's so smart." Miss Beardsley taught in junior high.

"Mignon, look at it this way," said Miss Beardsley. "If Joshua had a harelip, you'd have to make the best of it. Am I right?"

"A harelip would be a pleasure by comparison, and I don't care who knows it," said Miss Velma.

Miss Velma later told Frank Shay, the school principal, that I was a little sass-box, no more and no less.

"Mignon, what would you do if you had Albert Einstein in your class?" Frank Shay asked her.

"Who?" asked Miss Velma.

"Well, Thomas Edison then," said Mr. Shay.

"We got along just fine without the electric light and a lot cheaper, too," said Miss Velma.

I knew all this because a boy named Al Jordan told me. Al was a freshman at Pegasus, and he earned a few dollars each week by doing some typing for Mr. Shay.

Al was the one who introduced me to astronomy. I learned about the stars and other planets from him, and he was gentle. The kind ones and the gentle ones. Those I remember.

Al said Mr. Shay told Miss Velma that admittedly I was *difficult*, but he said, "Mignon, with a special boy like that you have to take special pains. It's worth it."

According to Al, Miss Velma then got red in the face and said, "Joshua Bland will die a drunkard's death, and you can mark my words on that," after which she flounced out of Mr. Shay's office.

Miss Velma came close to being right about me and booze, but I don't think that was because she had any special powers of prognostication. She based her prediction on the fact that a few months earlier she had asked each of us in the sixth grade what was the first word or words we had spoken.

There were *Dada*'s and *Mama*'s and *Baby-waby*'s till you couldn't rest.

When Miss Velma came to me, I thought of several satisfactory words that I wished had been my first, but I settled for the truth.

"The first words I ever spoke were *bourbon whiskey*," I said, "and I was only eight months old and could say the alphabet *forwards and backwards*."

That last I doubt, but it's true that my first words were *bourbon whiskey* at eight months.

"That'll be just about enough out of you, young man," said Miss Velma.

"Not only that," I said, "when I was a year and a half old I could say the Ten Commandments backwards, 'yretluda timmoc ton tlahs uoht.'"

Miss Velma did not speak for several moments; then she went on to Nadine Gidney, who sat behind me and whose first word had been *dolly*.

Anyway, the afternoon of the primates, which is how all this got started, Miss Velma was correcting English themes after school. I was reading *The Bengal Lancers*.

Both Miss Velma and I forgot the time.

At about five-thirty, she looked up, frowned, and said, "Why didn't you tell me you could go home half an hour ago?"

I rose from my desk, giving Miss Velma a look which seemed to me a more than adequate answer.

She allowed me to reach the door, then said, "It is quite obvious to me that nobody has taken down your pants in a long time and given you a good spanking where it would do the most good."

This time I had the last word, and I knew before I said it that it would be the last. I had already learned that there were certain things I could say to which people either would not or could not reply. This was one of those things.

I said to Miss Velma, "It is quite obvious to me that nobody has ever taken down your pants."

Then I left, taking my time about it.

On the way home, I felt ashamed of what I had said to Miss Velma—but not too ashamed.

I turned over in my mind the bitter knowledge that most people weren't grateful when I called their attention to a mistake in logic or an error of fact.

To the contrary, they were almost always angry. The fact was that neither Miss Velma nor anybody else in the sixth grade, or in all of New Athens as far as I knew—except maybe my father and Frank Shay—gave a damn whether man was a primate or not. The fact was that most people *preferred* to be ignorant, and if I wished to avoid censure and ridicule, it was better to keep my mouth shut about what I knew—or thought I knew. There was nothing to be ashamed of in doing that. After all, Galileo had recanted.

"So it doesn't move," I said aloud.

Irma Beardsley was coming in the opposite direction, and she smiled at me and said, "Little Alexander Hamilton was *always* talking to himself."

"So it doesn't move," I said again, walking on.

My father was home when I got there. He was sitting in the living room on a straight-backed chair, drinking a glass of bourbon. Mother was in Des Moines with Petrarch Pavan.

I said, "Hi, Pop," and went over and kissed him on the forehead.

He smiled at me and then, very solemnly, asked me to sit down. I did so, uneasily; I suspected from his manner that he had heard either about that afternoon's argument with Miss Velma or about what had happened a couple of days earlier.

The earlier seemed more likely. I was pretty sure Miss Velma hadn't had a chance to report our argument about the primates, and I knew she would never tell anyone what I had said about her pants.

"Frank Shay came to see me this afternoon," said my father.

"I'm sorry, Pop," I said, my worst suspicions confirmed. Pop had heard about the essay I wrote.

"Are you?" he said, taking a large swallow of the drink. "Let's hear your side of what happened."

"Well, it's nothing much. A couple days ago Miss Velma told us to write about our favorite kings."

I imitated the closed nasal tones of Miss Velma.

"'And then you can each read your little pieces aloud to the class,'" I imitated.

"Now what the hell's a little piece?" I asked my father. "She meant short, I guess, and she should have said *piece*, singular. I've about given up on her stupid grammatical mistakes. Anyway, it'd been a damn dull afternoon, and all I did was just liven it up a little."

"A vocabulary that consists almost entirely of curse words also has a habit of becoming dull," said my father, "but go on. I'm breathless. Which king did you choose?"

"Didn't Mr. Shay tell you?" I asked.

"You tell me," said my father.

"Louis the Bastard," I said, and my father laughed. So did I, with relief.

"How many times did you manage to say it?" he asked.

"Sixty-eight times in two pages," I said, and my father laughed again.

"She stopped me in the middle of the first page, and she gave me a flunk, which I don't think is fair. He *was* my favorite king."

"Really?" asked my father.

"Well, no. Not really. My favorite king is still King Arthur, I guess."

"So in a way what you wrote was a lie, wasn't it, and Miss Velma was perfectly justified in flunking you because you hadn't really carried out the assignment."

"Yes, sir," I said, and then, brightening, "but it was funny, wasn't it, Pop?"

"It was funny," said my father, "but I wonder if you really think it was worth it."

"No, sir," I said, looking at the cigarette burn on the carpet. "The other kids liked it, though."

"Oh, sure. A little temporary popularity is the cheapest thing in the world to buy."

Then he said, "I doubt very much if Miss Velma told Frank Shay. It makes her look too foolish, and nobody likes to look foolish, and everybody hurts easily, and everybody scars. Try to remember that, will you?"

I nodded, not looking at him.

"It will be very easy for you to hurt people, Josh," he said.

He put his hands on my shoulders and drew me close to him.

"I hope that I don't have to tell you that you've made a cheap joke at the expense of a silly old woman who hasn't got half the intelligence you've got but who has to earn her bread and butter by teaching. The fact that she's not suited to her job either by training or temperament or intellect doesn't excuse your showing off and being rude to her. Have you apologized to her?"

I ignored the tears that were running down my cheeks.

"I shall," I said.

"Will," said my father.

Then he added, "You'll be able to get away with a lot in your life. I hope you won't."

He paused so long I thought he had finished.

Finally, he said, "When you grow up, there's nobody around to punish you. There's just you."

He paused again, smiled and said, "My God, I get pompous. Gene Debs once told me that pomposity is one of the curses of always being right. I thought he was joking, but he wasn't. Gene was a fine man, but he had absolutely no sense of humor."

He sat very straight in his chair. My father was a formal man. He tried always to sit straight in a chair, and he wore his jacket to work even during July and August. When he was sober and he and I were alone, we wore ties and jackets at dinner, and we always ate in the dining room.

When mother was home, we usually ate in the kitchen.

My father took a short drink, then, "You remember those tests those fellows from Iowa City gave you?"

I said that I did. During the summer for reasons that are not important in this scene four young psychiatrists had come to New Athens from the Iowa Child Welfare Research Department in Iowa City and given me a series of tests.

"And you were asked not to tell anybody," said my father.

"I didn't tell anybody, Pop."

My father kept swishing what was left of the bourbon around in his glass; he spilled a little and rubbed the moisture into the carpet with his foot.

"Do you know what a genius is, Josh?" he asked.

"Sure. Michelangelo—Einstein—Shakespeare. People like that."

He looked at me for what seemed a long time, and then—irrelevantly, I thought—he asked, "Do you remember when you were in third grade, and I heard you crying in bed one night, and I came in to find out what you were crying about?"

"Yes, sir," I said. "I remember."

"And you said, 'I was thinking about how cruel the North was to the South after the Civil War.'"

"Yes, sir."

"You were ashamed of crying," he said, "but you shouldn't have been. Very brave and very good men often cry when men are cruel to each other. Lincoln might have cried if he'd lived after the war."

He finished what was left in his glass.

"You've got a first-class brain," he said, "and I hope you'll use it and develop it and be grateful for it. A man to whom God has given extraordinary endowments has extraordinary responsibilities. Wouldn't you say?"

"Yes, sir, *noblesse oblige*, I guess."

"*Noblesse oblige*, I guess," said my father. "A really first-rate man has first-rate emotions, too, in addition to the mind. Now pity's a fine emotion, properly channeled, and compassion, and anger at the right things."

I nodded, and my father said, "'We must watch them from their youth upward and make them perform actions in which they are most likely to forget or be deceived, and he who remembers and is not deceived is to be selected, and he who fails in the trial is to be rejected.' That's from Plato."

"I know," I said. "You told me."

My father nodded, very slowly; it was clear that there was something he had to say to me, and whatever it was, he didn't want to say it.

Father said, "You haven't read Mill yet, have you?"

I shook my head.

"'Aim at something noble,'" said my father. "'Make your system such that a great man may be formed by it, and there will be a manhood in your little men of which you do not dream.'"

"Yes, sir," I said. I said it quietly; I was suddenly frightened, not knowing why.

"You got 188 in those tests," my father said.

My throat felt dry and strange, and it was a while before I found a voice. Then I said, "Is that good? I didn't think I did any too well with all those planes."

"It's very good. It means that you—that you're a very gifted boy."

He rose unsteadily and started toward the kitchen, stumbling over the chair on which he had been sitting.

I said, "Pop, I've got another—confession to make."

He waited. I sighed, and then I told him about me and Miss Velma and the primates. I didn't mention what had happened after school.

"That's an entirely different matter from Louis the Bastard," my father said. "Never hesitate to defend what you know is right, and never apologize for having done it."

He was at the kitchen door when I asked, "Was that really good, getting 188 in those tests?"

"About the best it's possible to do," said my father. "The people in Iowa City say it's—history-making."

I whistled, pleased with myself.

"That makes me very happy," I said. "I'm glad."

"I am, too," said my father. "It'll be all over the papers in the morning."

"Oh boy."

My father came over to me, smelling of bourbon; he picked me up and swung me over his head the way I liked. Then he said, "God help you."

After that, he went into the kitchen to fix supper, but first he said he had to lie down for a little while, and he went to sleep.

I fixed my supper and ate alone. I didn't mind. I always read at the table when I was alone and as often as I could get away with it when I was not alone.

I ate two hamburgers and three hot dogs, all of them doused with both mustard and catsup. I drank a whole quart of milk and ate two good-sized pieces of a thick-crusted cherry pie which had been baked especially for me by my Aunt Mettabel.

While eating, I read over my unfinished novel, *Upsidedown Land*, and threw the pages in the waste-basket including those scenes in which a woman resembling Miss Velma was tortured by giants *sixteen feet tall.*

At that moment, the novel seemed to me a childish thing, particularly for somebody who'd just made history by scoring 188 in a series of tests given him by *four* psychologists.

After supper, I washed the dishes and went to see if my father was all right. He was snoring loudly.

I crossed the street and told my friend Hughie Larrabee about the tests.

"I got a score of 188," I said. "That's historic. It'll be in all the papers."

"Catch," said Hughie, throwing me a softball.

The next morning it was in all the papers, and nothing was ever the same after that.

I was already at school when Miss Velma got there.

I knew she must have read about me in *The Des Moines Register*. My picture was on the front page, and she had the *Register* under her arm. I waited for her to congratulate me, but she didn't. She didn't say a word.

Nevertheless, I said that I was sorry about Louis the Bastard. She nodded.

Then I made the mistake of adding, "And I'm especially sorry about saying what I said about your pants."

Miss Velma's face got red, and she raised her hand and slapped my face as hard as she could. Then she said, "Now cry, you little bastard. Now cry your goddamn eyes out."

Miss Velma was very active in the New Athens First Methodist Episcopal Church.

She leaned close to me and said, almost in a whisper, "I hate smart little bastards like you. I don't think you're a little boy. I think you're a goddamn midget in disguise."

She slapped me a second time and said, "Now get out of here but first look at me and let me see you cry."

I looked at her for a long time, but I didn't cry.

Then I started out of the room.

When I got near the door, "I'm glad I said what I did about your pants."

It was not much of an exit line, but I felt pretty good about it at the time.

Later, other people accused me of being a midget in disguise, and some of them were serious, and some of them were not.

I didn't know it, but I was about to leave Arnold School and what is inaccurately known as public education forever.

I expect I had better say something about how I got into Arnold School in the first place.

My first day at school is the kind of experience I remember in detail.

I had just turned four, and mother had somehow got me into the second grade at Arnold. There must have been tests of some kind, though perhaps not. Perhaps mother simply overwhelmed Frank Shay.

As is surely apparent now, mother's style of speaking was rather like the writing style of Macaulay—except that she would describe a skirmish among the Star sisters in terms Macaulay reserved for the Battle of Waterloo.

Possibly mother just took me to Arnold School and announced that I was ready for second grade.

Maybe Mr. Shay said, "Impossible."

If he did, then mother almost certainly issued one of her favorite manifestos. "There is no such word as *impossible* in my vocabulary, Mr. Shay."

When mother said something like that, the best thing to do was nod.

Anyway, however it was arranged, when I was four years old, there I was in second grade.

Of the teacher I remember, first, that she smelled of cologne and sweat. I remember that the desk assigned to me was too large for me and that I was too shy to ask for a book to sit on. I remember that the other children seemed like giants.

I remember that the teacher told me to go to the blackboard and write the figures four, six, and ten, and add them.

I knew that it would be difficult if not impossible for me to walk all the way to the blackboard, and I knew that once there I was too short to reach the blackboard without standing on tiptoe.

So from my seat I said, "Four, six, and ten are twenty."

"How'd you happen to guess that?" the teacher asked.

I said I hadn't guessed it, that I'd added it in my head.

"None of your smart-aleckness now," said the teacher. "I've heard all about you, and I won't take any of your sass around here. How do you expect me to believe something like you just said?"

"Because I said it, and I don't lie," I said. "I could do sums like that in my head when I was eleven months old."

"You're a little smart-aleck," said the teacher, "and I'll see that that smart-aleckness gets taken out of you before I send you home where you belong. You're not even old enough to be in kindergarten yet."

"I'm smart enough to be in fifth or sixth grade," I said, probably something I'd heard my mother tell Frank Shay.

"I want you to say you're sorry for lying about knowing those numbers," said the teacher. "You've worked that problem before, and you know it. Now say you're sorry for lying."

"I can't possibly say I'm sorry for something I didn't do," I said, then added, "but I will say this. I don't expect to learn anything around here. Not from you."

The teacher leaped from her desk, and she was almost immediately standing above me, smelling of sweat and cologne.

I looked very far up at her, and she said, "I don't want to hear another word out of you. Not another word."

Then she said, "Go stand in the corner until recess."

I stood in the corner until recess, feeling no remorse, feeling only what I was to feel very often again, a combination of self-pity and resentment.

That teacher heard few words out of me during the rest of the school year. I was, as Hughie later said, a quick learner, and one of the first things I learned in school was that the best answer to a question was, "I don't know."

That particular answer always pleased that particular teacher. "That's what I figured," she would say. "I figured you wasn't any smarter'n anybody else if that."

At recess that first day I hid in the cloak room, and after school I waited in the Boys until everybody else had gone home, then ran all the way to the house in which I lived. I ran very fast.

On the second day before I went to school I came downstairs for breakfast, fully dressed and wearing a Hallowe'en mask.

"What've you got that thing on for?" my mother asked.

"I'm going to wear it to school," I said.

"What in the world for?" asked my mother.

"Because I want to."

"Take it off."

I refused.

"You want to be the laughingstock of the whole school?" she asked.

"I am anyway," I said.

"Well, I'm not going to have you make a fool out of me," said my mother, and she ripped the mask from my face. In about six months I started having headaches, and Dr. Llewellyn sent me to an eye doctor. The eye doctor decided I was nearsighted, and I've worn glasses ever since. The glasses I've worn seemed to get bigger and bigger and cover an increasing area of my face.

I've worn many other masks, too. The beard, for one. Books, as I've said. Liquor, narcotics, and a sneer.

But I've never found anything that would have worked as well as that Hallowe'en mask.

Not much else about school. It was almost never more than a way to fill up the day.

I soon found out that to stay out of trouble it was not only better not to answer any questions, it was better not to ask any.

I remember some teacher, very angry, at a PTA meeting telling my mother, "He is always asking something that isn't in the book."

Her tone indicated that I was guilty of a crime on a level with high treason.

"If you ask me," this teacher said, "Joshua Bland thinks too much."

It's been a long time since anybody's been able to pin that rap on me.

I was a fast reader and always finished any classroom reading long before the others, so one day I brought *The Cyclopedia of Common Things* to school to keep me occupied.

The teacher wouldn't let me read it, though.

"I have absolutely no intention of encouraging cheating," she said.

I never knew what she meant.

There was a good art teacher at Arnold School, Milly Stanton, with red hair and very large breasts, and everybody said that she and Ed Clark, captain of the basketball team, were lovers. I don't know.

With Miss Stanton's help, I did a great deal of painting and drawing for about two years, and a watercolor of Aunt Mettabel's Spot took a prize at the Iowa State Fair.

"You may be a good artist one of these days," said Miss Stanton, "very, very good if you just keep at it."

I read all I could find about the lives of artists and at one time thought of cutting off my ear.

Then—I was seven—Miss Stanton took the whole class to Cedar Rapids to see an art exhibit. I remember there was a Picasso, and there were some Cezannes, and a Matisse. On the way back to New Athens in a school bus, I sat next to Miss Stanton, and I was silent for a long time.

Finally, Miss Stanton asked me what was wrong. I burst into tears and said, "You should never have told me my pictures are good. They aren't at all."

I never painted another picture—not from that day to this.

Oh. Once when I was in fifth grade we were asked to rate ourselves for achievement. This is what I wrote:

"People are always saying I have done a lot, but I don't think I've done much, not when I think of people like Charles Darwin and Galileo and people like that."

I don't know whether I was born that way or not, but from those two examples—and I could give a hundred others—it is obvious that at an early age I was competing with the entire human race, living and dead, and if I wasn't pretty certain that I'd come in first, I didn't compete.

So I withdrew from the real world. When I was a freshman at Pegasus, a young psychologist on the staff had a series of talks with me, and he gave me a sealed written report to take home to my mother. I remember every word:

...Joshua is unable to achieve and to lead on a level with his mental age. Because he is so young in calendar years, he finds it pleasant to imagine for himself a position of prestige ... At his age this is not especially dangerous, but if it continues it could lead to paranoia ... a psychosis more frequent among those with superior mentality than others. Paranoia often begins in frustrated childhood ambitions, along with delusions concerning the motives of others.

After I read the report, I tore it up. Mother never laid eyes on it.

And that's about all I'm going to say about school—except for what comes later on about Pegasus.

Actually, from the time I was about seven on, school was not very important. I was nearly seven years old when Petrarch Pavan entered my life.

I'll save Pavan for tomorrow, how he came to town and how my father left town.

It has begun to mist slightly. I have taken two pills.

I find myself thinking of my daughter Taffy. The hell of all this is that Taffy is going to spend the rest of her life paying for my foolish pride.

NOTES·DICTATED·ON·
THE·THIRD·DAY

(1) The golden glow

This is the third day, and I'm shocked at how little I've told. I must proceed very much faster. Otherwise, I'll never finish, and I must finish. I am leaving these tapes to the place in New Haven, along with enough money to set up a fellowship for a young psychiatrist interested in looking into what ailed me—and ever so many others I could name.

Not that I expect much. I believe that the sickness goes much deeper than anything that psychiatry can cope with. The very air is thick with it.

I would also like to have Taffy hear—or read—what I have said, but that decision is up to Dr. Baron.

As I said, I thought of Taffy before going to sleep last night, and I thought of her first thing when I woke up this morning.

Now comes the place where I talk about the man I am calling Petrarch Pavan. The name is clearly made up, and there are reasons for my choosing both parts of it, but those have nothing to do with this narrative.

Pavan arrived in New Athens late in August in 1928; he was the new head of the Fine Arts department of Pegasus.

For months after Pavan's appointment and before he got to town, both the college paper and the *Times-Dispatch* were filled with accounts of his accomplishments. It looked as if there was no place he had not been, nothing he had not done; and as if that were not enough, he was, as the local papers so often pointed out, "a member of one of America's first families." He came from a New England family that had arrived in this country on or before the *Mayflower*; one ancestor had helped write the Constitution and had been in Washington's cabinet, and a great-grandfather had been an unsuccessful candidate for vice-president of the United States. Pavan had spent a large part of his boyhood in Europe, and, after going through a series of American colleges, he had studied at various European institutions. He had in addition studied painting with ..., had been a music pupil of ..., writing apprentice with ..., was a close professional associate of ..., had served with distinction in ..., been on the faculty of ..., and more and more and more.

Pavan's picture appeared on the front page of the *Times–Dispatch* several times, but if I saw it, I don't remember. Mother must have, though; I have a feeling that even then she felt a stirring in her vital areas; even before Pavan got to town, Pavan had no doubt taken the place of Charles Farrell in her restless dreams.

She read everything about him—often aloud. Once toward the end of some journalistic effusion or other, I remember my father saying, "And he walks on water."

"What's that?" said mother. "What'd you say?"

"He must walk on water," Father said. "What else is there?"

Mother said, "If there is anything that I cannot stand, it is petty jealousy."

Another time, Father said, "I've been figuring it out, Celeste, and if he's spent all that time at all those colleges and universities and he's forty-three years old, he was at each of them for approximately a *year*."

"He is probably a man who wants to *share* himself," said mother. "You wouldn't understand a thing like that, Kendall."

I also remember Father saying, "If he's such a hot shot, what in God's name is he doing in a jerk-water town like this?"

"For his health," said mother. "I read it in the papers."

She had, too, and Pavan's health did have something to do with his being in New Athens.

He roared into town late in August—1928, as I've said. He came in a Pierce-Arrow roadster, painted red.

Pavan had about as much business behind the wheel of an automobile as—well, certain other people I could mention.

He made an immediate unfavorable impression on everybody who met him. Most people disliked him on sight, but with some it took a little longer.

The faculty at Pegasus was—as faculties are likely to be—loaded with persons who spoke with fraudulent accents, but Pavan's seemed to be even more fraudulent. He had the kind of sulky, high-pitched voice that I later learned to associate with certain types of homosexuals and with members of families of the New England area that have done nothing much but breed and live on the interest from their wealth for several generations.

Mother said, "I could listen to Pavan's voice for hours on end, and he'd never have to say *anything*. Like whatshername, that actress who was always reciting the multiplication tables and making you cry."

Pavan's voice had that effect on almost nobody else in New Athens.

But it wasn't the quality of his voice that aroused people's suspicions every time he spoke. There was something improbable about the man's entire personality. If he said, "Nice day," you felt like denying it. Or if he told you you were looking well—not that he ever did—you felt like rushing to the nearest mirror to see if you had broken out in a rash.

I never believed a word he said.

I was usually wrong, too. As far as I know, Pavan never told me a major lie. He omitted certain parts of the truth—always for good reason—but what he said was usually based on fact.

I think maybe my father came closest to summing him up. Once when mother was going on over Pavan, she said, "He's a man who's got absolutely everything—money, looks, personality. You name it; he's got it."

"You're wrong there," said my father. "There's one thing I'll name he hasn't got."

"What's that?" asked mother, an edge to her voice.

"Character," said father. "He hasn't got a *smidgin* of a character, Celeste."

What mother said back we needn't go into.

Let me give two examples of my own distrust of Petrarch Pavan, and then I'll bring him on scene.

First, Pavan claimed he had attended the University of Bologna, and he said that he had been graduated "the same year as my old friend George Jean Nathan." The year was 1905.

This was such a palpable lie that even mother, who usually hung on to Pavan's every word as if it were Holy Writ, would shrug her shoulders and say, "Now, Petrarch dear, aren't we storying just the teensiest bit about that?" She went through a long baby-talk period when she and Pavan were first married.

It doesn't matter why, but a few years ago, I was stuck in Bologna for a day. Out of malice and curiosity, I went to the University and, after immense difficulty and several bribes, I got hold of a partial class record for the year 1905. Two names stood out, those of Petrarch Pavan and George Jean Nathan.

Example Two. Pavan had little interest in news, probably because he disliked people, collectively as well as individually.

"Eventually, the race will destroy itself [this was in the early Thirties], and high time, too," he said.

Or, somewhat later, "I approve heartily of Adolf Hitler's method of treating the Jews. My only complaint is that he doesn't do the same for Gentiles."

Or, once I remember mother asking him, "Petrarch, you don't really like children, do you?"

"I despise children," said Pavan. "The children of today are the pimps, the prostitutes, and the gangsters of tomorrow."

"Now, Petrarch, remember little pitchers have big ears," said mother, nodding in my direction.

"That is not a child," said Pavan. "That is a monster in miniature."

All right. Pavan didn't like people, especially children, and he didn't care what went on in the world. Nevertheless, he did receive the Sunday edition of *The New York Times*.

In those days, the Sunday *Times* arrived in New Athens the following Wednesday. Wednesday was also the day I took my piano lessons, and the minute I walked into the parlor of the house on West Main where Pavan roomed and boarded (before he and mother were married, that is), I could tell whether it was going to be a good Wednesday or a bad Wednesday.

This is the way one good Wednesday went.

I got there a few minutes late. On a Bad Wednesday, this would have caused Pavan to say something like, "Myself, I think Stevenson, a minor writer at best, was wrong. Myself I think it is better to be dead than to be a fool. Particularly a tardy fool."

But on this day, Pavan had the *Times* open to the art section, and I could tell at once that he was happy with something. He pointed to a photograph of a statue of a girl. The caption over the picture said, "Tegg Wood Nymph." Beside the picture was a short, unpleasant evaluation of the latest exhibit of a sculptor named John Tegg. Among other things, the critic complained that Tegg had not "kept abreast of the times." His work was too literal, and so on.

Pavan looked approvingly at the criticism. "Of course not," he said. "Naturally not." He laughed. "Tegg was never a breast man, so how could he possibly keep abreast of the times?"

I also laughed, heartily, too heartily. I knew that if I played my cards right this could be a Wednesday when we wouldn't get to the piano until toward the end of the hour.

"She really a wood nymph, Pavan?" I asked.

"Wood nymph, my ass," said Pavan, gazing fondly at the bad notice for the Tegg exhibit. "That girl was a waitress at the Childs' on Fourteenth Street, and in addition to a commendable sexual liberality she stole odds and ends of food for us."

"Who's us?" I asked.

"John Tegg," said Pavan. "He and I and anywhere from four to five other hopefuls used to share a loft on West Fourth Street. Miss Wood Nymph there used to bed down with all of us, one at a time, of course. Usually. Her name was Chloe, and I remember once she brought home an entire apple pie in her bloomers. Waitresses wore bloomers in those days. The pie was still warm."

For a moment, he was back on West Fourth Street, and I said, "What were you going to be in those days, Pavan?"

"I could never decide," said Pavan. "I could have been anything, anything I set my heart on. I could out-sculpt, out-paint, out-play, out-compose, out-write and out-act the rest of them put together."

He thought about that, and he smiled.

I looked once more at the sculptured Chloe and said, "She certainly looks like a nice girl all right."

"Oh, she was a most accommodating girl," said Pavan. "She often brought us as many as four or five hard rolls stuck in her brassiere."

"What do you suppose ever happened to her?" I asked.

"Oh, I suspect the worst, acute respectability. I remember once when I asked her what her ambition was, she said, 'I'm going to roll around in the hay with you boys 'til I'm twenty, and then I'm going to marry a fella with a good job and a little something on the side.' The last I heard she'd been transferred to the Childs' on Broad Street. God knows what that led to."

He looked once more at the picture, and he smiled again.

"She insisted that the conversation be kept on a high moral plane. 'Don't talk dirty,' she'd say. 'It makes me sick to my tummy.' Yes, she was the kind of girl who used the word *tummy!*"

"I'm going to live in Greenwich Village when I grow up," I said, but Pavan didn't hear.

He said, "For a man with no talent, John Tegg has done remarkably well. I remember that first winter we were in Rome, Lorenzo—he was our teacher—Lorenzo said, 'Mr. Tegg, you might someday become an acceptable stone mason—though there is reason to doubt it—but a sculptor, never.'"

Pavan paused. "I was the one with talent," he said. "I had the future."

He rose. It was obvious that unless I could think of something the piano lesson would begin.

"How long were you in Rome, Pavan?" I asked.

Pavan shrugged and placed a book on the piano stool so that I could reach the keyboard.

"Tegg didn't get a very good review, did he, Pavan?" I asked.

"No, he did not," said Pavan, smiling.

"That make you happy?" I asked.

"Of course," said Pavan. "There is nothing in the world quite as satisfying as the golden glow we feel stealing over us when one of our friends gets a bad notice. Now get your ass over here."

I got my ass on the book; it was *Great Fires of History*.

"We'll begin with Chopin," said Pavan.

That was a good Wednesday. There weren't many of those.

Well, there you are. Typically, I have already described two incidents involving Pavan and haven't really gotten him on stage yet.

I remember every detail of the afternoon mother came home from an Artsy-Craftsy meeting; this must have been a week or so after Pavan arrived.

"At long last we have a first-rate mind in New Athens," said mother, taking off the long black gloves she wore on Artsy-Craftsy days; on Eastern Star days and evenings she wore long white gloves, and she went bare-handed to P.E.O. and Rebekah meetings.

My father continued reading.

"What a pleasure it is to have a brain of dimension in New Athens at last," said mother.

My father cleared his throat. I was reading *Dombey and Son*, and had just made up my mind that whenever I was big enough to have a dog of my own, I would name him Diogenes.

"Not only a brilliant brain but an all-around brain," said mother.

I stopped reading. I knew what a brain looked like, but I had never seen one. The way mother was talking it seemed as if she had encountered a brain without anyone attached to it, but the next sentence cleared that up.

"Petrarch Pavan is all I expected and more," said mother. "Kendall, are you listening?"

"How could I possibly avoid it?" said my father.

"A real Michelangelo," said my mother, "an all-around man, living here amongst us. He not only talked for the girls. He played for them, and while I always thought my piano was second to none, Petrarch Pavan gave me pause."

"That is something," said my father, returning to his book.

"Not only can he play, he paints, and he can act," mother said. "He has consented to appear opposite me in the community-theater production of *They Knew What They Wanted*."

She sighed happily. "At last we have a giant in our midst."

"For God's sake, Celeste," said my father, "are we or are we not going to have some supper?"

"Food," said mother, "at a time like this?"

"Oh God," said my father. "I'm going to scramble us some eggs. Want some, Josh?"

As I have said, Pavan was forty-three years old at the time he arrived in New Athens. Many years later during a miserable summer in New York I spent some time finding out about Petrarch Pavan and about the family from which he came and the reasons it was healthier for him to be in New Athens than in, say, New York—or, for the matter, a great many other places. That comes in due time.

He was actually forty-three, though.

Lincoln said that a man is responsible for what is written on his face after forty, but nothing at all was written on Pavan's. He was vaguely handsome; each feature was perfect and in the right place, but the total effect was upsetting. I hadn't read Dorian Gray at the time, but when I did—in England, I believe—I thought of Pavan at once.

Mother insisted that Pavan looked like Lord Byron, but I doubt that she had any idea what Byron looked like.

Pavan's hair was dark and wavy, and he wore it just enough too long so that you always felt that he needed a haircut. He was short—five-four, thereabouts—and had a well-proportioned figure. Not an ounce of extra weight on him, which was odd because he took no exercise at all. He never did any physical labor either.

I remember once, early in their relationship, mother asked him, pretty please with sugar on it, darling Petrarch, to bring her her portable typewriter.

"Celeste," said Pavan, "I do not carry. I am carried for."

From then on mother carried for him.

Pavan's skin was olive, his eyes brown and soft and large, and he had a club foot.

It is this last fact which has made it impossible for me ever to get through *Of Human Bondage*. I am in general fond of Maugham's work, but I never liked Philip Carey. He, too, made me think of Pavan.

I never cared for that tiresome whore Mildred either.

Around the time Pavan showed up at the college, a lady writer who called herself "Madame" Elinor Glyn showed up in Hollywood, and the Casino had her in a couple of two-reel shorts, one of which was called, "What is *It*?"

You can bet every woman in New Athens was at the Casino to find out, among them mother.

I remember once hearing mother say, "Petrarch, do you think I have *It*?"

"What in God's name is *It*?" asked Pavan.

"Oh, you know," said mother. "It's what Clara Bow's got. I found out all about *It*. I saw Madame Elinor Glyn in the movies."

Pavan said, "Celeste, be silent always when you doubt your senses."

I don't know about mother, but I guess Pavan had *It*. I know there were harpies in Artsy-Craftsy who thought that if those fools out in far Hollywood had any sense, they would have found a successor to Valentino right there in New Athens.

"Think of Valentino with a doctor of philosophy degree," said mother.

Pavan did not have a Ph.D. degree. What he did have, it turned out, was a B.A., of somewhat questionable origin. In addition to his Artsy-Craftsy appearances (fifty dollars an appearance), Pavan played the piano and lectured before other groups of women in and around New Athens.

Not only that, he agreed (mother's word, not mine) to take on a few piano students. "Only those with the most exceptional promise, of course."

That was where I came in.

I had been making noises on the piano since I was three years old. I learned the difference between the white keys and the black keys sitting on my mother's lap. When I was four, she had me before the Eastern Star girls. I played and sang a simplification of Beethoven's *Minuet in G*, "...fleecy clouds are drifting by, drifting by, in the sky, in the sky."

Between my unique performance at the Eastern Star and Pavan's arrival in town, I made no more public appearances, but I was at the upright in our living room an average of two hours a day.

Shortly after Pavan came, mother began saying things like, "I'm afraid you've gone about as far as you can go under my tutelage, sonny. If you have what I know you have, it would be wrong of me to hold you back."

That was such a strange way for mother to talk that I knew something was up. What was up was Pavan. He limped into the house one afternoon about six weeks after mother first mentioned him. Mother trailed not far behind.

"Pavan has consented to listen to you play," said mother. So I played. I can't remember what, and it is of no importance. When I finished, there was a vast silence, and finally mother, who was seated too close to Pavan on the davenport, said, "What do you think, Dr. Pavan? Sonny boy can certainly make that piano talk, can't he?"

"If sonny boy could make that piano talk, it would say, 'Sonny, take your goddamn clumsy hands off of me,'" said Pavan.

Mother burst into tears. Myself, I was delighted. It looked to me as if my piano-playing days were over.

"I guess that means that you won't agree to teach sonny," said mother.

"I didn't say that," said Pavan.

Later, over tea, Pavan said to me, "Your mother tells me you're a little genius."

"Tell Dr. Pavan about the Burma Shave ad," said mother, purring.

I sighed, then said, "'Roses are red, violets are blue, and Burma Shave is the One For You.'"

"He wasn't quite three years old, and I had no idea he could read," said mother. "Mr. Bland and sonny and I were driving to Montour one afternoon, and all of a sudden out of the clear blue sky, sonny read out that Burma Shave sign. We were absolutely flabbergasted. His father nearly ran into a tree." (My father was skunked.)

Mother paused for a reaction. There was none.

"Isn't that the most amazing thing you ever heard of?" she asked.

"No," said Pavan. "It is not. Sidis was reading *The Odyssey* in Greek at that age."

"Who?" said mother.

"Never mind," said Pavan. "How old is he?"

"Six," said mother. "Only six."

"Has he had calculus?" asked Pavan. Mother shook her head. "Trigonometry?" A sadder shake.

"Physics? Chemistry?"

"Only a little," said mother, meaning none.

"Greek? Latin?" Same answer.

Pavan shook his head sadly. "You've wasted a lot of time," he said. "It may be too late."

"Too late for what?" said mother.

"Never mind," said Pavan. Then he turned to me.

"I might agree to tutor you," he said. "I just might."

After that, he asked me a great many questions. I don't remember what they were about, but I do know that I'd gladly have confessed to anything.

Finally, Pavan turned back to mother. "It would be a lot of work," he said, "but he appears to have a good memory. We shall work together. We shall work very hard, and I shall brook no interference from you, Celeste."

"Why, of course not," said mother. "You know me better than that, Petrarch. But what did you have in mind?"

"What I have in mind is a national winner of the Harvey Jordan O'Conner Cranium Derby," said Pavan, "and ten thousand dollars."

Mother gasped with pleasure, sexual anticipation, and greed.

"Is it possible, do you suppose?"

"Ten thousand dollars," said Pavan.

Then he patted me on the head.

"We've got a little gold mine here," he said.

He took out his pipe and started stuffing it with a sweet-smelling tobacco. To this day, I cannot smell that tobacco without getting sick to my stomach.

For that matter I've yet to meet any pipe smoker I'd trust.

I might add here that Pavan didn't need the money; he always had plenty of money; his family saw to that. What appealed to Pavan was the sport involved. He was a born gambler, and he loved games of all kinds in which craft, skill, and cunning were involved.

He was good at them, too. After a year in New Athens, there wasn't anybody in town who'd play poker with him. He always won, and everybody was sure he cheated. I bet he didn't, though. I bet he never had to.

I have a feeling that in Pavan's mind I took the place of poker; I was a promising gamble. Not only that, I believe he saw in me a chance to make up for at least a few of his own past failures and defeats. I do know this. Pavan in his way did some of the same things that—as you'll see—were done to him in his childhood, and I in turn—by my false pride, by my neglect, by my inability to love, or, for that matter, forgive or turn the other cheek—did the same thing to my daughter Taffy. And she in turn....

And so it goes, on and on, hour after hour, century after century. Experience the great teacher? Don't you believe it. We learn nothing from history—and we learn less from experience.

Believe me, if there were another race, I'd join it. Since there isn't, for some time now I've had as little as possible to do with this one.

For instance, I seldom read a daily newspaper. I am too old and too tired to keep up with the day-by-day account of the avarice, cruelty, peanut-mindedness, and downright bastardy of your average, run-of-the-mill human being.

As I said earlier, bring on your bombs.

Back to the past now. Pavan began tutoring me early in October 1928.

On the night after his visit to our house, however, I heard this exchange between my parents.

Father: "Celeste, Pavan is a charlatan through and through, and you know it. I will not allow you and that fourflusher to exploit my son."

"*My* son," said mother. "*My* son. There is nothing whatever of you in sonny boy. Nothing. Pavan sensed that at once."

"I won't have you make a public spectacle out of Josh," said my father.

"Have you ever been able to stop me from doing anything I chose to do?" asked mother.

My father didn't answer.

"And I don't wish to discuss Pavan with you ever again," said mother. "Ever again."

I don't believe my father ever did mention Pavan again. He was always away from the house when Pavan came, and if he wasn't he left soon after. My father seemed to get smaller and drabber and quieter. After a while, he disappeared altogether.

As is surely obvious, I hated Pavan's guts when I knew him and, for that matter, hate the memory of him now, but I must admit that I learned from him certain things that I am grateful for knowing.

For instance, he loved the theater, and would talk for hours about plays he'd seen—in England, in France, in Greece, even in Russia.

He'd spent a summer at Provincetown, and he knew Eugene O'Neill.

"I think O'Neill writes very well," Pavan would say, "for an able-bodied seaman."

He was critical of everything and everybody.

"There hasn't been a great playwright in the world—really great—since Euripides."

"What about Shakespeare?" I once asked. Pavan was a reader-aloud of the Tragedies. He refused to pay any attention to the Comedies.

"William Shakespeare had a nice little talent," said Pavan, "if he had just taken the trouble to develop it."

Still, Pavan did make the theater sound exciting, and I suspect in a way he's responsible for the fact that I have made my living in it.

Pavan took me to the first *real* play I ever saw. I don't count the community-theater productions in which mother carried on, or the Tremayne Players, which I'll discuss later. What I mean is a play "with the original Broadway cast."

It was Katharine Cornell in *The Barretts of Wimpole Street*, and I saw it in the Shrine Auditorium in Des Moines. Because of the weather, Miss Cornell was late, but it didn't matter. I loved her and the play and the Shrine Auditorium.

On the way home in the Pierce-Arrow, mother said, "I wouldn't say she was an actress. I mean not compared with the great ones, but she does know how to project. We didn't have what I'd call good seats, Petrarch, but I could hear every word she said. *My* only trouble as I see it is I don't *project* enough."

There was no possible answer to this, and mother, after a moment, said, "Petrarch, what would you think if the community theater did *Candida* next season? I, of course..."

Pavan interrupted. "If the community theater did *Candida* next season, I, of course, would leave town."

Time passed, and there was no conversation at all. About the time Pavan was roaring into New Athens, I said, "Pavan, don't you ever wish you were back in New York where you could see all the plays and all?"

He didn't answer. I looked up at his face. He was close to tears.

Pavan also took me to all the traveling art exhibits that came to New Athens. If his judgments on playwrights were severe, his opinions of painters were murderous. To hear him tell it, there'd *never* been a good one. I'm exaggerating a little, but I remember looking at a Matisse and saying I liked it.

Pavan said, "That man should be prohibited by law from ever picking up a paint brush."

And once this sentence (can I have imagined it?): "Michelangelo did a quite satisfactory job on the Sistine Chapel."

On the other hand, once when we were in Cedar Rapids, Pavan took me to see the St. Paul's Methodist Church. It was built in 1913, and it looks more like Frank Lloyd Wright's Guggenheim Museum than any other building in this country. Not surprising, I suppose; it was designed by Louis Sullivan.

Pavan and I examined the church, inside and out, and when we'd finished, he asked me what I thought about it.

I used a favorite sentence of Hughie's. "Is that guy kidding, Pavan?"

Pavan looked angrily down at me. "You ignorant, corn-fed little barbarian bastard," he said. "You listen to me."

Then he took me to dinner at Bishop's Cafeteria, and he talked for at least an hour about architecture, ancient and modern. He had never been more eloquent nor, it seemed to me, more knowledgeable.

I was very impressed. I remember that, and I remember I said, "You ever want to be an architect, Pavan?"

It was a moment before he spoke. Then he said, "Yes, I did, among so many other things, but as my mother pointed out, I'd never be as good as the great ones—and so...."

He shrugged. He looked out at the dark street with its Saturday night crowds, mostly farmers and their families who, after they had finished shopping, would go to the picture show—usually a Ken Maynard or a Hoot Gibson and selected short subjects, a serial, and anywhere from twenty minutes to half an hour of advertisements.

"Iowa," said Pavan, sighing, and then he said, "Of all places in the world, *Iowa*."

He made it sound like a dirty word.

In addition to playing the piano, Pavan played the organ every Sunday in the college chapel.

He loved Bach. In fact, Johann Sebastian Bach was the only artist, living or dead, for whom Pavan ever expressed unqualified approval. He had made a pilgrimage to all the places Bach lived and worked, everywhere from Eisenach to Leipzig to Potsdam.

Moreover, Pavan spent a great deal of time working on the one thing in his life he hoped he might finish, what was to be the definitive biography of Bach. He had collected tons of notes, great wooden boxes filled with them. I also saw some of the pages he had written. He had a clear, forthright style that I admired.

Later, what he had written and his notes were destroyed. I expect he had planned it that way.

I was never in a class of Pavan's; so I can't comment on how he was in, say, "The History of Art—Caveman to Picasso." Otto Zorich, whom you'll meet in a moment, paraphrased a remark of Oscar Wilde's to describe him.

"Pavan, has learned everything, and he knows nothing," Otto said.

My own experience with Pavan as a teacher was more personal. All the time he was tutoring me, I spent at least five hours a day with him, and during those hours we worked very hard.

"Facts," Pavan kept saying. "We have to accumulate facts."

He would say, "You are stupid beyond belief, but perhaps there is some slight hope for you. Very slight. We shall once more conjugate the Greek verbs."

In June 1929 Pavan announced to the *Times-Dispatch* that I was a genius.

He said, "Joshua Bland was born with a reasonably high intelligence quotient. With my guidance, he has developed into a genius. Not, of course, that I did it alone. His mother, Celeste Bland, has been at my side the entire way."

True enough. *Heavenly* was always beside him.

Not long after that announcement, Pavan arranged—how I don't know—for the four graduate psychologists I've mentioned to come to New Athens to test me.

I've told about the results and what my father said.

What Pavan said was, "Celeste, next year the Harvey Jordan O'Conner champion will be the boy here."

Mother said, "Petrarch, I always knew I'd produce a child the like of which this town has never seen, but it took you to prove it to me."

A few days later, mother and Pavan took me to Iowa City, and there I was given the Thorndike tests for college freshmen, along with about five hundred eighteen- and nineteen-year-olds who were entering the university as freshmen.

I scored third from the highest.

The month of September 1929 was sultry in Iowa, not much happening anywhere except that the stock market was acting up a little.

President Hoover announced that there was nothing whatever to worry about. "The stock market is as sound as the dollar," he said.

In the Iowa papers I was a three-day sensation, and various predictable people acted in various predictable ways.

For instance, eight far-sighted members of the Iowa state legislature issued a joint statement denouncing the Iowa school system.

I was in no way unusual, these wise men declared. If the five hundred freshmen hadn't done as well as I, the schools of Iowa were to blame.

"Too much country club, not enough hickory stick," said one, a mortician from Red Oak who now graces the U.S. Senate.

He and the other seven, through a logic known only to themselves, recommended an immediate cut in the legislative appropriation for the state university.

Naturally, several reporters asked mother how I had happened, and she came forth with the one about how during her pregnancy she had thought only the largest thoughts, "and I ate a great deal of cottage cheese."

A scamp from the *Des Moines Register* dared to quote her verbatim on another matter. She said, "I and Petrarch Pavan are solely responsible for sonny boy." What about my father? "Mr. Bland had absolutely nothing to do with it, and you can quote me."

The scamp did, and mother threatened to sue.

She didn't, though, because the next morning the *Register* noted her claim of being misquoted, adding, "Mrs. Bland told this reporter, "I want an immediate refraction.""

Most of the newspaper stories said that I was a "regular boy" (they always said that), that I liked baseball, that I was popular with all my classmates at Arnold School, and so on. One story, in the *Cedar Rapids Gazette*, quoted me as saying, "I feel humble in the face of this God-given gift I seem to have."

A lady reporter wrote that. What I probably said was, "Nothing to it, toots."

There was a banquet in Iowa City at which I was guest of honor. Among others, a dean from the University of Chicago spoke. His subject was, "The Immensity of Intellectual Power," whatever that means.

Pictures were taken, and I remember at one point mother knelt beside me and gathered me to where her bosom would have been if she'd had one.

She said, "Joshua, my darling, from now on you belong to the ages."

And she said, "Joshua, I hope you make the most of today. It is your day, after all."

It wasn't, of course; it was her day. It was always her day.

During the evening, she did find time to give the dean a few hints on education.

I remember two sentences. She said, "I do not believe that I myself will ever become a great scholar, but sonny boy here proves beyond all doubt that I am a great teacher."

She paused for emphasis. She was the kind of pauser for emphasis somebody like Helen Hayes or Lynn Fontanne could have learned a lot from.

Then she said, "In the immortal words of the Bard of Avalon, 'Those who can, teach.'"

The dean said he had to catch a train.

While still in Iowa City, I was given the Army Alpha tests. I made a score of 188 on one and 174 on the other.... You'll come to how well I did twelve years later when I enlisted in the Army.

Anyway, as a result of the Army tests in Iowa City there were more pictures, more newspaper stories, and more crap.

That was when Pavan publicly announced, "We have here in our midst next year's winner of the Harvey Jordan O'Conner Cranium Derby."

Some reporter—those fellows are often very rude, you know— asked whether or not Pavan had any interest in the loot involved.

Mother answered for Pavan. She inhaled and said, "That sort of thing simply doesn't interest us. It will never be said of Celeste Bland that she exploited sonny for money."

Now the alert reader may have noticed that I haven't said a word about how I felt about this spurt of minor-league fame.

How I felt was that I couldn't get enough of it.

I can remember very clearly what I wrote in my diary. In fact I happen to have it right here:

Today I started keeping a scrapbook in what will undoubtedly be a continuing series which might very well be titled, *The Life and Times of Joshua Bland*. In this scrapbook, which, incidentally, I picked up at Woolworth's [meaning *snitched* it], I have pasted pictures of myself which appeared in the local newspapers as well as those that were in the *Des Moines Register*, *The Iowa City Press-Citizen*, and *The Daily Iowan*. It looks to me as if for the rest of my life I am going to be plagued by publicty. I shall simply have to make the best of it, I suppose.

If there were time, I'd go into my sermonette on what publicity does to you, and I mean whoever you are. As I've said, I've known a lot of people whose names are Household Words—Out There, in the theater, and in Wonderland, D. C., where the virus is often fatal.

In the theater I've seen it happen to dozens of perfectly nice kids. First, there is always that attractive blush of youthful surprise. "Who *me*? You mean *my* name's in Lennie Lyons' column? Gee whillikers...." Fade out. Fade in. Six months have passed. The above blusher is on the telephone.

Blusher: Riley? Blusher here. Riley, are you or are you not aware that you are being paid six hundred goddamn dollars every goddamn month to get my name in the papers? Well, listen, you drunken booze hound, I've read every column all week, and my name has only been mentioned twice—in *The National Enquirer*. And it's misspelled.

I'm sure there are exceptions. Did Einstein care? Does Schweitzer subscribe to a clipping service? Would St. Paul have been able to resist a certain capriciousness if he had been interviewed by one of those horn-rimmed demigirls doing the research for the cover story of *Time* Magazine?

Well, St. Paul might have avoided it, but I have known several cover stories, and, honest to God, most of them get to thinking they are God. Honest.

Anyway, as I say, when I started keeping a scrapbook of my personal publicity after I got back from Iowa City, I used to look it over before I fell asleep at night, thinking how next time I had a press conference I'd be faster on my feet and how when the pictures were taken, I'd remember that my left profile made my face look *stronger*.

But to get back to Iowa City. After the results of the Army Alpha tests had been announced and all possible publicity milked out of that, *Mummy*, Pavan, and I went back to New Athens. I remember that at the city limits we stopped for gas, and the frayed female who tended the pump kept staring at me.

Finally she said, "Ain't you the kid his picture was in all the papers?"

I modestly admitted it, and she begged for an autograph. So I condescendingly wrote my name on the back of an oil-stained map of Ohio. I found that as I wrote I made a few extra flourishes with the pen, a habit that continues to this day.

And then there was Horatio P. Baker.

Had we but known, at the very minute I was autographing Ohio, Horatio P. was sitting in our living room with my father.

Baker, who was easily the most genuine phoney I have ever come across, had the face of a kewpie doll that had been left out in the rain. He must have been in his mid-sixties at the time, but there was not a wrinkle on his round, red face nor was there hair on top of his round, red cranium. I don't know why no hair, but I do know why no wrinkles. In sixty-some years of existence not a thought had passed through the crevice Baker had instead of a brain.

Now enter Pavan and I. Mother was getting the bags out of the car.

Pavan nodded to Baker; he never seemed to notice my father.

"You've probably read what happened in Iowa City," Pavan said to Baker.

Father, sitting on the sofa next to Baker and drinking heavily, said nothing.

However, all four-feet-nine of Baker rose, and in a strained, high-pitched voice very much like that of John Gilbert, Baker said, "Greetings, Petrarch, and heartfelt felicitations."

To me he said, "I am President Horatio Phineas Baker of Pegasus College."

Then he said (you'll have to take my word for it once again, but, believe me, there are some things I just couldn't make up), "I have come to worship at the feet of the little master."

And then do you know what that fool did? He got down on his knees, and crawled toward me. I was all set to run, and then I got it. The little master was me.

By this time *Mummy* was in the doorway with our bags.

"Sonny," she said, quivering with delight. "That's President Baker."

"Mrs. Bland, I am honored," said Horatio P. Baker, and he continued crawling.

I know. I know. This is the part that always stops everybody. Everybody always says, "Bland, he couldn't have *crawled*," and I always say, "It was late September in the year of Our Lord 1929. Baker had on a Palm Beach suit, and he *crawled*."

When Baker got to where I was, he said, "Pegasus Experimental School welcomes you with open arms. You and Pegasus are destined for each other."

On his knees, Baker was eye-level with me. I looked him straight in the eye.

"We'll have to see about that," I said. "I don't believe we've met."

Alert readers may wonder how it is possible that in a town as small as New Athens I had never met Horatio P. Baker of Pegasus. I'll tell you how.

In the first place, in my day Riverdale Avenue was practically on the wrong side of the M. and St. L. railroad tracks, within two blocks of them. *Unforgivable.* In New Athens the people who ran Pegasus and, for that matter, the town—the more prosperous lawyers, the more successful doctors, the faculty members, and, of course, the Lavendar family—almost all lived on West Main Street. In New Athens the people who counted didn't belong to Eastern Star, the P.E.O., the Rebekahs, or the Woman's Club. The people who ran the Country Club, the Red Cross, the school board, and the town's politics didn't know and didn't care what mother did, but she cared desperately what they did.

Mother would have given an arm, a leg, and her eyeteeth to belong to the Atheneum Club, of which her own Artsy-Craftsy group was only a pale imitation. The Atheneum met once every two weeks in a barnlike club house on East Main, and papers were read:

Mrs. Robert Phelps, recently returned from Europe, read a paper on, "I Visited Hadrian's Villa—What Is Its Deeper Meaning?"

A Lavendar or a Lavendar-in-law was almost always president of the Atheneum and of the Country Club. Once every year mother tried to elbow her way into both, but she was blackballed every single time.

As if all that were not enough, in mother's day the People Who Really Counted in New Athens were no longer Methodists. They were Episcopalians: "We have left undone those things which we ought to have done; and we have done those things which we ought not to have done."

Thus—

"President Baker," mother shouted. "I've been dying to meet you." In her own mind she was at that very moment delivering a paper at the Atheneum, "Celeste Bland Looks At the World."

"Likewise, Mrs. Bland," said Educator Baker, getting up from the floor and brushing off his Palm Beach knees.

"What can we do for you?" mother wanted to know.

"The point is what I can do for you and for the little master here," said Baker, patting me on the head.

(2) The home of presidents

Louella has just brought me lunch.

She was bursting with self-importance. There is an article about Old South Friendly Road in *The Wall Street Journal*, and there is a picture of me taken a few years back when I was given the Henry Van Prang Award for Good Citizenship. That award is presented every twelve months to somebody whose name is known to the semi-literate, who has stayed out of jail, and has done nothing much to annoy the Power Elite lately. In 1955, since I met those three demanding qualifications, the mantle fell on me. Quite a mantle. In the picture I am grinning fatuously. I am drunk—on Scotch, champagne, brandy, and disgust.

I don't believe too many people in the grand ballroom of the Waldorf knew it, though, and I believe I delivered one of the most popular speeches ever made there. It was at the nadir end of a particularly nadir evening, and I got up and had the award pushed into my grimy fist after a great many words of no importance had been uttered by various people of no consequence.

In response I said all I was capable of saying. I said, "Thanks a lot, fellows," and sat down.

The applause was thunderous.

Anyway, the picture taken that night is the picture in *The Wall Street Journal* this morning.

Guess what the caption says. Right. The caption says, "Joshua Bland, stormy petrel, etc...." Where do those fellows get all their ideas, do you suppose? The *Daily News* always calls me "a stormy petrel," meaning I once was a trouble-maker. But no more, no more. Once a paper in Medicine Hat, Saskatchewan, said I was "a stormy pretzel." That is more like it.

God knows why *The Wall Street Journal* has decided to run an article on Old South Friendly Road. Summer doldrums, I guess.

The piece says The Road is "the home of nine presidents." True enough if you keep in mind that's a small *p* there. As I may have mentioned, we do have this one fellow who tried for the top spot in Wonderland, D. C., too often. He never made it, though, a fact which gives me some small faith in democratic government.

Our presidents are less exalted. Four of them are heads of corporations that turn out the kind of products Which Have Made This Country Great—mouthwashes, toothpastes, dandruff removers, beer, cigarettes, that sort of thing.

Our other five presidents are heads of advertising agencies whose overpaid jobs are to make us feel that we absolutely cannot do without a single one of the products Which Have Made This Country Great.

In addition, there are living on the road people whose names are Household Words, Davy Bronson, for instance, Pism C., a mealy-mouthed purveyor of misinformation on television I wouldn't name if you tore out my fingernails, and Ernestine Kraftall. Well, actually, Ernestine's *name* may not be familiar to you, but her *sounds* certainly are. Ernestine did baby cries in literally hundreds of radio shows, and then she was lucky enough to meet and *do* Mr. Kraftall, who owned all the tin in Chile and who only two years after marrying

Ernestine had a stroke and died, which is why Lloyd Barlow says in the village that mail is not *all* he delivers to Ernestine.... I see nothing whatever about *that* in *The Wall Street Journal*. Nor about the fact that in a non-Grecian urn on the mantel in her gracious living room Ernestine has the old man's ashes. She also has two copies of Joyce's *Ulysses*, one with the Matisse illustrations, the other bound in what looks to me like human skin. Knowing Ernestine as I do, I have often wondered if that skin ever contained Kraftall. Ernestine never likes to throw anything away. Is that discussed in *The Wall Street Journal*? It is *not*....

The article does say this, though:

> Some of the large estates on Old South Friendly Road are reminiscent of those so rapidly disappearing in England. A typical week end on one of those estates might include golf, fox hunting, and skeet shooting.

There is no mention of our most recent shooting, though. That took place on one of the smaller estates on Old South Friendly. Ram (right, *Ram*) Roman, who is only a *vice* president and, thus, probably doesn't really *belong*, shot his wife one night last October. Ram had just got back from Chicago, and, naturally, his first order of business was to clean his pistol in Mrs. Roman's bedroom, which is how Mrs. Roman got a very nasty leg and thigh wound. Fortunately, she has completely recovered, and the Bradley boy, whose father is president of Bradley Brewing, was only nicked in the shoulder. Young Bradley went home from the Romans' the minute he was dressed, and his mother attended to his minor shoulder wound.

Mrs. Roman was helping Billy Bradley with his homework at the time of the accident. Billy, then a sophomore in our frill-less local high school, is, I believe, planning to attend frillier Hotchkiss this fall.

About me, the *Journal* says:

> Stormy petrel Joshua Bland, Broadway producer and one-time prodigy, has dabbled in many activities. These include the making of several motion pictures, a short stay in Washington, D. C., as propagandist and lobbyist for a government subsidy to support a Federal theater. Of course, Bland is probably

best known for his wartime book, *Prodigy as Private*, which became one of the great best-sellers of all time and has since...

Enough of that.

(3) Is the sky the limit?

Back to the salt mines, back to me.

When I left off a few hours ago, Horatio P. Baker was patting me on the head and referring to me as little master. Well, the next week the little master entered Pegasus Experimental School.

Just before that happened, I remember this:

My father's voice saying, "Celeste, I choose to think you're joking about putting Josh in that school."

Mother's voice saying, "You choose to think wrong then."

Father, "Baker's a fake, and you know it."

"Horatio Phineas Baker is a respected, intelligent educator with a nationwide reputation."

"A nationwide reputation as the keeper of a combined bordello and reform school. He's just been through a very nasty scandal, and he wants Josh for a little whitewash publicity, and you know it."

"Kendall, *you* seem to know a great many things that the less fortunate among us do not know. For a man who has just lost a job, and I might add a job that you got in the first place only because I happen to have a little influence in this town, you take a great deal on yourself."

Now there is a gap in my memory. What follows may have been said at the same time—perhaps later.

Mother's voice saying, "As a matter of fact, you'll be a very good teacher."

Father, "Were you born with this capacity for self-delusion or did you have to learn it?"

Mother, "I am doing what I am doing because it is the best thing for sonny boy. As I have said many times before and as I will no doubt be called upon to say many times again, in my son's race for destiny, my only function is to serve."

"Oh God, oh God, oh God," said my father, but was there mockery or despair in his voice? I can't remember.

Mother, "Through my influence Horatio P. Baker has offered you a position in the journalism department at the college. Do you or do you not propose to accept it?"

"I'd rather die," said my father.

Said my mother, "Why don't you just do that? Why don't you just do that little thing?"

My father accepted the job in the journalism department at the college and doing that must have taken what was left of his pride.

"In your deepest relations there is only one test of what you profoundly want; that consists in what happens to you."

I can't remember where I first read that, or when, and I can't find it in *Bartlett's*, but it made a profound impression on me, and I've never questioned the truth of it. Never.

Charley put the same thing another way: "Nobody ever does anything to anybody. People do it to themselves."

Still, I always pitied my father. I still pity him.

There was also this:

Frank Shay, the principal at Arnold School, came to see my mother. I don't know where I was, but I heard—

Mr. Shay said, "Mrs. Bland, this is probably none of my business."

"When people preface their remarks with that statement, I find they are usually right," said mother.

"Well, fools rush in. I can't believe what I read, that you're going to send Josh to—*that* school. How old is he—not quite eight?"

"Not quite eight, and I'm going to send him to—*that* school."

"I wish you wouldn't," said Mr. Shay. "Joshua's an extraordinary boy. I'm fond of him. I think he might become an extraordinary man. I can't be sure I'm right, of course, but I'm not very impressed with—that school."

"I suppose you are impressed with the persons on *your* faculty. If you'd like I could tell you a thing or two about the private lives of some members of it."

"I wouldn't like."

"If that's all then, Mr. Shay...."

"Not quite all. I think Joshua ought to have a chance to learn along with other children more or less his own age. I think that's very important for him. He's a very withdrawn boy, and very lonely. I think it's important for someone like him to learn to communicate with other people. I'd like to keep him at Arnold School for one more year; we'll set up some special classes for him. I've already asked Miss Auerbach and Miss Parkinson, and they are willing..."

"Special classes in what?" asked mother. "Perversion?"

Mr. Shay did not reply.

Mother said, "If I ever need any advice on real-estate matters, I'll come to you, Mr. Shay. On matters of education, I believe a man like Horatio P. Baker might be considered somewhat more of an authority. You said a few minutes ago you weren't sure you were right. Well, I'm sure I'm right."

"That's an extraordinary human experience," said Mr. Shay. "I hope you'll treasure it."

Mother made a laughing sound.

A few days after my father took the job at the college I left Miss Velma's sixth-grade class and Arnold School forever.

A picture showing Miss Velma and me shaking hands appeared on the front page of the *Times-Dispatch*, and there was a story about Miss Velma and my classmates doing what was described as "saying their reluctant farewells to Young Bland." The story quoted Miss Velma as saying she was sure I would learn a very great deal at the Experimental School. It said she said it had been a privilege and a pleasure to have me in her class and that she was sure all of my little classmates would miss me.

The truth? When the *Times-Dispatch* reporter told Miss Velma he bet she'd miss having me in her class, she said, "No, I won't, and neither will any of them," meaning my little classmates.

She paused and added, "Now those crackpots [meaning the teachers at the Experimental School] are going to make that little brat [meaning me] into a real trouble-maker."

Is it any wonder I've never trusted newspapers? Or that one of the principal planks of the Bland Plan for Shaping Up the World has an entire section dealing with what has to be—but probably never will be—done about them?

I walked out of Miss Velma's class without a single regret. The girl in the wheelchair had died a few months earlier. Our house-keeper, Mrs. Hoadley, an enthusiastic funeral-goer, took me to the funeral, but I refused to look into the coffin. Mrs. Hoadley said that Lucille, if that was the girl's name, "looks very natural and her death's a blessing for all concerned when it comes to that."

Hughie, my only friend at Arnold School, still lived across the street from me. No problem.

The next day I was enrolled in the experimental school. President Baker made a speech; Pavan made a speech; mother announced that she would never forget any part of that day, and she didn't. Pictures were taken, and even *The Des Moines Register* made much of the fact that not only was I a prodigy; I was also the great-great-grandson of the founder of the original college. You see, Baker was getting two for the price of one.

I have a scrapbook, *My First Year At The Experimental School*, in front of me now. There is a full page of the pictures taken that first day. In one, standing a little apart from the rest of us and almost hidden by mother, is my father. I'd forgot how frail he was. He is looking at me, a half-smile on his face, not of pride, of puzzlement, I think, and maybe of hope. I may be reading too much into the picture, but I think he wanted me to turn and smile at him. I didn't, though. I was too busy smiling into the camera.

Now a few words about Pegasus College and its Experimental School:

I said some time back that the town of New Athens was founded by Robert Leith Kempton, my great-great-grandfather. He was one of a group of "educational missionaries" sent out from Andover Theological Seminary to set up colleges in the barbarian wilderness of Iowa. There were twelve altogether; they arrived in 1843 and were known as the "Iowa Band." Josiah Bushnell Grinnell and two others stayed in Davenport and set up Iowa College, which a few years later was moved to a settlement to the west and eventually became Grinnell College. I never did find out what happened to the rest of the "Iowa Band," but I know that R.L. spent a few days in Davenport and then in a flat-bottomed boat went upstream on the Iowa River until he came to a bend in the stream that pleased him. He decided to stop there and establish the college he had been sent west to set up.

I believe I said earlier that R.L. kept a journal. And I believe I also said that my grandfather passed that journal along to me, in addition to two books that had belonged to R.L., Emerson's *Essays* and *Walden*.

I still have the journal; it is sprinkled with quotations; R.L. was a bookish man. One of the early quotations is this one on the dead by Emily Bronte:

I lingered round them under that benign sky, watched the moss fluttering among the heath and the harebells, listened to the soft wind breathing through the grass, and wondered how anyone could ever imagine unquiet slumbers in the quiet earth.

Of the area in which New Athens was built R.L. wrote:

I spent the night here and this morning decided to remain. I shall be lonely, but I am used to that. Loneliness seems to me as necessary and natural a part of man's life as breathing ... This place is very beautiful, and I have decided to christen it New Athens. I feel that some day the love of God and of learning will be as free and natural in this spot as is the air.

For three years R.L. was the only white man in the area. The Indians were not hostile. They were of the Sac and Fox tribes, and I used to see their descendants around town when I was a boy—too lethargic ever to organize a massacre even if they felt like it.

By 1853, there was a small community of whites in the area; R.L. married one of them. She was the daughter of a Mormon who had stayed behind in Iowa rather than go on to share the bonanza swept up by the Mormons who looted Utah. R.L. wrote of my great-great-grandmother:

She is incapable of learning the difference between a goose and a gooseberry bush, but she is more at home out of doors than I am, and there is not a dog, a cat, a bird, or a horse, or a cow who does not know her.... She believes in the old ways; she never makes a call on anyone without taking a present of some kind.

When she died, R.L. wrote:

...We were as close as it is possible for two human beings to be, and in all the years she never shouted at me. She was the most generous woman I ever met, or now, of course, ever will. She was gentle of heart....

By 1857, New Athens had doubled in size, meaning it had a population of about two hundred people. In that year, R.L. and five other leaders of the First Methodist Episcopal Church set aside forty acres of land east of town, providing that "now and for all future time said forty acres of land be reserved exclusively for educational purposes."

The land is rather like that around Sloane's Station—which is no doubt one of the reasons I am here. The hills are soft and green, and for a few days every spring and a few more every fall the weather is not completely intolerable.

The six brought an architect all the way from New York City to design what in my youth was called Old Humphrey Hall, after another of the founders. It looks vaguely like the Parthenon. Frank Lloyd Wright, who once lectured at the college, said its existence was "the only reason I'd think twice before recommending that this town be dynamited off the face of the earth."

Two years after it was founded, two other buildings had been erected on the campus of Pegasus College; both are monstrously ugly, and I suppose R.L. was responsible, but, as he once wrote:

I have schooled myself in as many of the arts as I have had time for, but I am not, I am afraid, an extraordinary man. What a galling admission for a man to make. I mean extraordinary in the sense that Sydney Smith meant it: "The meaning of an extraordinary man is that he is eight men in one man; that he has as much wit as if he had no sense, and as much sense as if he had no wit; that his conduct is as judicious as if he were the dullest of human beings, and his imagination as brilliant as if he were irretrievably ruined." I shall, nevertheless, make the most of the endowments the Lord has given me....

By 1860, Pegasus had a staff of six, all newly ordained ministers, two of whom had gone to Yale, four to Andover Theological. The purpose of the college was "to train ministers of God and to increase the knowledge of and the practice of fine arts in our sovereign state of Iowa."

The motto was taken from Ralph Waldo Emerson's Phi Beta Kappa speech:

> The study of letters shall be no longer a name for pity, for doubt, and for sensual indulgence. The dread of man and the love of man shall be a wall of defense and wreath of joy around all. A nation of men for the first time will exist because each believes himself to be indulged by the Divine Soul which inspires all men.

R.L. was the first president of the college; he was president for forty years.

I would not care to say whether by the Rev. Sydney Smith's definition R.L. was an extraordinary man. I do know this; he and my grandfather, A. J., were the last Nineteenth-Century men in my family. If I had time—which I haven't—I'd go into a short discourse on the Nineteenth-Century fellow. Both R.L. and A.J. were in a sense failures; yet both had qualities which Aristotle had in mind when he defined the Magnificent Man; both despised small ends; both would have given their lives, their fortunes, and their sacred honor for the great cause. Both had a great regard for honor, and in that now neglected area both were indomitable. Both would have understood what E. M. Forster had in mind:

> ...and if I had to choose between betraying my country and betraying my friend, I hope I should have the guts to betray my country ... Such a choice would not have shocked Dante ... Dante places Brutus and Cassius in the low-est circle of Hell because they had chosen to betray their friend Julius Caesar rather than their country Rome...[2]

---

2   I was thinking of R.L. and of my grandfather when I was called before the Unmentionable Committee in Wonderland in 1949. My action there was one of the few proud moments in an almost wholly misspent life. I quoted Forster, "...I hope I should have the guts to betray my country." Then I took my stand on the Constitutional Amendment meant for standing on.

One of the tabloids had this headline, "...Broadway Producer Admits He would Betray Country."

Both had courage, and both possessed that rarest of Christian virtues, courtesy. Both were concerned with the matters of the mind and of the spirit; both despised quackery and avarice. Each in his way had qualities of great selflessness.

And that is all I have to say about the men of the Nineteenth Century who played so large a part in my life.

Unfortunately for R.L., Pegasus College never really caught on. I don't know why. Perhaps the Civil War was partly to blame. Half the faculty and three-fourths of the student body went off to fight in it and never came back.

R.L. was forty in 1861:

> I have prayed nightly that God will give me the strength to resist the temptation to throw everything aside and enlist on the side of right.

He did resist, and, of course, regretted it for the rest of his life.

In 1897, the bishop withdrew the church's support from the college. R.L. tried desperately to raise money to keep it going. He even went to Cadman Lavendar—a Twentieth-Century man I'll dispose of in a minute.

R.L. wrote:

> The man laughed at me. He is a barbarian. I said to him, "We have an obligation to keep the college open. An obligation to ourselves and our children." He said, "Kempton, my obligation to myself and to my children is to make money." Then he laughed. He said, "I'll take that forty acres of land off the hands of you Methodists." I said, "Never. That land is for educational purposes only." He said, "Never is a long time, Kempton." I left his house. I do not like such people, though I see many of his kind these days.

Many? Thank God R.L. died when he did. What would he think if he were living now, when this country is crawling with Lavendars? This *country?* This *world.*

This is the age of the absolute bastard, the unmitigated sonofabitch. This is the time of the non-committed, of root-hog-or-die, of looking out for Number One, of pull-up-the-ladder-mate-I'm-aboard, of up-yours-mac-I've-got-mine. This is the time of I-couldn't-care-less.

R.L. said it better, wrote it rather: "I sometimes think that God must despair of the activitites of His children."

The kind of world R.L. lived in, the kind of things he believed in are non-existent now. Why? I don't *know* why. I no longer care why. All I want is out.

What's that Ab? I'm shouting? No, I'm not, boy. What I'm doing is crying.

I'm back now. I took time out for a cold shower.
On with it.

Less than a year after the Methodists withdrew their support, Pegasus College closed its doors. Among the last entries in R.L.'s journals are these:

There is not a fiercer hell than the failure in a great object.

And:

By the rivers of Babylon, there we sat down, yea, we wept, when we remembered Zion. We hanged our harps upon the willows in the midst thereof. For there they that carried us away captive required of us a song; and they that wasted us required of us mirth, saying, Sing us one of the songs of Zion. How shall we sing the Lord's song in a strange land?

R.L.'s grave stands alone in one corner of the Pegasus campus. It is surrounded by a picket fence, and there is a plaque.

I used to spend a lot of time near that grave when I was a child. I hoped then and I hope now that R.L. has slumbered quietly in his quiet corner of the strange land that he tried to illuminate.

He should have known better. Given a choice between enlightenment and ignorance, your average run-of-the-mill human being will take the latter every time.

That reportress from the white man's *Ebony* said, "Don't you *like* people, Mr. Bland?"

I was just drunk enough to speak the truth. I said, "Good God, no."

Take my advice, citizens. The minute you hear somebody carrying on about how much he or she just *loves* people, check the lock on the hen house.

So much for R.L. We come now to the Lavendars, then on to the Pegasus I attended.

In 1860, Cadman Lavendar arrived at the same bend in the river which sixteen years earlier had attracted R.L. by its beauty. Cadman Lavendar didn't give a damn about beauty. What attracted him was the potential for profit. He wasn't in a strange land. He was right at home. He cheated; he lied; he stole; and he plundered. When he couldn't get what he wanted any other way, he bought it—at his own price, of course.

My grandfather once said that there wasn't a family in Athens County that Cad Lavendar hadn't stolen from. I believe it.

Naturally, Lavendar's grateful victims sent him to the state legislature, and he was so good at looting while serving in that body that he was elected governor. Twice.

When he died, the whole state went into mourning, for days. Three preachers carried on at his funeral.

I don't know what would have happened to New Athens or to Iowa if Cadman Lavendar hadn't left behind three sons and two daughters who were just as greedy and dishonest as he had been.

By 1921, which is when I entered screaming, the Lavendar family owned New Athens, lock, stock, and barrel, "A Lavendar Barrel is a Dependable Barrel."

Just about the only thing the Lavendars couldn't get their claws on was the forty-acre plot of farmland east of town which was for all time "...reserved exclusively for educational purposes."

They tried everything, first everything illegal, then, as a last resort, everything legal. They got nowhere. R.L. hadn't been a lawyer, but the deed he had drawn up was upheld in every court the Lavendars tested it in, including the Iowa Supreme Court.

So for more than twenty years Old Humphrey Hall and the other two buildings of what had been the campus of the original college stood there on the river bank, deserted and decaying. Except for one week out of every fifty-two. Then something called

Chatauqua came to town. Instead of being under a tent as they were in most towns, the programs were presented in Old Humphrey.

Horatio Phineas Baker arrived during that week, the last in August. The year was 1920.

Baker was made for the place and the time. He was then in his late thirties. He was an Elk, a Lion, a Rotarian, a thirty-second-degree Mason, a Kiwanian, a member of the American Legion, the V.F.W., and of an invidious little group called the Sons of Freedom.

Baker had been a book salesman (medical books of questionable authenticity), a minister (not ordained), an actor (in a down-at-the-heels stock company in Cleveland), a drug clerk, and a writer (a pale plagiarist of Zane Gray for the pulps).

He had failed in all of them. Then he was drafted into the U.S. Army, and he spent most of the last year of the First World War as a company clerk in an ordnance outfit. His front line was Paris.

Horatio Phineas Baker was never nearer to the actual fighting than, say, Versailles, but he had a fruity voice, a fatuous manner, and a way with a cliché. So the minute he stepped off the troop transport, he signed a contract with the Chatauqua people, and for two years after that he went across the country delivering his lecture, "Back From Hell and Lives to Tell It." He wore his khaki uniform and a trench coat, and, while he didn't actually claim to have been wounded, he limped on stage and off. I'm told there was never a dry eye. H.P. was one of several phoneys making a sob story out of the war on the Chatauqua circuit—"What I Saw at the Front," "A Yankee at Verdun," and "The Saddest Story Ever Told."

Horatio Phineas had a second lecture as well, this one delivered in a business suit, black, with a bow tie—"Is the Sky the Limit for the U.S.A.?" Baker's answer, no. There was heaven just beyond.

He was a great success on the Chatauqua circuit, which presented a kind of seven-day, in-person version of the *Reader's Digest* in small towns all over the country, lots of moral uplift, lots of crap. My own most vivid memory of Chatauqua is of a regurgitated version of *Carmen* in which the heroine entered carrying a milk pail. No drinking and no smoking in any Chatauqua program; so the setting of the opera had been changed from a cigarette factory to a dairy.

I have a feeling that the minute Horatio Phineas Baker walked out on the stage of Old Humphrey Hall, he knew he had found a home. I've said that he didn't have a brain in his head, but what he did have is worth just as much on the open market, probably more. He had a sure instinct for survival. He knew that the demand for war lectures delivered in uniform wasn't going to last long; he may even have guessed that the days of Chatauqua were limited. So H.P. kept his eyes open for the main chance, and that is how he and the Lavendars got together.

After he gave his talk, Baker was invited to the dark, ugly Lavendar house on West Main Street. His host was Jeremy Lavendar, the eldest son of Cadman and a widower, whose unpaid housekeeper was his daughter, a small, brown virgin of thirty named Laverna. Laverna had a habit of repeating what you said to her. "Beautiful day, Laverna." "Beautiful day." "Just murdered my uncle, Laverna." "Just murdered my uncle."

It was said in New Athens that Baker deflowered Laverna that first night; in any case, he cancelled the rest of his Chatauqua tour and stayed on in New Athens.

He and Laverna were married in October, and the following January—1921, the year I was born—Baker announced that Pegasus College was to be reopened. Baker had dreamed up a way to adhere to the provision that the forty acres be used 'exclusively for educational purposes' and at the same time make a quick buck for himself and for the Lavendar family, of which he had become a member.

Naturally, Baker, who had flimflammed a B.A. degree out of a cow college in Ohio, was president. The next member of the staff to be hired was a scoundrel I'll call Alfred L. Eckerman, one of the early practitioners of Public Relations, or Lying. Eckerman came up with two things absolutely essential to an institution like Pegasus—a gimmick and a slogan.

The slogan was: "Pegasus College. The Parthenon of the Prairies. A Very Special College for Very Special Young Men and Women."

The gimmick was this:

Eckerman, who until that time had never been west of the Hudson, rightly felt that New Athens was just far enough away from both coasts so that it would be a very attractive dumping ground for the delinquent brats of the rich and almost rich of, say, Los Angeles or San Francisco or, say, Philadelphia, Washington, or New York.

To make the place seem even more attractive, Eckerman decided that Pegasus had to be "exclusive," meaning the tuition would be ridiculously high. It was. Two thousand a year, a lot of money in those days. A great many people thought that at those prices Pegasus had to be first-rate. Our whole economy is based on that particular folk fantasy.

It seems redundant to add that the place was restricted. In an autobiography written twenty years later while he was dying of cancer, Eckerman wrote, "That last gave me special pleasure. It seemed to me the supreme joke on the solemn Iowa sods who were paying me."

Digression: During the depression—1932, I believe—it looked for a time as if Pegasus might have to close its doors. Not enough special students with the moola. Didn't happen, though. In what Iowa newspapers at the time called a triumph of democracy, the restriction against Jewish students was lifted.

"We only want the quiet ones, of course," said President Baker.

"Little Josh will be talking with his hands first thing we know," said mother.

Democracy's triumph didn't pay off any too well. As is so often the case. There were never many Jewish students at Pegasus. The few that came were mostly serious boys interested in chemistry. Through some accident, the college had a good chemistry department.

Even before Pegasus was opened, there were advertisements in such publications as *Harper's*, *Atlantic*, *Vogue*, and *Town and Country*. "The Parthenon of the Prairies.... Our Specialty is the Problem Boy and the Problem Girl." The picture showed (it still does) Old Humphrey Hall, and there is a caption, "...Only one of the many beautiful buildings on our lovely campus, deep in the rolling hills of fertile, fruitful Iowa."

The campus is beautiful; no doubt about it. There are gravelled walks and endless, carefully tended lawns, and beyond them fields with lazy cows and restless rows of corn and wheat.

The river which divides the campus and at the same time gives it unity is sometimes gray and sometimes brown. In the spring, the banks were and probably still are used for what might loosely be called romance. In the summer there are boats for hire, and an occasional sluggish catfish is caught. In the winter there is skating, and the boathouse is used for romance.

The fraternities and sororities are set a little away from the river, hideous mansions with Greek letters hanging out front.

The center of the campus is Old Humphrey Hall, and, except for it, all the buildings are vaguely Gothic and authentically ugly.

There is a huge stadium. In one of Baker's first speeches as president, he announced, "There is no such thing as a well-trained mind unless there is also a well-trained body." Most of the well-trained bodies came from the steel mills of Chicago and Gary, Indiana. They were always scholarship students, and there was one—an All-American—who spent four years on the campus. He arrived and left totally illiterate.

Naturally, there is a golf course, a polo grounds, a baseball diamond, a cricket field, and an enormous field house. There is even a library.

It seems unnecessary to add that the new Pegasus was enormously successful from the beginning. From 1921 until this moment, there have never been fewer than five hundred special young men and women in the college—except, as I've said, during a period of the depression.

The special young people enrolled have almost always been types who would have been in reformatories had they been born to poor parents.

In 1923, about two years after Pegasus was reopened, Baker—I guess it was—realized that Americans are just like the English in one respect, and unlike the French. Many of us don't really like children and, if we can possibly afford it, want to get them out from underfoot at the earliest possible moment. So Pegasus Experimental School was opened, a dumping ground for delinquents of high-school age.

It looked for a while as if Pegasus were going to be just about the biggest thing since the founding of Harvard.

Unfortunately, the hills of Iowa proved to be too fruitful, too fertile. In the year before I entered the Experimental School, four girls had left school hurriedly, all ostentatiously pregnant, and a Pegasus girl had died in Des Moines from an abortion.

During the furor over this unfortunate series of scandals, H. P. Baker decided I was needed in the Experimental School. As my father said, Pegasus needed a "little whitewash publicity."

I'll have some more to say about Pegasus later, but that's enough for now—except to add that it is accredited and that, since the library has about a hundred thousand books, it is probably possible to get some kind of education there.

I never did, though.

I went through the Experimental School in less than three years. I finished when I was eleven, a technical high-school graduate. I entered college the next fall.

At the time there was a lot in the papers about how they (meaning Baker, Mummy and Pavan) didn't want to push me too fast in college. So I didn't finish college until I was fifteen.

Right now let me say that in seven years, first in the Experimental School and later in the college, I almost never had a free hour in the library. I almost never read a book for pleasure—or, for that matter, enlightenment.

I simply didn't have time. I was always boning up for something—first, the Harvey Jordan O'Connor tests and, then, for my weekly appearances on the "Can You Top Them?" program.

I didn't have time to *learn* anything; all I ever did was memorize facts.

It was understood by the entire faculty that I was to get straight A's—no matter what.

I did, too, except that one rogue gave me a *D* in American history. I deserved a flunk.

At the end of the academic year, that renegade's resignation was accepted.

I have more than my share of opinions on education and, as you'll see, once made a furtive entrance into and quicker exit out of the field. What's more, I've spent time on quite a few campuses for one reason or another.

There is more genuine cynicism, more incompetence, laziness, and second-rateness among both the faculty members and the students on the average college campus than in any other organized group in our society.

There is more backbiting, too, more than in the theater, more than Out There, more than in the average advertising agency.

True, there are exceptions. I have an envious suspicion that some of the Ivy League colleges are exceptions and that so are two or three girls' colleges here in the East.

True, almost every campus has one or two or maybe three dedicated teachers. Agreed, a good teacher is the best kind of human being.

I go along with Shaw, though. Good teachers "actually do more harm than good, for they encourage us to believe that all school teachers are like that."

Now back to 1929. To December of that year. I apologize for the lengthy digression. I wanted to make clear what a fraud Pegasus was and I feel sure still is.

1929. By December I had been in the Experimental School since the previous September.

At the time I'm talking about, President Hoover had issued a statement saying that the national economy had never been in better shape. I know. I just looked it up.

The newspapers were filled with pictures of grinning Wall Street brokers saying that the market was just making a very healthy adjustment and that if the good people of the United States just realized it, they were indeed fortunate, and so forth. You know how Big People talk.

My father was saying nothing at all at the time. His face had turned a permanent gray, and his hair seemed to have got whiter; his eyes were always bloodshot and not always from liquor.

This was the time my father lost $7,500 in an unhappy investment in plastics. I have never forgot the sound of his voice when he said, "Oh, my God, hast Thou forsaken me?" Nor the terror I felt when I heard him cry.

There are some things that one human being should not say to another no matter what the provocation, but my mother said them all during the late fall and early winter of that year. Sometimes she screamed them; sometimes she said them in a contained cold voice.

Sometimes she said, "We are just going to forget the whole thing, and no matter what, even if we all end up in the poorhouse, we are never going to mention it again."

As I've indicated, what was never mentioned again was the worst. Every time she looked at you, her eyes mentioned it.

On a late December afternoon I'm going to tell you about now, my father had just returned from the campus. He had probably also finished his fifth of bourbon for the day.

He went into the bedroom mother had converted into a study for herself, and he said, "Happy New Year, Celeste."

I heard him. I was sitting in the living room, eating an apple, watching Hughie shovel the Larrabee front walk, listening to Myrt and Marge on the radio, and reading a volume of the complete works of Mark Twain, which my father had given me for Christmas.

I remember there had been a card in the first volume on which he had written, "Don't tell anybody, but I'm really Santa Claus."

Mother had said, "Kendall, I don't think that is even *remotely* humorous."

We had no nonsense about Santa in our house. When I was about two, my mother had said, "Joshua, if anybody tries to tell you there's a Santa Claus just simply explain the origin of the myth and say that intelligent people don't perculate *myths*."

For that matter, mother didn't approve of Mark Twain. She said that he had been a trivial man with a third-rate mind, but she did not absolutely prohibit my reading him, provided that I had already done my homework for the entire Christmas vacation, spent the required two hours daily at the piano, and finished the Greek and Latin and calculus lessons Pavan gave me five afternoons a week.

Mother added that as far as she was concerned, everything Twain wrote was the "*most errand nonsense*," particularly when I could and should have been reading the *Decline and Fall of the*

Roman Empire, a book I did not finish at the time nor have I in the eternity since nor will I in the few days remaining.

Her final words about Twain: "He was a Christian Scientist, and we all know what *they* are."

When I pointed out to her that Twain had written a whole book *attacking* Christian Science, mother said, "That is only a very clever attempt to conceal what is a well-known fact. It is proof that a man like that is not to be trusted."

Anyway, in answer to my father's New Year's greeting, she said, "Are you under the weather, Kendall?"

"I'm no drunker than usual," my father said, "and I'm wishing you a Happy New Year."

"Well, Happy New Year, Kendall," mother said, "but it's only December 28th."

"I know," said my father, "but I won't be here on the 31st."

I'm quite sure that mother didn't hear that. She missed most of what little my father had to say to her, her theory being that it couldn't possibly be important. Besides, at the time she was working on the speech she would deliver the next week at the state convention of the Eastern Star.

"Be good to Josh," said my father.

"Ladies of the Eastern Star," said my mother, "I am unworthy of the great honor you have, unsought, thrust upon me. Nevertheless, I will put my shoulders to the wheel, and together with the great team of girls you have elected to serve with me, we will win the race, come what may."

"God help us all," Father said.

That night I'd been asleep for several hours when I woke up, frightened. My father was standing beside the bed, looking down at me. I suppose he was drunk, but he was in charge of himself.

"Don't be scared," he said, seating himself on the bed beside me. "I've come to tell you good-bye."

Until then, I hadn't really believed he was serious about going away, but as I looked at his sad, defeated face, I knew. Finally I said, "Where you going?"

My father shrugged. "Just away," he said.

"Can I go with you?"

"Not now. Maybe later."

When I could speak again, I said, "Why you going away, Pop?"

"I'm tired of watching," said my father. "I don't like what I see."

I knew what he meant, or thought I did.

"If I stay here, I'll keep right on disintegrating," said my father. "If I don't—well, I may disintegrate anyway. I have to find out if there's any of me left. If there is, I'll try to come back and get you."

He paused for a long time. Then he said, "Would you like that?"

I nodded, forcing back the tears.

For a time, neither of us spoke. My father seemed to be searching for something to add, some words of comfort, or wisdom, or of love.

For that matter, so was I.

Finally, he said, "Do you know what my father said to me just before he died?"

I shook my head. I don't believe he had ever mentioned his father before.

"He said, 'Son, don't let the sonsabitches get you down. They'll try.' Then he turned over and died."

I didn't know whether I was supposed to laugh or not. So I just smiled a little. "What sonsabitches?" I asked.

"I think he meant life," said my father, "and all the sonsabitches you meet up with."

"Oh," I said. "There are a lot of sonsabitches around. I've certainly noticed that."

Then I said (it had just occurred to me), "He was my other grandfather, wasn't he?"

"Yes."

"Was he nice?"

"Very. I had a good childhood. Happy. A mother, a father, two brothers, a sister, all *nice*. I must have been at least twenty-nine before I realized that my father was right about all the sonsabitches."

"You're nice," I said.

"I'm afraid your judgment isn't very good on that subject. If I were nice, I'd stay and fight back, but I know I can't. Maybe this is the way."

"She's not nice."

"Josh," this severely, "didn't we agree never to talk about your mother behind her back?"

"I suppose," I said. Then, "How come you married her, Pop? And don't tell me I'm not old enough. She wasn't pregnant or anything like that, was she?"

My father smiled. "She wasn't pregnant or anything like that, and you're not too young to understand, but I'm not sure I know. You do a lot of things in your life you don't understand. Especially big things. Does that make any sense to you?"

"Yes, sir."

"Maybe it was weakness. I'm a weak man. Eugene Debs once said to me that the big evils of the world aren't greed or selfishness but weakness and incompetence. That answer your question?"

"I don't think so," I said, "but I'm willing to think about it."

He kissed me. "You're going to be awfully lonesome," he said.

"I sure will until you get back."

"I mean for the rest of your life," he said, his arms tightening around me. "Try to be kind to your mother. Try not to hate too many people for the wrong reasons, and try to be serious about something, and remember I love you."

Then he kissed me again.

I said, "Promise to come back and get me as soon as you can, Pop."

"If I can, I will. I promise."

He continued to hold me, and I concentrated on keeping my eyes open, but, eventually, I fell asleep. It was nearly dawn.

When I woke up, he was gone; there was a robin in the tree outside my window, but my father was gone. I cried; my mother cried, too, but we did not cry together. Each of us alone.

Father had got on the nine-twenty train for Chicago. He may or may not have gone that far; we never knew. Jed Durrell, the M. and St. L. ticket agent and station master in New Athens, believed my father had bought a ticket to Chicago.

"But I wouldn't want to swear it on a stack of Bibles one way or the other," Mr. Durrell told my mother.

Later, I heard him say *sotto voce* to Farleigh Henderson, a switchman, "If it'd been me and I was Kendall Bland I'd of bought me a one-way ticket to hell and figured I'd be better off at half the price in the long run, married to a hellion like that."

Mother didn't hear.

At the time Mr. Durrell was speaking, mother was testing her theory that father had been kidnapped.

"Though if I know Kendall, he would have resisted to the death," she said to Ella Finch, who had come with us to the railroad station. Ella was Worthy Vice Matron of the New Athens Eastern Star.

The only thing we ever found out for sure about Father is that he got beyond Cedar Rapids. He was seen that far by Corinne Slay, who was on the same coach but who had had to get off in Cedar Rapids.

Corinne, Elektra in the local Eastern Star and not fond of mother, said that Father looked happy as a lark.

This did not jibe with mother's final version of Pop's disappearance.

She finally decided that he had been stricken with a mysterious, incurable disease and that he did not want his loved ones, meaning her and me, to watch his painful lingering death.

"It was maligment, whatever it was," mother decided, and sometime later she said, "Thank God for Petrarch Pavan. At last, sonny, we have a brain we can look up to."

We never saw or heard from, or about, my father again.

Here I should probably spend some time discussing what his disappearance did to me and meant to me, but I've talked about that at length with several analysts. It was never either very interesting or very rewarding.

The fact is I didn't have time for brooding. I was almost immediately involved in training for the Harvey Jordan O'Conner Cranium Derby.

(4) The man who respected brains

Nobody who was around at the time can have forgotten the Cranium Derby (my name for it) or the man responsible for it, but in case some of you came in late, *The New Yorker* once published a profile of the man we're calling Harvey O'Conner. I'll tell you what I remember of it.

At the time the profile appeared (1930, I think) O'Conner was in his late sixties. He had been a cobbler in Warsaw, where his name had been Okonsky. How he got from Warsaw to New York or from Okonsky to O'Conner I haven't a clue. Or why Harvey Jordan.

I just know that he had started making children's shoes in the early 1920's and that they were very good shoes—"The Most Precious Shoes in all the World for the Most Precious Feet in all the World—Your Child's."

God and this country had been good to O'Conner, and he wanted to show his gratitude. *The New Yorker* reported that he had said, "Than brains there is nothing I have more respect for."

By this time, I feel pretty sure, the agency boys had stepped in. Surely it was they who thought of a nationwide series of competitions. "The Harvey Jordan O'Conner Cranium Derby."

The first prize for THIS YEAR'S MOST BRILLANT YOUNG AMERICAN (always in caps) was ten thousand dollars; second prize, five; third, twenty-five hundred; fourth, a thousand. There were eight honorable mentions, five hundred dollars each. Each winner, including those honorably mentioned, got twenty pairs of O'Conner shoes.

Naturally, the idea caught on. First, there was the loot involved; second, all kinds of worthy people were able to get themselves publicity by endorsing the awards because while there were (still are) plenty of prizes and plaques and encomiums for those who can throw a ball straight or lift a weight, there weren't (aren't) many for encouraging exercise of the brain—the memory, actually.

One interesting aspect of the awards was that there were no strings attached. By that I mean the money was given directly to the child who won it. It was assumed that it would be used for his education, but it didn't have to be.

Thus, all over the country there must have been a great many people like Petrarch Pavan casting covetous eyes on the O'Conner booty—and, as in Pavan's case, on the gamble involved and the approbation that went along with winning.

I'm not going to spend much time talking about my training for the competition. It was rough; that's about all that's necessary here.

There was a series of preliminary tests—first, the town of New Athens. There were half-a-dozen other contestants. I won easily. Then there was the county contest, then the state. I won both. After the last, as I've said, my picture was once more on the front page of *The Des Moines Register*, along with those of the two runners-up, a mouse-haired girl from Laurel who was glaring at the camera through two off-center eyes and a boy from Council Bluffs who is now one of the best cancer specialists in the country.

After that, tests were held to choose twelve finalists out of the forty-eight state winners. I was one of the twelve regional winners, and at that point all hell broke loose, not only in the house in which I lived but all over New Athens; for that matter all over Iowa.

About this time I realized something most people are probably born knowing.

Despite all the talk about how it matters not who wins or loses but how you play the game, I realized that nobody gave a damn how I played the game. What mattered was winning.

I had to be THIS YEAR'S MOST BRILLIANT YOUNG AMERICAN. There was a lot riding on it.

Don't think that I was a reluctant debutante; I wanted desperately to win. It's not good to want anything so much at nine.

I studied willingly, eagerly, and incessantly. As I've said, I got pale in the process, and, despite the *scientific* diet, I lost weight. I couldn't sleep at night; so I was given half a sleeping pill when I went to bed. I still couldn't sleep.

Nevertheless, a number of quite pleasant things happened.

I already had some local notoriety in New Athens, about on a par with that of Millicent Fairchild, *New Athens' Own Elocutionist*, or Tommy Updike, *The World's Second Greatest Magician, Retired*, or Leonard Best, who had acted on Broadway and wasn't safe around boys, and Torbert Somebody, who had drowned his wife in the cess-pool and got away with it.

After winning the regional Cranium Derby, I outshone them all. I even began being treated with a kind of reverence. At least that's the way I interpreted it.

Naturally, I wallowed in it, and in public I adopted a dreamy, far-off look which I felt was appropriate to a Cranium Champion. It worked, too.

For instance, I was in the Royal Kandy Kitchen having a hot fudge sundae one afternoon, and George Skondus, Prop., started to tell the girl who worked for him to brew up another urn of coffee.

"Shh," said the girl, pointing to me. "He's thinking."

I fingered the silver pencil behind my ear, the one sent to me by the governor of Iowa, and *thought*.

I passed Miss Velma on the street, and she smiled and spoke to me. "I like to think I have played some little part in your great success," she said, simpering.

"Oh, you did, Miss Velma," I said. "You did indeed."

"Now don't let me disturb you," she said, floating away. "I'm sure your little mind is just as busy as a little bee."

At Pegasus Experimental, I fell asleep in a class in Shakespeare, and I remember hearing the voice of the teacher, "Mr. Bland, if it's not too much trouble...."

I was half-asleep, but I remember saying, "Oh, what a rogue and peasant slave am I!"

It brought down the house.

"Why don't you go home and take a nice little nap?" said the teacher.

I went home, but I worked on my trigonometry instead. Pavan had said, "Trig's your only weak spot."

Even the attitude of the kids on the street seemed to change. Now when they called me "the Brain" or "Genius," there seemed to be respect rather than contempt in their voices.

"Hey, you really are a genius, aren't you?" said a tall, dark boy who was football captain at the college and who up to then, if he said anything to me, said, "Hey, Four Eyes!"

On this occasion he said, "I'll trade my strong back for your strong head any day of the week."

Grown-ups stopped me on the street, some to congratulate me, some to wish me good luck in the finals, some to ask for my autograph, some for advice.

"You think Hoover's right about this being just a temporary slump?" or, "What's your opinion of the gold standard?" or, "What's with those foreign countries that won't pay their war debts? If I didn't pay my debts, I'd be behind bars. Am I right?"

Did I answer these questions, many of which were keeping people in Wonderland, D. C., up at night?

You bet I did.

"Hoover's wrong," I said. "We are now entering what may be a very serious economic upheaval." (Before he left, Pop must have said so.) I said, "War debts and personal debts are by no means the same thing, and by declaring a moratorium on our war debts, President Hoover will simply be recognizing a very basic economic fact, namely, that..." and so on.

I forget my opinion on the gold standard, but I'm sure I had one.

The *Times-Dispatch* said, "This nine-year-old moppet has brought honor and glory to New Athens and is about to bring us more."

Moppet? I wrote a letter to the editor: "Sir: The word *moppet* means *baby*, *darling*, or *long-haired pet dog*. Which do you mean I am? Sincerely."

The letter was printed, and then it was reprinted and reprinted once again. You'd have thought I'd dashed off *Paradise Lost* during an otherwise unoccupied moment.

"The cutest thing I ever read," people said.

"He's a little genius is what he is," people said.

"He'll be President of the United States before he's twenty," people said, those who knew nothing whatever about the Constitution, which was most of the population of New Athens.

"Remember he was Pegasus-trained," President Horatio Phineas Baker kept chanting. "Pegasus trained him, and don't you ever forget it."

The girls in mother's woman's club started circulating a petition which suggested that it would be a good idea if the city council approved an appropriation for a statue in mother's honor—and, incidentally, mine.

It was to be called, "Mother and Child." Millicent Fairchild, who oozed a poetry of her own when she wasn't reciting other people's, went to the trouble of composing an epic to be inscribed on the base of the statue, just below *Mummy's* feet, as I recall. Fortunately, I am able to remember only the first lines: "Without a mother's hand to guide him, this lad would not so fortunate be."

And speaking of statues, the friendly folks who ran the Iowa Dairy Cattle Congress in Waterloo wrote asking for permission to have a butter statue of me included in the butter exhibit that fall. There was also going to be one of President Hoover and another of Grace Coolidge.

Mother agreed. "It'll be the very best kind of publicity. There is something so very wholesome about butter."

"Joshua Bland is good for New Athens, and New Athens is good for Joshua Bland," said the Chamber of Commerce.

All in all, the frenzy in town was the greatest it had been since Torbert Somebody went on trial for drowning his wife in the cesspool.

The *Times-Dispatch* ran a daily slogan under its masthead, "Fourteen Days Until Joshua Bland Wins the National Cranium Derby. Thirteen Days Until...." And so on.

A parade was planned, beginning at Riverdale Park, continuing all the way down Riverdale Avenue. The parade would stop in front of the dark house my great-great-grandfather had built and in which we lived. There bands from as far away as Keokuk would play; drum majors and drum majorettes would perform, and some Scottish bagpipers from Sioux City.

After the band concert, a U.S. Senator was going to speak, and then by radio from Washington the President of the United States, a former Iowan himself, was going to congratulate me. After which the mayor of New Athens, a Lavendar, of course, would, according to the official program, "honor young Bland with a presentation."

Can you imagine my mother during this period? Well, you must; I have no intention of describing her. If you think Marie Antoinette was perhaps a bit *arrogant*....

One example:

Mother went to the J. C. Penney store and bought me a dozen white shirts.

Then she said, "I'll want them delivered, of course."

The manager agreed, though Penney's didn't deliver. "I'll have them sent over in the morning."

"I want them delivered by you," said mother, "personally."

That is exactly what happened.

The climax of the day was to be a banquet at the Legion Memorial Hall at which mother, Pavan, Horatio Baker, and yours truly were to speak.

True, there was one slight technicality; I hadn't yet won, but Pavan had said, "I'll guarantee we've got a winner here; you can take my word for it."

Everybody took his word for it; his word fitted in with everybody's plans.

In all this gathering squall, one tempering straw—Hughie; I've told you about that *hoodlum* poisoning the cultural atmosphere of our nation.

I spent the day before taking the test in bed. Pavan and mother agreed it would be better if I didn't study that day.

A delegation came from Pegasus; they had some insane ceremony in mind, but I refused to see them. I was afraid that if somebody so much as touched me, some of the facts I had so painfully acquired would spill out.

That night I didn't sleep a wink, but I do remember getting down on my knees, and I remember exactly what I said, "Please God, if there is a god, let me win. Let me win. Let me win."

Then I tried to make a cheap little bargain with Him. I said, "God, if I win, I'll believe in You. I promise."

The test—like all others—was given in an empty classroom under the supervision of Dr. Philip Melrose, head of the political science department; he was a "derby trustee," and he was also an honest man.

Before Dr. Melrose and I went into the room, Pavan touched my shoulder and said, "Remember trig's your weakest spot; pay special attention to trig."

Mother said, "Aren't you going to wish him luck, Petrarch darling?"

"Luck is for superstitious fools," said Pavan. "I am more interested in trigonometry."

Mother said to me, "There is no such word as defeat in our vocabulary, is there, darling?" and she kissed me.

Horatio Phineas Baker said, "*You* have the honor of Pegasus on your small shoulders; just remember that."

Dr. Melrose winked at me and smiled; then we went into the empty classroom, and Melrose opened the sealed test papers.

I started writing at eight in the morning; by noon it seemed to me I had written the sum total of human knowledge, the sum total of mine, anyway. I had written all I knew about algebra, arithmetic, geometry, botany, chemistry, biology, physics, history, and so on. I didn't understand a lot of what I wrote, and I didn't remember it a week afterwards, but that day I did, and that day was all that mattered.

Shortly after twelve, I began the last test, literature, the one area in which I had nothing whatever to worry about. I can't remember how many questions there were, but I do remember that at the end of forty-five minutes, I had answered every one. I had even gone a second time over those few about which I had slight doubts.

At twelve-forty-six I raised my hand and announced that I was finished.

"You have another hour yet," said Dr. Melrose.

"I'm quite finished," I said. "To spend any more time would be silly."

As I went out the door of the classroom, there were several newspapermen and a couple of photographers, one of whom was

Jim Harkus. I smiled at Jim, and then I saw that there were two microphones, one from a Des Moines radio station, and one from New Athens' own 250-*powerful*-watt station.

I spoke into the microphones. I said, "It was a remarkably easy test. You can be assured I won."

After that, there was a two-week period before the results were announced.

During that time I didn't go to school. I relaxed; I slept around the clock for two days in a row; it snowed; Hughie and I threw snowballs and made a snowman. I worked on the speech I was going to give at the banquet in my honor and decided (probably with some help) what I would say after President Hoover had congratulated me from Washington.

I remember once Hughie said, "My mother says there is no such thing as a sure thing."

I said, "Hughie, I'm very fond of your mother, but in this instance—"

The telegram announcing the results of the test was to arrive from New York at four in the afternoon.

Shortly before then I got home from a long walk in the woods with Hughie and his dog. Hughie had been given a .22 for Christmas the year before, and we were technically hunting, but Hughie felt as I did about hunting, negative.

I was eating a sandwich and drinking a glass of milk when, a little after five, the Western Union boy arrived. Besides me in the room were Pavan, mother, Baker and Dr. Melrose.

Pavan tore the message from the boy's hand and ripped open the envelope.

I remember being frightened for the first time. Until that moment it honestly had not occurred to me that I might lose.

There were four uneasy pairs of eyes on Pavan's face as he read the message. His face went ashy, and then it went dark. He looked at me with loathing and contempt, and he took a step toward me. Then he crumpled the telegram and dropped it to the floor.

Mother scooped it up, unfolded it, and screamed. "*Honorable* Mention. *Dishonorable* mention more like." Then she began wailing.

Pavan walked to where I was, and I thought for a moment he was going to slap me, but he didn't.

"*Eleventh* place," he said.

"I'll never be able to face anybody for the rest of my life," mother screamed.

"Now, now," said President Baker. "One out of twelve in the entire country. That is nothing whatever to sniff upon. We must make the best of it, and we can. We will cancel the parade, to be sure, but we will go ahead with our little dinner. The photographers will take their pictures...."

"I'm sorry, boy," said Dr. Melrose.

What I did was throw up, all over the floor, all over the telegram, and then I sobbed, and then I fainted.

The banquet took place. I never asked nor was I told exactly what happened, but I can imagine some of it.

Mother, who only a few hours earlier had been positive she would never be able to face anyone as long as she lived, was there, and she spoke. Or am I being redundant?

Did she perhaps say, as she so often said later, "Now don't quote me as saying there is anything fishy about the O'Conner awards, but did it ever strike you that the winners are always *East*erners? And very often *Hebrews* to boot? And we all know what O'Conner's name was *originally*."

Mother said the word *East*erner in a way *The Chicago Tribune* would have admired. To her everything east of the Ohio River was populated exclusively by "dagoes, spicks and spans, and *Hebrews* of every description."

Pavan spoke at the dinner; so did President Baker. I don't know what they said either, and I do not care.

(5) A slight case of indigestion

While the banquet was going on, I was in St. Thomas Hospital, suffering from what the *Times-Dispatch* the next afternoon diagnosed as "a very slight case of indigestion."

Dr. Llewellyn said it was a nervous breakdown and recommended complete rest and relaxation for a month or six weeks.

The Mother Superior of the hospital, a very old woman who looked as if she had been the most beautiful woman in the world the day before yesterday, said, "All that's wrong with this little man is that he's all tuckered out."

I slept for days, sometimes under sedation, sometimes not. For days I spoke to no one except Dr. Llewellyn, the Mother Superior, and Sister Theresa, a nurse who played checkers with me and who often won. She was very young, not more than twenty, I'd guess, and her face was pink with blue eyes and a smile of compassion.

Most of the time I studied a watermark on the cream-colored ceiling of my room. Some days it was a butterfly, and some days it was a roc.

I wanted it to be a roc. I wanted to be carried away. It didn't matter where. Arabia? Okay. But was Arabia far enough? Would they know of my disgrace in Arabia?

Someone—could it have been Mother Superior—suggested that a psychiatrist should perhaps be brought from Chicago to talk with me.

"Nonsense," said Dr. Llewellyn. "Those people are all quacks. Psy-chiatrists, faith healers, Christian Scientists, birds of a feather."

Ah, yes. I remember I composed suicide notes without number, in poetry and in prose, short and long, but none contained the anger I felt, or the humiliation.

Finally, I settled on these words, never written on paper but to this day stenciled across my mind:

THE SONSABITCHES HAVE GOT ME DOWN. GOODBYE FROM THE DISHONORABLE ELEVENTH PLACE LOSER OF THE HARVEY JORDAN O'CONNER AWARDS.

I received flowers and books and candy and notes of condolence, but for two weeks I received no visitors. Orders from Dr. Llewellyn, although he said I could see my mother or Pavan. I said no to that; I didn't want to see either of them—ever again.

Hughie was my first visitor. I had so yearned to see him that the reality was a letdown. Partly the awkwardness came from the aroma of the disinfectant and the ether and whatever else it is that makes all hospitals smell the same.

And partly it was the awkwardness of youth.

Hughie brought me a book, a very expensive and beautiful edition of *The Pickwick Papers* which I still have.

"I tried reading it myself," he said, "but I just don't get it."

Then, shifting a little and swaying a little in embarrassment, he said, "Congratulations."

"On what?"

"For winning eleventh place in that contest," he said. "In the whole country. That's really something."

He meant it, too. To him I had done a remarkable thing.

"Yah," I said. "I did just dandy."

"You can't win all the ball games," said Hughie, and I felt the sting of tears in my eyes. I'm not sure Hughie noticed the tears, but I'm pretty sure that as he looked at me that day it was suddenly clear to him that I did have to win all the ball games, always. Finally, he said, "Hurry up and get out of here. I miss you."

And I said, "I'm glad you're my best friend, Hughie."

Several days later, Sister Theresa came to the door of my room and said, "Dear, your mother's here again; she's been crying."

I put a bookmark on whatever page of Sam Weller's adventures I was reading and said, "I don't want to see her. I don't even want to know she's here."

Sister Theresa just looked at me.

"Do I have to see her?" I asked.

Sister Theresa continued looking.

"All right," I said, "for your sake, but in ten minutes you come in here and say something to get her out of here. Promise?"

"She's right outside the door now," said Sister Theresa.

My mother looked very tired and very old; she seemed to have shrunk a little, and her face was red and streaked with tears; her eyes were bloodshot.

I turned my face to the wall, but I felt her seat herself by the bed and push a book toward me. It turned out to be *The World Of Christopher Robin*, which some years earlier I had been forbidden to read on the grounds that it was trash. Naturally, I had read it.

I felt the hard cover of the book pressing against me through the blankets.

Then Sister Theresa came in with a vase full of American Beauty roses with very long stems.

"Aren't they pretty?" she said. "A lovely present from your mother."

She put the roses on the table nearest my bed and left.

After a while, my mother said, "Darling, please look at me."

I didn't move.

"Darling," she said again, and there was a sound in her voice that I had not heard before. "Please."

"Forgive me," she said.

"I'm sorry for what I've done," she said. "Let's start all over again. Let's try."

"You'll have to forgive me sometime," she said.

She said, "Please, Joshua, please, please, please."

My hand reached out behind me and pushed the book to the floor, and then it pushed the vase with the flowers to the floor, which was marble. The vase broke, and I suppose some of the water spilled on her. I don't know.

After a while, I heard her rise, and I heard her leave, and neither of us ever spoke of what she had said that day or what I had done, and in this single instance I have to say that she never accused me of my failure.

When Sister Theresa came in a little later, she saw the broken glass and the wet book.

"Get that stuff out of here," I said.

I cannot describe the look she gave me. It was as if she had seen something in me that she had not known existed. She surely guessed what I had done, and as I have said she was very young and had perhaps come from a house in which there was love. I think she saw the hatred in my face, and it shocked her.

I imagine that she prayed for me and asked God to drive the cruelty and hatred from my heart.

The next morning she was outwardly as cheerful as ever, and that evening she beat me at checkers.

But there was a change in our relationship. I sensed that Sister Theresa had withdrawn from me.

Finally, this:

I felt nothing for my mother that night—no love, no tenderness, not even any pity, and I feel none now in telling what happened. I could not weep then, nor can I now.

God help me. Amen.

Pavan came to the hospital once, one afternoon. I don't remember why or how I agreed that he could come, none of that, but I do remember precisely what he said.... Have I mentioned that in my youth I could repeat an hour's lecture, word for word, for months afterward? Once in England I repeated one of Harold Laski's lectures for the master himself.

"Very ingenious," he said. "Very ingenious."

"Like the dancing dog, you mean," I said.

"Very ingenious," said Mr. Laski.

That was in England, when I was sixteen. What I'm talking about now is what happened in a hospital room in New Athens when I was nine.

Pavan seated himself by the bed, smoking that damnable pipe. He said, "Joshua, I'm not going to give you any cheap, cold comfort. I'm not even going to say you'll learn from this defeat or from all the others in store for you."

He paused; he tapped the dreadful pipe on his perfect, detestable white teeth.

"How old are you?" he asked.

"Nine," I said. "I'm nine years old. You know that."

"'The purest affection the heart can hold is the love of a nine year old.'" Then he laughed. "You don't love me, you little bastard," he said. I turned my face away. "Do you?" he asked.

"I hate you," I said.

That pleased him, too, and he laughed some more. "Do you love anybody?"

"No," I said.... I loved Hughie, but I was afraid to say that— or ashamed to. "You and that Larrabee boy," Pavan used to say. "A regular Damon and Pythias. Ah, well, sometimes they outgrow it. If you don't, you can go into interior decorating and support your mother and me in our declining years."

"I doubt you ever will be capable of love," said Pavan. "Well, join the party."

"What party is that?"

"The party of haters. I come from a long line of them. My father was one; he took me with him when he went to Vienna to be ana-lyzed by the master himself. The analysis lasted a long time and was very costly, but my father never learned how to love. Once he said to me, 'When your mother was seven months pregnant with you, I thought of pushing her down the stairs. Everytime I look at you I regret that I didn't.'"

He started toward the door, then turned. "My mother, no mean hater herself, once told me she wished I'd been born mute. She was right, too. To be glib and superficial—and charming. That's the fatal trio. You're not charming—but you'll learn."

Pavan was at the door when I asked, "What'd you want to be when you were a little boy, Pavan?"

"Why do you ask that?"

"Because I was trying to picture you as a little boy, and I couldn't."

Pavan smiled. "I was young once," he said, "but I doubt that I was ever a little boy. What did I want to be? Nothing much, I think. I've done one and a half of almost everything. But never two of anything. When you do two of something, you are no longer that bright, promising amateur. When you do two of anything, you must be judged, and I could never stand that."

He paused. "Besides," he said, "once I learned how to do it—whatever it was—it bored me."

He paused a moment. "You're like that too, I think. I thought maybe I could help you—or at least I like to think I thought maybe I could help you. I'm no longer sure. In any case, I failed."

From somewhere far off there came the sound of a fire engine.

"Some day I may be able to do you a favor," he said. "I'll try." Then he quickly limped from the room.

I'll never know whether Pavan's probable last act on earth was meant to be a favor to me or not. I rather suspect that it was.

I'll say this. Years later, when I pieced together some of the disjointed puzzle of Pavan's life, I pitied him. Not that I think highly of pity.

(6) He ain't thinking

It would be pleasant to say that the good citizens of New Athens forgave and forgot my disgrace, but they did neither.

On the campus of Pegasus, I was a pariah; I'd let them down. My defeat had besmirched the *honor* of the campus. How dare I? The football captain was the kindest. He said, "You put up a good show."

When I walked down East Main Street, which I did no more than was absolutely necessary, nobody any longer rushed up to me to ask what I thought about the gold standard. Most people hurried by me, their faces averted.

George Skondus of the Royal Kandy Kitchen was the only one who articulated how he felt. One day many weeks later when I came in for a hot-fudge sundae, he said, "How come you didn't win that O'Conner thing?"

I confessed that I didn't know why.

"We had this here pool on was you going to win or wasn't you," he said. "I put down five bucks says you was going to win. You let on like you was going to win."

He had me there. I had let on like I was going to win.

Skondus frowned and turned to the pimply girl with greasy hair who worked for him. "Make up another urn of coffee," he said, and then, just before the girl could reply, "and don't give me none of your lip about how he's *thinking*. He ain't *thinking*."

Two other items, and then we'll be done with the Harvey Jordan O'Conner awards:

(1) The five hundred dollars given to each winner of an honorable mention must have come. I forget how or when—or in what way it was spent. I do remember that the twenty pairs of shoes eventually arrived. Stamped across the large, abominable box were the awful words, "For a Prize Winner Of the Harvey Jordan O'Conner Cranium Derby. Twenty pairs of Precious Shoes for the Most Precious Pair of Feet in the World." Somebody—probably mother—put the box, unopened, into a closet. I never wore a single pair of the shoes. A couple of years later, in 1932, I believe, she gave the still unopened box to the Salvation Army. I'm sure those shoes were much appreciated that particular winter.

(2) The year after my disgrace, the body of a twelve-year-old girl who had placed fifth in the O'Conner awards was found in the Charles River the morning after the winners were announced. The drowning was believed to have been suicide.

As I recall, her father was a high-school biology teacher in Boston; naturally, he issued a statement to the press. He said, "My wife and I are very sorry this thing has happened. We devoted five years of our lives to getting our daughter ready for those examinations."

After the suicide, there was a period of great moralizing in the press, and the organizations of parents and teachers that had once so enthusiastically endorsed the awards started attacking them. Resolutions were passed; speeches were made, and editorials were written. There's nothing in the world more popular than a *moral* bandwagon.

That proud defender of the public virtue, *The New Athens Times-Dispatch* decided that the awards were:

...a shocking exploitation of youth for commercial purposes ... one of our distinguished local boys, Master Joshua Bland, at one time participated in the contests, but Master Bland, now one of the regular panel members of that estimable radio program "Can You Top Them?" did not take the contest seriously.

Nevertheless, he was one of the national winners. For a young man of Master Bland's intellectual attainments, such a sordid commercial enterprise...

And so forth.

The awards were cancelled, and a few years later the Harvey Jordan O'Conner shoe company went out of business—no more precious shoes for the most precious pairs of feet in the world.

I've often wondered what happened to O'Conner-Okonsky. Castigated to the end of his days, no doubt. How dare he respect nothing more than brains?

I can't remember much about the next couple of years. In fact, nothing of much importance happened until the summer at Aunt Mettabel's and Uncle Dick's that I've described.

Hughie and I spent a great deal of time together. Mother and Pavan didn't pay much attention to me during that time. She was getting her divorce from my father on the grounds of desertion, and she and Pavan were talking about getting married. He spent very little time in his furnished room on West Main, and for the first time in my life I heard the sounds of sex in the night. It didn't sound like much fun.

In the spring of 1933 while my mother and Pavan were getting ready for their honeymoon trip to Chicago, we heard "Can You Top Them?" on the radio for the first time.

I don't remember paying much attention, but I do remember that a bunch of (to me) nasty little smart-alecks were answering a lot of questions that seemed to me to be easy. I also remember Pavan's saying, "The boy here ought to be on that program."

Mother said, "Oh, I don't know, Petrarch. A thing like that, we'd have to give it some thought."

Pavan said, "I'll have to give it some thought."

You know what time it is? Five A.M. I have been dictating the whole night; yet I'm not really tired. I must get some sleep, though. I've got a lot of territory to cover yet. First of all, you'll have to get acquainted with Letty.

...In the few minutes before the pills take over.

I was married to Letty for almost eleven years.

There are a great many things about that period in my life which are very vivid in my mind—The Book, for instance, the war, the night my daughter Taffy was conceived, etc.

But I can remember almost none of the details of the life Letty and I had together. Isn't that incredible? Well, no, I suppose it isn't.

Schopenhauer was right: we do remember our victories; we do forget our defeats. I'll tell you something else he was right about. In *The Art of Controversy*, which I happen to admire and which I also happen to have right here, Schopenhauer says of argument:

...A last trick is to become personal, insulting, rude, as soon as you perceive that your opponent has the upper hand and that you are going to come off worst. It consists in passing from the subject of dispute as from a lost game to the disputant himself, and in some way attacking his person.

That's a perfect one-paragraph description of my marriage to Letty.

I have just yawned twice in succession. The pills are taking over. If two make me yawn, think of what fifty will do.

NOTES·DICTATED·
ON·THE·FOURTH·DAY

(1) The other side[3]

I opened my eyes at a little after eleven this morning. I wasn't refreshed, but I didn't feel too bad either.

After I drew the curtains from the wall of glass, I saw that the sun was shining brightly; there were a few indolent clouds, only one in the shape of a wolf. The series of green meadows stretched on until they reached the darker green hills, and the hills appeared to continue into eternity.

For a moment or an hour, however long it was, I sat on my bed, and in all I surveyed there was not a man, not a woman, not a child. I thought:

> I wandered lonely as a cloud
> That floats...

Once in college I questioned that line; I said that I thought it was silly. "I've never seen a lonely cloud," I said. "There's usually a whole skyful, or none, but there are never less than two or three together. Never."

Miss Forsberg, who taught English poetry, said, "Are you questioning the powers of one of the great lyric poets of all time?"

"If you put it that way, I guess so," I said.

"If you'd like to be excused, we'll excuse you," said Miss Forsberg, who had practically the entire football squad in her class. She never flunked a football player.

As I left the room, Miss Forsberg said, "There are two kinds of people in the world, poets and barbarians."

---

3   "We have heard only one side of the case; God has written all the books." —Samuel Butler.

"You ain't a kiddin', Miss Forsberg," said Bronco Nogarensco, who was from Gary, guard on the Pegasus team, and a poet.

"I wandered lonely as a cloud."

When I was in England, I asked Professor Lindsay if he'd ever seen a lonely cloud; he said he hadn't.

"What probably happened was this," said Lindsay. "Wordsworth wrote the third line first, and he had to find a word that rhymed with *crowd*."

"I wandered lonely as a cloud."

I thought about Charley. I thought about a late afternoon and an evening and a night of our life together. It was not like any of the others, but it was also not unlike any of the others.

I had been home that day, reading scripts, and I had come across one I loved—inexpertly put together but moving and true.

I came out of my study around five, and I read all of the play aloud to Charley, and I said, "What do you think? Could it be fixed?"

"It made me cry," she said. "I think it's worth trying."

"I'll try to get this boy to fix it," I said. "His agent says he's twenty and the self-proclaimed genius of lower MacDougal Street and a louse. Good writers are all sonsabitches, and so are a great many bad ones. Gives you something to think about, doesn't it?"

Charley poured us each a cup of coffee, and I thought nostalgically of my old boozing days, then banished the thought.

"Maria called," said Charley. "We talked for *hours*. She and Wiz want us to come for dinner on Saturday. Just us. I said yes. Okay?"

"Okay." It was through Wiz and Maria that I had met Charley.

Later, over our second cup of coffee—which, believe me, will never take the place of that second cocktail—I said, "What did Maria ever say about me?"

A moment passed; then Charley rose and went to the icebox.

"Steak for dinner?...Oh, she said how's Joshua. I said Joshua's fine. She said what's he doing. I said he is reading plays, and she said give him my love, and I said, See you Saturday. Around seven-thirty."

I waited.

"There's enough left-over beef stroganoff. Oh. Maria says Son John has discovered that you've played bridge with Suzy Parker. Parker is John's current passion; so you're in for an evening of grilling about her on Saturday."

I rose and went to the kitchen, standing for a moment in the black doorway.

Then I said, "Come off it, Charley. You know what I mean. What did Maria say about me when you and I first met and you told her that you might marry me."

Charley looked at me. I can only imagine what she saw in my face, but it can't have been pleasant.

"Stop it," she said.

I turned and started angrily away.

"Darling," said Charley. "What possible difference can it make tonight to know what Maria said two-and-a-half years ago?"

"None," I said. "But I asked."

"I really don't remember."

"I thought you were one who didn't lie."

Charley closed the freezer, and she poured herself some more coffee, and she said, "You want some?"

I didn't answer.

She came into the great room; she stood by the wall of glass, looking out at the graying hills and at the desolate end of a day in early summer, and she said, "Two-and-a-half years ago when you and I first met, Maria asked me what I thought of you, and I said I liked you a lot. She said so did she."

She drank some more coffee.

"Go on."

Charley turned and looked at me.

When she went on, some of the desolation had crept from the hills into her throat. She said, "Maria told me that every time she looked at you, she wanted to cry; she told me that you were destructive and wasteful of yourself and other people.... Please, darling."

"Go on."

"She said that you'd never forgive me if I fell in love with you, and she said you'd try to punish me for it. She said run don't walk to the nearest exit, and she said you'd break my heart. Now don't ask me any more because I'm going to cry, and I don't like that."

"Why didn't you run for the nearest exit?"

"Because, goddamn it, I did fall in love with you."

I went to her, and I kissed her. "I forgive you," I said, and I said, "I'm glad you fell in love with me."

She took my hand in hers, and she said, "Every morning when you wake out of that deep, drugged sleep, that open, bleeding subconscious of yours must say to itself, 'Now what am I going to do today so that he'll really get somebody to hurt him?'"

"It's not a subconscious," I said.

She rubbed her face against my hand, leaving the moist edge of a tear, and she said, "Oh, darling, God help you, and God help me, and God help us," and she said, "I didn't want to fall in love with you. I resisted for almost a week, and then I said to myself, 'Damn it to hell, I love the bastard,' and I still do. You break my heart at least once a day. I've given a lot of thought to the reasons, and I've decided that you're always so afraid somebody's going to hit you—that—you—hit first," and she said, "And don't say you're sorry again. I know you're sorry."

She wiped away the tears, and she said, "And now what would you like for dinner?"

I said, "I, of course, don't deserve you."

"We don't get what we deserve. We get what we get."

"I love you. You know that?"

"Uh-huh. I know that," said Charley, "and what I'm awfully glad about is that you don't hate me. How about lamb chops?"

We had lamb chops, and during dinner the moon appeared, orange and full. We turned off the lights, and the room became part of the out of doors. The furniture, the trees, the ground, the floor all were one. An affectionate breeze drifted down from the hills and through the house and then stole softly into the dark, delighted pines. Then we listened to some music, and we talked, until three, maybe later.

While Charley was warming the milk in the kitchen, she said, "My, you're nice."

"When I'm nice," I said.

"Yes," said Charley, "when you're nice."

On the way to bed, I said, "I didn't know Maria hated me that much."

I heard Charley's quick intake of breath.

I said, "Aren't you sorry you didn't take her advice? You still could, of course, run to the nearest exit, I mean. Why don't you?"

Charley ran into her bedroom, locking the door behind her.

"I wandered lonely as a cloud."

After I woke up this morning I was finally able to shut Charley out of my mind. I looked outside once more. I saw what seemed to be a chicken hawk circling very high above the bird bath, which was occupied by a family of robins.

The bird could have been a crow, I suppose, but it could not have been a bluebird.

I got up, went to the wall of glass, and as the bird started to circle down, I quickly closed the curtains.

Chronologically, the "Can you Top Them?" program comes here, but I'm just not up to it. Tomorrow maybe or the day after.

My memory of those weekly trips to Chicago is at the moment one dark, oblong blur. I hated every minute of it. I vomited once every week; I remember that, and I still feel the gorge rising in me every time I get even close to the City with the Inferiority Complex. It seems to me the sun didn't shine once when I was there.

(2) "The memory be green"

It clouded over a few minutes ago and now has begun to rain. Before getting on with Letty I'd like to try a green memory or two. There aren't many. Besides, I'll have to change this tape before I start with Letty. Letty will take at least one full tape, maybe two.

Okay.

Green Memory Number One. I once read the entire first act of *Hamlet* to Hughie, aloud, playing every part. I believe I was a pretty good Polonius, but then any ham can play that old bore.

I remember I paused triumphantly at the end of the act, just to catch my breath before plunging into Act Two. "What do you think of it, Hughie?" I asked.

Hughie was fishing in the river, as far away from the campus of Pegasus as we could walk. At first he didn't answer.

"Well, what do you think?" I repeated.

"That guy Hamlet is a bigger pain in the ass than Penrod," said Hughie.

From that day to this I have never been able to sit through a production of *Prince of Denmark*.

Green Memory Number Two. At about the same time came what might be called the Booth Tarkington period of my life. It won't take long, and I do want to tell about My First Date, with Mildred Bellamy.

Mildred was seventeen and a freshman at the New Athens Senior High School. She had been a freshman for two years.

Mildred was larger than any of the girls in her class and older than any of the boys. She was the daughter of a woman who worked at the canning factory—"Uncle George's Kidney Beans. They Will Like You, and You Will Like Them." Mavis Bellamy had had several husbands—some legal, some not—and most of them had left behind a child or two. Mildred came in the middle of a brood of fourteen.

Mildred was generously breasted, had a clouded complexion and a whine for a voice.

Hughie told me that every boy in Senior High who wanted to had had Mildred, including, Hughie indicated, himself.

There was another boy with us at the time. I can't remember who.

"I bet The Brain'd be afraid even to *ask* Mildred for a date," this boy said.

I said, "I don't bet, and I can think of a good many girls I'd rather spend the evening with than Mildred Bellamy."

The more I thought about it, though, the sounder the idea seemed. Why *not* ask Mildred for a date?

After all, she could only laugh and say no, and I was used to people laughing at my questions and saying no. So I had nothing to lose. What I had to gain (I hoped) was the chance to learn something about s-e-x.

True, I had read widely on the subject. For one thing, I was familiar with Krafft-Ebing, which was in the restricted room of the Pegasus library. As what Letty, years later, called the Belle of the Ball at Pegasus, I had my own key to the restricted room.

It was run on the honor system. You were only supposed to read what you'd been assigned to read.

Naturally, I read everything. However, I was familiar with the large difference between the textbook knowledge of a subject and laboratory experiments in other fields, and I thought I might as well try to use Mildred as my laboratory in the field of sex.

So, one afternoon, without a word to anybody, including Hughie, I marched down to the Rexall drugstore, and after walking up and down in front of the door a half-dozen times, I went in and bought a chocolate malted with an extra dipper of ice cream *and* an egg.

I dawdled over the malted and at the same time kept a watchful eye fixed on the drug counter. I didn't know the pharmacist and I hoped he didn't know me.

Finally, I paid for the malted. I even left a dime for the waitress. Then I slowly walked to the drug counter and stood in front of it, clearing my throat. The druggist, an elderly man, came in from the back room.

"What can I do for you, sonny?" he asked.

I cleared my throat again, and then in a loud stage whisper which must have carried far beyond the malted-milk machine where the waitress was, I said, "I want to buy some rubbers."

"For yourself?" the druggist asked.

I nodded vigorously.

"You're in the wrong place, sonny," the druggist said. "The kind of rubbers you want you get in a shoestore."

Was he serious? Was he making fun of me? I never knew. I turned and started goose-stepping out of the store, my face a bright vermilion.

Just before I reached the door, the waitress picked up the dime.

"Hey, kid," she said. "You forgot your dime."

I started running. I ran out of the door and for blocks beyond. I never went back to Rexall's, not all the time I was in New Athens.

After I went to bed that night, I decided that maybe it would be better if I didn't ask Mildred for a date.

At thirteen, I told myself, I was in no position to become the father of an Unwanted Child. Not only that. Suppose Mildred had one of the dread diseases I'd read about? Was even a *successful* laboratory experiment worth the dangers involved?

At first, I decided no, and then I changed my mind. What the hell? I had been reading *The Memoirs of Casanova* in the restricted room.

And hadn't he written, "...in my old age, I can find no other enjoyment but that which recollections of the past offer me"?

It looked to me as if I wouldn't have any recollections of the past if I didn't get started. By my age, Casanova was *a man of the world*, sexually and every other way.

So the next afternoon I was in the yard of the New Athens Senior High when Mildred came out.

Since we had a nodding acquaintance, I just said, "Hi," and she smiled, pleasantly, I thought, although her teeth were inadequate.

"Would you like to go see the Tremayne Players with me on Saturday night?" I asked. "It's *Sun-Up*."

The Tremayne Players were a stock company that had stopped over in New Athens for the winter.

Mildred looked down at me from a great height, and first, as I had expected, she giggled, and then she smiled and then she said, "It might be kind of fun at that for a change."

I never did know whether Mildred meant that I would be the change or the Tremayne Players would be. I didn't care. I extended the invitation on, let's say, a Wednesday, and between then and Saturday I spent all my spare time in the restricted room reading every sex book I could lay my hands on, memorizing certain—I hoped—crucial passages.

Came Saturday night. When I picked her up, Mildred was wearing a crepe de chine dress (it was January), underneath which she had on a pink slip but clearly no brassière. Her coat was thin and patched in two places.

I brought her a bunch of violets, and she almost cried. I suppose those were the first flowers anybody ever gave her—and possibly the last.

Sun-Up is a very sad play, and I always wept at movies and plays in those days. I still do, for that matter. The only emotions that never get a rise out of me are the real-life ones.

After the third-act curtain, Mildred and I edged our way out of the Odeon Theater.

Mildred, who had been restive during the entire performance, devoting her time to admiring and smoothing the corsage, said, "What were you blubbering about all the time?"

"The play," I said. "It was very sad."

"It was?" said Mildred, profoundly surprised. "What was sad?"

"Well, for one thing, when the mother and the girl got the telegram from the War Department saying that the son had been killed in the war. That was sad."

"The son was just Guy Templeton," said Mildred, naming the leading man, who had black curly hair, no chin, and no talent.

"I know," I said, "but in the play he was killed."

"He wasn't killed," said Mildred. "I seen him out in the alley between the acts, smoking a cigar."

Mildred adjusted the corsage. "A girl friend of mine's been out with him, and she says about half the time he's dead *drunk*. But he wasn't *dead*. So what was so sad?"

I smiled vaguely. I did not feel that this was the time to go into a discussion of the willing suspension of disbelief.

"This girl friend of mine says this Guy Templeton ain't all he's cracked up to be anyway," said Mildred.

"I expect you're right there," I said.

Then I suggested that Mildred and I take a taxi out to the Green Gables, which was bootleg and where the college kids went.

"We might have a beer or something," I said.

"Yah," said Mildred. "You and me and who else? Unless you're like this girl friend of mine claims. She claims you're a midget and wants me to ask you. You ain't no midget, are you?"

"Please," I said. "Please."

"I figured you wasn't," said Mildred. "If you'd a been a midget or something you wouldna been crying like that."

"Yah," I said in what I believed to be the manner of George Raft. "Yah, sure."

I would at that moment have given a lot to have had a cigarette. I would have lighted the match with my thumbnail, the way George Raft did in some movie. I could. I'd practiced.

However, I compromised by taking Mildred to the Royal Kandy Kitchen, where she had a butterscotch sundae with nuts and whipped cream. I had a chocolate malted—no egg. The whole deal set me back thirty cents.

Then I suggested that since there didn't seem to be much else to do we might as well start home (Mildred's), and why didn't we walk through Riverdale Park?

"Okay by me," said Mildred.

Just north of the empty swimming pool, I asked the crucial question.

"Would it be all right with you if I kissed you, Mildred?"

"You going to stand on a box or something?" asked Mildred, laughing, and then she said, "It might be kind of fun at that for a change."

She leaned over, and we kissed.

Now my father had kissed me, and so had Aunt Mettabel and Mrs. Hoadley, and my mother had often kissed me in public, but this was the first kiss in which I felt *sex* was involved.

I had expected quite a bit, and I was disappointed—perhaps because I was standing on tiptoe and straining every muscle, perhaps because it was January, and in January in Iowa it is very cold.

I don't know why. All I knew then was that kissing wasn't anywhere near what all the novelists had said, and for that matter, the poets didn't seem to me to have got it down right either. What kissing was was a lot of work.

However, I had my reputation to think of. So I felt of Mildred a little in the places I had read you were supposed to feel of girls.

The difference between literature and life had never seemed greater than at that moment.

I was still feeling when Mildred said, "You wasn't figgering on going the whole way, was you?"

I said, "Well, no not tonight. I mean we've hardly got acquainted yet."

Mildred could have laughed; she didn't; she seemed neither surprised nor disappointed. She just said, "That's what I figgered."

I stopped feeling her, and we walked on toward the shack just the wrong side of the M. and St. L. tracks that she shared with her mother, her numerous brothers and sisters and at various times the various husbands.

As we were waiting for a switch engine to clear the tracks, Mildred said, "It sure was nice of you to give me these violets," and she once more fondled them.

Later she said (not unkindly, merely observing), "You may be smart, but in some ways you ain't so bright."

On the sidewalk in front of the Bellamy place, she said that it had been lots of fun and again thanks for the posies.

I kissed her lightly near the beginning of her chin, and she said, "It's still news to me that play was sad."

I thanked her for a most enjoyable evening.

Naturally, I never told anybody, not even Hughie, everything that had happened between me and Mildred that evening, particularly not the part about the disappointing kiss and the conversation which followed.

But the next morning after Hughie got back from Mass I did describe to him a whole series of imaginary erotica that I claimed had taken place between Mildred and me, largely based on what I had read in Krafft-Ebing.

When I finished, Hughie, who had been listening intently, grinned at me. "Just who do you think you're kidding?" he asked.

"Nobody," I said, and we started laughing, and he said, "I didn't bang her neither. I was just saying that."

We laughed even harder after that, so hard in fact that Mrs. Larrabee, who was cooking Sunday dinner, came out to see what was up.

It was years before I made a real laboratory experiment in sex. If I read my Kinsey right—and, naturally, I turned to the autobiographical part first—I was somewhat retarded in this area.

The place was London, and my patient partner was a lady with a Cockney accent so pronounced that even a Professor Higgins would have despaired; she called herself Miss Hart—"That's what you my call my stige nime, ducks"—and she told me all about her daughter. In a convent. Her daughter didn't know what Miss Hart was up to, and Miss Hart wanted to keep her in the convent so that she would never know. Thus, Miss Hart had to charge a little more for her services than some of the other girls who were in it "just for a lark."

If memory serves—and, in my case, if memory does anything, it *serves*—Miss Hart's comment, after the event, was, "Don't worry, ducks. We all have to start somewhere." Something like that.

For weeks afterward I worried about every pimple that appeared anywhere on me, certain that I had the Dread Disease. I didn't, but I did decide that Lord Chesterfield (wasn't it?) was right—the position was ridiculous, the price preposterous, and the pleasure momentary.

I've often wondered what happened to Miss Hart, whose ambition (she said) was for her imaginary (I imagine) daughter to be presented to the King. "Many, many things more unusual than that have happened in Buckingham Palace, dearie."

I had a second sexual experience that same night in London. I'll discuss that in context.

Mildred? She married Gus Robertson, who used to pound a bass drum in the New Athens Senior High School Band and who, the last I knew, was pounding a beat for the New Athens Police Department. I'm told he's the cop who, when he found a dead dog on North Dubuque Street, moved the body to East Main before he made out his report. They say Gus couldn't spell D-u-b-u-q-u-e.

He and Mildred have nine children.

After Mildred, nearly three years passed during which I had only three or four dates. Once Hughie and I double-dated for a Hi-Y banquet. My date was Matty Hare, whom I've mentioned as editor of the Pegasus yearbook. Matty's palate was not completely cleft, but it leaned in that direction. She is now a senior researcher on a magazine I have no intention of naming, and she has called me several times over the years and left messages, which because of her palate condition have not always been too clear. I have never called back.

Once I had a date with a Marion Sokoloff, now one of the Biggest Literary Agents on Either Coast. I'll bet she weighs a good three hundred.

About all I remember about my only date with Marion is that when I picked her up at the Kappa house she opened the conversation by saying, "You are small, and I am large, but our souls are the same size."

I can't remember where the conversation went from there. Where could it?

Marion hasn't changed much in the years since. She's just about the most influential Zen person on the island of Manhattan. She has even been Out East where they thought it up.

I saw Marion at a party in New York not long ago. She greeted me by saying, "Joshua, dear, there are many roads up the mountain. I knew our paths would cross once more."

And later she said, "Just tell me this, if you will. Is there any connection between the washing of the clothes, the blowing out of the candle, and the twisting of the nose?"

I didn't answer. I disappeared in a puff of smoke, like wild geese flying.

(3) A hundred kinds of love[4]

I've just had lunch—if that's what you call a meal at five in the afternoon. I've taken two of the dexedrine pills, and they've done for me what they're supposed to do.

It's still raining—not too hard, though, and if I hadn't destroyed all the hi-fi records, I could shut out the sound of it.

Louella's going to put my dinner in the oven.... Now her bonnie lies over the ocean. Her bonnie lies over the sea. Oh, bring back, bring back....

---

4 "I've known a hundred kinds of love— All made the loved one rue."
—Emily Bronte.

Louella is very lonely. Luther died last year, a heart attack, and Henry, their only child, was in one of the few integrated divisions toward the end of the next-to-last Great War. Henry was reported missing in action one spring afternoon in 1945. They never found the body, and I like to believe that Henry is living Over There now, maybe Paris, perhaps the Casbah, integrating like mad.

Nevertheless, Louella misses him. Bring back. Bring back. Oh, bring back my bonnie to me. To me....

There's no escaping it. As well do it now as later. I'll tell you about Letty. We met in the winter of 1936, shortly after my fifteenth birthday. I was a senior at the college; Letty was a sophomore. She admitted to seventeen.

Letty was a "tithe" student. My great-great-grandfather and the five other Methodists who set up the original college had provided not only that the forty-acre plot of land east of New Athens had to be used for educational purposes but that one out of every ten students had to be a "tithe student," meaning tuition-free.

As I've indicated these were almost always football players, but, occasionally, somebody like Letty was allowed on the campus. Letty had been salutatorian of her high-school class. Although her grades at Pegasus weren't nearly as good, she still was in the upper ten per cent. That was the way she got to be a member of the Pi Beta Phi sorority. The sisters needed her grades to keep up the house average.

Pi Beta Phi was the second best sorority on the campus; the best was Kappa Kappa Gamma. That meant its members had the richest parents, were in general the prettiest, the bitchiest, and the most snobbish.

At the time we met, Letty's main claim to attention on the campus was the fact that she had been Angus MacDonald's date at the annual military ball. Angus had been Cadet Colonel, and he and Letty had walked into the military ball under a canopy of crossed swords held aloft by two lines of young men who on graduation became second lieutenants. Not too many years later large numbers of them were killed on one side of the world or another.

I was a militant pacifist at the time and had written an editorial for the college weekly demanding that the military ball be cancelled.

Since it wasn't, I wrote a second editorial saying that anybody who had *anything* to do with the military ball was "aiding and abetting the war lords and that clearly and definitely includes Angus MacDonald and Letty Novotny."

What I was doing at that particular Pi Phi dance is very clear in my mind.

It was my mother's idea, not original. She had pecked at another book, always a dangerous thing. As a result, she had me and Pavan on a diet consisting almost entirely of raw turnips.

"George Bernard Shaw says that turnips are the *original* brain food. He's *constantly* nibbling on one."

I've said she was a food nut. Turnips were about the eleventh original brain food to which I'd been subjected.

Another result of mother's looking into whatever book it was:

"I.Q. is important, Joshua, as we both know, but it isn't everything is it, dear?" This must have been in public; otherwise, there'd have been no "dear."

"We must learn to develop our social grace notes as well as our brain, mustn't we? The well-rounded man is the complete man, isn't he?"

I didn't argue with mother; by that time I knew better. I went to dances to develop my social grace notes, and the evening at the Pi Phi house must have been among my first.

I wasn't a good dancer then; I'm not now.

Worse yet, in those days I was very much shorter than most of the girls. Besides, they were on the lookout for potential husbands, and I was never thought of (except by Letty) as being in that category.

I remember around this time hearing a couple of girls discussing marriage and me.

One of them said, "Incredible as it may seem, some day somebody's going to marry The Brain."

The other said, "Sure, some bearded lady or maybe the Hilton Sisters." The Hilton Sisters, who had recently appeared at the Odeon, were a vaudeville team of Siamese twins.

At the dance that night, as always, several boys said things like, "Your mother know you're out, Genius?" or, "How come they're letting you wear long pants, Brain?" Witty, original things like that.

Somehow I did trap one girl into a waltz, during which she kept as far away from me as possible; I said, "Don't worry, Toots, my leprosy's not contagious." Something original and witty like *that*.

I remember that I spent a whole hour listening to the Pi Phi house mother, whose inappropriate name was Myrtle Swift, talk about her gallstones and her highly original lumbago.

Then Letty Novotny came up to me.

"Would you be aiding and abetting the war lords if you danced with me?" she asked. She also smiled; it was a pleasant smile. Later, she learned how to use it, and then it was no longer so pleasant.

I said that I would enjoy dancing with her.

It is difficult for me to remember the way Letty looked the last time I saw her, but the image of her that first evening is very clear in my mind.

First off, she was about my height, which was pleasant. Her hair was blond and soft. Her eyes were light blue. Her skin was clear and fair. Her mouth was too small and impatient, but the bones of her face were good. Her chin receded slightly, yet it somehow thrust itself at you, demanding that you declare it to be more than it was.

Not a pretty face but not an ugly one either.

There were thin, then almost imperceptible lines running from each side of Letty's nose to the edges of her mouth. George Banning once said that those were lines of dissatisfaction and anxiety. He said that Letty always looked and acted as if she were in too much of a hurry. He said that for that reason Letty would never achieve whatever it was she wanted to achieve. He said that the ones who did make it were always smart enough to hide their anxiety.

George was wrong about Letty.

Letty had come to the Pi Phi dance with Angus MacDonald, who in addition to having been a Cadet Colonel was captain of the swimming team. Angus had a square body and a square face into which every perfect feature fitted into a perfect cipher. He had a brown skin and brown hair and brown eyes. I was reminded of Angus's eyes a few years ago when I bought my first golden retriever, Prince Alexander. The Prince was beautiful, loving, and not bright, but his eyes were kind, and so were those of Angus, whose family owned MacDonald's, the next-to-largest department store in Des Moines.

I remember that during our first dance Letty, who danced beautifully, said, "You dance well—but oddly, if you don't mind my saying so."

"You want to stop?" I asked, heart-broken. I thought I had been doing well.

"Of course not," she said. "You're good, but your dancing is very—different. That's all."

I said, "Well, I've really only danced about two or three *real* dances in my whole life."

"What do you mean, *real* dances?"

I smiled at her, hoping for the best, and said, "I got a book out of the library, and it had diagrams of different dance steps. I memorized the diagrams and practiced some, but I've almost never danced with *anybody*."

"That's amazing," said Letty. I thought I detected admiration in her voice.

There is another exchange of that evening which floats through the years at me, the sound of my own voice (a combination of false basso and natural mezzo-soprano) and of Letty's (tight, controlled, very high-pitched).

Me: I take it you don't feel the slightest compunction about allowing your name to be used in the encouragement of cannon fodder.

Letty: Oh, for pity's sake, relax and lead.

I remember asking Letty if she planned to marry Angus MacDonald. She said she doubted it.

"Mama and Papa MacDonald don't want a scion of the MacDonald clan hooked up with anybody named Novotny."

She prounced *scion sky-un*, and I didn't think she'd mind being corrected the way most people did, so I said, "By the way, that word is pronounced *si-un*. At least that's the preferred pronunciation. It can be pronounced *si-on*, but never *sky-un*."

"Oh, is it?" said Letty, and she pronounced it correctly.

"Thanks," she added. "I always want to be told. When I say or do something wrong, I always want to know."

What I said was, "That's very commendable of you, and I might also add it's very rare."

Letty said, "Oh, I could snatch Angus Pangus if I wanted to work at it, but I'm not that interested."

I said, "I take it you're not in love with him then."

"Good God, no," said Letty.

Later, when Letty said that the *ass-me* of her ambition was to go to New York, I told her how to pronounce *acme*.

"What do you want to be in New York City?" I asked.

"The biggest they've got," said Letty.

At the end of the evening, Casanova Bland, temporary basso-profundo, said, "I don't suppose we could have a date sometime."

"I'd love it," said Letty, and it was like the day Hughie had said that if everything worked out, maybe we could be friends. I fell in love with Letty at that moment, or thought I did. My heart sang.

"Oh, wonderful," I said, somewhat falsetto.

"You're very interesting to talk to," said Letty.

I said, "In many circles I'm considered a bore."

"You're often outrageous, but you're definitely not a bore. Angus Pangus is always talking about some swimming meet or what a hot shot he is on the rifle range. *That's* boring."

"Angus MacDonald is barely average in intelligence," I said. "He can't help that, of course, but it does make him a perfect pawn for the munitions makers."

"You could take me to the art exhibit on Saturday afternoon," said Letty, "and then we could have dinner at Finch's and go to the French movie."

And so it was that on a December afternoon in 1936, Letty's and my odd association began. Letty planned the first date. It was ever thus—almost.

I'll tell you this about Letty and me in the beginning.

We almost always had a good time together.

For one thing, Letty had a quick, cruel gift as a mimic. She could be President and Mrs. Baker and Dean of Men Fletcher, the one who on the day he met me said, "I understand you're a boy prodigy. I don't like boy prodigies." And Miss Something Bartlett, an amiable scatterbrain who posed as dean of women.

Every year in her lecture on feminine hygiene, Dean Bartlett told the freshman girls, "Nice girls *know* where babies come from, but they never under any circumstances *reveal* that they know."

In her talk on "Girl-Boy Etiquette," Dean Bartlett used to say, "Girls, when you are with a boy, find the bond of common interest and hammer away."

Letty could also imitate Matty Hare, her sisters at the Pi Phi house *and*, when she found out how I stood on the subject, *mother*. There were those who, years later, Dr. Baron among them, suggested that Letty's imitation of *Mummy* came naturally; that in this case Letty wasn't acting. Maybe.

I just know that when I first knew her Letty made me laugh, and almost nobody ever had before—except Charlie Chaplin and the Marx Brothers and Mark Twain.

What's more, Letty and I always seemed to have an endless number of things to say to each other, or maybe I said and she listened. Letty was a good listener in those early days.

However, mostly what Letty and I had (from my point of view, anyway) was an easy naturalness together. Until I met Letty, the only people I ever felt at ease with were Hughie, the few teachers I've mentioned, and Aunt Mettabel and Uncle Dick. I hadn't yet been introduced to Jack Daniel, who for *years* made me feel at ease—and then some.

Letty's attitude toward me was vaguely admiring but by no means worshipful (fine by me), and she plucked eagerly at that part of what I knew that she felt would be useful to her. Letty never forgot anything she wanted to remember, and she was always shrewd in separating what for her purposes would be wheat and what would be chaff.

We went to all the art exhibits that were held on the campus, attended all the concerts, went to the weekly French movies at the Cameo, and even an occasional football game.

Letty to me: It doesn't matter if you don't like football or baseball. You have to know enough to be able to hold up your end of the conversation if they're being discussed.

Me to Letty: Nuts.

I tried to teach Letty Conversational French, not too successfully. Midwesterners in general aren't much good at speaking foreign languages. I happen to have a flawless accent in no tongue at all, including my own, and Letty—well, at the time I remember telling her that her accent was so poor she'd have trouble ordering a croissant on the Champs Elysées. In those days, I thought they spoke French on the Champs Elysées.

I never understood why Letty wanted to speak French anyway, since she had no aptitude for it.

Letty said of that what she said of other things. "You never know when it'll come in handy."

She was right; you never know. Letty, after much practice, learned how to pronounce *fraises des bois*.

When I first met her, Letty never wanted to talk about her past, or about her present, only about the future, her plans for which were specific and detailed.

For instance, Letty wanted to have lots of money. How much?

"Well, for one thing I'd like to be rich enough to have a different car for every day in the week."

She and her present husband Harry have only three cars, but they could easily *afford* four others.

Or, Letty would say, "I want to be able to buy anything in the world I want and never have to ask how much it costs."

Letty can now do that, and does.

Letty was always interested in the places I had been and in the people I had met. Nobody else in New Athens cared much—not even Hughie.

"Wherever you go, you just see more people," he used to say, "and we've got plenty of people right here."

But Letty was curious about everybody.

As I believe I said, on one trip to Iowa City, I shook the hand of Queen Marie of Rumania. When I mentioned this to Letty, years later, Letty said, "How was she dressed?" and "How did she bow, or does she just stand there while you bow?" and "If you hadn't known she was a queen, would you *know*?" and "How *old* was she?"

Even then, Letty always wanted to know how *old* everybody was.

The other "Can You Top Them?" participants and I once went Out There for a movie appearance, and I guess the best way to put it is that we were *exposed* to Norma Shearer.

"How *old* was Norma Shearer?" Letty asked. "I bet underneath all that makeup you couldn't tell a *thing*," and "They say she's such a *lady*; in Norma Shearer's case, what would you say that meant?" and "What did she have *on*?"

You see, Letty never knew whether or not the time might come when she'd have to know about queens, meeting one or being one, and if Miss Shearer was a lady, Letty wanted to know all about what that involved.

In the beginning, Letty was always vague about her parents.

"My father's dead," she would say. "He was Quaker Oats."

Her tone of voice when she said that prevented you—me, anyway—from inquiring further into the matter. It was clear from Letty's tone that while her father might not have been president of Quaker Oats, which was in Cedar Rapids, he certainly had been one of its top executives.

Whenever her mother was mentioned, Letty would say, "Mother travels a good bit," and when the Pi Phi sisters held their annual Mother's Day reception, Letty always regretfully announced that Mrs. Novotny would be unable to attend.

"I know Mother'd love to come," Letty would say, "but she's in *Florida*."

One did not ask *where* in Florida. One could tell by the way Letty said the word that it was not Miami Beach. *Palm* Beach, at least.

Letty's family name was unfortunate; there was no getting away from the uncomfortable fact of it, though. In Iowa at that time—and probably still—people from the part of Europe where *Novotny* is a common name were known as Bohunks.

Characteristically, however, Letty made or tried to make an asset of a liability. She would say, "I'm a Novotny, you know."

You knew; you nodded.

"My late grandfather was one of Eduard Beneš's closest friends and advisers in the early days of the Czech Republic," she would say.

When you heard that, you felt like a fool for not being privy to such an important historical fact. So you nodded again, vehemently.

Since Letty's magnate father and her statesman grandfather were dead, I decided that I simply had to meet her globe-trotting mother, and I had a feeling that that would take some doing.

I did it, though. Easy did it.

My campaign took place on a blustery March night, shortly after I had told Letty that I doubted if she would ever be able to master French verbs. Then, too casually, I said, "Your mother back yet, Letty?"

"Yes, she's back," said Letty, her mind on the future tense. "Why can't those lousy French have a simple language like English?"

I said, "As a matter of strict fact, English is perhaps the most difficult of the spoken languages, with the possible exception of Russian. I'll meet you at your place on Saturday after the debate."

"Okay," said Letty. "We'll go to the movies. It's Helen Twelvetrees."

Then, doing a slow take, she said, "You'll meet me where?"

"At your place," I said. "I've been aching to meet your mother, and since I'll be in Cedar Rapids on Saturday, this seems like the perfect opportunity."

"Heh, heh," said Letty. "Some fun. You'll meet me at the store."

Letty had a week-end and summer job at a Cedar Rapids department store, not, you understand, that she needed the money, "though a little pin money always comes in handy no matter what. I just want to learn merchandising. After all, we live in a mercantile society."

But I refused to meet Letty at the store. "I'll meet you at your place," I said, "After all, if our friendship is to mature, I will certainly want to meet your mother and vice versa, won't I?"

The argument that followed was short, somewhat acrimonious—though mild compared with many that followed—and I won.

"Okay, so meet my mother," said Letty. "Only, baby, don't tell people around the campus—well, you know."

"I know."

"And don't come 'til five-thirty. I'll be home from the store by then. Remember. Five-*thirty*. That doesn't mean five-*fifteen*."

I nodded. "Five-thirty," I said.

Letty should have known better. I arrived at the Novotny house at *four*-thirty.

Many years later I described that afternoon to Dr. Guenther, the Jungian.

"You know how punctual I am," I told him. "I'm always on time or early. Well, the afternoon I went to White Street to pick up Letty I was almost an hour early."

Dr. Guenther, Swiss and himself as punctual as one of their watches, was doing his best to master idiomatic English. He said, "Accidentally on purpose. Am I right?"

When I arrived at the Novotny house, I was feeling good. I was a member of the Pegasus debate team, and we had won our debate with Coe College.

While there had been another fellow on the team, I was sure I had carried the burden of the argument, which had to do with whether Hitler was going to help or hinder Germany. I was on the *hinder* side.

When I had asked Letty which street she lived on, she had said, "White Street, unfortunately."

At that time, early 1937, Grant Wood, who had been born near Cedar Rapids and had spent part of his youth there, had moved to Iowa City. Cedar Rapids then was a depressed, depressing overgrown country village. I am told that they have put up a couple of art galleries since, and there is always the really beautiful church that Louis Sullivan built, so the town may now resemble Versailles.

But in 1937 the street I've chosen to call White Street was not Cedar Rapids at its best. White was a block and a half from the railroad tracks and thus too close to the tracks, and on the wrong side.

At that time (and I imagine still) the houses on White were small, cheaply built, and in need of a coat of paint. Their tiny front windows faced on narrow strips of anemic earth on which nothing ever grew. A few scrawny trees were planted along the edges of the sidewalk.

The house in which Letty was born and raised was even older and smaller than most of the neighboring houses. It had most recently been painted a dirty brown, but that had not been so very recent. A good deal of the brown had chipped away, and in those places a hideous, mocking green showed through.

There was a loose board on the tiny front porch, and the board squeaked when I stepped on it.

A small, hand-lettered square of pasteboard beneath the gutted doorbell unnecessarily stated that the bell was out of order.

I knocked, and after a moment I saw a shadow through the cracked pane of frosted glass.

The door was opened a crack, and two dark, suspicious eyes stared out at me.

"I am Joshua Bland," I announced, blandly.

"I recognize," said a woman's voice, and the door opened wider. "I Letitia's mother."

The woman extended a rough, red hand, and I gave her mine. I smiled pleasantly at her. She was a short, plump woman with a broad Slavic face. Her eyes were brown. Her sparse gray hair was gathered into a tight bun at the nape of her neck, and she had just had a permanent wave or a marcel which had not yet been combed out.

She led me into the living room, her eyes surveying it with apprehensive dissatisfaction.

"You was early a little," she said, and then, indicating a blue overstuffed chair which had a design of birds in flight, she said, "Make yourself right to home."

I thanked her and sat down.

"You like a sandwich, something like that?" she asked, twisting her hands inside each other and out again.

I smiled and said, "No, thank you."

"You was early a little," Mrs. Novotny repeated, stating an unwelcome fact.

She stooped and scooped up a pair of discouraged pink bedroom slippers which were on the floor near the blue sofa. She held the slippers indecisively in her left hand, looking at them as if she weren't sure how they had got there. Her right hand brushed nonexistent crumbs from her apron, which was white with large red dots and very clean. She wore an equally clean red gingham house dress.

"A cup of coffee, something like that?" she asked hopefully.

I said that I would very much like a cup of coffee if it wasn't too much trouble.

Mrs. Novotny gratefully started to back from the room. She saw a comb on the sideboard. The comb was losing its wisdom teeth, and there was evidence that it had been used a lot; it was red. She grabbed it up and added it to the unwanted pink slippers she held in her left hand.

"You was early a little," she said a third time. "I wasn't finished with the redding up."

"Everything looks just fine to me," I said.

"Letty shown me your pitcher and that write-up in the papers," she said. "You're a very bright fellow. I can see that."

I smiled and thanked her for the compliment, which I shyly indicated was not deserved.

"This neighbor lady, Missus Donovan," she said, looking at me closely, "she said she bet you wasn't a day under thirty-five." Mrs. Novotny chuckled at Mrs. Donovan's preposterous idea, but I could tell she wanted to make sure I wasn't really thirty-five. People always thought that if I were thirty-five that would explain me.

"That is silly," I said.

"Letitia just worships the ground you walk on," she said.

She paused to let her meaning sink in. I nodded to indicate that it had.

"You sure you wouldn't like a sandwich?" she asked again. "I could run down to the store. Takes a minute only. Boiled ham?"

"Just the coffee, thanks," I said, and she backed into the kitchen, closing the door behind her.

I have forgotten nothing about that living room, which I examined closely while Mrs. Novotny was making the coffee.

Whenever I was most angry with Letty, I remembered that room. The memory never made me any less angry, and in the end when I hated Letty, I hated her no less because of it; still, it helped to keep that room in mind.

Now that Letty lives on Canyon Drive Out There in what she describes as a Modern French Provincial Home, which cost half a million dollars, part of her is still back there on White Street in Cedar Rapids.

Letty once said, "I started packing to leave White Street when I was one year old." She never really got away from it, though. Nobody ever escapes. Nobody can ever go far enough.

The room was small but very clean. There was a rag rug in the middle of the room, and there were large protective pieces of towelling on the stubby sofa and on the two overstuffed chairs. I felt sure that if I had not arrived early, the towelling would have been replaced by lace antimacassars.

The boards in the pine floor were wide, and there were wide spaces between them. The floor had been varnished, but there was still a look of despair about it.

A large, inexpertly tinted photograph of Letty hung on one of the walls, which were papered with an endless succession of no longer very red roses against a cream-colored background. The only other picture on the wall was, not unexpectedly, "The Song of the Lark." My Aunt Mettabel had the same picture, clipped from an issue of the *Delineator*.

The sideboard was from Grand Rapids. There was a bowl of wax fruit exactly in the middle and on one side a collection of orange glass elephants of graduated sizes. On the other side was the Novotny wedding photograph, also tinted, and I could see that

Letty resembled her father, whose face was thin and had a certain handsome grace. Part of it was hidden by a wide mustache.

I walked to the shelf hung in one corner of the room. On it was the complete Novotny library, Emily Post's *Etiquette*, the Holy Bible, bound in limp leatherette, and a Fanny Farmer cook book which looked as if it had never been opened. On the fly leaf of the last was scrawled, "To Mother. From Letty. Merry Xmas. And a Happy New Year. 1933."

Incongruously, there was also on the shelf a copy of Anna Louise Strong's *I Change Worlds*, a book about the brave new civilization the Soviets had invented.

I couldn't believe it, but the inscription was, "To Letty—Who Has Certainly Changed My World. Otto Z."

Otto Zorich. It couldn't be.

Otto was the Pegasus radical, and at the time I thought he was the greatest thing since the invention of the wheel. He was the youngest instructor in the art department, and he was a quite good artist in his own right. Some people said he was as good as Picasso; he wasn't, but he was younger than Picasso, and he was just as radical.

I took every class of his I could get into, and I kept waiting for him to ask me (a) to become a member of the Young Communist League and (b) to do something *daring*, like maybe blowing up the Rock Island railroad station just to prove I could be counted on When the Time Came.

Otto never did, though; he just ignored me, but I kept trying to impress him. One sentence I remember using several times in his presence was, "Do you think the Communists really go *far* enough, Dr. Zorich?"

Otto wasn't a Ph.D., but he was an admitted Marxist, a hinted Communist Party member, and a frequent target of some state legislator who needed a little free publicity. How and why President Horatio P. Baker put up with Otto I never did know.

Otto Zorich. He had even marched in a picket line in a *real* strike, and he had given this book to Letty, who had changed his world.

Would wonders never cease!

I was working away at Miss Strong's oracular prose when Mrs. Novotny came back into the room.

She was carrying a black tray on which were two cups and saucers, cream and sugar, and a huge pot of coffee. There was also a plate on which were several kinds of homemade cookies.

Mrs. Novotny had changed into a sateen dress that was surpassingly purple, and she had fluffed out the tight wave in her hair.

"You reading that book?" she asked as she put the tray on a walnut stand. She was clearly alarmed at my choice of reading matter.

"I was just thumbing through it," I said.

"That's just any old book," said Mrs. Novotny. "Can't remember where Letty got that old book."

"A present from Otto Zorich," I said.

Mrs. Novotny appeared to be dredging deep into her memory. "Otto Zorich," she said, and then, "Just some fella Letitia used to know. Long time ago. Very long time ago. I tell her, 'Letitia, you don't want to go around with no boys whose folks was in the old country born.' Have a cookie."

I helped myself to one of the cookies, which was made largely of butter.

"Have some more," said Mrs. Novotny. "There's plenty more where them come from. Plenty more."

She pushed my coffee toward me. Then she seated herself in the other overstuffed chair.

"Help yourself to some cream and sugar," she said, and I did.

She sat very straight on the edge of the chair, perhaps the way it said in Emily Post.

"Letty, she is very good girl," said Mrs. Novotny, stirring her coffee vigorously. "You like her?"

"Very much," I said, eating another of the buttery cookies. "These cookies practically melt in your mouth."

"Try another," said Mrs. Novotny. "Them with the poppy seeds."

I tried one with the poppy seeds. "Delicious," I said.

"Letty be home any minute now," said Mrs. Novotny. "She is very good cook. A girl with all the brains she's got, you wouldn't think maybe, but she is very good cook."

I said that I bet she was and took another of the cookies with the poppy seeds.

"Always got her nose stuck in a book," said Mrs. Novotny. "Never no time for the fellas." She smiled benignly at me. "I am glad she has met up with a smart fella like you."

I said that I was glad, too.

"Few years different in her age and yours don't make no difference one way or the other," said Mrs. Novotny. "Few years one way or the other."

I nodded, sampling a cookie cut in the shape of a star; it was delicious. I said so.

Since by this time it was clear that Mrs. Novotny was not quite the well-traveled woman of the world her daughter had indicated and Letty's father had probably not been quite as highly placed in the Quaker Oats hierarchy as his daughter's manner suggested, I thought it would do no harm to find out exactly how close to President Eduard Beneš of Czechoslovakia Letty's grandfather had been.

I believe I said, "President Beneš is certainly doing a wonderful job, isn't he, Mrs. Novotny?"

I believe Mrs. Novotny said, "I thought was Roosevelt president."

I do not know what I said in answer to that, but I do remember that Mrs. Novotny spoke several times—and warmly—of marriage, and she cited several instances in which an age differential had made no difference at all or had even *helped* some marriages, particularly when the *wife* was older.

There was more; I can't remember what.

Then Letty got home from work, and she was very upset when she saw me. "You're not supposed to be here for twenty minutes yet," she said. "You're always early. That's a very sure sign of a person's insecurity. How *long* have you been here?"

"Not long," I said. "But I've had time to read almost all of Otto Zorich's book about world-changing."

Letty glared at me. "Very funny," she said.

Then in the manner of a gracious lady distributing Thanksgiving largesse to the poor, Letty turned to her mother.

"Hello, mother dear," she said, kissing Mrs. Novotny on the forehead.

The tone and the gesture clearly startled Mrs. Novotny, who said, "You like a glass of milk, Letitia, cup of coffee?"

"No, mother," said Letty. "I'm going to dress. Immediately as of now, and you had better come button me up."

Mrs. Novotny nodded but didn't move.

"*Now*," said Letty, "and I mean it."

Her mother, puzzled but acquiescent, started toward the door behind Letty.

"I shall be only a minute, Joshua," said Letty.

"No hurry," I said. "I've got this fascinating book to read about everybody's world getting changed. The one by Otto Zorich."

"*Otto Zorich!*" said Mrs. Novotny. She said it the way people years later used to say, "*Sonny Tufts!*"

"Come on, mother dear," said Letty.

While they were gone, I read about Soviet Siberia, and from Anna Louise Strong's description of the place it sounded like something out of a Rudolf Friml operetta. Laughing peasants 'til you couldn't rest.

When Letty and I were ready to leave, Mrs. Novotny said she was sorry I couldn't stay for supper. I looked at Letty and said that I was, too, and that the cookies had been delicious.

Letty said for Heaven's sake it was getting late and quickly closed the door, more or less in her mother's face.

We walked to the sidewalk, and Letty turned to me angrily. "You rat," she said. "You came early just to *spy* on me."

"I like Otto Zorich's book," I said. "He's some writer, that Zorich."

"If there's anything I can't stand it's a spy," said Letty. "I'm glad they're shot. They deserve it."

I looked at her, and all of a sudden she was crying. They were honest tears, and it may have been then that Letty learned that they were her best weapon with me.

"I'm sorry," I said. "I'm really sorry." I handed her my handkerchief. "I wasn't spying on you, Letty. I like your mother."

"Oh, go to hell," said Letty, handing me back the handkerchief.

"What's all this about my not being able to stay for supper?" I asked.

"*Supper*," said Letty. "Other people have dinner. We have *supper*."

"I'll bet your mother's a good cook," I said.

"If you like beet soup and potato noodles and poppy seeds sprinkled all over everything," said Letty.

"How about goose with apple-and-sausage stuffing?"

"*That* we have *all* the time," said Letty.

"I love it. Are you a good cook? She says you are."

"Not me. She's tried to teach me, but I refuse to learn.[5] I'm going to *hire* cooks."

Letty walked on a few steps, and then she said, "Isn't it awful being ashamed of your own mother?"

"No," I said, "it's not awful. It's not at all unusual psychologically. Look at all the Greek tragedies."

Letty smiled at me, and she tossed her head in a way I was pretty sure she had practiced in front of a mirror. "You're a very nice boy, Josh," she said. "I don't know why the kids don't like you."

"Who cares about something like that?" I asked, caring.

"I'm going to get as far away from White Street as anybody can get," said Letty.

On the way to the movie after we left Bishop's Cafeteria, I asked Letty, "In what type way did you change Otto Zorich's world for him?"

"Please. Let's not talk about him," said Letty.

I made a rude sound. "How about changing my world after the show?"

"That's not funny. Not even remotely funny."

"And how about Angus MacDonald? Have you changed his world for him yet?"

"It's got Helen Twelvetrees," said Letty, speaking of the movie. "Some people think I look like her. Do you?"

---

5 Letty was right about that; she never learned to cook. One of the very early strains on our marriage was a casserole dish—"slops," I called it—consisting largely of tuna fish and corn flakes.

I said that the comparison was odious; I said Letty was twice as good-looking as Helen Twelvetrees.

When Letty and I got back to the house on White Street, there was a large pasteboard box next to the bowl of wax fruit on the sideboard, and on the box was a note written on a sheet of lined tablet paper:

"For Mr. Bland from Mother Novotny."

"Oh, God," said Letty. "It's probably about twelve dozen cookies and six fried chickens. Something ghastly like that. She's *always* putting fried chicken in my suitcase when I'm going back to school. I throw it out before I get to the Pi Phi house. All my dear sisters need is to find a little fried-chicken grease on my formal."

"It's not a *formal*," I said. "I've told you, and I happen to like fried chicken. Tell your mother thanks very much."

Then I started out, but I saw how Letty looked. So I went back, put down the box, took Letty in my arms and said, "I love you."

We kissed; I was beginning to understand why kissing was rated so highly.

"Your mother hates my guts," said Letty, "and so does your so-called friend Hughie."

"Give me another kiss," I said, in what seemed to me about the way Preston Foster had said it to Helen Twelvetrees in the movie.

Letty looked around the small room, and she said, "When I was a kid I used to think if I closed my eyes long enough, I'd find myself someplace else, but I never did."

"You will," I said. "I'll see to it."

"I want to get so far away nobody's ever heard of White Street or potato noodles," said Letty.

Well, Letty hasn't got quite that far, but I'll tell you this:

Once many years later when I was Out There Letty and I had dinner at Romanoff's. I forget why.

Letty ordered, and I said to the waiter, "Do you happen to have any potato noodles? I don't see any on the menu."

The waiter, who was probably a grand duke at least, gave me a very White Russian look, then shook his head.

"What in the *world* are potato noodles?" said Letty. "They sound like *fun!*"

I gave Letty a White Russian look.

"Oh, my God," said Letty. "I forgot I was with you."

She blushed, and then she laughed, nervously.

There will be more about my early relationship with Letty, but right now I'm going to skip quite a few years. I'm going to talk about where Letty has got to and how she's changed—if she's changed.

Two examples:

Example 1: A lunch Letty and I had in New York a little more than three years ago. The place, Twenty-One. It was a July afternoon.

I arrived on time, which was early. When Letty arrived half an hour later, she kissed me on the forehead and said, "Why in the world don't you shave all that hair off your face?"

I asked about my daughter Taffy. Letty said Taffy was fine. She said Taffy sent me her love.

I asked about Letty's second husband, Harry. Letty said that Harry sent his love.

Letty had two Gibsons, and I had three cups of coffee. I explained that I had become a member of Alcoholics Anonymous.

Letty said, "For God's sake." Then she said that I had been drunk the entire eleven years of our marriage, an exaggeration; she said that *she* had suggested several times that I join A.A., not so; she said that if I had joined A.A. *then* our marriage might have lasted, and so on, and so on.

Then she said a number of things, largely inaccurate, about A.A., and she said thank God Harry didn't drink. She said, "As a matter of fact, Harry is as different from you as day is from night. In every way."

What I did was nod.

Then Letty named several movie stars who are members of A.A. That concluded that part of her lecture; she sipped at the last of the second Gibson, and since I am a great believer in holding up my end of the conversation, I told two jokes.

Of the first, Letty said, "The way they tell it on the Coast is this," and she told it that way. Of my second joke, Letty said, "Is *that* just getting back here? Harry brought *that* back from the studio at least six months ago."

After that, we talked about nothing for a while, and then we had lunch.

During lunch, Letty kissed and was kissed by three other refugees from that Absurd Area. In addition to being big touchers, all of those people Out There are big kissers.

They all agreed—they always do—that the weather in New York was "just ghastly" and that there wasn't a play that was "worth seeing" and that you couldn't get a decent fresh fruit salad *anywhere* in town, and so on.

When the coffee arrived, I said, "Letty, I'm going to get married again."

Letty looked closely at me to see if I was serious. "Well," she said. "So that's the reason for the A.A. kick. Congratulations. Is it anybody I know? Or is it one of those glamor pusses of yours?"

"It's a woman named Charley Barr," I said.

Letty said, "Umm."

I said, "She's an editor at Highland House."

"How old is she?" asked Letty.

"Over thirty," I said, "only don't ask me how much over thirty because I don't know."

"Charley," said Letty. "That is an odd name."

"It's for Charlotte," I said.

"Oh. Where's Charlotte from?"

"Lansdowne," I said. "It's near Philadelphia."

"Very Main Line, I suppose," said Letty. "Up to her elbows in breeding. Very thin, very coltish, very Katie Hepburn. Right?"

"Not so far," I said, "but keep trying."

"Definitely over thirty, though."

"Definitely."

Letty thought this over for a moment, and then one of those odd actors with an odd name passed, and they kissed, and Letty told him who I was. He said, "I warn you; I'm going to be in one of your plays yet."

I nodded; Letty smiled, and I saw that although the dentists Out There are very clever, they have not been able to disguise the fact that Letty had not worn braces on her teeth when she was a girl.

The odd actor walked on, and Letty said, "I don't care what anybody says, I like him."

I said, "He's a regular All-American boy is what he is."

Letty sipped at her demitasse. She looked well. By *their* standards, which are not *my* standards, she was well dressed. She wore a lot of dark pancake, but you could see that the lines of dissatisfaction had deepened under the pancake and the suntan. Letty had on a dress that was burnt orange in color, and the cloth had a lot of urns stamped on it. Her hair, which has gone through a lot of alterations, was jet black, and it was piled in great loops on top of her head. The whole thing looked very precarious, and I kept hoping that Letty wouldn't move her head too far or too fast.

Letty's lipstick was very dark and quite wrong for her, and her nails were the same shade of orange as the dress. Her hands like her teeth showed the result of considerable expensive care, but they were still her mother's hands.

Letty put down her cup.

"Charlotte must be at least thirty-five," she said. "At least. Charlotte sounds like a brain. Is she?"

"Charley," I said. "Her name's Charley."

Letty laughed and, through much practice, the laugh sounded almost relaxed.

"She really sounds like a brain," said Letty. "You mean you've met your intellectual equal at last? Phi Beta Kappa? I.Q. 479? You probably should have married a brain the first time round, and I never was one. A brain. Well. Well."

I looked at Letty and waited, knowing there was to be more.

"I've often thought you might have been happier if you'd married that Matty Hare-lip or whatever her name was. She did have brains, and so what if you couldn't understand what she was saying?"

I did not respond.

"Is Charlotte pretty?" asked Letty.

"I think so," I said.

Letty examined my face. "No," she said, triumph in her voice. "No, Charlotte is not pretty. I can always tell what you mean. God knows I had time enough to learn. This her first go-round at the altar?"

"She's been married once before," I said.

"Well, they say you choose a second one just like the first one," she said, "though I must say Harry's as different from you as day and night. Every jot, tittle, and iota of him."

She laughed again. "Remember when I asked you what a jot was, and you said it was the same size as a tittle, only rounder?"

I said I remembered.

"Just don't ever forget the lovely times we used to have together," she said. "We almost never fought. Until the very end. Did we?"

I looked at her and saw that she believed what she was saying.

"I'm very glad for you," she said. "I hope you and Charlotte will be very happy together."

Then she glanced at the most expensive wrist watch money could buy and said that it was time for her to run. However, I didn't think she was through yet, and I was right.

"I hope you'll be very happy," she said again, and then she added, "You and I could never have made it. Not in one million years. Don't you agree?"

"Not in a million years."

"I think about it sometimes," said Letty, thinking about it. "You do, you know, once the tumult and shouting are all over. Don't you?"

"Sometimes."

"When we were first having our trouble, I used to think if we'd got married in a church or something like that everything would have been different. Of course, your trouble was you weren't ready to settle down yet. You had ants in your pants."

Having made up her mind about that, Letty started putting on a pair of white gloves that looked too white against the thin and mottled brown arms.

I had been waiting for the right time to say what I had on my mind, what had been my reason for asking Letty to have lunch with me, but I realized that, as always, there would never be a right time.

I tried the indirect approach. "I want you to meet Charley."

"I'd like very much to meet her sometime."

"How about having a drink with us? This afternoon or tomorrow afternoon before you have to catch your plane?"

"I'm terribly sorry, doll, but I'm all booked up. Maybe next time I'm in town. You going to live in the city?"

"In the country," I said, and I told her I had bought some land near Sloane's Station and was going to build a house there.

In some ways I may be smart, but I am not very bright.

"Oh," said Letty. "Oh, really."

I had never built a house in the country for Letty, and I could see that she was thinking of that.

She finished stretching the left glove, and then for a moment the burnt-orange nails of her right hand tapped an angry, familiar beat on the brown left arm.

I watched, and I waited.

"Have you seen *Pajama Game*?" asked Letty.

I said that I had. I didn't know what was coming, but I was ready for something.

"The man who wrote it's from Iowa, you know."

I said that I knew.

"He's really got it made, hasn't he?" she asked.

I said that the author seemed to be a very talented man and that he was certainly very successful.

"And you hate his guts," said Letty. "Anybody else from Iowa who succeeds, you hate their guts."

"All right, Letty. I hate his guts."

"Whatshisname, the man who wrote *Pajama Game*, is about your age, isn't he?"

"I guess so."

Letty's right hand gave another impatient yank to the left glove, and the arm-tapping was resumed.

"Did I tell you I met this terribly nice young director who's just come out?" asked Letty. "He's the one who's going to do the next Faulkner picture. What's its name? You know me and Faulkner."

"*Requiem for a Heavyweight Nun*," I said.

"That's the one," said Letty. "Anyway, you'd like this Georgie Campbell, and you know something: he went to Pegasus. Years after us, of course. I mean to him we're ancient history. He didn't even know *you'd* been there until I told him. I mean apparently they don't even talk about you any more. George Campbell. You'd like him. Terribly talented and terribly attractive, too. And not queer for a change. You know what this one terribly attractive queer boy said, the one that's always camping? Louis Arno, the dancer but he's married. He said being queer's just like communism. He said in the Thirties all the creative people were Communists and now they're all queer. Isn't that a hoot?"

I said that it was.

"*Anyhoo*, when I told George Campbell *when* we were at Pegasus he was very surprised. He said he never heard anybody say a *word* about you all the time he was on the campus. He also said you have certainly been stinking up quite a few theaters the last couple of years with the productions—"

"Is that all, Letty? Is that the end of the story?"

"Now you're getting mad. Just like always."

She smiled patiently at me. "My only point is you were the belle of the ball in college, and people like Georgie Campbell were hardly born yet, and now he's going to direct one of the biggest pictures—"

"I get the point, Letty," I said. "I understand what you're getting at."

It was as if I had not spoken.

"And Norman Levine," said Letty. "I mean whoever in the wide and shining world would have thought he'd get a Nobel prize— what was it for?"

"Inventing gunpowder," I said.

Letty didn't hear. "He had his picture on the cover of *Newsweek* and all those magazines. Normie and I used to date, you know."

"No, I didn't know," I said. "That is one I missed. Tell me."

"Well, I did," said Letty, believing it. "You've just forgotten, doll."

"Letty, would you mind not calling me doll?"

"He wanted to marry me. I used to invite him to all the Pi Phi dances before I had the great, good fortune of meeting you."

I knew perfectly well that Letty had not taken a chemistry major from the Bronx named Norman Levine to a Pi Phi party, but I didn't say so.

"He was always after me to marry him," said Letty. "He didn't like you. I remember that. All flash, I remember his saying. Joshua Bland is *all* flash."

I reached in my pocket for a cigarette and realized that my hands were trembling. Letty could still do it; she still knew how to get me.

I kept my hand in my pocket, and I said, "Well, maybe next time you're in New York we'll be able to get together, you and Charley and I."

"What kind of a house are you building?"

"Modern," I said, "mostly glass."

"It sounds sweet. I don't like glass, though; it's awfully hot. Unless you have air-conditioning, and you always hated air-conditioning. Are you going to have—"

"No," I said. "Neither of us like air-conditioning."

"Well, it's going to be awfully hot in July," said Letty, "and I've got to run and run. I'm late and late and late."

Then I said it, knowing better.

"Letty, Charley and I would like to have Taffy come and spend some time with us."

Letty smiled some, keeping her lips over the reconstructed teeth.

"Don't be silly, Joshua," she said.

"I don't think that's so silly," I said.

"The answer is no, and no *if*'s, *and*'s, or *but*'s about it. No."

"Would you mind telling me why?"

"Yes, I'd mind," said Letty, her voice getting a familiar edge to it.

If Letty and I still had been married, I would have stopped right there. During our marriage there was almost nothing I ever wanted enough to argue with Letty when her voice had that edge.

Letty said, "I believe we have been over this one million nine hundred and sixty-seven thousand times."

"Please," I said. "Just for a couple of weeks next summer."

"No," said Letty. "I'm sorry. Absolutely no."

A woman at the next table turned and looked at Letty, whose voice carries.

Letty said, "I am raising Taffy as a normal, healthy American girl, and Harry is a normal, healthy American father. And that is that. I am not going to have Taffy grow up with a screaming neurotic and an alcoholic to boot and you've tried staying on the wagon before, many, many times, I might add. And you have no moral or legal right to ask."

"All right, Letty."

"You've got off pretty easy—financially and every other way—as far as Taffy is concerned."

"All right, Letty."

"And don't you ever forget it."

The woman at the next table whispered something to her companion, who looked at Letty, smiled and nodded.

"I had enough on you to crucify you," said Letty, her voice on the rise. "Not to mention getting every cent you had to your name. Instead, I didn't even want to ask for *any* alimony."

She believed that, too.

I started to rise, and I felt the half-forgotten sting of tears that Letty was always able to bring to my eyes.

"All right then," said Letty. "No more talk about *adopting* Taffy."

I nodded and motioned for the check.

"I'm bringing Taffy up in a nice, normal, average American home," said Letty.

I signed the check, not looking at it.

"Did you hear what I'm saying?" Letty asked.

"All of Twenty-One has heard."

"You never want to listen to anything. That was one of your troubles. You never listened."

And so on.

At the top of the stairs, Letty said, "Let's not part bad friends."

I did not reply.

On the stairs, Letty met two other Prominent Personalities from Upsidedown Land. They commented on the fact that the theater was dead and the weather "just ghastly." A woman whose name

I can hardly forget said that she had just been at the Parke-Bernet galleries, where she had purchased a Dufy.

"Biggest Dufy in the world," she said. "Eighty-five thou."

"I'm on my way there right now," said Letty.

While I waited for my hat, Letty wanted to know where Charley and I were going on our honeymoon, and, since it no longer mattered, I said Paris.

"Have you got a good black-market man in Paris?"

"No."

"Harry's got the best there is," she said. "Our whole last trip practically didn't cost us a cent. Except for the money Harry lost the last night at Monte Carlo. He lost about eight thou in one night. But this black-market man he's got in Paris is the best there is. I'll give you his name and address."

"Goddamnit, no," I said.

But Letty was already writing something on a card with a gold fountain pen.

"Here," she said, shoving the card into my hand. "Maybe you'll change your mind later."

I let the card drop to the floor. A boy in uniform stooped and picked it up. He looked to see which of us to hand it to, then handed it to Letty, who looked at me again, shrugged, and put the card back in her purse.

As the man opened the door of her taxi, Letty said again, "Let's not part bad friends, Josh."

"So long, Letty," I said.

I started toward Fifth Avenue, and I heard her tell the driver, "Parke-Bernet and snap it up. I'm late."

And I thought that Letty had always been late and always would be, and I thought maybe they'd have the largest something or other still left. Maybe a Picasso, and Letty would buy it.

Letty was certainly not going to buy the second largest of anything. (Who would? Would you?) And the only trouble with the largest is that it would not be large enough. Nothing is ever large enough for Letty.

Then her cab passed, and a brown and white and orange stick waved at me, and a voice that carries shouted, "I wish you and Charlotte all the happiness there is in the world."

And that was what happened on the next-to-final time I saw Letty Bland Lowenstein *née* Novotny.

Example 2: My final encounter with Letty was early this summer. I was Out There. The reason is of no importance. I was up to no good; you can be sure of that.

I wanted to see Taffy; so I called Letty, and she said that Taffy was away at camp.

I said that I happened to have the afternoon free and would like to drive out to see Taffy, wherever she was.

Letty said, "Out of the question, doll. Taffy's in the High Sierras, accessible only by mule back, and I wouldn't let them let you in even if your vertigo let you get there. Come here for supper anyway. Harry's home."

When I had adjusted to my disappointment about Taffy, I said, "Supper. *Well.*"

"Sure, doll. Words like that are now part of my colorful Iowa past."

"Umm," I said.

"At seven," said Letty. "Harry'll be tickled to see you."

I knew that if there was one thing Harry would not be, it was tickled to see me.

Here I have to say the fewest possible words about Harry Lowenstein.

Harry's equivalent of White Street is somewhere in Brooklyn. I've been told that his first movies were circulated exclusively at bachelor parties, and I see no reason to doubt it. Harry, like my neighbor and enemy, Pism C., soon caught on to the fact that the big loot these days is in the Bible. If the Bible Book Biz is Big, Bible Show Biz is monstrous, and monstrous is what Harry's Epics are.

I have never seen a whole one, but I am occasionally trapped by a Coming Attraction, which is the best part of any movie anyway. Hughie Larrabee and I once wanted to open a movie theater that showed only Coming Attractions. I still think we had something there.

In a typical Harry Lowenstein Coming Attraction, the dialogue is what those people Out There, not one of whom has ever listened to anybody but himself, think is colloquial.

What's more, if you don't actually see J.C., you at least hear a lot of talk about him.

For instance, you'll see Paul—the one who got to be a saint—seated at a sidewalk cafe in Jerusalem. He is drinking a Coke. There's a tie-in; Paul drinks Coke, and the Coke people plug the picture. All clear?

Paul is drinking and fanning himself with a copy of *The Judea Daily News*. This helps Harry's Epic get an almost certain four stars in *The New York Daily News*. See how these things work out if God's on your side?

I might add that Paul has his shirt off; he is drinking and fanning. He's beat, man.

Now two hastily dressed girls pass. Paul eyes them. His mind is on conversion.

Judas enters.

Paul: Hi, Jude. Draw up a chair. I'll stand you to a Coke.

Judas takes off his shirt; he sits.

Paul: Where's He at?

Judas, shaking his head sadly: I've told Him to watch His step. If I've told Him once I've told him a dozen times that if He doesn't watch His step—

You get the idea; I do anyway, and as I say I've never seen a whole Lowenlet Production. That's the cute name Harry's thought up for his company, a combination of part of his name and part of Letty's.

Anyway, this is about Letty's second husband, a man who is kind to animals, mean to people, and humorless. All of them Out There are humorless, particularly those who write comedies. Also Harry is rich. As Croesus? I wouldn't put it past him.

At exactly seven-ten of the evening I'm discussing, I pushed a button on the door of the crypt inhabited by the Lowensteins.

After a few bars of Beethoven's *Ninth* on the door chimes, the Master of the House appeared at the door. He had just come in from the pool, and he was dripping, and there is a great deal of him to drip.

He invited me in, wrapping himself in a clearly colossal towel. He offered me a wet hand, which I touched. He asked if I was still on the A.A. kick and when I said I was he told a pale, exquisite Chinese girl in a maid's uniform that I would have coffee, black. Then he motioned me into a chair that must have been designed by somebody who had heard about sitting but who had never done any or seen any done.

Harry excused himself, and I nervously stirred the coffee the maid brought, trying not to look behind me.

When I am Out There, I am always afraid somebody is going to come up behind me, tap me on the shoulder and say, "Come on, Bland. The jig's up."

The Lowenstein living room is depressing, and it is ugly, and it is very large. If the Olympics are ever again held Out There, it would be a nifty place to have the track events.

As I think I mentioned, the house was not cheap.

"This house cost Letty and me half a mil," Harry once said. Personages Out There always tell you what they pay for things.

What I said to Harry was, "I can see that, and, believe me, it'd be cheap at half the price."

Harry narrowed his extremely narrow eyes. "How's that?" he asked.

"I'm just surprised a half-mil is all it cost," I said. "It looks to me like a three-quarters-of-a-mil house if it's a cent."

Harry looked closely at me, but he let it pass.

Harry can't tell about me. He once told Letty that all the hair on my face makes him nervous.

"I'm always afraid Bland's pulling my leg."

When Letty reported Harry's fear to me, I said, "You can absolutely guarantee Harry that I will never under any circumstances pull his leg."

Anyhow, the lovely Modern French Provincial Home the Lowensteins pig it in is the work of an architect whose name is known to me, but it surely cannot be known to the American Institute of Architects.

The furniture can best be described as awful, and on the evening I'm telling you about there was a Rouault on the wall which looked to me like the biggest Rouault in the world.

But back to the evening itself, back to an At Home with the Lowensteins.

When Harry came back into the living room, he was wearing a pair of pea-green trousers, chartreuse silk slippers, and a scarlet kimono which I believe he thought made him look like a mandarin but did not.

"Well, the Epic's in the can," he said, mixing himself a ginger ale and ice. He doesn't drink. Very few of them do.

"But there are still a few odds and ends before I want anyone to see it," he said. "I'm a perfectionist, you know."

I said I knew.

"You don't know what you're missing," said Harry. "The Italian government lent me their whole army. Eight thousand Wop soldiers in one scene alone. Nine casualties."

I nodded.

"It's the best thing I've ever done, and she's marvelous. I don't honestly think there ever has or ever will be a Mary Magdalene to equal hers. There's one scene where she's naked from the waist up, and I can quote Bible and verse to prove it. It'll tear your guts out," said Harry.

I said, "Harry, you don't really believe all this shit, do you?"

Harry turned and looked at me, and for a moment he was no longer playing the fool, the fool that a great many people along the way had at one time or another underestimated, including the fool he was then looking at. Harry had the handle; Harry had what it takes, and he also had my wife and my daughter.

He smiled the condescending smile of the winner, and he said, "We had a writer at the studio, and one night he got a little high at a party, and he said to me, 'Lowenstein, if you're so rich, why ain't you smart?' The next morning I got the sonofabitch fired, and he ain't worked in this town since."

He paused to be sure he had made his point, which he had, and then he went back to playing the role he has chosen for himself.

"It's Academy Award material if ever I've seen Academy Award material," said Harry. "I expect at least six awards."

I saw a dreamy look come into Harry's eyes; he was already composing his acceptance speech.

"I always knew I had it in me," he said, and then he said, "I didn't get a picture today. We'll just have to talk."

What Harry meant was that he would not be able to show a movie in the forty-seat theater he and Letty have in that Canyon Road mausoleum.

You see, most evenings Out There, you get up from the table, and before you can say Courvoisier those people are showing you a movie. That's about all they do after sundown, look at movies. All those stories you've read. Lies, all lies. Those people just look at movies in the evenings. They don't see these movies, but they keep right on looking at them.

"There's this one scene where you see His shadow and hear His voice," said Harry.

"Who handles that assignment?"

"Fabian," said Harry, "and that kid gives a performance that—"

For a moment there, I thought Harry might break down at the thought; fortunately, however, Letty then entered, upstage right. She was wearing a gunny sack and some diamonds and some rubies.

Harry kissed her lustily, and since they only despise each other, he said, "How's my sweetheart?"

His sweetheart passed a handkerchief across her lips and said that she was glad to see me.

Time passed. Dinner was served, and during dinner the following words were (among other words) spoken:

Harry: Bumblebee [that's Letty] and me care nothing whatsoever about money in any way, shape, or form. Do we, honeybun?

Honeybun struggled with a piece of beef stroganoff.

"Why," said Harry, "if we lost all our money tomorrow afternoon and had to move into a little $4oo-a-month bungalow in Brentwood, it wouldn't mean a thing to us. We'd just snap our fingers. That's what you have to do, Bland. Snap your fingers at adversity."

He snapped his fingers while I choked over a piece of stroganoff.

For the benefit of those who take over this charred peach after we have been dislodged, I would like to add that none of the Personages Out There know anything at all about food, and I have eaten many meals in Happyland that prove it.

In this instance, the Chinese cook—and we all know how clever those people are and what a sense of rhythm they have—had substituted pieces of Harry's old belts for the filet, but the cream was sour all right.

For dessert, we had *fraises des bois* and Devonshire cream.

"They were flown over the polar route," said Letty.

"I always knew those French lessons would come in handy sometime," I said.

"I liked you better when you were drinking," said Letty.

Later, during an eternal evening, Harry revealed that he had hired my neighbor and enemy Pism C. as technical adviser for his next picture.

"I'm paying him $8,000 a minute," said Harry. Maybe it was $8,000 a second. I'm not sure.

"Not that he cares about money," said Harry. "Money means no more to him than it does to us, does it, sugar plum?"

Sugar plum was silent.

"Nope. Every cent goes to charity," said Harry. "Every red cent."

I said that I knew that, that one of Pism C.'s favorite charities was just down the road from me.

A moment of silence passed, each of us searching for a way to fill in the vacuum.

Finally, I said to Harry, "This one going to have the dog in it?" I was testing one of my favorite ideas.

"What dog's that?" asked Harry, his voice sharpening.

"Well," I said, "a lot of Biblical scholars have tried to suppress the fact, apparently because they hate dogs, but the Dead Sea Scrolls *prove* beyond reasonable doubt that Jesus had a dog."

It was as if I had told Harry that all the stuff buried at Fort Knox was his, that all he had to do was cart it away.

"You're kidding," he said, his eyes popping.

"No," I said. "You've read the Edmund Wilson book, of course."

"What book's that?" asked Harry, grabbing at my arm, as they all do.

"Edmund Wilson," I said. "His book on the Dead Sea Scrolls *proves* that Jesus had a dog."

"Why wasn't I given a synopsis of that book?" said Harry. "*That* book is right up my alley. If I find out—well, there will be a shake-up in the story department, and you can quote—"

"A collie, as I recall," I said.

"Harry," said Letty. "He's joking."

"Joking," said Harry, getting his left eye back in its socket. "Joking about a thing like *that*?"

While Harry got his right eye back in its socket, Letty said, for a second time, "I liked you better when you were drinking."

After a while I said, "What's the name of the movie you and the reverend are working on, Harry?"

"Well," said Harry, releasing my arm, which to this day still has several small black-and-blue marks. "Well, I don't think jokes about Him and dogs are funny."

Then he assumed his Christlike pose. "What's it called?" he asked himself. Then he answered himself. "It's called, *The Thirty Pieces of Silver*."

"Nifty," I said.

"That's what I told Pism. I said that with a title like that all we have to do is open the box office in the morning."

"And Lord how the money rolls in," I said.

"That's the idea. You've got the idea," said Harry.

"What's the new epic about?"

Harry stopped pacing; he did the little fox-trot he does every time the odor of money assails his delighted nostrils. He looked down at the lighted expanse of his swimming pool (or else it was the Pacific Ocean; big anyway). He smiled on his tiled bathhouse, which is slightly larger than the house on White Street in which Letty was born and raised. He looked at the rolling lawn, at the weeds which in That Desert are mistaken for flowers; he checked the wall to see if the World's Largest Rouault was still there. It was.

Then Harry seated himself in his custom-built chair.

"What's it about?" he asked himself. Then he answered himself. "Well, it's about how people today are too materialistic-minded. Now you take your average movie-goer—"

I laughed; I couldn't help it.

"I liked you better when you were drinking," Letty said again.

A few minutes later, Letty volunteered to drive me to my hotel to pick up my suitcase and then on to the airport.

"Which car you going to take, sweetie?" asked Harry.

"The Imperial," said Letty. "Of course."

"You mean the lightweight car," said Harry, laughing.

Letty turned toward him and frowned. "No," she said, "not in front of Josh."

"You know much about cars, Bland?" asked Harry.

"You are asking the wrong man," said Letty. "His driver's license has been revoked, which is a blessing for all of us. Behind a wheel he was Murder, Inc."

"I mean, Bland, if you were asked, just in a general way," said Harry, "which would you say—"

"Harry," said Letty, her voice rising. "I'll leave you."

"I'll walk to the garage with you," said Harry.

"Harry," said Letty. "I warn you; I'll leave you."

Harry took my arm, and the three of us walked out to the garage. Harry went up to the Cadillac, which was his.

"Now listen to this, Bland," he said, slamming the door, hard.

I listened.

Letty walked to the Imperial, which was hers. "All right," she said to Harry. "You asked for it."

Then to me, "Josh, listen to this." She slammed the door of the Imperial, hard.

I listened.

Harry opened the door of the Cadillac again. "Bland," he said. "I want you to give this your best thinking."

He slammed the door again. "Now which of these two doors has the heavier slam, would you say?" he asked.

"Listen," said Letty, slamming the door of the Imperial a second time.

"Listen," said Harry, slamming the door of the Cadillac a third time.

"That's not fair," said Letty, running over to the Cadillac. Her voice was in full fury. "Here, let me," she said. She grabbed the Cadillac door from Harry and slammed it, lightly, I thought. Harry ran to the Imperial, slamming that door, lightly.

"What's your opinion, Bland?" he asked. "Which is the heavier car, would you say?"

I said, "I'm an old Stutz-Bearcat man myself."

"Listen," said Letty. "Just listen."

And so on. The argument got quite acrimonious toward the end, and Letty used a few words she must have learned either in her youth on White Street or from me, when I was discharged from the Army. Harry used a few, too.

Just keep in mind a fat boy from Brooklyn, aged fifty, and a thin girl from Cedar Rapids, aged an official forty or so, running from Cadillac to Imperial and back again, screaming epithets.

I can think of no better way to conclude this portion of my remarks on Happyland.

On the way to the airport, Letty, who had been quiet for an unusually long time, finally said, "I'm grateful to you for one thing, doll."

"Would you mind not calling me doll?"

Letty said, "You've been bitchy all evening and were positively mean to Harry. His feelings were hurt. I could tell."

"His what were hurt?"

Letty said, "As I've observed before, doll, I liked you better when you were drinking."

I said, "You're grateful to me for one thing. What?"

"If you hadn't come to the Pi Phi party, I might have married Angus MacDonald."

"Or Otto Zorich, whose world you changed."

"Don't you ever forget anything? I wouldn't have married *him* for anything in the world. I told you there wasn't a sincere bone in his body, and I was right. Whatever else you say about Harry, at least he's *sincere*."

"He is that," I said. "Whenever I think of Harry, the first word that comes to mind is *sincere*."

Letty ignored me. "Angus Pangus I could have had. I was in love with him if you remember."

I said that I remembered.

"Thank heaven I didn't, though," said Letty.

"Being married to MacDonald wouldn't be so bad. If you were, you'd probably at this very moment be driving a brand-new Imperial to or from your lovely home in Des Moines, a city in which there are so many splendored mansions."

"Are you kidding?" asked Letty. "After the war, Angus stayed in the Army, and he was killed in Korea. The family lost its money, and now Angus's widow, who was a Kappa and a bitch on wheels, is clerking in MacDonald's ladies' ready-to-wear, selling eight-ninety-eight dresses to the *hausfraus* of Des Moines. Deliver me."

"How'd you find all that out?"

I didn't need to look at her. I could feel the smile as Letty exposed her expensively rebuilt teeth. She said, "I always find out everything I need to know. You know that, doll."

There was a silence, and then I said, "Letty, how come you took up with me?"

It was a question I had asked before, and the answer had varied from time to time.

"I've often wondered," said Letty. "I really often wondered."

After a while, she said, "I thought you were going to be head of it all. I thought you really were on your way someplace rather special. I mean you had the brains. Or so I thought."

"How wrong can you be?"

"At one time I thought maybe I could help you," she said. "I thought with all I thought you had on the ball maybe you'd still need somebody to carry the water bucket. Namely me. I was pretty sure you were going to be world champion."

A few miles farther on I said, "Is it nice at Taffy's camp?"

"A lot of the stars send their kids there," said Letty.

"Oh," I said.

We drove into the airport, and Letty stopped the car.

"What do you think of Taffy?" she asked.

"I didn't see her," I said. "As I recall, she's away at camp."

"Last summer," said Letty, her voice rising a little. "You know what I mean. When you saw her in New York last summer."

"She seemed fine to me," I said. "Just fine. She's a very pretty girl. Takes after you."

"You think I botched it, don't you?"

"I try not to judge people any more."

"Ha," said Letty. "Ha, ha, ha."

I opened the door of the heavy car, and a brown hand reached for my bag.

"He's not ready yet," Letty snapped at the hand, and it withdrew. I gently closed the heavy door of the car.

"You always judge everybody," Letty went on. "Everybody in the whole world. And nobody but nobody ever measures up to your goddamn stratospheric standards. Including me. Including your daughter. That was always *our* trouble. I *never* measured up. Well, I've got news for you, buster. You never measured up to mine. *Never.* You're a failure, kiddo."

I picked up my bag and once more opened the door of the car.

"A failure," said Letty. "Ex-prodigy. Ex-genius. Ex-everything."

I said give my love to Taffy when she gets back from camp, and I said good-bye.

Letty shouted after me as she had done so many times before but as she will now never do again.

"You're a smug bastard, and you always were," she shouted.

Well, there you have it, the beginning of my relationship with Letty, and the end of it.

I would like to be around for a while afterwards, though.

I know exactly what Letty will say. First off, she will tell anybody who will listen that her intuition always told her that I would do something like what I am about to do.

"Why do you suppose I divorced him?" she will ask. "I knew even then that he was a very, very sick man. I didn't want my little Taffy around a man like that."

And, "At least four analysts have given up on him, you know. Absolutely threw up their hands and said that Joshua Bland ought to be behind bars. And he was behind bars up at that place in New Haven until George Banning *bribed* somebody to get him out."

And, "He was out here in June, you know. Since Taffy was in camp, I thought it was safe enough to invite him for supper. It was the *least* I could do. I always was kind to the poor thing. Anyway, he was on this A.A. kick, and I said to him at the time that at least when he was drinking he was *quiet*. When he was drinking he'd sometimes just sit all evening, never once opening his mouth. But *sober* it was yackety-yak all the time. None of the rest of us could get a word in edgeways. And he said several positively obscene things to Harry. Just to shock Harry. Joshua Bland was jealous just because Harry happens to be a deeply religious man who happens to be bringing a spiritual message to people all over the world who in most cases haven't had the advantages we've had."

And, "Josh wanted me to drive him to the airport, but I said no. I said absolutely no. I said he had better take a taxi. I was afraid of him and don't mind admitting it. He had threatened my life. Several times."

And at some point Letty is certain to repeat two sentences she has said before, often in my presence, "Joshua Bland was all flash, not an ounce of substance to him. I knew I'd made a mistake an hour after he'd bamboozled me into marrying him."

Oh, my death will provide excellent dinner conversation for Letty for a while, but not for long. Memory is short Out There, and after a few weeks or months, when Letty speaks of me, somebody is sure to ask, "Who was Joshua Bland?"

Letty has lived Out There long enough to know that if they have to ask *who*, they don't care *who*.

It is now after eleven.

The effect of the joy pills wore off hours ago.

I must say something about Taffy. I must. But not now.

Taffy was conceived in a moment of anger, and I am too tired to describe that moment now. Maybe later, maybe not. I have told only one other human being about that moment, Dr. Baron in

New Haven, whom I loved and hated and feared and despised and admired.

He only nodded, but I thought he went a little white.

Right now, I'd better have dinner, or supper, whatever it is. It's in the oven. I said that. Louella left it.

Ab is back, and it is later. How much later I don't know.

I didn't eat. What I did—well, there's no escaping the fact of it. I had a drink. My first since the night Charley left. As if there were such a thing as *a* drink. I had a hundred drinks the night Charley left me—and a hundred more the night after. Then I stopped. It was no longer any fun—if, in fact, it was ever any fun.

But now. I guess maybe it was the thought of Taffy that did it. Let's say that. Let's use that as an excuse. As if I ever needed one. As if I couldn't always find an excuse.

I went on my last long bender about a month before Charley and I were married. It lasted five nights and five days.

After a hundred and twenty hours of straight boozing, I was taken to Towns Hospital—never mind who took me—and there they dried me out, and then I joined the Society of the Sauceless, the Drink-and-Tell Club.

I never liked it, though, which, again, puts me out of step with the times. Why, Out There A.A. is even bigger than Zen; Out There, in addition to your osteopath-psychiatrist, you have to have a membership in Drink-and-Tell. People who can't even get into the Diners' Club get into the Sauceless Society.

I didn't tell Charley, who is A.A. for reasons that are hers to relate and not mine, but I hated every meeting. Why? Not sure. Mostly, I think because I simply do not care for public confessionals. Because I do not care for humble pie. Because I can not accept their God.

True. I did stop drinking, but I never came across anything to take its place. I found nothing to quiet the torment that rages within me.

Maybe they do; they say they do, but they say it too often and too loud. My grandfather used to tell me, "Never trust a man who's always praying in public."

"...I sinned, brothers and sisters, Oh, sistern and brethren, I used to drink four fifths a day; I used to, etc., etc., Glory Hallelujah! Look at me now. I'm dry now. Nobody knows the troubles I've seen. Nobody, and so on."

It always struck me that the A.A. people have a lot in common with the M.R. people. The Moral Rearmament folks gave me quite a rush when I was in England the first time. They never got to me, but I did attend several meetings, and they, too, used to spend very enjoyable evenings talking about what miserable sinners they had been. What's more, they all wanted to join damp hands.

The A.A. people don't hold hands. What the A.A. people do is smoke like chimneys and drink uncounted cups of black coffee, and they tell you, publicly and privately, what bad boys and girls they were when they were on the sauce. Want to know something, Ab? There isn't one of them who has had a good time since. Except when they're shooting off their mouths about what a bad time they had when they were having a good time. Well, you get the idea, Ab. I don't have to rub your nose in it, so to speak.

You like another drink, Ab?

Well, I would. Yes, I would. Thank you very, very much.

It's silly to waste this tumbler on beer. This is a vodka tumbler if ever I saw a vodka tumbler.... Leaves you breathless.

Look, Ab. There's a fire in the woods behind the main house over there on Olympus. Bet you Hebe and her worshippers are offering up a few sacrifices. Human, of course. That Hebe never lets go of anything but people.

I wonder if they'd like a volunteer.

Available. Slightly burnt sacrifice.

I ever tell you about that sign they had at Buchenwald, Ab? Be patient. Your trouble is you never learned patience, and that was my trouble, too.

Anyway, stick around; you'll see the point; Hebe's fire over there on Olympus reminds me of the day we got to Buchenwald.

The sign on the large crematorium, the sort of Willow Run of the place, said:

Not a horrible and distasteful worm will feed upon my corpse, but a clean fire will digest it. I have always loved warmth and light. Therefore, burn but do not bury me.

Isn't that a beautiful thought, Ab?

Please don't insist on going out, Ab. Pretty please.

Sacha Jackson isn't that sexy, and, anyway, Ab, sex isn't worth it, and you can quote me.

All right, go out then, you heartless sonofabitch, but don't ever come back. Go out and stay out.

I know; I know. We are all of us prisoners of our own skin, but for some of us the skin is thinner. Thinner skinner, and I do know the meaning of insouciance.

Ab has gone out.

Burn but do not bury me.

There was another sign they had on the small, family-size crematorium at Buchenwald:

Jedem Das Seine; loosely, *Everybody Gets What He Deserves.*

As has happened often before, a thought has sobered me, an awful memory:

When we got to Buchenwald, ten machine guns were mounted on the front gate, and the SS had started destroying seventy thousand human pieces of evidence.

They didn't finish, though; we got there ahead of schedule, by about an hour.

I myself killed two of the SS with their own machine guns; a major from Chicago, Illinois, stopped me by slapping my face and kneeing my groin. He said that I had gone out of my mind.

Others of the SS were hanged; some were cut up; many were mutilated; and a few were thrown into the bear pit by the GI's. But not one was burned, and not enough were killed, not by me or by anybody else.

Sometimes you wonder about those seventy thousand people who except for our arrival would have been dead.

You keep listening for their voices. At least I do. Seventy thousand voices are a lot of voices.

I suppose they've forgotten, though. I suppose they've forgiven. It's all the rage.

What I remember is the smell of death and of evil. What I remember is the row of waiting nooses and the crematoria and the cord-wood piles of dead and the bear pit and the skeletons that were hunched onto shelves like bottles of poison, skeletons that breathed.

I looked at them, and then I heard from them an awful sound, and I asked what it was, and my colonel, who was pale and later sick near the place I had been sick, said that the skeletons were cheering our arrival.

There were tears in his eyes, and anger, too, once he had got over not believing what he had heard and seen.

We all had to get over not believing, and then we all had to take our revenge, and then, forever after, we all had to remember.

I remember when the major from Chicago stopped me from killing any more of the SS, I said this, I think to myself though perhaps aloud:

"Whoever else forgets, I shall not forget; whoever else forgives, I shall not forgive; whoever else is silent, I shall not be silent."

I have not forgotten, but I have forgiven—as I suppose one must. My only wish for the Germans has been—is now—that they not be so forgiving of themselves. My wish has always been that one among them rise and say, "There is blood on my hands. I am guilty...I am responsible."

But I hear no such voice, and I have not spoken. Not me. This is a time of silence and of shame—and I am part of it.

Jedem Das Seine. Everybody Gets What He Deserves.

The grass grows very green in Buchenwald. I went back a few years ago. The fine, patriotic citizens of Weimar, which is a few miles away, have not forgotten that it existed. Those good people never knew.

Jedem Das Seine....

(4) Under the shadow[6]

I don't know what time it was when I passed out. I vaguely remember opening the curtains, and there was a rim of pale pink on Olympus, what was left of Hebe's fire. After that, the blackout came, and I must have fallen or slipped to the floor, a burning cigarette still in my hand. Why did it have to go out, do you suppose? Why couldn't the fire have spread the two feet to the curtain, and caught there? After that, there would have been no stopping it, and no saving me. That is what I was talking about, wasn't it?

Burn but do not bury me.

I have now taken a cold shower and, with two green pills inside me, I feel no more than normally depressed. This is not unusual; for years I used to get an early-evening buzz on, sleep for an hour, shower, and then go out on the town for the rest of the night.

I must get on. But I do have to report this. I had the dream again, just before I woke up and found myself on the red carpet.

I screamed at the same moment as always, and when I awoke, I was sweating, and both my hands were trying to get a hold on the carpet.

Eventually, I found the strength to rise, and supporting myself on the bottom bookshelves, I made it to the bathroom.

Afterward, I went to the closet where among a few other odds and ends I brought back from the war I found Nick Contino's cigarette lighter.

I held it in my hand for a while, remembering a day in December 1944, remembering the snow and the cold and the blood that seemed to be everywhere.

I remember cradling in my arms what was left of Nick. It had no head, and the once-brown arms were gray.

Sometime later two corpsmen came, and as they lifted the gray, headless thing onto a litter, Nick's cigarette lighter fell from a pocket, and I picked it up.

---

6 "Come in under the shadow of this rock, and I will show you fear in a handful of dust."—T. S. Eliot.

A third corpsman came then, and he saw the blood on me, and he saw the tears, and he held out his hand to me, and he said, "Come on, sergeant."

I looked down at the lighter I was holding, and I saw that it, too, was covered with blood.

It was then that I screamed, and in the dream, which has been recurring very often these last weeks, I scream at that same point.

Finally, on that dark December morning almost fifteen years ago, the corpsman put an arm around my shoulders and led me away.

I was still screaming.

I looked once more at the lighter and at the spot of rust which looks like blood.

After a while, I put the lighter back in the drawer and once more locked the closet.

(5) In which my career ends

As is surely apparent by now, I am a manic-depressive, in addition to all the other ailments. This is not a manic night.

After I locked up the lighter, I didn't feel like going on; so I glanced at a few scripts Pan had sent me "just in case you might be interested"—plays by old writers who have learned how to say it but who by this time have already said it and by young writers who haven't learned how and haven't got much to say anyway. Except for one girl. She is twenty-two; it is her first play, and there isn't an ounce of craftsmanship in it, but it has a good deal of vitality and urgency and a sense of the theater that you have to have by instinct; you can't learn it. I read only a few pages of the play; you can tell in a few pages, a few lines even. She's good, or could be.

But even if I weren't checking out, I wouldn't produce Miss Hopeful's play; a letter from Miss Hopeful's agent describes her: Miss Hopeful is from Virginia; she went to Randolph Macon; "You'd love her, Josh dear," the agent writes. Not so; I would hate her; I dislike even hearing about her. "Pretty and so unspoiled," writes the agent. "Knowing of your interest in developing new talent...she is so hoping that..."

Not me; no, Miss Hopeful. I have no interest in developing new talent; I have no desire to help anybody else become a Household Word or become rich and famous and indifferent. I watched my first playwright eat himself up in 1945, shortly after I got back from the wars. I watched him change from a sweet, callow boy of near-genius to a vain, self-abasing tyrannical monster.

Oh, he's writing still, and with great success, too. They say if he were to drop a hundred-dollar bill on the sidewalk, he couldn't afford to take the time to pick it up. I don't doubt it a bit. He is a virtuoso of the not-so-very unpopular cause, and he has won all the prizes there are—Emmies, Oscars, Christophers, and enough hams from the Barter Theater to open a delicatessen. The critics fall all over themselves in awarding him. You can see him on television, too; in fact, it is very difficult not to see him on television. He is always turning up with the collection of crotchets on "Guess My Racket." (I have never been on that program, but I did volunteer once. I wanted to turn the tables. I wanted the people on that panel to let me guess some of the things *they'd* do for money. They wouldn't let me, though....)

Yes, indeed. The Playwright I am credited with discovering is still around—a smile, a baritone voice, and a heart useful only for pumping blood. It is not only that his youth is behind him. Somewhere along the way he mislaid his identity, too. Even as I.

Sorry, Miss Hopeful. I've watched it happen too many times, and at first it made me angry, and then it made me sad, and after a while I turned my head and closed my eyes. Is what happened inevitable? I don't know. I do know I've never known anybody famous who wasn't also infamous.

It always hurts, too. In my youth, I used to think each disappointment would be easier to take: when I was twenty, I was sure that by the time I was thirty, a kind of callus would have grown over the hurting place; at thirty, I knew better, and at thirty-five, I was hanging on to Charley, knowing that if she let go of me, I would drown. Now I know it is never going to hurt any less, and I know that there is no way to untie the knot, and I know that even if there were, I wouldn't have the energy to do it.

For years now I have heard the whispered invitations from behind the door, and sometimes there is a tapping on the door, and of late *They* have been beating their fists against it.

I am now prepared to open the door, and accept.

I have gone full circle. "*Dis*honorable mention more like....No, you didn't darling; you did it for you. Everything was always for you."

I must now describe the years with "Can You Top Them?"

In 1933, when I was eleven years old, mother, Pavan, and I started commuting to Chicago almost every other week, sometimes more often. Occasionally we went farther.

There were five kids on the panel of the program—and Obadiah O'Ryan, the former vaudevillian who, because he had an I.Q. of about *minus* eighty was a very pleasant contrast to us five brats. O'Ryan asked the questions; we answered them. We, meaning an unending series of elderly children with atrocious manners, prodigious memories, and the kind of parents who under the Bland Plan for Shaping Up the World wouldn't be allowed to get near children, let alone breed them.

The program was broadcast on the radio forty times a year during the period I was on it; as a "regular" I appeared on it more often than any of the others except Lucille, an overdeveloped, strident little encyclopedia of nine who had as fully developed a case of penis envy as I've encountered in a lifetime of such encounters, and Ned Something, a dark-haired, gentle little boy of no more then eight who was born with total recall, a flair for figures, and, for parents, two of the most reprehensible human beings God ever let breathe.

Except for the time spent with Dielle Cranburg, the woman who ran the program and who was really very nice, the whole "Can You Top Them?" experience was a nightmare.

As I have said, I had always looked forward to the luxury of eating in a dining car on a train, but even that was not at all what I had expected. A typical meal:

"You're going to want a cheese sandwich," mother would tell me. "You don't need to look at a menu."

Then she would say to the waiter, "You mean a cheese sandwich is a *quarter*? That must be a misprint. And milk a *dime*? Impossible."

The waiter would shake his head. "No, ma'am, it's not a misprint."

"Highway robbery," mother would say. Then, "We'll have one cheese sandwich and a glass of milk."

When the sandwich came, mother always tested the bread, and three times out of four she'd send it back. "That's day-old bread," she would say. "Steward!" (Is this the same woman who only a short while before had insisted that *fresh* bread was responsible for most of the illnesses of the world, including rheumatism? It is indeed she. If anybody had had the courage to remind her of an inconsistency like this one, mother would have listened with bird-like intensity; then she would stretch her lips across her teeth and shake her head. "You are very much mistaken if you think I ever said a thing like *that*.")

When the steward came, mother would say, "He [meaning the waiter] is trying to palm day-old bread off on me, and the president of the Rock Island railroad it so happens is a very close personal friend of mine, and if you think for one minute..."

Sometimes the steward would try to argue with mother.

"Get me the conductor or whoever is in charge here," she would say. "I am not accustomed to dealing with underlings."

Mother was one of the very first take-me-to-your-leader people.

Usually, though, the steward had better sense than to open his mouth. The cheese sandwich would go back to the kitchen, and a few minutes later a cheese sandwich would emerge from the kitchen. I always felt it was the same cheese sandwich.

Mother always tested it. "That's more like it," she would say. "Don't try to palm your day-old bread off on me. I wasn't born yesterday, you know. Sonny, eat your sandwich.

"I'll just have this one little bite," she would add, taking half the sandwich.

That last was all right with me. I always had trouble choking down my half of the sandwich and swallowing my glass of milk.

"I don't believe in tipping," mother would tell the waiter as she paid the check. "Tipping is not the American way. Am I right?"

The waiter invariably said that mother was right.

I had looked forward to staying in hotels, but that was a let-down, too.

"We'll have one room," mother would say, "for the two of us."

"You and the little boy," the clerk would say, nodding, "and a single room for your husband?"

"Apparently you can't understand English," mother would say. "One room for myself and my husband. My son here sleeps with me, and we'll have the theatrical discount, of course. We're with 'Can You Top Them?' and judging by the business that has followed in our wake in other communities, you should be paying *us*."

That part about sleeping with mother, not so. I popped out of the womb, into a warming box, into a crib. I knew better than to get into bed with my mother when I was three weeks old. No, in hotels I slept on the floor. "One blanket's going to be enough for you," mother would say. "Heat travels down, you know."

God knows how many third-rate Chicago hotels we honored with our presence during the "Can You Top Them?" era. I don't believe we ever stayed in any of them more than once.

They'd have locked the doors.

Checking out, for instance—

Mother would say something like, "The bill has six telephone calls at ten cents each. I know for a fact that none of the three of us used the phone *once* since checking into this rattrap."

The cashier would say various things, and, finally, at the climax of the argument, mother would say, "Don't get impertinent with me, miss. I happen to be an old family friend of Mr. Kirkeby." (I don't even know if there was a Mr. Kirkeby, and I'm sure mother didn't either. Nowadays, mother would be flinging Mr. Hilton's name around.)

Finally, mother would say, "Get me the manager. Not the assistant manager or the assistant-assistant manager. I want the manager."

She would take a little notebook and the stub of a pencil out of her pocketbook; then she would say to the cashier, "And I want your name, miss. I will not forget any of this, and you can bet your bottom dollar on that."

Very often mother got sixty cents knocked off the bill. Believe me, it was cheap at half the price if you were a cashier or a hotel *manager*...

Sometimes, instead of objecting to the telephone charges, mother would say, "...and, furthermore, what is the meaning of this six-dollar-a-day rate? That's a mistake, of course. I asked for and was told that we had a four-dollar-a-day room, not to mention the theatrical discount to which we are entitled, in addition to which, judging by the business that has followed in our wake...."

Mother did have one minor come-uppance, on the first day she and I reported to the dark theater in Chicago in which the broadcasts and rehearsals for "Can You Top Them?" were held—when we were not on the road, that is. The office of Dielle Cranburg was in the same building.

Was the fog in Chicago always so dense? Was the angry wind blowing in from the lake always so angry? I didn't know; all I knew was I'd never been so cold.

Mother and I had walked all the way from the hotel to the theater, which was on a side street off Michigan Boulevard. By the time we got inside, I'd decided that both my hands and my ears would drop off. I didn't have on any mittens, nor a stocking cap. I was dressed in short pants; my knees were bare, and I had on a short jacket that wasn't warm enough. Mother had decided that mittens and a stocking cap made me look *countrified*.

"There is no reason to *advertise* the fact that you are from Iowa. We are at last going to have the opportunity to move among people of our own kind, and we must live up to it."

Little did she know.

If mother had thought she could get away with a Lord Fauntleroy haircut, I'd probably have had one, or else I'd have had the kind of boyish bob Jackie Coogan used to wear. By 1933, however, Jackie Coogan was a has-been; it was then Shirley Temple and Jackie *Cooper* time.

Anyway, this is what happened the first time mother marched me into Miss Cranburg's office. My teeth were still chattering, partly from the cold, partly from fear.

"Tell Miss Cranburg that Mother Bland and sonny boy are here," she announced to the secretary.

The secretary went into the inner office and emerged a few minutes later.

"Miss Cranburg will see the little boy," said the secretary. "She asks if you'd be kind enough to wait in the mothers' room, Mrs. Bland."

"In the *what*-room?" asked mother.

"In the room with the other mothers," said the secretary.

"I do not believe that you know to whom you are speaking," said mother, sweeping past the secretary and dragging me with her into Dielle Cranburg's office.

Miss Cranburg was seated behind a huge desk, and when she saw mother, she rose. She was a woman of forty, give or take a few years. She had a completely square figure; her arms and legs were the size and shape of four-by-fours, and her torso was like the trunk of a redwood tree. Her face was wide, disillusioned, plain to the point of ugliness, and altogether rather pleasant.

"Dielle, I'm delighted to see you again," said mother. "I'm Mother Bland, and this is sonny boy."

Miss Cranburg said nothing.

"You must remember me," said mother. "I was here last summer with my husband, Petrarch Pavan."

"Mrs. Bland, I must ask you to wait in the room with the other mothers," said Dielle Cranburg. Surprisingly, her voice was that of a sweet-tempered little girl. "I'd like to talk to Joshua alone," she said. "I will probably see you later in the day."

She went to a side door of her office and opened it. There must have been fifty mothers in the room just beyond, at least fifty, and there were even more of their terrifying offspring. Fifty women and fifty or more children, and there was not a sound coming from the room.

It was one of the most unsettling *sights* I ever saw, though. Fifty women sitting on straight-back chairs on both sides of a long, narrow room; each woman glaring at each other woman, and each with the excuse for her existence on a chair beside her. Each excuse stared straight ahead. There were maybe thirty blondined little girls with Shirley Temple curls, lipstick and rouge, bare knees and, as I was to learn, nasal voices and the worldliness of aging strumpets. There were at least twenty boys, many of them blondined and rouged and made up to look like Jackie Cooper. Little boys whose mothers had decided when they were born that no other woman would ever enter *his* life. In nine cases out of ten I doubt that any other woman ever did.

Once some newspaper took pictures of us. I haven't forgotten the caption over the page, "...the sound of childish laughter."

If there was one sound I never heard during all the time I appeared on "Can You Top Them?", it was that. God, I hate newspapers.

(For the record, nobody under eighteen has ever appeared in a production of Joshua Bland Enterprises, Inc. When I first started as a producer, I announced that it would be a waste of time—mine and theirs—for agents ever to send me plays in which there were parts for children....)

Anyway, Dielle Cranburg held open the door leading into the mother's room, and she said, "Mrs. Bland, it is one of the rules of this program that I insist on talking to the children alone. I know you won't mind waiting in here."

"*Mind*," said mother. "I absolutely refuse. I am not allowing my sonny boy to stay here without me. Heaven only knows what you might try to get him to *sign*."

Dielle smiled, tapping the twiglike fingers of her right hand on her left elbow.

"I never have and never will," said mother, vaguely, already beginning to waver.

Dielle Cranburg glanced at her wrist watch, which was somewhat larger than the dollar Ingersoll my father used to carry.

"You have thirty seconds to go to the mothers' room," said Dielle.

Mother gathered her dignity and her coat about her buttocks. I think she started to say, "I gather you don't know who I am," but she rightly decided that Dielle knew exactly who she was—and what. So she closed her mouth and went into the other room.

Dielle shut the door, then turned to me and smiled. "I'm sorry to have to be rude to your mother," she said.

I said, "I rather enjoyed it."

"Sit down, won't you?" said Dielle.

I did, on a chair next to her desk.

"Now tell me about yourself," she said. I imagine she was seeing how at ease I might be on the program. "What's your favorite hobby, for instance?"

"At the moment, architecture," I said. (Shades of Pavan.) "I like to look at beautiful buildings of all kinds, and I like to draw buildings of my own."

"Would you like to be an architect when you grow up?"

"Oh, no," I said, "not at all."

"Why?" asked Dielle.

"Well, in the first place architects don't make much money. That's because most people don't give a damn—I'm sorry, darn—where they live. In the second place most architects have to prostitute themselves. I mean most people don't *want* beautiful buildings. Most people *prefer* ugly buildings. It's one of the crosses architects have to bear. So they usually just prostitute themselves. It's very sad."

"What would you like to be then?" asked Dielle.

"A doctor, I guess," I said, "because they make lots of money and do lots of good in the world, and besides, they don't have to prostitute themselves—the way lawyers do, for instance." (I was naïve at eleven.)

"Have you ever listened to 'Can You Top Them?' on the radio?" asked Dielle.

"Oh, yes," I said. "I listen to it all the time. I think it's wonderful." (How little I've changed....)

"What do you really think of it?" asked Dielle.

"Not much," I said. "I mean I guess it's all right for what Mr. Mencken calls the boobs, but it's not the kind of thing *I'd* care to listen to on any regular basis." Pavan had bound copies of *Smart Set*, and I'd read practically every word H. L. Mencken had written up to then.

"How would you feel about being on it?"

"Well," I said, "I'd like to earn two hundred dollars a week."

(The above is perhaps the most precocious thing I ever said. In fact, that's the whole explanation for Out There, for television, for most of the crap printed in magazines, and so on. There isn't a pimp in any of those fields that would be seen dead looking at or listening to or reading the bilge he turns out for the boobs. Occasionally, a pimp tries to reform. Know what the boobs do then? The boobs demand more opiates. What's the answer? Don't ask me. I'm getting off the merry-go-round at the next stop.)

Not surprisingly, Dielle Cranburg decided I was exactly what she was looking for, and she was very kind to me the whole time I was on the program. Not only that, mother was never allowed in during any of the rehearsals, and, while she and the other mothers could attend the actual broadcast, Dielle told them, "You'll have to sit in the back, *way in back*."

By the way, don't think that all of the children on "Can You Top Them?" had Monstrous Mamas. No, some had Pernicious Papas. I still remember a day when I went into Dielle's office and saw standing in front of her desk a sturdy little boy who couldn't have been more than seven. He was weeping bitterly. A few minutes before, he had rushed off the stage during his first and last rehearsal. I guess he was terrified by the noise and confusion and by all the people.

Beside the frightened boy stood a tall, hard-faced, angry man, his father.

Dielle was saying to the father, "Some children just don't like to appear in public; it's nothing whatever against them."

"He'll appear on this program if I have to drag him on stage," said the father.

"Not on *this* program he won't," said Dielle.

She smiled at the little boy. "Good-bye, Philo," she said.

Philo cried even harder, and his father grabbed his arms and, lifting him off the floor, carried him from the room. A moment passed, and all we could hear were the frightened cries of the little boy and the angry voice of his father.

Dielle sighed, and then, half to herself, she said, "And, thus, another faggot is born."

I don't think Dielle ever guessed my terror. About a fourth of the time, we were on the road, broadcasting from cities other than Chicago. Wherever we went, though, there was always an audience in the theater of the kind of idiots who turn up for such events, and every time before I walked on stage, I went to the men's room and vomited.

That happened fifty-four times, and fifty-four times I then walked on stage, and as the idiot-applause reached my ears, I bowed, and I smiled, and I counted the house with my eyes.

Since this is the time for it, let me shamefacedly add that just a year after my last appearance, after the show had gone off the air, I stopped off in Chicago on the first lap of the trip to England.

The minute I got off the train, I grabbed a taxi and went to the theater off Michigan Boulevard, which was then unoccupied and dirty. I stood in front of the theater for several minutes, and during all that time nobody asked me for an autograph; nobody wanted to know if I really ate the same breakfast food as Jack Armstrong, the All-American boy (The Wheaties ads had said so). Nobody wanted to know whether I had had my picture taken with Shirley Temple; I had. Or whether I was in love with Baby Eileen, as had been reported in the columns. In fact, nobody noticed me at all.

Did I mind? You bet I did. I was heartbroken. But then I was on my way to New York, New York, and London, England, so I recovered. As I've said, my emotions, like those of most children, were extremely resilient.

Anyway, "Can You Top Them?" ended in late August 1936. No scandal. So far as I know, Dielle never gave anybody any answers. She didn't have to. As I remember them, the questions were never very complicated. We also each had our own dreadful specialty. I guess I've said that my memory used to be not only total but photographic. I'd be shown a dollar bill—just for a second—and then I would recite the eight figures and two letters in the serial number, forwards, backwards, and from the middle in each direction.... At that age, John Stuart Mill was translating Homer.

I'm not sure why the program went off the air. Maybe the sponsor didn't renew. Maybe the ratings had gone down—or were there ratings in those days? I don't remember.... A few years later the Quiz Kids came along, but I know nothing about them, though I once heard part of one of their broadcasts. I was in the Army, at Fort Jackson, South

Carolina. I got sick as a dog during the first five minutes and had to leave the service club where the program was turned on.

I still remember every detail of the final train ride back to New Athens. I remember mother sighing and saying, "I don't suppose I'll ever shop in Marshall Field's again as long as I live." She didn't either.

A moment passed. Mother said, "I knew the minute I walked into the office of that Cranburg woman that she had no understanding of show business, none whatsoever."

After another sigh, mother turned to me and said, "*Your* career is over, down the drain, up the chimney, and what have you. At fourteen."

She turned to Pavan, "What else is there, Petrarch?"

"Shut up, Celeste," said Pavan. "I'm reading."

Mother turned to me again. She was aching for a fight. "If you'd just tried a little harder, you could have been another Jackie Cooper." I had had a screen test when the whole gang from "Can You Top Them?" went Out There and made a short.

"I can't act," I said. "That's what the director told me."

"For that matter, I could have been another Norma Shearer," said mother, raising her voice so that the woman across the aisle could hear her.

"I'll miss Norma," said mother, having caught the woman's ear. "I'll never have another friend like her...."

(The day Norma Shearer shook hands with each member of the cast of "Can You Top Them?", mother stepped forward and said, "I'm an actress, too."

"On set," said the director.

"Excuse me," said Miss Shearer. They were shooting *Private Lives*.)

"A great lady," said mother. "Norma Shearer is a great lady."

The woman across the aisle, disbelieving, went back to her *True Story*.

Then mother had her final go at me. "I absolutely give up on you," she said. "Absolutely. I have given my all for you, but no more. No, sir. From now on I am going to look after my own interests."

"That's something to look forward to," I said, but I said it under my breath.

I must add that during the trip from Chicago back to New Athens, it looked to me as if my mother's prognosis was right. My career was behind me. All I had to look forward to was an anti-climactic senior year at Pegasus. What else was there?

(6) The irresistible end, or forgery as a fine art

Actually, my final year at Pegasus turned out to be the best.

There were several reasons for that: (1) I learned that the end sometimes does justify the means; (2) I had a good friend and a good teacher in a man named Orion Bernstein, and (3) Letty and I spent a great deal of time together, almost all of it enjoyable, and several times on the bank of the river, Letty came close to changing my world for me.

For the moment I've said more than enough about Letty; the forgery chronologically comes later, so I'll start out with these few words about Orion.

One day not long after our final return from Chicago, I heard mother tell Pavan, "I hear the new instructor in the philosophy department is one of the Chosen People and makes no bones about it."

"What's his name?" asked Pavan.

"Orion Bernstein," said mother, "and I hear he's bald as a baby."

"I'm taking his advanced philosophy," I said.

"I don't doubt," said mother. "I told you, Pavan, the way things are going at the college, sonny will be talking with his hands before you know it."

"Um," said Pavan, who was reading a book by E. M. Forster, the only living author he liked.

There were only half a dozen of us in Orion's Advanced Philosophy class, among them Norman Levine, a quiet, intense boy incapable of calling attention to himself. He's the one who won the Nobel Prize in chemistry a couple of years ago—and the one Letty wrongly remembered inviting to Pi Phi parties.

Orion himself was a small man; Letty said he was only two feet tall, but Letty hated him. He was five-six, I imagine, and everything about him was small. He had a long, melancholy face that might have interested Goya. He had a beak instead of a nose, and he was not bald, as mother had said. On his head was a soft, black fuzz that looked like something that might grow on the face of a dark young man who hadn't yet shaved. Somewhat above two of the largest, blackest, and brightest eyes I have ever encountered was a thin, single line of black hair that tilted across his forehead at about a sixty-degree angle. That single eyebrow gave his face the look of a man who has just encountered a most unexpected, pleasant surprise. His voice was soft, rather high-pitched, and in my memory never raised in anger.

The first day of class Orion Bernstein walked into the classroom, stood in front of his desk, and waited until we had got used to the sight of him and he had caught all six pairs of eyes.

Then he said, "Man is the measure of all things," and he turned to me.

"Mr. Bland, can you think?"

"Of course," I said, "I think, therefore, I am. I feel, therefore—"

"Can you prove to me that you can think or feel or that you are?" he asked, and he smiled. The teeth were uneven, and at least two were obstrusively not his own—the result of a childhood fight on the Lower East Side. The smile was extremely pleasant, though; it invited you to share in the enjoyment of a world—maybe even a universe—created especially for that purpose.

Orion did not think highly of people; yet I have never known anyone who enjoyed life quite as fully as he did. Nor anyone with the passion for knowledge or the enthusiasm for sharing it. Orion had read all the philosophers, and he had also read *Das Kapital*—the only man I ever came across who had—and Engels and Kropotkin and John Reed, etc. He had visited the Soviet Union, had spent a summer in Spain, and was tortured by the news that came from there the fall, winter, and spring I knew him.

He was not a Communist—"That would mean my having to call somebody like Otto Zorich *comrade*; I refuse." He was not an admirer of the Soviet Union—"They have succeeded in destroying the spirit of a people." He accepted neither the easy slogans of the left nor the easier shibboleths of the right. He was a man who accepted nobody's answer for any problem— "...we know the lies in all of them; we do not know what truth is."[7]

And yet he felt that he should be in Spain— "...He who has neither the courage to die nor the heart to live, who will neither resist nor fly, what can be done with him?"

In any case, I cannot remember whether or not on that first day I answered Orion's question about my existence, but I do know that I felt I was in for a stimulating nine months, and I was right. Orion must have walked a hundred miles that year in his Advanced Philosophy class, up and down, back and forth, his arms waving, words pouring out of him, his eyes surveying all of us, demanding that we be half what he expected us to be. I was often the devil's advocate in his class. Orion loved argument just as much as I did, and we would shout at each other; quarrel violently, and continue to like each other.

During the time I studied with Orion, September 1936 to June 1937, I read all the philosophers: Hume, particularly his auto-biography, "a collection of the most instructive and amusing lives ever published"; Descartes, partly because of his clear style but also because of his cynical turn of mind, which I mistakenly assumed to be typically French. I went part way with Santayana but never really liked him, and when his novel was published, *The Last Puritan,* I hated it with a passion; it was rubbish, I thought, high-sounding rubbish. I could never read Alfred North Whitehead; I just didn't understand what he was getting at.

"Never pretend to understand what you don't understand," Orion used to say, "and never let anybody tell you you *should* like something. You can educate your taste, but you can't change it. So

---

7   Many years later when I came across George Orwell's work for the first time—and I went through it all in one delighted interlude, the way I had earlier done with Balzac—I thought that the quality of Orwell's mind and the purity of his spirit were very much like Orion's. I do not know what Orion thought of the Spanish War after he got into it, but I have a hunch he would have felt somewhat the same way Orwell did. Not incidentally, I happen to think that Orwell's *Homage to Catalonia* is the only good book about the Spanish war and one of the best books about anything published in the Thirties.

trust it. Most people are afraid to admit they don't like what they don't understand. Which is why so much unintelligible crap gets accepted."

Naturally, mother did not like Orion, though I don't think she met him more than once or twice. Her first encounter with him was at the Bakers'. By this time, she had wormed her way into the Faculty Club—but not the Atheneum, never the Atheneum.

She was standing in a reception line not far from Mrs. Baker. Orion introduced himself.

"Of course," said mother. "You're the Hebrew."

"The Hebrew," said Mrs. Baker.

"No, ma'am," said Orion. "I'm the Jew."

"The Jew," said Mrs. Baker.

Later at home, mother said, "*Pushy*. Don't let him try to convert you, sonny. We all know what the Protocols of Zion are."

Once Orion, Letty, and I had dinner together at the Green Gables, the student hang-out on the edge of town. It was my idea, and a bad one. Letty tried to be pleasant to Orion because she knew he was important to me. She tried too hard.

The evening was over before it began. After coffee, Orion rose abruptly and said he had to work on his lecture for the next day's philosophy class. He said it had been a delightful evening and that he hoped he'd see a lot more of Letty, knowing he'd never see her again.

After he left, Letty was silent for a moment; then, in one of the few completely—or almost completely—frank moments in our life together, she said, "There are some people who take one look at you and see right through you. He's one of them. The minute we shook hands, I knew what he was thinking. He was thinking, 'I know who you are, tootsie-belle. I recognize your kind. Every time.'"

"What kind's that?" I asked.

"Let's go," said Letty.

I don't think Letty ever did mention Orion again. Except once. The scene above took place in the winter of 1937, late February, early March.

The scene that follows took place ten years later, in the spring of 1947. You might call it a typical at-home during our marriage.

We were living in a brownstone that I had bought on East 81st Street and had had remodeled at a cost of several million dollars.

Letty and I were having dinner alone, which was unusual. Because by then we couldn't stand the sight of each other, we managed to go some place or to have someone in almost every night of the week.

God knows what we were talking about—or, more likely, what Letty was talking about; it doesn't matter. What matters is that suddenly, out of nowhere, Letty said, "What ever happened to that so-called friend of yours, Orion Bernstein, or whatever his name was?"

I said that he had been killed in Spain during the war there.

Letty thought about that for a moment, and then she said, "He never liked me, did he?"

"Who knows?" I said diffidently. I knew what was up. I always knew when a storm was brewing.

"I'm asking you a question," said Letty. "He never liked me, did he?"

"No, Letty," I said, because if I lied the storm would be larger and louder and longer-lasting. "Orion never liked you. So what?"

Letty thought it over; she lighted a cigarette with a candle. She had been doing that ever since she had seen Luise Rainer do it in *The Great Ziegfeld*.

"Why not?" asked Letty. "Why didn't he like me?"

I paused for a moment, which infuriated her.

"Well?" she said, exhaling great clouds of smoke.

"I don't know," I said. "You didn't like him. What difference does it make? It was a long time ago. It was ten years ago, Letty."

Letty stamped out her cigarette with the force of a pile driver. "I just don't get it," she said. "I didn't like him, but I was nice to him. For your sake."

And she said, "None of your friends ever likes me. You always very carefully arrange that, don't you?"

There must have been more words along these general lines, and then, "We are going to take the place in East Hampton, aren't we?"

I said, "No, Letty, we are not going any place this summer unless you're willing to go to the Jersey shore in August. This summer we stay in town."

"Would it be too much if I asked why?"

"We've been through it a few times. Reason A, I can't afford to rent the place in East Hampton. Reason B, I have a play in rehearsal. Reason C, I happen to—"

"*You* happen to," said Letty. "*You.* What *you* want. What *you* feel. The fact that *you* may be stunting the physical and possibly the mental growth of *my* daughter by keeping her cooped up in—"

My turn. "In a brownstone house on East Eighty-first Street with a garden, said house having been remodeled at a cost to me of—"

That's enough. What's interesting here is that fantastic feminine ability, by no means restricted to Letty, of resurrecting the memory of a man ten years dead because she, Letty, wasn't going to go to an overpriced place on Long Island for the summer.

Don't ask me to explain it.

This particular *discussion*—what we might call the Bernstein-East Hampton colloquy—ended as follows:

Letty to me: You're a failure. A failure. A failure. You reached your peak when you were fifteen years old.

To that I said, "You've got something there. I was fifteen when I met you."

Letty threw a Meissen cup at me. It didn't hit me, though. Letty hit me only once with something she threw at me—a steak knife.

Back now to New Athens, the spring of 1937.

For the first time in my life—and I guess also the last—I had three friends at the same time. Naturally, none of the three liked any of the others.

Hughie of Orion: Odd-looking bird. He won't never win a beauty prize. What do you two guys ever find to talk about anyway?

"Ideas," I said, and I probably added, "Nothing you'd be interested in, Hughie."

Not long after the disastrous dinner with Letty and Orion at the Green Gables, I said to Orion, "You didn't like Letty, did you?"

"No," said Orion. "Is it required?"

"I like people to like each other," I said.

"Haven't I absolutely forbidden you to read Edgar Guest?" said Orion, giving me a look. Then he said, "Nobody who was anybody was ever *popular*. One of the things you have to learn—and the sooner the better—is that a great many perfectly nice, normal, intelligent people that you want desperately to like you hate your guts."

Now comes the forgery part.

I don't remember whether I've mentioned it or not, but I had a part-time job while I was at Pegasus, paid for by you taxpayers. It was under the National Youth Administration and just about as socialistic as you can get, and we could use several billion dollars' worth of something like that right now.

(Once when I was in Wonderland, testifying for a bill to set up a Federal theater, an idiot Congressman asked me if a thing like that wouldn't raise taxes. I said, "I most certainly hope so, Congressman." I said, "What I think we ought to do in this country is spend and spend and spend and tax and tax and tax." The Congressman went off with a heart attack a few weeks later; I like to think I may have contributed to that. You see, given a choice between raising the taxes of my enemy and neighbor, Pism C., and helping Tommy Barbori, the son of my barber in Sloane's Station and a very bright boy, get through Cornell—well, I'm for taking from Pism and giving to Tommy. Naturally, under the Bland plan for Shaping Up the World, there will be a hundred per cent inheritance tax. As I said one dark night last spring to another enemy and neighbor, Silas Marner, a fellow who was born with four or five silver spoons in his oversized mouth and ten or twelve million dollars in his grubby fists, "Let's you and me start out broke, Silas, and we'll see who ends up with the most.")

Anyway, during my last year at Pegasus, 1936-37, I had an N.Y.A. job; I corrected themes for an English teacher who also taught a class in Greek poetry, largely limited to the work of Sappho. Every other summer this particular teacher took her favorite girl pupil to the island of Lesbos. Believe me, she knew the way.

One day during Christmas vacation that year I was in Sappho's office correcting themes on the subject of "How I Hope to Spend My Christmas Vacation." There was the usual collection of absolute crap, tedious rewrites of Louisa May Alcott and dreary accounts of holiday activities that sounded like a Norman Rockwell painting. I read through them, restraining my impulse to write what I thought about them. Sappho was a C-grader; that is, she gave almost no A's—except to a few girls who also took Greek poetry—and almost no B's. She never flunked anybody.

I'd like to add here that one of the themes got an A-plus from me. It was about a *blue* Christmas tree in the front yard of a boy whose father was at the time a well-known director Out There. This boy's plan for Christmas vacation was to wait until everybody else had gone to sleep on Christmas eve, then get up, go out in the front yard, and, as he so elegantly put it, "water on that blue tree with all my might."

Later, Sappho and I had a heated argument about my grade on that theme; she marked the composition down to a C-minus. "We will have no vulgarity in this class," she wrote on it.

I still think I was right; that was an A-plus theme if ever I saw an A-plus theme.

Anyway, that afternoon after I'd finished grading the papers, I went through the stuff on Sappho's desk to see if there was any of her mail I hadn't read. (You Cub Scouts and Camp Fire girls are going to be shocked at this, but I have always read all mail that wasn't sealed, no matter who it belonged to. Not only that, if a steaming teakettle was handy, I often scanned what was sealed. I have always felt that the readers of other people's mail and eaves-droppers pick up a good deal of extremely useful information about themselves and other people.)

Under the blotter on Sappho's desk that afternoon was a let-ter from the University of London. London, England, that is. It was signed by a man named Hollis Lindsay, and it said that a few scholarships were available for "promising graduates of American colleges interested in philosophy and literature." All "reasonable liv-ing expenses" would be paid; the only cost to the fortunate young Americans would be their transportation to and from London.

I read the letter through once, and then I read it through a second time and a third. By that time, my hands were trembling, and my mouth was watering. Until then, I had had no idea what I was going to do after I was graduated from Pegasus in June. I would be not-quite sixteen, and both mother and Pavan agreed that I should stay in New Athens for another two years of graduate work. "After that," mother kept saying, "we'll have to see. We'll just have to see how things work out."

The last thing in the world I had any intention of doing was staying in New Athens for two more years.

The possibility of an all-expenses-except-transportation-paid trip to London seemed the perfect out. But how? Who would recommend me? Sappho? Not on your tintype. If I had been pretty and a girl, maybe, but I was a boy and not pretty. Orion? Possibly; he was fond of me; he thought I had a good mind, and he thought I ought to get out of town just as soon as I'd graduated. But would he recommend me for a year of study in London? I couldn't be sure, and in this I had to be absolutely sure.

Would President Baker recommend me? Not bloody likely. The longer I stayed at Pegasus, the more chance there was to milk a little more publicity out of me. Baker wasn't going to make any move to send me to London. Pavan? Ridiculous. Mother? Don't be silly.

Actually, it seems to me I was born with the knowledge that the only person you can count on in a pinch is *you*. In my mind on that December afternoon, there was only one thing to do. I had to recommend myself.

So I took the letter from under Sappho's blotter; I looked around and found a piece of paper with her signature on it, and then I turned off the lights and locked the office. That night I didn't go to sleep at all; I practiced writing Sappho's signature; by morning I had it down so pat that I would have sworn even the beady-eyed tellers at the Farmers' and Merchants' bank would have been unable to detect my forgery.

During the next week I learned how to forge two other signatures, those of President Baker and of Orion Bernstein. I hated myself for doing what I was doing, but I didn't hate myself enough not to do it.

I remember that at one point, I said to Orion, "Does the end *ever* justify the means?"

"Never," said Orion. "Never, never, never.... Unless, of course, the end is absolutely irresistible."

I spent days working on the three letters to Hollis Lindsay. The one signed by Sappho not only commended my scholarship in the field of *letters*; it also said that I was a promising poet with the sweet nature of Robert Browning and the talent of Keats, not to mention "Bland's outstanding accomplishments in the field of the short story."

The letter signed with President Baker's name concentrated on my character. The way Baker looked at it in my letter, if Jesus had been a contemporary of mine, He would have had to look to His laurels. The letter I signed with Orion's name was shorter, a little more formal, and most of what it said was more or less true.

When the three letters were finished, each in its way seemed to be a masterpiece. Stealing the letterheads to write the letters on was easy; I'd been a stationery thief from way back.

I forged the three names, took the letters to the post office, and off they went, along with my pagan prayers.

Did I lie awake nights worrying about the dark deed I'd done? I did not. I was too tired. I got up at dawn every morning, and I visited, first, Sappho's office, then Baker's, then Orion's. The campus postman made once-daily rounds very early, and he left the letters in a box outside the office of each of the three people whose signatures I had forged. I was looking for the replies from London.

I know; I know. The penalties for interfering with the U.S. mail are very severe, but the way I looked at it, the letters from London— should there be any—actually belonged to me because they would be in answer to the letters *I* had written. See how things work out in your mind once you start forging.

A week passed; then two, then three, four, and five. No letters from London. By that time I was just about as morose as I'd been in my whole life. I expected the F.B.I. at any moment.

Then, maybe six weeks after the forgery, I was in Orion's class for his lecture on Hegel. After the bell rang, Orion said, "Bland, stick around for a moment."

Did I sense that something was up? Did doubts and fears assail me? Not me.

Orion waited until everybody else had left the room. Then he put his lecture notes in his brief case. After that, he looked up and seemed to be aware of me for the first time.

"What are you doing here?" he asked.

"You asked me to stay," I said.

"Oh, did I?" said Orion. "I can't remember what I wanted. It must not have been very important. You can go."

I started toward the door, and Orion said, "Your thoughts about natural religion were very well thought out and very well expressed."

I said thank you.

"Oh, by the way," said Orion, his voice as casual as if he had been commenting on the weather, "I got an answer to my letter to my friend Hollis Lindsay."

I did not turn; I couldn't have if I'd wanted to. I didn't move a muscle; I didn't have any muscles left.

I could hear Orion Bernstein fumbling in his brief case, and he said, "I guess I neglected to mention that I spent three months at London University. Lindsay and I became very good friends. When I got the letter from him about the scholarships, I was going to recommend you; I just hadn't got around to it. Thanks, though."

I heard him unfold a letter, and I did manage to turn.

"Thanks for what?" I asked in a tiny voice.

"For saving me the trouble," said Orion.

Then he read this letter aloud:

Dear Orion:

Kathryn and I were pleased to hear from you, though I have to confess we were both surprised at the brief, businesslike tone of your letter. Please do write us a personal note; we are anxious to know how you are liking it in the wild and woolly west.

As for young Bland, he will, of course, be awarded one of the scholarships. We have also had enthusiastic recommendations from President Baker of Pegasus and from Miss — [Sappho]. He sounds like a very unusual young man for twenty, and...

Your friend,
Hollis Lindsay.

When Orion had finished refolding the letter and returning it, first, to the envelope and then, very slowly, to his brief case, he closed the brief case and locked it. Then he closed all the drawers of his desk and locked them.

After that he put on his hat and started out of the room, brushing past me as if he didn't know I was there.

"The letter came to my house," he said when he got to the door. "I guess that possibility never occurred to you." It hadn't.

He waited a moment, then asked, "Why did you say you were twenty?"

"I—didn't want them to—think I was a—freak," I said.

"Well, it's better to be smart and dishonest than stupid and dishonest," said Orion. "You'd better get over to the library and start boning up on positive religion."

He opened the door, and then he turned again and said, "By the way, what did I say in my letter?"

Through the tears I told him what I had written above his signature, and then I told him what I had written over Sappho's and Baker's signatures.

"I could have expressed it more gracefully," said Orion, "but not bad—for a twenty-year-old."

"What are you going to do about it?" I asked.

"What?"

"Are you going to—tell?"

"No," said Orion. "No, I'm not. If you're lucky, you may get away with it. If you're not...."

He left the sentence trembling in the air; then he said, "I may even write a second letter to Hollis saying that perhaps my first was a little less enthusiastic than it should have been."

"Orion—" I began, tears streaming down my face.

"Remember this, junior," said Orion, "the end never justifies the means."

"Unless, of course, the end is absolutely irresistible," I said.

Let me say here and now that in all the years since, I have never once regretted those three forgeries, never once.

Suppose I hadn't got away with it, you say; suppose I'd been caught. Well, there's only one answer to that. I did get away with it; I wasn't caught.

When I was in London, I once casually asked Hollis Lindsay if he'd ever answered the letters supposedly written by Baker and Sappho.

Hollis sighed. "I'm sorry," he said, "and deeply ashamed. I meant to, but I just never got around to it. Should I now, do you suppose?"

"I wouldn't," I told him. "I wouldn't bother."

"What puzzles me," said Hollis, "is how they could have thought you were *twenty*."

I didn't mention the scholarship to mother and Pavan: I knew exactly what they'd say; *no*. I discussed the whole thing with Orion, and he said, "Let me tell them."

"You can be sure they'll never let me go, let alone pay the transportation," I said.

"Yes, they will. I'm positive of it."

"How can you be so positive?"

Orion winked at me and said nothing.

I did tell Hughie and Letty about the scholarship, expecting them to be delighted. My knowledge of human nature is more extensive now.

Hughie said, "What do you want to go to England for? You'll just see more people, and there are plenty of people right here."

Letty said, "I wouldn't give two cents to go to England. Why *any*body should want to go to England...."

Not long after, Letty, who not only had to have everything *some*body else had but everything *any*body else had, came up with a scholarship of her own.

She had written a letter to a magazine I choose for dark reasons of my own and because of the laws of libel to call *Puberty*. They offered ten *scholarships* to "ten ambitious, intelligent undergraduate girls who want to learn the magazine business first-hand." That piece of humbug meant that *Puberty* was getting ten girls to work for the summer *free*. Letty was able to accept the honor only because she got free room and board in New York at the apartment of a former professor.

I didn't point this out to her, though. I already knew better than that.

In any case, in late June 1937, I was graduated from Pegasus. *The Cedar Rapids Gazette* called me "the youngest, smallest, and brightest college graduate in the history of Iowa."

I was valedictorian of the class—an honor of no consequence. Norman Levine, who was graduated at the same time and who has probably been among the half-dozen most valuable citizens this country has had in this century, got a high-*B* average.... You take your average valedictorian, and what are you going to do with him? Like Rhodes Scholars. Ever know a Rhodes Scholar who was worth a hill of beans?

Anyhow, I gave a speech at Commencement. The title was—forgive me—"I *Am* My Brother's Keeper."

I remember one sentence: "I am told I am a radical. Well, the word *radical* comes from the Latin word *radix* meaning *root*. If being a radical means to examine the roots of things to find out what is wrong with our society, then I am a radical."

I wouldn't bother quoting that pastiche if the American Legion newspaper in the state the next week hadn't had a banner headline saying, "Pegasus Prodigy Says He Is Communist."

I threatened to sue and got a retraction, but that's another story. I will add that when I was subpoenaed to appear before the Unmentionable Committee that headline was the trump card used against me. No more mention of the Unmentionable, but I do want to say this word in favor of the American Legion. For thirty-some years now, those boys have been against every idea and every human being in this country that was worth a damn. You can't knock consistency like that.

The week after graduation, Letty took off for New York.

Nowadays, Letty travels only by jet, and the fact that tourist-class passengers are allowed in the same plane as first-class passengers causes her some small discomfort. Not only that, an American

Airlines jet was recently eleven minutes late in its flight from New York to Los Angeles; Letty threatened to sue. The delay caused her to miss an appointment with the head fellow she is now consulting. This man isn't so much a head *doctor*; he is more what you might call a head *osteopath*. You don't have to tell him everything; you just tell him what you want to, and as I make it out, he *guesses* the rest.

Letty was in just as much of a hurry twenty-two years ago in New Athens, but her financial status compelled her to contain her impatience. She went to New York by Greyhound bus in thirty-six hours.

I reminded her of this recently, and she said, "Oh, *that* was really a *fun* trip. There's nothing like going by bus to get to know where America lives."

In that far away time Letty and I swore eternal fealty at the Greyhound station.

"Don't have relations with anybody else," she said. The request seemed to me unusual since as I've said I had not yet had *relations* with Letty.

"You wouldn't have any respect for me if I let you," said Letty.

I said, "My God. A law should be passed making it illegal to teach women how to read." (In the twenty-odd years that have passed since, I have given this idea much thought. I haven't changed my mind either. But let's get rid of the Nineteenth Amendment first. A step at a time. A step at a time....)

When Letty got on the bus, she said, "I'll see you in New York in August," and she said, "Don't even *think* about any other women," and she said, "Criss-cross your heart and hope to die," and she said, "And remember no— Right?"

I made the promise willingly enough. At the time, the opportunities along that line in New Athens were limited. In my case, anyway. And especially in the summer when the campus was deserted except for a few delinquents repeating courses and a handful of over-age high-school teachers working on advanced degrees. I do remember that one excessively unattractive instructor in the English Department, who had a runny nose and a collection of songs sung by a fellow named Dwight Fiske, kept wanting me to come to his room to listen to the Fiske records; not only that, Mr. Runny Nose kept wanting me to borrow his autographed copy of André Gide's *If It Die*.

I'm going to die not having read *If It Die*.

Between late June and mid-August when I left New Athens forever, I read a great deal in the college library, mostly about God and Jesus and Buddha and Mohammed. Nothing took.

I wrote Letty every day; she'd told me to. I got one letter from her. "Don't tell a soul, but I have no intention of going back to college next fall. Or ever. New York is the town for me, and I'm the girl for it...I'll see you in New York in August. Now in haste, in haste, in haste. Your only true love, Letty."

At the end of the first week in August, Orion Bernstein still hadn't spoken to Pavan and my mother about the money for my trip to England. I was in a real sweat.

Orion kept telling me to relax. "Relax!" I kept saying. "With my whole *future* at stake! What about my ship reservations and all?"

"You'll have no trouble getting on a ship in late August," said Orion, "but, if you want, I'll talk to Pavan and your mother today."

"But what'll you say?"

"I shall quote two lines from Alexander Pope's 'Epistle to Dr. Arbuthnot,'" said Orion.

"Which two?"

Orion displayed the two ostentatious teeth and said, "Josh, if I told you all I know, then you would know as much as I know."

Then he went off to the house on Riverdale Avenue in which I was born and raised.

Less than half an hour later, he returned to his office, where I was nervously waiting.

"It's all set," he said.

"Tell me."

"Some day you'll know," he said.

Orion said one other thing on the subject. He said, "A little blackmail now and then is useful to the best of men."

When I got back to the Riverdale Avenue house that night, mother and Pavan were sitting in the living room without any lights.

I turned the lights on and saw that mother had been crying, and Pavan looked even more wild-eyed than usual.

"Hi," I said, almost liking them. "I hear I'm going to England."

Mother said, "Only a Jew would stoop so low. I wish I was living in Germany at this very minute."

"Would you mind telling me what went on between you and Orion?" I said.

"Be quiet," said Pavan, and I was.

The next morning by the time I got up mother and Pavan had gone to Newton to a Star meeting, but under my plate was Pavan's check for a thousand dollars.

I raced to the Milhausen Travel Agency on East Main—combined with Treat Insurance, Notary Public, Legal Services, etc. Trude Milhausen hadn't actually booked a passage on a *boat* for some time. "The Lavendars use an *Eastern* agency, lah-de-dah. In Chicago." Trude thought she could manage it, though, and I chose the *Queen Mary*, third class.

When I left Trude's office I winked at myself in the dusty window of the Royal Kandy Kitchen.

"From now on," I said to myself, "the sky's the limit. You've got it made, kid. You've got the handle."

Then I went inside and ordered a triple chocolate malted with *two* raw eggs.

That night I said, "Thanks a lot for the check, Pavan."

Pavan said, "I never wish to hear it mentioned again as long as I live."

So far as I know, he never did.

(7) The sweeter fig[8]

We come now to what those of us in Show Biz call The Essential Scene. That is the scene which the playgoer has been led to expect and had damn well better get. It is often the second-act curtain, and

---

8 "If God had not made brown honey, men would think figs much sweeter than they do."—Exonphanes.

a play without it will probably close in New Haven. A play with it may also close in New Haven.

The Essential Scene here has to do with the last time my mother and I saw each other.

The farewell took place two days before I left New Athens for the next-to-last time. Mother was packing to go to Des Moines for some big do the Eastern Star was having. I went to the bedroom she shared with Pavan. She was humming and wrapping a white dress in tissue paper.

I stood in the doorway for a moment, and she turned but did not look at me.

She said, "I was just getting packed."

I said, "I thought maybe you might need some help."

She said, "No, thanks. I'm nearly finished."

"Oh."

"I'm not taking much, just this dress I'm wearing at the meeting and some odds and ends."

I said, "I hope the meeting goes all right."

"Well, thank you. That's very nice."

I said, "Well, I guess I'll be on my way to England when you get back from Des Moines."

She said, "Well, I hope you have a good time over there and learn a lot."

I said, "I will. Well, I guess I better get going. I'm going down to the library."

She said, "It won't be long, of course. Only a year."

"That's right," I said. "It won't be long."

I went to her and kissed her on the forehead, and she looked at me. Not only that; I believe she actually saw me.

What she saw I can only approximate, but something like this—a thin, nervous boy, small for his age and needing a haircut, always needing a haircut. The boy had a wide forehead, a smooth, girlish skin, and large, hungry brown eyes that dominated the face, not only because of their size but because the bent, scratched horn-rimmed glasses the boy wore magnified his eyes. The boy—someone said it of me, or wrote it—had the face of a disappointed octogenarian and the body of an underfed child. I wasn't underfed. I ate like a horse, but I just never got much taller, from the time I was about twelve—I exaggerate, but not much—until I was twenty-five or so; then I started expanding, horizontally.

I had socks with holes in them, and my shoestrings must have been broken; they almost always were. The shirt I wore was too large; all my clothes were bought with the mistaken hope that I'd grow into them, and my pants had a hole in the rear end, and I never wore underwear.

Altogether I must have been a sight only a mother could love, but not my mother. No, I think on that day as on all others mother was comparing the drab reality of me with the rosy vision of an imagined Jessica.

You can hardly blame her for being disappointed.

I'll tell you what I saw that day, too. My memory of my mother has always been of the way she looked then.

She was a small, dark woman with large, restless brown eyes, a narrow, petulant mouth that was almost never closed, and nervous hands. The hands gave the impression that they could continue to exist without being attached to their owner, that in fact she was only vaguely, if at all, aware of what the hands were up to.

It may seem strange, my dwelling on her hands, but I remember them more distinctly than anything else about her. At night, while she slept, her hands wandered clockwise and counterclockwise over the sheet or blanket that covered her.

God knows what made her tick; I've spent too much time and money trying to figure out what makes me tick to have any firm opinions on anyone else.

I know this. She was totally incapable of facing reality; she did not face a fact from the day she was born until the night she died....

I can't be quite sure about that last, of course, but I'm sure enough....

True, it wasn't easy to live in a house that had once—by a man running for the U.S. Senate and desperately in need of votes—been described as "the show place of the Middle West," but which in 1937 had a hamburger stand on one side and a gas station across the street. Three doors away a woman whose name mother never quite caught plied a furtive but nevertheless thriving trade. Mother lived in a past that probably never existed, and she was endowed with a terrifying energy. But no will, no energy, no force of nature could edge out the Lavendars in New Athens, and nothing could change the fact that, no matter what, mother would never be admitted to the Atheneum Club.

I mentioned near the beginning of this dissertation that I once went to the New Athens Country Club; I said that I was on exhibition, true enough. It happened during the time it looked as if I might win the Harvey Jordan O'Conner Cranium Derby.

After the festivities—a dinner, speeches, dancing to "Coon Sanders and His (I forget)"—mother not unexpectedly found herself seated next to the two Lavendar girls—one married, one not. Naturally, she had brought me along.

The conversation was not free-flowing, but that was the kind of thing that mother treated as a challenge.

For instance, mother said to the married sister, "I see by the *Times-Dispatch* you and your hubby are going to Europe this summer."

The Lavendar girl made affirmative noises in her throat, and the conversation lagged again.

"I said to sonny boy that it sounded like a wonderful itinerant," said mother, and then she giggled. "Though, of course, I don't understand why you're going *back*."

She paused and waited, and nothing happened.

Mother giggled again. "I said, 'It isn't as if they hadn't already *been* to Europe!'"

Still no response.

Mother said, "I certainly do admire the program you girls have planned for the Atheneum Club this winter."

The married Lavendar girl managed to catch the eye of her husband, who started toward her.

"We girls at the Arts and Crafts try very much the same sort of thing," said mother, "not in the same league, to be sure, but we try to discuss at least one worthwhile idea at every meeting."

The Lavendar husband was nearly there by then.

"I was saying to the girls just the other day that it would be more fun if the Atheneum and we could have a joint meeting," said mother. "I mean we could pool our resources, so to speak, and maybe have a covered-dish supper, and, after supper—"

Both Lavendar girls had risen by now, and the elder one said, "Please do excuse us, Mrs. Bland."

Mother also rose, expecting, I believe, to be introduced to the Lavendar son-in-law, who ran the canning factory. That did not happen.

"Very pleased to have met you, I'm sure," said mother. She said it to nobody. The Lavendars were gone.

"Come on, sonny," said mother. She grabbed my hand, holding it so tightly that it hurt.

Just before we reached the coat room, we heard the sound of laughter from the vicinity of the dance floor. I don't know what mother wanted to do, but I wanted to die. God is never so good.

Mother and I got our coats, and we walked out. Not a word was spoken on the way home that night. When we got out of the car, Pavan looked at mother, and, with surprise in his voice and as much tenderness as he was capable of, he said, "Why, Celeste, you've been crying."

Mother didn't answer him—the first time and probably the last time that happened.

But I am talking here about mother's and my good-bye. One hand was smoothing the tissue paper in which her white dress was wrapped. The other was picking at a stray thread on the bedspread.

"Never forget who your mother is," she said, apropos of nothing.

"I won't," I said.

"And never forget I gave up a very promising career to have you," she added, believing it.

"I won't," I said.

"I brought you into the world, and blood is thicker than water. Keep that in mind."

I nodded and said, "Well, so long, Mom. Take care of yourself."

She said, "You, too, and don't forget to write."

"I won't."

I turned and left the room, and as I walked down the hall I heard her singing, very softly, "When I'm calling you ... ooo-ooo-oooo ... ooo-oo-o. Will you answer true ... ooo-ooo-oooo ... ooo-oo-o?"

I stopped and listened, and then there was a silence, and then I heard my mother crying.

I started to go back to her room, but I didn't. I wasn't then— I never was—sure whether she was crying because the reality of me was going away or because the hoped-for Jessica had never appeared.

I guess maybe I didn't want to know. So I went to the library instead.

And that was the last time I ever saw my mother.

Next there will be two more short good-byes.

The afternoon before I left New Athens, I walked all over town. I think I knew I'd never be back.

I started at the river bank, at the place I'd always thought my great-great-grandfather had stopped. I looked into the blue haze of the late August afternoon, but no one beckoned me—no Marquette, no Joliet, no Hennepin.

I walked to Old Humphrey Hall, and for the last time I read the plaque my great-great-grandfather had placed on the wall: "The direction in which education starts a man will determine his future life. Plato. *The Republic*."

Norman Levine was at the organ; he was playing Bach. I stood behind him for a while, and when he'd finished, I said, "That was very good, Norman."

"Thanks," he said, politely enough. I realized, though, that Norman had been playing for his own pleasure and that while he was pleased with the compliment, he didn't have to have it. An audience was not required for everything he did, not in the way it was for me.... A girl whose name and face are forgotten, but whose voice and words are not, once told me, "Honey, you act as if people ought to be willing to buy tickets to watch you brush your teeth...."

As Norman started to play again, I walked quickly and quietly out of Old Humphrey.

I walked past all the rooms in which I had sat so briefly, listened so half-heartedly, and learned so little.

I walked past the football field, where in the golden late afternoon a group of scholarly young men were shouting guttural football signals at each other.

Then I came to a small, sad square of a building, the shabbiest on the campus; there in what must have been the tiniest cubbyhole was Orion Bernstein.... President Baker had often said, "Worthwhile education pays its way." Philosophy never once paid its way.

"Hi," said Orion, looking up from his book and raising the long, narrow strip of hair which served as an eyebrow. "All packed?"

"Nearly. I came to say good-bye. You won't be at the Baker party tonight."

"I shall never be at a Baker party, but I might come down to the station in the morning to lift you onto the train."

"Well—"

"Okay," said Orion. "I won't come then...."

"Pavan's taking me, and he's so nutsy."

"I won't come then."

I said, "I'm not good at saying good-bye."

"Nobody is."

"Or thanks. I'm very bad at saying thanks, but I'll never forget anything you taught me. You're the only teacher in this whole damn college I ever learned anything from, and if it weren't for you, I'd be rotting away here for the rest of my life."

Orion took a small book from his pocket and handed it to me. The book was *The Praise of Folly*, by Erasmus.

"It may take you years to understand it, or never," he said, displaying the two false teeth. "I hate a man that remembers what he reads. 'So drink heartily and live lustily, my most excellent disciple in folly.'"

I said, "Thank you, Orion. We are friends, aren't we? Best friends."

Orion Bernstein rose, and he touched my hand, and he made a small, soft fist and touched my shoulder with it, and he said, "Try to be something extraordinary," and he said, "Some day take a look at St. Matthew. Chapter Twenty-Five. Fourteenth Verse."

I nodded and turned and left the smallest office on the campus.

As soon as I got to the house on Riverdale Avenue, I looked up the parable of the talents. It was years before I understood it, though.

Now for the second and last good-bye.

I've already told how Hughie and I quarreled the night before I left for England, and I said that Pavan drove me to the station.

On the way, he started to speak several times, but each time he changed his mind.

When the train pulled into the station, Pavan and I got out of the car. I carried my two large suitcases, a bagful of books, and my portable typewriter. Even at the end, Pavan did not carry.

I said, "Well, Pavan, I guess this is it."

He nodded.

I said, "I want you to know I'm awfully grateful for everything you've done for me."

"Try not to be a fool all your life," said Pavan, and I realized that was all; that was his good-bye. So I got on the train, and I looked out the window. Pavan was still standing on the platform, looking as if there was still something he wanted to say, but whatever it was, I never knew.

As I've said, I also saw a shadow in the station behind Mr. Durrell, the station master and ticket agent, a shadow that could have been Hughie's.

The train started to pick up speed, and Pavan waved to me, and then we were passing the Pegasus campus. I saw Horatio Phineas Baker and the dean of men who didn't like boy prodigies.

I looked at them for a moment, hating them, and then I realized I didn't have to hate them any more, and I turned away. I even felt a little gratitude to that empty-headed man, H. P. Baker. In a way, he was responsible for the fact that I was going to England.

I never heard much about Pegasus after I left, though someone once told me that, after his retirement, President-Emeritus Baker took to wandering nude in the Shakespeare garden. He thought he was Ophelia.

When the train crossed the Mississippi, I said the old rhyme, "M-i-s, s-i-s, s-i-p-p i, oh, M-i-s, s-i-s, s-i-p-p-i."

I said it three times between Davenport and Moline.

As the train paused in Moline, I inhaled the free, exhilarating air. I exhaled, and I said to myself, "I'm free! I'm free! I'm free!"

Then a sobering thought occurred to me. I realized I wasn't free at all and never would be. I realized that for the rest of my life, wherever I went, whatever I did, I'd have to take me along.

And that's the end of the first part. The rest won't take nearly as long. Each year gets shorter, after all.

Not only that; there are several years in my life that I can't remember at all—an almost complete and not unpleasant blank from one New Year's Eve to another.

Good morning, Ab.

PART • TWO

NOTES·DICTATED·ON·THE·FIFTH·DAY

(1) One for the money

I spent a miserable morning. It was after seven when I stopped dictating, turned off the recorder, and took three pills.

I tested all the locks in the house, and from behind the curtain in the room that was Charley's I looked out into the stand of maple and larch and oak that belongs to Filmore Grayson. At first I thought I saw the shadow of a man standing there, watching this house. It was not, of course. It was the stump of a tree I hadn't noticed before.

The air was oppressive, very humid, with no breeze at all.

From the village came the wail of the morning train, and a lonely cow made a mooing sound from the Grayson field. Otherwise, nothing.

After an eternity or two, I turned from the glass wall and looked at what had been Charley's bed, which we had so often shared. I slept there for a time after she left, and at first there was the smell of her, and sometimes I held her pillow in my arms while I slept. After a week or so, the sweet, subtle smell—real or imagined—was gone. I tore her photograph into a thousand pieces and put them in the sewage disposal, and I never slept in her bed again.

This morning in my room the curtains were drawn, and I put on a sleep mask to shut out the rest of the light, but I had nothing to mute the sounds of the morning—the caws of a horde of complaining crows, the petulant quarrels of some angry jays, and somewhere a mourning dove.

And there was nothing to stay the black memories that beat against my mind—

Charley said, "I can't stand scenes, you know. I won't have them. I just won't."

Or she said, "Don't shout at me. I will not be shouted at."

Or, "Darling, please be kind to me, please."

...The headaches began perhaps three months before X's wife left him. He never told her because he knew she would advise him to go back to the doctor, and he had no intention of doing that, and he had no intention of returning to the place in Connecticut.

So X endured the daily torture in silence, and when the machine was set in motion in his head, he tried not to hear the sounds it made or feel the grinding motion of its wheels.

Once, after he had suffered a particularly humiliating defeat, there had been such a whirring and pounding in his head that even the softest voice tore at him, malevolently, violently.

That was why—or so he persuaded himself—he shouted at his wife when he got home from the city and the reason he went into his study, locking the door behind him.

He lay on the red couch, his face to the wall, his eyes closed. Great waves of misery swept over him and the pain was so intense that twice he came close to screaming. Once he almost went to the filing cabinet in which he had the bottle hidden.

He didn't scream, though, and he didn't take a drink, and for a moment he felt some little pride.

Several hours later, his wife came to the door and knocked, and X admitted her. She said there was cold roast beef for dinner if he wanted any.

He said, "I'm sorry I shouted at you."

She said, "I'm getting used to being shouted at, I guess."

X drew her to him, and they stood for a while, nearly one.

She put her hand on his trembling lips, and she said, "I just wish you'd let me get to you sometime. I always feel as if a great wall of glass keeps us apart. I don't know how it is on your side, but on my side it gets lonely."

X said, "Forgive me," or thought he did.

"What's wrong?" asked his wife.

Just then a gear in the machine in his head made a grinding noise, and X shuddered.

"What's wrong?" asked his wife.

"Nothing," he said.

He made a smile, and, just to be sure, he said again—if it was again, "Forgive me."

His wife said, "I forgive you. I forgave you the first time I met you because at the same time that I wanted to kill you, I wanted to kiss you. I was already in love with you, you bastard. Now come have some cold roast beef...."

This morning I also remembered something that happened during my second stay in London, the one I made as a soldier in 1944. I thought of a girl named Elisia, whose face I couldn't remember. But I could remember every word she said and the sound of her voice. I could remember what I said to her, too, and the quick, sharp intake of breath and the moaning sob that followed. I could remember how in the odd, broken voice with the accent that reminded me at best of Bergner and at worst of Luise Rainer she said, "You're in the wrong army. I don't care what color your uniform is. You're one of the enemy. You're one of them."

"Lisa," I said. "I'm frightened. I don't want to die."

"I hope you do," she said. "I very much hope you do, I hope you are killed by your own men. It would be just."

When she ran out of the room, she did not close the door behind her. It was Charley who closed the door behind her when she left me for the last time....

This morning, I thought of Letty, too. I thought of a night when I came home to the house on Eighty-first Street.

Letty was in the dark, listening to the record player. It was Sinatra, "Someone to Watch Over Me."

> I'm a little lamb who's lost in the wood.
> I know I could
> Always be good
> To one who'll watch over me.

"We're closing it tonight," I said.

"Oh," said Letty. The record ended, and there was the scratching sound made by the needle.

"I guess it's a lousy play," I said.

"I could have told you that," said Letty.

"Is that all you have to say?"

"Yes, I think that's all," said Letty.

She looked at me, and I saw that she had been crying. She said, "I was prepared to give you quite a bit once, but you didn't want it."

"When was that?" I asked. "That I don't remember."

"Now I give you the back of my hand."

"That's all you ever had to give anybody," I said.

Then she started crying again, and I said, "What's wrong with you? Can I do anything for you?"

"Yes," said Letty. "You can go to hell."

Later, I found out that Letty was in trouble at the magazine. This morning I thought, Suppose I had tried to talk to Letty that night—that one night—would it have mattered? Probably not. Almost certainly not. And yet, I thought, if I had I would at this moment of my despair, in this late summer of my discontent, have that to remember.

This morning, too, I thought of a day when—I couldn't have been more than five—I was coming up Riverdale Avenue with the newest and most beautiful kiddy-car in the world. A birthday present from my father.

An older boy whose name I've forgotten was sitting on the stoop of a slatternly house, watching me. I stopped, and I smiled at him, hopefully. He continued looking at whatever he was looking at.

"You like a jawbreaker?" I asked, starting toward him.

"Throw it," he said, and I did.

"You throw like a sissy," he said, putting the jawbreaker in his mouth.

"Would you like to play with my kiddy-car?" I asked.

He shook his head.

I went on a step or two, and then I said, "I'll *give* it to you if you'll play with me. I mean you can keep it forever, and if I ever wanted to borrow it, I'd ask, but you could say no."

He looked at me, amazed, and then he laughed. "Fuck off, you four-eyed little sissy," he said. "I wouldn't play with you if you gave me one million dollars cash money."

He took the jawbreaker out of his mouth, threw it on the ground, and went into the house. The jawbreaker was red, blood red.

Why is there so little kindness in the world, do you suppose? Why so much cruelty? Why so much hating? I wonder. Why so little compassion?

And why those awful waves of loathing that will some day soon engulf us all?

Why are we so afraid to hold out our hand to someone, and if a hand is held out, why are we afraid to take it? Can nothing be done about the paralyzing fear that is everywhere, inside us and out?

There were other memories after I went to bed this morning, but that's enough.

A little after nine, shortly after Louella came in, I was unconscious for about an hour. Then I woke. The machine was at work in my head. I tried not to hear the sound of it or feel the motion of its grinding gears; I did, though; I do now.

After breakfast, I went for a long walk, into the hills and beyond onto the great plateau where the man who was almost President now grazes his Black Angus.

I passed Miranda Greene, whose father is head of a committee the members of which include Russ Grierson. I believe their main objective is to return the Grand Canyon to private ownership, to a combine I've heard is controlled by the Hilton people or the Disney people.

Miranda was wearing a green cashmere sweater very nearly the color of her eyes, tight-fitting shorts, and she was barefoot. Every visible part of her was freckled, and although I am not by nature a freckle-admirer, I found myself for one instant almost irresistibly tempted to ask her if she is that way all over.

Miranda was walking through the meadow in my direction, and she managed to come very close to me, making sure I brushed her left breast. She is not particular in the men-and-boy department. Sidney Levinson, who hears about such things, says that Miranda is one of nine girls in the senior high school who had abortions this year. There was one miscarriage.

"I've been thinking about you," said Miranda. "We were sorry you didn't give the Commencement speech."

"I had nothing to say."

"Who's that ever stopped?" she asked. "It didn't stop—" She mentioned Pism C. by his real name.

"What'd he talk about?" I asked.

Miranda grinned toothily; she had a smear of lipstick on a front tooth. "The Three *C*'s," she said, "Chastity, Charity, and Christianity. He's gone ape for all three."

I smiled and started on.

"I hear you're all alone in that glass pad over there," said Miranda.

"Umm."

"I've got a couple things I want to talk over with you. I'm thinking of going into the theater."

"Um-um," I said, edging away.

"Well, give me a ring if you ever need company," said Miranda, and I walked on.

Miranda no doubt thinks that in the theater casting is done from a couch, and I'd be the last to deny that a large number of young women have got more than a headstart that way. Not to mention an increasing number of young men.

A little farther on, I saw Hilary Hansen lying on the grass near the Hansen tennis court. Hilary was drinking a tall, cool drink; he waved languidly at me. Hilary is off to Princeton next month, and I doubt that anyone there will ever know about the slight unpleasantness in which Hilary was involved this spring. Since Hilary's father, Herb, is president of the First National Bank in Sloane's Station, it really isn't surprising that Son Hilary was chosen to be treasurer of the senior prom committee, nor is it surprising that Hilary used the money that was supposed to pay for the orchestra to make a final payment on his M.G. It looked for a while there as if there'd be nothing but a jukebox at the prom, but Herb forked over the money Hilary had appropriated, and *The Sloane's Station Banner* reported that a good time was had by all at the dance. Naturally, Hilary is going to succeed his father at the bank.

As I passed, Herb himself was running the power mower over part of his lawn. Exercise. Herb has two gardeners.

He very carefully manipulated the mower so that he could avoid having to speak to me.

Louella, who has a lively interest in people and is, thus, a splendid gossip, says that Herb Hansen says that I am crazy as a loon.

I am not surprised, and Herb may be right.

Herb is angry with me because when his electronic computer made a mistake of two or three million dollars in my account, said mistake—naturally—in the First National's favor, I was gauche enough to point out this error.

Herb was furious with me.

"Impossible," he said. "It couldn't happen. Electronics don't make mistakes. The man said, and I've got papers to prove it."

I did not take the time to look into Herb's papers. I simply pointed out to him that if the error was not corrected within forty-eight hours I would sue him and destroy the non-mistake-making calculator with my bare hands. I added that in Eleventh-Century France bankers were shot for inefficiency and that I was sorry there wasn't such legislation on our own books and that the next time I was in Wonderland, D.C., I would ask our local Congressman, Fred Loomis, to introduce such a bill.

Herb said that I was quite a card, but that isn't what he really thinks I am.

You see, Herb is bitter. He bought several hundred acres of land in the neighborhood of Our Town when it looked as if his friend might become President of These United States. Herb figured that if his friend became President, his friend's house would become a national shrine. Herb then figured he could sell the land he had bought to the kind of cretins who want to live near the place a President lives when the President is not in the White House. Herb Hansen figured he would become a millionaire.

Well, as we all know, Herb figured wrong, about both his own financial future and his friend's political future, and this has left Herb very embittered.

Our Town is inhabited largely by bitter people, people whose faces are angry and resentful, people who look as if they'd been denied something they deserve.

I was thinking of that this afternoon as I walked past the indignant back of Herb Hansen. I was comparing the village near which I shall end my life with the village in which I began it, and

I was thinking that describing the way I got from New Athens to Sloane's Station is as good a way as any of explaining how I became *insouciant*.

So I'll begin this part of my description of the journey to indifference by saying something about Sloane's Station itself.

This afternoon I stood on the edge of the plateau and looked down into the valley in which the town is built.

The valley is beautiful; the town itself is uncompromisingly ugly.

Sloane's Station was named after General Franklyn Sloane, who brought a regiment of musketeers up here during the Revolutionary War. There was fighting all around Sloane, but he just sat there. He sat there nearly as long as Field Marshal Montgomery sat on his Caen during the summer of 1944.

Montgomery wrote a book of rationalization about his dilatory tactics, and I understand they're going to make a movie out of it, *The Montgomery Story*, which they're going to start the minute they finish *The Henry James Story*.

Fortunately, Sloane did not write a book. As is more often than not the case with men who attain his rank, he was almost totally illiterate, and there were fewer ghosts in those days.

Sloane was also a coward.

Most of his troops eventually deserted and went back to their farms. When the war ended, Sloane was almost the only one of Washington's generals who didn't get at least a Legion of Merit. Sloane didn't even get a Good Conduct Medal, and he wasn't invited to Philadephia for the Inauguration.

Nowadays they'd make him Chief of Staff.

After the Revolution, Sloane stayed right here, and there is a plaque on Old South Friendly Road marking the place he had his command post.

I'm told that in the Thirties, one of those mean, truthful historians—the Beards, Josephson, Woodward, one of those—made quite a case for his theory that Sloane was not only a coward but also a sympathizer with the British. This historian also claimed that George III rewarded Sloane by giving him enough money to buy up most of the land on which the village is now built.

Etta Ettinger, the bearded lady who runs the local library, told me she had never heard of any of those historians.

"Of course, Mr. Barlow and I burned all the Communist books," she said.

Eventually, Etta, who has the typical librarian's reluctance to getting a book off the shelf, produced a biography of General Sloane written by a great-great-granddaughter and very privately printed. I asked if I could borrow it, but Etta said no. She said I would have to eat it there.

So much for the man Sloane's Station is named after.

This afternoon, after I'd stood on the plateau for a long time, I came back here.

As I passed the Hansen place, Elspeth Ectoplasm was driving her twenty-year-old Rolls into the driveway. Elspeth works at the First National, and she may have been bringing Herb a sackful of embezzled funds.

Elspeth Ectoplasm is not her real name, of course; I am calling her that in what is probably a futile attempt to disguise her identity.

Miss Ectoplasm has a place above her neck where most people have a face, but in her case I feel that God or whoever it was got interrupted while assembling her and sent her out incomplete. No face.

All there is where a face would normally be is the small, mean mouth necessary to people who work directly with money—payroll people, bank employees, C.P.A.'s, people who disapprove expense accounts, hotel cashiers, that kind.

The day Ectoplasm and I were first aware of each other, she refused to cash a fifty-dollar personal check of mine.

As is my wont, I patiently explained to Elspeth that I had opened a six-thousand-dollar checking account in that very bank only three days before.

"You must have been out to lunch," I said, smiling pleasantly. "Otherwise, I'd have noticed you." (*Noticed* her?)

"I've heard all about that," said Elspeth. "I know they *say* you opened an account here, but that's as it may be. Your credit rating hasn't been checked yet, and the six-thousand-dollar check you claim you deposited hasn't even begun to clear."

She made her mouth look like a closed drawstring purse. "There are still many, many loose ends in your case," she said.

I swallowed a time or two. I don't believe my throat had ever been drier, and I hadn't had a sliver of sauce for months. I was a cub A.A. at the time.

"What do you mean my *case*?" I asked.

"*Case* is what I said, and *case* is what I mean," said the mouth, inhaling. Then it added, "It will be a week or more before we can honor *any* check of yours. *If* we do."

The mouth then dismissed me and my obviously rubber check.

I backed into the street, trembling. You see, for thirty-some years now I have never entered a bank without having all activity stop. Honest depositors edge away from me; guards finger their pistols to be sure they are loaded; tellers whisper anxiously to each other; vice presidents grab the latest F.B.I., bulletin on the most wanted man, and by the time I get to the teller's window, the president of the bank has pushed a button that double-locks the vaults.

True, nobody every *says* anything, but they can't pull the wool over my eyes. I know what they're thinking.

And at last Elspeth Ectoplasm had come right out and said it. I was a *case*.

As I reached Main Street that day, I figured she was already on the phone with J. Edgar.

Then I saw a man there'll be more about in this chronicle, John Barbori. John was gazing admiringly up at my beard. Obviously he did not recognize a public enemy when he saw one.

"I wonder could I ask you a personal question if you please, sir?" asked John.

I said that he could, and John asked, "Would you be so kind as to tell me who please trims your beard, sir?"

I told him the name of the place in New York, and John sighed. "I could do it better by far and at half the price," he said.

I agreed to let him try and the next week he came out to the house, trimmed my beard, and cut my hair, and he has been doing it ever since, better by far and at half the price.

Back to Elspeth driving into Herb's place. I'll say this for her; she treats Herb Hansen with the contempt he deserves.

"Hansen," she'll say. "How about running over to Poole's and getting me a nice, cold Coke?"

Know what Hansen does? He runs over to Poole's and gets Elspeth a Coke. Elspeth's family has been in Sloane's Station at least two generations longer than Herb's has. I expect Herb thinks that if he runs enough errands for Elspeth, he'll be invited to the Ectoplasm mausoleum on Calm Drive, where a handful of old-timers hold out against the twentieth century and us interlopers on The Road. Herb will never make it to Calm Drive, though, not in a million years.

Herb, the third generation of banking crooks in this area, is just as much an interloper to the handful of Ectoplasms in Sloane's Station as anybody else on the Road. They say Elspeth's mother has a Social Register by the telephone; she won't even talk on the phone to you if your pedigree isn't up to snuff.

You may wonder how with all that breeding Mother Ectoplasm allows Elspeth to work in a *bank*. I'll tell you how; Mother Ectoplasm would starve to death if Elspeth weren't *in trade*. So Mother Ectoplasm pretends that Elspeth is doing charitable work. My God, the lies people need to live by.

Except for Old South Friendly Road, Sloane's Station would be just another sagging New York village—a little better than Patterson, a little more run-down than Brewster, considerably less turn-of-the-century than Pawling.

The Road winds through the foothills of the Berkshires and is lined on either side with meadows, beyond which the hills stretch endlessly on. Very beautiful.

Among the first to notice the beauty was Geoffrey Rawleigh, an assistant secretary of state in the administration of George Washington. Rawleigh had also been a colonel at Valley Forge and was, I gather, a good one. In addition, as has so rarely been true of people around here, Rawleigh had both character and taste.

The Georgian house he built is handsome and is beautifully preserved. Since the death last year of the last Rawleigh descendant, it has been the cause of considerable controversy. I'll come to that in a minute, too.

I don't believe anybody paid much attention to The Road after Rawleigh's death until the early 1920's.

Then Charles F. N. Doran, who had made a fortune selling defective rifles in the first crusade to make the world safe, etc., bought a hundred acres of land on either side of The Road. Next, he built a house that cost an immense amount of money and is certainly hideous enough to justify it.

After that, Doran married Sarah Jane Somethingorother.

Now there isn't a woman on this road you'd feel safe meeting in a dark alley, but Sarah Jane is the most dangerous of the lot. In the first place, she's *tiny*. Already trouble. Second, she has a soft, Southern-type accent and those two first names. Triple trouble. I have yet to meet a Southern woman with two first names that wasn't a man-eater. Three, Sarah Jane was in the Ziegfeld Follies. I've known far more than my share of these ex-Follies sweethearts, too. The sure instinct for the jugular that got them into the Follies in the first place stays right with them to the end, and by the time they get to be around fifty, their looks are gone, but their stilettos are still at the ready, sharper and more deadly than ever. Four, after her days in the Follies Sarah Jane was, for a short time, an executive in the New York department-store jungle. She kneed her way to a vice presidency. We've got a lot of those in this area, too. Those and retired New York's finest police women. The latter come two by two, and while they do not reproduce, they sure as hell multiply, and we all know what they do to a community, running down property values, pushing honest people off the sidewalk, spreading arthritis.

As I say, Sarah Jane didn't come up here with a girl friend; she nabbed Charles F. N.

But can you imagine a more terrifying combination of characteristics in a woman, tiny, two first names, Southern with an accent that butter wouldn't melt, a term in the Follies, *and* experience as a department store in-fighter. Any one of those would be enough to send an honest man looking for a storm cellar, but all of them! *Murder.*

After Sarah Jane got Charles F. N. under legal obligation to her, she sent him off to the city every day to work on her fortune and his coronary, and she went into the real-estate business up here.

God knows how she did it, but in about ten years she managed to persuade a large number of the types that have Made This Country Great that the only way they could prove that they had it made was to buy a hunk of overpriced property on Old South Friendly Road. As a result, The Road is just about the biggest success symbol in this country, and as I believe I said there are more people here whose names are Household Words than just about any place in the United States, with the possible exception of a certain boulevard Out There. I wouldn't know whether they've got more sonsabitches or we have. Pretty even, I should guess.

In the history of the world there has seldom been a more imposing collection of brigands, fourflushers, and people you want to get out of the way of in case they want something on the other side of the room.... What am I doing here? Very simple. I like to live among my own kind.

The widows run The Road. Naturally. Husbands have to run so fast to try to pay off the mortgage that they hardly ever live beyond fifty-eight, fifty-nine, around there. I don't know how old the widows live to be. None of them has died yet.

But let me repeat. Sarah Jane Doran is the most lethal of the lot. She's the one who during the Recent Unpleasantness in Wonderland, D.C., used to greet me on the streets of Sloane's Station by saying, "Well, well, and how's your friend Alger Hiss today?"

Need I add that all the residents of the Road are Episcopalians—except me and my friend Davy Bronson?

The new padre has called on me twice; once I hid in the bathroom, and the other time I lay flat on the floor of my study for more than twenty minutes while that mealy-mouthed fraud walked around the house, looking at it and for me. The Reverend K. L. M. C. Michaelson never found me, though, nor will he. Nobody with four initials will ever find me, and I wouldn't trust a *three*-initial person with an Ingersoll.

But this is big Episcopalian country, and the things they have done that they ought not to have done, I don't even like to think.

The only covenants any of them know anything about are restrictive. That's why there's all the uproar about Davy wanting to buy the Rawleigh place.

Davy had spent a couple summers in rented houses near Pawling, and one day when he was visiting Charley and me, he saw the Rawleigh house and decided he wanted it. What Davy wants he gets. He went immediately to the executor of the Rawleigh estate and made a down payment.

That did it. Within twenty-four hours a Committee to Save the Old Rawleigh Place was formed. Guess who was chairman? Right. Sarah Jane Doran.

For months Hermia Brader has been screaming in *The Sloane's Station Banner* that, "Unless Something is Done Now, the Rawleigh Place Will Go Forever," and, "Is Nothing Sacred in Sloane's Station—NOT EVEN TRADITION?" and, "Where WILL WE TAKE OUR STAND?"

I have the answers to those two questions. I know Hermia won't print them, but I'll record them anyway:

(A) The *last* thing that is sacred in Sloane's Station is tradition; what is sacred is *moola*.

(B) Nowhere. People who live on the Road got where they are by not taking stands on anything ever. You don't get to be a president by taking a stand, and you certainly don't get to be President.

Last week the *Banner* had a front-page story about Davy. The story was fifteen lines in all, framed in a black border, like a funeral notice.

Davy, who had just finished a flick, had been in what Hermia called a *disgraceful altercation* with a newspaper photographer. The implication is that the photographer is slowly dying because of internal injuries inflicted on him by Davy.

Davy spent last Monday evening and a large part of the night pub-crawling on Sunset Boulevard accompanied by an almost Miss America of four or five years ago.

Hermia concluded her inconclusive account of what happened by saying that Davy, "who was demonstrably intoxicated, is presently engaged in an attempt to take over one of Sloane's Station's hallowed shrines, the Rawleigh estate."

Davy is a fifth-a-day man most of the time, but he has never been demonstrably drunk in his life. The more he drinks the more he retreats into his hated self.

If Hermia were just a few years younger, I bet she could get herself a nifty job on one of the news magazines.

What really happened last Monday was that a newspaper photographer tried to take a picture of Davy and Miss Almost-America as they were coming out of one of those questionable places on The Strip. Davy had been drinking, and so had Miss Almost-America, who is married to a third assistant prat-boy at one of the studios.

Words were exchanged on the subject of picture-taking, and Davy, gallantly protecting his companion, kneed the photographer in the groin.

There were a number of righteous editorials in the tabloids all last week. The implication is that Davy has come out in favor of repealing the Bill of Rights. There is nothing more self-righteous than a *newspaper*.

This is a battle in which, along with all other battles, I find myself uncommitted. If Davy Bronson doesn't want his picture taken, he should have gone into some other line of work, like becoming a Trappist monk. By now he should be used to the fact that when he beds down someplace, maids and bellboys and hotel clerks being what they are, his picture and that of his bed companion or his drinking companion are going to appear on the front pages. So Davy might as well relax.

On the other hand, newspaper photographers—a motley crew at best—act as if they had just flushed out the Holy Grail when they try to take such pictures, and when a photographer's groin gets kneed by somebody like Davy, the screams of anguish are as loud as if the Magna Charta were about to be violated. I've told you; I don't like newspapers. I don't like the people who work for them either, especially *reporters* and *photographers*.

Which brings me back to the *Banner*. Hermia, who would have made a simply wonderful Nazi, and Mrs. Doran and a few others of my enemies and neighbors are angry with Davy not only because he used to be named Bronstein. He has added insult to injury by contributing $15,000 to help build the new hospital this county needs and is getting despite the opposition of everybody who lives on The Road.

"I'd rather die than be treated by a socialized doctor," Sarah Jane Doran said at the protest meeting against the hospital. What she meant is that the hospital is going to raise taxes one-tenth of one per cent.

Davy is also a large contributor to the Community Chest; he helped set up a music scholarship fund at the frill-less high school, and he has even contributed several hundred dollars to the library presided over by Etta Ettinger.

"We don't welcome that kind of money," said Etta, but I noticed she slipped the check into a very safe place, her brassière.

"As far as I'm concerned, he should be tarred and feathered and ridden out of town on a rail," Ernestine Kraftall said in the supermarket the other day. "I do not like immorality flung in my face."

I've mentioned that there is talk and considerable circumstantial evidence—like finding a trout in the milk—that Lloyd Barlow delivers something besides the mail at Ernestine's every morning. The thought of Lloyd and Ernestine each getting what the other deserves causes me some brief joy when I think of it.

Well, there you are. Is it any wonder the Road dwellers are manning the barricades to keep Davy away?

Not only is he guilty of all I've mentioned. There are these additional counts against him:

While he is by no means the richest of us on The Road, he started out with less and acquired more of what most people around here think they want, money and notoriety—or fame, same thing.

As Lolly Parsons has so often pointed out, Davy's name and Davy's face are known from Racine to Rangoon. He has been married to three immensely beautiful women who are almost as famous as he is, and he has bedded down with a great many other delectable dishes, many of them also famous.

Moreover, Davy is intolerably good-looking; he has translucent blue eyes, curling brown hair, a nose that turns up at the end, and an engaging smile of great warmth. He is intelligent; he can and does read; he is gallant, and he is kind to those needing kindness.

Even my secretary Pan, who claims to have founded and to be the president of the I-Hate-All-Celebrities Club, adores Davy.

"Hello, Miss Pan," he will say in that quiet voice that has done no harm at all in keeping him at the top of the box-office favorites.

There is a formality in Davy's manner with women, a hint that if the lady—and all women are ladies to Davy—will only oblige him by asking him, he will gladly rush off to defend her honor. What's more, his manner implies that should it be necessary to give his life in the process—why, no matter. The pleasure will be all his.

Davy means it, too. He is nearly guileless.

"Little Miranda wouldn't be safe with a man like that loose on Old South Friendly," Miranda's father told Hermia in Poole's the other day.

Miranda is five-nine in her stocking feet, all muscle, too. Who wouldn't be safe if Miranda Green were loose on Old South Friendly is Davy.

Well, you can see why the friendly residents of Old South Friendly are circulating a petition.

The petition is circuitously worded, but its intent is clear enough. It calls on the executors of the Rawleigh estate to stand firm for a White-Protestant America. I need hardly add that one of the first names signed to it is that of Pism C.

If the petition doesn't work (and it won't), there is talk of getting up a fund. Twenty residents of the Road would each contribute $10,000 to buy the Rawleigh place and make it into a museum, as Hermia Brader puts it, "a glorious monument to our glorious Christian past."

That won't work either. Given the choice between putting up and shutting up, the people on South Friendly will do neither.

And so Davy will spend a fortune to buy the Rawleigh house and grounds, and he will spend another to keep both just as they were, only more so, and whenever he is not Out There he will live in the Rawleigh house, hoping to find what he will never find. Serenity.

When I first got back from The War, Davy—well, he wasn't serene, I guess, but he was surely the best jazz pianist around New York and the best who'd been around for some time. On the rare nights when I was sober enough to make it, I used to go wherever he was to hear him. One night I unfortunately brought George Banning along, and George asked Davy a question—the same question George a few years earlier had asked me. I had said *yes* to the question, and so did Davy, and both of us were wrong.

There will be no pianos in the Rawleigh mansion when Davy is there, no hi-fi, no music of any kind. Davy gets physically ill when he hears music of any kind—especially if it's any good.

But so much now for Davy and so much for The Road.

Now that we've gone full circle, I'll say the few promised words on the village of Sloane's Station. Eventually we get to everything around here; you just have to be patient.

First, the villagers love Davy. He is the only one of us trespassers on the Road the villagers forgive. Well, he and Charley really. They loved Charley, too.

But Davy, who keeps his hurts and his self-hatred and resentments hidden behind a very bland exterior, is a real, live movie star, and he lives up to that expectation in every way, including the red slacks he often wears, the cream-colored Thunderbird he drives, and the girls on his arm whose hair is sometimes scarlet and sometimes lavender.

For the rest of us the villagers have the kind of contempt year-round people have for vacationers in a summer resort.

Since the brewery closed eight years ago, we on the Road are the economic mainstay of Sloane's Station. The villagers never had it so good. Of course, they hate those of us responsible for their prosperity. They invent malicious stories about us, which because they are dull-witted and unimaginative are not nearly as malicious or as interesting as the truth.

We conspicuous consumers on The Road have, of course, changed the character of Sloane's Station. The village used to be surrounded by dairy farms. Now the farms are the phoney kind Pism C. has, mostly income-tax dodges of one kind or another, and the only cows around are Black Angus, a breed that might be all right if it weren't for the people who own most of them. Like French poodles.

The stores in the village cater almost exclusively to us Road dwellers. Mr. Bert's, for instance, Hats and Original Creations, his friend Mr. Jim, who has Only Old Originals, and the Gristede's and the Fancy Foods, Inc., and the shelf of books on Zen at Poole's—not to mention the butcher shop where you can get perfectly grand ground horse meat for only twelve dollars and fifty cents a pound.

NOTES·DICTATED·ON·THE·FIFTH·DAY

There is Dugan's Tavern, filled with the smell of dirty old men, urine, and dead beer; there is what we lovingly call The Arm Pit, now closed but with a sign in front sadly proclaiming that final lie, "Movies Are Better Than Ever." There is Loretta's Diner, our local coffeehouse, no checkers, no newspapers, no intellectual exchange but a place where you can find out more than you have any business knowing about the bed habits of the people in and around town. It takes about ten minutes from the time anything disreputable happens anywhere in this county until it is being malevolently and inaccurately dissected in Loretta's. Ten minutes. I know somebody who's timed it.

There is Donaldson's, "Undertaking with Distinction." There are those who say Henry Donaldson undertook Agatha Donaldson, his wife, before she was quite prepared for it; officially, though, Agatha died of a most unexpected heart attack, and since that happy event, Henry has been shacking up with the Gulwilling girls, the forty-year-old identical twins who run the most outrageously expensive restaurant in this part of the country.

That's about it. Sloane's Station might be Your Town instead of Our Town. Every time I walk down Main Street I get a queasy feeling in the pit of my stomach. You wouldn't think there was as much meanness in the entire world as you see in the first dozen faces you look at. There isn't a man or a woman among them you could trust to hold a watch if you were leaving the room. As for the children, the ones that are any good leave town by the first train as soon as they are able to toddle; the rest stay on, middle-aged at twenty, elderly at twenty-five; and since they have never lived at all, death is a mere formality.

But, as I said, they loved Charley. I give them that. For that matter, so did The Road dwellers. Charley doesn't count popularity. She just expects people to be better than they are, which often causes them to be.

For instance, one day last winter as she was driving me to the station, she waved happily at Mr. Voegler, the only widower on the Road, and he waved at her, even smiling a little. He did not acknowledge my presence.

"Voegler's an unmitigated bastard," I said to Charley.

"I suppose," she said, "but maybe he'd like to be mitigated a little. I bet nobody ever talks to him. He scares people."

"He's got his own personal, private crematorium for the two of us in his backyard," I said.

"Like you," said Charley. "You scare people."

Yes, I thought, Adolphus Voegler, multi-millionaire manufacturer of ball-bearings, misanthrope, supporter of lunatic causes, writer of hysterical letters. Like me.

Once this spring while I was in New York over night, Voegler asked Charley to dinner, and she accepted. Yes, she went. She said that when Voegler showed her the photograph of Mrs. Voegler, who had died nearly fifteen years earlier of cancer, the old man's eyes were moist. At that time, he had just bought the house on The Road, and they were about to move in when they found out.

"When I got home I cried, too," said Charley. "Fifteen years ago, and I didn't even know her. Ridiculous."

"Ridiculous," I said.

In the village, Charley frequently took the time to stop in at Loretta's; she would order coffee and doughnuts and stay on to do what Loretta calls *chewing the fat.*

Charley knows the first and last names of just about all the villagers—except for those who have no last names, like Mr. Bert.

I'll bet there isn't anybody in the village or on The Road who doesn't miss Charley. That is the one thing I have in common with all of them.

But now I've got to get on with the story of me, of how I became totally *insouciant.* Because the account of my journey to Old South Friendly Road, a place I despise, among people I loathe, is the story of that part of my life which begins after I left New Athens—the part for which I can no longer blame my mother or, in fact, anybody else at all. Except me. I did it, citizens. I did it all to me.

I used to look back on my life and wonder which was my one big mistake, my most important wrong decision. Which the fatal step? Which the turn beyond which there was no turning back?

Then, as I've said, one day not too many years ago I looked at myself in the mirror and saw that there was no reflection. I realized that I was completely gone, and I realized that there had never been any turning back. Each small deceit, each tiny treachery, each rationalized lie, each dirty deed over the dirty hours and days and weeks and years had altogether made me what I had become.

(2) The happiest year

Now I'm going back briefly to the morning in August twenty-two years ago when I breathed in the free air of Moline, Illinois.

It's odd the trivial odds and ends of shadow that make up memory. I remember a man with a broad, vacant face who sat across the aisle from me in the Rock Island coach.

"Where you headed, sonny?" he said.

I said, "I'm going to London, England, alone, to study philosophy."

"Heh-heh," said the man, and he went back to reading his *Police Gazette*.

A few minutes later he got up and moved to another seat, and when he got off the train in Chicago, he looked at me strangely and whispered something to the man ahead of him.

"I'm a goddamn midget in disguise," I shouted after him. "They call me Tom Thumb, though that is not my real name. Just ask for LeRoy Lilliput, and they'll let you into the side show free of charge."

It was, of course, raining in Chicago that day, and there was fog coming in from the lake. On little cat's feet, my ass; not once.

As I've said, I went almost immediately to the theater from which "Can You Top Them?" had been broadcast. After a while, regretting my lost youth and my misspent future, I left. I looked in the phone book as I had always done before when I was in Chicago.

I had hoped to see my father's name there, but I didn't. I looked at every face I passed, too, and once I saw a man just ahead—a slight, white-haired man who walked with the list of the never-quite sober. I ran to the man, but it was not my father.

That afternoon as the train left the city I kept looking out the window, hoping for a miracle which didn't happen.

After the city was well behind me, I cried.

I went from Chicago to New York on the Twentieth Century, which cost a little more but came close to living up to expectations, one of the very last things in my life that ever did.

I was disappointed at not seeing any movie stars; from all I had read, I at least expected Shirley Temple, whom I hated. Not even a Shirley Temple, though. There was, however, a woman who in the dusk looked rather like Sally Eilers.

I went into the diner, my first such experience without mother; it was great.

The only thing I was absolutely sure of was that I would not have the cheese sandwich. I have not had one since.

A man named Alonzo first suggested the children's menu, and I gave him a look that I would have made pretty withering if Alonzo had not been a Negro. He then gave me the regular menu, and I glanced at it, then ordered the *filet mignon* because it was the most expensive.

I told Alonzo that I was going to England and why, and he didn't laugh. We talked about the war in Spain; we were sure the Loyalists would win, and we exchanged views on literature. Alonzo told me that Uncle Remus was a crypto-Fascist, even worse than Uncle Tom, who was just a plain Fascist. I had found both uncles a bore, but what Alonzo said pleased me because up to then I had thought you had to like all Negroes, in or out of books. I gave Alonzo a dollar tip, but the minute I did I got scared that he might think I was either a crypto-Fascist or a plain one.

He didn't seem to, though; he pocketed the money rather quickly and apologized for having given me the children's menu.

I went into the club car and ordered a ginger ale. A man with a white mustache and eyes the color of an early morning sky in spring talked to me about anthropology. He taught at Columbia and knew John Dewey and Irwin Edman, both of whom I had read and liked. The man had a recognizable inner tranquility which even then I recognized as rare and enviable.

A little later a woman with the blondest hair I had ever seen came over and sat next to me. She was a little drunk, and she had been watching me curiously for some time.

She said, "You're the cutest little dwarf I ever did see. I been listening to you, honey, and for a midget you're just as bright as a button. You in show biz?"

I believe I told her that it might *behoove* (*behoove* was a word I used often in those days) behoove her to learn the difference between a midget and a dwarf but that I was neither, that I was not in show business, that I was in fact on my way to London, England—

The blonde said, "How'd a good-looking little dwarf like you ever learn a line like that?"

That night, in the womblike upper berth, I remembered the last morning I had spent with my father, realizing, I think, that I would never see him again. I thought of my mother and of her unending efforts to make me an extension of herself and of the fact that she had never once succeeded. I thought of the endless series of *if*'s in my mother's life—*if* the agents in Chicago hadn't been such rapscallions and Hebrews to boot, *if* she hadn't married my father, *if* I had been a girl, *if* I'd studied harder and won the Cranium Derby, and on and forever on. To her dying day I don't think my mother ever realized that each step in life, either the most careless or the least careless step, is the result of the step directly before, and there are no *if*'s. Life is a series of conjunctions, a succession of *and*'s and *but*'s. I thought of the man temporarily named Pavan, who had done one and a half of nearly everything but never two of anything, a man who bored easily, who had never really tried anything difficult, a man for whom what was difficult for most people was easy.

"I'm not going to be like him," I decided. "That's for sure."

I am, though; I am very much like him.

I thought of all the rapacious and dreary people at Pegasus and, when it came to that, just about everywhere else I'd been. I thought, surely the world is not made up of such greedy dullards. I was wrong about that, too.

I thought of New York and London, golden and waiting, just for me.

I didn't realize that Hughie had been right; all I would find wherever I went was just more people—but, as I've said, I did realize that wherever I went *I'd* always be along.

I didn't realize that whether I would be looking at the Venus de Milo or the Great Sphinx or the Champs Elysées at twilight on an April evening, my inevitable first reaction would always be the same. I would sigh a small, sad sigh, and I would say to myself, "Oh. Is that all it is?"

Letty and I were alike in that. Charley was different. I think the happiest time we ever had was our honeymoon in Europe.

I remember when we were in the bus from Orly to Esplanade Les Invalides, Charley, loving every moment of the ride, saying, "Oh, isn't this *fun*?" and, "Goodie, there's the Eiffel Tower," and of Notre Dame, "Oh, my, it's even more beautiful than I expected," and, "Oh darling, thank you, I'll never forget any of this. Thank you." Her childish delight infected several of the other passengers, who smiled, sharing her innocent pleasure.

"I'm going to love everything about Paris," said Charley, taking my hand.

A young Englishman sat on the seat facing us; he was close to a caricature of the blond Oxford undergraduate who always proudly needs a haircut. He stood Charley's exuberance as long as he could, but, finally, he said, "Paris, my dear, is a big, bloody, expensive bore."

Charley looked quickly at him humiliating him with the pity in her eyes, and he turned away, embarrassed. I've always been like that boy, and I was unhappily never able to share Charley's enthusiasms. "You can't ever really share anything," she once said. "You can't share any of yourself, and that's why you can't even bring yourself to ever *like* anything or anybody."

But that was very much later. As I've mentioned, I didn't have that bitter knowledge of myself the first time I went to New York.

I have read all the accounts of the country boy in New York for the first time, including several by more observant and sensitive and far more talented men than I, and none of them ever gave me much. So I'm going to give only the most cursory account of my own first day in the City.

I know this. I'd been in many cities while traveling with "Can You Top Them?", including the short stay Out There that I mentioned, but I had never been to New York, and when I stepped out of Grand Central the next morning, I knew I was home at last. We were meant for each other, the City and I. I looked up at the windows from which, when the time came, I knew people would shower me with ticker tape; I looked at those who would beg for my autograph, who were, even though they didn't know it yet, going to cheer and applaud me.

I checked my bags at the station, and then I took a sight-seeing bus, and then I walked, for miles, I guess. Everything I saw pleased and challenged and delighted me. Like all malcontent hicks, I knew New York was what I had to conquer; it was New York that had to be at my feet. There wasn't another place in the country that mattered a tinker's dam.

I thought of something Letty had once said. When I'd asked, "What do you want to be in New York City?" she had said, "The biggest they've got."

I knew that bright, hot August morning in 1937 that I had to be the biggest, too. The biggest what? Oh, that didn't matter, in either Letty's case or my own. Size was what counted.

Late that afternoon I checked into a decent midtown hotel recommended by the taxi driver who had brought me and my bags from the station. I remember this exchange between me and the clerk:

He said, "You're from Iowa, huh? I saw the picture, *State Fair.* Pretty good picture."

I smiled tolerantly. "Of course it doesn't bear the slightest resemblance to reality," I said.

I pointed to my bags. "I shall require those immediately."

When I got to my room, I had a moment of panic. I felt completely alone and very scared. I thought of Hughie and wanted to call him and ask for his shoe size and ask had it been his shadow I saw in the station and would he please forgive me. I wanted to call mother and ask how the Eastern Star meeting had gone in Des Moines. I wanted to call Pavan and once more hear his disjointed talk about whatever came to his disjointed mind. I would even have settled for calling that befuddled idiot, Mrs. Horatio P. Baker. "Just murdered my uncle, Mrs. Baker," I wanted to say, or her husband. "Between you and I, President Baker...."

I thought of the river, brown and sluggish on an afternoon like this; I thought of Humphrey Hall with its smell of summer and of my great-great-grandfather's dream; I thought of the whispering stream in Mettabel and Dick's back yard and of Spot and of the horses that missed me and of Orion and even Mignon Velma. I remembered them all, enemy and friend, with affection and nostalgia.

Then I called Letty, and she told me what subway to take to get to Morningside Heights. Then she said, "I tell you something funny? I've been homesick. Isn't that a hoot, an absolute hoot? I wouldn't go back there for five hundred million dollars, but I've been homesick."

I agreed that that was an absolute hoot.

Professor Durr and his wife, with whom Letty was staying, are of little importance; I may have said Durr was head of the Fine Arts department before Pavan came. He was a gentle man; he was also the fattest man I have ever seen. He looked like the cartoons of William Howard Taft. His wife was blonde and very Germanic, both in appearance and in manner. At dinner that evening, she talked almost exclusively about what great things Hitler was doing for Germany and about a man named Joe McWilliams who was then a street-corner orator in Yorkville but who, according to Mrs. Durr, was straight on his way to the White House.

I was happily able to keep my mouth shut, perhaps because I was holding Letty's hand under the table.

Afterward, Letty and I went to the Radio City Music Hall, and, since neither of us knew we weren't supposed to like the Rockettes, we did. Then we went to the Oak Room of the Plaza. My idea. I knew all about the Plaza, having several times read *The Great Gatsby*.

I wanted to act like a Fitzgerald character but considering my age and size didn't feel up to it; so I ordered a Coke. Letty, who looked older than her age, had a daiquiri. "With loads of ice," she said, "and *Gordon's* gin."

"Oh, baby," she said. "We'll make the big time; just you wait."

"You've been going to too many movies, Letty," I said, "though I admit we could make sweet music together, you and I."

After we left the Plaza, we took the subway back to Morningside Heights, and I remember Letty said, "I love New York. I'm never going back to Iowa. Never. Never. Never."

"Aren't you going to get your degree?" I asked.

"Not this kid. I haven't got time. Besides, you'll be the educated one in our family. You haven't had relations with anybody have you?"

I swore I hadn't, but since Letty and I had never discussed marriage, I didn't know what to say to the *our-family* talk.

Letty was looking hard at me, as if she hadn't ever really seen me before, and she said, "You know something? You're not even bad-looking."

I nodded modestly and ran a finger over the palm of her hand; I'd heard that was supposed to be very sexy.

"Until I met you I thought geniuses were clumsy or had big heads or something," Letty said.

I said, "I'm not a genius. I simply have a very good memory and a reasonably high I.Q."

Letty kept looking at me. "Actually, you're quite good-looking. You look a little like you could be Tyrone Power's kid brother."

I said, "I think you're nice, Letty. I think you're the nicest girl I ever met."

"You do, don't you, darling?" said Letty, and then she kissed me on the cheek. "Don't ever stop thinking that. Ever. Ever. Ever."

"Don't worry," I said. "I won't." Then I said, "I love you, you know."

It seemed to me to be the kind of thing called for under the circumstances, or maybe I even believed it.

"You mean it? You really mean it?"

"I love you beyond any doubt, reasonable or otherwise," I said.

"It's lovely, being loved," said Letty. "It's absolutely lovely."

She held my hand very tight. "I don't ever want to get old," she said.

"Like Mrs. Moonlight in that play? She was very unhappy."

"No. Not like that. Like Jane Wyatt in that movie we saw. Remember? And Margaret Sullavan in *Only Yesterday*. Remember how you cried?"

I said I remembered, and I kissed Letty, and just before we got off the subway, she said, "Golly, it's wonderful being us. I'm going to get Myrtle Frump's job on the magazine, and you're going to be president of the whole works, I'll bet. And people are going to look at me and say, 'Know who *she* is? She is Mrs. President of the whole works!'"

Letty and I kissed a good deal on the walk from the subway to the Durr apartment. It looked to me as if my world was about to be changed, but that, as I've indicated, had to wait until I got to London. The Durrs were home and were up when we got back. Mrs. Durr was reading *Mein Kampf* in German.

Letty took the next morning off from work and came to the ship to see me off. As I've said, it was the *Queen Mary*, and I was traveling third class. Letty had bought a bottle of champagne, and we drank it in my cramped cabin. Then we went to inspect the luxury of first class.

After we had finished examining what was available to our betters, Letty took my hand and said, "Let's go on deck."

We did, the first-class deck.

"I hate that dinky little cabin you're in," said Letty. "It's so cramped, and you'll probably get a roommate that smells."

We brushed shoulders with a fabulously pretty girl who couldn't be—

"Isn't that ...?" I asked.

Letty nodded. "She'd better get herself another henna rinse before *she* gets to England."

We stood for a while at the railing, and I realized that if I said a word I'd break into tears.

"When we get rich," said Letty, "I'm going to drink champagne and eat *paté de foie gras* and caviar *all* the time."

I said, "You'd better learn how to pronounce *paté de foie gras* before you start eating it; besides, if you eat it *all* the time, you'll break out in pimples," and I said, "I'll miss you, Letty. I wish you were going with me."

"I'll wait for you," said Letty. "You can count on that. I'll wait for you, but when I go to Europe, I'm going right. You know what I mean?"

"You mean in the Deflowering of the Maidens Suite?" That was what we had called the largest and most luxurious of the first-class suites.

Letty giggled and nodded.

Then a precise, not-quite (I learned) public-school voice on the loudspeaker said that it was time for all ashore, etc.

Letty leaned over and kissed me very hard. "I'll wait," she said. "I'll be waiting. Hurry back."

Then she said, "And, remember, don't have relations with any-body. Promise."

I promised; that was the first of many promises to Letty that I broke.

"Don't forget to write," she said.

She gave me a quick forehead kiss, and she ran.

I watched her on the pier as long as was possible. Her bright yellow hat and the lighter yellow dress were still visible when every-thing else on the pier had become a long, gray blur.

Then I cried a little in pleasurable self-pity.

I watched the first waves, and then I turned and was going to go below. On the way, an efficient-looking middle-aged steward passed me, turned and said, "Begging your pardon, young man, but are you a first-class passenger?"

I said, "No. Would you like to clap me in irons?"

When I got back to my cabin, an old man was lying, fully clothed, on the upper bunk, his face to the wall. I could tell by the scarred cardboard suitcase on the floor and by the shiny black suit that he had on that the old man was very poor.

He turned toward me as I came in, and I smiled at him. "Hello, sir," I said. "My name is Joshua Bland. I imagine that we are to be cabin mates."

The old man looked at me, then, without speaking, turned back toward the wall. He had a thin, tired face and completely white hair, and when on a rough day it was necessary to keep the port-hole closed, he was the kind of cabin mate Letty had predicted. He smelled. So far as I know he neither washed nor took off his clothes, not even his shoes and socks, during the entire voyage.

"Wouldn't you rather have the lower berth?" I asked. "It's much more comfortable, and I really don't care one way or the other."

There was no reply; so I put my bag on the lower berth and started unpacking.

"Which drawers do you want to use, sir?" I asked. There was no reply; so I used the bottom two. The old man never unpacked his suitcase.

The steward told me that the old man's name was Antonio Ronaldo. He had come to the United States from Naples when he was a boy, and now in what I guessed were his seventies (though I wasn't much good at guessing ages in those days) he was meeting a brother in England, and the brother was going to take him to Naples, appropriately to die. The steward said he thought the old man had made his living in New York by shining shoes.

It was a lonely voyage, and it seemed to me very long. In the dining room, I hid behind that old reliable, a book, and after the first day or two, no one spoke to me, not even the people at my table.

I played a few games of deck tennis with a dull English boy who had just spent a year with his divorced father, a doorman at the Waldorf. He was a very phlegmatic, uninteresting boy, which surprised me. I had the illusion that all the English were absolutely fascinating. He was no better at deck tennis than I was, which was terrible.

I wrote letters, one every day to Letty. They were very good letters, unlike the letters I wrote her later, which became famous. The letters I wrote later were dishonest; the ones I wrote on the way to England were ingenuous, adolescent, and often foolish, but they were serious, nakedly honest, and sometimes embarrassingly revealing. Letty took them with her when she left me; I can't imagine why, but it's just as well. I'd as soon not remember how, beneath the rather flashy exterior I wore to protect myself from injury, I was really quite a nice boy. My instincts were not tempered by compromise or dulled by wear; my emotions were raw and innocent and ran very deep.

I wrote to Hughie and apologized for our last day together, and I wrote to Orion Bernstein, expressing my gratitude for what he had done for me, and I wrote to mother and Pavan, saying nothing.

I watched the ocean for hours on end, and I tried to love it as Conrad had—and, in his way, Melville. I never succeeded, though; the ocean bored me.

The cliffs of Dover were dingier than I had expected, and the day the *Queen Mary* arrived at Southampton, all of England seemed to me to be very gray, very damp, and very foggy. It reminded me of Chicago.

The old man who shared my cabin hadn't said a word the whole time. He was always on his bunk; so far as I know he left it only to go to the toilet. He so seldom moved that I several times wondered if he might be dead.

One day when the weather had been especially bad and the sea very rough, I asked if I could bring him something from the dining room, but he didn't answer.

The steward said he had brought the old man soup several times but that it had never been touched.

The last morning of the voyage, shortly after our arrival at Southampton, I said, "Good-bye, sir. It's been awfully nice knowing you."

The old man still didn't turn.

Feeling that what I had said was inadequate, I stopped at the door of the cabin.

"I wish we'd had more of a chance to talk," I said.

Still no movement or sound from the upper berth.

So I left the cabin and never saw my cabin mate again.

While I was in England, I thought very often of the old man. I kept hoping that he had made it to Naples and that he'd died happy. I was reading philosophy, and I was sure that if I studied hard enough and long enough I'd discover why he had wanted to go back to the place he was born just to die.

I never found out. I did, however, spend the happiest, most nearly satisfying nine months of my life, and you know something? I remember very little of it.

I have never been able to recall many of the pleasures of my life for long. On the other hand, the pain I've suffered always rushed back, every second of it to be suffered through a second time, a third, sometimes a hundredth. I'm not sure why.

I know nothing makes me more *uncomfortable* than happiness. I invariably break out in a guilty rash. Is it because the disciples of that odd psychopath John Calvin got to me so early?

Surely that is one of the reasons the minute things start going well, I start getting worried. I know that They've got a knockout blow all ready and waiting for me. "Look at him," They say, nudging each other and grinning malevolently, "*He's* happy. Well, We'll soon put a stop to that. We'll fix his wagon."

They do, too. Always.

Who are They? Why, myself, of course, in several easily recognized disguises.

The only disguise I need mention at the moment is my hypochondria. For instance, in the midst of what was probably the most pleasurable period I've had lately, I felt a sharp stab of pain in the small of my back. *Of course*, I said to myself, cancer. I almost immediately drove back here and saw Sid Levinson, who has nursed me through several imagined brain tumors, heart attacks, strokes, and cancers. It turned out the pain in my back was a stiffness caused by sitting too long in one position in the Schubert Theater in New Haven. That and the fact that Charley and I were about to be married. Plus the feeling that the play was not only going to be a hit; it was probably also good. (It won that year's Critics Award.) Intolerable.

Well, you see. What I'm getting at, going the usual long way round, is that a large part of what happened to me during my first stay in England is gone from my mind.

I know this. That was the first time in my life—and very nearly the last—when I was on my own, when nobody really expected anything of me. Nobody cared how young I was or how much notoriety I had had at *The Parthenon of the Prairies*, or that some columnist had reported that I and a thirteen-year-old harridan named Baby Eileen were in love, or that I had endorsed Wheaties at ten.

At London University I was just another student, a little smaller than most, a little more arrogant and vociferous, but, since I was one of a handful of Americans, perhaps only typical.

There were lectures, brilliant, tedious, largely mediocre. I could attend all or none; nobody cared. I quickly discovered who knew what he was talking about and who had taken the trouble to learn to express himself clearly, and I never missed a lecture of the good ones—Harold Laski, for instance, who was always both stimulating and entertaining.

There were libraries, including the British Museum, but nobody had any interest in seeing to it that I visited them or read any of the books in them or whether, having read the books, I understood or digested the ideas in them. I found out that in discussing an abstract idea, I was as good as most, but there were some who were very much better. I worked hard, especially at the course in logic taught by Hollis Lindsay.

I like to think that instead of having to dominate every discussion, my usual pattern, I did as well as I could considering the size and shape of my mind. Usually, you see, then and now, if I couldn't dominate, I wouldn't take part. If I wasn't positive I'd win the game, I wouldn't play the game.

I had friends—

Cedric Hathaway, a teddy bear of a man with a growth of yellow, wirelike stuff on his head, and cheeks as red as fire. He was eighteen and had already had a book of highly praised poems published; he seemed to write a poem every day, and he always read it aloud to anyone who would listen, including me. The poems were often very good, too, and all of us who listened were sure Cedric Hathaway would win a Nobel Prize some day, but Cedric said that would involve his having to live too long. "In which case, they might make me poet laureate. I'd *far* rather die."

Years later when I heard Dylan Thomas read I was reminded of Hathaway, though Cedric's voice was less melodious, possibly because he was a Yorkshireman instead of Welsh. Perhaps the same enemy of promise as Thomas's kept Cedric from a Nobel Prize; I've wondered.

Lee Bullet was in one of my classes; I remember almost nothing about him—except that he mocked everything, especially himself. Early in the war he wrote an extraordinary book about being a fighter pilot; shortly after the book was published, he was shot down over France, thus achieving a kind of temporary immortality which he would have loathed.

Gerald Martin—an insincere, pushy little man of twenty—who has since become an actor, a playwright, and a character in New

York and London, as famous in his inconsequential way as the Schweppes man. The main thing I remember about Martin is that when you had tea with him he never ordered a bun or a muffin. He'd take half of yours. "You aren't going to eat *all* of that, are you?" he'd ask, his tone indicating that if you did you would be guilty of greed. At that time my insecurities always forced me to say, "Heavens, no, Gerald. You take it." He would, too; every time.

A couple of years ago Gerald invited me to the Plaza for drinks. When we'd finished talking—I forget what about—there was an interminable wait while neither of us reached for the check. Finally, in perhaps the stillest, smallest voice ever heard in the Oak Room, Gerald said, "Am I host?" My reply was remarkably loud, unbearably clear. "That you are," I said.

Don't try to tell me all that analysis hasn't paid off.

There were many others I knew, liked or hated. I see some other faces and recall other deeds, but mostly I remember the almost unending flow of words. We talked—talked in Lyons Corner Houses, in obscure saloons, in abandoned classrooms, in grimy restaurants in Soho, in attic rooms, in houses in Mayfair, and, often, at the Lindsays'. God knows whether the talk was better or worse than the kind going on in colleges now. It was different. We didn't yearn for safety. Heaven forbid. *Safety!* We demanded danger. But were we also unselfish? Probably not. Were we kind? I doubt it.

I do know that we seldom listened to each other. Few of us ever heard the question; we were too busy preparing our answer.

That's about all. As I've said, I held a few hands at Moral Rearmament meetings, but the hands were too sweaty for my taste and the incidence of halitosis too nearly unanimous. I did take the Oxford Oath, three times, swearing I'd never bear arms in a foreign war. At the same time, I wanted desperately to go to Spain. I said so, often too. I may even have thought I meant it. Considering my age and my size, that might have brought down the house. It never did. Possibly because everybody else was too busy telling how he couldn't wait to shoot a Fascist bastard just as soon as, and so forth.

Silent, intense young men who never talked at all kept disappearing from various of my classes, and later they were often said to be in Spain. There were many young Communists among the students, and they were always picketing and protesting and circulating petitions. I ached to be asked to join them, but I never was.

I spent the first four months in London in a dank, gloomy boarding house not far from Bloomsbury Square. I can't remember any of the other boarders—bank clerks, widows, and reedy young men who worked in the tie department at Harrod's or Simpson's.

I remember that the maid-of-all-work appeared at my bedroom door with a pot of tea every morning at seven, and at seven-thirty she brought me a kettle of hot water for a bath, which by the time I took it in the frigid bathroom was never more than lukewarm.

I shivered all through the winter. I am a hothouse flower by nature and really only comfortable when the temperature is around eighty. I doubt if I was ever any place—except the theater—where it got above sixty.

I remember that for five months in that dismal digs we had Brussels sprouts for supper five evenings a week. On Tuesdays and Thursdays we had cauliflower.

I remember that the meals were served forth with a foolish flourish by two sisters named Stanton who every evening wore the same black, long-sleeved dresses that smelled of decay and sweat and in which, both proudly announced, they planned to be buried.

That's all except for a few words about the theater and the Lindsays. The former is important if only because I've made my living in the theater ever since The War.

I started going to the theater that winter in London because it was really the only place I could keep warm. If the play was a hit, that is, with the theater packed.

Don't worry; I'm not one of your the-theater-is-a-shrine fellows. You're not going to get anything from me about the quickening beat of my heart in that hushed moment when the lights are dimmed, just before the curtain goes up.

Nonsense. I like going to plays, good ones and bad ones; I often enjoy myself; I have at rare times been moved and enlightened and even somewhat changed by what I saw, but I'm just as likely to bust out crying at the latest rewrite of *East Lynne* as at the new offering by an annoyed young man of forty whose main trouble is he doesn't like girls.

This theater-is-a-shrine stuff is mostly spread by sentimental liars who write highly successful autobiographies that are about as dependable as a Ouija board. Of course, actors, not a one of whom has an I.Q. of above eighty, get all weepy when they talk about The Theater, but then we all know that actors shouldn't be allowed out when they're not on stage.

The other people in the theater come in two types: (a) those manic-depressives with the neurotic necessity to justify themselves to themselves with something outside themselves and (b) racketeers of one kind or another who are about as sentimental as the Mafia.

Once in a distant city in a far-off land I went to a professional free-for-all. God knows why. Maybe it was raining, and if there's one thing I do know it's when to come in out of the rain. Anyway, however it happened, there I was when twelve boozy, paunchy old bums straight off Skid Row were pushed into the ring together. They started hitting each other, more or less at random. One of the most nauseating exhibitions I have ever seen. You might ask, if I was so nauseated, did I walk out? No. I stayed until the end. It seems to me now that the ring was knee-deep in bodies and blood. Finally, only one frazzled old boozer was still upright, and the referee held up his palsied arm. The *winnah*.

As the *winnah* was being led out of the ring, he slipped—on some blood, no doubt—and fell flat on his ass. That's when I left.

Well, that's the closest I can come to describing what the theater is like. A barbaric free-for-all in which should you ever win, you are for sure going to fall flat on your face or your ass.[9]

That's enough. I went to the theater in London that winter to keep warm. And I can't think of a better reason.

---

9 I have never been a purveyor of the cuddly anecdotes those concerned with theatrical shenanigans tell about each other—what Ethel said to her children that day in Central Park, what Alfred said to Lynn about her dress and what Lynn said back, that kind of thing. The only theatrical story I ever heard that hit the nail on the head had to do with the two fellows cleaning the cage of a herd of elephants that had been *sick*. One of the fellows said, "Another day like this and I'm getting out of Show Biz."

Late in January 1938, I received a letter from Orion Bernstein. I have it before me now, yellow and coffee-stained but intact:

My dear Joshua:
   Hollis Lindsay writes me that you are doing well, which pleases me.
   The last night you were in my cubbyhole in New Athens, I had many things to say to you, but communication between friends is very difficult, not to say impossible. I wanted to tell you that I believe you can possibly become something rather special. I can't tell you how or in what way. I do know that you have remarkable endowments. I wish I could tell you how best to make use of them, but I cannot.
   I have always sensed in you a great dissatisfaction, with yourself, with your environment, with your fellow human beings. You are very quick to anger and to blame, and you once said to me, "In my whole life nothing's been even half as good as I expected it to be." You were then—what? Fourteen? That sad sentence would have been understandable coming from an aging cynic—but at fourteen?
   That kind of bitter dissatisfaction—well, it could be very dangerous. It could lead—a single for-instance—to your deciding that since whatever you accomplish will always turn out to be dross, not gold, why bother? Why even try?
   I have known a few not-much-above average men who have fulfilled themselves, who became important, useful human beings. But you. You have both a head and a heart. How unusual. What an irresistible combination. What a challenge to make use of both. But will you? I will be deeply interested.
   Last winter when you wrote the thesis on "Societies—Utopian and Otherwise" for my class, I could tell that you were really very excited by having read most of the first-rate thinkers on the subject, from Plato to Sir Thomas More to Walter Lippmann and, having distilled their thoughts, by having made a contribution, however small, of your own. Even though nobody except me read your paper—which, as I said, was extremely good—I think you had some inkling of just how exciting the disciplines of scholarship can be. And the rewards of a difficult piece of work well done.
   What comes to you easily you will despise and you will also despise yourself and perhaps the rest of mankind. A man must esteem himself to be complete.
   End of lecture.
   I am going off to Spain—still by no means totally committed. Why am I going then? I guess because I believe with Holmes—the Justice—that, "A man must take part in the actions and passions of his time lest he be judged not to have lived."
   I shall do my best not to die in Spain.
   I do not look forward to dying, nor do I think I will, if called on, do it especially well. The people I've known who've made a fetish of meeting it bravely were mostly sentimental fools. My own feeling is that it should be done with a minimum of pain.

I cannot help comparing myself as we all do with the men and women I have known. Whatever the score, I have had an extremely fortunate and happy life. If I had been tortured by ambition, I would have gone further and achieved more, but I think that I would have understood far less and surely would have missed happiness. I hope very much that you achieve it. Since we are unique personalities, we cannot pass on to each other effective recipes for the great thing, the wonderful dish which we so ardently desire to whip together, to cook and to enjoy. But I wish you good luck.

Very sincerely yours,
Orion Bernstein.

P.S. If I find out what truth is, I'll drop you a line.

Less than two months after I got the letter, Hollis Lindsay received word that Orion, despite doing his best, had died in Spain. We tried to find out how and where—shot by the enemy, by a dissident comrade; dead of malaria, malnutrition, gangrene, boredom, or disgust? We never knew. Still, I envied him his death and wondered if he had found out what truth was.

It is fashionable now to dismiss and deprecate the several hundred young men of the International Brigade who died in Spain. I knew Orion well and was acquainted with several young Englishmen who died there. At the time I thought them rather noble and, for that matter, still do, but then I am foolish and old-fashioned, and am unwilling to rewrite history for the convenience of the moment.

And now for the Lindsays.

I met Hollis Lindsay the first day I was at the University, and we got along beautifully from the start, our friendship greatly helped, of course, by a mutual affection for Orion.

Hollis Lindsay was fifty; he was a tall man with the bearing of a professional army officer, possibly Prussian; he wore glasses with lenses of binocular thickness; his dark gray hair was in a modified crew cut, and he always carried a swagger stick. God and Hollis alone knew why the swagger stick.

Never was a man's appearance less like the man. Hollis Lindsay was a pacifist; he spoke softly; he was patient, diffident, and while not humble, possessed of great humility. He was incapable of being unkind. He had only to see a face or to hear a name to remember it. He had a deep faith in the potentialities of people, and since he believed that everyone was better than he was, all who knew him tried their best not to disappoint him; as a result, quite commonplace people often found that they could temporarily become almost as remarkable as Hollis Lindsay thought them to be. He was incapable of malice and, seemingly, of anger, and since he was unable to contradict anyone, fools laughed at him and went about getting their own way and then found that Hollis, without trying, had prevailed, but even those who had acceded to his wishes without realizing it, loved him not in spite of that fact but because of it.

I have not forgotten his gentle gray eyes, or the wide range of his mind, or the quality of his goodness. Since we meet so few good people in our lives, and since we are so suspicious of goodness when we find it, I'm sure I will be accused of exaggerating. A bad man; no trouble at all. We are born prepared to believe the worst of everybody. Nothing pleases us more than to discover the duplicity of a friend; such a discovery makes it easier for us to live with ourselves for another twenty-four hours.

But I must insist. Hollis Lindsay was a good man.

I dictated the above without consulting the diary I kept in England. I have now done so, and the memory of Hollis Lindsay and what I wrote about him twenty-some years ago are startlingly similar. In April 1938, not long before I took the Housman book to the Lindsay house at Land's End (mentioned much earlier in this peripatetic record), I wrote in my diary:

I have never before really met anybody I'd like to be like. At least not anybody I really thought I *could* be like. I couldn't have been *like* Hughie if I'd tried for a million years, or like Orion, when it comes to that, but I do think that if I tried very hard for a very long time, I might some day be half as good a man as Hollis Lindsay is.

It is very late now—I am tired and depressed, but I must go on. I now count the time left by the hours.

These few further thoughts about Hollis. He was not widely known. I doubt that it occurred to him that men and women—ah yes, indeed—would kick and claw and knife each other to get their names in print, but then he was complete in himself, and those with the compulsion to get famous never are.

He was one of the few people I've ever known who really loved teaching. He was stimulating without being deliberately controversial. I've known many of the latter, and for reasons I've never taken the trouble to analyze, they almost always turn eccentric, and along about forty-five they get to be campus characters and are never worth a damn as teachers after that. Hollis Lindsay was not like that; he was a solid, hard-working scholar with an ability to penetrate and pass on the meaning of the most obscure prose and the most puzzling idea. I sometimes suspected that the philosophers might not always have agreed with his interpretation of their ideas, but no matter. He not only didn't expect his students to agree with him; he was disappointed if they did. Because he knew a great deal about all of his students and because he cared not only about what they did in class but before and after, we all worked hard not to disappoint him.

Kathryn Lindsay was in her late forties, but she had the trim figure of a woman ten years younger. She never seemed to pay any attention to her appearance, but her dresses must have come from Paris. I've yet to see an English dress that my Aunt Mettabel couldn't have made better out of a pattern from *Delineator*. Kathryn Lindsay's long brown hair curled naturally around her ears. She had blue-green eyes and the English complexion which, when not overdone, brings beauty to the plainest face.

Mrs. Lindsay was not plain; her features were strong but feminine, and she had the high cheekbones that in my youth I associated with good breeding. Since then I've had gutter girls in plays of mine who have the same facial bone structure. Breeding often has nothing to do with it. It's still great to have if you're a woman, though.

But it was not Kathryn Lindsay's appearance that I found most appealing. She had something I had never up to then known in a woman, something I have rarely come across since.

Composure is the word that comes closest to describing what I mean. *Serenity* will do. *Equanimity. Calm.* They all come close, but this is one of many cases where one word or even several won't communicate my meaning. You either know what I mean or you don't.

If you do, then you also know that the quality is unmistakable. You cannot walk into a room without recognizing it at once if a woman there has it. Since I have spent most of my life among women who can't even relax in the grave, I am a connoisseur of the quality.

Let me hurriedly say that it has nothing whatever to do with *charm*. New York City is armed to the teeth with *charming* women, all of them working at it, day and night, asleep or awake, in and out of bed. I'll say this. In bed *charm* is—well, frankly, I'd rather she ate an apple. And as someone who had always suffered from morning dyspepsia and, for a large part of my life, acute hangover as well, I'd rather have breakfast with a leper than with a woman who's working at being *charming*.

In any case, Kathryn Lindsay had—let's settle on the word—*composure*. Hers and Hollis's only child, Ronnie, had died a few years earlier. If I ever knew how, I have blotted the information out of my mind.

There was a photograph of Ronnie on Kathryn's dressing table; he was a good-looking boy, taking more after his mother than his father, though the face was very *manly*. (I hate the word *virile*. Ah there, Dr. Baron.)

Ronnie was very much missed by the Lindsays, but when they spoke of him, it was with a loving regret at his death, not the disguised necrophilia often so popular among parents who've lost a child.

The Lindsays lived on a street the name of which I have carefully forgotten. It is not far from Marble Arch. The Street is short and lined with horse-chestnut trees and lindens. The houses were small, but no two were alike. The Lindsay house was brick, three stories high and cheerful. When there was sun, it bathed every room.

From the time I arrived in London, I always had tea once a week with the Lindsays, and I usually spent Sunday there, too. There were usually other students and sometimes other professors and people who wrote good books and criticism for the better weeklies and some painters and composers and musicians, a few politicians; the Lindsays were members of the Liberal Party. The groups were never self-consciously put together; they simply happened. The Lindsays liked to have people around them, and people liked to be around them. It seems to me there was always laughter in the house and always the sound of happy conversation.

Those who are made uncomfortable when told of a paragon will be pleased to know that in my eyes Hollis Lindsay did have one major fault; he was excessively fond of *rambling*. Now the English *ramble* isn't as hearty as the German hike, and, thank God, there is seldom any *singing*; nevertheless, so far as I'm concerned, walking is a solitary pastime. Two people, maybe, if they're very fond of each other; more than two, a mob.

Hollis, on the other hand, went for a *ramble* someplace near London almost every Sunday morning in the spring of 1938. He usually was accompanied by as many as half-a-dozen students. I went once or twice, but I much preferred to stay home with Kathryn Lindsay, who was also anti-ramble.

"When you come home, we'll want to hear all about it, dear," she would say, kissing her husband on the cheek. Then she and I would spend a quiet day together. Being composed, she was not a compulsive talker. At the time I wasn't either; but since she was almost the first woman I'd ever known who when I spoke to her didn't seem to have her mind on more important matters, I would sometimes tell her what was on my mind, knowing she would be interested because she liked me. In her whole life she had probably never actively disliked anybody. I also knew that nothing I ever said would shock or surprise her, and I never had to worry that she'd laugh at me.

She spoke of Ronnie, who had been a healthy, happy boy, athletic, but not to the point of a fetish, studious, but not a grind, popular, but not needing it, considerate, particularly to his parents but, like his father, kind to all human beings, etc., etc.

The more I heard about him, the more I hated his guts, and this may be another instance in which memory distorts. I suspect Kathryn Lindsay didn't volunteer information about Ronnie; I'll bet I asked.

I remember this. "Was Ronnie an extrovert?" I once asked.

Kathryn Lindsay said, "Good Heavens. I don't believe in those silly classifications of people. Do you?"

"Some people are more *extro* and other more *intro*," I said. "It's all a matter of degree."

"Well, I expect Ronnie was a bit more *extro*," said Mrs. Lindsay, "but no more than was healthy."

"As a general rule, I don't care much for extroverts," I said.

Anything else? Well, yes. The Lindsay house was the fourth and the last house I knew very well in which there was love. They were wonderful together. You couldn't be with them more than two minutes without knowing that they loved each other and, equally important, were unfailingly considerate of each other.

They must have had quarrels; that's only human. Isn't it? As I've indicated earlier, I'm inclined to make universal truths out of my limited observations. I simply cannot imagine a married couple that doesn't quarrel.

That's like Charley's childhood. She would say, "Every time you talk about that misery of a childhood you had, I think about how absolutely perfect my first fifteen years were. Really, they were magnificent. I don't remember anybody ever shouting at anybody. Ever. We lived in a great big house all filled with tender loving-kindness. Just what Doctor Spock ordered." Then she'd look at me. "Don't you believe me?" she'd ask. "Sure," I said. "Of course. I *believe* you." I never did, though; I just thought she remembered it wrong.

The news of Orion Bernstein's death in Spain reached Hollis Lindsay in mid-March.

London was very gloomy at that time. I guess it always is in March—but in 1938 especially so. Hitler had marched into Austria, and no one had stopped him. It was clear to everyone—with the possible exception of the people in charge of the government—that Czechoslovakia was next. There was a sense of doom, a feeling that the sooner the war came the better, along with a forlorn hope that perhaps what appeared to be inevitable was not inevitable, and maybe if the peace would last just a little longer—as one of the girls I knew put it, "Hitler might get cancer; there's always that."

Anyway, even before I heard about Orion's death, I was feeling depressed and for the first time since my arrival in London, I was achingly lonely.

I didn't cry the afternoon Hollis told me that Orion was dead.
He drove me to the sagging digs I've described, and when I started
to get out of the car, he said, "You know what you're going to do?
You're going to come and live with Kathryn and me for a while."

That's when I burst into tears.

We went up to my room, followed by the Sisters Stanton and
the maid-of-all-work.

"You ladies have a beautiful house here," Hollis Lindsay told
the Sisters Stanton, "but this boy needs a mother and father, and my
wife and I are going to try to be that to him, at least for a time. So
I'm taking him home to live with us."

He paid the Stantons a month's rent, overtipped the maid, and
helped me pack my belongings, which weren't many.

I cried like a two-year-old the whole time, but that night and
all the nights in London that followed, save the last, I stayed in the
last house of happiness I have known.... Except this one, of course,
but only for a little while. I saw to that....

It seems to me now in looking back on it that the sun began
shining the morning after I moved into the Lindsay house and that
it didn't stop until the morning I realized I had to punish them for
being kind to me.

For that offense I destroyed what was most precious to each of
them.

Why is it that everyone I have touched in my life, however
briefly, has been the worse for it? Why must I destroy? What makes
it necessary for me to hate? For what reason are there those like me
condemned to walk the earth incapable of love of self or any other?

And why is the night so suddenly black? What happened to the
moon? Where are the stars?

And why has what was only a moment ago a benign breeze
turned into a rapacious wind? And is it thunder just beyond the
horizon or is what I hear the tired, erratic beat of my cold heart?

My hands tremble now; the skin on my arms is gooseflesh,
and my blood is ice. I never told anyone except the doctor in New
Haven what I did. Eventually, I understood the reason for it—but I
did not learn how to stop myself from doing it again.

There's only one way to stop me, and I'm coming to that.

It is now two in the morning. I have been talking into this damn thing for more than twelve hours. My throat is raw from all the cigarettes I've smoked these last few days, and my voice is nearly gone.

I've taken two sleeping pills, and all the doors are locked. It has begun to rain again, a harsh, vindictive rain, and the shadow that could be a man is not a man. He wouldn't be standing out there in this kind of weather. Would he?

You can never be completely sure, of course. I slid open the glass door, and I shouted out into the night. "All right, you bastards. Let's get it over with. I'm here. I'm here."

Then I closed the door, very quickly, ashamed of myself. I locked it, too. I know there is no one out there and that there won't be. I know that the misery is within me, but that knowledge does nothing whatever to relieve the pain.

There is only one way to escape. There are fifty-four pills left.

NOTES·DICTATED·ON·THE·SIXTH·DAY

(1) Three to make ready

I took a third pill after I went to bed, but it didn't put me to sleep. It only deadened a little of the pain.

Sometime after dawn, the rain stopped; the sky grew pink with promise, and I fell into a restless doze for an hour or so. Three days now and two nights.

When I awoke, the promise was gone. The sky has turned black, mottled with slate. It is as if the sun has forever forsaken it.

The air is moist and hot and oppressive, and there is the smell of putrescence and of rot, and in my mouth is the sour taste of all the cigarettes smoked, all the drinks drunk, all the lies told and believed and lived with, and all the bitter bile caused by the twin diseases, failure and success.

At what point did I finally disappear, do you suppose? When was what is encased in this assembly of bones no longer me?

It was on a morning like this that I repaid the Lindsays for loving me.

Had there been in them some malice, some suggestion that they felt I was not and never could be what their dead son had been, I would have done all in my then considerable power to make them replace the dim gray vision of the dead with the golden vision of the alive.

But since that was not necessary, since they did not compare us, since they loved me as much as they had loved Ronnie, I had to make them pay.

I think I knew as I did it that for the rest of my life during certain dark hours, voices would pursue me. I believe I was even then aware that always just beyond reality I would hear awful secrets being exchanged. I think I knew that there would be only one way to escape the sibilance. I wonder how it is possible to have avoided for twenty-two years what was inevitable from the beginning.

They know that, of course. *They* have forgotten nothing, These people who pursue me. Their plan is perfection itself. *They* will not let me escape a moment of the suffering.

Louella has just invaded my privacy and despair. I told her to stay out, but she wouldn't. She burst into the room and made that dangerous clucking noise women always make when they are about to do something you don't want done but which they want to do and will at great personal sacrifice do *for your own good*.

Louella pulled back the curtains and slid open the glass door.

"Isn't this better than all that old dark and cigarette smell?" she asked.

I had to admit that it was. Sometimes they're right in these matters.

I looked out and saw that even in the gloom Charley's shock-yellow day lilies are out, looking arrogantly beautiful.

Louella wanted to give me some lunch, and I said no. She said I needed some food on my stomach, and I said, "Goddamn it to hell, I don't want anything to eat."

Then, as before, I apologized for having shouted at her and for swearing.

"I don't pay your shouting no never mind," said Louella. "I know you don't mean half what you say. If that."

"Well, you're wrong," I said. "I mean all I say."

Louella insisted Ab and I go for a walk, and, since she had to red up in here, I agreed. Ab had already started on the walk when I made up my mind.

While we were gone, I crowded the thoughts of London and of the Lindsays out of my mind; I thought of Charley and wondered if she was in Philadelphia or in New York and wondered if she had gone back to her job at Highland House and wondered if, after I am gone, she will remember me as I was or as she thought I might be.

I thought of the picture of her brother Cal, and I realized—isn't it odd that it has only now occurred to me?—that Cal's photograph in a way played much the same part in my life that Ronnie Lindsay's had.

The first time Charley and I went to the theater together, I picked her up at her apartment. Naturally, I noticed the photograph immediately. It was in a silver frame on a bookshelf.

"Who's the blond charmer?" I asked.

"My brother Cal," said Charley.

"Good. I was afraid he was competition. He looks like the late Leslie Howard, or are you too young to remember the late Leslie Howard?"

"I saw *Gone with the Wind* nineteen times and *Intermezzo* thirty-four. Are you shocked? I'm sure it's very neurotic."

"Probably," I said. "He older then you?"

"He was. Five years. He's been dead for twenty-three."

"Oh," I said.

Charley did not then know me well enough to recognize the symptoms. She didn't realize that a door had slammed shut in my mind.

"Tell me about him," I said.

"Not now," said Charley. "Not if I'm going to make everybody in the theater gasp with astonishment and admiration when I walk down the aisle with the handsomest, nicest, sweetest producer in all of New York."

I said, "I thought you were going to the theater with me," and then I kissed her and stroked her hair. Charley has very soft hair, the color of mahogany.

Later, of course, I'd have insisted; later, there would have been anger and recriminations, but that night, early in our relationship, I wanted Charley so desperately that I managed to keep silent.

I don't mean only that I wanted to go to bed with her; I mean that I wanted her in every way; I mean that I wanted her to want me just as much, and for always, and yet even then, wanting her and wanting her to want me, I knew in the outer reaches of my mind that the moment I got what I wanted, I would no longer value it.

But that night I forced myself to look away from the photograph of her long-dead brother, and I said, testing, testing, "He must have been quite a guy, your brother Cal."

"Oh, he was," said Charley. "I warn you right here and now that I'm going to make him sound like a god because he was one. Or so I choose to think."

"It's very hard to compete with gods."

I was being careful, but there must have been a certain harsh resonance in my voice because Charley raised her head from my shoulder, and she gave me a quick, apprehensive look and said, "What do you mean, *compete*? Are you joking?"

"Sure," I said, kissing her forehead.

"I hope so," she said, and then she smiled. "Because, darling, love's one of the areas you don't compete in. You either are loved, or you aren't, and there's no need to shove. There's plenty of room for everybody."

She took my hand and kissed it. Then she rose and walked toward the bedroom. Have I said that she walked as if she was being propelled by a slight wind at the small of her back? I read that someplace about someone, I forget, but that's the way Charley walks. At the bedroom door, she turned and smiled. I've told you about her smile—no reserve behind it, no holding back, and always it is completely spontaneous. Charley has never practiced smiling in front of a mirror, and when she laughs, the sound does not ring in her own ears, and she is not always listening to the sound of her own voice. She has a beautiful voice, and I'm a voice man.

Charley's voice is rather low-pitched but not harsh, not like the voices of several girls who've been in plays I've produced. Charley never wanted to be or tried to be a boy.

"Give me five minutes and I'll make what meager improvements on nature are possible," said Charley.

I finished my drink while she was dressing and made myself another, stronger drink, and as I passed the bookshelf, I stood for a long time in front of that picture.

"You son of a bitch," I said to the picture. "You smug bastard. You in your Ivy suit that looks as if you'd been born in it. I'll bet you were born with a silver-spoon, Main-Line accent. I bet if you were alive now, every time you looked at me, I'd have to glance at my fly to see if it was open."

I turned the picture half away so that from where I sat on the sofa, my competition would not be looking at me.

If Charley noticed, she never mentioned it.

On my walk this morning I thought of the way Cal's photograph had looked on that shelf, both before I turned it and after. I thought of the two-volume edition of *Bleak House* beside it. On the flyleaf of Volume One was inscribed, "To That Other Charley, My Dear Sister, From Her Loving Brother, Cal."

When I first read the inscription, I thought, how Louisa May Alcott, how proper, how Main Line, how secure, how intolerable. I hated his very bones then, and I do now, at this moment.

When Charley came here, she either did not bring the picture in the silver frame, or she hid it very well.

I looked everywhere, in all the drawers and all the cabinets, in her trunk, in the basement, in the matched luggage I gave her, in her purse, even in the kitchen. I thought perhaps she had hidden it in one of the cook books.

I never found it, though, and I never found the book with the Louisa May Alcott inscription.

I haven't told you all about the night Charley left me; I couldn't then, and I'm not sure I can now, but I can say this much more:

On the last night X shouted, "I told you I couldn't be Cal."

"Oh, my," said Charley. "I do feel sorry for you. I pity you, too."

"But you don't love me any more," said X.

"No," said Charley, "not for quite some time now. 'Love has its limits of endurance,' and said limits have long since been passed and passed again."

"I'll always love you," said X. "Always."

"No. What you'll love is the idea of loving me, and knowing you can't, you'll hate yourself a little more. You hate yourself a lot, and then you have to hate everybody who happens to be nearby. If there's nobody else after I leave, maybe you'll start kicking Ab. I don't know. Or maybe you'll run outside and kick trees. Or stick your head in an oven. Or take a drink. Or a million drinks. Oh, you'll go out with a flourish all right, banging and whimpering both at the same time. Only I'll read about it in the papers. I don't want to see it."

"You must hate me quite a bit," said X.

"Yes, I do. Quite a bit, and I hate myself for it. I hate myself for wanting to make you as black and blue inside as I am."

"I didn't know," said X's voice.

"How could you possibly know? You haven't once ever looked at me—or listened to me. You don't look at anybody or listen to anybody."

"I need you," said X. "I really need you."

"No, you don't. What you need is a housekeeper who'll sleep with you when it suits your fancy and take your abuse when it suits your fancy—and receive your tenderness when it suits your fancy."

"I told you I couldn't be Cal," X said again. His voice had the sound of chalk on slate.

"Good-bye," said his wife.

"I wish to Christ he wasn't dead," said X. "Who can compete with a dead man? I bet if the truth were known, he was a bastard. I bet if he were around now he'd be a worse bastard than your brother Colin. That bastard. I wish he were dead, but as for competing—anybody can compete with that bastard. Colin."

"You can't even make me angry any more," said X's wife, "and you can't make me strike back because I'm out of words. There've been so many words in our life together. I may be silent for the rest of my life."

"Colin," said X, "that cheap, stuck-up..."

After his wife left, X shouted at the trees, and then he ran out into the woods, and he kicked a tree, just as the woman who was his wife had said he would, and then he lay on the ground on the pine needles, and he shed all the tears he had saved from his childhood, and, after that, a blackness opened, and a blackness closed, and there was nothing.

When I got back from my walk this morning, I dictated the part about Cal's picture and about Charley's leaving me, and then I did an insane thing. I did this....

I've mentioned that Charley was born and raised in Lansdowne, one of the Main-Line towns outside Philadelphia. Her live brother—her *breathing* brother, let's say—still lives there, and I had a feeling that Charley might have gone there to recover from the ordeals of Las Vegas.

So, half an hour ago, I called Lansdowne. The Master of Ballantrae himself answered the phone. Don't I have the luck, though.

Colin—ought to be spelled *Colon*—is a wheel in—wouldn't you know?—the Pennsylvania Company for Assurances on Lives and the Granting of Annuities. Where else?

It seems hardly necessary to add that the bastard's voice is very deep, very assured, the perfect voice for the perfect man. Colin is tall, in great physical shape—who wouldn't be with all that soccer?—forty, blond, and in possession of the looks they hand out at Yale along with a B.A. Thus, a prominent Adam's apple. "Such fine reserve and noble reticence." That is Colin all over, and then some.

Anyway, I disguised my voice—or thought I did—and asked if Miss Barr was there.

A moment passed; Colin cleared his Yale throat, and I feel sure the Yale Adam's apple moved up, then down again as he swallowed; then the Yale voice said, "Bland, my sister either is or is not here and you either have or have not been drinking. The latter is none of my business, and the former is none of your business. If you ever again attempt to communicate with my sister in any way, I shall personally see to it that you are put in an institution, which is where you belong, and failing that, I shall personally kill you. In cold blood."

Then he hung up.

When I asked the operator to call back, the line was busy. I suspect that reticent Colin had left the phone off the hook.

Why did I do it, do you suppose? And speaking of supposing, do you suppose Charley is at dear Colin's? I do. I'll bet that's exactly where she is.

I have never been at noble Colin's noble house, and he has never been in this ignoble one, and if you want the truth—and that's what you've been getting—the reason Charley and I were married in the

American Embassy in Paris is so that I wouldn't have to have Colin at the wedding. I never told Charley, and I don't think she suspected.

And so, the last, futile telephone call made, I will continue. I must.

I want now to describe, as accurately and with as few flourishes as possible, what happened on the last day I was in the Lindsay house and give enough background to explain the enormity of what I did. Not excuse it; I could never do that.

As I've already said Hollis Lindsay brought me home to stay with him and Kathryn late in the afternoon on a gloomy day in mid-March.

Kathryn was in the living room, a low, pleasant rectangle gleaming with fresh paint, soft shades of green and yellow which even on a day like that made the room seem cheerful and inviting. There were pictures on the wall, mostly modern and mostly by little-known artists, many of them friends of the Lindsays. There was a collection of Chinese sculpture on the mantel; Kathryn was an expert on Chinese art. She had written a master's on some period or other.

There was a wood fire, and on a side table a tray of glasses, a siphon, and a bottle of whisky.

The room looked like something I'd been waiting a long time to get into. This was clearly the room in which I should have spent my childhood and it was only through some accident of fate that I hadn't. Home at last, I thought; after all this time, I'm home. I'd been in the Lindsay living room before, but only as a transient, a guest along with others. This was different. I was near something so exciting that I hardly dared breathe.

I felt the wild flutter of hope in my heart.

Kathryn Lindsay, who was sitting on a blue divan that accidentally came close to matching her eyes, looked up from her book and saw Hollis and me. "What a very pleasant surprise," she said.

"Joshua is going to stay with us for a while," said Hollis.

Kathryn rose and came to me, stooping to kiss me on the forehead.

"How perfectly wonderful," she said. "You'll have Ronnie's room."

The flutter contracted into a small, silent ball of fear.

"Who's Ronnie?" I asked.

"Our son," said Hollis. "He's dead."

I felt the flutter once more, but very much weaker.... Later, I thought what Kathryn Lindsay said that first night was part of the trouble; I thought, Perhaps if she'd said "the spare room" or "the guest room," things would have been different. I know better now. Or should I say I always knew better but now can admit it? Kathryn and Hollis both tried to get me to change the room. "You surely can't want to keep it *exactly* the way it was when it was Ronnie's," Kathryn said. "Yes, I do," I said, "exactly." "But you wouldn't have things this way if you'd been doing it," Hollis would say. "Sounds silly," I'd say, "but I would have. Believe me I would."

So I changed nothing. Even when I did something as simple as picking up a book, I was careful to put the book back exactly where it had been.

You understand why, don't you?

The room was small, the walls the color of *café au lait*. There were several pictures of horses, both photographs and paintings. Ronnie had loved horses.

Also on the walls was a print of Vermeer's "The Girl with a Red Hat."

There was a shelf of books, the Waverley novels, a set of Dickens, bird books and others about natural history, books about chess, Tolstoy's stories about his childhood, and a Bible. The Lindsays were agnostics.

It seems to me there were always flowers in the room, daffodils, tulips, anemones.

And Ronnie's butterfly collection.

Kathryn once told me, "When Ronnie was fourteen, he stopped collecting butterflies. He'd made up his mind it was cruel, and he was ashamed. He kept the collection to remind him of his cruelty. 'Otherwise, I might forget,' he said. That was so typical of him. Which is why I treasure the collection."

Don't misunderstand me. Or the Lindsays. They hadn't kept the room as a temple to Ronnie's memory. They hadn't changed it simply because until I came along there'd been no reason to. They didn't talk about him all the time either. As I said, almost all I learned about Ronnie I found out by asking.

The shrine was in my mind, not the room itself. Sometimes I'd wake up in the morning, and in that brief interval before my mind returned from whatever black place it had been, I would imagine that perhaps while I slept....

I would run to the mirror, not daring to hope.

The result was always the same. The reflection in the mirror was of my face, my hated face.

I've mentioned the photograph of Ronnie on Kathryn's dressing table. It was the last ever taken of him and, when I was alone in the house, I used to study it at length. One day when I was having my hair cut at a place near Piccadilly, I had it done exactly the way Ronnie's was in the picture. Ronnie's face was longer and very much thinner than mine, and I took to sucking in my cheeks when I was with Kathryn and Hollis, and, when I spoke, my accent became a faint Iowa imitation of an English boy with a public-school education.

What's more, I often expressed a lively interest in horses, but when the Lindsays suggested that I might like to go riding in Hyde Park, I declined on some grounds or other. Nevertheless, I did mention that experts in the field felt that I was nearly without a peer as a *currier* of horses.

If Kathryn and Hollis were aware of what I was doing, they never mentioned it. I doubt that they were.

I shall say no more on the subject except that during the five weeks I was with the Lindsays, I often went without my glasses. Ronnie hadn't needed any.

Without glasses, my world becomes a blur of soft, half-familiar shadows, and I was always bumping into things. I was black and blue all over.

Sometimes in my mind that spring I was Ronnie, sometimes his younger brother, and sometimes—though rarely—I persuaded myself that the Lindsays loved me for myself alone. Despite my many imperfections.

These further facts:

Among Kathryn's collection of Chinese statues was a small, terra-cotta figure of a shaman, Han dynasty. I don't know whether it was valuable or not, but it was old, made about the time of Christ, and it was cherished by Kathryn. She had got it in Hong Kong when she and Hollis were there on their honeymoon.

"It's the only *possession* I'd be heartbroken at losing," she said. "I don't in general value *things*."

Hollis didn't much value things either, but he had a collection of pipes of which he was fond, including a meerschaum, which was a special favorite.

During the time I was with the Lindsays, we went to their cottage near Land's End twice, maybe three times. Once was the golden day I took the book of Housman's poems to them.

In London, all our days were very much alike, as I suspect they are likely to be in a happy household. So far as the Lindsays were concerned, I was a member of the family; so far as I was concerned, we were always separated—by something sometimes gossamer thin, but, more often, something as thick and impenetrable as unbreakable frosted plate glass.

They had invited me to go to Greece with them in June, and I had just enough money left to do it. There have been few things in my life that I've looked forward to quite as eagerly. Not only that; it looked as if my fellowship might be renewed for another year.

In moments of rue and regret since, I've often wondered, Suppose I had gone to Greece? How would my life have been if I'd stayed on at the University for another year, living with the Lindsays, being loved by them, perhaps even breaking through the gossamer screen?

I know the answer, of course. No different at all except in detail.

Now we come to that last day and the afternoon and evening preceding it.

It was a bank-holiday week end, in April. The Lindsays left on Thursday afternoon for the cottage at Land's End; I was going after a class I had on Friday morning.

I hadn't been alone in the house before, and neither Kathryn nor Hollis wanted to go without me, but I insisted.

I said good-bye to Kathryn in her dressing room, the photograph of Ronnie just behind us. She was going to meet Hollis at the station.

"Now you're sure you're going to be all right?" she said.

"Of course. What could happen?"

"Your supper's in the icebox, cold but really rather pleasant for this time of year. The chicken's good anyway. Why don't you have it in the garden? Sometimes I think it's rather exciting eating alone. Not all the time, but once in a rare while. And there are eggs and some of that lovely Westphalia ham from Harrod's for breakfast, and we'll meet you at the station."

"I had a friend who told me I'd be spoiled rotten while I was in England," I said. "Little did he know."

She laughed with real delight. "It has been such a pleasure spoiling you," she said. "Just magnificent, and Hollis and I are going to keep right on doing it. And we've got a whole two months in Greece and a whole year after that. My, we're lucky."

"I'm the lucky one," I said.

She kissed me. "Darling, promise me something, will you? If anything at all happens, call us, will you?"

"I'm not exactly a child, you know."

"I know," she said, kissing me again, "but you're so—oh, so vulnerable, so exposed. I sometimes think you're nothing but a great big, open, bleeding wound."

"You've been nice to me," I said. "I'll be grateful for the rest of my life, and I'll never, never forget it."

"This is only the beginning, darling."

She gave me a quick forehead kiss, then rose, glancing at the photograph of her dead son. "Oh, my, I wish Ronnie were still alive. You and he would have had such times together."

I felt a flow of adrenalin, blood, and resentment rise to my face. "Those all-around boy types never had much time for me," I said. "I know that from bitter experience."

I saw a tiny glint of moisture in Kathryn's eyes. She once more brought me close to her. "Ronnie wasn't an all-around boy," she said. "That description makes him sound—oh, I don't know—like some awful picture in a magazine. He was really quite ordinary but quite sweet, and my son. You'd have liked him, and he'd have liked you, just as much as we do, and now there's the taxi."

I carried her bag to the taxi, and we kissed once more.

Her last words to me were, "Don't forget to lock the front door, darling."

As soon as the cab was driven off, I hurried back into the house. I knew Kathryn would be waving until it went around the corner, but I didn't look. I have never liked the piece of death even the most casual good-bye represents.

That evening, I ate the cold chicken in the garden, and I had the wireless turned on very loud in the kitchen. Some BBC musicians were playing the Archduke Trio of Beethoven. I had never heard it before, and it was many years before I allowed myself to hear it again.

After dark, I rinsed and wiped my dishes and then got ready for bed. Just before turning off my light, I went into Kathryn Lindsay's dressing room and looked at the photograph of Ronnie, hating the thin, handsome face, the wide, unspectacled eyes, the strong, sensuous mouth, the proud tilt of the chin. I despised him for his looks but, even more, for having two insurmountable advantages over me, being the Lindsays' son and being dead.

But it was a mild night and perhaps because of that or because I had a week end and a summer and a year to look forward to, I forgave him.

"They'll forget all about you yet," I told the photograph, and then I went back to my room and went to bed, falling asleep almost at once.

The next morning I woke up feeling completely happy. The sun was shining, and I had breakfast in the garden, surrounded by the bright, varied colors of the spring. The forecast had been for a beautiful week end, and that morning was all blue and green and golden.

I went to class and took the test, then walked all the way back to the Lindsay house, a considerable distance. I sang all the way.

When I got back, there was a cable under the door, addressed to me. It said:

YOUR MOTHER AND MR. PAVAN WERE BURNED TO DEATH LAST NIGHT IN A FIRE WHICH COMPLETELY DESTROYED YOUR GREAT GREAT GRANDFATHER'S HOUSE OUR LOVE AND SYMPATHY DEAR WE WISH WE COULD BE WITH YOU YOUR AUNT METTABEL AND UNCLE DICK.

I read the cablegram a second time, still feeling nothing.

After that, I counted the words, realizing that my aunt must have been extremely upset to have used so many words. I folded the cable into the breast pocket of my jacket, experiencing for the first time the total aloneness I've described earlier in this narrative.

In addition, on that spring morning in London I felt as if somebody had stripped all the skin from my flesh with the single stroke of a sharp knife, beginning at the back of my head.

I went to my room and packed all my things into my two suitcases. I returned my portable typewriter to its case and locked it. I went to the green-and-yellow living room to see if I had left anything there. I saw nothing except the expensive table lighter I'd got for Kathryn and Hollis on their twenty-fifth wedding anniversary two weeks before. I put that in a pocket of my jacket.

I started out of the room. Then on the mantel I saw the terracotta shaman dating back to the birth of Christ. I picked it up and, without a moment's hesitation, tossed it through the open window. When it hit the flagstones, it shattered into dozens of pieces. I went to Hollis's study and picked up the meerschaum pipe. I broke that into enough pieces so that it couldn't possibly be repaired. I threw the pieces into the fireplace, then picked up the rack and threw that and the other pipes into the fireplace, too. Not all of the pipes broke.

I went to Kathryn's dressing room and took Ronnie's photograph out of the frame. I folded it and put it in a side pocket of my jacket.

Then I went to the room that could never have been mine and put the butterfly collection in one of the suitcases. I gave the room a final look, knowing, I think, that for the rest of my life every detail of it would be as clear in my mind as a still wet fresco.

I picked up my two suitcases and the typewriter case and walked to the hall. There I put the key to the front door on a table and went out of the house for the last time.

I left the front door unlocked.

On the way to the corner, where I got a taxi, two small tears escaped from my eyes. They dried almost immediately in the warm spring air.

(2) The universal secret[10]

I got out of the cab in Piccadilly and checked into a small, drab hotel not far from the circus. The sheets on the narrow bed were yellow-brown with age and with many washings and were stained with the familiar and the not-familiar.

That was the night I brought the Miss Hart I've mentioned to my room.

After Miss Hart had gone, I walked through the streets for hours. Toward dawn, a boy named Billy and I came into the room.

Not a second of what followed is gone from my mind, not even the color of the light that shone in through the transom, or the intricate shadow of a spiderweb reflected on the dusty glass.

It was broad daylight when I fell asleep.

When I awoke, Billy was gone; so were two of the shirts I'd bought at Harrod's, a sweater I'd got for Hughie, and the ten pounds I'd had in my wallet. So was my first and for a long time my last pair of tailormade shoes. The two hundred dollars in traveler's checks I had hidden in the typewriter case were still there.

The thefts meant very little to me. In fact, I believe I welcomed them. In a way, the fact of them made it unnecessary for me to feel the great mortification required of me. In a way, I had already been punished.

I also decided that of all the sins in which the earth abounds, sexual transgressions of one kind or another rank near the bottom of the list.

Of the two experiences I had had that night and that morning, who was the worse for them? Certainly not Miss Hart, surely not

---

10 "Most of us, if you will pardon me for betraying the universal secret, have at some time or other, discovered in ourselves a readiness to stray far, ever so far, on the wrong road."—Conrad.

Billy. Both were, in fact, somewhat the richer for them. Myself? I had learned a lesson at reasonably small cost.

In any case, that morning in London I made a moral rule for myself that has worked fairly well for me, though I wouldn't recommend it to anyone else. The rule: Be as good as you can under the circumstances.

I should also explain here that my first two sexual experiences were disappointing. All the rest have been, too. For a long time I kept on hoping, though. I'd have settled for any kind of love—a woman, a man, a child, a goat, a snake, a stone. I just never discovered the secret—but not through lack of trying.

I went through the motions, but no matter what their sex or shape or species when they came to my bed or I went to theirs, none ever gave me what I was looking for. Or vice, of course. Or versa.

I've been inhaling and exhaling for twenty million minutes, give or take a few tens of thousands, and for no more than—let's say— twenty of them have I ever felt that combination of pleasure and passion which is presumably what all the shouting has been about.

My pleasure and my passion have been reserved for hating; I never had enough energy left over for love.

That morning I had breakfast in the Piccadilly Corner House, and during breakfast I thought of getting on a train, going to Land's End, and explaining to the Lindsays what I had done. They'd have forgiven me—willingly, gladly, grateful for the chance.

I couldn't do that, though. Don't you see? I could never do that.

I went to a travel agency in the Strand and exchanged my Cunard Line ticket for passage on a Dutch ship that was sailing from Southampton that same afternoon.

Just before I boarded the ship, I sent a cablegram to Letty saying that I was on my way back to New York and would she please meet me.

Irrational, you say? Absurd? Stupid? Preposterous?

Why, of course. What are you, a new boy? Don't you see that that's the story of my life? Don't you realize that what I know intellectually and what I can cope with emotionally are as twain as—well, yes, East and West.

Don't you see that if I were not a born self-punisher it wouldn't be necessary for me to deal out to myself the final punishment day after tomorrow?

I want to say here that the fact that I knew Letty would meet me when I got back to New York was very important to me, and I have always been grateful for that.

Once very much later when Letty and I were calling each other names in court, and having them all repeated in the *New York Daily News*, I tried to explain to George Banning the reason I would always be grateful to Letty. I didn't even come close to making him understand.

"You know why she met the boat, don't you, boy-o?" said George, who had not long before put considerable money into an O'Casey revival.

"No," I said. "I was married to Letty for nearly eleven years, and I never knew why she took up with me in the first place."

"Loot," said George. "She wasn't interested in what was in your pants. It was what was going to be in your pants' pocket that interested that young lady. She saw in you the Main Chance. She never cared a tinker's dam for you, boy-o."

"George," I said, "shut up."

Of the trip home from England, there is not much to say.

One morning when there was a kind of somber grandeur to the sea, I threw overboard Ronnie's butterfly collection and, after a very long time, the pieces of his photograph. The wind blew some of them back into my face.

Having done that, I returned to my cabin and started to write a letter to the Lindsays, explaining why I thought I had done what I did. I worked at that letter off and on for a year, but I never finished it.

I never heard from the Lindsays again, and they never heard from me.

I've been in London many times since, but I've never gone near the Lindsay house, or what was their house. Most of the time

I've even been afraid to go listen to the zealots near Marble Arch, because the Lindsays used to go there.

I said much earlier that I have always been a great maker of lists. I made one on my way back to New York that spring. It was called *What I Want to Do With My Life.* I can remember almost none of it, which is just as well. You'll see from these two embarrassing fragments that it was hopelessly adolescent:

Try to be Nicer to People: Remember, if you hadn't turned around the morning you met Hughie, you'd never have noticed that he was smiling.

Try to be Happy: Then you will make other people happy.... As I've said, there have been odds and ends of happiness since. Charley again. Isn't it incredible, come to think of it, how short a time ago she and I were happy—or seemed to be? Only last April, when the air was new, when every tender leaf breathed a message of hope, when in the evenings she and I would sit in the living room, the only light that of the moon on the hills. April when what we had seemed to be eternal....

But no more of that. Besides, this tape is at an end.

After changing the tape, I had one of Louella's omelets. Superb. Then, after she had finished redding up the dirty dishes, I made a decision that has been nagging at me for some time.

Surprising how easy, now that I no longer give a damn.

I said, "Louella, would you please call John and ask him to come out here as soon as he can?"

"But this isn't his regular day."

"I know that, but I want him to come out anyway."

"What do you want him to do, Mr. Bland?"

I then said what I had made up my mind to say. I said, "I want him to shave off my beard."

"You're making a joke, Mr. Bland," said Louella. "You can't mean what you're saying. John is going to be very mad in every way."

"We all have our little disappointments. Call him. You needn't tell him what I want."

I've described how I met John and that he has been cutting my hair and trimming my beard ever since.

John is here now. Louella is warning me that she is escorting him to my study. "Brighten the corner where you are. Someone far from harbor you may guide across the bar. Brighten the corner where you are."

John has gone. What happened was this:

He came in carrying the little black bag in which he keeps his tools. He put his bag on my desk, looked at me approvingly, and said, "You are looking like one million dollars at least, Mr. Bland."

He gazed affectionately at my beard.

"Every time I look at your beard I know how Michelangelo must have felt. Not that I am comparing a beard in any way with the Sistine Chapel. You want a little trim?"

Before I could answer, John added, "The beard is becoming very popular. Your picture in the newspapers and all has had no small part in that, I'm sure."

"It's the beatniks, John."

"The whatniks?"

I smiled and said quietly, "Shave it off, John."

John's moist eyes were at first incredulous. "You are making a joke," he said.

"Shave it off, John," I said, louder.

"Oh, no, Mr. Bland," said John, and he repeated the words as he tied the bib around my neck.

"I'm sorry," I said.

John waited one long, hopeful moment, and then he reached for his scissors. Moaning softly, he started to work. Once in a while, I heard the breathed, garlicky curses of the artist affronted.

When John finished, he looked at me sadly, shook his head, and, saying nothing, handed me a mirror.

I pushed the mirror away, my hand trembling.

"You don't look like Mr. Bland any more," said John.

"Thank you very much for doing it, John," I said.

John nodded glumly and put away his tools; he snapped the black bag shut and pointed to the piles of dark brown hair on the carpet.

"You want me to sweep that up?" he asked.

I shook my head. I said no; I said, "One part should be burnt, one chopped up, and the rest thrown to the wind."

Then I took a five-dollar bill from a drawer in the desk, handing it to John. He pushed it aside.

"No, thank you, Mr. Bland," he said. "Taking money for doing a thing like that would make me feel like a whore lady."

He picked up his bag and started for the door.

"Good-bye, Mr. Bland," he said.

I said, "Good-bye, John, and thank you."

I think somehow he realized that we had said our last good-bye.

After John had gone, I rose, went to the door, and locked it.

I could hear John and Louella having a low, conspiratorial conversation in the kitchen. John's voice rose and fell, rose and fell, and there was the soft murmur of Louella's agreement, followed by a sharper sound from John, who must have been describing how I looked. I could not make out the words, but the sound was not flattering.

Shortly after John left, Ab came up on the deck. His tail wagged happily. I slid open the door, and he came in. He seemed to recognize me without the beard, but I can't be positive. There is something devious in his character, particularly if he suspects there may be a piece of dog candy in somebody's pocket. Anybody's pocket.

Ab shoved his head under my damp hand, and, after he finished the dog candy, I gave him enough petting to last through a short nap.

His simple needs of love and food fulfilled, he then crawled under the divan and went to sleep.

I have just looked at the clock in my bedroom. I was tempted to look at myself in the mirror, but I didn't.

My God. Is it possible? I have only a little more than forty-eight hours left. At the end, as always, I am pursued by time, and in the end, as always, it will defeat me.

I've said that when I was in fifth grade I compared myself to Darwin and Galileo and "people like that." Naturally, as I said, I found myself and my achievements sadly deficient.

On my eighteenth birthday, a dark and dismal day, I concluded—don't laugh—that life had already passed me by, that the salt had lost its savor, that no matter what happened I'd never really *care* again, not for anything or anybody.

I was married to Letty then, and her present to me on that day was a beautiful, very expensive set of *The Golden Bough* I'd lusted for, and on a card she had written the following:

At 37, Samuel Butler wrote his first novel, *Erewhon*.
Abraham was 80 when his first son, Isaac, was born.
Ambrose Bierce accomplished his most famous achievement, disappearing in Mexico, when he was 71.
Mohammed founded—yes, Mohammedanism—when he was 52.
Engelbert Humperdinck's dream of becoming head of the Berlin Meisterschule was realized at 48.
Napoleon was unable to retire from public life until he was 46.
America had to wait to be discovered until Columbus was 46.
The Origin of Species flowed from Charles Darwin's pen when he was 50.
At 43 Alfred Adler broke from Sigmund Freud and founded the school of Individual Psychology.
Not before he was 40 was Paul Revere able to take a spectacular horse ride.
By the time he was 36 William Jennings Bryan had gathered enough momentum to deliver a speech about the Cross of Gold.
And Baffin Bay was not discovered until William Baffin was 32.
Happy Eighteenth (18) birthday, darling.

Letty

But do you see what I mean by being pursued by time? And being defeated by it?

Aesop had my kind taped a good five hundred years before Christ. I'm the racing hare all right, and since the tortoises that surrounded me never gave me much competition, I stopped off too often, refreshing myself with booze and other narcotics. I once figured I'd spent at least ten years of my life completely skunked—not all the time, you understand, but night after night for years, week ends, once two entire months. There have been many other time-wasting, destructive diversions.

I've brought the clock in here now. I want to watch the disappearance of these final hours, and I must try to do what I've never done up to now. I must try to use them well.

I will not sleep between now and then. The circles under my eyes will disappear with the rest of me.

I have nine of the *green-for-glory* pills left. I have just taken two.

In a few minutes I'll be sorry that Bach wrote the *B-Minor Mass*, knowing that if he hadn't, I could. I've always known I could write *King Lear*, if I'd just had the time.

> Oh, Dexedrine, dear Dexedrine.
> You soothe my spleen...

And so on. To be sung to the tune of "Sweet Genevieve."

(3) The open question[11]

I'll return now to the time I got back to New York from England— May, 1938, I think it was. I'm not sure any more. The dates are going. I was seventeen, I think, though I could have been sixteen.

Letty was in the customs shed waiting for me in front of my luggage. She looked very beautiful, or so it seemed to me; she was all in red, and her eyes were very blue. In appearance at least, there was no longer anything of White Street in her. True, she looked very much like a thousand other girls you could see any afternoon on Fifth Avenue, but after nearly nine months in England, that fact was remarkable and wonderful.

"Hi," she said. "Welcome home."

I put down my typewriter case, took her in my arms, and kissed her.

---

11   "Is not marriage an open question ... such as are in the institution wish to get out, and such as are out wish to get in."—Emerson.

"My, it's good to see you," said Letty, and she seemed to mean it. I'm afraid I burst into tears.

"For God's sake stop blubbering and get your bags," said Letty. "I've got to get back to work."

I did as I was ordered.

Letty said, "I'm sorry about your mother, though if you ask me and you didn't you're just as well off. She never liked me anyway."

I picked up my typewriter case, and Letty said, "Did she?"

I hadn't yet learned to roll with the punch. I said, "As a matter of fact, Letty, she never even mentioned you."

What mother said—the only time she ever did mention Letty—was this, "Darling, when I advised you to develop your social grace notes, I didn't expect you to take up with every Tom, Dick, and Harry on the campus."

I said, "Mother, I've been going with girls, not boys. One girl in particular—"

"I don't want to hear about it," said mother. "I know all about that peasant woman, whatever her name is, from Cedar Rapids."

I said, "Her name's Letty Novotny, and I'd like to invite her for supper sometime."

"I have no intention of entertaining *peasants* in this house where royalty has been entertained," said mother.

"What royalty was that?" I asked.

"Well, Queen Marie, for one," said mother. "We certainly entertained her in Iowa City." In Iowa City I had shaken the hand of the Queen of Rumania, and she had said, "He looks just like a little man, doesn't he?"

Mother had tried a curtsy but given it up mid-curtsy. "Your Highness," she said. "I'm its mother."

But we never had Queen Marie at our house. Or Letty either.

As Letty and I started away from the customs shed that afternoon, Letty said, "Don't worry, baby. I'll take care of you."

In retrospect, the evening of the first night Letty and I spent together seems embarrassingly absurd.

She said that I could stay in her apartment on Charles Street, "for the time being." She had a day bed in the living room.

That first night we had candles and champagne and *paté de foie gras*, all of which I'd got at various places in The Village while Letty was still at work. I also got a bottle of red wine and a cold roast chicken, and Letty and I sat on the floor and ate off her coffee table, and we talked. It was as if we'd never finish saying all that we had to say to each other. Never. We both had been homesick for a home neither of us had had, but that night we pretended we had. That night we were temporarily back in New Athens.

I expect that of the two of us Letty was the worse off. I'd had the Lindsays, after all, but Letty hadn't had anybody, except her colleagues at the magazine. Women never have cared much for Letty, particularly those forced to work with her. I remember one editor of *Puberty* saying of Letty, "She was always trying, very trying, night and day."

That night, time and distance lent an air of enchantment to a place we both hated and to people we were either indifferent to or disliked. Mrs. Horatio P. Baker, for instance, became not a doltish harridan but an amusing eccentric, a character out of a play like *You Can't Take It With You.*

We laughed so hard that, after a while, we lay on the floor, exhausted.

The enchantment we shared was also in large part due to the champagne, the red wine and, later, the Scotch Letty provided.

I'd had sherry with the Lindsays and an occasional glass of wine on the ship coming back to New York, but I'd never been drunk before. I believe I realized right then and there that in booze I'd found a friend for life. But I may exaggerate; I usually do.

Anyway, while Letty was making up the day bed, I reminded her that Gertrude Stein had once said that a dawn could be very beautiful depending on which end of the day you saw it from, and that, too, struck us as hilarious. We fell—Letty or I, who knows— into each other's arms, and in a few minutes Letty led me to the bedroom.

I remember very little of what followed, except that at one point Letty said, "You haven't had relations with anybody else, have you?"

I shook my head, and Letty said, "Well, I certainly hope not. Especially in England."

I also discovered that, not surprisingly, in world-changing as in dancing Letty tended to lead.

The summer that followed was the strangest of my life.

I remember that I got a letter from Aunt Mettabel. She described the fire and mother's and Pavan's funeral in some detail. I read only part of it. Then I put it away to read later. I never did, though. I don't even know what happened to it.

(4) My brother the wolf

Not long after I got back to New York, two men from an insurance company came to interview me. As I said very much earlier, in the last real conversation Pavan and I ever had—when I was in the hospital after the O'Conner fiasco—he said that he might some day be able to do me a favor. The favor—I think—turned out to be a double-indemnity life insurance policy on himself and mother. A hundred thousand dollars, and I was the sole beneficiary.

Whatever else can be said about Pavan, there is always that.

The insurance men asked me a great many questions, and I gave them a great many soft, evasive answers. In my own mind I was sure that Pavan had set fire to the house and, indirectly, to himself and mother. I didn't tell the gumshoes from the insurance company that, though. I told them nothing—not even that every time I took a piano lesson from Pavan, I sat on a book called *Great Fires of History*. Nevertheless, every time I thought of it, I laughed.

Had I got the hundred thousand dollars, knowing that it had been dishonestly come by, would my conscience have bothered me? Not for a second.... I might add here that at a time when there is a great deal of tedious talk going around about morality, I decline to join in. People who *talk* a lot about morality or who *write* about it all the time seldom know much about the real thing. This is especially true of newspaper people, editorial writers in particular. Myself, in addition to the moral code I've mentioned earlier—Be as good as you can under the circumstances—I feel this way. I would take whatever I could get away with from any large corporation— certainly any insurance company. What's more, I have one of the best income-tax men in the business. He has—I believe—robbed the federal government blind on my returns. With my blessing. I will continue to be in favor of bilking the government so long as— to use only one example—there is that twenty-seven-and-a-half per cent depletion allowance on oil wells.

I wouldn't rob a sweet old lady, though, and that often causes me some problems. You take Abercrombie and Fitch. Once through a mix-up too ridiculous to go into here, Abercrombie sent me *five* cashmere sweaters but only billed me for one. I went through hell for a week. Was Abercrombie a sweet old lady or a giant corporation? Finally I settled on the sweet-old-lady classification, largely because I have always liked Abercrombie. I returned four of the sweaters, but I also wrote a short note to them warning them that if they get any bigger....

Anyway, during that summer I pieced together most of what I know about Petrarch Pavan. I found it out partly by reading and partly from a cousin of Petrarch's who is now involved with the United Nations. I'd better not name him.

As I've said, Pavan's family was a very old one, and not too many years ago there was a thinly disguised fictional biography of it, written by somebody like Frances Parkinson Keyes. I wouldn't have thought it was possible for me to read through more than a thousand pages of the grayest prose since *Uncle Tom's Cabin*, but, by God, I did. Fascinating. The hero-narrator was Petrarch Pavan. The gray lady didn't understand him, but then neither did I.

Pavan was the last direct descendant of the man who'd got the clan started in this hemisphere. As I also mentioned, the ancestor was in on the drafting of the Constitution and in Washington's cabinet. The Pavans were Huguenots to begin with.

By the time Pavan came along—he was born in 1885—there wasn't much juice left in the family. Petrarch's father appears to have been a fussy, inadequate little man who found fulfillment by clipping coupons, and I gather if he'd been born in a different economic status, paper dolls would have done as well.

Pavan's mother—née Mary Finnerty—had been his father's secretary in the office in downtown Boston that the old man visited when he couldn't think of anything else to do. I should think she was the kind of woman The Road abounds with. As you'll see in a moment, she knew Henry Adams, and I've always thought that maybe Adams had her in the back of his mind when he said of his wife, "She rules me, as only American women rule men, and I cower before her."

In any case, it soon became apparent to Mary Finnerty Pavan that the kind of thing she had in mind could not be done in Boston. So she and her husband, Lucien, moved to New York, to a brownstone on upper Fifth Avenue.

You see, what Mary planned to be was the Perle Mesta of her day, and she succeeded. They always do.

Pavan was born in that brownstone, and by 1885 his mother's parties were already *famous*. People smart enough to know better elbowed each other out of the way to get an invitation. (This is a phenomenon that is an absolute mystery to me. I have never in my life gone to even the most infamous party except under duress and very often under the influence of alcohol as well.)

Not so with the turn-of-the-century movers and shakers who went to Mary F. Pavan's get-togethers. The lady writer I referred to above gives the guest list for a dinner party presided over by the fictional Mrs. Pavan. Jay Gould was there, William Howard Taft, William Dean Howells *and* Mark Twain, John LaFarge, Henry Adams, his brother Brooks, Arnold Bennett, who was in this country on a lecture tour, Charles Dana Gibson, Lincoln Steffens, Ida Tarbell, and the younger Oliver Wendell Holmes.

Mary F. Pavan was not only a social climber; she was also—and this is, I suppose, to her credit—a woman who had an enormous respect for "people who do things."

Is it any wonder that Pavan did one and a half of almost everything but seldom finished two of anything? Did he try to paint a picture? He could never be a John LaFarge or a Charles Dana Gibson. Did he write a poem? Vachel Lindsay had done it better. Did he want to act? He could never compete with Mary's friends the Barrymores.

Pavan's cousin said this, "Petrarch was tortured by his own inadequacies, and if he temporarily forgot them, his mother reminded him.... If there was one thing in the world Mary didn't have time for, it was a baby, particularly a boy baby with a clubfoot. That's why she was always shipping him off to Europe."

The lady writer said, "His childhood was spent with the creative giants of that age—writers, artists, journalists, musicians, actors, politicians. He was told that what these people had done he could never hope to equal, and he was told that since he could not, he was of no earthly use."

Pavan might even have survived that kind of childhood; he might, I think, have become one of those perennial students, an eternal undergraduate, working on some vague project or other if, after he had returned from Europe in 1906, he had not gone back to Cambridge for perhaps the third time to audit some courses in a Harvard graduate school. He was twenty-one years old and possessed of a questionable Bachelor of Arts degree from—as I've said—the University of Bologna.

He was there until 1909, the year in which the whole academic world was watching the progress of five Harvard undergraduates; 1909 was "the year of the prodigies" at Harvard. One of them, W. J. Sidies, was nine years old at the time.

In one of his rare moments of self-revelation, Pavan once said to me, "When I was at Harvard for the last time, I felt like a broken failure of a man. I once met Boris Sidies at a party; he was the father of W.J., and he asked me what I was doing there. I told him what I was doing, which was nothing much, and he said, 'And how old are you?' I said, 'Twenty-four,' and he said, 'Oh my, you are retarded, aren't you?' I left Harvard and Cambridge the next day."

What Pavan did not tell me I learned during the summer of 1938 in New York. I learned that he set fire to the rooming house in which he had been living. There was very little damage, and no hint of what had happened appeared in the newspapers, but Pavan was firmly told never to come back to Massachusetts. He never did.

After Cambridge, Pavan left a small, burning memento of his stay wherever he went. He never stayed anywhere more than a year or two, and, although I don't know this for sure, I have a feeling that wherever he went, he was asked not to come back.

By the time Pavan got to New Athens, there weren't very many places left to go.

I should add here that Horatio P. Baker must have known all about Pavan's record when he invited him to become a member of the Pegasus faculty. Orion Bernstein certainly did. Baker didn't care; he had hired a man to head the Fine Arts department who—to use his favorite phrase—"has a nationwide reputation." Reputation was worth more than merit to Baker.

As for Orion Bernstein, he made use of his knowledge about Pavan. The afternoon he went to see my mother and Pavan to persuade them that they should let me go to England, he told me he was going to quote two lines of Pope's. They must have been these:

Fire in each eye, and papers in each hand.
They rave, recite, and madden round the band.

Whatever Orion said, Pavan got the message.

I should add these further facts about Pavan. Mary F. Pavan died in 1917, just ten years before her son reached New Athens in that red Pierce-Arrow. Pavan was in Europe at the time of her death, and when newspaper men told him that she was dead, he was quoted as saying, "Why couldn't she have done that thirty years ago?"

He did not go back for the funeral, but among others present were Henry Adams and Edith Wharton, who was no doubt gathering material for a new novel.

When Pavan did return from Europe about three years later, apparently one of his first acts was to set fire to the brownstone on upper Fifth Avenue. The place was gutted from the basement, where it started, to the fifth floor, and there was an investigation, even though there was no insurance. The investigation was halted quite suddenly, and Pavan left New York. He never went back there either.

After that, Pavan taught at colleges in Canada, in Oregon, in Texas, in North Dakota, and then he came to Pegasus, and he must have known from the beginning that New Athens represented the last stop.

The rest I've said: how he met mother or, more likely, how mother managed to meet him and, as soon as she could manage it, how she brought him to me.

God knows what Pavan thought of mother and her shabby pretensions. He must have found her ludicrous, somewhat pathetic, and possibly even pitiable. He was not kind to her, but she loved every cut and begged for more. Not only that, he gave her as much happiness as she had any right to expect—and probably a whole lot more.

I should put this on the record, too. Pavan never once talked about his family or about his childhood, and he seldom mentioned any of the famous and important people he had known.

Mother's wildest dream would have been answered if she could have been asked to join the Atheneum Club in New Athens. Pavan was asked; he refused. He told one of the Lavendars, "I could if I wished have been a member of the real Atheneum Club. I refused. Can you think of any reason I should agree to join a twelfth-rate substitute in this godforsaken wilderness?"

I am only guessing here, but as I've indicated I think what Pavan really had in mind was that in me there was a chance to get back at the Harvard class of 1909 and possibly to make up for all his failures of the past.

If I had been the national winner of the Harvey Jordan O'Conner award, perhaps some of his frustrations would have been dissipated. I don't know. Maybe as I suggested earlier it was just that I represented a gamble to him, and he loved gambling.

I don't know what Pavan thought of Henry Adams, but two things Adams said come as close as anything I know to summing up Pavan's own point of view of the world and its people.

Adams once told John Hay:

I am fairly tired—bored beyond endurance—by the world we live in and its ideals and am ready to say so, not violently, but kindly, as one rubs salt into the back of a flogged sailor as though one loved him.

And this, Adams to a woman named Cameron:

The book is coming along rapidly and will announce the immediate dissolution of the world. My brother Brooks grumbles because I won't make it quicker.

Pavan's own final comment on the world was to set fire to the house on Riverdale Avenue that had once been called "the showplace of the Middle West."

It is certainly not surprising that he took mother with him to a violent, not a kindly grave, but I have always been rather amazed that he tried at the same time to make me a rich man.

He failed in that, too. After a long investigation in the summer of 1938, the insurance company ruled against paying me anything.

They never did prove that the fire had been set, though, and a series of dishonest lawyers tried to get me to sue. I refused.

What was left of the Pavan money went to the cousin who is now with the United Nations.

That's all on the subject of Petrarch Pavan, without whom and so on. Except to add that Pavan was perfectly right when he said he and I were very much alike.

I am still very much like him, even to the slight limp I picked up in the war. But do I, as I said earlier, still hate his guts? I don't know. Not as much as I hate my own, I guess.

(5) A marriage made in heaven

Toward the end of the summer of 1938, I did get $4,000, what was left of my mother's money after all the bills had been paid. I decided to spend that money to pay for a year of study at Columbia, philosophy again.

I was tired the whole summer, seized by an *ennui* almost as strong as that which took hold of me at the beginning of this one, twenty-one years later. Not even going to Columbia interested me much.

I used to sleep the clock around, and I spent a lot of time on the roof of the Charles Street apartment house, soaking up sun.

I read incessantly, sometimes in the apartment or on the roof, sometimes in that odd and wonderful place, the main reading room of the New York Public Library.

I reread the whole of Dostoevsky; I have never felt more at home with any author.

In the evenings during that very long summer, Letty and I went for walks, and we went to foreign movies, and we went to parties in the Village at which we sat on the floor and drank wine and plotted revolution.

We sang songs about the Peat Bog soldiers, and we dreamed we saw Joe Hill last night alive as you and me.

We got the truth in *The Daily Worker* and *New Masses*, since you obviously couldn't understand the capitalist press. I joined the Young Communist League and was a card-carrying, dues-paying member until two days after the nonaggression pact. At that point I tore up the card and stopped paying dues; I also realized that for quite a long time what I'd been at Y.C.L. meetings was not subversive but bored.

I remember that during the summer Letty and I went to a rally at Madison Square Garden where a blind man who had just come back from Spain made what seemed the most moving speech I had ever heard. I still think it was.

He read a poem written by an American boy killed over there. I remember the first two lines—

> Comrades, the battle is bloody and the war is long.
> Still, let us climb the gray hills and charge the guns.

I remember that the speaker said that the last words he had heard before he was blinded were, "*No Pasaran.*"

The Garden was packed, and we all chanted it with him: "*No Pasaran.* They Shall Not Pass."

I contributed fifty dollars which I could ill-afford to the Loyalist cause. At least I was told that was what it was for. After writing out the check, I felt as if I myself were climbing the gray hills, charging the guns.

It occurs to me that perhaps I should say this further word about Letty's and my relationship.

That summer was the last time there was any sort of communication between us. We shared our loneliness. That is about all.

"We're just two hicks from Iowa," Letty used to say. "We've got that in common. At least."

Marriage? We talked about it. We discussed it with about as much animation as we reserved for the weather.

Letty would say, "You're too young. I'd be arrested." Or, "I don't think I'll ever marry you. Every time I look at you I'm reminded of White Street."

And once she said, "We'll wait until you've finished your year at Columbia. Then we'll see."

I never got to Columbia, though. Two days before registration Letty found out she was pregnant. *They* had been at work again.

Both of us must have thought about an abortion; I did anyway, but I never mentioned it.

Letty told me about the pregnancy at dinner, and when she had finished I got up from the table and went to where she was and kissed her.

"I guess we better hurry up and get married," I said.

"I guess we better had," said Letty.

Then she started crying, and I said, "Everything will be just wonderful, darling. Really."

And I said, "I like children, you know." And I said, "I love you, Letty."

I knew as I said those sentences that they were not true. I did not love Letty; I did not like children, and I didn't think for a minute that everything would be wonderful.

Maybe that was the trouble; maybe you ought to start a marriage with one or two illusions. Small ones.

The next day I telephoned Aunt Mettabel, who had been named my guardian in mother's will. After some argument—the details of which are unimportant—she agreed to send me a telegram giving me permission to marry Letty.

The day after that, Letty and I went to White Plains, where we were married by a slightly sozzled justice of the peace, in his office, next door to a urinal.

I showed the J.P. Aunt Mettabel's telegram, but I doubt that he could read it. He asked me how old I was; I said I was eighteen. True, I didn't look it; I looked about fifteen.

Letty and I had our wedding supper alone in the Oyster Bar at Grand Central, and in the subway on the way back to Charles Street, I realized that Letty hadn't entered our marriage with what you could truthfully call a romantic view of it.

She said, "Well, Junior Genius, where do you go from here?"

I said, "What do you mean by that? I mean I'm going to Columbia. I mean this doesn't change that, does it?"

Letty gave me a look. "What were you planning to use for money? What's left of the $4,000 to support me and a baby on? I'll have to quit my job, or has that occurred to you?"

I said, "I see what you mean."

She said, "I'm very glad," and then she said, "Some people may think you're Albert Einstein, but I'm not one of those people."

I said, "My, isn't this fun."

Letty said, "Oh, go to hell," and then she cried.

And so our marriage began.

Anyway, I did not go to Columbia. I went to a teacher's employment agency on Times Square and with the teacher's certificate they'd thrown in with the degree at Pegasus I was able to line up a job teaching seventh grade in a delightful little village I'm going to call Upstate.

I guess I should have realized there was something a little odd about a town that didn't have a seventh-grade teacher in mid-September, but I didn't. Besides, I couldn't afford to be choosy.

(6) The eye-opener and other matters

Upstate, population four thousand.

I went alone. Letty was going to join me in December, shortly before Christmas.

I found three *light-housekeeping* rooms in a disheveled house not far from the school. It belonged to an addlehead named Mrs. Junius L. Harrington the Second. Junius the Second, lucky man, was dead, and Mrs. Harrington took in what she called "paying guests."

"Think of me as your happy hostess, Mr. Bland," she said. "Think of yourself as my delighted guest."

The rooms consisted of a dark closet-kitchenette with a sink and an electric plate. There was a bed-sitting room with one window. Period.

Those of you who are clever at mathematics may think this adds up to one room, not three. Not so. I mentioned this matter to Mrs. Harrington, and she said, "It's very simple. The kitchen. One room. Am I right?"

I nodded.

"Then there is this room, which is both a living room and a bedroom. One and two are three. Am I right?"

"You are right, Mrs. Harrington," I said.

I shared a bathroom with a Mr. Moorehead who, according to my happy hostess, was just as clean as he could be and no trouble at all to anyone. Mr. Moorehead was an engineer on the New York Central, and I never once got a look at him.

I have no idea whether I was a good teacher; I expect not. I was too young, too lonely, too filled with self-pity, and too frightened. I had two boys in my class who were just as big as I was and one who was bigger.

As for the self-pity, I was convinced I was a failure. On my seventeenth birthday, the Upstate weekly, whatever it was called, had an article on me. I was referred to as "a former boy prodigy."

That proved it, I kept thinking. At seventeen, already a has-been. How right my mother had been. My future was behind me.

However, I do have this to say in my favor as a teacher. I cared, and I tried. None of my colleagues did.

The Upstate school in which I taught did have one distinction, its principal. I remember writing Letty that he would have been a splendid Storm Trooper. He was cruel to his staff and even crueler to the children. During that year he slapped one little girl so hard she lost her hearing in one ear.

There was some slight difficulty about that, very slight really. The girl's family moved away, and the principal went right on kicking, beating, and slapping.

I believe it was during my brief tenure in Upstate that I was for the first time referred to as "a stormy petrel."

That was because of a complaint lodged against me by the manager of the local J. C. Penney store.

What'd I do?

Well, instead of just reading Shakespeare, we acted it, shades of Miss Auerbach back in New Athens. The kids even memorized their parts. Right now I don't remember which plays we did, but I do remember that the daughter of the above-mentioned manager said the word *strumpet* in front of Mama, Papa, and a group of friends.

For reasons that are nobody's business I happen to know that said manager was a regular visitor at a bordello in a town not far from Upstate. However, he was also a deacon in the Lutheran church. If Lutherans have deacons. A high-mucky-muck of some kind.

Thus, the complaint. He claimed I had corrupted his daughter. Not Shakespeare. Bland.

Well, I got out of that one alive, partly, I imagine, because they were fresh out of hemlock in Upstate. Also because getting a replacement for me was next to impossible.

But then I compounded my crime. I read parts of *Sister Carrie*, *A Lost Lady*, and *Gatsby* aloud to my class. I had a pretty seditious point in so doing. I wanted to prove reading could be *enjoyable*, or Books Don't Bite.... Ridiculous.

After that, my days were numbered.

The end came a few weeks later in a class in Current Events. Somebody asked me what I thought about the Spanish Civil War. Well, if there was one thing I was not capable of during this period, it was keeping an opinion to myself—of softening it for public consumption. I described how I felt about that war, emotionally and with partisanship.

I added that the Franco side of the war was well covered by the newspapers of the area. True enough. I believe I concluded my remarks by quoting Justice Holmes: "The test of an idea is its ability to get itself accepted in the marketplace of public opinion."

That did it. The next Sunday I was denounced from the pulpit by both priests in Upstate, and on the Monday following, the school board fired me—without a hearing—by a vote of nine to nothing.

I issued a statement which never saw the light of day, but I happen to have a copy handy.

I said, "The school board of Upstate consists of ignorant, arrogant bigots. There are schools in Upstate only because schools are required by law, and, besides, schools keep the children out from underfoot a large part of the day. But as for learning anything, there's about as much chance of that in Upstate as there is in Nazi Germany."

My, I was young. I left town by the next train.

Oh, this. I was pleased and flattered that a handful of my thirty-five seventh-graders talked about going out on a strike if I weren't rehired. I wasn't, and they didn't, but the talk alone was quite enough, considering what year it was and considering the kind of place Upstate was.

What's more, I was additionally delighted a couple of years ago when a girl who'd been one of the strike leaders had a novel published. It was a good novel, and the dedication was this:

For Joshua Bland, Who Opened My Eyes.

When I got back to New York from Upstate, there were stories about my dismissal in all the New York papers, and the *New York Post* had an editorial rather mistily comparing me to Martin Luther and Galileo.

I went to the apartment on Charles Street feeling rather heroic. "You acted like a damn fool," said Letty. "A childish damn fool." Since what she said was true, I was furious. I slapped her, and she said, "In other words, I'm right." I slapped her again, even harder.

Later, Letty said, "What are you planning to do now, bird brain?"

And she added, "You had better do something and do it very damn quick because I have no intention of going back to Cedar Rapids to have your baby."

Letty did not have to go back to Cedar Rapids. In February, she had a miscarriage.

I was in Indianapolis on that day, lecturing at the Indian. Woman's Club.

Why was I lecturing—or, in Letty's words, "Letchering. He used to lay them in the aisles"?

Like almost everybody else in the world, I had had to accept the first money-making opportunity that came along—in my case, a lecture tour. I was billed as "FIFTEEN-YEAR-OLD PRODIGY TELLS ALL ABOUT AMERICAN YOUTH. ARE THEY READY TO FIGHT?"

Fifteen yet.

The fee was $500 for fifty minutes of nothing much, a question period, and an endless amount of surfeiting hospitality.

What was my answer to a question that was keeping General Marshall, among others, awake nights? It was the only answer any group of organized women would have been willing to pay $500 to hear. It was, *Maybe.*

Every time I stood up in front of the foolish females paying good money to hear my foolish remarks, I couldn't help thinking that they'd have been better off at home, making babies, chopping down trees, or ploughing fields.

But no, they wanted culture. The effortless way. And that was where I came in.

Bored, idle females. This country is bursting at the seams with them. They've got the constitutions of healthy horses; and, as a beady-eyed actor once observed, they never die. They are always sick, but they never die.

As I've told you, The Road is populated almost exclusively by widows.

Have you any idea of the sound made by five hundred of these culture-seekers gathered in a single room, not a one with a thought in her head?

Secret weapon? We have got the most powerful secret weapon in the world. All we have to do is record a roomful of that sound and if anybody gets Fresh With Us, let 'er rip.

I don't think we'd even have to turn up the volume.

.t a little more than two years lecturing, getting
.s, getting over hangovers and making new ones,
., eating their dreadful food, saying things of monu-
.gnificance, and getting paid for it.

.ne $500 per appearance, an agent, whose name I have care-
full, .locked from my memory, took half, and I paid most of my
own expenses.

I did other things between the time I got fired by the Upstate
school board and the beginning of The War. I'm sure the white
man's *Ebony* is right; I must have wandered in and out of fourteen
lines of work, maybe more.

About the only thing I missed doing was working for the
benevolent corporation.

I was once interviewed for a corporation job—*what* doesn't
matter—and the interview seemed to go well enough until the chief
interviewer said, "Then there are the tests, of course."

"What tests are those?" I asked.

"Well, the tests are to find out if you're—well-adjusted, if you'd
fit into the Youdknow Family. That kind of test. They only take three
days."

Something must have shown on my face because the interviewer said, "You don't have any objection to *that*, do you?"

I said, "Why, of course not. Not as long as I have a chance to
test you people first."

I didn't get the job.

Around this time, the Japanese or Franklin Roosevelt or whoever it was bombed Pearl Harbor.

Among other things, that event marked the unofficial end of
my marriage to Letty.

You must not think, by the way, that because I am able to
choose as illustrative only a few rather dreadful hours of Letty's and
my marriage that we were miserable the whole time or that there
was constant warfare between us. Not so. More often than not when

Letty and I were alone, we managed to be indifferent to each other. What's more, we arranged it so that we almost never were alone.

After the war, the fact of Taffy kept us together for a while. We both clung to the idea that two miserable, mismated people should pretend not to be "for the sake of the child." I believe I said something about that medieval notion earlier. If not, I'll say it here. No child has ever been helped by being in the trenches in a household at war. And I speak as the scarred veteran of two such households, the one I was born into and the one I helped create and maintain for my daughter Taffy.

May God forgive me that last.

I'll say this for Letty and me; we never had scenes while Taffy was around. But I doubt that that mattered. Children are like seismographs in this area, and if there is hatred in a household, it drips from the walls; it has a sour smell. A minor eruption between a father and mother at midnight is recorded in the mind of a sleeping child. I know.

I shall get back to The War in a minute, but this is how it went on the night Letty and I decided—if that's the word—on a divorce.

The time, mid-July 1949. Taffy was at a friend's for the night. She was not quite five. Letty was gone for the evening.

We were living in the brownstone on East Eighty-first Street. It was a very hot night, and there was no air-conditioning in the house, one of the few matters in which I had prevailed.

It had been a bad day, a day of crisis—though as I say that, I wonder when, if ever, there was any other kind.

I had been reading. At the same time I had been wondering how it was that a dozen people of intelligence, ability, and experience could put on a play that they loved and that had been loved in Paris and London and had run for more than two years in both places; yet when it opened in New York, every critic in town had leaped on it with frenzied fury, and the play had closed after *two nights*.

I came out of my study and started padding around the living room, looking for a coffin nail. At the time I was paying for five or six dozen cartons of cigarettes every week. But whenever I looked for one, one was not available.

I picked up several gold and silver boxes that were encrusted with diamonds and rubies. The boxes had been bought by Letty—paid for by me, of course—on the pretext that they would contain coffin nails. But did they ever? They did not. Except at gatherings at which whiskey-drinking, cigarette-stealing locusts descended on me, eating, drinking, and smoking me out of house and home. At such times those boxes were always loaded with coffin nails.

Not that night, though. I hurled several jeweled boxes to the floor. I pulled open drawers and flung some of them to the floor. I shouted for the maid. Naturally it was her night out. It always was.

I went to the kitchen. The cook had, of course, gone to bed. She was no doubt lying awake deciding how the next day she would manage to render inedible several hundred dollars' worth of the most expensive stuff Gristede's had to offer.

I continued jerking open drawers, including those containing the silver the cook and maid hadn't got around to looting.

Finally, I looked in the icebox. No coffin nails in there either.

I was about to start emptying the freezer when Letty came into the kitchen.

"Would you mind letting me know what is going on here?" she asked.

I said, "As I should think any goddamn fool could plainly see, I am looking for a goddamn cigarette."

Letty opened her purse, which was made of the most expensive brocades and had a platinum clasp. She took out a brand of cigarettes I happen to loathe and threw them to me.

Then she went into the living room. I followed her, inhaling furiously. She stooped and picked up one of the diamond-encrusted boxes. She put it on a coffee table worth an emperor's ransom.

"Did you have fun with your little temper tantrum?" she asked.

I exhaled furiously. "Where the hell have you been?" I asked, a fairly standard greeting in the household since Letty had met a man named Harry Lowenstein.

"Out," said Letty. "Did Taffy call?"

"Yes, at nine."

Letty lifted her eyebrows, but I didn't go on.

"I guess if she called, she's all right," said Letty. "Well, I'm going to bed."

She started out of the room.

I said, "When was it we decided not to share anything with each other, not even the information on where or with whom we are spending our evenings?"

"You didn't ask. I didn't know you were interested. I happen to have been with Harry Lowenstein."

I waited for her to say where, but she didn't.

Finally, I said, "Mr. Lowenstein seems to be doing a good deal of flitting from coast to coast these days."

Letty took a second pack of the brand of cigarettes I despise from her purse. She lighted one with a cigarette lighter that cost enough to keep Tiffany's in business for another ten years or so.

"I wouldn't use the word *flit* where Harry's concerned," she said. "He's quite a man in every way."

I should have left it there. I should have allowed myself some little pride, but I didn't. I never once did.

"Have you been sleeping with him?"

"Of course. Quite often. I enjoy a little sex once in a while."

"I guess you know this is the end."

"Is it? I've been hoping you'd say so. I'll get the divorce. I'll get it in Mexico."

Once more, I should have known when to stop. I didn't. I don't.

I said, "It's none of my business, of course, but why that particular hairy ape?"

"It's none of your business, but I'll be glad to tell you. I've shopped around quite a bit in the several thousand years I've been married to you, and Harry seems to be just about what I have always had in mind. Fortunately, he's as different from you as day is from night. In the first place, he's a success, not a failure; he's on the way up, not on the way down, and in the second place, he is all man, or as nearly all man as they come. I find that refreshing. Just for a change."

On the step leading out of the living room, Letty said, "Yes sir, Harry was born knowing what sex is."

"I won't let you have Taffy," I said.

"Just you try to stop me," said Letty. "Just you make the slightest move in that direction, and I'll make it impossible for you ever to set foot in Sardi's again as long as you live."

Then she went to bed.

I got drunk that night, just for a change. At the time I was only getting drunk every other night, a habit I quickly altered.

I moved out of the house before Letty got up the next morning and, thus, left behind many things I really wanted.

I never got back to the house because Letty got a court order restraining me. She said I had threatened her life.

And, when I tried to get custody of Taffy, Letty said things in court that made it difficult for me to have the courage to walk the streets at midnight without wearing dark glasses or carrying a brief case in which there was nothing but a fifth of comfort-giving Jack Daniel. Letty, among other things, swore that in addition to threatening her life, I had threatened Taffy's.

You may have read about it. As I've said, the *Daily News* carried a full account.

The things Letty did not say in court but suggested in an affidavit were what the tabloids had such a good time with.

Once in a moment of guilty despair, I told Letty about my last night in London and about my two companions. She, naturally, never forgot. Letty never forgot anything she needed to remember.

After that, Letty, in angry moments of her own, would mention that confession, and she tiptoed around it in her affidavit.

She also alluded to a young actor who had been very anxious to play a part in the first play I produced. He didn't, but Letty knew that he was trying, and she knew how hard he was trying. She realized that the actor had seen something in me that I did not dare to see in myself. Eventually, the actor went Out There, and he is now a leading swashbuckler in all those swashbuckling movies I take the trouble never to see. On his part, there was never more than a few not-too-veiled hints, and on my part there was always an elaborate pretense of not understanding what he was getting at.

Finally, in an angry scene I ordered the actor out of my office. He looked at me, smiled, and said, "I've got plenty of time. I'll wait." He knew.

I knew, too. I knew that nobody ever made a pass at anybody if the passee wasn't receptive. That hasn't happened once in the history of the race. I am sure of it. Not once. The not-so-very delicate relationship between the passer and the passee is another of the minor areas of knowledge that I happen to have researched rather thoroughly.

The following has happened since I dictated that last sentence.

I went to the large, flat rock on the hill, and I sat on it for a while. I don't know how long, but first I laughed, and then great sobs tore at me. Ab moaned and crawled into my arms and made comforting sounds. He licked my wet face with his rough, friendly tongue, and, after however long it was, I could not sob any more. Not even the dry tears would come, and the rock grew cold, and a cloud hid the moon.

A vindictive wind sprang up from somewhere and pursued Ab and me as we raced back into the house.

Ab rushed into the room ahead of me, and so did some of the wind, but I got the glass door closed, shutting it out.

Then it began to rain.

In this room now, even with the curtains drawn, there are the sounds of wind and of rain and of tired, lost souls wandering the night, searching for refuge and forgiveness.

If I am to get through the remaining hours, I need one happy memory. However small.

In the disorganized file of my mind, there must be one that will help me through the dark time until dawn....

There is this, out of context, perhaps adding to the confusion, but essential to me right now. Doesn't every murderer get a last wish, before the gallows, before the gas chamber, before oblivion?

(7) The memory

In the beginning, when I first knew Charley, there were some perfect days, not many, but of the few, not a detail is forgotten.

This one was more than three years ago. It was a Sunday, a week or so after the night Charley agreed to marry me.

We slept until noon, in my apartment on the East River, and then, while Charley read the *Times*, part of it aloud, I cooked breakfast.

I remember she said, "You don't even trust me to scramble an egg."

"I most certainly do not," I said.

The breakfast was magnificent.... Have I said that I am a good cook? I might if I'd played my cards right have become an acceptable second chef in a first-rate restaurant. Duncan Hines would have hated me (turn-about seems fair play), but Michelin would have given the kind of place I'd have agreed to work in at least a three-star rating.

"Which cook book do you think I should buy?" asked Charley as we stacked the dishes in the washer.

"This one," I said, handing her a large package. In it were both volumes of the *Gourmet* book, and the inscription on the flyleaf was:

For Charley—Who After Absorbing This Will Be the World's Best Cook and Who Is Already the World's Loveliest Human Being.

"How sweet you are," she said. "How really very sweet. How do you manage to keep this fact such a closely guarded secret?"

"My sweetness is only in the eyes of the beholder," I said, and I kissed her.

In the afternoon, we decided—I decided, Charley agreed—to go for a drive and have dinner in the country.

I had planned the whole thing very carefully, even to what Charley would say when I asked, as I did, "Where should we go?"

"That's entirely up to you," she said. "I plan to make no more decisions of any kind as long as I live."

So I brought her here.

As we approached Sloane's Station, I kept saying, "I don't think much of this country, do you? I like Connecticut."

"Are you crazy? Connecticut's self-conscious. Artsy-craftsy, groomed, and *cute*. This is real country. I love it."

We stopped in a town for gas. Was it Brewster?

"At any rate, you've got to admit Connecticut's got better towns," I said.

"I admit nothing of the kind," said Charley. "You mean places like New Canaan, all those fat asses wandering around in their Bermuda shorts and all that planned, phoney elegance? Ugh. The only nice things in New Canaan are the modern houses."

"Not what you'd call a clean town, this one," I said.

"It's the very best dirt," said Charley. "It's good, clean dirt."

I drove on, and then we got off Route 22 and onto Old South Friendly Road, and I pointed out where Pism C. lives and where the man who was almost President lives and where Mr. Nice, Normal Author has his house.

"Lots of sonsabitches on this road," I said.

"That cannot be denied, but there are lots of those everywhere, and it's beautiful country."

After a while, I said, "I want to show you something," and I turned the car into this road. I stopped at the end of the road, near where this house is now.

"What's all this?" asked Charley as I got out of the car.

"This land belongs to a friend of mine," I said. "He's thinking of building."

I held open the door, and Charley walked to the place where the deck now is; she looked across the hazy afternoon hills and at the occasional clumps of Virginia creeper just then turning red and at the sky and the trees against it, and she said, "It's beautiful. It's really beautiful."

"This guy wants to build a house here," I said.

"Oh, look," said Charley, not hearing. She pointed to Old South Friendly Road. "The cars, just the right distance away, just the size of cars on an electric train."

"I think it's a ridiculous place to build a house," I repeated.

"Are you kidding?" asked Charley. "Who owns this place anyway?"

I named the man from whom I had bought it.

"He's a very lucky man," said Charley.

She walked to where the back of the house now is and beyond into the stand of pines.

"I'd build a modern house," she said, "mostly glass, with the bedrooms facing the pines. He got a large family?"

"Only himself and his wife."

"Oh, definitely in the pines then. With glass walls it'd be like waking up in the woods. I used to go to camp in the Ramapos when I was a girl, and it'd be just like that, waking up here. That magic time of day, very early in the morning, waking up, hearing the birds exchange the scandals of the night, seeing that the trees all look as if they had had a restful sleep, seeing that the sky has somehow become a brighter blue than yesterday, seeing that you can very nearly touch the clouds. It was always the very best time of day, before anybody else got awake and before those hearty, healthy counselors started ordering us around."

She came over to me. I was standing where the kitchen now is.

"Oh, darling," she said gently. "Could we try to find a place something like this?"

"It's awfully isolated," I said. "If I were Out There, you'd get very lonely."

"No, I wouldn't."

"And scared. Tramps and all that."

"Tramps and all that haven't worried me since I was four years old, and, really, I wouldn't get lonely if I knew you were coming back. I only get lonely, really lonely, when I think of spending the rest of my life alone."

She led me to what is now the middle of the living room, and she said, "Just look. This whole wall could be glass, looking out over those hills and fields. The view'd never be the same twice, and think of the fall. Oh, I suppose the land around here costs about ten million dollars an acre, but couldn't we ask in the village? How much did your friend pay? Oh, wouldn't it be wonderful, though."

She sounded like a twelve-year-old, and the bright blue eyes shone. Her hand in mine felt small and very at home and very warm and wonderful.

And I thought, Why didn't somebody tell me what it was like? I thought, Oh God, if there is a God, help me make her happy, and I felt tears in my eyes.

"...you weren't even listening," said Charley.

"I was so," I said. "You were saying that we ought to build a glass house in a place something like this."

"I said a lot more, too, all of it of great importance and terribly interesting. But what do you think?"

She looked up at me and gave me a queer, sudden grin. "Here I chatter on. You may hate this whole area, and anyway it's probably impossible."

"I don't hate this whole area. In fact, I think this right here would be a nice spot for a house, and I doubt if we'd be able to find anything half as good, so I guess what we ought to do is just build our house right here."

She looked sharply at me. "What do you mean by that?" she asked.

"Well," I said. "You see I happen to be the one who owns this property, and I was thinking if you liked it at all we might build a house right here."

I stopped and looked at her, and she was crying.

"You're such a bastard," she said. "Give me your goddamn handkerchief."

We made love that afternoon in the pine woods on a bed of needles, and in the evening we had dinner at a French place in Mount Kisco, and on the way home we played "I love my love because—," and we sang all the songs either of us had ever learned.

When I dropped Charley at her apartment house, she said, "What an absolutely wonderful day. Thank you."

I said, "It was okay if you like wonderful days."

She said, "I'd about given up hope of ever having such a day."

And she said, "I'm awfully glad you showed up," and she said, "When I was a little girl and something particularly marvelous happened, I used to close my eyes and say, 'Please, God, keep it always now.'"

"I'm going to try very hard to make you happy," I said. "I think we've got a very good chance to make it."

"At this moment, I'd be willing to make book on it," said Charley, "and won't it be wonderful. Two shy, sick, middle-aged people in love—and incredibly happy, thank you very much."

"I'm going to try very, very hard," I said again.

"Do that. Do that not so little thing."

Did I say a *happy* memory?

Well, no more of that childish nonsense.

Time is really pressing now. I have left the rest of tonight, tomorrow and part of Saturday.

I've got so much more to say, too. Letty was right, as she so often was. She said that if I ever did produce an autobiography I should call it, *Exit, Talking.*

This further fact. A little while ago I did what I've avoided doing since John was here late this afternoon. I looked in the bathroom mirror.

I saw in the mirror the face of a soft, middle-aged man with the taste of ashes in his mouth. I have more of a chin than most men I know who wear beards, but otherwise there is no feature in the face that is either very attractive or very memorable. The naked mouth is somewhat too small, and there is a suggestion of petulance to it. The lines on either side are those of someone who has laughed a lot or frowned a lot. As is the case with the lines around the wide, brown, frightened eyes. A closer look shows beyond any doubt that the lines are not those of a laughing man. It is a quite typical face for a resident of The Road. It is the face of a man who feels he has been denied something he deserves.

This, too. The face reminded me of someone I didn't or don't like—besides myself, I mean. It took me a while to remember, and then I did. Except for the long, red scar on my right cheek, I look almost exactly the way my mother looked the last time I saw her.

Louella was amazed to find me up when she arrived for work this morning. She didn't know I haven't gone to bed—and won't.

While she cleaned up in here, vacuuming up all the hair on the floor, and made breakfast, I took one of the capsules and a green pill. Then I showered and shaved. I'd forgot that I used to have to look at myself in the mirror *every* morning.

The accumulation of capsules and pills inside me is beginning to have an effect. Rather more than I want. I'm starting to feel the way I did when I'd fast for several days. The first time was a period when I was imitating—feebly, to be sure—the idiot who said that nothing human was alien to him. Who was it? In any case, fasting was one of the human experiences I tried. Another time—actually, another of several times—while shopping around for a god that I could live and die with compatibly, I studied the mystics. Then, too, I fasted.

About the third day without food, I'd start to feel the way I do now—as if my head had detached itself from my body and was floating a foot or so above my neck.

At the same time, I'd lose my sense of perspective; I have now.

Louella brought me orange juice, a sweet roll, and coffee.

She looked at me oddly, as if the sight of my naked face embarrassed her.

"I wouldn't know you from Adam, Mr. Bland," she said. "If I was to pass you on the street, I wouldn't know you from Adam."

Her tone indicated that she's just as glad such is the case. I must do something about Louella today. I must think up some perfectly ordinary excuse for giving her some time off. I don't want Louella to be the first to find me.

Just now, I picked up the porcelain pot to pour some coffee in my cup. Except I poured the coffee on the table and on me. A bad burn—but I didn't even feel it. I mean if I didn't know, I wouldn't know.

"You all right, Mr. Bland?" asked Louella.

I assured her that I was, but she's suspicious. She probably thinks I've been drinking, which is just as well.

I've had coffee now and smoked a cigarette. It burned my hand a little, or else the match.

I've taken a second shower, a very cold one; I feel better. I believe I'll be all right, though my head is still semi-detached.

This seems as good a place as any to tell you about The Book.

The Book happened during the war, but it had nothing to do with the war.

My condition being what it is at the moment, I may forsake the literal now and again.

About The Book, it isn't only the pills. The experience itself had an unreal quality.

The war itself was real enough—the first time I jumped out of a plane, for example. Not a moment of that gone from my mind. The day I was dropped into France, for example two. All of it preserved in my memory, like a fly in amber. The day the Bulge began. The day Nick was killed.

But The Book first.

Since The Book wouldn't have happened if I hadn't been in the Army, here is how I got in the Army.

I enlisted the day after Pearl Harbor.

There was a long line of men—most of them boys, really—waiting to get into Grand Central Palace.

For the boys, it was a game, a lark, a chance to play hooky for an indefinite period.

For the men, assuming there's something that separates them from the boys, it was a chance to escape from a wife, a job, creditors, boredom. Mostly boredom. In my case, it was a combination of the first, the second, and the third.

Patriotism, you say? What has that ever been except a fancy rationalization for what I've just said?

Anyhow, after waiting in line a long time, I finally got into Grand Central Palace and, in the words of a friend, took off my clothes, jigged, stooped, squatted, wet into a bottle, held up my right hand, and became a soldier.

Then I walked to the apartment on East Sixty-sixth Street that Letty and I shared when I had the bad luck to be in New York.

I'd been away for several weeks, but Letty and I at that time were not even going through the motions of being glad to see each other.

I told her that in a burst of patriotic enthusiasm I had enlisted in the Army, and she said, "Exactly what am I supposed to do to support myself? Take to the streets?"

I said, "I don't care what you do, but I wouldn't take to the streets if I were you. You're not the type that would attract many customers."

Letty picked up what was nearest at hand, a steak knife, and she threw it at me. It hit me, too. Where? Near the jugular vein; where else?

I fainted, and I bled a lot and for a long time, until after the doctor sewed me up.

No real harm done, though. The scar on my right cheek is not Letty's responsibility. No, Letty has left many marks on me. The bruises that will go up in smoke in a few days are largely self-inflicted, but Letty contributed her share.

The scar on my cheek? That badge of honor—the only one; why did I cover it up so long, do you suppose—was a gift from an SS lieutenant.

I believe the possibility that she might have killed me with that steak knife terrified Letty because during the few days before I left for my induction station, Fort Dix, Letty kissed me and petted me and asked me to promise that while I was in the Army I would write to her every day.

The more she whispered sweet nothings into my ear, the more I hated her. Nevertheless, I promised to write her, twice a week.

I did, too.

The morning before I left for Fort Dix Letty kissed me good-bye at the station, and I remember her saying, "Everything will be different when you get back, baby. Everything."

I said, "I hope you're right."

Letty said, "I love you, Josh. I really do."

I said, "Good-bye, Lets. Take care."

She said, "Write to me. You promised. Twice a week."

I said, "I promise."

I slept on the train, but I also did some thinking. I decided that my life with Letty was over; it was only a question of admitting it, and I also decided that in the vast anonymity of the Army I'd be able to *think.*

I remember something I said to myself that morning. I said, "In the Army I'll have a chance to find out who I am. My trouble is I don't know who I am."

Could I actually have been *twenty?*

At Dix I took the Army General Classification Test, which was very nearly the same test I'd taken twelve years before in Iowa City. At that time, if you remember, I got a score of 186. At Dix, my score was 132.

Some incompetents from the public-relations office at Dix rushed over with photographers to get a story and pictures, and the news of my disintegration made page one of the *Newark Evening News* and page 86 of *The New York Times.*

Psychologists and analysts who ought to have been serving prison sentences issued statements, as the quacks in this field often do, "Is Intelligence Variable?" they demanded. "Is Joshua Bland a *Fluke?*"

Myself, at times I thought I had just been *tired* when I took the tests at Dix. At other and more frequent times I concluded I was a fluke, that at last I was exposed as the fraud I had always been.

I still don't know and now never will and neither, thank God, will anybody else.

An elderly, very pleasant colonel had a long interview with me. He asked me what I wanted to do in the Army. Since I had been assured by dozens of men who knew just as much about it as I did that I'd never get the assignment I wanted, I told the colonel that I yearned to be an Infantry soldier.

To my great surprise and chagrin he made a check mark on my 201 file, and within twenty-four hours I was on my way to Fort Jackson, South Carolina. Assignment, Infantry.

At the time, I hated the colonel's guts; I'd been perfectly sure I would be sent to some cushy job in the Pentagon. I had always wanted to spend some time in Washington, particularly in wartime.

I may have been a *fluke*, but I knew perfectly well that if I was stationed in Washington, I could sit in the bar at the Mayflower and tell everybody who came along that if I'd had my way, I'd be *fighting*. Instead here I was cooped up in the Pentagon. Talk about your snafus.

Actually, for reasons that I'll go into in the next section, The War, I got to be very grateful to the colonel.

At Jackson, nobody gave a damn what I had got in my General Classification Test. Down there I was a body with a serial number—33170247. I was sent off as a replacement in a National Guard outfit, most of whose members were from the hills of Tennessee.

To my great surprise and delight, I liked them immediately. What's more important, after a while they got used to me.

Basic was tough for me. For one thing, I have always had a difficult time remembering which is my right hand and which the left. I took to carrying a small stone in my right hand—but, very often, on the drill field I forgot. Was my right hand the one with the stone in it? Or was it the left?

Twice a week, true to promise, I went to the service club and wrote a letter to Letty.

I was surrounded by an extraordinary group of men for whom I had the greatest admiration and affection, but I could share none of the experience with Letty. So I improvised. I invented a group of preposterous cut-ups, of cuddly-cute trainees who were laughing and frolicking their way through basic. They couldn't *wait* to get at Hitler and the Japs.

I sent this fiction off to Letty every Wednesday and Sunday night, and that is how The Book happened.

Letty decided that the letters I was writing her were absolutely hilarious. Don't ask me why.

She took them with her wherever she went during the early months of 1942—to the Colony for lunch, to every dinner she attended, and so on. I understand you couldn't stop her. She read every letter aloud, with gestures.

One evening—and here, friends, was my downfall—she took some of the letters to a dismal gathering of the almost rich and very nearly famous.

Among those in that lugubrious group was a man I'm calling Proudly Presents. He's the fellow who issues the novels erupted by the woman I've called America's Foremost Lady Novelist. Proudly has no sense of humor whatsoever and has proved it on many public and private occasions. When Letty read my letters, he proved it once more by laughing his fool head off.

Then, his voice atremble, his arms akimbo, Proudly came up to Letty and asked her if there were any more such letters.

Letty said, yes, *closets full*.

Presents cleared his throat. I know he did, even though I wasn't there at the time. Whenever the smell of money drifts toward the carefully attuned nose of Proudly, he clears his throat. I don't know why. People just do different things when they sniff loot. I could give you a long list. One man I know whistles; Letty's present husband, Harry, does a little half-foxtrot. I hum.

Anyway, "*Closets full?*" asked P.P.

Letty nodded. "Closets full."

I'll bet you dollars to doughnuts Proudly then cleared his throat a second time.

After that, he said—solemnly, I'm sure, for he is another of the solemn ones—that those letters were not only gems of wit, etc. He said that unless he missed his guess and he almost never missed his guess, those letters could become more famous than the letters George Bernard Shaw wrote to Ellen Terry.

Here he must have paused, allowing Letty to decide that Ellen Terry couldn't hold a candle to her.

Then P.P. almost certainly added, "I consider it my duty as a publisher to bring those letters to the very much wider audience they deserve."

I have heard P.P. say that sentence with minor variations many times. What it means is that P.P. has spotted the chance to make another fortune.

His judgment in this respect is flawless. He wouldn't know a good book if he accidentally came on one, but he does know a moneymaker when he smells it. That is the reason Proudly Presents has been able to follow the late J. P. Morgan's sensible advice. P.P. has bought several yachts without having to inquire into the price.

Anyway, Letty brought the closetfuls of nonsense I had written into P.P.'s office. There a neuter lip-reader stuck in a few commas and semicolons, and even before the letters were published, they were better known than the Shaw-Terry correspondence. You see what I had written fitted into everybody's plans in the spring and summer of 1942. The letters *proved* that the war we had just stumbled into was going to be *fun*. They proved not only that the Army would make a man out of you. It was a lot of laughs, too.

Magazine editors fought duels over the questionable privilege of being the first to print portions of *Prodigy as Private* before it appeared in book form.

Finally, the white man's *Ebony* paid through the nose and did publish some of it. Let's call that magazine *Reek*.

A short digression here. I can't resist. After Charley left me, I tried one evening to ease some of the pain by taking a very pretty girl to dinner. Her name is of no importance; all that matters is that she was willing to go to any length to appear in an on-Broadway play.

During the course of a pleasant dinner and what promised to be a fine evening, I said something about Pearl Harbor. Who knows what? I was *talking*.

"What's Pearl Harbor?" asked my companion.

I blanched a little, but I told her.

"Oh," she said. "Well, I never was very good at history."

I forgave her that, but as the taxi stopped in front of her apartment house, I said something about the fact that the Katzenjammer Kids in Wonderland, D.C., were going to sink us all, and she nodded, emphatically. Girls like that always do.

Then, impulsive fool that I am, I said, "Who's the first President you remember, Randy?"

Randy thought a minute; then she said, "Well, I sort of remember Truman."

I stared at her; I saw she wasn't joking.

I said, "Good night, Randy."

She said, "Aren't you coming up for a night cap or anything?"

I said, "Uh-uh," and I said again, "Good-bye, Randy."

Then I left, on the double....

Anyway, The Book was published in the very distant past, on June 25, 1942.

The Army gave me a two-week leave so that I could be in New York on that historic day.

I arrived on June 19, accompanied by a photographer from *Life* and a researcher who was all girl and a yard wide. She had been on the train with me for two days and most of two nights.

There were several 4-F newspaper men waiting for me at the station, and there were many photographers, and there was Letty. She ran up, threw herself in my arms, and kissed me, publicly, lustily, almost as if she were glad to see me.

"Thank God, you're safe," she said.

I said, "Fort Jackson isn't exactly Corregidor, you know."

Letty laughed fit to kill, and my brilliant little riposte appeared in papers all over the country the next morning.

You see, if you're famous, you don't have to be witty or wise; all you have is to be.

My silly face, overseas cap resting comfortably on both ears, was not only spread all over the jacket of the foolish volume Proudly Presents was issuing the next week. It also appeared on the cover of *Life*, *Collier's*, *See*, *Peek*, *Reek*, etc., etc., and on the inside pages of *Vogue*, *Harper's Bazaar*, and God knows how many other excuses to waste paper.

Famous. A Household Word. At last. People were talking about *me*.

Is it necessary to add that Proudly Presents was also at the station to greet me? He clutched me in one hand and a copy of The Book in the other. Then, grinning in the direction of the cameras, he said, "In my humble opinion it is the patriotic duty of every patriotic American to buy this patriotic book."

He made no mention of the patriotic profit involved.

Now you may think that the critics exposed this fraud when The Book was published. Not a bit of it. The first thing everybody loses when there's a war on is his common sense, and common sense is not a quality most critics are overly endowed with in the most peaceful times.

Instead of attacking the infamy, the critics fell all over each other in praising The Book and me. The Writers' War Board gave it their full endorsement. They said that reading it was as important to the war effort as gas rationing.

More?

Well, let's put it this way. I should have been arrested for taking money under false pretenses, but I wasn't.

No. My father had it right, citizens. I was so trivial that I was rewarded handsomely. I was loved and petted and cherished. I was quoted and misquoted; I was compared to Tolstoy and Shakespeare and Louisa M. Alcott.

And letters. Well, to give you one for-instance, on a single day in the late summer of that year, a staff sergeant at Fort Jackson brought me four hundred and twenty-six letters from girls who proposed marriage or I could have it without obligation.

In fact, it seems to me that in the summer and fall and winter of 1942 the only person in the universe who knew what dreck The Book was was me.

I forgot, though; you'll see.

These further words:

In a little less than eighteen months The Book sold more than a million copies in a hard-cover edition. It has now sold many hundreds of millions more in soft-cover editions in this country alone, and it is still selling.

It has been published in every spoken language and in several unspeakable ones. It is as well known in postwar Japan as the atomic bomb, and it is better liked. The Germans roared over it. They are roaring still. It proves they're right. War is more fun than a barrel of monkeys.

That is another reason I don't care for them.

The Book has been digested, condensed and regurgitated. It has been read to the blind and been put into Braille for them. It has been reduced to simplified English, a job that took very little work. An idiot child of forty-seven did something with it in iambic pentameter. Portions of it have been read into recording machines by such varied personalities as Tab Hunter, Rock Hudson, Red Buttons, Milton Berle, Yva Sumac, Johnnie Ray, Georges Jessel and Raft, Sarah Churchill, several first ladies of the American Theater, and Estelle Schultz, who after a most minor operation in Stockholm, changed his given name to Esmond. Schultz recorded it in both sexes and toured with it as a one-woman and then as a one-man show.

The Book was converted into what was incorrectly called a legitimate play, which, while not as good as *Abie's Irish Rose*, lasted longer.

The next time round it became what was advertised as a musical. It opened shortly after *South Pacific* but outlasted it by years. The damn thing might be running still if the actor singing the leading role had not dropped dead on stage while going through the loathsome motions for the millionth time.

I have no idea how many road companies have bamboozled how many millions of boobies into parting with as much as $16.80 to sit in on performances, musical and non-musical, of the biggest hoax since the Cardiff Giant. Juveniles have become grandfathers while touring in the leading role. Both the musical and what is referred to as the legitimate version have been performed for eternities in the West End in London and in theaters in Rome and Paris and Berlin.

Naturally, several dreadful movies have been made out of material contained in The Book. From some I received discredit and cash. In other cases, the expensive and untalented persons involved simply lifted my material and changed it ever so slightly, like making the Infantry private (me) into a WAC.

All of these filmed versions, legal and pirated, caused persons with no ability of any kind to become members of the power elite.

And it is not over.

I am nearly over, but *It* may never end.

I shall say nothing about the ninety-minute version or the many hour versions that have appeared on television or about the series still assaulting the public decency every Friday night from eight-thirty until nine.

Enough?

Well, there is more, but that is all I can keep down on an empty stomach.

You might be interested to know that I dedicated The Book to Letty:

To my dear wife Letty—without whom I might have been an honest man.

People thought the dedication was funny as a crutch.

When Letty and I got into the divorce courts, Letty asked for and got what was left of the royalties.

It couldn't have happened to a nicer girl.

I have said that I arrived in New York from Fort Jackson on the morning of June 19, 1942.

That evening Letty and I had dinner at the tax-deductible apartment on Park Avenue which belonged to Mr. and Mrs. Proudly Presents.

It was the first party of its kind I ever attended, and I wish to God it had been the last. Everybody in the place either was well known or was on the make to be.

Let's be fair. The only people who are more dreadful than obscure people are celebrities, or near-celebrities. I have never known anybody whose name has appeared in Walter Winchell's column that I'd throw a life preserver to if he was drowning.

Believe me it takes one to know one.

There were many what you might call creative people there, playwrights, novelists, painters, musicians, and, if you include actors in that category, actors.

The conversation was on about the same level as that at a faculty tea in New Athens. There was not a name mentioned that was not accompanied by a detailed dossier on his or her sleeping habits and companions, and it turned out that practically everybody who was anybody in New York either was *queer* or about to turn *queer* or already was and just too chicken to admit it. (After fourteen years in the theater, I'm not sure they weren't right about that.)

It turned out, too, that nobody had any talent except people within earshot. "Whatever happened to *him*?" they screamed. "Oh, he *never* had any talent," they screamed back. I realized at once that my mother would have been right at home at such a party.

Everybody admired me, though. People said, "What you are, young man—whatshisname, Veronica—is *lucky*." No talent, but lots of luck. I got the message.

Or they said, "I certainly plan to lose no time in reading your little book—whatsitcalled, Marilyn?"

What's more, everybody was simply green with envy at my good fortune in being in the Army. Everybody was *jealous* of me because I was going to have the opportunity to give my life in the fight against Fascism. There was practically nobody at that party who hadn't been a very active member of Fight for Freedom or the Committee to Defend America by Aiding the Allies; they had all made speeches on street corners, in telephone booths, over the radio, or at Madison Square Garden, demanding that the United States get in there and fight.

And just as soon as they finished their next book or play or concert tour or mural they were going to join up. If, that is, the Commander-in-Chief would let them. It turned out the Commander-in-Chief had *personally* told each and every one of them that each and every one of them was doing more for the war effort by writing books and plays and going on concert tours and painting murals than he would be able to do in uniform.

Among those present was a girl who had all the money in the world, and she was married to a man who looked very much like Whistler's Mother. There were also several individuals celebrated (though not by me) as wits. I remember only one comment. One of the wits said that a man at the Columbia Broadcasting System had a most amusing way of answering the telephone.

He was *implored* to tell us how the fellow at CBS answered the phone.

The wit was pretty well broken up before he got it out, but he finally managed. "He says, 'This is me,'" said the wit, and this remark caused several people to laugh so heartily that the chocolate soufflé fell.

That gives you a pretty fair idea of the intellectual caliber of the evening.

Proudly Presents, assisted by Mrs. Presents, who more than held up her end of the conversation, talked mostly about liter-a-cha. P.P. was and is the biggest author-dropper I've ever come across. He is also a president dropper, a Hollywood producer dropper, and a continent dropper.

Proudly several times made it clear that he was not in publishing for *money*. He said that if it was *money* he was interested in, he would have gone into some other line of work, and so on.

When he said that, I clapped my right hand on my wallet and kept it there for the rest of the evening.

At one point, Proudly turned to me, and he twinkled at me. I honestly can't think of any word that describes what he did better than *twinkled*.

He twinkled at me, and he said, "You won't need an agent, of course. None of my writers *ever* have *agents*."

I wasn't any too sure what *agents* did, but I could tell from P.P.'s tone that being one was just about as low as you could sink.

"I'll handle the whole thing," said Proudly, "including the movie sale, and there'll be a movie sale, because I personally have alerted all of my friends in Hollywood, from A to Zanuck."

Here Proudly laughed far more than was necessary, and so did several of the wits.

"I'll take only the usual twenty per cent plus the agent's commission," said Presents, quickly.

"As a special favor to you," he added, slowly.

Friends, fathers, brothers, I was more than half-drunk; I was twenty-and-a-half years old, and I knew very little about publishing, but I did know a portentous pickpocket when I met one. I was, as you may have guessed, born tired and filled with bile.

I said, "Why don't you just take it all and save yourself all that bookkeeping?"

Proudly chuckled madly at that, and he said that it was that kind of youthful impudence that gave what he was going to call Our Book its stamp of authentic genius, and so on.

As Letty and I left, Proudly said he hoped we would be his guests at his place in Oyster Bay over the week end. I said we'd let him know, and he said, "Now don't you worry about a thing, son. And *remember*. You don't need an *agent*. Think of me as your father."

In the elevator, I took out my wallet and counted the bills in it.

"You looked to see if anything's gone from your purse?" I asked Letty.

"What's that supposed to mean?"

"Well, who knows what Proudly Presents was doing when he *claimed* he was on the telephone with the Pope? It was the Pope, wasn't it? I meant to ask him, was it Alexander or Pius? I bet you a man with all the connections Proudly Presents has got probably talks to Alexander Pope very day. He no doubt talks to Alexander the Great every day, too. Must cost a pretty penny because it's a very long way to where Alexander Pope and Alexander the Great are, but I'll tell you who it doesn't cost a pretty penny. Proudly Presents."

Letty glared at me, inclining her head in the direction of the elevator operator, a man in his declining years, who seemed to be having a violent coughing spell.

When we got outside of the Presents' apartment house, which was a little larger and more lavish than Buckingham Palace, Letty said, "You have been absolutely abominable the *entire* evening in addition to being drunk. Proudly Presents just happens to be one of the most charming and cultured and cultivated and generous people in the entire city of New York."

"He's a pompous pirate, and you know it. There isn't a generous bone in his body, and he's got the charm of Dr. Goebbels."

"You don't even seem to be grateful. It's a great honor and a privilege to be on Proudly Presents' list, and, besides, you'll probably make a lot of money."

"That last part has the ring of truth," I said. "The word *money* is the first true word you've spoken all evening."

"It's a very good book," said Letty.

I cupped my hand to my ear and pretended to be listening very carefully to something, but Letty wouldn't ask what I was listening to. Letty had learned better.

So I told her what I was listening to.

"That twirling sound you hear is Count Tolstoy turning over in his grave," I said.

"You have already reached a great many more people than Tolstoy—" Letty began, and I started laughing.

By that time, the doorman had our cab, and I don't remember what Letty did. She probably went into one of her long, silent sulks.

Letty had given up the East Side apartment and was living in a cubbyhole on West Twelfth Street, but, for convenience sake during my leave, we were staying at the Waldorf in a suite paid for by Proudly, or so he claimed. I was sure the money would be taken out of my royalties.

When we got back to the hotel, there was a telegram from Cedar Rapids, addressed to Letty.

She tore it open, read it, and I could see her face going pink with anger.

Letty's mother, who had already done so much to be forgiven for, had committed the final indignity. Mrs. Novotny had died at the beginning of a two-week period when Letty was about to cash in on her mistaken marriage to me. Letty had been about to spend two weeks being the wife of the most famous enlisted man in the U.S. Army.

"Now of all times," said Letty, crushing the telegram and throwing it to the floor.

I picked it up, read it, and said, "It was rather thoughtless of her."

Then Letty cried, and she said, "I'm so ashamed."

I took her in my arms, and I stroked her hair, and I kissed her, and I said, "Don't be ashamed, darling."

"It's so awful," said Letty. "I always wanted her to be something she wasn't. I wanted her to be tall and have good bones and blue-gray hair and look like the mothers of those awful Pi Phi bitches who were always looking down their noses at me. I never was very nice to her, and I was so ashamed of her, and she knew it. I'm really very bad."

"There is no such thing as a bad girl," I said, and then Letty laughed and at the same time cried. That night for the first time in a long time and for the last time ever, we were close to each other.

The next morning, with the help of a good-natured corporal in the Army Transportation Office at Grand Central Palace, I managed to get Letty on a coach that took her back to the place she had been running so fast to get away from, White Street in Cedar Rapids, Iowa.

She said, "Don't do anything I wouldn't do, darling," and then she tried a smile, and then she cried again.

On my way back to the Waldorf, I thought of Letty's mother holding those preposterous pink bedroom slippers in one hand and the red comb in the other, and I laughed, rather hysterically.

Then a newspaper truck passed, and on it was a poster with a blown-up photograph of me in uniform, a little larger than life-size.

"*Corporal Bland Blasts Pentagon*," the poster said.

In somewhat smaller type, no more than a foot high, the poster added, "*Most Famous Enlisted Man in U.S. Army Gives Low-Down on Army Life. Exclusive in the* World-Telegram."

This was the result of an interview I'd had with a *World-Telegram* reporter the evening before.

I can no longer remember just how I *blasted* the Pentagon, but I'm sure it was about something terribly fundamental, like how wrong I thought it was that enlisted men had to make hospital corners on their bunks.

I watched the truck until it was out of sight, then stopped in front of a dress shop. I looked in a mirror in the window and adjusted my garrison cap to a jauntier angle. Several people glanced at me with a puzzled look of what I took to be half-recognition.

Then a woman came up to me, wanting to know did I know where the Graybar Building was. When I told her, she looked curiously at me.

"Don't I know you from somewheres?" she said. "You got a very familiar face."

"I'm Corporal Bland," I said, familiarly, and if the woman had been listening at all carefully, she would have heard the blare of trumpets and the respectful roll of drums in the background.

She wasn't listening, though. She said, "I'm sorry. I must of mistook you for somebody else.

Then that fool woman wandered dazedly off in the direction of the Graybar Building, little realizing that I had taken out the fountain pen given to me by Proudly Presents, who had no doubt paid for it out of my money.

I had been prepared to give that woman an autograph.

After she left, I kept thinking about what Presents and ever so many other pleasant, perceptive people had said about me in the twenty-four or so hours since I had arrived in New York from Fort Jackson.

For instance, the worldly, pipe-smoking editor of *Reek* had said that my letters proved beyond any doubt that I had the mind of a philosopher; he had also said that *Reek* would publish anything I wrote, including my laundry list. All I had to do was ask.

He added that *Reek* was *proud, yes proud* to add me to the friendly family of friendly contributors and would pay me two thousand friendly dollars for every friendly contribution.

As I left him, this friendly editor said, "I just want to shake your hand once more, Corporal Bland. I am honored to shake your hand."

He honored himself for quite some time, and while his palm was slightly damp, I didn't mind basking in his reflected honor.

The New York story editor of—let's call it—Miracle Pictures had told me that if the Miracle people were just lucky enough to have the honor of making a movie out of *Prodigy as Private* they would be content never to make another picture; they would be satisfied to rest on their—well, laurels.

Moreover, he had said, "This is the first time in my life that I have been privileged to be present at the birth of a classic—and I am grateful for it. It makes me feel all humble inside."

I had told Letty that this fellow was a charlatan with halitosis, but, thinking it over on my way back to the Waldorf that morning, I decided that perhaps I had been too harsh. The man undeniably had bad breath, but a charlatan? Perhaps not.

"I laughed," the Miracle man had said. "I laughed until I cried, and you've never seen Shakespeare do that to me, have you?"

I had to admit I had never seen Shakespeare do that to him.

I thought of Proudly Presents, and I forgave him his transgressions.

After all, Proudly did recognize me for what I had always fancied myself as being, an amusing, *impudent genius.*

Everybody who was anybody recognized me as something special. Since this only confirmed what I already knew, why should I deny it?

Having gone that far, I started worrying. What worried me was whether people recognized just *how* special I was. Well, just in case, I'd have to demonstrate it; that was all.

I walked through the massive ugliness of the Waldorf lobby, picturing General Marshall trembling in his boots because of my *blasts* at the Pentagon.

At the desk I picked up my key and a few messages, and I was starting toward the bank of elevators when a small, dark man stepped up to me.

"You are Corporal Bland," he said, his manner indicating that he had spent a drab lifetime waiting for the pleasure of this moment.

"I am," I condescendingly agreed.

"My name is George Bansky the agent," the man said.

George Bansky the agent was about five-four and small-boned; he had a ring of dark hair on his oversize head; his face was round; his eyes were enormous and somewhat sad, but at the same time his large, sensuous mouth gave the impression of being admiringly amused by me.

His nose was enormous. It defied me to ignore it, and I did not. What I did do was try not to think about Cyrano or the story about Mrs. Dwight Morrow asking J. P. Morgan if he wanted milk or lemon with his nose.

George then had and still has a habit of leaning very close when he talks to you, and his nose is mouth-level on me. In the old days, I always used to feel a nearly irresistible urge to bite it, but I never did.

Altogether, George was not then a man one would overlook. He has often told me that in those days people seeing him for the first time did not ask, "Who's that?" They invariably wanted to know, "What's that?"—which is what George wanted them to ask.

"George Bansky the agent," George repeated, and he handed me his card and said, "I was wondering could we have a small, little talk someplace."

I was then new to city ways and city slickers, but I knew a fourflusher when I saw one.

Nevertheless, I was courteous. I ostentatiously glanced at my PX watch.

"I'm terribly sorry," I said, "but I have an appointment with Ambrosine Coy, the radio interviewer, in exactly twelve minutes, and I have to get cleaned up."

During that period in New York, I never kept anybody guessing about whom I had an appointment with. I named names.

Actually, my appointment was with Ambrosine's assistant.

However, I politely glanced at the card of George Bansky the agent. The type was plain Gothic, and the pasteboard was not of the best quality.

"Ambrosine is a very, very close personal friend of mine since the days when she first arrived in Gotham from Indianapolis some twenty years ago," Bansky was saying.

I sniffed inwardly at the obvious lie and said that if Mr. Bansky would please excuse me I would try to call him sometime.

"Of course, of course," he said, and I once more started toward the elevators. I was thinking that Proudly Presents had been so right about one thing. Being an agent *was* just about as low as you could sink.

Then George said, "I was only wanting to ask you one small little question, which is whether or not you would be interested in becoming a millionaire."

I immediately answered George's question in my mind. I said, Yes, and that was where I made my big mistake.

Meantime, George Bansky the agent was adding that perhaps after I had had my chat with his old and very dear friend, Ambrosine, I would agree to give him a small, little tinkle on the telephone.

Then he left.

I thought of shouting after him, but I didn't. It didn't seem to me that shouting would become a future millionaire.

I caught the next elevator, went to my room, showered, shaved, and put on the gabardine uniform which made me look almost like an officer. Then I went down to the Waldorf coffee shop and met Ambrosine's assistant, who was one of those terribly hearty women you are liable to run into in New York and Out There if you don't watch your step.

As I've said, there are a lot of them around Sloane's Station too. They are like red ants, and lots of them are named Freddy and Joe and Mike, and an incredible number are named Mona. I don't know why, but if the Rockefeller people just put their thinking caps on they are going to find this whole phenomenon is something it's worth spending a little money to look into.

Ambrosine's assistant was named Mona, last name Hearty, as I recall.

Toward the end of the interview, I took out George's card and asked Mona Hearty if she had ever heard of a George Bansky the agent.

"Is George romancing you?" she asked.

"He has spoken to me, as have many others."

"Grab him," said Mona. "Don't hold out for marriage. George has got more in his pinky than William Morris and MCA put together. If he wants you, you've practically got your first million in the bank already."

Then she rose, shook my hand, bruising it only a little, and said not to worry about my radio chat with Miss Coy the next morning. She said Miss Coy knew how to make folks feel at home, about which she was wrong. If there is one thing Ambrosine makes you feel, it is not at home.

I said, "Thanks, Mona," and I returned to my suite, on the double. I picked up the phone and gave the operator the number that was printed on George's card.

When I got through to him, I explained that I was really very busy but that I might be able to put aside a few minutes for him *sometime* during my stay in New York.

George said he realized that I was a very, very busy young man. He said that he realized there wasn't the smallest chance of it, and it was a foolish question to ask the most famous enlisted man in the

U.S. Army, but he was a foolish man and would ask anyway. Was there the smallest remote chance that I would be free for a small, little drink with him that afternoon?

I said that, well, I could probably *get* free, my tone indicating that to do so I would have to cancel my appointment with the Joint Chiefs of Staff.

George said that made him very, very happy indeed. Then he apologetically asked whether or not Twenty-One would be satisfactory with me as a meeting place.

I had never been to Twenty-One; I had never heard of Twenty-One, but I said, "Why, of course. I rather like Twenty-One."

We arranged to meet there at five. I found the address in the phone book.

By six that afternoon, my marriage to George had been consummated.

George had not been anxious, nor, as I had feared, had he been *pushy*. George had simply explained to me that he didn't represent just any writers, and he mentioned the names of several to me impressive writers, many of whom he said had begged him to represent them. He said these writers were no doubt very, very fine human beings, but George Bansky the agent was simply not interested in representing *journeyman* writers, even though such *journeymen* might make a very, very great deal of money for themselves and for George.

George was strictly interested in quality, he said; his sole concern was with literature, and if George had been an agent at the time of Stendhal, George would have wanted Stendhal on his small, select list of happy clients.

He paused for a moment to allow me to absorb this fact.

Then George, his voice trembling only a little, said, "Joshua Bland, I would like to add your name to my small, select list of happy clients."

I started to speak, but George lifted an admonishing hand.

"Wait, Bland," he said. "Think it over, but remember this. I know you are not interested in money as such, but I would be less than fair if I did not say that if you and I were associated together, the association would be very, very profitable indeed for both of us."

George said that he realized I would want to give a great deal of thought to a matter as serious as this. He wanted me to take however long I needed to make up my mind, however long, a week, a month, even a year if need be. However long. It might even be, though George had to chuckle at the thought, it might even be that I would allow myself to fall into the hands (he said *hands*, but his tone indicated *clutches*) of one of the *factories*. William Morris or MCA, one of *those*, though he George Bansky thought that that would be the gravest possible error on my part.

"If you're not producing *money-makers* for people like *that*," said George, "they drop you like a cold potato. They are not only not *interested* in *art*. They are *opposed* to *art*."

George breathed deeply. "Those are not the methods of George Bansky the agent," he said. "I am definitely not interested in a few measly tens of thousands here, a few tens of thousands there. I take the long view. I want two things for you. I want you to produce art, and I want you to make a million dollars, after taxes, and you certainly can't knock either of those, can you?"

I hurriedly said that I certainly could not and would not knock either of them, but I did diffidently mention the fact that only the night before Mr. Proudly Presents had said that in *my* case an agent was unnecessary. I said that Mr. Proudly Presents had *assured* me that it was his privilege and his pleasure to take care of the tedious trivialities of, for instance, a motion-picture sale.

"Proudly *Presents*," said George, and he laughed. He laughed a long time. Then he wiped his mouth with his handkerchief, and he said, "Forgive me for laughing, Bland, but I couldn't help myself in this instance. *Proudly* Presents."

He laughed some more and wiped his mouth some more. Then he took an envelope and a stub of pencil from his pocket, and while I waded into another Manhattan, George scribbled some figures on the back of an envelope.

"After all, in this area Proudly Presents is a *publisher*," said George, smiling tolerantly, as if at the antics of an idiot child of seven.

Then he looked up from his figuring. "Taking into account all you have told me about extra rights, magazine sales, syndication, all of that, I figure Proudly has *already* cost you in the neighborhood of fifty or sixty thousand dollars. *Already. At least.*"

George smiled pityingly at me.

"That is the reason people out in Hollywood just laugh at a publisher like Proudly Presents trying to act as an *agent*, too. Not to mention the ethics of the matter."

The way George sounded it looked to me as if, given a choice between pimping and trying to publish and act as an agent at the same time, pimping was the better deal.

George carefully folded his handkerchief and put it back into his breast pocket.

"Not that I am saying Proudly Presents is not as honest as the day is long," George added, his manner indicating that it was a wonder to him Presents wasn't in Alcatraz.

"Proudly and I have been acquainted for many years," George went on. "I knew him when he was still hustling for nickels and dimes on Seventh Avenue, long before he picked up that Harvard-type accent he's got now."

George then turned toward the waiter, and my heart dropped a good distance. I was afraid George was going to pay the check and dismiss me for having been stupid enough even to listen to Proudly talk about acting as my agent.

However, George ordered another round of drinks, and I took a deep breath and started talking very fast. I told George that I didn't really need time to think over his generous offer, that I wanted to sign just as soon as possible, provided, of course, he was *really sure* he wanted to add my name to his small, select list of happy clients.

How soon did George think he could work me in? I asked, anxiously, afraid that I might have to wait for somebody like Stendhal to die.

Well, I was very, very lucky that afternoon.

It turned out George had hoped I might make a decision like the one I had just made, and being an optimist, he had been presumptuous enough to bring along four copies of a contract with him, my name all typed in.

All I had to do was sign, four times, though George was sure that I would want to read the contract over, including the small print, because he knew that—

I quickly took a sip of my fifth Manhattan.

I said, "I don't need to do that, Mr. Bansky. I trust you, and you trust me, and I see absolutely no nec—"

I signed, using the pen Proudly Presents had given me. It was clear to me that through dishonesty or incompetence or both Presents was costing me money every second he continued to represent me, not to mention the fact that I was still afraid that George might change his mind about me.

When I had finished signing all four contracts, George shook my hand, and he said that this was a day neither of us would ever forget.

Then he said, "Now let's get down to brass tacks."

George pushed his nose very close to me.

"We can't afford to waste any more time," he said. "The iron ain't gonna get no hotter than it is at this minute."

I wanted another Manhattan, but George made no move to buy me one. I recognized that a subtle but unmistakable change in our relationship had already taken place.

George was jotting down a list of things, very quickly, and he started humming something I thought might be an ancient Hebrew chant of some kind. I asked George what it was.

"That," said George, "is an old American folk song. It is entitled, 'There may be flies on some of you guys, but there ain't no flies on me.'"

I have been on George's no longer small, never very happy list of clients ever since.

Quite a long time after I had signed with him, George said, "I knew right away that you and I were meant for each other. I observed that first morning in the Waldorf lobby that you were a kid on the make."

Know what Proudly Presents said when I told him I had signed with George?

He said, "Not *George Bansky!* Of all the agents in the wide and shining—why, that man is no more and no less than a common criminal. If you *had* to have an agent, which I carefully explained to you you did not have to have with me in charge of the annoying little trivialities like film sales, etc., but if you *insisted*, which none of *my* authors ever does, I have a very close friend who is one of the very best agents in the business, but George *Bansky.*"

"Mr. Bansky spoke very well of you, Mr. Presents," I said.

"I've *asked* you as a boy I think of as my son to call me Proudly," said Presents, shuddering a little. "George *Bansky.*"

This is as good a place as any to add that there is a lot of George in Proudly, and vice versa, but there is one major difference between the two men. When George spins a lie, he never for a minute believes it; the minute Proudly utters a fast one, it becomes Holy Writ simply because he, Proudly, said it. I prefer the Georges of the world.

I do have to add that I became somewhat disillusioned with George a few days after I had signed up.

The occasion was a cocktail party given in my behalf and probably at my expense by Presents and *Reek.* George had not been invited.

As guest of honor, I was pretty much *on* the whole time at the cocktail party, and I felt it absolutely mandatory to have an opinion on everything. At that time, I'd have felt naked without one.

I demanded an immediate opening of a second front and called for an instantaneous landing on the Japanese mainland, and so on. I remember one of my *pronunciamentos.* I said, "The sooner we *fight* this war, the sooner well win it, and I should think that George C. Marshall would have the *sense* to see that."

Several of the guests nodded vehemently, and a man who looked like Ernest Hemingway said he couldn't agree with me more.

The fellow wasn't Hemingway, but there was among the guests an honest-to-God writer.

This writer and I naturally settled down in a quiet corner to discuss art and literature, as writers do.

I was silently rehearsing some sharp and penetrating observations on the works of Proust and Dostoyevsky when the other writer opened the conversation.

"Who's your agent, Bland?" he asked.

Since George had told me that he had absolutely refused to represent this fellow whom George had dismissed as a *journeyman* writer, I was proud to reply, "I've just signed with George Bansky."

"Well, good luck, Bland," said this writer, not seeming at all envious. "You could do worse. A kid like you might have ended up with a real crook, and George isn't a *real* crook. I mean he wouldn't steal money from you unless he was pretty damn sure he could get away with it."

I smiled, pitying this *journeyman* writer for his small-minded jealousy. Meantime, he drank quite a bit of his drink, *fast*, a habit I have since observed in many other writers.

"George give you that hanky-panky about Stendhal and literature, his small, select list and all that crap?" this journeyman alcoholic demanded, grabbing another drink from a passing tray.

I didn't answer. I simply took a very small sip of my own drink.

"Agents are all alike," said this inebriate. "They're all a bunch of crooks, but I have to admit George's hanky-panky about Stendhal is pretty impressive the first time you hear it. I might have fallen for it myself if I hadn't already been nailed to the cross by Sid Kaplan. Where'd George take you for lunch? Twenty-One?"

A waiter forced a drink on me, and I said, with the utmost dignity, "Mr. Bansky and I had cocktails at the Twenty-One Club."

"Well, you got the A treatment, all right; hell, you ought to, you'll make him a fortune with that one lucky shot of yours. How long you in for?"

I decided that as long as the waiter had forced another drink on me, I might as well sip a little; I did, and I said, "I beg your pardon?"

"How many years has George got you signed up for?"

"The contract is a mere formality," I said. "Any time I am dissatisfied Mr. Bansky *wants* me to leave the agency. He doesn't *want* unhappy clients on *his* list."

That sot laughed so hard he spilled some of his drink on the beige wall-to-wall carpet in Proudly Presents' tax-deductible apartment.

"George tell you that?" this alcoholic scrivener demanded.

No answer seemed necessary.

"I bet George's got you nailed down for life plus ninety-nine years," the journeyman added. "You just ever *try* leaving, son. George'll hang on to you just as long as you keep making him money. The minute you stop, he'll drop you like a hot potato."

Later, after the journeyman and I had completed our discussion of art and literature, I went straight back to the Waldorf and for the first time read my contract with George straight through. The journeyman was right. I had indeed signed with George for life plus ninety-nine years, but I was relieved to find that it was no worse.

It might have been the electric chair.

George was right about one thing, though. I did make a million dollars, *before* taxes.

God knows what ever happened to it, to art, to me, or, for that matter, to Stendhal.

Let me add here that a long time later I finally got up enough courage to ask George if he would mind telling me what he meant when he referred to a writer as being a *journeyman*.

"Not at all," said George, who by then was no longer George Bansky the agent but George Banning, artists' representative.

"A *journeyman* writer is a writer represented by an agent other than myself."

I was in New York for ten days after George and I first met, and where money was involved, George took over everything, including Proudly Presents.

"Never speak the word *money* to that man again," said George, "and if he so much as looks as if he might be going to *mention* the subject, get in touch with me, and if I am not *immediately* available, call the police."

There was a great to-do in the columns about how the movie companies were falling all over each other to buy the rights to *Prodigy as Private*, and I was pleased.

One day, a little surprised that George had not been discussing these fascinating details with me, I dropped into his office and asked which company had made the highest bid.

"I'll let you know when it's time for us to discuss it," said George, who appeared to be very busy.

"Now look here," I said. "This happens to be my business."

George looked across his desk at me. It was and still is a desk at which Governor Winthrop is alleged to have sat. George's wife, Shirley, picked that desk up for less than nothing at a cute little place near West Tisbury, Massachusetts, where the two boys who run the place just aren't aware what they have and where somebody like Shirley who really *knows* antiques can and does take advantage of them.

"Nobody's made a firm bid for the book yet," said George.

I went pale. "But I read in Mr. Leonard Lyons' column—" I began.

"That's just stuff I planted in the columns," said George. "The highest *firm* offer is from Monogram, one of those places, for $100,000. That's just a little joke."

I believe I sank into a chair.

"But Miracle offered *$500,000* a week ago to Proudly Presents," I managed to say, "and *he* turned it down."

"Miracle-Schmiracle," said George, his eyes and his mind returning to whatever he was reading. Clearly, I was dismissed.

"Now look here—" I started to say.

"Don't you have some place to go?" asked George, and I realized then that there was under the velvet glove the required iron hand.

"What about a lovely matinee?" George asked. "There's *The Son of Mrs. Miniver* at the Music Hall."

I stalked angrily out, slamming the door, but not too hard. That afternoon I saw *Casablanca* for the seventh time, and that evening I appeared on the stage of the Roxy and sold war bonds.

Four days later Metro-Goldwyn-Mayer promised to pay half of what was buried at Fort Knox for the movie rights to *Prodigy as Private*. As I recall, they threw in Greer Garson and Myrna Loy as bonuses.

The day after that George arranged a deal with the Queens Syndicate by which I allowed an illiterate hack employed by them to write a daily newspaper homily to which my name, rank, and serial number would be signed.

The Queens people wanted my name; they had no interest in my ideas, although they said they had no objection if from time to time I wanted to send them *suggestions* for the column.

I remember I was worried about whether or not I would be able to approve what was written. The answer was I would not. The Queens people pointed out that I was in the Army and that I might be shipped overseas, etc.

I started to insist. Then I noticed that George was rolling his eyes heavenward, his manner indicating that if I didn't keep my big mouth shut, the federal government and the Queens people would be able to keep what little was left at Fort Knox.

I signed immediately, and that's how it went.

Everybody interviewed me, *everybody.* Their faces and most of their names are gone now, but I do remember a girl from Antioch College who was on temporary duty at, I believe, *Mademoiselle.*

She entered my foxhole at the Waldorf, sat down, unfurled four thick stenographer's notebooks, took five freshly sharpened No. 2 pencils from her ample purse, lifted one, leaned confidently toward me and said, "Corporal Bland, I am here to plumb you to the very depths."

I don't remember that girl's name, but I do hope she's made out all right.

Almost forgot. How could I?

I met Mrs. Roosevelt, and my long-distance love for her was greatly enhanced when I met her. She said to me, "If you're ever in Washington, do let us know. We'd love to have you come for dinner."

It wasn't until I got back to the Waldorf that I realized she meant the White House. I've never been so pleased with myself, or so flattered.

I never made it, but it didn't matter. The invitation itself was enough; she'd meant it.

George and his wife, Shirley, took me to a night club, Café Society Uptown, and people stood and applauded when the master of ceremonies told them who I was.

I stayed seated and nodded, giving them my twenty-eight-tooth celebrity smile.

Mildred Bailey sang "Ole Rockin' Chair's Got Me" at my request.

I applauded so loud that she sang it a second time, and then a third, and the M.C., one of the chuckly ones, said that somebody ought to write a song, "Prodigy as Private."

Later, somebody did, and a great many bad singers recorded it. So did a good singer, Frank Sinatra. It was a lousy song, but I thought it compared favorably with some of Bach's better efforts. Not only that, I made a great deal of money out of it.

As is surely apparent by now, while I may not have chased the Bitch Goddess, once she had climbed into bed with me, I made no effort to kick her out. In fact, I did my best to keep her entertained so she'd stick around for a while.

I talked to Letty in Cedar Rapids on the telephone. She said that she hated missing all the excitement, and she said she hoped I realized who was responsible for my success. I said that I did, and Letty said she was settling her mother's *estate*, by which she meant she was selling the sad, small house on White Street in which she'd been born and raised.

Later, I discovered that as soon as Letty sold the house, White Street disappeared from her memory. After that, Letty persuaded herself that she had been born and brought up in a white clapboard house on Elm Street, U.S.A. What's more, Letty now really believes that her father was a vice president of Quaker Oats, and she remembers her mother as a tall, well-boned woman with blue-gray hair—and a world traveler.

One other item about my stay in New York during the time The Book was published. The night I left to go back to Fort Jackson, there was a bond rally in the grand ballroom of the Waldorf. Tallulah Bankhead, Grover Whalen, and others spoke, including me. I auctioned off the packet of letters which had become The Book. A Merchant of Death bought the letters. *Bought!* He invested a hundred thousand dollars' worth of easily earned money in a sure thing at the usual rates of interest.

Anyway, after the Merchant of Death wrote out his check, he and I had our pictures taken. We shook hands and laughed at nothing and sat down. From the applause, you'd have thought the two of us had established a beachhead in Normandy. There was even some cheering.

Now comes something which even after all these years embarrasses me every time I think of it.

The master of ceremonies at this affair was an actor, a very famous one who specializes in playing Presidents of the United States, dead ones, or else he plays people who would like to be President but are just too pure to make it.

Anyway, Mr. President Player was master of ceremonies at the Waldorf wing-ding I'm describing.

Before the whole thing started, he asked me where I was going afterwards, and I said I was taking a late train back to Fort Jackson.

"You mean you're going from here straight back to the *wars*?" asked P.P. (not to be confused with Proudly Presents, another phoney from way back.)

"Well, I wouldn't put it that way," I said.

P.P. said, "Look, I have a marvelous idea. We'll have you *last*. I'll fix it with Talloo; she's very patriotic and she's stopped drinking. You last and after you've made your little talk and sold your letters, you can leave right from the ballroom for the *wars. Immediately.* I'll have everybody stand and applaud. There won't be a dry eye in the house."

"But I'm only going to Fort Jackson," I said.

And I believe I added, "Look, guys are getting killed. You can't crap around with the *war*. I won't do it."

Maybe I didn't say that, though. As I've mentioned repeatedly, my memory—like Letty's—is always deciding in my favor.

Whatever I said, P.P. didn't hear. He was composing what *he* was going to say. In this non-listening age, actors listen the least of anybody. In fact, they never listen at all unless you're telling them how great they are and how, by comparison, somebody like Richard Burbage or Sarah Bernhardt couldn't act their way out of a paper bag.

All right. As described above, the Merchant of Death and I did our act and had our pictures taken, showing teeth. The applause started, and we sat down.

At what you might call the peak of the applause, P.P. got up and made that ridiculous gesture actors and politicians make to quiet down applause. You know, both hands above their heads in a kind of swimming motion. Only you always know they don't want the applause to quiet down too fast.

P.P. had been getting more presidential all evening, and by this time you'd have thought he was turning down a draft for a fifth term.

"Ladies and gentlemen," he said, his voice trembling, the way he did it in that play where as Thomas Jefferson the entire Declaration of Independence came to him in a flash.

"Ladies and gentlemen," said P.P. or Thomas Jefferson. "In a moment I'm going to ask all of you to stand because we are present at a very solemn occasion. Let us please have complete silence."

There were sounds of "shhing" all over the place, and I felt the small hairs at the back of my neck rise, and I felt a vermilion flush creep over my face. I knew what the sonofabitch was up to.

Mr. President Player made another silencing gesture, and eventually everybody did quiet down, even the waiters who were serving booze to the lushes.

P.P. said, "There is only one among us here tonight who is really *fighting* this *war*, who may at any moment be called upon to give his life—"

Here he paused, and for a moment it looked as if he would be overcome with fraudulent emotion. This was bad acting in the grand style, but you want to know something? A lot of fifty-year-old dames who thought their sun tan made them look forty got out pieces of lace and started blowing into them. I tell you, during a war you can get away with *anything*.

Somewhere a man coughed, and P.P. looked in that direction and frowned. It was obvious that he considered the cougher a Hitler supporter.

After one of the memorable pauses of our time, P.P. cleared his throat of a lifetime's accumulation of phlegm. That took a good ninety seconds.

"I refer, of course, to the only real soldier among us tonight," he said, tremolo.

Here several merchants of death comforted their consciences by getting a little misty-eyed, and several of their leather-skinned wives broke down completely.

President Player turned toward me, his right hand raised for silence. "Stand, Corporal Bland," he said. "Rise and be paid homage."

Oh, my God.

P.P. motioned for the whole kit and kaboodle of those patriotic profiteers to rise, and they did. Not a dry eye anywhere.

They were all applauding, waiting for me to get to my feet. What would you have done under the circumstances? Announced that the whole thing was a fraud, that you were on your way back to Fort Jackson, South Carolina, which was a lot safer than the Waldorf? Like hell you would. You'd have done just what I did.

What I did was, first, look for an escape hatch under the speakers' table. Finding none, I rose.

P.P. motioned for silence, but not everybody quieted down. There was a ripple of applause, the way there sometimes is at concerts at the end of a movement when some dolts wishfully think the thing is over and start clapping. Said dolts always get stared at by the dreadful people who *really know music*. The applauders always want to die right on the spot but never do. I know because I've often been an applauder at the wrong place and always want to die.

Anyway, this night at the Waldorf, Mr. President Player gave a White House frown in the direction of the applauders. Then using the voice he uses every time he plays Abraham Lincoln's[12] death scene, he said, "I want all of you to wish this brave young warrior hail and farewell. Hail and *farewell*."

By this time, P.P. had his handkerchief out, and he gave his nose a presidential blow.

"God bless you, Corporal Bland," he said. "God bless you and keep you."

Well, I knew an exit line when I heard one; besides which, when the God-blessing starts, I get out. On the double.

---

12 One of the minor but nonetheless vital planks in the Bland Plan for Shaping Up the World is a proposal for a twenty-year moratorium on plays, novels, and especially speeches about Abraham Lincoln. What's happened to Lincoln is that one of the most interesting men ever to get in the White House has been reduced to a stupefying bore, especially by the writers who get all mixed up when they start writing about Lincoln and get to thinking they're writing about themselves. They will be forbidden even to *think* about Lincoln.

As I started off the platform, the band began playing "God Bless America," and people applauded and shouted and cheered. Then, just before I got to the door, P.P. stopped the music and made another silencing gesture.

"Corporal Bland..." he said. I turned.

"Corporal Bland, the only way we poor civilians can show our appreciation for the supreme sacrifice you are making is by buying another million dollars' worth of bonds—and I said a *million*. Am I right, folks?"

"Right," shouted a thousand addle-pated, folksy bond buyers, and then they applauded some more, either themselves or me. I never knew.

George Bansky the agent, was waiting for me by the elevator. "Not a dry eye in the house," said George.

I believe I had the grace to blush.

The applause continued, and by that time the band was playing, "Praise the Lord and Pass the Ammunition."

"Let's get the hell out of here before they start playing 'White Cliffs of Dover,'" I said to George.

George nodded. "What time's your train?" he asked.

"One-thirty."

"It's now ten-thirty," said George, "and since you are about to make the supreme sacrifice, how about coming up to my place for a drink? I'm a summer bachelor. Shirley has taken the kids to Long Island."

"I told him not to do that," I said, inclining my head in the direction of P.P. and the applauders. "I guess I didn't tell him hard enough, though."

George placed an affectionate hand on my shoulder. "In some ways you're not a bad kid," he said.

"Is it all right with you if I get drunk?" I asked.

"Under the circumstances, what else is there?" said George.

At that time George and Shirley had an apartment on upper Park Avenue, at Eighty-ninth. It was a large gloomy place, hideous beyond belief. The entire six-room apartment was cluttered—too many tables, too many chairs, too much bric-a-brac, too much everything. There were many bouquets of artificial sweet peas. There was an immense number of lamps, many of them with fringed shades, and the dark floors were covered with rag rugs and woven rugs and vaguely Oriental rugs and rugs of mysterious origin. The impression I got from the whole apartment was that Shirley had gone into a very bad furniture store and said, "I want several of everything expensive."

There were also candlesticks everywhere you turned. Shirley at that time collected candlesticks.

She also collected silver match boxes. Believe me, there wasn't a bare space in the whole six rooms of that dank apartment.

"You've got a nice place here," I said to George.

"So I hear," said George.

"Sure," I said. "It's very nice."

George handed me a very dark rye and water, and he poured a Coke for himself.

"That was quite a performance President Player put on," he said, naming the actor.

"I wish he hadn't," I said, drinking.

"But at the same time it had its pleasant aspects, didn't it?" said George.

"I suppose."

"Look, kid," said George. "Nobody ever gets too embarrassed when a thousand or so VIP's wearing their best bib and tucker get up and applaud him."

"But it was so phoney," I said.

"Baby doll, six months from now, looking back on this night, all you're going to remember is how that clapping sounded and that it was for you. You'll forget why they were applauding, or else you'll decide it was because you made such a good speech or something. Applause is very easy to get used to and as impossible to get over as cancer."

"I suppose," I said, working on my drink.

Believe me, I know," said George. From behind his nose he looked closely at me, and he smiled. George has a good smile.

"You're a good kid, and I'm going to give you some advice. The nice thing about advice is that it flatters the ego of the giver, and there is never the slightest chance that the givee will pay any attention to it. First, may I ask you a couple questions?"

I nodded.

"You going to fight this war or sell war bonds?"

"I'll do whatever they tell me, I suppose."

"There were a couple brown-nosing idiots from the bond division of the Treasury Department there tonight. They wanted to catch your act. You were okay. They're going to ask you to go on a tour, making speeches, selling bonds. Applause every night, and they'll put you up at the best hotels. Oh, it'll be quite a thing."

"I'd hate it," I said, finishing the dark drink.

"No," said George, taking my glass and walking to the bar, "you probably wouldn't. You might even like it. You see, one of the troubles with the race—the human race—as now constituted is that it goes around telling itself it's feeling all kinds of things it isn't feeling at all but thinks it ought to feel. Am I clear?"

"Crystal," I said.

"My advice to you would be to try and get overseas someplace where there's some honest-to-God fighting going on. If you don't, you'll spend the rest of your life regretting it. You'll regret missing the greatest common experience—maybe except for the depression—that your generation is going to have."

George handed me a second, even darker drink.

"I won't say combat will make a man out of you," said George. "That's ridiculous. What it might do is to enable you to find out some rather valuable things about yourself that you never even suspected before."

I nodded into the glass. "I can see that," I said.

"What are you going to do after the war, assuming, of course, you don't make the supreme sacrifice?"

I shrugged. "I don't know. It seems to me I've tried a little bit of everything already. I've taught. I've lectured. You know. After about six months, I always say, 'Okay, I know all about *this*. So what else is new?' Or does that make any sense?"

"Sure," said George. "A good deal."

"You see, I sort of enjoyed all of them until I learned the ropes, and then I got bored. I bore easy."

"And master of none, and you're twenty."

"Almost twenty-one."

"My God," said George, and he started to say something else but then didn't.

"You going to write another book?" he asked, after a time, "or do you figure you've already written a book?"

"Well, I don't know. I didn't think much of the book, you know, not at first. It was just those letters, but everybody seems to think I can write."

"Here's where I lose a client," said George. "You see, I don't think you can write."

I looked away from him, and, since what he said was true, I felt my gorge rising.

"Not yet anyway," said George. "You see, I think it takes a long time to learn to write, maybe as long as it takes to learn how to play the violin. Nobody ever says he knows he could play the violin if he just had the time.

"Kid, that thing you've wrought. That's not a book. At least not to me. To me a book is—well, forgive me—something almost sacred. *Prodigy as Private* is a lucky piece of merchandise. That's all, and because a lot of fools get even sillier during a war, you're being compared with Thucydides and Stevie Crane and Hank Beyle, none of which you are. Yet. Or maybe ever."

"I suppose not," I said, hoping I hadn't let myself get too red in the face.

"What you did is get a lucky ticket in the national lottery, and your getting it has nothing to do with talent or hard work or purity of heart. All it's got to do with is luck. Now if I figure it right, you'll have maybe as much as a hundred and fifty thousand bucks, after taxes, from this particular lottery ticket. Go fight your war; try not to get killed, and when you get back take that hundred and fifty thousand bucks and go someplace and decide what you want to do with the two-thirds of your life still left."

"Oh, that's very good advice," I said. "I mean it, *very* good."

"I was really talking to myself, as all givers of advice do," said George.

He looked closely at me. "You're miffed because of what I said about the book," he said. "Well, I'm glad I said it. You see, I spend most of my life telling middle-aged misfits that their every word or gesture is godlike. I thought maybe you were young enough—well, my error."

"Not at all. I'm very grateful," I said, lying, and thinking that George was, after all, nothing but an agent and that Proudly Presents had certainly been right about one thing. Proudly had said that George had no taste, and, I thought, what George had just said about The Book certainly proved that. I thought, George's opinion certainly couldn't compare with that of the lady who had written a most enthusiastic review for a literary-type magazine. I had met that lady, whose body ran largely to breast and who was wearing a snug lavender sweater when I met her at a cocktail party. She had said, "I just *loved* that book of yours. That book of yours is literature, and, believe me, if there is one thing I can spot it's literature."

Then she whinnied happily and pushed one of the purple-covered, melonlike things at me.

Oh, no, I thought, George Bansky the agent may know his business, but he does *not* know literature.

And yet. And yet—that familiar, mystifying ambivalence. I was grateful to George for his honesty; I knew that he had said what he had said because he liked me, and I knew that in the society of sycophants in which I had spent the previous two weeks there was very little sincerity, and no affection.

I thought, "It is terribly hard to fight against these double thoughts."

And so, grateful to George for his honesty, forgiving his bad judgment, and hating his guts for telling the truth, I said, "Could I have another drink, please?"

That was the first time in my life I had ever asked anybody for another drink. Not the last, though—by no means the last.

"Help yourself," said George.

I bumped into a table, knocked over two pairs of candlesticks, and a silver match box on the way to the liquor cabinet.

There was a crudely tinted photograph on a sideboard, showing Shirley with a pretty little girl of about four and a dark, brooding boy of six or seven.

"Those your children?" I asked George, making the drink as strong as I thought was permissible and polite.

"Nina and Jonathan," said George. He walked to the sideboard and picked up the picture.

"They're nice-looking kids," I said.

George looked at the picture and nodded. "When Hitler gets through with us, there won't be a lot of us left," he said. "And these two, I should be teaching them about their God and their history. But Shirley—oh, no—she wants me to change my name; she wants me to get my nose bobbed; she wishes to interfere with my syntax. 'There's nothing whatever to be ashamed of, being a Jew,' she keeps saying, 'but we don't have to be blatant about it.' 'Blatant, my dear Shirley,' I tell her. 'That is what we should be.'"

George carefully put the picture back down on the sideboard.

"Those kids will be as American as blueberry pie." (As I've said, he was completely right about that.) "Among the first pieces of legislation that will be passed after this war will be a law declaring individuality unconstitutional. If we win, that is."

There was a moment, and then he said, "My mother wanted me to be a rabbi. What am I? A flesh peddler. A panderer for persons of small consequence."

"I'm told you're the best agent in the business," I said, pitying George and being condescending.

"Hitler's the best in his line of work, too," he said, and he looked at his watch. "Drink up."

He put on the homburg he wore in those days.

"Forgive me for telling you my troubles," he said. "And you understand I'm not blaming Shirley. If it hadn't been Shirley, I'd have found somebody just like her to make me do what I claim I hate doing. Let's go."

At the station, I remember telling George that I was grateful for everything he'd done for me.

"Look, kid," he said, "in the flesh pots I work in, nobody ever does anybody any favors."

I said that nevertheless I was glad I was a client of his and always would be.

George said, "I'll remind you of that when you start claiming I corrupted you."

Then he winked at me and left.

That was seventeen years ago.

NOTES·DICTATED·ON·THE· SEVENTH·AND·EIGHTH·DAYS

(1) The size of emptiness

Three of the final hours have vanished since I said that last sentence. I'll never finish what I started out to say, but then did I ever finish what I started out to say?... Isn't it odd that I can face death as indifferently as life? Isn't it odd that no one in all the world will really care? Isn't it odd that not a tear will be shed? And no words will be spoken; no incantations will be said. There have been lies enough in my life; let me go to the first of the final fires in truthful silence.

I'll go on now. Another ninety seconds have disappeared. What is the shape of nothing? What is the size of emptiness?

What happened during the three lost hours was this.

When I finished the account of The Book and of my last night in New York with George, I put my head on the desk for a moment and, despite the green pills and the capsules and the coffee and the cigarettes, I slept for more than two hours.

Then Louella woke me. Russell Grierson had called. He and George are coming up tomorrow, just as I planned. When the papers are signed, I'll have finished my worldly duties, and at five in the afternoon I will take all the pills that I have managed to accumulate through lies on my part and greed on the part of a whore doctor who gave me a prescription for the pills. All I had to do to get the prescription was leave a hundred-dollar bill on the mantel. You can get one of these medical streetwalkers to do just about anything these days. They'll even swear on a stack of Bibles and hundred-dollar bills that cigarettes are good for you. Is there anything people won't do for money, do you suppose? At Pegasus we used to have a song, "He will do it every time, for a nickel or a dime." Do what? You name it; he'll do it. Who? Why, Everyman, of course. And speaking of cigarettes, I do want to pass on to posterity a nifty idea I thought up for one of the coffin-nail outfits. This particular one is always handing out coupons, and if you get enough coupons to get a cancer, they'll send you a lot of stuff you wouldn't want to send as gifts to a Polish wedding. Anyway, my idea was that these coffin-nail folks advertise that if you'd just collect four million coupons, they'd send you something that would really come in handy, an iron lung. The damn fools didn't even answer my letter.

Anyway, everything is falling into place, very neatly, very neatly indeed.

I've just finished my next-to-last lunch—canned soup, a slice of bread, and a glass of milk. I ate at the black table in the living room.

It's a beautiful afternoon. The Virginia creeper has completely turned now, spots of scarlet wherever you look. It won't be long until the first frost, and that's another of the many things I won't mind missing. I hate the fall. It has always made me think of age and of pain and death.

Charley doesn't agree. She likes the fall best. I remember her saying—not all at once, over a period of time—but I remember it all. Yes, all. It seems to me at the moment I can remember every word Charley ever said to me.... "Spring is sort of—oh, I don't know. A lick and a promise. It's beautiful, but then there's the whole summer coming up, and you plan all the things you're going to do. You're going to practice—at least three hours a day, and maybe, if all goes well, by fall you will be able to listen to yourself without wincing. True, you've been saying that to yourself for—quite a few years now, but then, who knows, this summer may be the one when a miracle happens. What's more *this* summer you are going to read all the books you promised yourself to read *last* summer. If God is good, you may even finish *Remembrance of*....

"What's more, you're going to learn how to cook and—then fall comes along, and it turns out all you are is a few months older and tireder—no better as a musician because you didn't practice enough—no wiser because you didn't read enough—no better as a cook because.... And you think, Oh, my God, I can't stand another winter—not this year ... I'll kill myself first—and then you look out—and it's so beautiful, so incredibly beautiful—that you feel you can and will be able to go through it all—because there is going to be another spring—and *next* summer...."

I remember the night I asked Charley to marry me. We'd been to hear *Rosenkavalier* at the City Center, and we were walking to my place, slowly, quite silently, saddened and delighted by the experience we had just had.

After we'd walked several blocks, I said what I had been trying to get up enough courage to say for a long time. "I don't suppose you'd consider marrying me."

"I've already considered it," said Charley.

"Deciding what?"

"Deciding that I'd say no."

"Any special reason? I mean besides the fact that you detest me?"

"Several special reasons. Every reason there is. Reason number one, I have been married, and I made a botch of it, and it wasn't only because I was a drunkard."

"He drove you to drink," I said.

"Nobody ever drove a drunk to drink, not as long as he knows where the bottle is."

"*Several* special reasons."

"Reason number two," said Charley. "I think it's impossible for any two people to live together day in and day out, night out and night in. I believe it's a crime against nature."

I started to say something, but Charley said, "Be quiet, Bland, Charley Barr is speaking. Reason number three, I think it *might* be possible for two people to get married and stay married if they were physically and mentally healthy, twenty years old, and had nothing to do but work at being married. Not to mention having a family of twelve."

"You left out love," I said, and Charley said nothing.

"I'm lonely, Charley, and so are you," I said. "Besides, it's my last chance to go steady, and besides—"

I waited once more for Charley to say something, but she didn't. After a moment, I said, "When I was in the Army, I said to myself,

'I'm not going to blow this one. This is the one I follow through on'—and I did. I did, Charley—my love."

For a moment I thought Charley was going to cry, but she didn't do that either.

What happened was that we kissed. We were on Fifty-ninth, near Madison Avenue. People stared, and some even stopped to look at us. Not only because that area is mostly a snarling area, people and traffic. But a going-on-middle-aged man with a beard kissing a small, graceful woman in a red hat. How perverse!

"I do love you, you know," said Charley.

"I love you," I said, and I brought her hand to my mouth, and I said, "Oh, my, I do love you. I do. I really do, and I'm very glad you're fond of me."

"I love you," said Charley.

"I'll settle for your putting up with me," I said.

"I love you," said Charley. "Don't you believe that?"

"I'll try," I said, "but after all these years of the other, it's hard to get used to."

"I love you," she said. "Believe that."

"I believe that," I said, kissing her.

I never did believe it, though, not once.

That's how it began. You know how it ended.

I must get on, first with what I haven't said yet. Then I've got to clear up a few of the many loose ends of my loosely lived life.

First, Louella. I haven't mentioned the imaginary Nepal trip to her. Too much trouble; Louella makes too much of a ceremony of packing for me to want to go through with it for a trip I have no intention of taking.

On the other hand, I don't want Louella to be the first to find my body. So—

A little while ago when Louella came in, I said, "Louella, if you had a vacation, what would you do with it?"

"I don't know, Mr. Bland," said Louella, treating the apparently idle question idly. "Go down to New York, I suppose. My cousin and his wife are always after me. They go to this place on the Jersey shore week ends."

"Well," I said, "why don't you take the eight-thirty-two train to New York in the morning, and don't come back here until next week?"

"I couldn't do that, Mr. Bland. Who'd take care of you all that time, and Mr. Banning and Mr. Grierson coming up here tomorrow afternoon and all."

"I'm going back to New York with them, and they aren't going to be here for a meal or anything. All they'll want is some booze. Now you do as I tell you and no back talk."

There was more conversation, but Louella finally agreed, and now she has gone. I kissed her on the forehead and wished I could say some final word of wisdom or farewell but I knew if I tried a sob would escape my throat.

So I just said, "Louella, have a good time."

She said, "You, too, Mr. Bland. I'll see you Monday."

I held her hand for an extra second, and she looked at me, oddly, I thought, as if she sensed some finality in my words.

She said, "You're too nice to me, Mr. Bland, and always have been. I told my sister, I said, 'I wouldn't want to work for nobody else except Mr. Bland, shouting and all. That man's spoiled me rotten.'"

Then she got into Carrie McCarthy's taxi, and Carrie drove her away for the last time.

I won't see Carrie again either, nor hear that grating, raucous voice, ticking off all the village scandal, real and imagined. Oh, I suppose Carrie isn't so bad. Carrie was married to the wrong man, a tall, thin man with the mean mouth of the instinctively cruel. I'm told that he never talked to Carrie, although he sometimes beat her. Carrie had to talk to somebody; so she started gossiping.

It says here.

My God, it's a good thing I'm leaving tomorrow night. If I stuck around much longer, I'd become *lovable*. I've known several *lovable* old men. They spend their lives cheating, lying, stealing, knifing, destroying, and then they retire and get *lovable*. They get scared that there might be a God, after all.

Let us continue to face facts here; let us not get carried away.

Fact Number One. The reason Louella is so fond of me is that I have in fact spoiled her rotten. Since Charley left, Louella hasn't done a day's work. Louella has spent a large part of her time sitting on her can, reading my collection of mysteries. She gets through one a day, and Louella is a lip-reader, a slow lip-reader.

There's dust an inch thick in Charley's bedroom, and lately Louella has been too tuckered out to turn on the dish washer. The other day I came into the living room and Louella was running the vacuum cleaner, *sitting down.*

She was a little embarrassed. "I've just been plumb worn out lately, Mr. Bland," she said. "I don't know what's got into me."

I know what's got into her, a disease even more common than heart ailment, laziness. I kept my diagnosis to myself, though.

Fact Number Two. However she got that way, Carrie McCarthy is a small-minded, malicious defamer of character, and she has done and will continue to do a great deal of harm in and around Sloane's Station.

Thank God, I am going before I start saying things like, "He's all right, once you get to know him."

With fewer exceptions than can be counted on the fingers of my right hand, the more I got to know people the more the dark, devious sides of their natures showed up.

Ab has just come back from his late-afternoon inspection of the woods and fields. All's well, and he has had his petting and is sleeping the sleep of the just.

I've got to do something about that dog. I can't send him to the vet's. He hates that place with the same terrified passion I have for the place in New Haven where I spent eleven months behind bars. I don't care if they were the very best bars. I was miserable.

It's five in the afternoon....

"Five in the afternoon, and death laid eggs in the wound."

Just twenty-four hours now. Among the categories I won't have time to go into is *People I Wouldn't Have Missed Knowing.*

For Ab's sake and maybe also my own I just called one of that miniscule group, Sid Levinson.

I've seen Sid and Adah only once since Charley left. At their house. It was quite painful. Adah, Sid's wife and easily the nicest woman in this country—a position for which the competition is admittedly small—couldn't help showing that, when the time came, she had to join the sorority of women and be on Charley's side. The way she did it was by not mentioning Charley all evening and—I thought—by being cloyingly nice to me. Anyway, whatever the reason, the evening was a bust. They've asked me to come back twice since, but I've made excuses.

It doesn't seem possible. It's been fourteen years since Sid walked into that ward in the hospital in Paris, glanced down his great nose at me, and said, "You'll always limp, but we won't have to replace the leg."

Sid works very hard in New Kensington, about twenty miles north of here. He has cajoled, goaded, and kicked the town, and, for that matter, this whole county and its people forward, and some deprecate and some appreciate and some love and some despise him.

"They asked me to join the Rotary Club; I don't think they wanted to. I'm too goddamn loud, and pushy, but you have to say this for me. I don't insist on being liked. Anyway, I joined the goddamn Rotary Club, and now they want me to be president. I must do something outrageous immediately."

Just now, I told Sid about the trip to Nepal I'm supposed to be taking and asked him if he'd take care of Ab while I'm gone. He agreed.

"How long you going to be gone?"

"Not long," I said.

"How've you been?"

"Busy."

"Well, I hope so," said Sid. "You've sure as hell neglected your friends. These friends anyway."

He paused a moment, then said, "Adah got a call from Charley this morning. She's back in New York."

"Well, good," I said.

"Like to talk to Adah?"

"No, thanks. I'm really busy, Sid."

"How about a small game of chess this evening? I happen to have one of my rare opportunities to live it up. The kids are at their grandmother's, and Adah in a moment of weakness invited those worn-out strumpets she calls the girls for an evening of bridge. Spring me."

"Sorry, Sid. I'm up to my navel—"

"Okay, okay, I'm pushy, but I'm not that pushy. I'll pick up your damn dog around noon, day after tomorrow."

"Thanks, I'm very grateful," I said, and then I said, "How is Charley?"

"Good and lonely," said Sid, "and Adah says hello."

"Love to Adah," I said, and I made a sound in my throat which meant good-bye, and hung up.

Good and lonely. Well, Charley was good and lonely before she met up with me, and she will be good and lonely after tomorrow. More so or less so? The hell of it is I don't think my departure from the planet will matter one way or the other to Charley.

"I don't know just how you'll do it, but you'll go out with a flourish all right, banging and whimpering both at the same time, and I'm glad I'm going to miss it."

Twenty-three hours more, and now I've added fuel to the flame. I've swallowed a capsule.

I'll finish up The War now. I'll go back to July 1942.

I've described how George saw me off at Penn Station. Through some skulduggery—I forget on whose part—I had a lower berth to myself. Such are the rewards of fame. On my first trip to Jackson I had been assigned to share a lower berth with an obese boy with bad teeth and an advanced case of either athlete's foot or Chinese rot. I sat up both nights.

On that second and last trip to Jackson, I was alone, really alone, for the first time in two weeks, and I had not yet discovered any of the fifty-seven varieties of pills to knock me out. So I *thought*. I thought about The Book and what effect its success had had on me and what all the adulation and applause had meant. I decided that like liquor, applause and adulation were things I could take or leave alone. I was wrong about liquor, too.

I'll say this. The most immediate effect the success of The Book had on me was to give me a psychopathic fear of exposing myself on paper. For several years I broke out in a cold sweat every time I even touched a piece of paper, including newsprint. I haven't quite recovered yet.

The money was nice, though. Money always is. Cashmere jackets, for instance, one of the first signs of conspicuous consumption. I not only bought one the second I got back to New York from the Army; I bought six. I kept telling myself how after all that rough OD I needed something soft against my tender skin.

I also had a dozen pairs of tailormade shoes sewn together for my sensitive feet. I had walked halfway across Europe in a pair of combat boots. Not a blister. The first day I put on the first pair of hand-sewn shoes I limped from the place on East Eighty-first Street to George's office on West Forty-eighth. I got a blister on each heel.

I have a feeling that that fact is loaded with symbolism.

However, I started out to discuss what the success of The Book meant to me—aside from the money—and I believe I ought to make it clear that I am not a success-knocker. I've always felt it was better to be a success than a failure, but you know me. I'm living in the wrong century. These days if you write a play or a book about how you just can't stand your million-dollar bank account and how you wish you was back in that nice, dirty old slum you was brought up in, why, you have likely got a hit on your hands. I know. I produced one.

Let me add here that one of the reasons I particularly dislike it Out There is that all of those people sit around their corrupting swimming pools of an afternoon sounding off about how they miss their slums. I've noticed none of them ever goes back, though; no, what they do is take a cool, corrupting dip in the pool.

And of an evening Out There, should you have the guts to defy the unwritten law against walking in Beverly Hills, you will come across at least six former truck drivers in cashmere jackets getting into or out of white convertibles.

You know what these truck drivers say if you make the mistake of allowing them to speak to you? They say, "My God, the income-tax problems I've had this year. I ain't been happy since I was driving that ol' truck for, etc."

I have several times told these individuals that I have not been happy since they stopped driving trucks either, but they always think I'm joking.

I tell you. In my opinion, Southern California and Mississippi should be asked to leave. Together.[13]

But back now to Fort Jackson, where my days were numbered.

Nothing was the same anyway. I had changed, and so had everyone's attitude toward me. I was no longer ASN 33170247; I was CORPORAL JOSHUA BLAND.

For instance, I was met at the station by a major in Public Relations, and I was driven back to the post in a staff car. There was a bunch of kids outside the gate; there'd been a story in the Columbia paper about my return, and these kids wanted my autograph. What's more, when I got back to my company area, the first sergeant and the captain wanted me to autograph copies of The Book.

---

13   Some of those not familiar with the ways and byways Out There and with my own reputation for painful, devil-take-the-hindmost accuracy may feel that in one or two small instances in this area I have exaggerated.

People who don't know often say to me, "Come off it, Bland. People are people everywhere. What about the *little* people Out There?"

Little people?

Let me give you an example.

Because of the corrupt judicial system I have mentioned, I cannot drive a car and must submit myself to the mercy of taxi drivers. Out There everybody behind the wheel of a taxi is either a potential actor or a potential writer, and many are both.

I am often taken for a person in Show Biz; God knows why, but, very often, before the talentless drivers have shifted into second they are telling me about the play they are writing or, even worse, they are *acting* at me.

I try to mislead them; if they ask what line of work I am in, I say, "I'm in wallpaper," which often buys me as much as a thirty-second silence.

But the only really successful technique I found to silence those fellows was to have a little card printed that I handed to them as I got in the cab.

The card said, "I am deaf and dumb and cannot read lips. My destination is—."

Destination written in.

The card worked well most of the time. But not always. Once an individual who couldn't even sing as well as Mario Lanza bellowed at me all the way from the Beverly Hills Hotel to Television City.

Being deaf as well as dumb, there wasn't a goddamn thing I could do or say.

But don't talk to me about the little people Out There.

Not unexpectedly, the men in my company no longer considered me one of them. They treated me with an uncomfortable combination of deference and contempt. The contempt I understood. For instance, when the company went on a three-day hike, I was excused. Instead, I made a series of recordings for the Armed Forces Network. I read passages from The Book.

Then, too, when there was any visiting brass on the post, I was served forth, celebrity with coffee. There is no group that makes more of a damn fool of itself over anybody whose name has been in the paper than Army brass. I don't know why this is, but I expect it has something to do with the drab lives those fellows lead between wars. Plus the fact that Army officers as a group are just about the dullest bunch you're likely to encounter anywhere.

I remember one night we had a four-star general for supper, along with the filet; at the enlisted men's mess it was creamed chipped beef on toast, topped with mashed potatoes, peaches, corn bread and butter, and carrots and peas.

The visiting general allowed as how it was most unusual to see a corporal having dinner at the senior officers' mess.

"Bland here isn't really a corporal," said a chicken colonel. True enough; I was so embarrassed I could hardly finish my second filet.

In the middle of August (1942), the expected happened. I was handed God knows how many copies of a mimeographed order from the Secretary of War, directing me to appear at the Pentagon in the office of General So-and-So. To proceed by first available military aircraft.

The night before I left Jackson, I did get a bunch of the Tennesseans from my outfit to agree to do the rounds of the bars in Columbia; we must have heard the Tommy Dorsey arrangement of "I'll Never Smile Again" a dozen times or more on as many jukeboxes.

I wasn't allowed to buy any of them a drink the whole time, and I didn't know why.

Not long before V-J Day, I saw one of those men at a sidewalk café in Paris. He had been a buck sergeant when I knew him at Jackson. Now, more than three years later, he had simply added a stripe to his sleeve. I remember that he was tall, sparely built, and that he spoke in the nasal accents of the hill people. His hair had been bleached blond by the sun, and his wind-roughened face displayed two great fans of wrinkles when he smiled, which was often. That day in Paris we had quite a few drinks together, and we talked about what had happened in the company I'd temporarily been a member of. It had landed in Normandy shortly after D-Day, and it had missed very few major battles after that. The sergeant was one of two or three originals still left. Finally, with the courage of cognac, I asked him why on that last night I was at Jackson he and the others wouldn't let me buy them a drink.

"Well, I'll tell you, Lieutenant, sir," he said. "It was something you said. When we stopped in that first bar, you said, 'All the drinks are on me tonight, fellows.'"

I nodded, and I said, "And—"

"Well," said the sergeant. "The next thing you said was, 'Don't worry. I can afford it. I'm rich.'"

"I see what you mean," I said.

Twenty-four hours after leaving Jackson, I reported at the office of General So-and-So in the Pentagon.

The general was one of those rough, basically decent, often dangerous men who are a fairly standard product of the Trade School on the Hudson. During wartime, when they can order people around and no questions asked, they look like pillars of steel. In peacetime, when questions are possible, they turn out to be soft, quivering mountains of uncertainty.

Don't misunderstand me; the good ones they turn out at West Point are very good men indeed. I'll tell you about one in a minute.

But the ordinary West Point graduate—well, sir, if Clemenceau was right, and he was, about war being too important to leave to the generals, what about the peace? No, sir. Under the Bland Plan, there would be plenty of civil liberties for almost everybody—except professional military men. They wouldn't be allowed to do much of anything except drill and do calisthenics. And no talking. Except to each other.

As I've indicated, General So-and-So was depressingly typical. He was sparsely educated, narrow-minded, prejudiced against all foreigners and all minorities, suspicious of most civilians, and mildly paranoid. I expect if his paranoia had been a little more advanced, somebody would have written a book about him, insisting that we need fellows like him to watch out for the welfare of our grandmothers.

In August 1942 when I reported to So-and-So's office he was not in yet. There was a captain behind the desk, a husky, ruddy-faced man who looked like a great many other people and like nobody.

I came to a very sharp attention. I have been told that my attention was a sight to behold. There had been men at Jackson who thought I ought to charge admission. All I know is I put all of me into it.

My salute was also distinctive.

"Corporal Joshua Bland reporting as—" I said.

The captain brushed a cowlick off his farmer's forehead.

"Oh, for God's sake, relax," he said.

He stood, revealing a small, proudly worn potbelly, and he extended a rough, reddened hand.

"I'm Russ Grierson," he said. "I'm from Boone, Iowa. You're from New Athens. Glad to meet a fellow corn-husker. Welcome aboard."

He indicated a straight-back chair. "Take a load off your feet, kiddo," he said. "I got to buzz the chief. I wake him up every morning at eight. He had a rough night last night."

He placed the call and in that flat, rural voice he said, "Hi there, chiefie boy. This is Russ-boy. Wake up and hear the birdies sing, huh?"

As I listened to the captain talk to the four-star general whose aide he was, I thought of that other corn-husker, Hughie Larrabee; I knew what Hughie would have said, "Is that guy kidding?"

I've known Russ for many years now, and I know he's not kidding, but I have yet to make up my mind whether Russ just happened or whether he has modeled himself after one of the less successful creations of, say, Sinclair Lewis.

Russ's rube accent has remained uncorrupted, and he tells any new acquaintance within half an hour, "I'm not one of your hoity-toity Ivy-League types. I went to a cow college, Iowa State, and my motto is, 'Root hog or die.'"

Having delivered himself of that sentiment, Russ always bares his yellowed teeth. He has made a joke.

"If the truth were known, about half to three-quarters of those Ivy-League fellows are faggots anyhow," Russ will often add, frequently to a graduate of one of the Ivy-League colleges or to a homosexual.

Through the years a great many bright boys from Ivy-League schools have listened to Russ's tasteless remarks and have looked at his Iowa-State-College face and at the disarming, tawny smile, and have to their peril ignored him.

The Ivy-League boys have gone ahead and elbowed and kneed their way ahead of other Ivy-League boys. They have stepped all over each other and got in each other's way and frequently eliminated each other.

All Russ has ever seemed to do is watch and wait and smile.

People with complex minds often find it difficult to understand men like Russ, who has a simple mind but who is by no means simple-minded. People Russ has passed along the way have married the wrong woman, have taken the wrong mistress, fallen into the wrong bed, given way to anger or petulance or sloth or fatigue. They have scratched or knifed the wrong back, have surrendered to liquor or fat or gardening, have taken time out to play in string quartets or read great books or popular books or bad books, have gone to concerts or to the theater or have paused to enjoy their children. Not Russ, not ever.

Russ's simple mind selected his simple goal early, and he has never changed his mind or his goal, and has never wavered from that goal.

It is not true that Russ's barber in the RCA building goes to a lot of trouble to retain Russ's cowlick. As Russ would be the first to tell you, his thick brown hair is just naturally stubborn.

And it is not true that Russ uses a special roughening lotion on his large hands. Russ has his father's hands; Russ's father farmed a hundred and sixty acres of Iowa land near Boone until he dropped dead of a heart attack at seventy-six.

Some of Russ's many enemies say that his suits come from a theatrical costumer. Don't you believe it. Russ buys his double-breasted suits at the J. C. Penney store in Ames, Iowa, and he wears them because he likes them. Russ makes an annual trip to Ames.

Fortunately, Russ married well. Grace is a perfect wife for him, and for all I know maybe their marriage was made in Heaven. Grace's father was the Lutheran minister in Lincoln, Iowa. So she was born with an automatic *in* Up There.

She and Russ met when they were both in college at Ames. She was a Home Economics major, though as a survivor of many of her meals, I refuse to believe she ever studied cooking.

Since those long-ago days at Iowa State, Grace has physically spread out in all directions. Elizabeth Arden cannot do much about Grace's figure. Grace goes to *Last Chance* or whatever it's called at least four times a year; she always goes hoping for a miracle, but it has not yet happened.

From all the evidence at hand, I doubt very much that this is the age of miracles.

Except for her shape, though, Grace has not changed at all since leaving Ames.

Diplomats and statesmen and wits and writers of good books and good plays and actors and artists of talent and renown have sat at Grace's dinner table and in Grace's living room, and these people have frequently said interesting and challenging and amusing things to Grace. I have heard them. I myself have said interesting things to Grace, but Grace was always waiting for an opening, and for a woman of her size and age, she is remarkably adept at leaping into a very small one.

Before you have drawn a breath, Grace is telling you about her two unremarkable daughters, one of whom has a left eye that seems to be looking at you but is actually staring at the fellow across the table. The other daughter suffers from a galloping case of baldness.

Or Grace is discussing her health, consistently and uninterestingly bad, or she is letting you in on what she said to Chancellor Adenauer the last time she and Russ were in Bonn.

"He had a sore throat, and I told him that the only thing in the world to do with a sore throat is to rub it with goose grease and drink a lot of water. I said, 'Nature's way is God's way, and no two ways about it.'"

Grace has been very nearly everywhere, but she has seen and heard nothing. Grace might as well never have left the Lutheran manse in Lincoln, Iowa.

It seems redundant to add that in 1958 Russell, Grace, Penelope, the daughter with the eye problem, and Prudence, the one with the hair problem, were chosen as "The American Family of the Year." An expertly and imaginatively retouched group photograph of them was published just about everywhere in this country, and I understand contraband copies were even smuggled behind the Iron Curtain as an example of "that family best exemplifying the American ideal and the American dream."

The four Griersons, of course, had a very enjoyable evening at the White House.

Well. I have gone on, and you have probably already heard more than enough about the Griersons. I just couldn't resist adding my own beady insight into so famous a foursome.

You want to know what Russ will say when the papers have been signed tomorrow afternoon?

I am sure of almost nothing any more, but about this I am positive.

When the liquidation is legal and complete, Russell will extend his farmer's hand, and he will say, "Josh, boy, there's nothing personal in all this, you know, and no hard feelings. Am I right?"

I haven't decided what I'll do or say when those particular bromides are uttered tomorrow, but I'm pretty sure I'll be thinking of a suicide club I dreamed up at a much earlier time when life was crowding in on me. The club never came to much, but it had a motto that I liked, "Don't go alone. Take somebody with you."

Let me, nonetheless, be clear on one point. When I very much needed his help, Russ Grierson—surely the most "other-directed" man of this other-directed time and place—risked what was most important to him to do me a favor.

I'm going back to the morning in August 1942 when I reported to the Pentagon. General So-and-So arrived around nine, and he looked like a man who had had a rough night.

Russ introduced me to the general, and the general gave me the smile they teach you at the Point. He followed that with the Military Handshake.

"You're a very, very lucky young man," he said. "We're going to send you on a bond tour. You'll get the A treatment, my boy, the best hotels, the best filets for dinner, and the best girls—well, for the evening."

He gave me a military wink. "How does that strike you?"

I wasn't up on how a corporal addresses a four-star general; so I improvised. As I recall, I said, "Sir, do you really want to know?"

If there was anything the general wanted, it was not to know, but he said, "Of course, of course, corporal. Speak up."

Notice how all of a sudden I wasn't "boy" any more? I was *corporal*. Well, you ask a silly question....

I said, "Sir, begging your pardon, I'd rather not go on any bond tour. I—I'd like to be in a combat unit, sir. You see, well, I've given the whole thing a lot of thought, and it seems to me if you're a soldier—"

The general cleared his throat in a military manner. He said, "Captain Grierson, take this soldier over to Treasury—"

"Thank you very much, sir," I said, giving him a salute.

The general returned the salute, and with it he gave me a smile that he might have used when sending a condemned soldier off to Leavenworth.

Oh. Just before Russell and I reached the door, the general said, "Did you speak to this soldier about those books?"

"I shall, sir," said Russell.

General So-and-So must have taken top honors in the course in Military Free-Loading at the Point. You know what he wanted? He wanted six copies of *Prodigy as Private. Autographed.* (That is not at all unusual. People who've got too much sense to ask for a free legal opinion from a lawyer and who wouldn't dream of being taste-less enough to ask a doctor for a gratis diagnosis of what ails them think nothing at all of asking an author for a free book. Usually they say something like, "And you can write your name in it, too, if you want to....")

Anyway, I *bought* six copies of *P. as P.*, autographed them, and sent them off to General So-and-So. What thanks did I get? None.

I was accompanied on the bond tour by another product of the Point. Let's call him Captain Anonymous. Members of the Anonymous family have been getting four years of free room and board at West Point for several generations now. Judging by the captain, that is all they have been getting.

At first glance, Anonymous looked like a model for a recruiting poster, but a second glance at those wide-set blue eyes showed you that there was nothing but empty space behind them. I have watched robins in the pine trees over there who have twice the brain power Anonymous has.

Captain Anonymous had been assigned to me after botching a number of assignments, the last of them being at the WAC training headquarters at Fort Des Moines, Iowa. Anonymous was supply officer, a job which is generally about as taxing on the intellect as egg-candling.

And, indeed, all might have gone well if the WAC contingent at Fort Des Moines hadn't run out of an item not included in most Army supply rooms, brassières.

The commanding officer took up the brassière matter with Anonymous, and he promised to work on it immediately.

But days passed, weeks, then months. Still no brassières. By that time the matter was serious. It looked as if the lack of brassières for WAC's at Fort Des Moines might be as costly to the war effort as the strike at North American Aviation. A colonel from the Inspector General's office flew all the way out from Wonderland, D.C., to look into the matter.

Halfway through his inspection of the Fort Des Moines warehouse, the I.G. colonel pointed to an entire section of the building which was overflowing with boxes, arranged in order, *Cup A*, *Cup B*, *Cup C*, *Cup D*, *Dixie Cup*.

The I.G. colonel turned to Anonymous. "Captain, what do you call those?" he asked.

At least that is the way it was told to me on a starry night in St. Louis not many months later, and I feel that if it didn't happen, it should have.

I was the next assignment for Anonymous after Fort Des Moines.

It was impossible to dislike the captain. There was nothing to dislike. It is also impossible to believe that Gelett Burgess could have written *The Man Who Wasn't There* without knowing Anonymous.

I took care of everything, transportation, reservations, time schedules. Everything.

Anonymous kept himself occupied with the Zane Grey novels he carried in his B-4 bag. He wouldn't let anybody handle that bag. "I don't like to tempt people," he'd say.

I guess Anonymous must have been the biggest fan Zane Grey ever had; he was the kind of admirer all authors must dream about. For instance, Anonymous had read *Riders of the Purple Sage* forty-four times.

"And you find something new in it every time," I remember saying.

Anonymous's face broke into the sweet, gullible smile of a four-year-old just complimented on the sand castle he'd built.

"How'd you know a thing like that?" he asked. "You must of read it yourself."

I remember once—in Seattle, I think—when Anonymous had bungled some simple assignment I'd trusted him with, I said testily, "Captain, what are you going to be when you grow up?"

Anonymous contorted his blank, beautiful face into thought. Finally, brightening, he said, "Well, I know what I'd like to be. I'd like to be a cowboy."

Then a terrible thing happened; an idea crossed his face. "But I am grown up," said Anonymous.

You can take it from there.... From time to time in my life in describing individuals like Anonymous I have been accused of exaggerating or magnifying or pasquinading. I plead not guilty. I haven't done it. Nature exaggerates, magnifies, and pasquinades. All I do is sit there. What I say is you can't improve on nature. Not when you're dealing with the Captain Anonymouses of the world. Or should I say the General Anonymouses? You see, Anonymous has been promoted.

I should say here that if Anonymous had had the requisite number of marbles he would have noticed that on the bond tour in addition to the best hotels, the best filets, and best girls, his charge was also getting an increasing amount of the best booze. I was hitting the bottle, any bottle, with increasing regularity. I hated every second of that bond tour, and I convinced myself—a pushover—that I needed to be ossified to go through with it.

Several times I swayed perceptibly when I stood up and said, "Ladies and gentlemen, as a soldier, I want to tell you how valuable to the war effort it is for each and every one of you...."

I honestly don't think Anonymous noticed. "Just listen to this," he'd say, reading me a Grey paragraph in which the most memorable line would be something like, "Me, Injun Joe. Me no like white man."

"What do you think of that?" Anonymous would ask, breathlessly eager.

"They just don't write like that any more," I'd say.

Well, the inevitable happened. It happened, quite appropriately, Out There. That fact may account for some of my antagonism toward that flowering desert.

In the morning of what we'll call the final day, I got the letter I mentioned some time ago, the one from my Aunt Mettabel, enclosing the clipping from the *New Athens Times-Dispatch* which announced that Hughie Larrabee had been killed in the Solomons.

When I had finished crying, I started drinking.

The bond-selling banquet that evening was at the same place I was staying, the Beverly Hills Hotel. The evening was one when those people went all out. The King was there, the First Lady, several ladies-in-waiting, and people like Louis B. Mayer, Trigger, Babies Leroy and Peggy, Sonny Tufts, several Cecil B. DeMilles, Pin-Up Girls of world renown, and Boy Actors who because of hernias, broken eardrums, homosexuality, flat feet, and long-term contracts had been found 4-F.

There were many speeches, and there were many acts. And by the time my turn came, a cool five million dollars had been noisily invested.

Now during the course of the evening I had been adding fuel to the day's fire by getting into the wine when it was white and when it was red. Not only that, I had snifted considerable brandy.

The master of ceremonies, who is sort of an actor and sort of a singer and profitably untalented in both areas, sensed that I was under the weather, but Anonymous said I never touched a drop.

So I was introduced.

For weeks, in hotel rooms and restaurants and on trains and airplanes, I had been mentally outlining a rather brilliant speech about war bonds and bond buyers and all of the sanctimony that went with them.

Alas, it was not to be. I rose, undulating, and then I became ill, as ill as I had been at the time of the Harvey Jordan O'Conner fiasco, and in the same way. I was ill in front of and on some of several billion dollars' worth of talent.

Anonymous and a bellboy got me to bed.

The next morning, feeling that now-familiar combination of remorse, self-hatred, and despair, I was on my way back to Wonderland, D.C., by plane. Anonymous sat beside me, rereading *Riders of the Purple Sage*.

He was silent the whole way; he was like a sullen small boy wrongfully convicted of rifling his mother's purse.

Over Cleveland, I said, "Captain, read me that part again where the Indian—"

Anonymous interrupted me, saying something which, even after all these years, I remember. He said, "Corporal, under the circumstances I don't think you're fit to listen to Zane Grey."

When we got to the Pentagon, Anonymous was the first to be called into General So-and-So's office. He was there for at least half an hour.

I sat in the outer office with Russ Grierson.

"What do you think they'll do to him?" I asked.

Russ said, "Well, they might strip him of all rank and ship him off as a motor-pool attendant in the Persian Gulf Command, but I doubt that they will. The West Point Benevolent and Protective Association will take care of Junior."

A few minutes later, Anonymous, white and drawn, emerged from So-and-So's office.

He started to the door, not looking at me, and I said, "Captain, will I be seeing you again?"

He said—and I was proud of him—"I'll do my level best to prevent it."

I worried about Anonymous, but I needn't have. Anonymous was given a Legion of Merit, with cluster, and transferred to the Army's haven for the hopelessly incompetent, the Public Information office. Since then he has, not unexpectedly, gone onward and upward. He was for several years in charge of our civil-defense program, but now he has been transferred. Anonymous now has three stars, and he is in charge of our hydrogen-bomb policy.

General So-and-So was sitting at this desk, poker-faced and poker-assed, when I came to attention in front of it.

I saluted and said what you say. I'll bet ten minutes passed before So-and-So returned my salute. Then, without putting me at ease (impossible anyway), he said, "You realize that you have disgraced the uniform of the United States Army."

I nodded.

"You realize that by being drunk on duty you have committed a court-martial offense?"

I nodded again.

"I didn't quite hear you," said So-and-So.

I said, "Yes, sir, I realize that by being drunk on duty so to speak I have, sir, committed a court-martial offense, and I realize, sir, that I have disgraced the uniform of the United States Army."

"I don't know what to do with you," said the general. "What would you suggest?"

"Well, sir, there's always the firing squad," I said. I had had a couple snorts before reporting to the Pentagon.

General So-and-So frowned.

Captain Russell Grierson, who was standing beside me, swallowed twice, and then in an odd, withdrawn voice, he said, "Sir, you recall that the corporal wanted to be assigned to a combat unit before he even went on this bond tour."

The general must have been one of the outstanding Military Pausers ever to graduate from the Point. He paused lengthily, his face turning mauve. Then he looked at his aide.

"Captain, I don't recall asking for that particular information."

Russell said, "No, sir, you didn't, but I do think that fact should be taken into account."

The general paused again, and then, his voice tight with anger, he said, "Captain, are you asking for a transfer to the South Pacific?"

"No, sir, but, as you know, sir, these new paratroop outfits they're setting up are looking for volunteers."

The general thought that over. Finally, he turned toward me and said, "I was thinking of suggesting that you volunteer for a paratroop assignment."

"Yes, sir," I said.

"Captain," said the general. "See that orders are cut transferring this man to the —th Regiment at Camp Tuckahoe, Georgia."

"Yes, sir," said Russell.

The general turned to me, a smile of accomplishment on his face.

"Well, well, well," he said. "How do you think you're going to like jumping out of airplanes?"

"I'll do my best, sir," I said, "despite my vertigo."

"Vertigo? What's that?" asked So-and-So.

I told him, and he smiled. "I'm very glad to hear it," he said. "I hope it's painful."

"Yes, sir," I said.

The next morning I was on my way to Camp Tuckahoe, Georgia.

Now what Russ Grierson did in So-and-So's office for me may not seem like much but, believe me, it took a lot of courage, and I'll always be grateful. He was risking a lot. The West Point Benevolent and Protective Association doesn't look after R.O.T.C. graduates of

Iowa State College. Russ could easily have wound up the war as a second lieutenant in the South Pacific, and his rank meant a great deal to Russell, and so did his being in the Pentagon.

Why did he speak up for me, then? I was at that time a most casual acquaintance.

I once asked Russ that question, and he said, "We're both from Iowa, aren't we?"

Of all the lunatic loyalties.

I have never had any such feeling. For instance, once for reasons of no importance I was in Pasadena on *Iowa Day*. I left town immediately.

Before I get to Camp Tuckahoe, let me say that the man who became my partner and is about to become my successor has now extended his loyalty beyond the borders of Iowa. His loyalty now includes every one of These Great United States of Ours. Now, as Russ is the first to admit, "All I have to do is pick up the phone, and there's J. Edgar."

It's true, too, and that is one of the reasons that during the Recent Unpleasantness, Russ was so very valuable to a radio and television network I wouldn't name if you tore out my fingernails.

As a former commander of the Advertising Post of the American Legion, Russ is both knowing and well-known in the upper strata of the higher patriotism clique. Thus, it was only good business for Jonathan Haverford, president of Blank Network and about the most liberal noisemaker you would ever want to meet, to make Russ vice president in charge of unpleasantness. Russ's job was twofold: (a) to keep undesirables from entering your home and my home via the television screen and (b) to keep the knowledge of what he was doing from Haverford. You see, Haverford is not only a member of the national committee of the American Civil Liberties Union and on the board of directors of Americans for Democratic Small Talk, he is just about the biggest free-speech maker north of Mississippi and east of the Mississippi.

In more ways than one, Haverford reminds me of my mother; it is very difficult to have a gathering of any size anywhere without having Haverford show up, prepared to speak freely and for nothing.

Haverford is, as you might guess, a self-made man. He started at the bottom in Blank, as a second vice president, and he would not have made it to the top except through hard work, native ability, and the death of his father, founder of Blank and chairman of its board of directors.

Haverford thinks of himself as a real radical ("I sometimes wonder if I'm not just a little too radical for my own good"); he was very, very, very anti-black list in the big black list days in the industry. If he said it once, he said it a hundred times, "I am against all lists, black, red, white, yellow, gray, and pink. That is not our way. That is not the democratic method of doing business."

It is speeches like that which have Made This Country Great.

But you can see what a spot Russ was in. Russ operated the biggest, blackest, longest, most inclusive list in the industry, and he did it without letting the network's left hand know what the right hand was up to.

You see, left-handed Jonathan Haverford is a Big Person, and Big People aren't like the rest of us. For one thing, Big People make their own rules.

One rule was that Russ be very, very friendly with the late Senator from Wisconsin but not ever mention that friendship to Mr. Haverford, who went all over the country making speeches attacking the Senator. Jonathan Haverford didn't even want to know that on the death of the Senator, Russ sent a very handsome wreath of bronze chyrsanthemums from Max Schling's, even though the network paid for the wreath.

You've got to be very fast on your feet in these areas. Big People don't have time to wait for the slower-footed and -witted among us.

Russell is not slow-witted, and as I've said he has learned to be fast on his feet, but Russell made one big mistake.

He thought that Jonathan Haverford would be grateful for the dirty, secret job Russ dirtily and secretly performed. Russ hadn't learned a lesson I picked up, along with a lot else, in the Thirties. When the strike is over, won or lost, the fink is the first to go. Nobody really likes a fink, not even other finks.

And so it was that when the Recent Unpleasantness simmered down, Russ got fired. One morning, along with his sizable monthly pay check from the network, Russ got two months' severance pay and a little note from J. Haverford saying that, regretfully, Russell's vice presidency was being eliminated.

The letter had been dictated by Haverford but not read by him. It was signed in his absence by his secretary. Jonathan Haverford was at that moment in St. Louis accepting a plaque from Americans All Out For Virtue.

In accepting the plaque, Haverford, whose speeches usually get coast-to-coast coverage on Blank, said, "This is a big, big country, a country big enough for all kinds of people and all kinds of ideas."

That speech, which we might call Liberal Noise A, ends with these stirring words, "Let us all say, as our forefathers said ... and sacred honor, and thank you for recognizing as those of us at Blank have ... eternal vigilance."

Haverford is another of the people on our side who I wish were on their side. He was also one of The Crusaders, and for that I have never forgiven him.

Russ came to see me shortly after he got his notice from the network. He said he had been trying for weeks to get in to see Haverford, but Haverford was always off someplace casting a medal for himself.

"I think I at least deserve an explanation, don't you?" Russ asked me. I said that I did.

"Do you understand it?" asked Russ.

I said that I did, and I explained it, referring to Haverford in words not normally heard in *any* company.

A few days later Russ came to work at Bland Enterprises, temporarily. He's been there ever since. He has a sure instinct for what will appeal to the small-minded people like himself whose expense accounts support the New York theater. No honest man can afford to go to the theater at his own expense.

I might add that Russ has learned a great deal since he got that dismissal note from Haverford. As I believe I have said, Russell is someday going to own it all.

It is nearly midnight—the last midnight. I feel oddly relaxed, tired, to be sure, but it is the kind of fatigue I have had those few times in my life when I have finished some difficult, demanding job and can get to bed early.

The effect of the green pills and the capsules has dwindled, and I am pleased that I am experiencing none of the panic I thought might seize me in the hours before the definitive dawn. None of the terror that overwhelmed me on the bright day in Georgia when I first jumped out of a moving airplane, none of the near-hysteria I felt as I climbed into a C-47 on a rainy June night a little more than fifteen years ago.

We owe God a death? Well, of course. My own debt is long overdue. You see, someone died for me on a certain afternoon in Belgium an eternity or so ago.

I will try in these next few hours to tell what I must tell as exactly as I can. I won't use any of the pills that—as surely you've noticed—heighten emotion, deepen the memory of love, intensify the memory of hate, eliminate grays, darken blacks, and strengthen whites.

No, this is just me talking, a stranger and afraid. As always.

I want to talk first about the time I spent at Camp Tuckahoe, Georgia.

It seems almost obscene to say so, but I was never more at peace with myself than during the nearly thirteen months I spent in those dark Georgian hills, from early November 1942 until mid-December 1943. Obscene because in addition to learning how to jump out of a moving airplane, I was learning how to kill and teaching other men to do it.

I'm reasonably sure I must have been the only man in the regiment who hadn't honestly volunteered for paratroop duty.

Men who volunteer for anything in the Army are suspect and rightly so, I imagine. They are likely to be fuck-ups, misfits, and troublemakers, or all three. That was true of most of the men who came to Tuckahoe. Among them were fools and fanatics and braggarts and show-offs. Many were simple romantics who, under different circumstances, would have offered themselves to climb the mountain nobody else had, or to look for El Dorado, or to be the first to try to reach the moon. A few wanted the extra jump-pay. Many were proving that they had hitherto unsuspected resources, or were escaping from something or somebody—a tedious job, a domineering wife, a too-protective family.

None of them was average or uninteresting, nor were they ever tractable.

Shortly after our arrival at Tuckahoe, each of us was interviewed by the commanding officer, Colonel Julian. After that interview, a large number of volunteers were sent back to the induction centers they'd come from.

I never knew how I managed to survive that interview with the colonel. I was and still am unbelievably grateful that I did. So what I say about Colonel Julian may be dismissed as prejudiced. It is.

I have said that when the Point turns out a good man, there is none better. The colonel was the best.

He was a thin, graceful man, about thirty-five, I should imagine. Every movement he made gave the impression of a well-oiled, intricate machine built for the exact thing it was then doing.

He had a sharp-featured, ugly face, and his deep, green-blue eyes examined your soul every time he looked at you—and found it wanting.

He was a showman; the best officers always are. Not a ham. MacArthur was a ham. Patton was too fond of vainglory and vulgarity for my taste, but Georgie Patton, warts and all, exuded a pride of outfit that seemed to reach every man in the Third Army. Not easy on an Army level.

Colonel Julian did that for our regiment. He felt strongly about cowardice, too, though I cannot imagine any circumstance that would have caused him to slap a man. He had a high regard for the dignity of the individual.

We'd stand shivering in the cold, gray Georgia dawn, and the colonel would scream at us, "Who's the best?"

And we'd scream back, "We are."

Childish, to be sure; but maybe necessary for such an infantile pursuit as war. All I know is I was one of the loudest shouters. My teeth were chattering so violently I thought they'd drop out, but, by God, I shouted.

The colonel was very much more than a first-rate actor and an efficient perpetual-motion machine. He was what they boast of turning out at the Point but almost never do, a gentleman and a scholar.

After his death at Bastogne, a group of us—a dozen, more or less—were in a warm basement that was under artillery fire. The talk began slowly, shyly, as such conversations do. What surprised us was that there was not a man present who didn't have a personal example of some unexpected kindness of the colonel's. What's more, there was not a man among the dozen or so who had ever mentioned the kindness while the colonel lived. Why? Each of us in his own way said, "I didn't think he'd want me to."

I suspect that what was true of those few of us in that bombarded basement was true of nearly every man in the regiment.

In our first interview, the colonel, after a great many other questions probing the degree of my neuroses, said, "You ever jumped out of an airplane?"

I confessed to my shame that I hadn't.

He said, "Well, you will. You haven't got a fear of heights, or anything like that, have you?"

I quickly said, "Oh, no, sir. Not at all."

I said it too quickly.

The colonel looked closely at me. "Have you ever?" he asked.

I said, "Well, a little, you know. When I was a kid. It's like the measles and the mumps. You get over it."

"Oh, do you?" he said.

That was one of the times his eyes unwrapped my soul and discovered it wasn't up to much but agreed to give it another chance.

"Well, you're on probation here," said the colonel. "I'll expect you to do twice as well as anybody else. Got that straight?"

"Yes, sir," I said. I drew myself up to attention and saluted him.

"For God's sake, relax a little," said the colonel, saluting back. "It makes me nervous just to look at you."

Later, I found out that the colonel had made about four hundred parachute jumps. Somebody asked him why, and he was quoted as saying he did it because he was afraid of parachuting.

There were many things about parachuting that terrorized me; in fact, at the moment I can't think of anything that didn't.

One source of panic was the fact that each of us had to pack his own chute. In general, the idea was sound enough. A man is likely to take more trouble with the chute his own life depends on.

But I doubt if in the history of aviation there has ever been anyone less qualified by nature to wrap up a parachute than Chicken-licken.

I believe I said earlier that I've always found it tough deciding which is my right hand, which my left.

What I did not say is that, in addition, I am a mechanical moron. Not only that, although I approach *things* with patience, fortitude, and hope, *things* do not respond in kind. Oh, no. *Things* lie waiting for me to come along. Sometimes they wait for centuries. For instance, once in a country beyond the sea I picked up a vase so old that Lucrezia Borgia may have hidden some of her poisoned darts in it. Now understand this. I didn't volunteer to pick up that vase. My hostess asked me to bring it to her. I am always the perfect guest, so I foolishly agreed.

Naturally, I no more than touched that vase than it shattered into six thousand pieces.

My hostess, of course, laughed merrily and said she was *hoping* somebody would do that. She said she had *never* liked that vase.

They always say things like that. "Oh, goodie, you mean you burned a hole in the Chippendale table *and* in the Renaissance chair? Goodie. Goodie." They chuckle at your caprices, and they say, "I couldn't care less. Think nothing of it. Come have another drink." I wish they wouldn't.

Anyway, one thing I know about both my right and my left hands is that they break things, and they are incapable of either tying or untying knots. And as for wrapping packages—well, the only packages that I have ever wrapped for mailing have been refused by the post office.

So much for the background. Now early in April 1943, our whole regiment went to the parachute school at Fort Benning.

I have blacked out a good deal of that unhappy memory, but I do recall that after about the sixth lecture and demonstration, the sergeant instructing us came around to examine our work. I thought that by concentration and hard work I had wrapped up a pretty good chute. The sergeant looked at it long and hard, and then he said, "Okay, now. Let's stop kidding and get down to work."

Our first jump out of an honest-to-God airplane was to take place on April 27, 1943. Not a second of the forty-eight hours preceding that event is gone from my mind.

I asked at least a dozen people to examine the parachute I had packed; some adjusted this, and others adjusted that. Finally, it was pronounced safe. *Safe?* I knew damn good and well that that chute was just waiting for me to jump out of the plane. Then it would show me who was boss.

Except that I was positive I'd never be able to make the jump in the first place.

I was number-three man in my plane, and when the time came, I went to the open door and stood there for a century or two, and then I turned, my face awash with tears, my body dripping sweat and near my mouth white flecks of fear. I opened my mouth to say, "I can't," and then an inner force I'd never used before and have seldom used since took over. It pushed me out of the plane.

I'm not sure what happened next. I blacked out the minute my body left the plane, and when I came to, my chute was opening, and I was drifting toward the green, friendly earth. I was alive; I had demanded the impossible of myself—and achieved it.

There were other men floating on either side of me, and I shouted at them. Heaven knows what. They shouted back at me. Heaven knows what.

When I reached the ground, I lay there for what seemed like a long time, meaning possibly a minute.

Then I rose, started folding my chute, and said to anybody, "There really isn't anything to it, is there?"

I attach no importance to jumping out of an airplane. It seems to me, in fact, to be an adolescent exercise. I attach no undue importance to physical courage either. It's a nice thing to have, like being able to play the piano. It's the man with moral guts I keep looking for. And seldom find.

What I'm getting at here is that it seems to me a pity that war is the only pastime yet devised that demands that a man be bigger than he had any notion he could be. That fact must be one of the many reasons for war's popularity. Oh, it is popular, you know. Next to sex, there is nothing men enjoy more. Particularly in retrospect.

I've known men who, given a choice, would swear off sex.

A couple years back I like a fool agreed to speak at a regimental reunion. I have neither the time nor the wish to discuss the emotions I went through that night.

But I want to say this. In the midst of the boozy meanderings that served me as a speech, I said, "How many of you guys look back on your worst day of combat with nostalgia? Raise your right hand."

Every hand in the room was raised, including my own.

That's all I have to say about jumping out of airplanes. Except that from April 27, 1943, until the present I have never suffered from vertigo. Other, more deadly diseases, but no vertigo.

I learned how to do a great many other very difficult things during the time I was at Tuckahoe. Most of those skills have fled me now, but I learned how to read a map and operate a radio and hike thirty miles and, most important of all, how to take orders and, equally difficult, how to give them without playing the role of the martinet, an acting assignment that I can fulfill as naturally as I breathe.

It seems to me that during the whole time there was nothing I was asked to do that I could do, and yet there was nothing I was asked to do that I did not do.

You think I romanticize? Possibly, though I've just consulted a diary I kept that year. This entry:

I got a letter from Letty. The usual crap. She's been to some damn thing at the Waldorf, and she met all kinds of famous people. She wishes I'd been there. She knows I'd *just love it*. What a crock. Letty and I are finished. What Letty wants she can have—but not with me. I don't know what I want yet. But it is not to be found at the Waldorf....

The platoon went on a twenty-mile hike today, most of the time on the double. We rode back, but, when we got back, we had a couple hours of drill. It's amazing. I'm not even *tired*.

Now we come to Nick and Susan Continos who, except for Hughie Larrabee and Davy Bronson, were the best friends I've ever had.

They had a two-room apartment in a town I'll call Christopher, Georgia, not far from Tuckahoe. Christopher was—and I'm sure still is—populated largely by a collection of thieves and pickpockets as small of mind and as mean of spirit as my enemies and neighbors on Old South Friendly Road. With this difference: the friendly folks on this road wouldn't rob you and knife you in the back unless there was a little something in it. Say, fifty bucks or so. The people in Christopher would do anything listed in the criminal code for the sheer pleasure of doing it, and those people had thought up crimes that weren't even classified yet.

Nick and Susan paid a hundred and eight dollars a month for two rooms that combined wouldn't have made one decent closet. Their landlady, a harpy who could have played any of the three witches in *Macbeth* without makeup, was fond of saying, "I'd do anything for you two kids. Going off to war and all. I ought to be paying you to live here if I didn't have my expenses and all. For the war effort."

Nevertheless, Susan made the dingy hole seem livable—pleasant even, and every minute I wasn't on duty at Tuckahoe, I was with Nick and Susan. And with Aristotle, their son.

Nick was a captain and a company commander, not my company. He was an honors graduate in political science from the University of California.

In our outfit, the standing operating procedure of the manual was in general disregarded. Nobody paid much attention to the non-fraternization policy dealing with enlisted men and officers. It was like that with paratroopers generally. And nobody ever made an issue of it. The brass recognized that the paratroops had an unusual assignment and, happily, allowed us to act in as unusual a manner as we wished. Which was usually most unusual.

Nick planned to go into politics after the war. His ambition was not limitless. He would have settled for being President of the United States.

"Although world government's the only real hope, and, believe me, I am not going to be a coy candidate. If they ask me to head it up and it looks as if I'm the best qualified candidate, which I wouldn't doubt judging from the competition I've seen so far, I'll take it."

With Nick you could never be sure whether he was serious or not.

He'd say, "Look, chum, I've been reading *The New York Times* very carefully every day since I was fifteen years old, and most of that time it looked to me as if I was the only sane man on the face of the earth, and if you think that ever gave me any comfort, you're off your rocker."

Although he planned to make politics his career, Nick did not court popularity. He wanted you to like him—who doesn't want that?—but only for the right reasons.

Ours was by no means a slack regiment, but Nick was the most demanding disciplinarian. He accepted no compromises, no jobs half done or simply well done. Each job—his own included—had to be done better than anybody had ever done it before. He was vituperative by nature, particularly when confronted with the sleazy, the slip-shod, the second-rate.

He was intolerant of error. For instance, very early in the days of Tuckahoe I was in his day room at the same time as a two-star general who was visiting camp on an inspection tour. The general was expressing some opinion or other. Nick interrupted. "Now, general," he said. "If you'll just think about it, you'll see how wrong you are. Let me set you straight on that."

That was not at all unusual. How he avoided a court-martial I'll never know, but he did, which is even more astounding when you consider that Nick committed the unforgivable sin of almost always being right.

I can explain how he kept out of the guardhouse only by suggesting that his manner was never arrogant. It was that of someone sorry to see you fall into error and anxious, for your sake, to set you straight.

Nick took it for granted that people should perform perfectly at all times, and when they did so, it never occurred to him that they expected to be complimented for it.

Just one example; there are hundreds.

When he arrived at Tuckahoe, he was assigned a jeep driver, "Happy" Sullivan. Happy was a tall, good-looking blond boy with a disposition of almost unlimited amiability.

That first day Happy was driving Nick someplace when the jeep broke down. Nick was sitting beside Happy, studying a manual.

"Sir, what do you want me to do?" asked Happy.

"About what?" asked Nick, looking up.

"About the jeep, sir," said Happy. "It's stopped."

"Yes, I've observed that," said Nick. "Get it started."

Happy gave Nick a smile that up to then had probably got him just about everything he wanted. "Sir," he said, "I've never looked inside the hood of a jeep my whole life through."

Nick gave Happy a surely-you-are-joking look and climbed down from the jeep.

"This is Wednesday afternoon, 1620," said Nick. "On Saturday at 0800 sharp I want you to be at my office with this jeep. I will then watch while you take the motor apart and put it back together again."

On Saturday at 0800 Happy, whose biggest problem up 'til then had probably been getting a *C* in an algebra exam, took the motor of that jeep apart and, while Nick watched, put it back together again.

I have a feeling Happy probably had stayed up all of three nights learning how to go through with that performance. When he finished, he looked at Nick, smiling hopefully. If Happy had had a tail, he would have wagged it.

Nick got into the jeep. "Now you can drive me to the colonel's office," he said.

This is the sentimental part. Until December 28, 1944, when Nick was killed, Happy was his only driver. Their esteem for each other, while never to my knowledge expressed, was so pronounced that if you rode with them, you could almost touch it.

After Nick's death, Happy never drove a jeep again. He asked to be and was assigned as a rifleman in my platoon. I remember that shortly afterward I started to say something to him.

"Happy—" I began.

He interrupted fiercely. "My name is Arthur," he said. "I don't want anybody ever to call me Happy again."

End of sentimental part.

And this man, Captain Nick Continos, wanted to be a *politician*, you ask? Yes, sir. Nick was the one—I guess every outfit had one—who in our outfit carried Thucydides with him the whole way, in Greek.

I remember Nick saying once, "Politics is the art of the possible? Bull. Some *practical* man thought that up.

"Politics is the art of leadership," he said. "Politics is the art of persuasion, of enlightenment. Politics is the art of convincing people that they are capable of greatness."

"Okay, okay," I said. "Whatever you run for, you've got one vote."

"Two," said Susan.

"*Practical* men," said Nick. "I have yet to meet a *practical* man that was worth the powder and shot it'd take to blow him up. If it weren't for *im*practical men, we'd still be debating whether it was safe to live anywhere besides a cave."

"Hear, hear, Demosthenes," I said.

I remember once sitting in on a lecture he gave on some phase of field communications. Colonel Julian was there that day, too. After the lecture the colonel came up to Nick.

"Well done, Continos," he said. "You certainly gave it to them straight. I just hope none of it was over the heads of any of the men."

"If it was, sir," said Nick, "then the men whose heads it was over will have to grow taller."

Nick had at least one great political advantage, in addition to his eloquence.

He was very good-looking. He had dark, curling hair and the kind of skin that had been so darkened by the California sun that it didn't fade all the time we were at Tuckahoe or in Europe. He was tall, had very white teeth, and a smile of dazzling brilliance and warmth.

Susan would have been a sure-fire Miss America if she'd gone in for that sort of thing. The sort of thing she went in for was history; she was Phi Beta Kappa and had all kinds of other academic honors.

Aristotle was—not surprisingly—a child of unusual beauty and extreme good nature.

Children frighten me. They recognize me for what I am at a glance. I always say something that even the densest child instantly recognizes as nonsense. The night I met Aristotle I said, "Well, well. Look it here. What do they call you, Art?"

Art, who was two years old, treated my foolishness with a contemptuous silence.

"His name is Aristotle," said Nick, "and I don't want anyone ever to call him Art. Aristotle is a proud name, and it means something."

There were many good officers in our outfit, many, but I believe that—with the exception of the colonel—Nick was the best. He could, had he chosen, have gone straight up and, very probably, by the time the war ended had himself at least a regiment. But he did not so choose.

"To guys on the line, it's 'we or they,' and once you get above company level, it's not 'we' any more, it's 'they.'" That's the reason Nick stayed with Able Company from the beginning of our training at Tuckahoe until he was killed in Belgium.

Nick hated the Army, and he hated the war with an angry passion—more, I'd say, than anyone I ever knew. Yet unlike most of the more intellectual of my friends—who wanted Hitler beat but whose dignity was affronted when they were called on to help (you can put me in that category)—Nick felt that since he had to be in the Army, he had to do a good job in the Army.

"I hate every part of it," he'd say, "every waking hour of it. I do indeed hate war, but that's the name of the game, and when you're in it, you'd better play it."

And that's all I'm going to say for now on the people I spent most of my time with during the best and happiest thirteen months of my life. I had one furlough during that time. Happily, it occurred when Letty was in Chicago on some urgent foolishness or other for *Puberty*.

Nick and Susan didn't have time to go all the way back to California; so they invited me to go with them to New Orleans. We were there for three outrageously happy days.

In late December 1943, the outfit got orders to move to the port of embarkation, which was near Camp Miles Standish in Massachusetts. We arrived on January 1, 1944.

Nick and I wangled a twenty-four-hour pass to Boston for the day before we sailed. Susan was already there.

Against my better judgment I telegraphed Letty.

I prayed that she wouldn't get the telegram or that the press of business at the magazine would make it impossible for her to come or that she'd feel the way I did about our marriage, that it was over, that it had been over before it began, and that the sooner she and I went our separate ways the better.

I prayed that on my last evening before sailing off to the wars I could have dinner with Nick and Susan, as had happened so often before, and that I'd then be able to go to the room I'd reserved at the Somerset and spend the last night in a real bed. Alone. It had been a long time since I had been alone, and I had learned to cherish privacy, as you do in the Army.

You can't count on God in a pinch.

I got an almost instantaneous reply from Letty. It said:

Meet you at the Somerset around noon can't wait to see you and oh darling does your being in Boston mean what I hope it doesn't millions of kisses and all the love there is Letty.

Different people remember different things—faces, smiles, a nervous habit, a way of walking, a gesture. Myself, as I have said, I'm a voice man. I remembered Letty's voice—too high-pitched, too tight, too loud, and too much of it.

As I came out of the elevator into the lobby of the Somerset Hotel that morning, I saw sitting in an overstuffed chair a trim, brown-haired woman wearing a clearly expensive black dress, a long string of matched pearls, and shoes that looked expensive but uncomfortable. Her right leg was thrown over the left and made a continuous, small swing, in and out, out and in. It was the movement of a restless, impatient woman, but it meant nothing to me.

This may be difficult to believe, but it's true. I glanced at the woman, whose face was partially hidden by a copy of *Vogue*, and then I went to the desk and gave my name.

Letty heard me, and I heard her voice. She rose from the chair and rushed toward me. She said, "My God, darling, you're here."

She rushed into my arms, and I kissed the stranger I had married.

"You've dyed your hair," I said, and before she could ask, "It's very becoming. It really is."

"Let me look at you," said Letty, and she did.

"I'm not sure I'd have recognized you," she said. "You've changed."

Nobody sees in himself what others see in him, either physically or in any other way; so I can only guess what Letty saw that day. I know this; I was leaner and harder and stronger of body than I had ever been before—or, for that matter, would ever be again. I was more sure of myself; I even walked with an air of confidence. I had been walking the way paratroopers should walk—or think they should walk—for so long that it almost came natural to me. But it was not only the walk. For the first time in my life—and, once more, the last—I knew my job; I knew there was nothing technical I'd be called on to do that I couldn't do. And—no false modesty here; we're telling the truth today—I felt as certain as I had any right to that when people started shooting at me I would be all right. I wouldn't run. I had too much respect for the men I'd spent a year in training with and too much respect for myself.

I had told myself very early in the training, "I'm not going to blow this one; this is the one I follow through on." I had followed through.

Letty took a long, neither-approving-nor-disapproving look at me, and she said, "Well, I have to admit that if I didn't know better, I'd think I was looking at an honest-to-God soldier."

In the past, a remark like that would have drawn at least a few drops of blood, because in the past, however Letty deprecated me, I agreed with her, and more.

Not that day, though. I said, "If the guys in my platoon heard you call me a soldier, they'd clean up on you. Soldiers are Infantrymen. Paratroopers are—well, we think rather godlike."

"What do you do, besides jump out of airplanes?"

"I'm a platoon sergeant," I said.

"Who would ever have believed it? George Vertigo himself jumping out of airplanes."

"We have parachutes," I said, "and if the first one doesn't open, you can always take it back and get a new one."

"Well, what's the schedule for the day?"

"We're going to have dinner with a buddy of mine, Nick Continos, and his wife, Susan. They're very special people."

"Oh," said Letty. "Special in what way?"

"At the Parker House. At seven. What'll we do in the meantime?"

"How long have you got?"

"I have to be back at camp first thing in the morning."

"You mean we aren't even going to have dinner alone? You mean I came all the way from New York in a filthy day coach just to have dinner with you and some people I've never met, and then we hop into bed, and I go back to New York in a filthy day coach, and that's all?"

"Letty, stop it. Let's have a drink."

Sudden tears appeared in Letty's eyes. I have never forgotten that because I had never brought tears to Letty's eyes before. I'd tried, very hard.

She put her arm in mine, and she said, "I'm sorry. I'm tired."

As we started toward the bar, she said, "You look marvelous, darling. All hard and military and, oh hell, kind of *gallant*. That's a word I never thought I'd use. I'm very proud of you, and you frighten me."

"I hope I have that effect on the Germans," I said.

Letty and I had two or three drinks, and we talked, and we went for a long walk, and, for a while, for a few minutes here and there, it was a little like the first evening I'd seen Letty in New York, just before sailing on my first trip to England.

Everything went well until we met Nick and Susan at the Parker House. I saw at once that Letty was going to dislike them and show it, and she did both.

The dinner was a nightmare, although I'm fairly certain that at first Nick and Susan didn't notice. They were an entity of two, sufficient unto each other. I doubt that they realized how much it showed, or how cold and alone it made you feel to be outside.

Letty was unpleasant all during dinner. I don't know why. I've thought about it, but I never came up with any very good answers. No one but Letty will ever know what fears she felt that night, what envy, what chills, what regret.

One example will be enough, more than enough. Over coffee she said, "Darling [that was me], did I tell you this story I heard about the couple that went to this hotel they'd been at on their honeymoon for their silver wedding anniversary?"

"Yes, you told me," I said, very quickly.

"Well, anyway," said Letty. "The wife got undressed and hopped into bed, and then he went to the bathroom and got undressed, and when he came out in his altogether, she took one look at him, and she said, 'When I married you, you looked like a Greek god. Now you look like a goddamn Greek.'"

What do you do? What do you ever do?

A flush crept into Nick's dark face, and Susan looked puzzled and then frightened, and then she said, "We're all terrified, Mrs. Bland. We pretend to be brave and unconcerned and we tell ourselves that it's happening to everybody else and there's nothing special about us, but there is something special about us. We're us, and we're scared."

"I'm used to being alone," said Letty. "It doesn't bother me in the least."

After that, the waiter brought the check.

I kissed Susan good-bye; I wouldn't see her the next morning. She said, "Don't let anything happen to him, Josh."

If she had not seen too many bad movies that had women cry-
ing when their husbands went off to the wars, she might have cried.
She didn't, though. I bet she didn't cry until after Nick and I left for
Camp Miles Standish the next morning.

I said, "I'll look after Nick. You look after Aristotle."

Letty said, "I'm very pleased to have met the both of you, I'm
sure."

She made her voice very Iowa when she said it, and I was sure
it was a sentence her mother had used, a sentence that had made
Letty cringe.

Why? I never figured that out either.

In the taxi on the way back to the hotel, I didn't say a word to
Letty, and she didn't say a word to me.

When we got in the room, I slammed the door and locked it,
and then I grabbed the collar of the black dress, tearing it. I brought
Letty close to me and began slapping her, first one cheek and then
the other, in rapid succession.

When my arm got tired, I stopped and released Letty. There
was a large, scarlet spot on each cheek, but she didn't cry. Not then.
She'd cried that morning over nothing, but not that night over
something. Who knows? Who knows why?

She went to the dressing table and took off her pearl necklace
and then started taking off her earrings. "He's very handsome, isn't
he?" she said. "And how fortunate that he's Greek. The Greeks have
an affinity for that sort of thing, don't they?"

I walked toward her, two steps at a time, but I did not reach
her before she had a chance to say, "Susan didn't even seem to be
jealous, but then she's not very bright. Have you made a pass at him
yet?"

I made a fist with my hand and hit her hard in the mouth,
drawing blood, and then I knocked her to the floor.

That was the night my daughter Taffy was conceived.

Taffy was born in September, during the time I was involved
in one of the bloodiest fiascos of the war. The latter was in Holland,
the former in New York Hospital.

I didn't know I had a daughter until mid-November. The telegram from Letty and a number of letters were waiting at Camp Mourmelon in France when what was left of my outfit got there.

I never told Nick that I had a daughter. I never told anybody.

The rest of what I have to say about the war—and there won't be much—I'm going to postpone for a few minutes.

It will be dawn soon; all the stars but one are gone. It is the last star in the sky, but it happens to be the first I have seen tonight, and I have just wished on it.

Was it St. Francis who said that the unselfish wish of a selfish man has a very special place in the sight of God?

I wish my daughter well. I wish that she would want the right things in her life and that she would get some of them.

I want to tell now about the last afternoon I will ever spend with Taffy. I have a point to make. I'll tell about the afternoon and then make the point.

The time is June of last year, 1958.

Taffy and Letty were at *that* hotel. Some of the preposterous personages from Out There stay at the Waldorf Towers when they are in New York, but those squares who have been told it is square to stay at the Waldorf Towers stay at *that* hotel. I won't name it; they'd sue.

I don't know what to make of all this, but The People from Looking-glass Land always stay at the same hotel wherever they are—the Connaught in London, the George V in Paris, the Excelsior in Rome, and tiresomely and forever on.

On the day I'm telling about, Taffy's stepfather, Harry Lowenstein, was in Rome, making the epic I've already dismissed.

It had been arranged weeks earlier that I would be allowed to spend the afternoon with Taffy, and when I arrived in the lobby of the hotel, I picked up a house phone and asked for Letty's suite.

A lady operator asked for my name; and then she asked whether I was *personally* acquainted with Mrs. Lowenstein and was I expected.

I quickly answered yes to both questions, but I could see that she was still suspiciously examining me through the glass partition which separated us. She was a plump, doltish-looking creature who reminded me of Letty's house mother at the Pi Phi house in New Athens. I wondered if she had gallstones and how was her lumbago.

She said they had to be so awfully careful in a hotel like this one. She said they had mostly a California clee-un-tell, and she said there were more teen-age delinquents and more plain and fancy nuts trying to crash into the hotel than you could shake a stick at.

It was clear that she considered me a fancy nut, possibly because of the beard.

"I used to be Peter the Hermit," I told her.

"Was that on television or in the movies?" she asked, reverentially.

"The silents," I said. "They're coming back, you know."

She said that was nice. And then she plugged in.

I heard her tell Letty my qualifications.

A man who looked for all the world like Gary Cooper and a woman looking for all the world like Maria Schell emerged from the elevator. I could have touched them both if I'd brought along a ten-foot pole.

Eventually, Letty's voice said, "Josh, I haven't seen you in a coon's age."

"Two years ago at Twenty-One," I said, and I said, "Thank you for letting me see Taffy."

"Charlotte's not with you, is she?" asked Letty. "You know you promised—"

"I'm alone. Shall I come up?"

"No, doll. I'll send Taffy down. I'm being pounded black and blue by a Finnish brutess. Maybe I'll see you later. You two have a good time."

Taffy was wearing the first flesh-colored lipstick I had ever seen, and she had on a dress that looked like the dresses the models in *Vogue* were wearing at the time.

Taffy was nearly fourteen.

"Hello there," she said, extending a thin, pale hand that seemed to be without bones. Her accent was a little like the one Deborah Kerr has developed through the years, though I detected a trace of Katharine Hepburn as well.

I took the embarrassingly fragile hand.

"Hello, Taffy," I said. "You look very pretty."

She did, if what I could make out behind the lipstick was true. Her eyes were dark blue; they were like my father's eyes, and Taffy's hair was like that of her mother when I first met Letty at the Pi Phi dance.

"You look very pretty," I said again.

"Thank you, kind sir." Then abruptly, "Do you mind if I don't call you anything?"

I wasn't sure what she meant, but I said I didn't mind.

"I mean calling you Josh is so sort of *outré*," she said. "I mean all the kids whose mothers go by Spock or some square like that are *encouraged* to call their parents by their first names. That kind of jazz. And I call Harry Dad."

"Well," I said.

We walked outside, and an obsequious doorman said, "Would you like a cab, Miss Lowenstein?"

Taffy looked at me, and I said, "Let's walk a little. It's such a magnificent day."

"No thanks, Donald," Taffy told the doorman, and to me she said, "Usually I can't *stand* New York weather."

We walked to the corner, and I said, "That's a very pretty dress."

"It's a Mainbocher," said Taffy. "Dad tried to get them to make me a Dior when he was in Paris. He had my measurements and a picture of me and all. You know they don't make dresses for my age?"

"That seems odd."

"Dick Lombardi makes most of my clothes. He's queer, but he's terribly nice," said Taffy.

"What would you like to do this afternoon?" I asked.

"I always let my dates decide that," said Taffy with a touch of coyness.

"It's a beautiful afternoon," I said.

It was, too. There were until recently days in New York when I still had the same foolish enthusiasm for the city that I had at fifteen when I was a hick from Iowa on the first step of an odyssey which I was sure would result in my remaking the world in my own image.

The afternoon with Taffy was very much like the first afternoon, gold and warm, the air soft and fresh.

"Would you like to go to a matinee?" I asked. "I didn't get tickets because I didn't know what you've seen, but I could. Have you seen *Two for the Seesaw*?"

"A bore if ever I saw a bore," said Taffy. "It's *ghastly*."

"I rather like it," I said, and then I suggested the boat trip around Manhattan Island. Taffy had been. I suggested, first, the Central Park Zoo and then the Bronx Zoo. Taffy had been. I suggested a ride through Central Park in a carriage. Taffy said the horses smelled.

Finally I said, "Would you like to go to the Music Hall?"

"I will if you want to."

A cab slowed down; the driver looked questiongly at me, and I shook my head. "Taffy, I want to do what you want to do."

"Well, I've seen the picture. At Jennifer's and David's, and I can't *stand* the Rockettes."

I reached for her hand, but she managed to avoid my touch.

"Let's start out at Rumpelmayer's and plan our itinerary over a sundae of some kind. How does that strike you?"

Taffy smiled at the street. "Is it like Wil Wright's?"

"A little."

"I think that would be rather pleasant," she said.

We crossed the street with the green light, our hands not touching.

"Isn't there anything you'd especially like to do?" I asked as she was finishing her strawberry sundae.

"You're the boss," said Taffy.

After a moment, I asked, "How's your sundae?"

"It's okay."

"But not as good as Wil Wright's?"

"It's okay."

Taffy ate another mouthful, slowly crumbling a wafer between the thumb and forefinger of her left hand.

"You know the Wil Wright's on Sunset?" she asked. "Near the Chateau Marmont. Harry calls the Chateau the French Rat. It's where all the odd balls from New York stay."

I nodded, not mentioning that among the odd balls who stayed there was sometimes myself.

"Well, anyway," said Taffy, "in this Wil Wright's down the street they've got this sign that says banana splits are a dollar apiece, and then it says, 'Only One to a Customer.' I had one last winter, and I still wasn't filled up, and I asked Dad to get me another, and he tried to order it, and one of the waitresses started to give him a hard time and all. She was a real square from squaresville. Dad had to tell her that the sign was a gag. Can you imagine not knowing that? Anyway, she finally brought me a second."

Taffy pushed from her what was left of the sundae.

"I couldn't finish the second one, though," she said.

I smiled, then reached over and touched her long blond hair again. She looked nervously across the table at me and quickly brought a crumb of the wafer to her mouth and ate it.

"You've got very fine hair," I said. "It's soft, like your mother's."

"It needs a shampoo," said Taffy, running her left hand through it, being careful to avoid my hand. "This woman comes every Thursday when I'm home. Right after school."

"How do you like school?"

"The teachers are all squares. Without exception. It's the best school in Beverly Hills, but you can't blame them. Considering how much they make who but a square'd teach?"

I finished my black and white, and then I brightly asked, "Have you ever been to Chinatown?"

"In San Francisco," said Taffy, disposing of all Chinatowns everywhere.

"You know what I bet you'd like? I bet you'd like the Cloisters."

"What's that?"

I told Taffy what the Cloisters were and where. Taffy looked at the tiny jeweled wrist watch which was a smaller version of the watch her mother had worn at Twenty-One and in its class clearly the most expensive watch money could buy.

"I think the Cloisters would be loads of fun," said Taffy, "but honestly I don't think we've got time. I forgot to mention that Mother wants me back at the hotel at four. Valentina's coming over at four. So I've got to get back there in less than an hour."

I started to say that I had thought we had the whole afternoon, and I started to say that it was only a few minutes after two, but I said neither. I asked Taffy if she would like to walk down Fifth Avenue, and she said that that would be just fine.

As we stood in front of Bergdorf's, Taffy said, "New York's a bore when you come right down to it, everything all scrunched together."

"Bullock's Wilshire is nice," I said.

"Bullock's Wilshire is the utmost," said Taffy.

We did some window shopping, and at Tiffany's there was a tiny diamond tree on which were hung six good-sized rubies. Taffy said that a star whose name she mentioned had rubies worth a quarter of a million dollars but that the star just threw them around.

"You'd think they were just red glass the way she throws them around," said Taffy.

We went into the basement at Brentano's. It was my idea, and I asked Taffy if she read much.

"Some," she said. "Dad gets all these synopses of books. They're a lot shorter than the *Reader's Digest* even."

I bought several books for myself, and Taffy said, "Mother says you always had your nose stuck in some book."

"I used to read a lot," I admitted.

"Dad doesn't read much," said Taffy. "He says nobody ever got rich hanging around the New York Public Library."

Taffy waited for a response, and, since there was none, she added, "That's a joke."

I smiled.

"Wouldn't you like something?" I asked. I picked up a collection of short stories. "How about this?" I asked, handing it to Taffy.

Taffy looked critically at the table of contents. "I think this Aldoos Huxley used to work for Dad," she said.

I told her how to pronounce Huxley's first name.

"Oh," said Taffy.

She handed the book back to me. "*Edgar Allan Poe*," she said. "We have him in school. No *thanks*."

Just before we left the basement, Taffy came across a collection of essays about the late James Dean. There was a picture of Dean on the cover, and there was also a death's head. A professor at Columbia had written a scholarly introduction, and there was a long piece by Sartre.

"I'll take this if it's all right," said Taffy.

As I paid for the books, Taffy said, "We had all the kids on my birthday, and we had sort of a Jimmy Dean festival, you know in our little theater." (As I believe I've already mentioned, the Lowensteins have a forty-seat theater in the lovely home they have Out There.) "We showed all of *East of Eden* and parts of *Giant* and a reel of *Rebel Without a Cause*," said Taffy. "It lasted six hours. Lolly had it in her column. You see that?"

I looked down at Taffy, and, with great difficulty, I said that I had missed that particular item in Miss Parsons' column.

Taffy and I walked back to the hotel along Lexington Avenue. We stopped in front of the Seagram's Building, and I asked her what she thought of it.

"It's all dirty-looking," she said. "Everything in New York's all dirty-looking."

I said that the Seagram's Building seemed to me to be very beautiful and tried to tell her why. She didn't want to know.

Later, I said, "Taffy, I haven't been a very good father to you."

It wasn't a question, and Taffy didn't treat it as one.

"I know it's very late," I told her, "but somehow I'd like to help you."

"What could you do?" asked Taffy.

"I don't know," I said, "but perhaps I could talk to you and try to help you find something I've never found and your mother's never found and perhaps your Dad hasn't found either."

"Like what?" asked Taffy. There was a definite note of suspicion in her voice.

"Well, like happiness, for one thing," I said. "Saint Augustine said that that was the great purpose of a man's life. I hope very much that you achieve it. Or come close to it. Or at the very least have an interesting search for it. It can be very interesting, you know."

Taffy looked down at the death's head on the cover of the book she carried.

"Nobody's ever completely achieved it," I said, "but some men and women have made some very good tries, and some of them have written about their tries. It sometimes helps to read and talk about what they've written."

Taffy ran a pale, boneless hand over the photograph of the pale, boneless face of the dead James Dean.

"Could I tell you something a very wise man once wrote to me?" I asked.

The blond head nodded.

"This man wrote, 'I cannot help comparing myself as we all do with the men and women I have known. Whatever the score, I have had an extremely fortunate and happy life. If I had been tortured by ambition, I would have gone further and achieved more, but I think that I would have understood far less and surely would have missed happiness. I hope very much that you achieve it. Since we are unique personalities, we cannot pass on to each other effective recipes for the great thing, the wonderful dish which we so ardently desire to whip together, to cook, and to enjoy. But I wish you good luck.'"

I paused a moment and then, quite softly, said, "I wish you good luck, Taffy."

She did not look up, but I felt that perhaps I had reached something within her.

She said, "How'd you remember all that from a letter?"

"I suppose it's because it's the nicest thing anybody ever wrote to me."

"Oh."

"Taffy, could I talk to you sometimes—and—oh, perhaps suggest some things you might like reading?"

Taffy turned over the Dean book. There was an identical death's head on the back cover and the same photograph of the dead boy.

"All that reading and talking hasn't helped you much," said Taffy, stating a fact.

That was when I wept. The tears hid themselves behind my hornrimmed glasses and then slipped in silent shame into my beard.

"No, it hasn't helped me much," I said, "but the failure was mine."

"Mother said I wasn't supposed to talk to you about stuff like this. She said you'd want to talk about stuff like this. She said you always did."

"Okay, Taffy. We won't."

We went into the hotel lobby behind a man I at first thought was George Raft, and I wanted to tell him that I had long ago learned a very important thing from him. I had learned how to light a match with my thumbnail.

Then the man turned, and I could see that it was not George Raft.

"Who's that?" I asked Taffy.

Taffy looked at the man, shrugged and shook her head.

"He looks like George Raft," I said.

"Not if you've ever seen George Raft he doesn't," said Taffy, adding, "Bill Holden and John Wayne are both staying here."

"And Gary Cooper and Maria Schell," I said.

"No kid," said Taffy, and she asked if I wanted to come up.

I said no. I said I'd better be shoving off.

"Well, then, thank you, darl," said Taffy, and she lifted her face and planted a quick, dry kiss somewhere near my chin.

"Thank you, darl," she said. "I've decided to call you darl. Short for darling. That's what Natalie Wood calls Bob Wagner."

She smiled, and it was a pleasant smile, nearly warm and almost natural. For a moment Taffy looked the way her mother had looked when I first saw her.

"I'm afraid you didn't have a very good time," I said, realizing that Taffy had probably never had a good time and that she probably never would.

"Don't be sil," said Taffy. "It was loads of fun, and we'll have to do it again sometime when we're both on the same coast."

The doors of one of the elevators opened, and Taffy ran toward it.

"Thank you, darl," she said. "Thanks a mil."

After leaving the hotel, I walked through Central Park for an hour or more, and then I took a taxi to Grand Central.

In the taxi I wept a second time, not bothering to hide the tears. *Mea culpa. Mea maxima culpa.*

As I said, the June afternoon I have just described was the last time I shall ever spend with my daughter, but I didn't know it at the time. I still hoped there would some day be a way of reaching her, and at Christmas last winter, I faced a standard dilemma of this time—what to send to the child who has everything, except, of course, love.

I gave the problem a lot of thought, and Charley and I discussed it oftener than any of the rest of our Christmas dilemmas.

Finally, early in December I was once more in the bountiful basement at Brentano's, and I saw a soft-cover collection of modern poems I'd once owned and loved and then lent or lost. I bought two copies, one for Taffy, one for me.

On the flyleaf of Taffy's I wrote, "For Taffy—I once more wish you good luck," and under that I wrote a line from a poem by Robert Lowell, "Stand and live. The dove has brought an olive branch."

In early January, I got this note written in red ink, on the most expensive stationery money can buy, "Darl—thanks for the lovely book. I liked a lot of the poems, but the flawless one is 'One Step Backward' by Robert Frost. Is Frost considered any good?"

It is this letter from Taffy that I brought back from the office with me on my final journey home the other day.

In February, I sent Taffy a copy of Frost's collected poems and wrote her that he was considered very good.

I hoped for an answer and in my heart composed a few—"Dear Darl—please come to my coast—or I will come to yours. We must talk about Saint Augustine. Harry never even heard of Robert Frost...." "Dearest Dad—'We may chance something like a star to stay our minds and be staid.' My dearest love. Your ever-loving daughter." And so on.

But there was never an answer.

I am leaving Taffy some money. Having said that sentence, my stomach trembles. All the forlorn failures leave money. Money is what the unloving leave behind for the unloved. What a shabby inheritance.

Taffy needs affection and appreciation; Taffy needed a childhood, and after the war I tried for a while to give her that, but I didn't try hard enough or often enough or long enough. And if there were to be a tombstone, that might serve: "...1921-1959. He never tried anything hard enough nor often enough nor long enough."

My daughter Taffy, the girl wearing flesh-colored lipstick, the girl in the Mainbocher dress, is a very unhappy girl, and she will be a very unhappy woman, and she will make some man or some series of men very unhappy, too.

Taffy is very much like her mother; she, like Letty, is going to spend a lot of time looking for peace of mind. She won't find it, though; her mother hasn't.

I believe that Letty thought that peace of mind might be one of the by-products of her winning the race, peace of mind and a few gold-tipped laurel leaves.

Well, gold-tipped laurel leaves are for sale in any of a number of stores along Wilshire Boulevard, and if you absolutely insist, you can have platinum tips.

But peace of mind is simply not available. Letty has looked everywhere, including Bullock's, which is the utmost. Letty has bought and even read most of the peace-of-mind books, including those ghost-written for my enemy and neighbor, Pism C.

No peace of mind, though, not even after years of sessions with that Canyon Drive analyst whose name is as well known as that of Albert Schweitzer and who makes a lot more money. Dr. Canyon Drive has worked wonders with more stars than you can shake a stick at. A lot of stars get to be around forty or so, and they start to wondering who they are. Dr. Drive tells them who they are, which is nobody.

I have no idea what Dr. Drive told Letty, but whatever it was, it didn't help at all. When she sits, Letty still puts her right leg over her left knee, and the right leg still makes that continuous, small swing of discontent, in and out, out and in.

Now Letty has discovered that what she wanted and got isn't enough, and so, she is angry. All of them Out There are angry. That's the reason they spend so much time in the sun. They seem to feel that if they just lie in the sun long enough, the turmoil will bake away.

To be sure, they hope they'll get immortal, too. After all, what's the use of being a *god* if you have to *die*. Just like *people*.

But then, maybe I'm wrong. Maybe Taffy will be all right. As Letty says she is bringing our daughter up in a healthy, normal American home. And you can't knock that, not if you're a healthy, normal American, you can't.

And that's the end of my comment on Taffy.

The point?

The point is that on that June afternoon last year, Taffy made me cry. I thought I'd forgotten how.

Mea culpa. Mea maxima culpa.

A mourning dove has lighted on the flat rock on the hill out there, now another, and a third. Charley used to put bird seed on that rock, but it is bare now.

With a disappointed whistle of wings, the doves leave, one, and another, and the last.

A moment passes, and then from the woods comes the sound of mourning. They are always mourning, those doves. In the mornings and in the evenings they mourn, and sometimes in the late afternoon.

They are not mourning death, you understand. It is life that is making them mourn.

The vise has been placed around my head again. I might have expected that, I suppose.

The screws are being tightened now. A little at a time. It is not only the pain, you see; it is the waiting for pain, too. The combination is almost unendurable.

They are going to spare me nothing; I see that now.

The sky is the color of slate, and a wind has entered the woods from behind. I can see it there quite clearly now, waiting for the signal to spring.

It will rain. Why, of course, I could have told you that had you asked. That was part of the plan; it always has been; from the very beginning They planned rain for this last day.

So. It will rain. I have opened the glass door, and the gray smell of death creeps into the room.

I see now that none of the sentence will be commuted. No second of the punishment will be set aside. I had hoped that They might suspend some small part of it—on the grounds of good behavior, or impending death. They can always find an excuse for leniency if They want to.

But not in my case. Oh, no. In my case, there are no mitigating circumstances. Not one.

What puzzles me is this:

With all the records in Their possession, with all the books They have filled with Their notes, with all the endless recordings of what I have said and thought, there must surely be evidence enough to condemn me. Why must They prolong the torture by putting Their damnable machine back in my head? Today of all days. Is there to be not a moment of peace, not even at the end?

Listen—I'll confess. I'll confess. Don't you hear me?

But no. That would be too easy. The waiting is part of the punishment, the waiting and the watching.

Half an hour has passed since I dictated those last words. *Mea culpa*, I said. *Mea maxima culpa.*

Since then I have shaved and showered, and I confess that I felt a certain sensuous joy in both. The first of everything is always the best—and the last, I suppose.

I looked in the mirror at the body which has given me so little pain and so little joy. I looked at the soft cipher of a face, at the assembly-line chin, at the curved, petulant lips, at the straight nothing of a nose, at the desperate, defeated brown eyes, at the white, lightly wrinkled forehead, at the carefully combed, thinning brown hair. I fingered the subdued anger of the scar on my cheek and felt a moment of foolish pride.

I clothed my body for this final sibilant day—the slacks from Saks, the silk shirt from Sulka, the shoes from—indeed—St. Tropez.

Then I took a pill and a capsule, squeezed orange juice, and made coffee.

In a little less than five hours George and Russell will be here; in a little less than eight, I will not.

Have I mentioned that it looks like rain? Well, let it rain. I am determined not to be depressed. Not today.

"This feeling of yours about the rain," Dr. Baron used to say. "It is nothing whatever to worry about. It's all in your head."

He would laugh, and I would look at a watermark on the ceiling, which sometimes had the shape of a cloud or a wolf's head or a tear. Sometimes it had the shape of rue, and sometimes it was round, like regret.

I must get on with this now.

I still have four tapes. More than enough. *Four?* Isn't that odd? I'd have sworn there were five. No. One. Two. Three. Four.

Well, no matter. I must have changed tapes just before taking my shower. I don't remember. I guess I was tireder than I realized.

Back now to the morning in January 1944 when I said good-bye to Letty in a room of the Somerset Hotel in Boston—a morning rather like this one—colder but perhaps a little less dismal.

It was not yet dawn when the girl at the switchboard called me. I was on the sofa, covered with a sheet. Letty was asleep on the bed; her lip, where I had struck her with my fist, was swollen and had turned purple.

I shaved and dressed and, before leaving her, I leaned over the bed and said, "Good-bye, Letty. Be good."

She opened her eyes and looked at me, and through the swollen, discolored lips she said, "I'm going to pray when you're gone. I'm going to pray that you get killed. I want you to die. I want you to die more than I can ever remember wanting anything before, and that's a lot."

"I'll do my best to oblige you, Letty," I said, and then I left for the wars.

A little less than five months later another woman said almost the same thing to me. In London, shortly before D-Day, a girl named Elisia said, "I hope you are killed by your own men. It would be right."

I left the United States, that raw January morning in 1944, absolutely sure that Letty's wish would come true—maybe desiring it. I don't believe that's usual. From what I have read and what I've heard from other soldiers the opposite seems to be more normal. Both before and during combat most men seem to feel that anyone and everyone else will be killed—but not you, not indispensable, kindly you. They wouldn't dare. God couldn't be that careless.

I don't mean just stolid, lethargic men have this feeling, the ones lucky enough not to be cursed with imagination. Nick, for instance. I honestly don't believe it ever occurred to him that he might die.

"You and I've got too much to give the world," he'd say, "too much to do."

Could he honestly believe that, knowing how accidental, how meaningless death in combat was? Was that the lie he had to tell himself to keep on doing what he had to do?

I can't be sure. I do know that he felt strongly that when the war ended, men like himself would be necessary.

"I've got to be around to keep the bull-shit artists from taking over everything," he'd say. "They've got about ninety-nine per cent of everything as it is."

I don't mean to suggest that the fact that Nick felt he ought to be around when the war ended made him any less courageous or kept him from doing what he had to do—and more. But, like most good soldiers, he took very few unnecessary chances and those only when somebody needed him.

All of us hated the war; we hated it with an intensity that before we took part in it we would not have thought possible.

And no one hated it more than Nick.

I remember a June afternoon in Normandy.

We were dug in in a cemetery not far from St. Lô. At first, there had been a few jokes about that, none of them very funny. There was the platoon I belonged to and, I believe, parts of two others, about forty of us all told. Nick had come by, and not long after he got there, we got pinned down by artillery fire.

None of our dead had been buried, and where shells had struck the French graves, coffins had spilled out their contents, mostly bones but in a few cases bodies that were not completely decomposed. Not far off were the bodies of several cows.

The day was warm, and the air was still, and it got to be evening, but the shelling continued.

After dark, Nick crawled over to where I was and took a light from my cigarette, being careful to keep his hand over the lighted end. His hand trembled violently, but he wasn't ashamed of that. If, in fact, he was aware of it.

He was silent for a while, inhaling the smoke. Then he said, "I wish they could bottle that smell. I wish they'd bottle about ten thousand bottles of that smell, and along about twenty years from now when they start getting us ready for the next one, it ought to be unbottled, a little at a time. Not all at once. Just a little at a time."

He finished the cigarette. "I pray to God I won't forget any of it," he said.

Then he crawled over the body of a corporal who had been split down the middle by a direct artillery hit, and went back to the command post.

But that came later.

Our transport arrived in England on a gray morning in late January, and of the time between then and June I remember almost nothing.

All of us knew that we would be dropped into France several hours before the Infantry landed. That knowledge haunted us— each in a different way.

The feeling was similar to that we experienced before we first jumped out of a plane at Benning, but it was much more intense. In Georgia, we knew that men had jumped out of planes before and no harm done, and what man has done....

But leaping out of a plane at night, landing in an alien land on top of the enemy. That was something else again. I don't believe any of us had a waking moment when this fear of the untried wasn't with us.

I was reading Malraux's *Man's Fate*, and I kept returning to this passage, time after time after time:

A sound of deep breathing, the same as that of sleep, began to rise from the ground—breathing through their noses, their jaws clenched with anguish, motionless now, all those who were not yet dead were waiting for the whistle.

As each dark day gave way to each darker evening and each black night, all of us during that desolate winter and spring were simply waiting for the whistle. We lived on the surface because that was the only way we could live; we joked too much and laughed too loud, and we all had thoughts and emotions we could not share with anyone.

Nick and I were very close, as close I think as two human beings can be; we each knew a very great deal about what the other was all about, but we never mentioned the panic that sometimes assailed us.

We had gone to London together several times, but I arranged to spend the last one alone. Nick never asked why. I expect he knew.

One of my intentions in London was to have a girl. Nick had not been unfaithful to Susan up to then, and he wasn't later, not even when we shared a desperate forty-eight hours in Paris.

I should say here that Nick never mentioned Letty to me, nor that last supper at the Parker House.

I'd written Letty maybe four letters in as many months, none of them much more than, "I am fine. I hope you are the same."

Letty wrote regularly, twice a week, on Wednesday night and Sunday. "Dearest darling," each began, and then something like, "I miss you more than you can possibly imagine."

She never mentioned that she was pregnant.

Until now, I've never told anybody about Elisia, not even Dr. Baron. I met Elisia in a bar near Albert Hall, after a recital at which I heard Beethoven's Waldstein sonata for the first time.

It was on the first night of my pass. Elisia came back to the hotel with me, and she stayed for the following three days and all of the nights except the last.

It is difficult after all these years to recapture so fleeting an experience; yet there are moments of it—good and bad—which are more vivid than any of my whole life.

If Elisia had a last name, I forgot it. Maybe she never told me. Maybe I never asked. She was Elisia; I was Joshua. It has been like that many times since. First names only.

Elisia's voice. To be sure. She said she was Polish. Her accent was quite pronounced, entrancingly so, or so it seemed to me. The voice was soft—even at the end, it was soft—and with an incredible range. One of the pleasantest voices I ever encountered—until Charley's.

She was beautiful—tall, blond, and blue eyes so dark that they sometimes seemed to be black.

I have mentioned, too, that she had a kind of queenly grace. She walked as if she had invented walking, as if all the people up to then had just somehow managed to get from one place to another. Elisia had found you could make an art out of it.

I would lie in bed watching her. "Would you mind walking?" I would say. "I like to watch you."

Except for what I did at the end, ours was not, I suppose, a very unusual wartime romance. But the intensity of it was something I had not known before and have not since. As if love-making had begun with us. As if, when we were done with it for the last time, no one would ever again reach such a peak of joy.

It seems to me that for the first twenty-four hours we did nothing but make love and laugh at what we felt was inspired non-sense and then make love again. Those twenty climactic, passionate moments I mentioned earlier occurred during this period.

Elisia knew that the invasion was not far off; everybody in the world knew that, and she knew that I would be part of it.

Later, we walked through the grim streets, holding hands, and talking, and several times we stopped in chapels and prayed. She was Catholic.

I told Elisia something about myself, and I said I wanted to know all about her, each breathing moment. She was a Polish princess, she said, and she talked about the great halls of the castle in which she had been born, about the gardens, about the huge forests on the estate, about the parties, about the governesses, and then about the sister who had been killed in an air raid, about the brother shot by the Nazis, about the mother who had disappeared when the Germans came, no one knew where. She talked about how she had been raped a dozen times the day the soldiers came and how, after many delays, she arrived at a camp near the Swiss border and how one morning, with the help of a nun, she had escaped into Switzerland, and how, along with several Polish soldiers, she had been smuggled into England.

I've not forgotten a detail of what Elisia told me. As she spoke, I managed for the first time in months not to think about the fact that I was about to jump into France.

I never told Elisia that our third night together would be the last, but she knew, I think, and on the final afternoon, after a long walk, we stopped at St. Martin's and prayed once more.

She left me there. I had given her some money, and she was going to buy what she could to make the last dinner one that we both would remember.

I watched her go, loving her more than I had dreamed possible. I left the chapel some time later and walked some more. I wanted to buy her a farewell gift, but that wasn't easy in those days. The stores were bare and desolate-looking.

I finally stopped at that old reliable, a book store, Foyle's. I looked through several books, and then I picked up a recently published one called—let's say—*Polish Princess*. I didn't have to read much to see that there was Elisia's whole story. She had appropriated every detail of it, some of it word for word.

I bought the book, and, as has happened so many times since, I stood outside myself, watching myself prepare to destroy something precious. Knowing that something of myself would be destroyed, too, but incapable of stopping myself.

I felt the fresh flow of adrenalin in my veins; I felt the blood rush to my face; I felt the stronger, more emphatic beat of my heart; I felt my throat go dry.

Then, book in hand, I got in a taxi and returned to the hotel.

Elisia had gone to wherever she lived and had changed her clothes. She was wearing a beautiful dinner dress, deep red and expensive-looking. She wore long, pearl earrings. There was champagne in ice on the table, and someplace she had found a tiny jar of paté.

When I came in the room, she looked up at me and smiled.

"We'll have a banquet, like the old days," she said.

My hand threw the book on the table.

"What page did you steal that line from?" I asked.

Elisia looked at the book, and her face went white. She drew her breath in quickly, and then both a moan and a sob tore at her. Even her wide, warm mouth had lost its color.

"Couldn't you at least have done me the courtesy of thinking up an original story?" I asked.

"Why did you do that?" asked Elisia. "Why did you have to do that?"

A wild look came into her eyes, and she got her coat.

"You're in the wrong army," she said. "I don't care what color your uniform is. You're one of the enemy."

I took a step toward her. "I shouldn't have said it," I said. "I'm sorry. I don't care who you are. I love you."

A scream escaped from her throat, and there were tears in the distraught blue eyes.

"Lisa," I said. "I'm frightened. I don't want to die."

"I hope you do," she said. "I very much hope you do. I hope you are killed by your own men. It would be just."

She ran out of the room, not closing the door, and I heard her savage steps as she ran down the hall.

I picked up the book and went to the door. I threw the book after her. "Here," I said. "You may want to brush up on your lies before you tell them again."

The elevator came, and before she entered it, she looked at me once more, and I realized that I had taken from her something which—for whatever reason—she had had to have to survive.

Knowing that, what did I do?

I went back into the hotel room, and with damp, trembling hands packed my bag. I smashed the bottle of champagne, and then I left the room. The book was still on the floor in the hallway; I started to pick it up and then changed my mind.

Was there one day in all my life when I was kind? Can anyone tell me that? One day in all those many days when I was kind to everyone I met and saw?

If there were evidence of it, I think They might stop torturing me.

There would have to be documents, of course; statements would have to be sworn to, and I'm sure those able to swear to such statements—if there were ever any such—are dead now or someplace far beyond reach.

Besides, even if such affidavits were possible, they would no doubt be dismissed as inconclusive.

You can see how difficult such a thing would be. Impossible, really.

No. I must wait.

What I don't understand is why They must watch me in the meantime. What good does it do? This thing in my head records my every movement, every thought I have. Why do they have to watch, too?

Are there shifts of Them, do you suppose? And do They know that I am aware of their presence? Perhaps They don't care. Those people often don't.

It is the same with asking Their names. They usually won't tell you, and They treat the question itself with a shrug of impatience. Should you persist with what is, after all, a perfectly logical, even essential inquiry, They will push at you and say come along now let's not make any trouble or We'll have to speak to him about you. The use of the word *him* is very interesting in this context because They will not identify *him*, and if you persist They will tell you that you know who They mean but you do not know.

I remember once when I insisted on knowing, a woman slapped me. I know she did, although later no one would believe me when I said so.

My enemy must have immense wealth and unlimited power. But is he (if it is a man) a stranger? Is he someone I have casually passed on the street and never met?

Or is it someone known to me, someone posing as a friend, a very close friend?

One thing is sure; I can trust no one.

I once thought I had guessed the identity of my enemy, and I shouted the name.

But then a man with a sword came, and there was pain, and the blackness followed.

Afterwards, I could not remember the name, and no one would tell me. It is very cleverly worked out, you see; even to the ringing of the bells. That too. I should have expected it.

What has happened is this. In addition to the wheels, They have put bells in the machine in my head, the same bells.

The din cannot be endured. It is quite unbearable, really. Quite.

Oh, my God, hast Thou abandoned me?

There were bells in the distant place in which X spent some time. They rang every afternoon at five.

X was in a gray room which the sun never reached. The room had no door, and from a single window came a bar of shadow that fell across his face late in the day, heavy there, binding him, like the chains which bound him to the hard, narrow cot. The chains sometimes were heavy and sometimes were not, but until the end there was no key to unlock them.

There was a picture on the wall which X remembered from somewhere else.

X could never make out what the picture was, though it was only an arm's length away. The picture sometimes pleased and sometimes annoyed and sometimes soothed and sometimes frightened him. It was at times familiar, at other times strange; often it was an enemy, and once—though he could not remember the circumstances—it was a friend.

The spot of red against the blue was the sun at high noon in a desert sky and was blood on the blue-white snow of a December day and was a face, sometimes threatening, and once—but when?—benign.

There were initials on one corner of the picture, but from where X lay he could not read them.

There was little else in the room, a chair the color of a distant forest fire or of a city in flames or of a house burning.

Sometimes a man sat on the red chair and looked at X and questioned him closely and tried to decide about the punishment.

There was a bureau in the room on which were a set of well-made brushes and a comb that could have been silver. There were initials on the backs of the brushes and on the silver comb if it was silver. X could not, however, decipher them because the chain across his throat made it impossible for him to raise his head.

But there was no mirror in the room, unless it was hidden someplace, which was likely. They often hid things, but X was determined not to look for the mirror, and he did not, nor did he ask about it.

For some time X did not speak at all. They had taken his voice along with his clothes when they brought him to the place.

In addition to the prosecutor if it was the prosecutor or the executioner if it was he, others came to the room.

They came dressed in blue and in white, and those who did not carry guns had spears in their hands, and some had sweaters that enveloped X. The ones with the spears and the sweaters were the most dangerous because they often smiled and spoke soft lies which had the ring of truth.

All of them were hale, and all of them were hearty, and all of them spoke as if to a child or someone dying. Except for her. She did not.

The other women were silly and ugly and loud and unpleasant; they often came in pairs, speaking of friends unknown to X and of lovers known only to themselves; they spoke of quarrels and of jealousy and of nothing. They spoke as if he were not present in the room.

Or, which was worse, they said of X not to X but to each other that X was looking well, that X would be up and around any day now, and they said that X was a sly one, and they said that X would have to give them tickets to the execution if it was the execution they spoke of, and they spoke of parts they had played which were different from the parts they were now playing.

X hated all of them, the women wearing white and the men dressed in blue and the man who sat on the flaming chair, making endless, damning notes. But he did not hate her. She, too, wore white, but she wore it with pride; the others smelled of death and drugs; she was surrounded by the odor of spring violets and of a rose from some far-off place X had dreamed of visiting. She had blue eyes and pink cheeks and lips that were red with health and good humor. She always said "Good afternoon" or "Good morning" or "Good evening," calling X mister and using the name they must have given him when he was brought into the place. He did not recognize the name.

"I'm Miss Lawrence," the woman said. She did not speak to him with a tone of condescension. She did not ask how he was, seeming to know; she did not tell him that *he* or *we* was or were feeling better. She did not ask if he wanted anything, her manner indicating that she was sure that when he did want something he would tell her.

X was sure that she would have pleasure in bringing him whatever it was that he wanted, but, though he tried, he could think of nothing.

When she left him, she said, "Good-bye. I'll see you tomorrow afternoon."

If it was Friday (and without her saying what she said X would not have known what day it was), she would say, "Good-bye. See you Monday."

He found himself looking forward to her visits during the long dead days he was in the place, and she reminded him of someone. He could not think who.

On an afternoon when there was almost sun in the tiny patch of sky and when there was the smell of spring and of promise in the air, she came in, saying, "Good afternoon, and isn't it really. So beautiful."

That was when the bell rang, as it did every day, usually while she was in the room, just before the bar of shadow came.

"Why does the bell ring?" he asked.

It must have been he. There was no one in the room except himself and Miss Lawrence. He was pleased with the question; it meant they had brought back his voice.

"Oh, that means it's time for people to come in from outside," she said.

"What people?" asked X. He was pleased with the sound of the voice, deep, not too loud, the voice of someone who heard other people; the voice was dry, though, as if They had kept it in a box, away from the air and light.

"The other patients," she said.

"This is a hospital then," said X, and questions marched into his head and stood at attention, waiting to be recognized.

"Partly that," she said, and she smiled, "and sort of a college and a country club. You'll see. Here you've been cooped up in this room; you'll see."

"Will they let me out?" he asked, too quickly, the note of impatience and eagerness too apparent. "I mean it would be pleasant," he said, slowly, covering up for his stupidity.

"Of course," she said. "At least I'm almost certain Dr. Baron will want you to be up and around. You'd just have to ask him."

He knew better than to ask who Dr. Baron was. It was that kind of question that would trap him.

"I certainly hope so," he said, keeping his tone noncommittal. "It would be nice."

Then he smiled, and he said, "You remind me of someone," and as he said the words he knew who. "Someone named Theresa."

"That's a very nice name," she said.

"What's yours?"

"Celeste," she said, "which I'm afraid means *heavenly*."

The demon beneath the cot screamed an awful scream, and X rose, pursued by the scream.

"You lie, you lie, you lie," someone shrieked. The voice was that of someone in agony.

The hag with the painted face backed quickly from the room.

The screaming went on and on; X thought it would never stop.

After the man with the sword had left, the executioner came and stood over X. With a traitorous leer, he said, "Miss Lawrence says you tried to hurt her. Now why should you want to do a foolish thing like that?"

And more and more and on and that, too, and we thought, and I hoped, and set back, and such progress, and that, and that, and now and such a good patient, and this.

X turned away from the executioner.

Someone had spilled drops of water beside him on the pillow, or else it was rain, or the dew.

The sky grew dark outside the window, and the light disappeared, and the sudden menacing wind screamed an epithet, and a bird shouted an obscenity.

X pulled the damp pillow over his head to shut out the sounds, and the orderly procession in his head became a howling mob.

Sometime later the executioner left, taking with him the voice, and X was alone once more, except at an arm's length away an inflamed eye stared at him from a sea of mucus.

The woman with the full red lips and the innocent blue eyes never returned, nor did the hag with the painted face.

The new one was plain and severe and had the broad body of a heavyweight. She had brown teeth and brown eyes, and she smelled of brown soap and brown bottles of disinfectant. She had stubby yellow fingers and a network of green veins circled the short, shapeless legs.

"My name is Helen Pound," she said, "and I brook no nonsense from my patients. Is that clear?"

"Brook," said X.

Then he said:

> By brooks too broad for leaping
> The lightfoot boys are laid;
> The rose-lipt girls are sleeping
> In fields where roses fade.

"No nonsense," she said a second time.

X never spoke to her again; it was weeks before the voice was returned again, and there was never any mirror in the room.

The bells continued, however, and at times, hearing the whispers and the short, sharp bursts of laughter outside his window, X wished he could join the members of the country club, if it was that, or the students at the college, if it was a college.

The man who sat in the vermilion chair began to smile, and after a while the executioner stopped coming.

There was a picture on the wall, a child's toy balloon, red, in a baby-blue sky.

I was outside when the telephone rang.

By the time I got back to the house, whoever it was had hung up. I have a feeling it may have been George, to say that he and Russell are starting.

Well, no matter. If they have just started, they'll be here in a little less than three hours. Plenty of time for the rag-ends of observation and recall still ahead.

I have just come back from a short walk, and this is where some slight confusion occurs.

I looked at the clock before I slid open the glass panel; I do remember that. It was then shortly after one, or so I thought. I am surely mistaken, though, because I don't believe I could have been out of the house more than five minutes, maybe ten. Yet, when I limped back in here, it was almost two.

I think what happened is this. The fall I'm about to tell about caused me to black out temporarily; thus, the confusion.

In any case, as I slid open the glass panel to go outside, there was a short, impatient mumble of thunder, and then a streak of lightning tore at the sky.

Suddenly, from deep in the woods, I heard Ab howl. It was a howl of anguish, not of triumph, and as the rain began, I started to run toward the sound.

As I ran through the woods, shouting for Ab, vengeful branches of larch and beech trees reached for me, their sharp claws tearing angrily at my face.

Once I stumbled and fell into a bed of poison ivy. I righted myself and ran on.

A little further on, my left foot sank into the grasping mud of the almost dry stream bed north of the house.

I went on, but, after a dozen or so steps, my left ankle turned in a lurking rabbit hole, and I could run no more.

By that time it was raining hard.

I lay on the ground for a while, my head in the quickly dampening grass and weeds. As I say, it is not impossible that I blacked out for a few minutes.

In any case, after however long it was, Ab ran up to me, his right paw carried off the ground and bleeding. He must have cut it on a piece of broken glass. There are no traps in these woods.

I finally found the strength to rise, and Ab and I, two cripples, made it back here to the house.

I was on the deck when I realized that the ringing in my ears which I had thought was caused by the fall was really the telephone.

By the time I picked up the receiver, whoever it was had, as I told you, hung up.

Well. I must continue.

There are only three tapes left. I had thought there were four. I guess I finished the previous one in describing my last evening with Elisia.

I have been at this damnable dictating for so long now that I go through certain motions automatically. I don't remember taking that tape off the machine or putting this one on.

Unless, of course, there has been someone in this room.

I have washed Ab's paw. The cut is small and deep, and I put some iodine on it. He moaned with the smart of the pain, but now he is asleep at my feet.

I put a kettle of water on to heat, and I have locked all the doors. Just to be safe. Have I said that I now carry all the keys in a ring attached to my belt?

It is difficult for me to keep track of what I have and have not mentioned.

There is also a certain confusion about time in my mind. I must be extremely careful while George and Russell are here. The least said the better.

I dried myself and changed my clothes, and now I am soaking my ankle. The scratches on my face are hardly noticeable.

Three tapes. I must use them to advantage.

I could write a whole book about my experiences from the June night when we landed in France until the February day in Alsace when the war ended for me.

But I have almost nothing more to say about combat. Better men than I have said it, yet have not said it, not even the best of them, not even Shakespeare, who romanticized it.

I remember Nick once said, "I don't like to take issue with Henry the Fifth, but have you ever given any really careful thought to that speech about St. Crispin's Day? 'The fewer men, the greater share of honor'? *Kings* always talk like that, but I'll bet there wasn't another man on the battlefield—at least none under the rank of duke—who wouldn't have settled for a little less honor and a few more men. I have a feeling that honor on the battlefield is one of the few things everybody is willing and even anxious to share. 'We few—we happy few.' Myself, in situations like that, I always say, the more the merrier. We happier many."

Even Tolstoy. The peace parts of that book. Wonderful. Reading them, you say to yourself, "I was never there, and I don't know anybody who was in Russia at the time, but I *know* that's the way it was." I never can figure out how or why I know, but I always get a strange, wonderful stirring in my stomach or gut area when I read such truth.

But the war parts of the Count's book. Nope. Not for me. Not a stir and no more feeling of validity than the accounts of D-Day written from the Dorchester Hotel in London.

Occasionally in a letter home a literate enlisted man or a sensitive junior officer would get it down right. Once in a moment of postwar optimism I got together a collection of such letters. They were published shortly after the President then in Wonderland fired the General then in charge of things in Korea. The book sold about nine hundred copies. It made dandy Christmas cards that year—twenty-nine cents each, remaindered. I sent out more than a thousand, and there are still a good many in that closet over there.

That's all. Except for Nick's letter, a few paragraphs hence.

My own war ended in February 1945, not long after I got a battlefield commission. I was wounded on a mission in Alsace which was like any other mission, except that it was safer than most. We lost very few men in Alsace.

I reached a house on a side street before the others. The house was deserted; we all knew that, but the deserted house, like the shotgun that isn't loaded, is the most dangerous.

There was a wounded SS lieutenant in an upstairs bedroom. He fired and hit me in the left leg. I then fired three times, and I thought he was dead. I went to the bed, but there was just enough life in him for him to be able to raise himself, lift a bayonet, and slash my cheek.

Happy (Arthur) Sullivan fired a fourth, final shot into the lieutenant's head. I might have done that if I hadn't fainted at the sight of my own blood.

That night I was evacuated to a rear-echelon hospital, thus ending my physical participation in the last of the old-fashioned Marquess-of-Queensberry wars.

The captain in the Medics who took twenty stitches in my cheek was pretty well gone at the time he did it—on Calvados, as I recall. The captain, who when I first knew him had been an apple-cheeked graduate of the University of Iowa school of medicine with maybe a year as a G.P. behind him, had started laying into the booze since he had presided over a human barbecue at Bastogne some weeks before.

In any case, his condition accounts for an inept stitching job on my cheek and that in turn accounts for the scar.

This further note on the captain. In July, at Berchtesgaden, where our outfit was then stationed, the captain, using some kind of surgical instrument, killed himself. I heard from somebody that he made more than a hundred cuts on his body. It must have taken him quite a long time to die, and he must have wanted it that way and wanted a maximum of pain as he did it. I think I know why.

As I believe I have already said, Nick was killed shortly after the battle for Bastogne was over. It happened when we were on a mission not far outside the gates of that town. He was decapitated by an eighty-eight.

I wrote Susan, telling her as much as I thought she would want to know about what happened. I also sent along the letter that Nick had written to Aristotle; it was in his jacket.

Susan's answer to my letter said, "...I feel as if part of myself had died, and so must you."

I felt more than that. As I've indicated, I felt that Nick had died my death for me. Because when I first heard the sickening whine of the eighty-eight, I ran.

This is the letter Nick wrote his son three days before his death:

Dearest Aristotle:

The Stars and Stripes has arrived, and already what has happened here at Bastogne is being written about in terms of a U.S.C. football game. *Already.* Some ex-sports reporter wrote in Paris that at the beginning of the battle, one of us said, "They've got us surrounded—the poor bastards."

Believe me, no one said that.

I expect that what has happened in this town will become one of those legends which are among the greatest enemies of civilization.

When the Germans demanded that we surrender, our general said, "Nuts," and I imagine that will become part of the standard Fourth of July repertoire.

I wish the general's answer had been less colorful.

You may wonder whether I am not proud to have been in such a battle. No, not proud. To be sure, it was necessary for us to hold this town; when a war is allowed to happen, you must win it, but there is no pride in me. I am ashamed of many things that happened here. I am ashamed of almost all I have done since I landed in France.

What I did in Normandy and in Holland and now here is a denial of everything I have tried to teach you—a denial of love, of compassion, of human dignity, of life.

It seems to me there will always be wars unless, when they are over, the victor says with the vanquished, We have done an evil thing. Together. We are all guilty.

Whitman said—I am the man. I suffered. I was there.

Yes, I am the man. I suffered. I was here.

Should I not survive this war, I hope you will never forget that the man for whom you are named believed that the duty of man is to devote himself to great ends.

With love to you and your mother,

Two years ago, I made the painful, necessary journey back to Bastogne.

I visited the graves of Nick and Colonel Julian and several of many other friends who died there. The cemetery is well kept, with flowers on many of the graves, placed there either by Belgians or American tourists. I wasn't sure.

I saw the monument just outside the town. On its base:

...Seldom has more American blood been shed in the course of a single action.

The monument is simple, beautiful as such things go, but if I could have, I would have torn it down with my bare hands and erected another statue outside Bastogne—a statue of the bloody, headless thing that was left when an eighty-eight had done with my friend.

On the day I was in Bastogne, Germans were everywhere, taking endless pictures and pointing out where they had done their noble deeds.

I was in Paris in a general hospital on the day the war in Europe ended. I felt relieved, weary, done in; I felt a vague lassitude that lasted for months. I felt a great sorrow at all the waste; I thought what a pity that I was alive while Nick, a better and more valuable man than I would ever be, was dead; I felt ashamed to be alive, and then, of course, I admitted I was glad.

I looked at the photograph of a small, rather pretty baby named Taffy whose picture Letty had sent me. I told myself I was pleased that I had a daughter, but then I stopped lying. I was not pleased. I could not pretend that Taffy had been conceived in love, and I could not tell myself the lie that her existence would help me love Letty or help Letty love or even tolerate me.

I thought, "I am one of those who have created, even if it be but a world of agony."

I thought, I will never have to jump out of an airplane again, and I will never have to fire a gun or toss a hand grenade, or sleep in the mud, or lie in the snow, or smell a putrefying body, or kill a man. I will never again hear the sound of a gun being fired by an enemy, or the whine of a bullet aimed at me—that incredible sound: You're shooting at *me*? You mean you want *me* to die?

I thought for the rest of my life I will probably never be as good a man as I was in the war, never so hard, never so disciplined, never so selfless.

I had often been selfless since the day I reported at Camp Tuckahoe, since I met a selfless man named Julian and another named Nick Continos, both selflessly and unavoidably dead. I thought, I selflessly jumped out of an airplane when I was selfishly scared. I thought, I selflessly landed in France. I thought, Selflessly I killed men in Normandy and Holland and Belgium and Germany, always selfishly afraid and ashamed. I thought, Oh Lord, let me somehow, sometime be selfless again.

I thought, Oh God, help me to love my daughter, help me to be kind to her; I thought, Oh God, help me to endure with patience the woman I married.

On that day the balconies of the hospital were crowded with men looking down at the exuberant mobs on the street and up at the planes dropping flares in celebration.

Sidney Levinson, Major, Med. Det., stopped by to talk with me, and a little later a man in a wheel chair paused by my bed, handing me a bottle of cognac. Both Sidney and I drank from it.

The man who had no legs and only one arm, said, "I hear that sonofabitch is dead." He meant Hitler.

Then he said, "Well, I hope the bastard was as scared as I was when the SS got at me," and then he said, "I wish it had been a little slower," and then he said, "You guys in the Bulge?"

I said that I was.

"Well, sir," said the man in the wheel chair, "we were cut off in this little town, and it was cold as hell. There was snow on the ground, and I was lying in the snow in a gully when I saw a German officer and six other Krauts start running from one side of a field to the other side about two hundred yards in front of me. I had the officer in the sights of my M-1 just when he started climbing over a fence. I squeezed the trigger, and this Kraut just kind of folded across the fence, pressing his hands against his belly and screaming real high-pitched, like a hurt rabbit. I stood that for about five minutes; then I shot the bastard again, and he stopped yelling."

He paused, thoughtfully. "You know," he said, "that was the first time I ever killed a man on Christmas day."

Then he wheeled himself off.

After a moment of silence, Sid said, "I'm going to get us a magnum of champagne."

Later, when the magnum was almost gone, they started singing "God Bless America," but Sid and I didn't join in. Not that day.

A few days later, a general came to the hospital and gave me a medal and read a citation.

The general was the one who had oranges flown in from North Africa for his senior officers' mess.

In the summer of that year, wearing a brand-new beard and a limp, I made a journey across Europe on assignment from the Historical Division of the Army. I visited many cities, or what was left of many cities, and it was always the same city. I wrote a series of widely published magazine articles describing what I saw.

I do not apologize for those articles, but another man in an outfit like mine said it better, in one paragraph:

We who had fought this war could feel no pride. Victors and vanquished, all were one. We were one with the crowds moving silently along the boulevards of Paris, the old women hunting through the still ruins of Cologne, the bodies piled like yellow cordwood at Dachau, the dreadful vacant eyes of the beaten German soldiers, the white graves and the black crosses and the haunting melancholy of our hearts. All, all were one; all were the ghastly horrors of what we had known, of what we had helped to do. [14]

By August, it became impossible to avoid going back to the States.

I was at Camp Lucky Strike waiting for transportation back when the atom bomb was dropped on Hiroshima. I didn't leave my tent for nearly forty-eight hours.

I cannot now even begin to recapture the horror I felt, but I can honestly say that I experienced such a sense of shame and guilt and revulsion that, if I had known how, I believe I would have renounced my citizenship.

---

14   Laurence Critchell. *Four Stars in Hell.*

At another time, in another place, what my country had done would not, I suppose, have shocked me any more than it did most Americans, but having just finished a pilgrimage across a continent of carnage, the decision to add such an awful magnitude to war seemed to me indefensible; for that matter, it still does. I never forgave the strutting little man responsible.

What's that you say, Ab? You say he meant well.

Well, don't say it to me.

Most of the trouble in the world is caused by well-meaning small men.

The gesture of protest I made at Lucky Strike seems rather juvenile in retrospect, but it's one of the few deeds of my life for which I have no apologies. I returned my medal to the War Department, along with a letter. The letter compared our crime with the crimes of Buchenwald and Dachau and Auschwitz.

A reporter for one of the networks was visiting Lucky Strike at the time, and I got the letter to him. It created quite an uproar. There was some talk in Wonderland of court-martialing me, but that was all it ever came to—talk.

As a result of the hullabaloo, I became a pariah at Lucky Strike. Most of the men there either had no feeling at all about the bomb or were understandably grateful for its ending the war. These were men who had been all over Europe, but they had learned nothing. They might as well never have left Oskaloosa. Except, of course, for the brief, joyous pleasure some of them had had in meeting the Germans. Most soldiers *loved* the Germans—couldn't *stand* the British, the French, the Italians, the Wogs, etc.

Half of Lucky Strike concluded that I was bucking for a Section Eight; the other half that I was a Communist, particularly those clerk-typists and loafers in the Finance Department who thought our Infantry ought to have pushed right on to Moscow.

My letter did have one happy result, though. As a result of it an Army sergeant from Bismarck, North Dakota, came to my tent late one afternoon. He was a tall, loose-jointed boy with deep dark eyes and something in him that saints and the greatest artists must have. Jesus must have had it. *Innocence? Incorruptibility? Purity?*

I don't know; I just know that he was without any of the defenses most of us surround ourselves with to keep from getting hurt too much.

I will call him The Playwright. He had an enormous package under one arm, and he stood in the doorway of my tent for a minute, holding his overseas cap in one large, brown hand.

"I beg your pardon, sir," he said. "I read in *The Stars and Stripes* about what you did."

"Are you going to hit me or pat me on the back?" I said.

"The latter, sir," said the Playwright, and then he pushed the package, which was wrapped in grease-stained brown paper, toward me.

"Is it a book?" I asked. "*The Rover Boys at Normandy Beach* or *D-Day Was Fun*? Or is it one of the serious ones with all the four-letter words?"

The Playwright's face reddened, and he reached for the package. "I'm sorry I bothered you," he said.

"I'm sorry," I said, keeping the package out of his reach. "I suffer from running off at the mouth."

I untied the package. Inside was a manuscript, written with a pen in a large, loose, readable hand, largely on lined tablet paper. It was held together by paper clips, and on the first page were the words, "*My Enemy Is Dead!* A Play in Five Acts by Laurence L. Powell."

I looked up at the open face of the sergeant; he had the naked, hopeful look of a newly delivered mother whose baby was about to be judged. It was a look I have come to know very well. It is one that all good writers have when you are about to examine their work. Many bad writers have it, too, often a little more so.

"Of course I'll read it," I said. "Of course, five acts—"

"Shakespeare liked five acts," said the Playwright.

"What's the title—a quote?"

"Whitman," he said:

Beautiful that war and all its deeds of courage must in time be utterly lost,
That the hands of the sisters Death and Night incessantly softly wash
again and ever again this soiled world;
For my enemy is dead, a man divine as myself is dead.

He paused, and then with a smile that held nothing back, he said, "I'm not at all sure it is a play. For one thing I've never seen a real play."

"Surely you're joking."

"No. Well, not in New York anyway," The Playwright said. "I never got to New York before we got shipped. However, I saw Helen Hayes in *Harriet* in Omaha. And I played the lead in my senior class play, *Craig's Wife*. I was Craig."

"But surely you've *read* a play or two."

"Oh, yes. Just about every play ever published. Especially the Greeks."

I smiled for the first time in days. I said, "What's *My Enemy Is Dead* all about?"

I didn't know it at the time, but that's the one that always gets them. "Well," they say, "it's about this guy, see—"

It didn't get The Playwright, though. He said, "It's about the sovereignty of the individual in war."

"Oh, I like that," I said. "I like that very much."

The subject was one I'd given a great deal of thought to. I had wondered what I would have done if I had been a member of the crew that dropped the bomb—either the one on Hiroshima or the one at Nagasaki. Would I have refused? Probably not. If I had been a German, would I have been one of the many who refused to admit either any guilt or any responsibility for what had happened in the previous fifteen years? Probably.

"I don't promise to like your play just because I like the subject, though," I said.

"You'll like it," said The Playwright. "It's a good play."

I did like the play. I liked it so much that I decided I wanted to have something to do with seeing that it got on the stage without mangling. Since I had no talent for, or training in, the theater, I decided to become a producer. I didn't know exactly what a producer did, but I had met one the night I was at Proudly Presents' place, one of the outstanding frauds on hand that fraudulent evening. I decided that if that fellow could do it, so could I.

It may seem odd that what turned out to be such a major decision in my life was made so casually. I don't think so. As I've said, people delude themselves if they think that they have much control over what happens to them.

I became a producer because in a particular place at a particular time a man brought me a play—and because I liked it.

I hadn't up to then been giving much thought to what I was going to do after the war. In combat, I had lived from second to second, with no past and no future. In the hospital I had been too tired to give much thought to the future, and on my pilgrimage to the ruins of Europe, I had been too depressed.

By the time I got to Camp Lucky Strike, it was obvious that I had to go home, that I had a daughter to support and a wife to maintain in a style that wasn't even dreamed of in the place she was born and raised. The money from The Book was still pouring in, but that wasn't going to last forever.

The theater looked to me like a place in which I could maybe make a fast buck—and possibly say something at the same time.

Anyway, when I got back to New York from overseas in late August, just fourteen years ago now, George Banning was at the dock to meet me.

He embraced me; he congratulated me on the beard, and he said, "You look enough like Jesus H. Christ to be his kid brother, and now what?"

I said, "George, what does a theatrical producer do?"

"Most of them are lucky if they stay out of jail," said George. "Why do you ask?"

"Because I'm planning to become one," I said.

George said, "Oh, my God. Combat fatigue. You're joking, of course."

"No," I said. "I have in my B-4 bag a play in five acts that will win all the prizes and also happens to be moving and honest—"

"Moving," said George. "*Honest.* Now I see what they mean when they say you soldiers talk dirty."

"Moving and honest, and I am going to produce it."

"Oh, my God," said George. "You are a masochist."

I did produce the play, and it became enormously successful, critically and financially. It ran for more than two years, its popularity greatly enhanced by the fact that the harridans in the D.A.R. passed their usual resolution denouncing it; Westbrook Pegler called on J. Edgar Hoover to stop it; and Hoover's people said they'd be glad to, only they needed more money. Their Congressional appropriation was doubled the next year. The bulging adolescents in the American Legion had a picket line in front of the theater for several months, and twice I got letters from lunatics who threatened to blow up the theater.

This much more about The Playwright. When he came to New York, after a brief post-Army vacation on his father's wheat farm in North Dakota, George presented him with a contract, which he signed without bothering with the small print.

When we were ready to go to work on his second play, I took him to lunch at Sardi's. He was wearing a suit woven by some nuns in Irkutsk out of the thread left over when they had finished the Emperor's Robe. His shoes were made of llama skin and had to be thrown away after one wearing.

He twice sent back his Eggs Benedict; once they were too hard, and once they were too soft.

When two maiden ladies from Grand Rapids came up to tell him how much they had liked My Enemy Is Dead, he sighed the sigh of the put-upon. "My God, will I never be allowed a moment's peace?" he said.

I told him that one of the theater's most talented young directors, a chap who had only been thirty years old for about four years, was interested in the new play. The Playwright said, "That has-been. I should think he would be."

Over the coffee, he said, "Okay, Bland. Let's you and me talk turkey. Now if you and Banning think for one minute you're going to get away with highway robbery the way you did last time you've got another think coming."

That's about enough.

I will mention The Playwright only once more in what little is left of this narrative. He has gone a long way from Camp Lucky Strike and from his father's farm near Bismarck, but whether that journey has been up, down, or sideways, you couldn't prove by me.

To get back to the time immediately following the Second World War, I've said that George came to meet me when I got back to New York.

Letty was, to use a word loosely, waiting for me in the Park Avenue apartment with Taffy, then not quite a year old. She was a pretty baby, and as I awkwardly held her in my arms, I tried to feel proud, but I didn't. I felt fear and shame, and, of course, I was afraid I would drop her.

When the nurse took her from me, I was relieved.

Not very much later I went to the first of the several analysts I've consulted. I reported in three times a week for almost two years. Very often I had two or three Martinis before arriving at Dr. Wyatt's office. It was during this period that I started changing from a man who occasionally drinks a little too much to a morose heavy drinker. The sullen alcoholic came later.

At the end of two years, Dr. Wyatt dismissed me. He said I was wasting the time of both of us, and my money, and that if I ever seriously decided to be analyzed, he was in the phone book.

I kept trying with Taffy, but I never got remotely close to her. I used to try to blame my failure on the war and on the fact that I hadn't been with her during the first crucial months of her life, but I knew better than that. I knew that millions of men had come home to babies they had never seen and that they loved the babies and were loved. I am not much for intuition, but I felt then that the tiny, blue-eyed assortment of flesh and skin and bones sensed my disquiet. But then who knows? Who ever knows?

I remember this. Taffy was a very self-contained baby just as she is now a very self-contained girl. She seldom cried, but on those rare occasions when she did, I used to go to her room and sit beside her crib. I never stopped her from crying, though; she seemed to cry her fill, and then she would turn away from me and fall asleep.

Letty never heard her cry; Letty had become a two-pill-a-night woman.

My relationship with Letty after I got back from the war was neither better nor worse than it had been before I went.

At dinner the first night Letty at one point said, "Why in the world did you grow a beard?"

"In the hospital it was easier not to shave, and, besides, I've always hated shaving."

"Well, I've always hated beards, and if the truth were known, I think there might be an explanation a little more basic than that for your growing it."

Later that first night, she said, "You certainly took your time about getting back."

I said, "I'm sorry I didn't get killed, Letty. Next war I'll try harder."

Then, as had happened many times before and as would happen many times again, Letty started crying, and she came to kiss me, and for a while we simulated love.

I was seldom home in the months that followed. I produced three plays that year, all three extremely successful. It never happened again.

A week or so after I got back from overseas I went to Washington to see Nick's widow and his son. Susan had taken a small apartment there, and she had a job in the book department at Woodward and Lothrop.

When I called her at the store, she sounded pleasant but a little annoyed, as if I had interrupted her in the midst of something important.

She asked me to come by the apartment, which was on Connecticut Avenue.

"Sixish," she said.

Susan kissed me when I arrived, but there seemed to be a coolness in her manner. At first, I thought I imagined it, but then I realized I hadn't.

I didn't know the reason until later.

She looked more than a year and a half older. There were purple shadows under her eyes; she had put on a few pounds around the waist and hips, and the sheer joy of being alive that she and Nick had both had was gone. Nevertheless, she still looked illegally beautiful.... If you want the truth, and at this late hour it seems foolish to withhold this final measure of my humiliation, I had hoped that perhaps Susan might fall in love with me. I cringe as I say it, but I have said it. I hoped that Susan and I might get married. I thought that I would take Taffy and—Oh, yes. I know precisely what my wish means. It has been clinically analyzed by myself and by experts....

Aristotle came in a few minutes after I got there, a small, serious boy of four with very dark skin and curly dark hair that needed cutting.

He didn't remember me, and I could think of nothing to say to him. He had a toy model of a B-24, and he was bombing the living-room rug with it. "Whoosh," he would say. "Whoosh. I'm leveling their cities, Mom."

I thought of Nick's hatred of toy guns and lead soldiers and what he called "the whole, subtle, profitable, successful preparation of another generation of boys willing and anxious to die gallantly for some senseless cause or other."

Susan said, "Art, you'd better get washed up for supper."

He nodded politely and went off.

"Art's what they call him at school," said Susan. "You know what lousy little conformists kids are. Anyway, I've bowed to the inevitable. Don't you think that's the best thing?"

I said that it unquestionably was.

Susan took my glass and made me another drink.

"I haven't shown Art the letter," she said, handing me the drink. "I asked—several people, and they seemed to feel he was pretty young."

"I've got Nick's Thucydides and his lighter," I said. "I knew he'd want you—and the boy to have them."

"No," said Susan. "I don't want them. Does that shock you?"

"No. I don't guess so."

She seated herself in a shabby, overstuffed chair that was a considerable distance from the couch I was sitting on.

"I've tried to forget Nick," she said. "Isn't that the best thing, don't you think?"

I said that it unquestionably was.

"I couldn't cry when the telegram came. Or when I got your letter. I think I was even relieved that it was over. I knew Nick would be killed. He asked so much of himself and of everybody else. But I couldn't cry. That's why I didn't go back to California. Everything would have reminded me, and I've got to go on living, and so has Aristotle. Don't you think that's true?"

I started to say that it unquestionably was, and then the doorbell rang, and Susan admitted one of those very young Air Force lieutenant-colonels.

Colonel Cranston was tall, blond, and very assured. He impressed me as the kind of man who had been born knowing all he needed to know about himself and able to cope with what he knew. He was a bomber pilot, and his chest was covered with ribbons he had been awarded for services performed in the South Pacific. Several of the ribbons had meaning.

He was from Pasadena, and he had known Susan when he was a senior in high school and she was a junior in college.

"Old enough to be his mother," said Susan, and I had the feeling that if I hadn't been there she'd have kissed him. The colonel struck me as a man who would never demand the impossible, of himself or anyone else.

The colonel, whose first name was Don, said that he had not known Nick.

"He was older than me, and besides, he wasn't the kind of guy—well, to tell you the truth Nick was the kind of guy that gives me the heebie-jeebies. I don't know why."

It turned out the colonel was what he called "one of your Army brats." His people, he added, had been graduated from the Point for several generations. Three, to be exact.

He had read about my returning my decoration to the War Department. "My father was very upset," he said, pleasantly enough. "He said it's a good thing not everybody does something like that."

His father was in G-2, a major general.

"Dropping that bomb saved a lot of American lives," said the colonel. "I guess you had to be out in the Pacific to understand that."

He wasn't being rude or critical. He was simply explaining; he was thinking, slowly and aloud.

"I suppose if Nick had been around, he'd have done some crazy thing like that," said the colonel.

I had one more drink, which the colonel fixed. Susan didn't have to tell him in which cupboard in the kitchen she kept the liquor.

While he got into the bourbon he went into a long, reasonably articulate monologue concerned with who in the State Department was responsible for preventing our army from going straight into Berlin and then beyond into Stalingrad. He was wrong about who was responsible for the decision about Berlin, but I didn't mention it.

Susan listened to his every word with the same devoted attention she had always had for what Nick said, and when I rose to leave, she seemed also to have forgotten I was there. She was, as Nick had once rightly observed, a one-man woman, one at a time.

She said she would call Art in for me to say good-bye, but I told her that was not necessary. I said I didn't want to interrupt his homework. She said something about now that I knew the way, and I said, sure thing, I'd let her know the very next time I was in town, but we both knew we were saying our last good-bye.

I had meant to tell her that if she needed anything, with Art in school and all, but with Colonel Cranston there, such an offer did not seem necessary.

The colonel gave me a hard, glad-to-have-met-you handshake.

When Susan and the colonel were married, about six months later, I was in England. I sent them a pair of silver candlesticks which I got at a shop near Regent Street. They were almost exactly like a pair Nick had wanted to buy once when we were in London on leave. He couldn't afford them at the time.

The colonel was shot down in the Korean War, just beyond the Yalu River. He was one of the few—if not the only—West Point graduate who broadcast for the Chinese. After his release, he resigned his commission. He and Susan are now back in Pasadena, and he has an important job at an aircraft factory.

(You must understand I do not blame the colonel for the broadcasts. Isn't there a Hebrew saying, something about how you must not condemn a man until you have stood where he has stood? I should have remembered that more often in my life....)

I have often wondered if Aristotle ever read the letter his father sent him. Aristotle will enter West Point this fall.

I have mentioned this great disarray about time. Some time has passed since I dictated that about Aristotle at West Point. How much I don't know.

After I had finished, I decided to do what I should have done years ago. I went to the woods and buried Nick's cigarette lighter. Or thought I did.

The man in the woods—if there has ever been a man in the woods—was gone. I felt sure of it. I watched and waited for several minutes. The slightest movement would have betrayed him because the air was still as death. Not a shadow stirred anywhere. There was not even the sound of a breath withheld. For a moment the steel band around my head felt lighter than usual.

Can you understand the feeling I had? How for one part of a moment I was able to feel that hope was possible once more?

Then I covered the mound where I had put the lighter. The sharpest eye could not have detected the spot.

I came back into this house immediately. I am sure it was immediately. I locked all of the doors again. Then I looked from behind the curtains to see if anyone was watching the house. No one.

I tested all the doors a second time. They were still locked. As I've said, I now carry the keys at my waist; the keys were still there.

And yet this—

Despite all the precautions I have described, someone has been in the house, some enemy of mine. Someone watched me bury that lighter, and then someone dug it up and brought it into this room.

The lighter is there now, on that table, no more than three feet from this desk. It is beside what might at first appear to be an innocent, half-smoked pack of cigarettes. They happen to be an English brand I never smoke, which, in fact, I detest. But the cigarettes are unimportant. They are only a malicious caprice of Theirs.

It is the lighter They want me to see.

It is a common enough lighter, but it has one distinction that is its alone. There is the spot on it that looks like blood but is not blood. That's how I know that the lighter I buried in the woods not fifteen minutes ago is now back in this room.

Oh, They are clever, these people, these enemies of mine.

I could give endless examples, but one will do. I have had all the locks on the doors in this house changed—within the not-too-distant past. Yet They always get in, and They always leave behind some fiendish evidence of Their having been here.

The lighter, for one thing. And the half-smoked pack of cigarettes. It can be there for only one purpose, to remind me of someone I betrayed.

Elisia smoked that brand of cigarettes.

The whole thing has some purpose in Their plan, but what?

I know They will come, soon, I think. But in the meantime why can't They let me alone? Why must They continually remind me that I am under surveillance?

And why in such diabolical ways?

Two memories more, only two. There are only these two tapes left.

Hurriedly then. There is someone coming this afternoon. George, I think, and Russell. I have papers to sign. After that, they will leave, thinking I am about to take a journey to the ends of the earth.

At the hour I would be boarding that plane, I shall take the fifty pills.

I need that eternity of sleep. My bones ache with fatigue, and a little while ago I found myself crying, over nothing, I think. Or at the waste of me and the decay of me. I can't remember.

I've mentioned The Crusaders several times in this narrative.

I came back from Europe, having not yet renounced optimism, determined that the death of men like Nick must somehow be given a meaning.

Each of The Crusaders in his own way had a debt of some kind to pay off.

First, there was Wiz Fenichel.

How and where we met I can no longer remember nor is it of any importance.

What is important is that both of us felt that the wrongs of the world could be righted. We gathered around us a handful of what seemed to be like-minded men, all of them also just out of uniform, and for more than two years we all sat at a table—naturally, it was round—and made plans for the future that so clearly belonged to us.

While we waited to take over the management of the universe, we sent the people who were then botching it numerous fretful injunctions.

We also waited, somewhat impatiently, for the millions of fellow crusaders who were about to line up behind us—or beside us; we were extremely democratic.

"I mean, after all," Wiz used to say, "guys aren't just going to go home and *forget*. Not after fighting a war like that one. They're going to want some very fundamental changes made. They'll insist on it."

Actually, nobody insisted on anything—except us, we impatient few, we temporal band of brothers.

After being discharged from whichever service it was, most veterans went home, made down payments on cars and houses and babies and put on weight, turning to the sports pages again. They didn't join The Crusaders; they joined the local post of the American Legion, which had a bar.

At the time I hated them—but no longer. Maybe they were wiser than we were.

In any case, soon enough, even *The New York Times* stopped printing the exhortations we Crusaders sent out, and the one or two

Congressmen who had been friendly to us stopped bothering to have our statements printed in the *Record*.

Since the grail was so clearly beyond our collective reach and since each of us had his own down payments of one kind or another to make, we drifted off, one by embarrassed one, to pursue our separate, less ephemeral destinies.

The night the members of the round table formally disbanded, we had dinner at a place that served excellent Martinis, and we all had too many, and we all pledged eternal fealty to each other and to the bright dream that had brought us together in the first place.

Eternal is a long time; so is a decade.

A word about some of the other Crusaders:

The Playwright was one. I've disposed of him. Jonathan Haverford was another. No further comment.

There was also a man whose professors at Princeton felt had one of the best analytic minds they'd encountered in some time. He majored in economics—and at the time I knew him he was daring, clear-eyed, and honest; I'll call him The Economist.

There was a man who was interested in politics; he was a Yale graduate, had been a Rhodes Scholar, had a great many military decorations, including one pinned on him by the King of England. He had a real sense of the necessity for public service; he was a good speaker, had a quick wit, and people instinctively seemed to like and trust him.

So did we, but we didn't think he had much of a political future. Too pure, we thought, too uncompromising. Somebody wrote that in him our postwar generation had found a conscience and a voice. He was The Idealist.

As for Wiz Fenichel, he had gone to Yale Law School before the war, mostly because his father had insisted. Wiz's father is a partner in a big, prosperous midtown law firm. Wiz spent a year there before the war. At that time, Wiz must have been like a thousand other well-to-do, presentable, intelligent young men around New York who go to a great many parties, football games, and night clubs.

During the war, Wiz had been the commander of a destroyer; it was sunk by the Japanese, and Wiz and five other men were the only survivors; they spent twenty-four days in a rubber boat before they were picked up. Two of the other men died in a hospital on Guadalcanal, and Wiz's right leg was amputated.

When he got back to New York sometime after V-J Day, Wiz had done a great deal of thinking and a great deal of reading. The Crusaders was his idea.

He had decided not to go back to his father's law firm. Like so many other men I knew at the time, Wiz had found that life was too capricious to spend the rest of it doing something that he didn't respect and that he felt didn't make use of the best in him.

Sometime earlier I discussed my own feeling for the way I decided to make my living after the war. In these last minutes, let me softly say that I did—as George has pointed out—approach the theater as a kind of shrine. I was honest enough with myself and familiar enough with myself to know that I was not a creative man, and at the time I did feel—quite deeply—that I could in my own eyes justify my existence if I managed to get a few plays on the stage that spoke the truth and spoke it eloquently.

I brought back many memories from the war, and I've talked about some of them. I have held this one back because I was afraid that it might disappear if I so much as mentioned it. Now it doesn't matter.

One July afternoon in Paris after V-E day I was by some accident in the Gare de l'Est at a time when several hundred French prisoners returned from Germany. There must have been more than a thousand wives and children and sweethearts waiting to meet them.

I watched when the gates were opened and when the two groups flowed into each other's arms. There were tears and laughter and pure exultation. The whole station exuded waves of love—waves so real they became something almost physical, something you could touch.

I looked on with awe and envy and regret. I felt then and feel now that I was witnessing something very special and very precious.

"*That's* what life can be like," I thought. "*That's* what it's meant to be. There should be love in the world so real you can touch it. If you can just find that—once."

I didn't, of course; that's why I'm here now.

Someone to whom I once mentioned that moment in the Gare de l'Est said, "Within a week, all the love had dissipated itself, of course. Anybody can be good in the big moments. It's the boredom of day-by-day existence that dulls and cripples. Boredom and bills; that is the deadly combination."

Who said that? I don't remember.... Unless I said it myself.

You will have to forgive me. My mind is wandering. I must force it back once more. I have just listened to the last few minutes on this tape, and I see that I started to talk about Wiz Fenichel coming back from the war, then interrupted myself.

I'll go on with Wiz.

In the series of hospitals in which he spent a year and a half, Wiz had discovered that he had an interest in and an aptitude for pure mathematics. So after the war he enrolled at Columbia under the G.I. Bill to study math.

I don't know what pure mathematics is, but I have a great regard for almost all pure passions.

Anyway, while he was at Columbia, making speeches and writing magazine articles and getting himself a reputation as a firebrand and a troublemaker, Wiz invited a handful of us to join The Crusaders.

There were others in the group, but I've given a fair sampling. We were delighted when the girls' magazine I mentioned at the beginning of this narrative said that we were—"Today's Hopefuls, Tomorrow's Leaders."

We couldn't have agreed more, and we drew up a statement of intentions that looked into every facet of society.

Wiz and I continued to see each other for a while after The Crusaders disbanded, but, again like so many other men I knew, after a year at Columbia, Wiz gave up his passion and settled for what was practical. He went back to his father's firm, which has a lot of theatrical clients. I never was one, however. I believe it would have embarrassed Wiz; I know it would have embarrassed me. The memory of the night Wiz told me what he was going to do was too vivid.

We were in a Third Avenue bar.

"I'm dropping out of school," Wiz said.

"Don't you like it?"

"I like it well enough, but, Josh, I'm thirty years old."

"So. You've got forty years yet. At least."

"Too late," said Wiz. "Maybe if I'd started at twenty instead of wasting all that time at law school. Besides, my mind's atrophied."

"Three weeks ago you were telling me how you'd never been so excited."

Wiz finished his drink, and we ordered another round, and after a while Wiz said, "Josh, my dad's getting old, and he wants to see me settled. He's spent his whole life building up a firm with the idea that eventually I'd take over. It seems—well, selfish...."

He let the sentence trail off, and I said, "If you really believe that, Wiz, okay, but I don't think you do, and I think when you're forty you're going to look back on the time at Columbia and hate yourself and hate your father—not much, because you're a nice guy—but some."

"Maybe," said Wiz. "Maybe you're right."

A little later he finished his drink and went off, and that was the last time we were alone together.

Wiz didn't abandon me, though. I abandoned him.

I was going to have an episode called *How I Got Rid of My Friends*. There isn't time, but what happened between him and me is typical. Wiz married Maria, a nice girl just out of Bennington. I was near the end of my marriage to a girl not long out of Cedar Rapids.

Wiz and Maria had a child; they moved to Norwalk and had another and then a third. I got involved in a very nasty divorce; I went Out There several times; I went on numerous prolonged bats, and I suffered through a series of failures both professional and private.

Wiz and Maria sent me Christmas cards; I never sent them any. They invited me to parties. I usually accepted the invitations, then on the day of the party would have my secretary Pan send a telegram, or telephone saying that I had come down with an incurable disease or had joined the Foreign Legion. I rid myself of many friends that way. My social ambivalence—wanting to be invited everywhere but never wanting to go anywhere—is one of the many ambivalences I've spent long, expensive sessions discussing with the men who tried to lead me out of the wilderness. Never with any success, though. The minute I started to see the light, I'd change analysts.

Once, after Letty and I were divorced, I invited Maria and Wiz to dinner. I was then living in a simple apartment overlooking the East River. Rent about $20,000 a month, as I recall. Technically I lived alone, but a girl with purple hair occasionally flew in from Out There for a few days. With her there it was still just about the same as being alone.

The night Wiz and Maria came to dinner, I was in a bar on Eighth Avenue. I had forgot I invited them, but the girl with purple hair was there.

I don't even like to think about the kind of evening it must have been. The girl with purple hair was not much of a conversationalist. She was always saying something to me like, "Now tell me all about the steel mine strike."

That night she ordered sandwiches from the delicatessen, and she and Wiz and Maria ate on the marble coffee table. Wiz and Maria left early.

And so it was that I got rid of Wiz and Maria. In different ways but in the same way, I got rid of all the others. Not deliberately; yet what happened I suppose I meant to happen. I have been careless of people.

Years passed, five or six of them, and then one morning three years ago Pan came into my office to say that a Mr. Fenichel was on the phone.

"Who?" I asked. In these last moments let us be kind. Let us say my mind was on other matters.

I picked up the phone, and a precise Hotchkiss-Yale voice said, "Hi, Josh. I'm going to be forty on Saturday. How about coming out and helping me through the barricades?"

I mumbled something, and then Maria got on the phone.

"Please do come," Maria said. "People are coming from all over, and all the boys who were in the group. Now please come, and don't send a telegram at the last minute saying you can't, and don't have your secretary call and say you've come down with something. Come."

I said that I would, instantly regretting it.

And this is the last memory we will have time for.

I hadn't yet lost my license, and as I drove up the Merritt Parkway that night, I kept thinking of all the one-time friends, now enemies, who would be at Wiz's. I knew that there would be a heavy air of hostility in the house in Norwalk, and I knew that I would see in each face a measure of my own failure and of broken promises—theirs and mine.

For instance, before I went to Wonderland to appear before the Unpleasantness Committee, I had written a letter to The Idealist, who had by then become a Senator. I had asked him if I could see him the night before I made my appearance; after all, he was a colleague of the Lord High Executioner. At the time, I hadn't decided what to do when they got me on the chopping block, and I was terrified. Six weeks after I had appeared, I got an answer to my letter, on Senate stationery.

My dear Josh—

In some way, your letter got mislaid, and only yesterday ... I am sorry ... I followed with interest your testimony before ... I have myself not yet made up ... considering the size and scope of the menace in this ... I hope very much ... in memory of the old days....

Six months later, I wrote back,

Dear Senator—

I have just come across yours of the ... It was lurking under a pile of second-class mail. I followed with interest your sudden illness on the day that ...

and your absence from the Senate during the debate on such crucial issues as ... and your speeches before such groups as.... Your voice had never been more eloquent, nor, I am sure, has your conscience ever been clearer.... In memory of the old days....

No answer to that one.

And there was the telegram I sent to The Economist after he had made a speech before those grand guys in the National Association of Manufacturers. In his speech, he had said, "... in *perlous* times like these, we must put our shoulders to the wheel and as *'mercuns* back Our Great Leader...."

In my telegram, which The Economist didn't answer either, I said, "... Have read account of your speech in the *Times*. Surely you were misquoted."

And then The Playwright, in accepting an Oscar or an Emmy (I can never keep them straight), said "...If Euripides were alive today, he would be out here in Hollywood, which is to the America of the twentieth century what Florence was to the Italy of the Renaissance."

Through shenanigans I won't go into, I got a copy of The Playwright's latest movie script—one of those written at the time Those People decided that since movies obviously were never going to be any *better*, they could at least be *dirtier*.

I mailed the script and the manuscript copy of *My Enemy Is Dead*, which The Playwright had given me, to his Out There address on Upper Golden Drive. I also sent along a note saying, "Dear Rip—You *do* write better since you moved to Florence."

You can see what I mean about my feelings the night I went to Wiz Fenichel's fortieth-birthday party.

And you won't be surprised to hear that on the way to Norwalk that night I had a very long talk with the only friend I ever had who never disappointed me, Jack Daniel.

By the time I got off the parkway, the bottle was half-empty.

Wiz's house was large, and it was freshly painted, and it looked expensive and was beautifully kept and very unattractive. It had been built in the Twenties.

I must have driven up and down in front of that house a dozen times before I got up enough courage to turn in the drive. Needless to say, Daniel held my hand.

Finally, I did go in, and each stone of the driveway looked as if it had just been polished. An open-faced boy in coveralls said he would park my car.

Wiz himself opened the door. He was a little paler than I remembered him, and his forehead was an extra, not unattractive height. He still looked like a man who could make a comfortable living modeling suits cut in the Ivy manner.

He shook my hand, and he said he was glad to see me, and I put the small, square package I had brought on the table with all the other packages. Maria kissed me and said what she already must have said fifty times that night. She said that she was especially glad to see me. As a mother of three, she seemed not to have changed at all, and she managed the large gathering with easy competence. There were three maids and two bartenders, one of whom circulated with a tray of drinks.

I was the last to arrive; there was no time to meet anyone. There was only time for two quick drinks, the second a double.

We had dinner on the huge lawn with its formal, unin-spired plant architecture. We were eight at each table, and there seemed to be one waiter for every two people, like policemen in Portugal.

By that time, Jack Daniel was no longer holding my hand; he was buzzing my head. About that time, I got into the wine.

There were three types of people there that night, ex-Crusaders, friends of Wiz's from law-school days and beyond, and the folks from Show Biz who are now his clients. Wiz's father sat beside him, looking exactly like what he is, a man who will take on any client if the bank account is big enough, and next to him was Wiz's mother, a sweet, vague woman who has a habit of disappearing while you look at her.

Myself, I was a Committee of One, the undesirable fourth type of person there.

The man on my left was a fellow you see on television all the time, softest touch on Broadway and a folksy, earthy sonofabitch. He turned to me at one point and said, "Have you read Dante's *Inferno* lately?"

I confessed with a blush of shame and of booze that I had not.

"You don't remember who the lowest circle of hell is reserved for then?" said the student-philosopher, using the Socratic method of teaching.

A waiter finished filling my glass with the red, and I took a hefty sip.

"I know who it ought to be reserved for," I said, looking at him. Let's call him Cuddles. "You."

Cuddles got all red in the face, though he hadn't touched a drop of the stuff. You'd be surprised how many absolute bastards there are who don't drink.

I remember very little else about the conversation at dinner. In my area the Show Biz folks were mostly telling each other how much they admired each other. In Show Biz Each almost always admires Other—unless, by chance, Other has stepped out of the room—"I don't care what the critics say, *You* were superb. *You* were simply *marvelous.*"

I hardly noticed the woman on Maria's left; I was at the next table. I knew there was a woman in the chair by Maria, but all I knew of her appearance was that she was short, not young, not old, not pretty, just pleasant-looking.

I was aware that she had said almost nothing during dinner, and Wiz once affectionately called out, "Charley, stop interrupting."

Charley laughed, a small liquid laugh. Very shy, I thought.

After dessert and coffee, there was the kind of forced hilarity that seems to be required on such occasions. Many guests—far too many—had written humorous poems about Wiz, about birthdays, and about middle age. Each of the poets read his contribution aloud. None of them would have caused Ogden Nash any discomfort.

My own turn came close to last, and when I rose, there was a moment of uneasy silence as I discovered that it would be better for all concerned if I put what I was going to read on the table and supported myself on the back of my chair.

I said, "I wish to read something that was written more than ten years ago, in the fall of 1945."

I spoke slowly, too slowly, I imagine, but as I spoke, my head cleared—as it had before with an effort of great will—and the words emerged clearly, each with a kind of proud independence.

"What I am going to read was a collaborative effort," I said. "It is not what any one of the eight men who wrote it had in mind, and yet it reflected the ideas of all of us."

I paused. I had the breathless, undivided attention of at least five other men than myself.

I looked down at the paper, and then, although every word was engraved both on my memory and my heart, I read, "A Statement of Intentions...."

I paused again, and I saw that a member of the Senate of the United States had caught the eye of The Economist.

I continued:

We the undersigned are combat veterans of the Second World War. We neither won nor lost that war; we fought it, and we survived it, and as survivors we feel a sacred obligation to those men who did not...

I looked up, but by then the lawn and the people and the lights and the night were one vast misty blur.

I went on, from memory:

...A sacred obligation not only to those who were our comrades in arms but to those who were said to be our enemies. It is very difficult to die when you are young and a soldier; it is often painful, too, and it is always very lonely. The loneliness and the pain are neither more nor less intense when you are German, and it was as difficult for a Japanese soldier to die on a nameless island of the Pacific as it was for an American...

I hesitated again, and I looked at the woman named Charley; and I saw that her face was gentle, and I saw that she was crying.

...We who survived this war lost something of ourselves in fighting it. We did what we had to do, but that does not make what we did the less obscene. Killing is obscene. In whatever place and at whatever time and for whatever reason, it is obscene for one man to kill another. In so doing, some part of our dignity has been lost to us forever...

And so it is that, obsessed by our guilt and haunted by our obligation, we, like other men before us, pledge our lives, our liberty, and our sacred honor to make sure in whatever way we can and at whatever cost to ourselves and to others—that there will never be another war.

We believe that wars are not caused by small groups of evil men. We believe that wars are caused by all men who are selfish, by all men who tell less than the truth, by all men who put comfort above duty, by all men who place personal position ahead of public responsibility...

And so on this fifth day of October, 1945, we the undersigned, offering our faith in our beliefs and in ourselves, do declare that we believe it to be our individual as well as our joint responsibility to devote ourselves to these principles:

I paused for a moment to swallow the thing in my throat, and then, with no warning—I burst into tears. Say it was the wine; say it was the bourbon; say it was the disappointment in myself, in the others who were there that night, in everybody everywhere.

Say what you will. I cried for a full minute, maybe longer, and during that time I was unable to move.

Then I found the strength to turn and walk away, and someone—I didn't then know who—applauded; a few others joined in, but then, whatever the mood I had created, whatever the memory I had evoked, was gone. We were back in a formal, rather ugly garden in Norwalk, Connecticut, and it was the present, not the past, and what we had been gave way to what we had become.

Maria said something to somebody. Her voice was stilted and strange.

As I passed the wife of the man who may be our next President, she drew a white cashmere shawl around her shoulders and adjusted her spine to reflect her disapproval—as if I had done her some personal damage.

After that, her husband rose and in a voice that was filled with Presidential resonance he said, "Those are very beautiful words we just heard, and I for one am proud and happy I had some part in writing them. That's why I'm in politics; that's why I'm in the Senate of the United States, and that's why some folks are saying ..."

I couldn't see him, but I feel he must have grinned at his audience and maybe winked at them. Several people laughed.

"... some folks are saying I ought to think about going for the top spot."

The applause was general and enthusiastic this time.

"What I say is, we'll just have to see," said the man who had in mind a rent-free four years in a house on Pennsylvania Avenue.

"We will just have to see."

More applause, more laughter.

"But I'll tell you this," he went on. "When the chips are down, it's not what you say; it's what you do that counts, and that's especially true when we're dealing with a man like Nikki and I guess you all know who I mean."

There were cries of "Hear, hear."

"However," said the man who—surely you knew—was once called the voice and the conscience of the generation that fought the Second World War, "I'm not here tonight to talk politics. In fact, as you folks know I'm spending about three-fourths of my time not talkin' politics."

The folks knew.

"I want to propose a toast to my oldest and best friend—a man who's just findin' out that life does begin at forty, as the feller said, a man who..."

By the time Mr. Presidential Caliber had finished toasting Wiz, I was in the car lot.

The boy who had parked my car was gone, probably inside eating. I couldn't have got the car out under the best of circumstances, and I didn't even try. I got in, leaned back, and closed my eyes. I went to sleep almost at once, and I slept for nearly two hours.

When I woke up, the boy was back, but I decided to return to the party. Why? Well, first let me explain why not.

Not to apologize to Maria for having been somewhat drunk and disorderly at dinner; the hell with that. You have a party with the kind of crowd that was there that night, and you are lucky if you have only one d. and d.: you may get a dozen. That's the name of the game.

And not to congratulate Wiz on being forty. Anybody can get to be forty. What's more, I didn't want Wiz's thanks for the present I'd brought him. Wiz, years before, had mentioned to me that Michelangelo had written a book on mathematics that had been published only in Italy; once in Italy I bought it for him. For sentimental reasons? Oh, no. I bought it because I wanted Wiz to see it on his desk when he was sitting there holding the hand of some aging tenth lady of the American theater. I wanted that book to remind him that he had once been something more than an average, run-of-the-mill whore lawyer. From all I heard Wiz did more than hold the hand of many of his female clients. From all I heard Wiz's bedroom popularity was not only due to the fact that he was a reasonably good-looking man. It was also due to the fact that he discarded his right leg in the South Pacific. I mean whatever else you say it's a bit different.

And from what I heard, Maria, knowing of Wiz's wandering eye and the popularity of his detachable leg, was not averse to an occasional roll in the hay with the garbage collector. Tonight, though, I thought, the evening being overcast with sentiment and booze, Wiz and Maria would probably forget all that, and after the party—well, you only get to be forty once, you know. So I was a little drunk and disorderly at dinner. So what? There are worse things, and in case anybody wants me to name five, I'll comply with pleasure—a hundred if you'd like.

Nor was I going back to the party to speak to any of the other Crusaders Turned Finks. I had nothing whatever to say to any of them. I thought, If a great tidal wave were to sweep in from the Sound at this moment, and envelop them all—us all—it would have my endorsement and blessing.

What, then, did I go back for? Why, to find out who the hell it was who had applauded.

I went toward the terrace; I stood a little away and watched the men who had once sat at a round table and I saw that except for Wiz, none of the Crusader-Finks could get as close to the table as they had ten years before.

Mr. Presidential Caliber was *on*: He had once been a man who looked on almost everything sharply and wittily, but not that night. Oh no, he was being very solemn that night and very obtuse. Calvin Coolidge once said, "The American people want a solemn ass for President," and he was in a position to know.

P.C. was solemnly saying there are two sides to every question, which happens to be a goddamn lie. What's more, P.C. was saying you had to go very slow on civil rights; otherwise, you might upset the apple cart. What's more, P.C. was saying, although he wouldn't want to be quoted on this and he was sure the fellows understood, he knew several of the oil people *personally*, and as for that twenty-seven-and-a-half per cent depletion allowance that Wiz had asked about and he was glad Wiz had asked that question—well, you had to understand that there have to be *inducements* for those oil men. This tax allowance on the surface might seem a little unfair, but without it the oil men would stop being oil men; they would go into some other line of work, and he was sure Wiz knew how important oil was to the national defense, particularly in view of the situation in the Near East, and so on.

All of the Crusader-Finks were leaning forward, appearing to listen; they weren't, though; what they were doing was seeing their pictures on the front page of the *Times* the morning after they had attended the Inauguration as personal guests of P.C. and Mrs. P.C.

I walked on and listened for a moment as The Economist explained to somebody why it was that a man in his position had to support both the National Association of Manufacturers and Americans for Democratic Action.

I didn't listen long, though, but as I walked on I did say, "Stewardess, bring me a vomit bag if you please."

The Economist looked up; he saw me; he shrugged, rolled his eyes, and shook his head, and then he continued talking to whoever it was he was talking to, an elm tree, I think.

The Playwright was seated at a table with two bull dykes, one named Mike and the other named Mona; they are big television producers and writers, and The Playwright was telling them how much he admired their work, and then he started telling them about *his* work, something about the fact that he was writing a situation tragedy for television, and that it was in the grand tradition of Euripides and they had tested Judith Anderson but had finally decided on Jayne Mansfield, who was more talented anyway.

I called for another vomit bag.

"Stewardess," I said, aloud, "this one's all full-up."

The Playwright didn't turn, but one of the dykes did. Boy, would she like to have got me in a dark alley.

I wandered on, and I stood in the darkness for a time, smoking a cigarette. I thought of The Idealist turned Presidential Caliber, of the clear-eyed Economist turned Nothing, of The Playwright turned...

I thought, Now let's be fair, Bland; you have a reputation for fairness. Let's look at things from their point of view.

Okay, I said, their p.o.v. Well, they have in their nostrils the smell of festering lilies; after all, they know it is far worse than weeds; not only that, when they wake up in the middle of the night, feeling a sharp pain in the soul area, they know that there is no cure for what ails them. There is not a salve or a potion or a drug that will lessen any of the pain.

Then I thought, Are you kidding, Bland? Is your brain softening faster than your arteries are hardening? Their p.o.v. Why, there isn't one of them who hasn't been able to justify every compromise, lie, evasion, duplicity, and deceit. Pain in the soul area? Don't be a horse's ass. They've forgotten they've got a soul, and when they wake up in the middle of the night, all they think is, Who'm I going to do in tomorrow? Or, Semper Fi, George. I'm getting mine while the getting's good. Or, the more pious among them, The Lord helps them that help themselves. It says so in the Bible, and you can't argue with the Bible. I forget what page it's on, but...

And should there ever be a niggle of memory of the time they were selfless, they will look back on it with shame—

"Look, the world can only afford about one Albert Schweitzer at a time, and from all I hear he's not exactly..."

"Look, that stuff's okay for kids, but I've got a family to support..."

"Look, you've got to face facts. You can't change human nature, and the sooner you find that out..."

Or, "Look, I'm not Jesus H. Christ."

And so on. And so on.

Then I thought, Having purged themselves of discomfort, the bastards will roll over and sleep the sleep of the self-justified.

And then I thought, Look who's talking. When have you been Christlike lately? What have you done for anybody lately?

And I thought, Why was so strange an animal as man ever created?

And I thought, Is it your business?

No, I thought, it is not.

And I thought, Who's that ever stopped?

I finished the cigarette, and, since the lawn was so well-tailored, I scattered the ashes, Army fashion, and I put the thread of white paper in the pocket of my jacket.

I walked toward a bench in the darkness on the far side of the lawn. As I reached it, a soft voice said, "Hello, Mr. Bland."

I said, "You don't happen to have a spare vomit bag on you, do you?"

And that was how Charley and I met.

George and Russell ought to be here at any moment now. The rain has slacked off, and the sun has come out. No doubt someplace there is a rainbow. I do not want to see it.

Eight minutes of three, eight minutes before the invariably punctual George and Russell, a man who is always on time because he believes in all the small virtues, will come up the drive.

I have just time to tell about the rest of the night I met Charley. It seems to me now that from the beginning I planned that this would come at the end.

At the risk of sounding eighteen, I'll say that the talk Charley and I had that night was the kind I'd forgotten existed. I hadn't talked *with* anybody for years—*in the direction of*, *at*, but not *with*.

Eighteen again. We shared a great many opinions—oh, trivial things—that *The Great Gatsby* is a better novel than *Tender Is the*

Night, that Rodgers and Hart were wonderful and Rodgers and Hammerstein a pity, that *Marty* told us far more than we wanted to know about a butcher, that democracy may be a workable system, but it hadn't worked for quite some time, and so on.

Nothing at all fundamental, you understand, just something rather pleasant. The fundamentals came later.

I said, "My God, I haven't had a drink for hours. What would you like?"

I rose, and Charley said, "Nothing, thanks. I'm an alcoholic."

I started to say, but I did not say, "So am I, but I haven't come right out and admitted it until this minute."

I paused, and then I said, "I guess my love of the stuff was pretty obvious to everybody at dinner."

Charley smiled, and I lighted a cigarette for her.

I said, "You were the one that applauded."

She said, "Uh-huh."

I said, "Let's get married at once."

She said, "I had the feeling you wrote most of it."

I said, "Why in the world would you think that?"

She said, "Because I know quite a few writers, and I recognize the special tone that creeps into their voices.... Anyway, I liked it."

I explained to her my theory that the guests at the party came in three categories. "Which are you?" I asked.

"An old friend of Maria's," said Charley.

We talked about Maria for a while, and at one point I said, "She happy?"

"How could she be?" said Charley. "She's neither stupid nor insensitive."

I said, "Is there a Mr. Barr?"

She said, "There was once."

We talked about the Crusaders, and I explained the Bland Theory of Crusader Turned Fink, and I said, "I expect too much of people, I guess."

"So does God," said Charley.

I said, "What's your opinion of your average, run-of-the-mill human being?"

"Well," said Charley, "I doubt very much that *we're* what He had in mind."

It seemed only a few minutes later when we heard the sound of good-byes, doors being slammed, wonderful-times being repeated, and cars being driven off.

It had been a long time since I had wanted to prolong any conversation, years, in fact, but, finally, I rose and said, "Would you really like to see *My Fair Lady*?"

"Really."

"You say what night."

"Almost any. I'm almost always available."

"Tuesday. I'll pick you up. Where?"

She told me, and I said, "I'll pick you up at six."

I left her sitting on the bench; she was staying the night. As I walked to the house, I realized that I had had a very good time, and I wanted to go back and tell Charley that that was rare, and thanks.

I didn't, of course. I was afraid if I did she wouldn't be there. I was always afraid of that, and in the end I arranged it so she wouldn't be.

I said good-bye to Maria, and she said, "How did you and my friend Charley get along?"

"I'm taking her to *My Fair Lady*," I said.

"Be careful of her," said Maria. "She's an easy bruiser."

"So am I," I said. "She and I ought to get along fine.... Say good-bye to Wiz."

Driving back to the city in the June dawn three years ago, I thought of Charley. I had enjoyed talking with her, and I knew she had enjoyed talking with me, because that is one of the things you always know. I realized that I didn't really know what she looked like. I had seen her tears at dinner, and I had seen her face when I lighted a cigarette for her, but I couldn't have described her if someone had asked me to.

And I realized I didn't care; I liked her; that was all, and enough. I thought, If I can just make her happy...I thought, If you blow this one, boy, there'll never be another....

I said aloud, "Oh God, please don't let me fail again."

And even as I said it, I knew that I would somehow manage to fail.

Russ's car is coming up the drive, and if I get through the next hour safely, I will never have to fail at anything again.

(2) The final tape

I took the first ten pills about ten minutes ago, remembering; I swallowed them down, two at a time, five swallows along with plenty of life-giving vodka to ease them on their way.

Twenty now.

That's thirty, and I want to be *it* because I like hiding, and I do not like to count to ten if I am not *it*.

I have now swallowed ten more of the pills, and I am it, and I am ready and not coming.

Now the final ten, which is the vodka and is vortex, but the man who said hello meaning good-bye was a man who could hear remembering, because it had the color of loneliness and the sound of waiting.

I know more or less what will happen next. I discussed the whole thing with Sid Levinson several weeks ago. I told him I wanted to know for a play I was producing. For a few minutes I will feel tired, relaxed, just pleasantly drowsy, the way I might feel having finished a hard day's work. After that, I will yawn and what *is* will start separating from what *was*, mind from matter, substance from shadow. Then my mind will start to wander, rational and irrational, and I will yawn, and in the end, all of me will down, but before that there will be dream, and there will be nightmares, and there will be the sound of good-bye.

George and Russ have gone. They were here but have gone, and I will tell you what they said because they whispered when they shouted.

There was a man named George, who is my keeper and is also my friend and who is an agent of God, and there was Russ, and then there were none.

There were papers that were sheets of sleep, but so is snow in the morning if no one has walked on it, and there were no people, and there were no people anywhere, and the man who was there said don't let the sonsabitches get you down. I've certainly noticed that, and the man who was there said it was easy, the fifty pills, he said to himself because there was no one. Simple, the man said, and it has the size of easiness squared.

The two men who were there before blue came, and they pounded on the door, and at first the man who was there but not sure it was them. He knew he could never be fire, because they wore many disguises, and a friend is an enemy, and they speak in shouts when they whisper, and then they came in if they went out. They stayed and they stayed if they arrived, and now if they were there the man who was there was blue because they were gone, and...

And, oh, it is amazing how easy it is, and what I don't understand is why it isn't more popular. That's the secret, I suppose; it is that they whispered behind the closed doors, and good night. They were saying that death is easy, and that is not life that is, and that is why they always laugh behind the door, because they have the secret.

I looked at my will, which was paper and not steel, and George said, "Are you going to live?"

And I said, "We all have to live sometime, George," and die, good-bye, why.

And the man behind the nose said that the man who was there would die for years yet, and the man said and it is this, I want Davy Bronson to read the funeral oration of Pericles to the Athenians, and George said if it was nice, for god's sake why, and the man who was X who was there said because that's what my grandfather wanted read at his funeral, and the sonsabitches wouldn't let them because they are all sonsabitches, and I said then I want Davy to play, because he knew and was good at musical before you corrupted him George, and I said Davy can play any damn thing he wants to as long as it's not sacred, and I said, I've got a little list of songs right here, George, and I said, Russ, this ought to interest you, Russ. You're a lisp expert, and the sonofabitch who is going to inherit me and the earth and the meek, my ass Russell, I said. The meek are going to get screwed by people like you Russ I said I said you are a meek screwer George and you know all about lisps don't you and the meek and you got it screwed too.

Russ yellowed his teeth and said it was a little nip that had not hurt me because I had been drinking before they came because if I had been drinking I thought they will not find me strange and remembering.

My God, this is easy, like rolling off a log. I tell you if you're planning one, and a little vodka shall lead them with fifty pills. They are waiting in the snow there, for you.

Oh yes, I said to George, I want Davy to play for my going-away party, as long as it isn't sacred, and as long as it says nothing about Jesus or God or any of those people I do not like those people I said, George Davy, and I said, there'll be a hot town in the old town tonight would be nice for the going away or I would like to hang around Piccadilly Underground and you know that one George and roll me over in the clover that's what I want when I am moaning at the bar none of your goddamn carrying on George I said and I said, George, you looked better with your nose, and I said, I loved that nose; that nose looked like something you got up on Broadway where it is square times and I said I always wanted to bite that nose George and you don't now look like anything or anybody and George said, "I'll drive you to the airport," and I said, "No, you won't, George, because I am going to be driven to the airport by a girl with purple hair and you have no hair and no nose and you are not nice. I never liked you, George," I said.

And George, noseless and without and in, sighed and said, "Have the William Morris people been at you again?"

And I said, "That's the principle of the thing, George, and the principle is the thing to make money with, George."

And I said, "Davy used to be a good musician, George, and you corrupted him George. You said Davy want to make dollars like a million and that is why you are not nice because of me same question." Higamus and hogamus.

And George said, "Nobody ever corrupted God, and you are better than anybody with six cups of coffee, black or you are going nowhere, purple hair or no purple hair."

And I said, or whatever and then, "That is not good enough any more, George; you won't get by with that one, not any more, and I said, George what you are is a question-asker, but you are not a Socrates, and you are not a philosopher, and you are nothing, but you ask people questions, and you corrupt the little children, and I said, you are just as bad as any of them, and all, and I said, you are nicer than they are, George, but you are not nice, and I said, you are not Socrates but you are a corrupter of youth and you are not nice George."

And then I signed, and then I signed, and I said, "Taffy is going to have more money than anybody, George, but I don't like her, and I don't love her, and nobody is lover, and she will never love anybody but she has all the money in the world and as a meek screwer George isn't that the pattern George isn't that the way George pardon me while I do you in because I have as they say a family in the normal healthy American way and aren't we, George."

And then I said, "You are an unprofitable servant, George," and I said, "There will be weeping and gnashing of teeth, but what is the parable of the talents."

And the man who was nowhere and the man who was nobody said, "No hard feelings, old boy," and he said, "I mean you let's shake," and he said, "I am going to miss you, and have a nice trip, and Grace is going to miss you."

I said and I said, "Russ, for the last half-hour or more you have been listening and witnessing I said the goddamnedest display of patience since the Sermon on the Mount, and if you want to know what I think, and you don't but I do, I said, you have never missed anybody because you have got a corncob where your heart ought to be," and I said, "Grace hasn't missed anything since she missed her last period and that is a very long time ago and I said, Get out of my house, you period-missing sonofabitch, I said.

And he went, and he went, and he said, "I'll wait for you in the car, George."

And I said, "George, if that bastard shows any sign of missing me, call the police."

And George said, "I hate saying good-bye," and even then he said, "I predict, and you will be back within the month."

And he to say good-bye, and I do not like him, and he is principally unprincipled, but I did not want the door to close for the last time for a minute anyway because They are waiting worse and more when you are alone, and I said, George, once in the war in a place in the snow where no one had walked there were little children who were with the enemy which was not my German and you know what George I told him in this because the children in the snow and it was I remember playing long ago and far away if it was in a box and warm. And I said, George, the children said good-bye when they meant hello, and the children were with my German because the children said good-bye meaning hello that made me cry for years and I am almost crying now I said because I am a phoney sonofabitch when it comes to crying, George, but so are you, noseless, and I said the enemies could be forgiven, George, because Jesus did, but the children were alone in the snow, saying good-bye when they meant hello.

And the man who was the agent of George said, "I will miss you anyway, and I hope you don't mind," and he said, "You sure that dame is going to take you to the airport," and I said yes and of course she will be here any minute I said and hello George meaning good-bye.

And I said, "You are the worst of all, George," and I said, "You knew how to be good, and you learned how not to and whoever said and I said, the one in the car, the one out there are not knowing because he never knew and you are as bad as him two of a kind and so on."

George said, and he said hello, but he meant good-bye, and the door closed because it could not open again, but love flew in the window when there was money, and money, and that has been.

I heard their voices, or the man who was there heard, and I thought, I will never hear a voice again, except my own, and I thought, I do not care, oh I do not care, and I do not care less, and could not, I thought I do not like people said I to myself said I, and I don't like people who like silbert and sullivan, and I do not like french poodle people because a french poodle people is a bastard everywhere always especially if he is of the poodle persuasion and if he is a poodle he has hatred in his corncob and I regret that I have but one life which I would not give for my country and that is not except for the general who said *merde* because he was French and nobody else ever said that about life and giving and country and that because that is why the absolute sonsabitches make up.

I just took a cold shower. Two minutes, all of it standing in the rain, and it is dripping, but I am not dressing; I entered naked, and I have been revived and was alone, and I am leaving naked and alone, and wasn't there a box in the womb and wasn't there death in the box lurking there.

Fastard, said the man, and the man said faster, and he is the man and no face had he but he was there the man he said is not here nor there because he is gone and where is my father said the boy there is a robin redbreast but there is no father and he said dear father come home but did not. He said, the mother cried, and the boy cried, and they both cried, but the father did not weep, and he did not gnash his teeth, because he was not there. He was gone, and he was gone, and left was only a robin, and he was a child again, but there was no father.

Faster, faster said the queen, and said the queen this is a slow country, but the man with no face went faster because there was a robin redbreast in the room and the boy said where is my father and boy was afraid because there was no box and no pink blanket and no father but there was a little girl, and she said faster, and she said I'll take two of everything, and the biggest they've got and the biggest there is, and two, and double, and I couldn't finish the second, she said, but the first was square, she said, and they went around and around and, and a man with no face listened, and another man who was not the same man but had no face said, Have a biscuit, and the girl who was not named said, I'm not supposed to talk to you about things like that, and then the girl whose hair was the color of good-bye said, I am swimming, and she was in a lake of tears with a soul where the swan should be, and the man reached for her, and the man reached again because the fog that swept into the room was gray and red, and there was a man who could hear remembering but could not reach the girl. The man who could see remembering heard a jawbreaker and he saw, remembering, a vermilion chair, and the duke was Louis the Bastard, and the spots were there on snow and sheets that slept, and there was a grave, and the man who could taste remembering said there is the face of a woman who has drowned in the lake of salt tears, and there was a man with no face. The man spoke a name, and no other, and his hair was white, but he had no name, but he was small and no remembering because the man who was dead but not gone is a father with forgiveness because there is no god, who is the father.

Father, forgive me, he said, because I am not the holy ghost, and I am alone, but the father could not forgive because he is asleep and he is white, and there is everywhere.

There is no forgiving, and the man said the sound of memory is the color of waiting, and the man who could see remembering heard the morning of a day with colors, all of them red, because there was Jesus and good-bye, but there was no father. Only the father could forgive, and a little girl shall lead them, but there is no father to forgive, because the sleep that knits up, and there will be tomorrow and tomorrow because there is no father to forgive, and there is a robin redbreast said the boy who was asleep awake, and where is my father, he said, and the mother said he is gone, and then there were more white sheets and more snow on which there had been no people. My name is Ronnie said the man with no face, but I am not a father, he said, because there are double of him but none of him to forgive and it is hello here.

The man who was there said, I search, father, and there is a robin in the tree, but he has no father and no forgiveness, and when the hand lifted him from the box he was afraid, and he said it is cold in the outside, but give me your hand because I am cold, father, and naked, father, and the snow is white, father, and I am a hand reaching into a box and out for the door because he said I am afraid in the dark, and I am the son in the dark, and I am the father but not forgiveness, because the father who never came and came home and came not and said there is no forgiveness, but always there is loneliness, and father, forgive, said the man and father forgive, and I am sleep and snow, and I am naked, and I am alone, and I am not god because there is no god, who is the father and could forgive.

The man who was there was tired, and the man who would not be forgiven was at the door, and the man raised the tired body from the naked floor, and, without forgiveness, the naked man's hand reached the door, but the man was tired and weak, and without forgiveness, and there was everywhere snow and there were acres of sleep, and white and no people to walk in the sleep, and he said, "Forgive me, father," and he said, father, and he said, I'm afraid in the dark and I'm alone in the dark, and I fear, he said, because I am not forgiven, and the man who could see remembering saw that there was everywhere loneliness, which is the color of everything and of nothing....

Readers' Guide for
A Gay and Melancholy Sound

Discussion Questions

1. What is the significance of the title? How can a song be both gay and melancholy?

2. How would your feelings about *A Gay and Melancholy Sound* be different if it were written with a third-person narrator?

3. There is an eternal debate among psychologists about the relative importance of nature and nurture in human development. When you look at the character of Joshua, which do you think had the most influence on him?

4. Is there a particular scene in the novel that you feel best reflects Joshua's character?

5. This novel was first published in 1961, more than half a century ago, and the story mostly takes place in the first sixty years of the twentieth century. Leaving aside the specific historical events it describes, such as World War II, how might it have been different if it had been set in 2011?

Suggestions for Further Reading

If you'd like to try more fiction by Miller, the two novels I'd highly recommend are *Reunion* and *A Secret Understanding*. They're both very different from *A Gay and Melancholy Sound*, but equally good.

Other books, both fiction and nonfiction, that you might want to try, include:

If you enjoyed the autobiography as novel approach that Miller took, you'll probably also want to read Pete Dexter's fabulous novel, *Spooner*.

In Nick Hornby's humorous and touching novel *A Long Way Down*, he introduces four characters who find themselves on the same London rooftop on New Year's Eve, each bent on suicide. They reluctantly decide to help each other regain the will to live, and thus an odd and unlikely quartet forms.

Christopher Isherwood's *A Single Man* is an incredibly poignant novel that spans twenty-four hours of the life of George, a middle-aged gay man mourning the death of his partner. It was, of course, popularized by the movie of the same name starring Colin Firth.

In *Night Falls Fast: Understanding Suicide*, clinical psychologist Kay Redfield Jamison writes from her own experience with manic depression and suicide attempts about why people choose to end their own lives.

Reif Larsen's *The Selected Works of T. S. Spivet: A Novel* is the story of boy genius T. S. Spivet, who sets out on a cross-country adventure when he finds out he's won the prestigious Baird Award for his cartography talents.

Two excellent memoirs about depression are *Darkness Visible* by William Styron and Andrew Solomon's *The Noonday Demon*.

Joan Wickersham's *The Suicide Index: Putting My Father's Death in Order* is a moving memoir in which the author struggles to make sense of her father's suicide.

About the Author

Merle Miller was born on May 17, 1919 in Montour, Iowa, and grew up in Marshalltown, Iowa. He attended the University of Iowa and the London School of Economics. He joined the US Army Air Corps during World War II, where he worked as an editor of *Yank*. His best-known books are his biographies of three presidents: *Plain Speaking: An Oral History of Harry Truman*; *Lyndon: An Oral Biography*; and *Ike the Soldier: As They Knew Him*. His novels include *That Winter*, *The Sure Thing*, *Reunion*, *A Secret Understanding*, *A Gay and Melancholy Sound*, *What Happened*, *Island 49*, and *A Day in Late September*. He also wrote *We Dropped the A-Bomb*, *The Judges and the Judged*, *Only You, Dick Daring!*, about his experiences writing a television pilot for CBS starring Barbara Stanwyck and Jackie Cooper, and *On Being Different*, an expansion of his 1971 article for the *New York Times Magazine* entitled "What It Means to Be a Homosexual." He died in 1986.

About Nancy Pearl

Nancy Pearl is a librarian and life-long reader. She regularly comments on books on National Public Radio's *Morning Edition*. Her books include 2003's *Book Lust: Recommended Reading for Every Mood, Moment, and Reason*; 2005's *More Book Lust: 1,000 New Reading Recommendations for Every Mood, Moment, and Reason; Book Crush: For Kids and Teens: Recommended Reading for Every Mood, Moment, and Interest*, published in 2007; and 2010's *Book Lust To Go: Recommended Reading for Travelers, Vagabonds, and Dreamers*. Among her many awards and honors are the 2011 Librarian of the Year Award from *Library Journal*; the 2011 Lifetime Achievement Award from the Pacific Northwest Booksellers Association; the 2010 Margaret E. Monroe Award from the Reference and Users Services Association of the American Library Association; and the 2004 Women's National Book Association Award, given to "a living American woman who ...has done meritorious work in the world of books beyond the duties or responsibilities of her profession or occupation."

About Book Lust Rediscoveries

Book Lust Rediscoveries is a series devoted to reprinting some of best (and now out of print) novels originally published between 1960 and 2000. Each book is personally selected by Nancy Pearl and includes an introduction by her, as well as discussion questions for book groups and a list of recommended further reading.